JUN -- 2013

W9-BMT-888

A FIC DUNBAR, PAUL LAURENCE
Dunbar, Paul Laurence
The Collected Novels of Paul Laurence

Georgia Law requires Library materials
to be returned or replacement costs paid.
Failure to comply with this law
is a misdemeanor. (O.C.G.A. 20-5-53)

THE COLLECTED NOVELS OF
Paul Laurence Du

CLAYTON COUNTY LIBRARY SYSTEM
FOREST PARK BRANCH
4813
FOREST PARK, GEORGIA 30297-1824

THE COLLECTED NOVELS OF

Paul Laurence Dunbar

Edited by
Herbert Woodward Martin,
Ronald Primeau,
and Gene Andrew Jarrett

Ohio University Press   *Athens*

CLAYTON COUNTY LIBRARY SYSTEM
FOREST PARK BRANCH
4812 WEST STREET
FOREST PARK, GA 30297-1824

Ohio University Press, Athens, Ohio 45701
www.ohioswallow.com
© 2009 by Ohio University Press
All rights reserved

To obtain permission to quote, reprint, or otherwise reproduce or distribute material
from Ohio University Press publications, please contact our rights and permissions department at (740) 593-1154 or (740) 593-4536 (fax).

Printed in the United States of America
Ohio University Press books are printed on acid-free paper ⊗ ™

First paperback printing in 2012
ISBN 978-0-8214-2007-2

HARDCOVER 18 17 16 15 14 13 12 11 10 09   5 4 3 2 1
PAPERBACK 20 19 18 17 16 15 14 13 12   5 4 3 2 1

Library of Congress Cataloging-in-Publication Data

Dunbar, Paul Laurence, 1872–1906.
  [Novels]
  The collected novels of Paul Laurence Dunbar / edited by Herbert Woodward Martin,
Ronald Primeau, and Gene Andrew Jarrett.
      p. cm.
  Includes bibliographical references.
  ISBN 978-0-8214-1859-8 (hc : alk. paper)
  I. Martin, Herbert Woodward. II. Primeau, Ronald. III. Jarrett, Gene Andrew, 1975–
IV. Dunbar, Paul Laurence, 1872–1906. Uncalled. V. Dunbar, Paul Laurence, 1872–1906.
Love of Landry. VI. Dunbar, Paul Laurence, 1872–1906. Fanatics. VII. Dunbar, Paul
Laurence, 1872–1906. Sport of the gods. VIII. Title.
  PS1556.A4 2009
  813'.4—dc22
                         2009026163

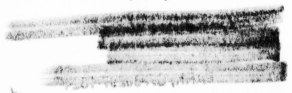

Contents

Introduction

In the prime of his literary career, Paul Laurence Dunbar (1872–1906) published four novels: *The Uncalled* (1898), *The Love of Landry* (1900), *The Fanatics* (1901), and *The Sport of the Gods* (1902). Despite widespread critical interest in Dunbar's writing during his time and ever since his death more than a century ago, the novels have largely been subordinated to his short stories and especially to his poetry. Between 1890 and 1905, he wrote slightly more than one hundred short stories, which he published either in collected volumes or individually in periodicals, and for which he earned some acclaim.[1] During this period, he also wrote hundreds of poems and published them in similar forms. His skills as a poet, rather than his skills as a fiction writer, were primarily responsible for his ascent to fame in the United States and abroad. In *Harper's Weekly,* the influential American magazine of culture and letters, William Dean Howells's praise of the black dialect in Dunbar's second book of poems, *Majors and Minors* (1896), triggered the avalanche of acclaim.[2] For the rest of his literary career, Dunbar was the de facto "Negro poet laureate," the first African American poet born after slavery to become an international phenomenon, and this reputation superseded the fact that he demonstrated expertise in writing fiction as well as songs, plays, and essays. Furthermore, ever since his death, Dunbar's reputation as an important American poet has remained relatively intact. While the numerous reprintings and constant circulation of his poems have stimulated the enthusiasm of general readers and the criticism of scholars, the novels Dunbar published during his lifetime—although reprinted, circulated, read, and studied, too—are usually an afterthought in the argument for his stature in American literary history.[3]

The Collected Novels of Paul Laurence Dunbar aims to redress this imbalance. Although not the first publication to transcribe, correct, standardize, and reprint a novel by Dunbar, it is the first to apply uniform editing to all four novels and collect them in one volume. This collection shows that his novels, as clearly as his short stories and poetry, reflect his exceptional literary talent, giving readers an equal opportunity to explore the characters, landscape, atmosphere, and visionary sensibilities of a preeminent African American writer. This general introduction and the subsequent introductions to the individual novels describe the major forms and themes of the novels, placing them in the proper contexts of Dunbar's creativity, his professional career, and American literary history. Each novel explores, in varying degrees, the issues of race, class, politics, region, morality, and spirituality. The first three novels, given their focus on white main characters, together challenge the long-standing assumption that African American authors should cast only blacks as main characters and as messengers of racial justice.

Although several collections of Dunbar's writings have been published, including not only the poems and the short stories but his plays, essays, and letters as well, only a few can claim to represent comprehensive and definitive sources. The fact that Dunbar's oeuvre spans hundreds of pages across these volumes testifies to his astonishing productivity. Despite having lived only thirty-three years, and despite having been a professional writer (that is, earning substantial money from his writings) for little more than a decade, he published fourteen books of poetry, four books of short stories, four novels, and many songs, dramatic works, short stories, poems, and political essays in newspapers or magazines. Publication of Dunbar's collected works in each genre testifies to the collective depth of our appreciation of his writings and our desire to preserve them, in their best and most convenient forms, for current and future generations to appreciate and preserve as well.

Neither Dunbar nor his contemporaries probably could have predicted that, at the turn into the twentieth-first century, his diverse range of writings, not only his poetry, would continue to live on and to intrigue so many readers. Indeed, in his own time, his efforts to experiment with different literary genres and styles beyond the black dialect poetry that launched his career were often met with disapproval, indifference, or at best faint praise. Much of that work in dialect was popular, though often for commercial reasons that were narrow and delimiting; Dunbar felt compelled to create work guaranteed to produce financial profit while continuing to seek critical recognition. Consequently, public expectations, which exploited racial stereotypes and celebrated literary expressions of racial authenticity, constrained and troubled Dunbar. Thus, his contemporaries simplistically reduced most of what we now see as Dunbar's innovative achievements. If ever there was a price for success, the African American writer once an elevator operator from Dayton surely paid it.

The centenary year 1972 marked the (relatively reluctant) emergence of academic interest in Dunbar. The Centenary Conference on Paul Laurence Dunbar held at the University of California at Irvine resulted in the landmark collection of essays edited by Jay Martin, *A Singer in the Dawn: Reinterpretations of Paul Laurence Dunbar* (1975). The centenary also featured a celebration at the University of Dayton, where Margaret Walker, an African American poet, introduced the academic community to the sophisticated ways of reading Dunbar that she and three generations of parents and grandparents outside the academy had been practicing for decades. The long-overdue attention to the complexity of Dunbar's poetry that ensued from such conferences and celebrations began to unravel the myth, originating with Howells in 1896, that only Dunbar's dialect verse was worthy of praise. It was a myth of racial authenticity that prefigured the labeling of African American poets of the twentieth century, who include the poets of the 1920s Harlem Renaissance (Countee Cullen, Langston Hughes, Claude McKay, and James Weldon Johnson), the 1930s and 1940s modernist movement (Gwendolyn Brooks and Melvin Tolson), as well as the 1960s and 1970s Black Arts Movement (Amiri Baraka, Sonia Sanchez, and Nikki Giovanni). As in these cases, Dunbar's renditions of dialect were long assumed to be either praiseworthy authentic folklore or demeaning minstrelsy, depending on one's perspective. Only archival research and a confidently post–Black Arts, post–black pride notion of African American literature were able to guide our attention to Dunbar's nondialect poetry (of which he wrote approximately as much as his dialect poetry). Similarly, we have been able to turn our attention to Dunbar's short stories and novels, among other writings, that also defy expectations.

A nuanced portrait of Dunbar has thus finally emerged. He was a writer who liked to try his hand at diverse literary genres, and was very good at each attempt. He was a writer concerned with matters of great historical import and significant social issues, and his essays are now read with keen interest. He was a writer whose poems are now reconnected to their contexts of imagination and production, thanks to the fact that a wide range of the poems have in the last four decades been read and performed with new insights. He was a fascinating dramatist who wrote comedies and musicals that sometimes fell into the minstrel traps and other times satirized the stereotyping with savvy and clout. He was also a writer who experimented with the British comedy of manners and, in *Herrick*, with incorporating what he had seen while living in London. In every case, he demonstrated a talent for trying anything once and doing it justice.[4]

With the publication of *The Collected Novels of Paul Laurence Dunbar*, the time has arrived for all four of Dunbar's novels, not only *The Sport of the Gods*, to receive the attention they too deserve. Dunbar's production of four novels between 1898 and 1902 is a notable achievement for a writer in the latter part of his twenties. Indeed, one of the novels, *The Sport of the Gods*, remains in print, and scholars tend to read it alongside the novels of other African American writers of racial uplift, including Sutton Griggs, Pauline Hopkins, and Frances Ellen Watkins Harper, and of Anglo-American writers now identified with the literary tradition of naturalism, including Frank Norris, Theodore Dreiser, and Stephen Crane. Admittedly, *The Sport of the Gods* reflects a refined development of plot and characters that an author of his fourth novel, not his first, is more capable of accomplishing. This literary maturity, in addition to the novel's more conventional portrayals of race, is arguably in part responsible for its popularity and continued commercial availability. But the recurring overemphasis of these qualities has also neglected evidence of Dunbar's promise or talent in the first three novels. In bringing all four novels together, this volume invites readers to recognize the patterns that both unite and distinguish them. For example, Dunbar was writing and publishing the novels at an extraordinary rate, and he was just as invested in writing esteemed literature as he was in making money. To what extent does such biographical information support or undermine the literary value of the novels?

A long view of Dunbar's life and career may bring us closer to a grasp of what Dunbar was thinking as he wrote the novels. Dunbar was born in Dayton, Ohio, the son of former Kentucky slaves whose tales of their antebellum experiences inspired the vernacular language and themes of his creative writing. He grew up in a period following Reconstruction known as Southern Redemption to disaffected white residents of the former Confederate states. In the mid-1870s, this group spear-headed the rollback of black civil rights that included the political disenfranchise-ment and racial segregation of blacks in public life. The social terror and political setbacks that blacks faced during the Jim Crow era have led scholars to call this period the nadir in African Americans' quest for political and social rights fol-lowing emancipation. Despite victory in the Civil War and the formal mandates of Radical Reconstruction, which helped protect their entitlement to national citi-zenship, blacks now realized that their racial progress faced a politically uphill and violent battle.

Dunbar responded to this atmosphere of racial unrest by publishing essays in local newspapers, such as the *Dayton Tattler*. One essay, appearing in 1890 in this paper, implored local black readers to buy the paper to "espouse the spirit of hon-est republicanism." Another essay, published in 1893 in the *Chicago Record,* ar-gued that the black press facilitated black political progress, also known as racial uplift. Similarly themed essays—printed in the *Toledo Journal,* the *Philadelphia Times,* and the *New York Times*—appeared over the next decade. His foray into political journalism illustrated his sensitivity to the conditions of black commu-nities across the country. Yet the approach also anticipated the irony inherent in his literary talent, critical reception, and commercial success, all of which often contradicted his original political sensibilities.

The June 27, 1896, issue of *Harper's Weekly* in which William Dean Howells, the preeminent critic of American literature and culture, effusively praised Dunbar's second collection of poetry, *Majors and Minors,* marked a breakthrough for the au-thor. (Dunbar's first collection, *Oak and Ivy,* arrived without fanfare.) Commenting on the portrait that served as the frontispiece of Dunbar's collection, Howells ap-preciated the ostensibly dark-skinned author as "the pure African type." Howells enthusiastically praised the poems written in dialect, which he felt represented ex-clusively black vernacular. Truth be told, the dialect poems reflected various re-gional and ethnic, not only black, dialects. The dialect poems also amounted to only a quarter of the book's poems; the other three-quarters were prayers, lyrics, odes, ballads, and sonnets in formal English. Nonetheless, the dialect poems, in Howells's eyes, represented Dunbar when he was "most himself," and through them readers could enjoy an authentic window into the black community. Coinci-dentally, the orthography of black dialect was a hallmark of popular American literature at the time, thanks mainly to the commercial success of white writers of the postbellum "plantation tradition," especially Joel Chandler Harris and Thomas Nelson Page.

Most critics reviewing *Majors and Minors* followed in Howells's influential footsteps. They similarly lauded Dunbar's dialect poems, contrary to the bulk of evidence—including *Oak and Ivy, Majors and Minors, Lyrics of Lowly Life, Lyrics of the Hearthside, Lyrics of Love and Laughter,* and *Lyrics of Sunshine and Shadow*—that the fledgling black writer was most interested in writing poems in formal English. The critical neglect of Dunbar's poems in formal English resulted from the overwhelming commercial popularity of the dialect poems included in these books, as well as such poems he published in magazines and performed in public. (To be fair to both critics and his public, he did not exactly oppose the financial incentives of this popularity. He needed the money.) The dialect poems often painted sentimental and romantic images of Negroes in the aesthetic tradition of mid- to late-nineteenth-century blackface minstrelsy, which appealed to the desire of many whites to return to the antebellum culture of blacks' supposed docility and subservience. Dunbar's dialect poems also ran counter to the prevailing signs of black political progress not only in the real world but also in the African American literature of racial uplift, written by Frances Ellen Watkins Harper, Pauline Hopkins, W.E.B. Du Bois, and, in some cases, Charles W. Chesnutt and Dunbar himself.

Some of Dunbar's dialect poems, however, belong to the literary tradition of racial uplift: even as they may have perpetuated black stereotypes to achieve a mass appeal, they criticized racial injustice in subtle ways. For example, a poem that Howells lauds in his review, "When Malindy Sings," focuses on the extent to which a woman's talent as a singer captivates anyone who hears her. Buried beneath the poem's dense dialect, sentimental aura, and minstrel imagery (such as the banjo player) is the reference to Malindy's song, "Swing Low, Sweet Chariot." This "Negro spiritual" was first sung by slaves and, for generations, passed down among blacks as a melody of religious hope and civil rights activism.

In the preface to a 1922 collection of African American poetry, James Weldon Johnson laments that the "qualities that gave [black dialect poetry] vogue— tenderness, sentimentality, homely humor, genial optimism—are the very qualities that now bring disparagement on it." Johnson assesses Dunbar's legacy in these terms to cast him aside, to create room in the canon of African American poetry for himself, Langston Hughes, and Claude McKay, writers who became representatives of the Harlem, or New Negro, Renaissance. However, the allegation could not undermine the fact that Dunbar's orthographic dexterity with dialect and his thematic ironies inspired these and other writers of their generation to hone their skills in representing black vernacular while delivering subtle political messages.

In addition to poetry, Dunbar wrote or published in the second half of his life more than one hundred short stories, many of them in four books, *Folks from Dixie, The Strength of Gideon and Other Stories, In Old Plantation Days,* and *The Heart of Happy Hollow.* As the titles suggest, several stories in the books sympathize with antebellum racial politics and representations. Yet some also break from these themes, illustrating the cultural, political, and religious complexities of black communities, and humanizing blacks in ways that the formal exigencies of Dunbar's poems may not always have permitted. Dunbar's four novels are equally experimental in examining the naturalistic impact of the environment on human agency. The first three—*The Uncalled, The Love of Landry,* and *The Fanatics*— use whites as main characters to tell stories, respectively, about spiritual regeneration and redemption, about the stricture of social convention, and about the morality of the Civil War. In contrast, the last novel, *The Sport of the Gods,* returns to the conventional form of African American literary realism by using a black protagonist to describe the cultural, regional, and ideological differences that fracture black communities.

To say the least, the reviews of all these works were mixed, showing the degree that Dunbar's experiments with literary form and theme contradicted mainstream critical and commercial demands. One century after his death, however, many critics and scholars have come to agree that his prodigious talent and versatility as a writer, and his sophistication and diplomacy in racial politics, deserve high admiration and further academic study, even as his career also suggests that he negotiated a personal crisis. Evidently, his creative loyalties were torn between, on the one hand, demonstrating his commitment to black political progress and, on the other hand, writing what prominent literary critics and publishers expected of him and of black writers in general. The standard biographies of Dunbar by Virginia Cunningham, Benjamin Brawley, Addison Gayle Jr., Peter Revell, Felton O. Best, and Eleanor Alexander support this assessment, but a closer look at his writings, including his novels, may also reveal the nuances of his life and career.

Even as he sometimes succumbed to the pressures of commercial demand, Dunbar sought nonetheless to maintain the integrity of his literary identity by seriously incorporating elements of his autobiography while modifying the literary conventions of naturalism, realism, romanticism, and even the racist plantation tradition. To begin with, *The Uncalled*, which is set in small-town Ohio, features a minister struggling against Puritan constraints who very well might be a stand-in for Dunbar himself. By the time he published this novel, Dunbar's proclivity to thread autobiography through his creative writing was already seen in such characters as the preacher of "An Ante-Bellum Sermon," a famous poem he included in *Majors and Minors*, or the poet Robert Herrick in Dunbar's long-lost play, *Herrick, An Imaginative Comedy in Three Acts*. Upon the release of *The Uncalled*, Dunbar came down with tuberculosis; while convalescing in Colorado, he contrived a love story that is, once again, autobiographical in its allusion to a maturing and satirical twenty-eight-year-old man against the backdrop of chameleonic train porters who, like Dunbar, dissemble as "good darkies." *The Fanatics* of a year later is a messy though fascinating social commentary on the Civil War, based on his research as well as on the stories handed down from his father, Joshua Dunbar, who fought in the war on behalf of the Fifty-fifth Massachusetts Colored Infantry and the Fifth Massachusetts Colored Cavalry. Finally, *The Sport of the Gods* tells the story of a young black man's moral decline as he transitions from the South to New York City, recalling both the pejorative connotation of the city in *The Uncalled* and Dunbar's own observations recorded four years earlier, in his 1898 essay, "The Negroes of the Tenderloin: Paul Laurence Dunbar Sees Peril for His Race in Life in the City." Autobiography had inspired Dunbar's writing to such a degree that, had he not become gravely ill and died a little more than three years after the release of *The Sport of the Gods*, he might in his maturity have written more novels, and his legacy might have been that of a novelist who happened to have written poetry earlier in his career.

Aside from strengthening our grasp of the novels, this collection also lays the groundwork for connecting them to Dunbar's other important writings. The political awareness and intellectual tenacity exhibited in Dunbar's novels, for example, are consistent with the social protest of his essays and the satire of his plays and musicals. These writings support the ironic thesis of Dunbar's classic poem, "We Wear the Mask," first published in *Majors and Minors*, for they highlight his long-lasting investment in the themes of black resistance and empowerment, even as his literary expressions consistently sought to appease racist public disaffection from such themes. This double move represents the mask of irony Dunbar mastered so well, both for the sake of making money and for the sake of communicating racial-political messages as subtly as possible. Gregory L. Candela, in his essay "We Wear the Mask: Irony in Dunbar's *The Sport of the Gods*," expounds on this point by identifying multiple levels of ironic masks in Dunbar's most famous novel.[5] While both naturalistic and melodramatic, *The Sport of the Gods*, like Dunbar's first three novels, enables Dunbar to wear "a Juvenalian mask" in order to present his "knowing assessment of his country's failings." Further, Thomas L. Morgan, in his essay "The City as Refuge: Constructing Urban Blackness in Paul Laurence Dunbar's *The Sport of the Gods* and James Weldon Johnson's *The Autobiography of an Ex-Colored* Man," illuminates how the setting of the city helped Dunbar "challenge realism's reified pastoral caricaturizations of blacks" and imagine "an alternate space for theorizing black subjectivity."[6] From Cincinnati in *The Uncalled* to New York in *The Sport of the Gods*, Dunbar created environments, at once realistic and imaginary, in which he could reconfigure black characters beyond the bounds of agrarian stereotypes, romantic melodrama, or minstrel ridicule. Morgan finds that "America's pastorally inflected beliefs about African Americans functioned as the glass ceiling" encountered by African American novelists of Dunbar's time. In those busy but short years between 1898 and 1902, Dunbar's novels indicated that he too was dealing with that ceiling.

Thus, we can only speculate on the progress Dunbar might have made had he lived longer. More certain is his seminal influence on the twentieth-century African American writers who followed him into the American canon. *The Collected Novels of Paul Laurence Dunbar* allows readers to assess Dunbar's life, literature, and legacy, hoping to stimulate interest and debate among students, teachers, scholars, and general readers for generations to come.

Notes

1. For more information on Dunbar's short stories, see Gene Andrew Jarrett and Thomas Lewis Morgan's introduction to *The Complete Stories of Paul Laurence Dunbar*, ed. Jarrett and Morgan (Athens: Ohio University Press, 2005), xv–xliii.

2. For more information on Dunbar's poems, see Joanne M. Braxton's introduction to *The Collected Poetry of Paul Laurence Dunbar*, ed. Braxton (Charlottesville: University of Virginia Press, 1993), ix–xxxvi. Also see chapter 1 of Gene Andrew Jarrett, *Deans and Truants: Race and Realism in African American Literature* (Philadelphia: University of Pennsylvania Press, 2007).

3. To put the scarcity of academic interest in Dunbar's novels in perspective, a recent search (in 2009) of the Modern Language Association's *MLA International Bibliography,* which indexes each year about 66,000 scholarly books and articles on the subject of literature dating as far back as 1926, revealed that, of the 140 scholarly items focused exclusively or significantly on Dunbar, only 21 (or 15 percent) dealt with his novels. Of these 21 items, an overwhelming 17 (or 81 percent) dealt with his final novel, *The Sport of the Gods,* which, coincidentally, is the only novel to feature mostly black main characters and, like *The Fanatics,* concentrates on racial politics.

4. For more information on the variety of Dunbar's literary writings, see Herbert Woodward Martin and Ronald Primeau, eds., *In His Own Voice: The Dramatic and Other Collected Works of Paul Laurence Dunbar* (Athens: Ohio University Press, 2002).

5. See Gregory L. Candela, "We Wear the Mask: Irony in Dunbar's *The Sport of the Gods,*" *American Literature* 48, no. 1 (March 1976): 60–72.

6. See Thomas Lewis Morgan, "The City as Refuge: Constructing Urban Blackness in Paul Laurence Dunbar's *The Sport of the Gods* and James Weldon Johnson's *The Autobiography of an Ex-Colored Man,*" *African American Review* 38, no. 2 (Summer 2004): 213–37.

Editors' Note

The four novels written by Paul Laurence Dunbar have reappeared more than once and in a variety of forms since their original publications. Dunbar's first and fourth novels, *The Uncalled* and *The Sport of the Gods*, first appeared in their entireties in the May 1898 and the May 1901 issues of *Lippincott's Monthly Magazine*. Otherwise, the entire novels have been printed or reprinted as separate books or in larger collections of Dunbar's writings. According to the Library of Congress and to official copyright records, Dodd, Mead, and Company was the first to print all four novels in book form in the United States. Under its imprint, *The Uncalled* appeared in 1898, *The Love of Landry* in 1900, *The Fanatics* in 1901, and *The Sport of the Gods* in 1902. Corresponding versions of the novels appeared abroad around the same time. According to Eugene W. Metcalf Jr., in his foundational 1975 bibliography of Paul Laurence Dunbar's writings, *The Uncalled* emerged in Toronto under the imprint of G. N. Morang Company in 1898, as well as in London under Service and Patton in 1899, while *The Sport of the Gods* emerged with a new title, *The Jest of Fate*, in London under Jarrold and Sons in 1902.

In the United States, the reprinted novels were often photoreproductions of the texts of the original editions. The first novel by Dunbar *not* published by Dodd, Mead, and Company was *The Uncalled*, which the International Association of Newspapers and Authors published in 1901. A little more than half a century later, the novels have generally reappeared around the same time, with the same set of publishers, although the fourth has resurfaced more than the others as an individual book or as part of a larger collection of Dunbar's writings. In 1969, the Negro Universities Press reprinted *The Uncalled, The Love of Landry*, and *The Fanatics*, coinciding with the academic rise of Black Studies and the related interest in establishing a marketplace for African American literature. In the same year, McGrath Publishing Company released the first novel, Arno Press released the fourth, and Mnemosyne Publishing Incorporated released all four. In 1970, Literature House published Dunbar's first three novels, while Collier Books republished the fourth; and two years later, AMS Press reprinted the first novel. More recently, aside from a publication of *The Fanatics* by Copley Publishing Group in 2001, *The Sport of the Gods* has contributed the most to Dunbar's reputation as a novelist. Dodd, Mead, and Company published it in 1975 (along with Dunbar's other writings) and in 1981; Mentor in 1992 (along with two other African American novels); Signet Classic in 1999; Modern Library in 2005 (along with Dunbar's other writings); and Dover in 2008.

The Collected Novels of Paul Laurence Dunbar is the first book to include all four of Dunbar's novels. The following versions of *The Uncalled, The Love of Landry, The Fanatics*, and *The Sport of the Gods* are based on Mnemosyne's 1969 reproductions of the texts of the novels' original editions. In the process of collecting the novels, we, the editors, decided to alter minimally their original texts. Specifically, we chose only to correct obvious errors in typography, spelling, and syntax and to standardize in subtle ways, according to present-day American usage, some of the archaic and confusing idiosyncrasies in Dunbar's hyphenation and contraction of words. The novels are presented in the chronological order of their publications.

THE UNCALLED

Introduction

FROM FEBRUARY TO AUGUST 1897, Paul Laurence Dunbar lectured and recited poems in London, Bournemouth, and other cities in England, capitalizing on his international stature as "Poet Laureate of the Negro Race," which he owed in large part to William Dean Howells's review of his poetry in *Harper's Weekly* on June 27, 1896. During the second month of the tour, Dunbar began to write his first novel, *The Uncalled*, published in book form in 1898, about a young man who resists his hometown's general insistence that his immoral ancestry predestines him for social failure. The novel demonstrates Dunbar's awareness of the generic tension between realism and naturalism. Certainly, Dunbar, among other accomplished American fiction writers of his day, knew the style of literary realism —namely, economic characterization, spare prose, streamlined exposition, and reportorial observation. Yet, his novel—along with other evidence, such as his letters to his lover, Alice Ruth Moore, and to his editors and literary peers—also suggests a simultaneous awareness of the rise of naturalism in American literary culture at the turn of the twentieth century, best theorized in the essays of Frank Norris and exhibited in the novels of Norris, Stephen Crane, Hamlin Garland, Kate Chopin, and Theodore Dreiser.

At the turn into the twentieth century, the distinctions between realism and naturalism—as well as their developmental succession and points of overlap— help reveal the importance of *The Uncalled* to this special historical moment in American literary culture. The theories and literatures of realism (and sometimes naturalism) purport objective readings and renditions of the local world. Naturalism features a more clairvoyantly omniscient narration that not only reports human actions and interactions but also asserts an uncompromising thesis: that the will governing these actions and interactions necessarily succumbs to the powerful influence of inborn character flaws, broad environmental forces, or both. The fates of human beings, then, are not decided by the agency of free will but rather are predetermined by powers beyond human control.

The distinction between the two genres should not distract us from the fundamental hypothesis that American naturalism evolved from American realism, as William Dean Howells, Stephen Crane, and Frank Norris had observed in their interviews and writings of the 1890s. (This intellectual movement from realism to naturalism is peculiar to American literary culture in the last decade of the nineteenth century. Critics a decade or two earlier insisted on a reversal of the relationship and on a broadly Western, transatlantic genealogy, whereby realism comes after, not before, naturalism. Indeed, Howells in his 1892 book, *Criticism and Fiction*, disparaged the naturalism of the French writer Emile Zola and used it as a foil to derive the tenets of realism.) Naturalism arguably refocused realism to confront the cultures and ideologies of American modernity, such as the social behaviors and attitudes brought about by the emergence of cities across the nation. In this sense, Dunbar's *The Uncalled* serves a threefold transitional function: as a point of generic transition from realism to naturalism, of formal transition from purported objectivity to unabashed subjectivity of narration and characterization, and of thematic transition from rural local-color to urban culture.

Indeed, any account of the formative stage of American literary naturalism must include Dunbar, beginning with *The Uncalled*. The novel not only engages literary naturalism per se but also accommodates the ideas of human uplift and redemption that run counter to the genre's tragic conventions. The novel is deterministic on its face—thanks to the title, *The Uncalled*—and probes the issues of spirituality, heritage, destiny, and the environment to explain social marginality and moral turpitude. Aside from a perceptive book review in the *New York Times* about the naturalist qualities of *The Uncalled,* American critics bemoaned Dunbar's departure from the minstrel variety of American literature and his embrace of the excessive didacticism, or the lack of reportorial objectivity, in naturalism. In contrast, the British press appreciated his literary experimentation and the novel's other merits.

Moreover, American critics of American literature at the turn of the twentieth century were racially exclusive. Howells and other critics categorized white writers, especially Crane and Norris, as the quintessential writers of literary naturalism. This categorization is a problem, for it illustrates the extent to which the cultural expectations of what blacks could and should write about blinded critics to Dunbar's excellence as a naturalist writer. The properties of *The Uncalled* suggest that, prior to Norris and Dreiser, Dunbar was already experimenting with literary ways of stretching realism in naturalist directions.

Indeed, naturalism provided the rhetorical and thematic means for Dunbar to tell the story of Frederick Brent. In the first part of the novel, Frederick (who also goes by Fred) accepts the Dexter community's conclusion that Methodist scruples and formal education can wash away the indignity of his birth and upbringing. Fred's mother, Margaret, was a housewife stigmatized for living in the dilapidated, lower-class section of Dexter and for marrying an abusive and often inebriated husband, Tom Brent. As an adolescent, Fred struggles through the divorce of his parents, the death of his mother, and the flight of his father. An unmarried and churchgoing woman, Miss Hester Prime, volunteers to discipline the motherless boy, overseeing his moral maturation with a biblical whip. Under her guardianship, Fred privately negotiates, and expresses anxiety over, the social and moral politics of conformity in his hometown, while she tries to steer him toward what she considers his calling: a professional future in Dexter's Methodist church.

At a key, climactic moment in the novel, when Fred matriculates at divinity school and prepares to deliver a sermon to a Dexter congregation, we see the extent to which his cynical view of the town's moral hypocrisy, which enables them to judge him, compromises his theological beliefs, spiritual purity, and personal happiness. In Fred's eyes, Dexter tends to equate his inheritance of familial blood with an inheritance of his parents' shameful morals and values. In predetermining his fate by interpreting his blood, however, Dexter has also created a self-fulfilling prophecy: the town always has the potential of willing this prophecy into reality by spreading rumors that the Brent family has lowered the town's ethical standards. In his struggle with such hypocrisy, Fred cries to himself, just prior to his sermon: "Is it Fate, God, or the devil that pursues me so?" *The Uncalled* illuminates Fred's engagement in a willful battle against the ideas and images of social determinism, as he rises from Dexter's "mean streets," flees his hometown when he can no longer deal with the hypocrisy, and encounters desolation in Cincinnati. While Fred searches for a boardinghouse in the city, he observes drunken adults and impoverished children lining the streets. The images horrify Fred, because they remind him of his family stigma, and rekindle his concern over whether he remains on a predetermined path toward tragedy.

Thanks to its thematic focus on human uplift and redemption, *The Uncalled* justifies Dunbar's association with the white and black authors of his era—namely, Howells, Edith Wharton, Frances E. W. Harper, and Pauline Hopkins—who were grappling with the pragmatics of social and moral uplift. The story line of intemperance in *The Uncalled* guides Dunbar's exploration of this theme. Once Fred finds his boardinghouse in Cincinnati, for example, he meets a young clerk, Mr. Perkins, who invites him to the nightclub of shame and sin, Meyer's Beer-Garden and Variety Hall. At the door of the club, Fred encounters an old man who tries to dissuade him and others from entering the club. The old man encourages them to attend a meeting later that night about the need for public temperance. Fred decides to attend the temperance meeting. There, for the attendees, the old man recounts his life, portraying himself as a man who, ultimately, has been elevated from his earlier squalor. At that moment, Fred realizes that the old man is Tom Brent, his own father, who then confesses that he plans to return to Dexter to make amends with his wife (who he does not yet know has died) and his son. The subplots of moral self-reform and spiritual regeneration, as they pertain to both Tom and Fred Brent, conclude with redemption overcoming tragedy.

Ultimately, Fred demonstrates the will to overcome his fate, despite the curse of his family. Tom Brent, after returning to Dexter, falls ill. Mr. Hodges learns of Mr. Brent's predicament and takes the sick man into his home; he then sends a telegram to Fred urging his return to Dexter. On his deathbed, in the home of Mr. and Mrs. Hodges—indeed, in the very room where Fred once slept under their guardianship—Mr. Brent repents before his son. At this final moment, after Fred blames his father for "ruining" his life by leaving him "a heritage of shame and evil," the son forgives the father. Fred then returns to Cincinnati, where he tries to clarify his relationship with God by attending a Congregational church and working in the name of "poor humanity." He commits himself to moral and spiritual autodidacticism, but it is a self-regeneration not entirely in biblical terms, as Miss Hester Prime would have liked: "I've been to a better school than the Bible Seminary. I haven't got many religious rules and formulas, but I'm trying to live straight and do what is right."

In Cincinnati, the sign of Fred's liberation from tradition, religion, and history is his newfound joy in having a girlfriend, Alice, who fills his life with happiness and emotional security. Alice helps Fred consummate not only his detachment from Dexter, but his maturation in the modern world as well. In this regard, the naturalism of *The Uncalled* represents not only a transition from local-color realism but also a slight break with the canon of naturalism, including Norris and especially Dreiser, which privileged men and their political interests, while characterizing women subjects in fiction as impeding male progress toward modernity. It illustrates the importance of individual will in overcoming environmental forces, even within the city. It shows how Fred can embrace modern civilization not despite but because of a respect for—or an anticipation of interaction with—a woman in his life. It presents a remarkable story of the human spirit, and resists portraying Fred, and even his father, as insurmountably degenerate. It is not a novel of tragedy, but a novel of triumph.

The Uncalled

Dedicated to my wife

Chapter 1

IT WAS ABOUT SIX O'CLOCK of a winter's morning. In the eastern sky faint streaks of gray had come and were succeeded by flashes of red, crimson-cloaked heralds of the coming day. It had snowed the day before, but a warm wind had sprung up during the night, and the snow had partially melted, leaving the earth showing through in ugly patches of yellow clay and sooty mud. Half despoiled of their white mantle, though with enough of it left to stand out in bold contrast to the bare places, the houses loomed up, black, dripping, and hideous. Every once in a while the wind caught the water as it trickled from the eaves, and sent it flying abroad in a chill unsparkling spray. The morning came in, cold, damp, and dismal.

At the end of a short, dirty street in the meanest part of the small Ohio town of Dexter stood a house more sagging and dilapidated in appearance than its disreputable fellows. From the foundation the walls converged to the roof, which seemed to hold its place less by virtue of nails and rafters than by faith. The whole aspect of the dwelling, if dwelling it could be called, was as if, conscious of its own meanness, it was shrinking away from its neighbors and into itself. A sickly light gleamed from one of the windows. As the dawn came into the sky, a woman came to the door and looked out. She was a slim woman, and her straggling, dusty-colored hair hung about an unpleasant sallow face. She shaded her eyes with her hand, as if the faint light could hurt those cold, steel-gray orbs. "It's mornin'," she said to those within. "I'll have to be goin' along to git my man's breakfast: he goes to work at six o'clock, and I 'ain't got a thing cooked in the house fur him. Some o' the rest o' you'll have to stay an' lay her out." She went back in and closed the door behind her.

"La, Mis' Warren, you ain't a-goin' a'ready? Why, there's everything to be done here yit: Margar't's to be laid out, an' this house has to be put into some kind of order before the undertaker comes."

"I should like to know what else I'm a-goin' to do, Mis' Austin. Charity begins at home. My man's got to go to work, an' he's got to have his breakfast: there's cares fur the livin' as well as fur the dead, I say, an' I don't believe in tryin' to be so good to them that's gone that you furgit them that's with you."

Mrs. Austin pinched up her shriveled face a bit more as she replied, "Well, somebody ought to stay. I know I can't, fur I've got a ter'ble big washin' waitin' fur me at home, an' it's been two nights sence I've had any sleep to speak of, watchin' here. I'm purty near broke down."

"That's jest what I've been a-sayin'," repeated Mrs. Warren. "There's cares fur the livin' as well as fur the dead; you'd ought to take care o' yoreself: first thing you know you'll be flat o' yore own back."

A few other women joined their voices in the general protest against staying. It was for all the world as if they had been anxious to see the poor woman out of the world, and, now that they knew her to be gone, had no further concern for her. All had something to do, either husbands to get off to work or labors of their own to perform.

A little woman with a weak voice finally changed the current of talk by saying, "Well, I guess I kin stay: there's some cold things at home that my man kin git, an' the childern'll git off to school by themselves. They'll all understand."

"That's right, Melissy Davis," said a hard-faced woman who had gone on about some work she was doing, without taking any notice of the clamorous deserters, "an' I'll stay with you. I guess I've got about as much work to do as any of you," she added, casting a cold glance at the women who were now wrapped up and ready to depart, "an' I wasn't so much of a friend of Margar't's as some of you, neither, but on an occasion like this I know what dooty is." And Miss Hester Prime closed her lips in a very decided fashion.

"Oh, well, some folks is so well off in money an' time that they kin afford to be liberal with a pore creature like Margar't, even ef they didn't have nothin' to do with her before she died."

Miss Prime's face grew sterner as she replied, "Margar't Brent wasn't my kind durin' life, an' that I make no bones o' sayin' here an' now; but when she got down on the bed of affliction I done what I could fur her along with the best of you; an' you, Mandy Warren, that's seen me here day in an' day out, ought to be the last one to deny that. Furthermore, I didn't advise her to leave her husband, as some people did, but I did put in a word an' help her to work so's to try to keep her straight afterwards, though it ain't fur me to be a-braggin' about what I done, even to offset them that didn't do nothin'."

This parting shot told, and Mrs. Warren flared up like a wax light. "It's a wonder yore old tracts an' the help you give her didn't keep her sober sometimes."

"Ef I couldn't keep her sober, I wasn't one o' them that set an' took part with her when she was gittin' drunk."

"'Sh! 'sh!" broke in Mrs. Davis: "ef I was you two I wouldn't go on that way. Margar't's dead an' gone now, an' what's past is past. Pore soul, she had a hard enough time almost to drive her to destruction; but it's all over now, an' we ought to put her away as peaceful as possible."

The women who had all been in such a hurry had waited at the prospect of an altercation, but, seeing it about to blow over, they bethought themselves of their neglected homes and husbands, and passed out behind the still irate Mrs. Warren, who paused long enough in earshot to say, "I hope that spiteful old maid'll have her hands full."

The scene within the room which the women had just left was anything but an inviting one. The place was miserably dirty. Margaret had never been a particularly neat housewife, even in her well days. The old rag carpet which disfigured the floor was worn into shreds and blotched with grease, for the chamber was cooking- and dining- as well as sleeping-room. A stove, red with rust, struggled to send forth some heat. The oily black kerosene lamp showed a sickly yellow flame through the grimy chimney.

On a pallet in one corner lay a child sleeping. On the bed, covered with a dingy sheet, lay the stark form out of which the miserable life had so lately passed.

The women opened the blinds, blew out the light, and began performing the necessary duties for the dead.

"Anyhow, let her body go clean before her Maker," said Miss Hester Prime, severely.

"Don't be too hard on the pore soul, Miss Hester," returned Mrs. Davis. "She had a hard time of it. I knowed Margar't when she wasn't so low down as in her last days."

"She oughtn't never to 'a' left her husband."

"Oh, ef you'd 'a' knowed him as I did, Miss Hester, you wouldn't never say that. He was a brute: sich beatin's as he used to give her when he was in liquor you never heerd tell of."

"That was hard, but as long as he was a husband he was a protection to her name."

"True enough. Protection is a good dish, but a beatin's a purty bitter sauce to take with it."

"I wonder what's ever become of Brent."

"Lord knows. No one 'ain't heerd hide ner hair o' him sence he went away from town. People thought that he was a-hangin' around tryin' to git a chance to kill Mag after she got her divorce from him, but all at once he packed off without sayin' a word to anybody. I guess he's drunk himself to death by this time."

When they had finished with Margaret, the women set to work to clean up the house. The city physician who had attended the dead woman in her last hours had reported the case for county burial, and the undertaker was momentarily expected.

"We'll have to git the child up an' git his pallet out of the way, so the floor kin be swept."

"A body hates to wake the pore little motherless dear."

"Perhaps, after all, the child is better off without her example."

"Yes, Miss Hester, perhaps; but a mother, after all, is a mother."

"Even sich a one as this?"

"Even sich a one as this."

Mrs. Davis bent over the child, and was about to lift him, when he stirred, opened his eyes, and sat up of his own accord. He appeared about five years of age. He might have been a handsome child, but hardship and poor feeding had taken away his infantile plumpness, and he looked old and haggard, even beneath the grime on his face. The kindly woman lifted him up and began to dress him.

"I want my mamma," said the child.

Neither of the women answered: there was something tugging at their heartstrings that killed speech.

Finally the little woman said, "I don't know ef we did right to let him sleep through it all, but then it was sich a horrible death."

When she had finished dressing the child, she led him to the bed and showed him his mother's face. He touched it with his little grimy finger, and then, as if, young as he was, the realization of his bereavement had fully come to him, he burst into tears.

Miss Hester turned her face away, but Mrs. Davis did not try to conceal her tears. She took the boy up in her arms and comforted him the best she could.

"Don't cry, Freddie," she said; "don't cry; mamma's—restin'. Ef you don't care, Miss Prime, I'll take him over home an' give him some breakfast, an' leave him with my oldest girl, Sophy. She kin stay out o' school today. I'll bring you back a cup o' tea, too; that is, ef you ain't afeared—"

"Afeared o' what?" exclaimed Miss Prime, turning on her.

"Well, you know, Miss Hester, bein' left, alone—ah—some people air funny about—"

"I'm no fool, Melissy Davis. Take the child an' go on."

Miss Hester was glad of the chance to be sharp. It covered the weakness to which she had almost given way at sight of the child's grief. She bustled on about her work when Mrs. Davis was gone, but her brow was knit into a wrinkle of deep thought. "A mother is a mother, after all," she mused aloud, "even sich a one."

Chapter 2

FOR HASTE, FOR UNADULTERATED despatch, commend me to the county burying. The body politic is busy and has no time to waste on an inert human body. It does its duty to its own interest and to the pauper dead when the body is dropped with all celerity into the ground. The county is philosophical: it says, "Poor devil, the world was unkind to him: he'll be glad to get out of it: we'll be doing him a favor to put him at the earliest moment out of sight and sound and feeling of the things that wounded him. Then, too, the quicker the cheaper, and that will make it easier on the taxpayers." This latter is so comforting! So the order is written, the funeral is rushed through, and the county goes home to its dinner, feeling well satisfied with itself—so potent are the consolations of philosophy at so many hundreds per year.

To this general order poor Margaret's funeral proved no exception. The morning after her decease she was shrouded and laid in her cheap pine coffin to await those last services which, in a provincial town, are the meed of saint and sinner alike. The room in which she lay was very clean—unnaturally so—from the attention of Miss Prime. Clean muslin curtains had been put up at the windows, and the one cracked mirror which the house possessed had been covered with white cloth. The lace-like carpet had been taken off the floor, and the boards had been scrubbed white. The little stove in the corner, now cold, was no longer red with rust. In a tumbler on a little table at Margaret's head stood the only floral offering that gave a touch of tenderness to the grim scene—a bunch of homegrown scarlet and white geraniums. Some woman had robbed her wintered room of this bit of brightness for the memory of the dead. The perfume of the flowers mingled heavily with the faint odor which pervades the chamber of death—an odor that is like the reminiscence of sorrow.

Like a spirit of order, with solemn face and quiet tread, Miss Hester moved about the room, placing one thing here, another there, but ever doing or changing something, all with maidenly neatness. What a childish fancy this is of humanity's, tiptoeing and whispering in the presence of death, as if one by an incautious word or a hasty step might wake the sleeper from such deep repose!

The service had been set for two o'clock in the afternoon. One or two women had already come in to "sit," but by half-past one the general congregation began to arrive and to take their places. They were mostly women. The hour of the day was partially responsible for this; but then men do not go to funerals anyway, if they can help it. They do not revel, like their sisters, in the exquisite pleasure of sorrow. Most of the women had known pain and loss themselves, and came with ready sympathy, willing, nay, anxious to be moved to tears. Some of them came dragging by one hand children, dressed stiffly, uncomfortably, and ludicrously—a medley of soiled ribbons, big collars, wide bows, and very short knickerbockers. The youngsters were mostly curious and ill-mannered, and ever and anon one had to be slapped by its mother into sniveling decorum. Mrs. Davis came in with one of her own children and leading the dead woman's boy by the hand. At this a buzz of whispered conversation began.

"Pore little dear," said one, as she settled the bow more securely under her own boy's sailor collar—"pore little dear, he's all alone in the world."

"I never did see in all my life sich a young child look so sad," said another.

"H'm!" put in a third; "in this world pore motherless children has plenty o' reason to look sad, I tell you."

She brushed the tears off the cheek of her little son whom she had slapped a moment before. She was tender now.

One woman bent down and whispered into her child's ear as she pointed with one cotton-gloved finger, "See, Johnny, see little Freddie, there; he 'ain't got no mother no more. Pore little Freddie! ain't you sorry fur him?" The child nodded, and gazed with open-eyed wonder at "little Freddie" as if he were a new species.

The curtains, stirred by the blast through the loose windows, flapped dismally, and the people drew their wraps about them, for the fireless room was cold. Steadily, insistently, the hive-like drone of conversation murmured on.

"I wonder who's a-goin' to preach the funeral," asked one.

"Oh, Mr. Simpson, of the Methodist Church, of course: she used to go to that church years ago, you know, before she backslid."

"That's jest what I've allus said about people that falls from grace. You know the last state o' that man is worse than the first."

"Ah, that's true enough."

"It's a-puttin' yore hand to the ploughshare an' then turnin' back."

"I wonder what the preacher'll have to say fur her. It's a mighty hard case to preach about."

"I'm wonderin' too what he'll say, an' where he'll preach her."

"Well, it's hard to tell. You know the Methodists believe that there's 'salvation to be found between the stirrup an' the ground.'"

"It's a mighty comfortin' doctern, too."

"An' then they do say that she left some dyin' testimony; though I 'ain't never heerd tell the straight of it."

"He can't preach her into heaven, o' course, after her life. Leastways, it don't hardly seem like it would be right an' proper."

"Well, I don't think he kin preach her into hell, neither. After a woman has gone through all that pore Margar't has, it seems to me that the Lord ought to give her some consideration, even if men don't."

"I do declare, Seely Matthews, with yore free thinkin' an' free speakin', you're put' nigh a infidel."

"No, I ain't no infidel, neither, but I ain't one o' them that sings, 'When all thy mercies, O my God,' and thinks o' the Lord as if He was a great big cruel man."

"Well, I don't neither; but—"

"'Sh! 'sh!"

The woman's declaration of principle was cut short by the entrance of the minister, the Rev. Mr. Simpson. He was a tall, gaunt man, in a coat of rusty black. His hair, of an indeterminate color, was slightly mixed with gray. A pair of bright gray eyes looked out from underneath bushy eyebrows. His lips were close set. His bony hands were large and ungainly. The Rev. Mr. Simpson had been a carpenter before he was "called." He went immediately to the stand where lay the Bible and hymnbook. He was followed by a man who had entered with him—a man with soft eyes and a kindly face. He was as tall as the pastor, and slender, but without the other's gauntness. He was evidently a church official of some standing.

With strange inappropriateness, the preacher selected and gave out the hymn:

> Sister, thou wast mild and lovely,
> Gentle as the summer's breeze.

With some misgivings, it was carried through in the wavering treble of the women and the straggling bass of the few men: then the kindly-faced man, whom the preacher addressed as "Brother Hodges," knelt and offered prayer. The supplication was very tender and childlike. Even by the light of faith he did not seek to penetrate the veil of divine intention, nor did he throw his javelin of prayer straight against the Deity's armor of eternal reserve. He left all to God, as a child lays its burden at its father's feet, and many eyes were moist as the people rose from their knees.

The sermon was a noisy and rather inconsequential effort. The preacher had little to say, but he roared that little out in a harsh, unmusical voice accompanied by much slapping of his hands and pounding of the table. Towards the end he lowered his voice and began to play upon the feelings of his willing hearers, and when he had won his meed of sobs and tears, when he had sufficiently probed old wounds and made them bleed afresh, when he had conjured up dead sorrows from the grave, when he had obscured the sun of heavenly hope with the vapors of earthly grief, he sat down, satisfied.

The people went forward, some curiously, some with sympathy, to look their last on the miserable dead. Mrs. Davis led the weeping child forward and held him up for a last gaze on his mother's face. The poor geraniums were wiped and laid by the dead hands, and then the undertaker glided in like a stealthy, black-garmented ghost. He screwed the pine-top down, and the coffin was borne out to the hearse. He clucked to his horses, and, with Brother Hodges and the preacher in front, and Mrs. Davis, Miss Prime, and the motherless boy behind, the little funeral train moved down the street towards the graveyard, a common but pathetic spectacle.

Mrs. Warren had remained behind to attend to the house. She watched the short procession out of sight. "I guess Margar't didn't have no linen worth havin'," she said to herself, "but I'll jest look." And look she did, but without success. In disappointment and disgust she went out and took the streamer of dusty black and dingy white crape from the door where it had fluttered, and, bringing it in, laid it on the empty trestles, that the undertaker might find it when he came for them. She took the cloth off the mirror, and then, with one searching look around to see that she had missed nothing worth taking, she went out, closing and locking the door behind her.

"I guess I'm as much entitled to anything Mag had as anyone else," said Mrs. Warren.

Chapter 3

BY COMMON CONSENT, AND without the formality of publication or proclamation, the women had agreed to meet on the day after the funeral for the purpose of discussing what was best to be done with the boy Fred. From the moment that Mrs. Davis had taken charge of him, he had shown a love for her and confidence in her care that had thoroughly touched that good woman's heart. She would have liked nothing better than to keep him herself. But there were already five hungry little Davises, and any avoidable addition to the family was out of the question. To be sure, in the course of time there were two more added to the number, but that was unavoidable, and is neither here nor there. The good woman sat looking at the boy the night after his mother had been laid away. He sat upon the floor among her own children, playing in the happy forgetfulness of extreme youth. But to the mother's keen eye there was still a vague sadness in his bearing. Involuntarily, the scene and conditions were changed, and, instead of poor Margaret, she herself had passed away and was lying out there in a new-made grave in bleak and dreary Woodland. She thought how her own bairns would be as motherless and forlorn as the child before her, and yet not quite, either, for they had a father who loved them in his own quiet undemonstrative way. This should have consoled her in the sorrows she had conjured up, but, like a woman, she thought of the father helpless and lonely when she had gone, with the children huddled cheerlessly about him, and a veil of tears came between her and the youngsters on the floor. With a great rush of tenderness, she went and picked the motherless boy up and laid his head on her breast.

"Pore Freddie," she said, "I wish you could stay here all the time and play with the other little ones."

The child looked up at her with wondering eyes. "I kin stay till mamma comes back," he answered.

"But, Freddie dear, mamma won't come back any more. She's"—the woman hesitated—"she's in heaven."

"I want my mamma to come back," moaned the child. "I don't want her to stay in heaven."

"But you mustn't cry, Freddie; an', some day, you kin go an' see mamma."

The child's curiosity got the better of his grief. He asked, "Is heaven far, Mis' Davis?"

"Yes, dear, awful far," she answered. But she was wrong. Heaven is not far from the warm heart and tender hands of a good woman.

The child's head drooped, and he drowsed in her arms.

"Put him to bed, Melissy—pore little fellow," said her husband in husky tones. He had been listening and watching them around the edge of his paper. The child slept on, while the woman undressed him and laid him in the bed.

On the morrow the women dropped in one by one, until a half-dozen or more were there, to plan the boy's future. They were all poor, and most of them had families of their own. But all hoped that there might be some plan devised whereby Margaret's boy might find a refuge without going to the orphans' asylum, an institution which is the detestation of women. Mrs. Davis, in expressing her feelings, expressed those of all the others: "I hate so to think of the pore little feller goin' to one o' them childern's homes. The boys goin' around in them there drab clothes o' theirs allus look like pris'ners to me, an' they ain't much better off."

"An' then childern do learn so much weekedness in them places from the older ones," put in another.

"Oh, as fur that matter, he'll learn devilment soon enough anywhere," snapped Mrs. Warren, "with that owdacious father o' his before him. I wouldn't take the child by no means, though his mother an' me was friends, fur blood's bound to tell, an' with sich blood as he's got in him I don't know what he'll come to, an' I'm shore I don't want to be a-raisin' no gallus-birds."

The women felt rather relieved that Mrs. Warren so signally washed her hands of Freddie. That was one danger he had escaped. The woman in question had, as she said, been a close friend of Margaret's, and, as such, an aider in her habits of intemperance. It had been apprehended that her association with the mother might lead her to take the child.

"I'd like to take Freddie myself," Mrs. Davis began again, "but with my five, an' John out o' work half the time, another mouth to feed an' another pair o' feet to cover would mean a whole lot. Though I do think that ef I was dead an' my childern was sent to that miserable orphans' home, I'd turn over in my grave."

"It's a pity we don't know some good family that 'ain't got no childern that 'ud take him an' bring him up as their own son," said a little woman who took *The Hearthside*.

"Sich people ain't growin' on trees no place about Dexter," Mrs. Warren sniffed.

"Well, I'm sure I've read of sich things. Ef the child was in a book it 'ud happen to him, but he ain't. He's a flesh and blood youngster an' a-livin' in Dexter."

"You couldn't give us no idee what to do, could you, Mis' Austin?"

"Lord love you, Mis' Davis, I've jest been a-settin' here purty nigh a-thinkin' my head off, but I 'ain't seen a gleam of light yit. You know how I feel an' jest how glad I'd be to do something, but then my man growls about the three we've got."

"That's jest the way with my man," said the little woman who took her ideas of life from the literature in *The Hearthside*. "He allus says that pore folks oughtn't to have so many childern."

"Well, it's a blessin' that Margar't didn't have no more, fur goodness knows it's hard enough disposin' o' this one."

Just then a tap came at Mrs. Davis's door, and she opened it to admit Miss Hester Prime.

"I'm ruther late gittin' here," said the newcomer, "but I've been a-neglectin' my work so in the last couple o' days that I've had a power of it to do today to ketch up."

"Oh, we're so glad you've come!" said one of the women. "Mebbe you kin help us out of our fix. We're in sich a fix about little Freddie."

"We don't want to send the pore little dear to the childern's home," broke in another.

"It's sich an awful place fur young childern—"

"An' they do look so pitiful—"

"An' learn so much weekedness."

And, as is the manner of women in council, they all began talking at once, pouring into the newcomer's ears all the suggestions and objections, hopes and fears, that had been made or urged during their conference.

To it all Miss Hester listened, and there was a soft glow on her face the while; but then she had been walking, which may account for the flush. The child, all unconscious that his destiny was being settled, was playing with two of the little Davises at the other end of the room. The three days of good food, good treatment, and pleasant surroundings had told on him, and he looked less forlorn and more like the child that he was. He was clean. His brown eyes were sparkling with amusement, and his brown hair was brushed up into the damp "roach" so dear to a woman's heart. He was, thus, a far less forbidding sight than on the morning of his mother's death, when, dingy and haggard, he rose from his dirty pallet. As she listened to the varied remarks of her associates, Miss Hester allowed her eyes to wander to the child's face, and for a moment a tenderer expression grew about her lips, but in an instant it was gone, and, as if she had been near committing herself to folly, she made amends by drawing her countenance into more than its usually severe lines.

Mrs. Warren, who was always ready with a stab, and who had not forgotten her encounter of two days ago, spoke up with a little malicious laugh. "Miss Hester 'ain't got no family: mebbe she might take the child. 'Pears like she ought to be fond o' childern."

Mrs. Davis immediately came to the rescue. "We don't expect no sich thing of Miss Hester. She's never been around childern, an' don't know nothin' about takin' keer o' them; an' boys air hard to manage, anyhow."

"Oh, I should think Miss Hester could manage 'most anything," was the sneering rejoinder.

The women were aghast at such insolence. They didn't know what the effect might be on Miss Prime. They looked at her in alarm. Her cold gray eye impaled Mrs. Warren for an instant only, and then, paying no more attention to her, she said quietly, "I was thinkin' this whole matter over while I was finishin' up my work to come here, an', says I to myself, 'Now there's Melissy Davis—she's the very one that 'ud be a mother to that child,' says I, 'an' she'd bring him up right as a child should be brought up.' I don't know no more mannerly, nice-appearin' childern in this neighborhood, or the whole town, fur that matter, than Melissy's—'"

"Oh, Miss Hester!" faltered Mrs. Davis.

But Miss Prime went on, unheeding the interruption. "Thinks I, 'Melissy's got a houseful already, an' she can't take another.' Then you comes into my mind, Mis' Austin, an' says I, 'La me! she's got three herself, an' is young yit; she'll have her hands full to look after her own family.' Well, I thought of you all, an' some of you had families, an' some of you had to go out fur day's work; an' then there's some people's hands I wouldn't want to see the child fall into." (This with an annihilating glance in Mrs. Warren's direction.) "You know what the Bible says about the sins of the father; well, that child needs proper raisin': so in this way the Lord showed it to me that it was my dooty to take up the burden myself."

First there was an absolute silence of utter astonishment, and then, "Oh, Miss Hester!" broke from a full chorus of voices.

"You don't reelly mean it, Miss Hester?" said Mrs. Davis.

"I do that; but I want you all to understand that it ain't a matter of pleasure or desire with me; it's dooty. Ef I see a chance to save a soul from perdition an' don't take it, I am responsible, myself, to the Lord for that soul."

The women were almost too astounded to speak, Mrs. Warren not less than the rest of them. She had made her suggestion in derision, and here it was being acted upon in sober earnest. She was entirely routed.

"Now, Melissy, ef there ain't no one that disagrees with me, you might as well pack up what few things the child has, an' I'll take him along."

No one objected, and the few things were packed up. "Come, Freddie," said Mrs. Davis tremulously, "get on yore hat." The child obeyed. "You're a-goin' to be Miss Hester's little boy now. You must be good."

Miss Prime held out her hand to him, but the child drew back and held to his protectress's skirt. A hurt expression came into the spinster's face. It was as if the great sacrifice she was making was being belittled and rejected by a child. Mrs. Warren laughed openly.

"Come, Freddie, be nice now, dear; go with Miss Hester."

"I want to stay with you," cried the child.

"Pore little dear!" chorused the women.

"But Mis' Davis can't keep the little boy; now he must go with Miss Prime, an' sometimes he kin come an' see Mis' Davis an' play with John an' Harriet. Won't that be nice?"

"I want to stay with you."

"Come, Frederick," said Miss Prime.

"Go now, like a good boy," repeated Mrs. Davis. "Here's a copper fur you; take it in yore little hand—that's a man. Now kiss me good-bye. Kiss John an' Harriet."

The child, seeing that he must go, had given up resistance, and, doing as he was bidden, took Miss Prime's hand, sobbingly. Some of us do not learn so soon to bow to the inevitable.

"Good-bye, ladies. I must git back to my work," said Miss Hester.

"Good-bye, good-bye, Miss Hester," came the echo.

The moment the door closed behind her and her charge, there was a volley of remarks:

"Oh, I do hope she'll be good to him."

"I wonder how she'll manage him."

"Pore child, he didn't want to go at all."

"Who'd have thought it of Miss Hester?"

"I wish I could have kept him myself," said Mrs. Davis, tearfully. "It hurt my heart to see him cling to me so."

"Never you mind, Melissy Davis; you've done yore whole dooty as well as you could."

Mrs. Warren rose and put her shawl over her head preparatory to going. "As fur my part," she said, "I'd 'a' ruther seen that child in the childern's home, devilment or no devilment, than where he is. He won't dare to breathe from this hour on."

The women were silent for a moment, and then Mrs. Davis said, "Well, Miss Hester's well-meanin'."

Chapter 4

AT THE TOP OF the mean street on which Margaret's house was situated, and looking down upon its meaner neighbors in much the same way that its mistress looked upon the denizens of the street, stood Miss Prime's cottage. It was not on the mean street—it would have disdained to be—but sat exactly facing it in prim watchfulness over the unsavory thoroughfare which ran at right angles. The cottage was one and a half stories in height, and the upper half-story had two windows in front that looked out like a pair of accusing eyes. It was painted a dull lead color. In summer the front yard was filled with flowers, hollyhocks, bachelor's-buttons, sweet-william, and a dozen other varieties of blooms. But they were planted with such exactness and straightness that the poor flowers looked cramped and artificial and stiff as a party of angular ladies dressed in bombazine. Here was no riot nor abandon in growth. Everything had its place, and stayed therein or was plucked up.

"I jest can't abide to see flowers growin' every which way," Miss Prime used to remark, "fur all the world like a neighborhood with different people's children traipsin' through everybody else's house. Everything in order, is my motto."

Miss Hester had nearly arrived at her fortieth milestone; and she effected the paradox of looking both younger and older than her age. Younger, because she had always taken excellent care of herself. Her form had still much of the roundness of youth, and her step was sprightly and firm. She looked older than her age, because of the strong lines in her face, the determined set of her lips, and the general air of knowledge and self-sufficiency which pervaded her whole being. Throughout her life she had sacrificed everything to duty, whether it was the yearning of her own heart or the feelings of those who loved her. In the world about her she saw so much of froth and frivolity that she tried to balance matters by being especially staid and stern herself. She did not consider that in the seesaw of life it takes more than one person to toss up the weight of the world's wickedness. Her existence was governed by rigid rules, from which she never departed.

It is hard to explain just what Miss Hester's position was among the denizens of the poorer quarter. She was liked and disliked, admired and feared. She would descend upon her victims with unasked counsel and undesired tracts. Her voice was a trumpet of scathing invective against their shiftlessness, their untidiness, and their immorality, but her hand was as a horn of plenty in straitened times, and her presence in sickness was a comfort. She made no pretence to being good-hearted; in fact, she resented the term as applied to herself. It was all duty with her.

Up through the now dismantled garden to the prim cottage she led the boy Fred. The child had not spoken a word since he had left the house of his friend. His little heart seemed to be suddenly chilled within him. Miss Hester had been equally silent. Her manner was constrained and embarrassed. She had, indeed, tried to find some words of soothing and encouragement to say to the child, such as she had heard Melissa Davis use; but she could not. They were not a part of her life's vocabulary. Several times she had essayed to speak, but the sentences that formed in her mind seemed so absurd and awkward that she felt them better unsaid.

It is true that every natural woman has the maternal instinct, but unless she has felt the soft face of a babe at her breast and looked down into its eyes as it drew its life from her life, she can know nothing of that freemasonry of womanhood which, by some secret means too deep and subtle for the knowledge of outsiders, wins the love of childhood. It is not so with men, because the childish mind does not demand so much of them, even though they be fathers. To be convinced, look about you and see how many more bachelors than maids are favorites with children.

Once within the house, Miss Hester was at an entire loss as to what to do with her charge. She placed him in a chair, where he sat disconsolately. She went to the bookshelves and laid her hand upon "Pilgrim's Progress"; then she reflected that Freddie was just five years old, and she allowed a smile to pass over her face. But her perplexity instantly chased the expression away. "How on airth am I a-goin' to do any work?" she asked herself. "I'm shore I can't set down an' tell that child stories all the time, as I've heerd tell o' folks doin'. What shall I do with him?" She had had a vague idea that the time of children was taken up in some way. She knew, of course, that they had to be washed and dressed, that they had to eat three times a day, and after all to sleep; but what was to be done with them in the meantime?

"Oh," sighed the poor woman, "if he was only old enough to go to school!" The wish was not entirely unmotherly, as motherhood goes in these days, for it is not an unusual thing for mothers to send their babes off to kindergarten as soon as they begin to babble, in order to be relieved of the responsibility of their care. But neither wishes nor hopes availed. It was a living, present situation with which Miss Hester had to grapple. Suddenly she bethought herself that children like pictures, and she secured from the shelf a copy of the "Bible Looking-Glass." This she opened and spread out on the child's knees. He glanced at it a moment or two, and then began to turn the leaves, his eyes riveted on the engravings. Miss Hester congratulated herself, and slipped out to work. The thought came to her, of course, that the novelty of "Bible Looking-Glasses" couldn't remain for ever, but she put the idea by in scorn. "Sufficient unto the day is the evil thereof." The book was good while it lasted. It entertained the child and gave him valuable moral lessons. This was the woman's point of view. To Fred there was no suggestion of moral lessons. It was merely a lot of very fine pictures, and when Miss Prime had gone he relaxed some of his disconsolate stiffness and entered into the contemplation of them with childish zest. His guardian, however, did not abandon her vigilance, and in a few minutes she peeped through the door from the kitchen, where she was working, to see how her charge got on. The sight which met her eyes made her nearly drop the cup which she held in her hand and with which she had been measuring out flour for a cupcake. With the book spread out before him, Freddie was lying flat on his stomach on the floor, with his little heels contentedly kicking the air. His attitude was the expression of the acme of childish satisfaction.

Miss Prime's idea of floors was that they were to be walked on, scrubbed, measured, and carpeted; she did not remember in all the extent of her experience to have seen one used as a reading-desk before. But she withdrew without a word: the child was quiet, and that was much.

About this time, anyone observing the cottage would have seen an old-fashioned phaeton, to which a plump old nag was hitched, driven up to the door and halted, and a man alight and enter at the gate. If the observer had been at Margaret's funeral, he would instantly have recognized the man as the Rev. Mr. Simpson's assistant, Mr. Hodges. The man walked deliberately around to the kitchen, and, tapping at the door, opened it without ceremony and went in, calling out, "Miss Hester, Miss Hester, I'm a-runnin' right in on you."

"I do declare, 'Liphalet Hodges, you do beat all fur droppin' in on a body at unexpected times."

"Well, I guess you're right. My comin' 's a good deal like the second comin' o' the Son o' man'll be. I guess you're right."

To Miss Prime, Eliphalet Hodges was always unexpected, although he had been dropping in this way before her mother and father died, twenty years gone.

"Well, I 'low, 'Liphalet, that you've heerd the news."

"There ain't no grass grows under the feet of the talkers in this town, I tell you."

"Dear me! a body can't turn aroun' without settin' a whole forest of tongues a-waggin' every which way."

"Oh, well, Miss Hester, we got to 'low that to yore sex. The women folks must talk."

"My sex! It ain't my sex only: I know plenty o' men in this town who air bigger gossips 'n the women. I'll warrant you didn't git this piece o' news from no woman."

"Well, mebbe I didn't, but I ca'c'late there wa'n't no men there to git it fust hand."

"Oh, I'll be bound some o' the women had to go an' tell a man the fust thing: some women can't git along without the men."

"An' then, ag'in, some of 'em kin, Miss Hester; some of 'em kin."

"You'd jest as well start out an' say what you want to say without a-beatin' about the bush. I know, jest as well as I know I'm a-livin', that you've come to tell me that I was a fool fur takin' that child. 'Liphalet, don't pertend: I know it."

"Oh, no, Miss Hester; I wouldn't dast do nothin' like that; you know, 'He that calleth his brother a fool is in danger o' hell fire,' an' I 'low the Lord don't make it no easier when it happens to be a sister. No, Miss Hester, you know yore own business best, an' you've got along this fur without bein' guided by people. I guess you'll git through; but a child, Miss Hester, don't you think that it's a leetle bit resky?"

"Resky? I don't see why. The child ain't a-goin' to eat me or burn the house down."

"No, no—none o' that—I don't mean that at all; but then, you see, you 'ain't never had no—that is—you 'ain't had much experunce in the bringin' up o' children, specially boys."

"Much! I 'ain't had none. But I've been brought up."

"That's true, that's true, an' a mighty good job yore mother made of it, too. I don't know of no spryer or stirrin'er woman around here at yore age."

"At my age! 'Liphalet, you do talk as ef I was about fifty."

"Well, ef I do, I ain't a sayin' what I want to say, so I'd better hush. Where is the little fellow?"

For answer, Miss Prime pushed the door open and bade him peep. Freddie was still upon the floor, absorbed in his book. The man's face lighted up: he pulled the door to long enough to say, "I tell you, Miss Hester, that boy's a-goin' to make a great reader or a speaker or somethin'. Jest look how wrapped up he is in that book."

"Well, I do hope an' pray to goodness that he'll make somethin' better than his father ever made."

"Ef he don't under yore trainin', it'll be because there ain't nothin' in him.— Come here, Freddie," called Hodges, pushing the door open, and holding out his hand with a smile. The child got up from the floor and came and put his hand in the outstretched one.

"Well, I declare!" exclaimed Miss Hester. "I tried my level best to git that child to make up with me, an' he wouldn't."

"It's jest like I say, Miss Hester: you 'ain't never had no experunce in raisin' childern."

"An' how many have you ever raised, 'Liphalet?"

The bachelor acknowledged defeat by a sheepish smile, and turned again to the child. "You want to go a-ridin' in my buggy, Freddie?"

"Yes, sir," said the child, unhesitatingly.

"All right; Uncle 'Liph'll take him out fur a while. Git his hat an' wrap him up, Miss Hester, so Jack Frost can't ketch him."

The man stood smiling down into the child's face: the boy, smiling back, tightened his grasp on the big hand. They were friends from that moment, Eliphalet Hodges and Fred.

They went out to the old phaeton, with Miss Prime's parting injunction ringing after them, "Don't keep that child out in the cold too long, 'Liphalet, an' bring him back here croupy."

"Oh, now, don't you trouble yourself, Miss Hester: me an' Freddie air a-goin' to git along all right. We ain't a-goin' to freeze, air we, Freddie, boy? Ah, not by a long sight; not ef Uncle 'Liph knows hisself."

All the time the genial man was talking, he was tucking the lap-robe snugly about the child and making him comfortable. Then he clucked to the old mare, and they rattled away.

There was a far-away look in Miss Prime's eyes as she watched them till they turned the corner and were out of sight. "I never did see sich a man as 'Liphalet Hodges. Why, a body'd think that he'd been married an' raised a whole houseful o' childern. He's worse'n a old hen. An' it's marvelous the way Frederick took to him. Everybody calls the child Freddie. I must learn to call him that: it will make him feel more home-like, though it does sound foolish."

She went on with her work, but it was interrupted every now and then by strange fits of abstraction and reverie, an unusual thing for this bustling and practical spinster. But then there are few of us but have had our hopes and dreams, and it would be unfair to think that Miss Hester was an exception. For once she had broken through her own discipline, and in her own kitchen was spending precious moments in dreams, and all because a man and a child had rattled away in a rickety buggy.

Chapter 5

"Goodness gracious, Mis' Smith," exclaimed Mrs. Martin, rushing excitedly into the house of her next-door neighbor, "you'd ought to seen what I seen jest now."

"Do tell, Mis' Martin! What on airth was it?"

"Oh, I'm shore you'd never guess in the wide, wide world."

"An' I'm jest as shore that I ain't a-goin' to pester my head tryin' to: so go on an' tell me what it was."

"Lawsy me! what next'll happen, an' what does things mean, anyhow?"

"I can't tell you. Fur my part, I 'ain't heerd what 'things' air yit." Mrs. Smith was getting angry.

"My! Mis' Smith, don't git so impatient. Give me time to git my breath: it'll be enough, when I do tell you, to take away yore breath, jest like it did mine."

"Sallie Martin, you do beat all fur keepin' a body on the hooks."

"'T ain't my fault, Mis' Smith. I declare I'm too astonished to speak. You know I was a-standin' in my window, not a-thinkin' nor expectin' nothin', jest like any person would, you know—"

"Yes, yes; go on."

"I was jest a-lookin' down the street, careless, when who should I see drive up to Miss Prime's door, an' hitch his hoss an' go in, but Brother 'Liphalet Hodges!"

"Well, sakes alive, Sallie Martin, I hope you ain't a-considerin' that strange. Why, you could 'a' seen that very same sight any time these fifteen years."

"But wait a minute till I tell you. I ain't done yit, by no means. The strange part 'ain't come. I thought I'd jest wait at the window and see how long Brother Hodges would stay: not that it was any o' my bus'ness, of course, or that I wanted to be a spyin' on anybody, but sorter fur—fur cur'osity, you know."

"Cert'n'y," said Mrs. Smith, feelingly. She could sympathize with such a sentiment.

"Well, after a while he come out a-smilin' as pleasant as a basket o' chips; an' I like to fell through the winder, fur he was a-leadin' by the hand—who do you suppose?"

"I 'ain't got a mortal idea who," said Mrs. Smith, "unless it was Miss Hester, an' they're married at last."

"No, indeed, 't wa'n't her. It was that little Brent boy that his mother died the other day."

"Sallie Martin, what air you a-tellin' me?"

"It's the gospel truth, Melviny Smith, as shore as I'm a-settin' here. Now what does it mean?"

"The good Lord only knows. Leadin' that little Brent boy? Ef it wasn't you a-settin' there tellin' me this, Mis' Martin, I wouldn't believe it. You don't supposed Hodges has took him to raise, do you?"

"How in the name of mercy is he goin' to raise a child, when there ain't no women folks about his house 'ceptin' old Marier, an' she so blind an' rheumaticky that she kin sca'cely git about?"

"Well, what's he a-doin' with the child, then?"

"That's jest what I'm a-goin' to find out. I'm a-goin' down to Miss Prime's. Len' me yore shawl, Melviny."

"You ain't never goin' to dare to ask her, air you?"

"You jest trust me to find things out without givin' myself away. I won't never let her know what I want right out, but I'll talk it out o' her."

"What a woman you air, Sallie Martin!" said Mrs. Smith, admiringly. "But do hurry back an' tell me what she says: I'm jest dyin' to know."

"I'll be back in little or no time, because I can't stay, nohow."

Mrs. Martin threw the borrowed shawl over her head and set off down the street. She and her friend were not dwellers on the mean street, and so they could pretend to so nearly an equal social footing with Miss Prime as to admit of an occasional neighborly call.

Through the window Miss Prime saw her visitor approaching, and a grim smile curved the corners of her mouth. "Comin' fur news," muttered the spinster. "She'll git all she wants before she goes." But there was no trace of suspicion in her manner as she opened the door at Mrs. Martin's rap.

"Hey oh, Miss Hester, busy as usual, I see."

"Yes, indeed. People that try to do their dooty 'ain't got much time fur rest in this world."

"No, indeed; it's dig, dig, dig, and work, work, work."

"Take off yore shawl an' set down, Sallie. It's a wonder you don't take yore death o' cold or git plum full o' neuralgy, a-runnin' around in this weather with nothin' but a shawl over yore head."

"La, Miss Hester, they say that worthless people's hard to kill. It ain't allus true, though, fur there was poor Margar't Brent, she wasn't worth much, but my! she went out like a match."

"Yes, but matches don't go out until their time ef they're held down right; an' it's jest so with people."

"That's true enough, Miss Hester. Was you to Margar't's funeral?"

"Oh, yes, I went."

"Did you go out to the cimetery?"

"Oomph huh."

"Did she look natural?"

"Jest as natural as one could expect after a hard life an' a hard death."

"Pore Margar't!" Miss Martin sighed. There was a long and embarrassed silence. Miss Prime's lips were compressed, and she seemed more aggressively busy than usual. She bustled about as if every minute were her last one. She brushed off tables, set chairs to rights, and tried the golden-brown cupcake with a straw to see if it were done. Her visitor positively writhed with curiosity and discomfiture. Finally she began again. "Margar't only had one child, didn't she?"

"Yes, that was all."

"Pore little lamb. Motherless childern has a hard time of it."

"Indeed, most of 'em do."

"Do you know what's become of the child, Miss Hester?"

"Yes, I do, Sallie Martin, an' you do too, or you wouldn't be a-settin' there beatin' about the bush, askin' me all these questions."

This sudden outburst gave Mrs. Martin quite a turn, but she exclaimed, "I declare to goodness, Miss Hester, I 'ain't heerd a livin' thing about it, only—"

She checked herself, but her relentless hostess caught at the word and demanded, "Only what, Mis' Martin?"

"Well, I seen Brother 'Liphalet Hodges takin' him away from here in his buggy—"

"An' so you come down to see what was what, eh, so's you could be the first to tell the neighborhood?"

"Now, Miss Hester, you know that I ain't one o' them that talks, but I do feel sich an interest in the pore motherless child, an' when I seen Brother Hodges a-takin' him away, I thought perhaps he was a-goin' to take him to raise."

"Well, Brother Hodges ain't a-goin' to take him to raise."

"Mercy sakes! Miss Hester, don't git mad, but who is?"

"I am, that's who."

"Miss Prime, what air you a-sayin'? You shorely don't mean it. What kin you do with a child?"

"I kin train him up in the way he ought to go, an' keep him out o' other people's houses an' the street."

"Well, o' course, that's somethin'," said Mrs. Martin, weakly.

"Somethin'? Why, it's everything."

The visitor had now gotten the information for which she was looking, and was anxious to be gone. She was absolutely bursting with her news.

"Well, I must be goin'," she said, replacing her shawl and standing in embarrassed indecision. "I only run in fur a minute. I hope you 'ain't got no hard feelin's at my inquisitiveness."

"Not a bit of it. You wanted to know, an' you come and asked, that's all."

"I hope you'll git along all right with the child."

"I sha'n't stop at hopin'. I shall take the matter to the Lord in prayer."

"Yes, He knows best. Good-bye, Miss Hester."

"Good-bye, Sallie; come in ag'in." The invitation sounded a little bit sarcastic, and once more the grim smile played about Miss Prime's mouth.

"I 'low," she observed to herself, as she took the cake from the oven for the last time, tried it, and set it on the table—"I 'low that I did give Sallie Martin one turn. I never did see sich a woman fur pryin' into other folks' business."

Swift are the wings of gossip, and swift were the feet of Mrs. Sallie Martin as she hurried back to tell the news to her impatient friend, who listened speechless with enjoyment and astonishment.

"Who would 'a' thought you could 'a' talked it out o' her so?" she gasped.

"Oh, I led her right along tell she told me everything," said Mrs. Martin, with a complacency which, remembering her reception, she was far from feeling.

Shortly after her departure, and while, no doubt, reinforced by Mrs. Smith, she was still watching at the window, 'Liphalet Hodges drove leisurely up to the door again.

"Well, Freddie," he said, as he helped the child to alight, "we've had a great time together, we have, an' we ain't frozen, neither: I told Miss Prime that she needn't be afeared. Don't drop yore jumpin'-jack, now, an' be keerful an' don't git yore hands on yore apron, 'cause they're kind o' sticky. Miss Hester 'u'd take our heads off ef we come back dirty."

The child's arms were full of toys—a jumping-jack, a climbing monkey, a popgun, and the etceteras of childish amusement—and his pockets and cheeks bulged with candy.

"La, 'Liphalet," exclaimed Miss Prime, when she saw them, "what on airth have you been a-buyin' that child—jumpin'-jacks an' sich things? They ain't a bit o' good, 'ceptin' to litter up a house an' put lightness in childern's minds. Freddie, what's that on yore apron? Goodness me! an' look at them hands—candy! 'Liphalet Hodges, I did give you credit fur better jedgment than this. Candy is the cause o' more aches an' pains than poison; an' some of it's reely colored with ars'nic. How do you expect a child to grow up healthy an' with sound teeth when you feed him on candy?"

"Now, Miss Hester, now, now, now. I don't want to be a-interferin' with yore bus'ness; but it's jest like I said before, an' I will stick to it, you 'ain't never had no experunce in raisin' children. They can't git along jest on meat an' bread an' jam: they need candy—an'—ah—candy—an' sich things." Mr. Hodges ended lamely, looking rather guiltily at the boy's bulging pockets. "A little bit ain't a-goin' to hurt no child."

"'Liphalet, I've got a dooty to perform towards this motherless child, an' I ain't a-goin' to let no foolish notion keep me from performin' it."

"Miss Hester, I'm a-tryin' to follow Him that was a father to the fatherless an' a husband to the widow—strange, that was made only to the widow—an' I've got somethin' of a idee o' dooty myself. You may think I'm purty presumptuous, but

I've took a notion into my head to kind o' help along a-raisin' Freddie. I ain't a-goin' to question yore authority, or nothin', but I thought mebbe you'd len' me the child once in a while to kind o' lighten up that old lonesome place o' mine: I know that Freddie won't object."

"Oh, 'Liphalet, do go 'long: I scarcely know whether you air a man or a child, sometimes."

"There's One that says, 'Except you become as a little child'—"

"'Liphalet, will you go 'long home?"

"I 'spect I'd better be gittin' along.—Goodbye, Freddie; be a good boy, an' some day I'll take you up to my house an' let you ride old Bess around.—Goodbye, Miss Hester." And as he passed out to his buggy he whistled tenderly something that was whistled when he was a boy.

Chapter 6

THE LIFE OF ONE boy is much like that of another. They all have their joys and their griefs, their triumphs and their failures, their loves and their hates, their friends and their foes, much as men have them in that maturer life of which the days of youth are an epitome. It would be rather an uninteresting task, and an entirely thankless one, to follow in detail the career of Frederick Brent as he grew from childhood to youth. But in order to understand certain traits that developed in his character, it will be necessary to note some, at least, of the circumstances that influenced his early life.

While Miss Prime grew to care for him in her own unemotional way, she had her own notions of how a boy should be trained, and those notions seemed to embody the repression of every natural impulse. She reasoned thus: "Human beings are by nature evil: evil must be crushed: *ergo*, everything natural must be crushed." In pursuance of this principle, she followed out a deliberate course of restriction, which, had it not been for the combating influence of Eliphalet Hodges, would have dwarfed the mental powers of the boy and cramped his soul beyond endurance. When he came of an age to play marbles, he was forbidden to play, because it was, to Miss Hester's mind, a species of gambling. Swimming was too dangerous to be for a moment considered. Fishing, without necessity, was wanton cruelty. Flying kites was foolishness and a waste of time.

The boy had shown an aptitude at his lessons that had created in his guardian's mind some ambition for him, and she held him down to his books with rigid assiduity. He was naturally studious, but the feeling that he was being driven made his tasks repellent, although he performed them without outward sign of rebellion, while he fumed within.

His greatest relaxations were his trips to and from his old friend Hodges. If Miss Prime crushed him, this gentle soul comforted him and smoothed out his ruffled feelings. It was this influence that kept him from despair. Away from his guardian, he was as if a chain that galled his flesh had been removed. And yet he could not hate Miss Hester, for it was constantly impressed upon him that all was being done for his good, and the word "duty" was burned like a fiery cross upon his heart and brain.

There is a bit of the pagan in every natural boy, and to give him too much to reverence taxes his powers until they are worn and impotent by the time he reaches manhood. Under Miss Hester's tutelage too many things became sacred to Fred Brent. It was wicked to cough in church, as it was a sacrilege to play with a hymn-book. His training was the apotheosis of the nonessential. But, after all, there is no rebel like Nature. She is an iconoclast.

When he was less than ten years old, an incident occurred that will in a measure indicate the manner of his treatment. Miss Prime's prescription for making a good boy was two parts punishment, two parts admonition, and six parts prayer. Accordingly, as the watchful and sympathetic neighbors said, "she an' that pore child fairly lived in church."

It was one class-meeting night, and, as usual, the boy and his guardian were sitting side by side at church. It was the habit of some of the congregation to bring their outside controversies into the classroom under the guise of testimonies or exhortations, and there to air their views where their opponents could not answer them. One such was Daniel Hastings. The trait had so developed in him that whenever he rose to speak, the question ran around, "I wonder who Dan'l's a-goin' to rake over the coals now." On this day he had been having a tilt with his old-time enemy, Thomas Donaldson, over the advent into Dexter of a young homœopathic doctor. With characteristic stubbornness, Dan'l had held that there was no good in any but the old-school medical men, and he sneered at the idea of anybody's being cured with sugar, as he contemptuously termed the pellets and powders affected by the new school. Thomas, who was considered something of a wit and who sustained his reputation by the perpetration of certain timeworn puns, had replied that other hogs were sugar-cured, and why not Dan'l? This had turned the laugh on Hastings, and he went home from the corner grocery, where the men were congregated, in high dudgeon.

Still smarting with the memory of his defeat, when he rose to speak that evening, he cast a glance full of unfriendly significance at his opponent and launched into a fiery exhortation on true religion. "Some folks' religion," he said, "is like sugar, all sweetness and no power; but I want my religion like I want my medicine: I want it strong, an' I want it bitter, so's I'll know I've got it." In Fred Brent the sense of humor had not been entirely crushed, and the expression was too much for his gravity. He bowed his head and covered his mouth with his hand. He made no sound, but there were three pairs of eyes that saw the movement—

Miss Prime's, Eliphalet Hodges', and the Rev. Mr. Simpson's. Miss Prime's gaze was horrified, Mr. Simpson's stern; but in the eye of Mr. Hodges there was a most ungodly twinkle.

When Dan'l Hastings had finished his exhortation—which was in reality an arraignment of Thomas Donaldson's medical heresies—and sat down, the Rev. Mr. Simpson arose, and, bending an accusing glance upon the shrinking boy, began: "I perceive on the part of some of the younger members of the congregation a disposition towards levity. The house of God is not the place to find amusement. I never see young people deriding their elders without thinking of the awful lesson taught by the Lord's judgment upon those wicked youths whom the she-bears devoured. I never see a child laughing in church without trembling in spirit for his future. Some of the men whom I have seen in prison, condemned to death or a life of confinement, have begun their careers in this way, showing disrespect for their elders and for the church. Beware, young people, who think you are smart and laugh and titter in the sanctuary; there is a prison waiting for you, there is a hell yawning for you. Behold, there is death in the pot!"

With a terrible look at the boy, Mr. Simpson sat down. There was much craning of necks and gazing about, but few in the church would have known to whom the pastor's remarks were addressed had not Miss Prime, at their conclusion, sighed in an injured way, and, rising with set lips, led the culprit out, as a criminal is led to the scaffold. How the boy suffered as, with flaming face, he walked down the aisle to the door, the cynosure of all eyes! He saw in the faces about him the accusation of having done a terrible thing, something unheard of and more wicked than he could understand. He felt revolted, child as he was, at the religion that made so much of his fault. Inwardly, he vowed that he would never "get religion" or go into a church when he was big enough to have his own way.

They had not gone far when a step approached them from behind, and Eliphalet Hodges joined them. Miss Prime turned tragically at his greeting, and broke out, "Don't reproach me 'Liphalet; it ain't no trainin' o' mine that's perduced a child that laughs at old folks in the Lord's house."

"I ain't a-goin' to reproach you, Miss Hester, never you fear; I ain't a-goin' to say a word ag'in' yore trainin'; but I jest thought I'd ask you not to be too hard on Freddie. You know that Dan'l is kind o' tryin' sometimes even to the gravity of older people; an' childern will be childern; they 'ain't got the sense, nor—nor—the deceit to keep a smooth face when they're a-laughin' all in their innards."

Miss Prime turned upon him in righteous wrath. "'Liphalet," she exclaimed, "I think it's enough fur this child to struggle ag'inst natural sin, without encouragin' him by makin' excuses fur him."

"It ain't my intention nor my desire to set a bad example before nobody, especially the young lambs of the flock, but I ain't a-goin' to blame Freddie fur doin' what many another of us wanted to do."

"'Deed an' double, that is fine talk fur you, 'Liphalet Hodges! you a trustee of the church, an' been a class-leader, a-holdin' up fur sich onregenerate carryin's-on."

"I ain't a-holdin' up fur nothin', Miss Hester, 'ceptin' nature an' the very couldn't-help-it-ness o' the thing altogether. I ain't a boy no more, by a good many years, but there's times when I've set under Dan'l Hastings's testimonies jest mortally cramped to laugh; an' ef it's so with a man, how will it be with a pore innercent child? I ain't a-excusin' natural sin in nobody. It wa'n't so much Freddie's natural sin as it was Dan'l's natural funniness." And there was something very like a chuckle in 'Liphalet's throat.

"'Liphalet, the devil's been puttin' fleas into yore ear, but I ain't a-goin' to let you argy me out o' none o' my settled convictions, although the Old Man's put plenty of argyment into yore head. That's his way o' capturin' a soul.—Walk on ahead, Frederick, an' don't be list'nan'. I'll 'tend to yore case later on."

"It's funny to me, Miss Hester, how it is that Christians know so much more about the devil's ways than they do about the Lord's. They're allus a-sayin', 'the Lord moves in a mysterious way,' but they kin allus put their finger on the devil."

"'Liphalet Hodges, that's a slur!"

"I ain't a-meanin' it as no slur, Miss Hester; but most Christians do seem to have a powerful fondness for the devil. I notice that they're allus admirin' his work an' praisin' up his sharpness, an' they'd be monstrous disappointed ef he didn't git as many souls as they expect."

"Well, after all the years that I've been a-workin' in the church an' a-tryin' to let my light so shine before the world, I didn't think that you'd be the one to throw out hints about my Christianity. But we all have our burdens to bear, an' I'm a-goin' to bear mine the best I kin, an' do my dooty, whatever comes of it." And Miss Hester gave another sigh of injured rectitude.

"I see, Miss Hester, that you're jest bent an' bound not to see what I mean, so I might as well go home."

"I think my mind ain't givin' way yit, an' I believe that I do understand plain words; but I ain't a-bearin' you no grudge. You've spoke yore mind, an' it's all right."

"But I hope there ain't no hard feelin's, after all these years."

"Oh, 'Liphalet, it ain't a part of even my pore weak religion to bear hard feelin's towards no one, no matter how they treat me. I'm jest tryin' to bear my cross an' suffer fur the Lord's sake."

"But I hope I ain't a-givin' you no cross to bear. I ain't never doubted yore goodness or yore Christianity: I only thought that mebbe yore methods, yore methods—"

Miss Prime's lips were drawn into a line. She divided that line to say, "I know what the Scriptures say: 'If thy right hand offend thee'—"

"Hester, Hester!" he cried, stretching out his hands to her.

"Good-night, Brother Hodges. I must go in." She turned and left him standing at the gate with a hurt look in his face.

On going into the house, Miss Hester did not immediately 'tend to Fred, as she had promised. Instead, she left him and went into her own room where she remained awhile. When she came out, her lips were no less set, but her eyes were red.

It is hardly to be supposed that she had been indulging in that solace of woman's woes, a good cry.

"Take off yore jacket, Freddie," she said, calmly, taking down a switch from over the clothespress. "I'm a-goin' to whip you; but, remember, I ain't a-punishin' you because I'm mad. It's fur the purpose of instruction. It's fur yore own good."

Fred received his dressing-down without a whimper. He was too angry to cry. This Miss Prime took as a mark of especial depravity. In fact, the boy had been unable to discover any difference between an instructive and a vindictive whipping. It was perfectly clear in his guardian's mind, no doubt, but a cherry switch knows no such distinctions.

This incident only prepared Fred Brent for a further infraction of his guardian's rules the next day. One of Miss Prime's strictest orders had to do with fighting. Whatever the boys did to Fred, he was never to resent it. He must come to her, and she would go to the boy's mother. What an order to give a boy with muscles and fists and Nature strong within him! But, save for the telling, it had been obeyed, although it is hard to feel one's self an unwilling coward, a prig, and the laughingstock of one's fellows. But when, on the day after his unjust punishment, and while still stung by the sense of wrong, one of the petty schoolboy tyrants began to taunt him, he turned upon the young scamp and thrashed him soundly. His tormentor was not more hurt than surprised. Like most of his class, he was a tattler. The matter got to the teacher's ears, and that night Fred carried home an ominous-looking note. In his heart he believed that it meant another application of cherry switch, either instructive or vindictive, but he did not care. He had done the natural thing, and Nature rewards us for obeying her laws by making us happy or stoical. He had gone up in the estimation of his schoolfellows, even the thrashed one, and he felt a reckless joy. He would welcome a whipping. It would bring him back memories of what he had given Billy Tompkins. "Wouldn't Miss Hester be surprised," he thought, "if I should laugh out while she is whipping me?" And he laughed at the very thought. He was full of pleasure at himself. He had satisfied the impulse within him for once, and it made him happy.

Miss Prime read the ominous note, and looked at her charge thoughtfully. Fred glanced expectantly in the direction of the top of the clothespress. But she only said, "Go out an' git in yore kindlin', Freddie; git yore chores done, an' then come in to supper." Her voice was menacingly quiet. The boy had learned to read the signs of her face too well to think that he was to get off so easily as this. Evidently, he would "get it" after supper, or Miss Prime had some new, refined mode of punishment in store for him. But what was it? He cudgeled his brain in vain, as he finished his chores, and at table he could hardly eat for wondering. But he might have spared himself his pains, for he learned all too soon.

Immediately after supper he was bidden to put on his cap and come along. Miss Prime took him by the hand. "I'm a-goin' to take you," she said, "to beg Willie Tompkins's pardon fur the way you did him."

Did the woman know what it meant to the boy? She could not, or her heart would have turned against the cruelty. Fred was aghast. Beg his pardon! A whipping was a thousand times better: indeed, it would be a mercy. He began to protest, but was speedily silenced. The enforced silence, however, did not cool his anger. He had done what other boys did. He had acted in the only way that it seemed a boy could act under the circumstances, and he had expected to be punished as his fellows were; but this—this was awful. He clinched his hands until the nails dug into the palms. His face was as pale as death. He sweated with the consuming fire of impotent rage. He wished that he might run away somewhere where he could hide and tear things and swear. For a moment only he entertained the thought, and then a look into the determined face of the woman at his side drove the thought away. To his childish eyes, distorted by resentment, she was an implacable and relentless monster who would follow him with punishment anywhere he might go.

And now they were at Billy Tompkins's door. They had passed through, and he found himself saying mechanically the words which Miss Prime put into his mouth, while his tormentor grinned from beside his mother's chair. Then, after a few words between the women, in which he heard from Mrs. Tompkins the mysterious words, "Oh, I don't blame you, Miss Hester; I know that blood will tell," they passed out, and the grinning face of Billy Tompkins was the last thing that Fred saw. It followed him home. The hot tears fell from his eyes, but they did not quench the flames that were consuming him. There is nothing so terrible as the just anger of a child—terrible in its very powerlessness. Polyphemus is a giant, though the mountain hold him down.

Next morning, when Fred went to school, Billy Tompkins with a crowd of boys about was waiting to deride him; but at sight of his face they stopped. He walked straight up to his enemy and began striking him with all his might.

"She made me beg your pardon, did she?" he gasped between the blows; "well, you take that for it, and that." The boys had fallen back, and Billy was attempting to defend himself.

"Mebbe she'll make me do it again tonight. If she does, I'll give you some more o' this tomorrow, and every time I have to beg your pardon. Do you hear?"

The boys cheered lustily, and Billy Tompkins, completely whipped and ashamed, slunk away.

That night no report of the fight went home. Fred Brent held the master hand.

In life it is sometimes God and sometimes the devil that comes to the aid of oppressed humanity. From the means, it is often hard to tell whose handiwork are the results.

Chapter 7

CYNICS AND FOOLS LAUGH at calf-love. Youth, which is wiser, treats it more seriously. When the boy begins to think of a girl, instead of girls, he displays the first budding signs of a real, growing manhood. The first passion may be but the enthusiasm of discovery. Sometimes it is not. At times it dies, as fleeting enthusiasms do. Again it lives, and becomes a blessing, a curse, or a memory. Who shall say, that the first half-sweet pang that strikes a boy's heart in the presence of the dear first girl is any less strong, intoxicating, and real to him than that which prompts him to take the full-grown woman to wife? With factitious sincerity we quote, "The boy is father to the man," and then refuse to believe that the qualities, emotions, and passions of the man are inherited from this same boy—are just the growth, the development, of what was embryonic in him.

Nothing is more serious, more pleasant, and more diverting withal, than a boy's brooding or exultation—one is the complement of the other—over his first girl. As, to a great extent, a man is molded by the woman he marries, so to no less a degree is a boy's character turned and shaped by the girl he adores. Either he descends to her level, or she draws him up, unconsciously, perhaps, to her own plane. Girls are missionaries who convert boys. Boys are mostly heathens. When a boy has a girl, he remembers to put on his cuffs and collars, and he doesn't put his necktie into his pocket on the way to school.

In a boy's life, the having of a girl is the setting up of an ideal. It is the new element, the higher something which abashes the unabashed, and makes John, who caused Henry's nose to bleed, tremble when little Mary stamps her foot. It is like an atheist's finding God, the sudden recognition of a higher and purer force against which all that he knows is powerless. Why doesn't John bully Mary? It would be infinitely easier than his former exploit with Henry. But he doesn't. He blushes in her presence, brings her the best apples, out of which heretofore he has enjoined the boys not to "take a hog-bite," and, even though the parental garden grow none, comes by flowers for her in some way, queer boyish bouquets where dandelions press shoulders with spring-beauties, daffodils, and roses—strange democracy of flowerdom. He feels older and stronger.

In Fred's case the object of adoration was no less a person than Elizabeth Simpson, the minister's daughter. From early childhood they had seen and known each other at school, and between them had sprung up a warm childish friendship, apparently because their ways home lay along the same route. In such companionship the years sped; but Fred was a diffident boy, and he was seventeen and Elizabeth near the same before he began to feel those promptings which made him blushingly offer to carry her book for her as far as he went. She had hesitated, refused, and then assented, as is the manner of her sex and years. It had become a settled thing for them to walk home together, he bearing her burdens, and doing for her any other little service that occurred to his boyish sense of gallantry.

Without will of his own, and without returning the favor, he had grown in the Rev. Mr. Simpson's esteem. This was due mostly to his guardian's excellent work. In spite of his rebellion, training and environment had brought him greatly under her control, and when she began to admonish him about his lost condition spiritually she had been able to awaken a sort of superstitious anxiety in the boy's breast. When Miss Prime perceived that this had been accomplished, she went forthwith to her pastor and unburdened her heart.

"Brother Simpson," said she, "I feel that the Lord has appointed me an instrument in His hands for bringin' a soul into the kingdom." The minister put the tips of his fingers together and sighed piously and encouragingly. "I have been laborin' with Freddie in the sperrit of Christian industry, an' I believe that I have finally brought him to a realizin' sense of his sinfulness."

"H'm-m," said the minister. "Bless the Lord for this evidence of the activity of His people. Go on, sister."

"Freddie has at last come to the conclusion that hell is his lot unless he flees unto the mountain and seeks salvation."

"Bless the Lord for this."

"Now, Brother Simpson, I have done my part as fur as the Lord has showed me, except to ask you to come and wrastle with that boy."

"Let not thy heart be troubled, Sister Prime, for I will come as you ask me, and I will wrastle with that boy as Jacob did of old with the angel."

"Oh, Brother Simpson, I knowed you'd come. I know jest how you feel about pore wanderin' souls, an' I'm so glad to have yore strong arm and yore wisdom a-helpin' me."

"I hope, my sister, that the Lord may smile upon my poor labors, and permit us to snatch this boy as a brand from eternal burning."

"We shall have to labor in the sperrit, Brother Simpson."

"Yes, and with the understanding of the truth in our hearts and minds."

"I'm shore I feel mighty uplifted by comin' here today. Do come up to dinner Sunday, dear Brother Simpson, after preachin'."

"I will come, Sister Prime, I will come. I know by experience the worth of the table which the Lord provides for you, and then at the same season I may be able to sound this sinful boy as to his spiritual state and to drop some seed into the ground which the Lord has mercifully prepared for our harvest. Good-bye, sister, good-bye. I shall not forget, Sunday after preaching."

In accordance with his promise, the Rev. Mr. Simpson began to labor with Fred, with the result of driving him into a condition of dogged revolt, which only Miss Prime's persistence finally overcame. When revival time came round, as, sure as death it must come, Fred regularly went to the mourners' bench, mourned his few days until he had worked himself into the proper state, and then, somewhat too coldly, it is true, for his anxious guardian, "got religion."

On the visit next after this which Mr. Simpson paid to Miss Prime, he took occasion to say, "Ah, my sister, I am so glad that you pointed me to that lost lamb of the house of Israel, and I am thanking the Maker every day that He blessed my efforts to bring the straying one into the fold. Ah, there is more joy over the one lamb that is found than over the ninety and nine that went not astray!"

Mr. Simpson's parishioner acquiesced, but she had some doubts in her mind as to whose efforts the Lord had blessed. She felt a little bit selfish. She wanted to be the author of everything good that came to Fred. But she did not argue with Mr. Simpson. There are some concessions which one must make to one's pastor.

From this time on the preacher was Fred's friend, and plied him with good advice in the usual friendly way; but the boy bore it well, for Elizabeth smiled on him, and what boy would not bear a father's tongue for a girl's eyes?

The girl was like her mother, dark and slender and gentle. She had none of her father's bigness or bumptiousness. Her eyes were large and of a shade that was neither black nor brown. Her hair was very decidedly black. Her face was small, and round with the plumpness of youth, but one instinctively felt, in looking at it, that its lines might easily fall into thinness, even pitifulness, at the first touch of woman's sorrow. She was not, nor did she look to be, a strong girl. But her very weakness was the source of secret delight to the boy, for it made him feel her dependence on him. When they were together and some girlish fear made her cling to his arm, his heart swelled with pride and a something else that he could not understand and could not have described. Had anyone told him that he was going through the half-sweet, half-painful, timid, but gallant first stages of love, he would have resented the imputation with blushes. His whole training would have made him think of such a thing with terror. He had learned never to speak of girls at home, for any reference to them by him was sure to bring forth from Miss Prime an instant and strong rebuke.

"Freddie," was the exclamation that gave his first unsuspecting remarks pause, "you're a-gittin' too fresh: you'd better be a-mindin' of yore studies, instead o' thinkin' about girls. Girls ain't a-goin' to make you pass yore examination, an', besides, you're a-gettin' mannish; fur boys o' yore age to be a-talkin' about girls is mannish, do you hear, sir? You're a-beginnin' to feel yore keepin' too strong. Don't let me hear no more sich talk out o' you."

There never was a manly boy in the world whom the word "mannish," when applied to him, did not crush. It is a horrid word, nasty and full of ugly import. Fred was subdued by it, and so kept silence about his female friends. Happy is the boy who dares at home to pour out his heart about the girls he knows and likes, and thrice unhappy he who through mistaken zeal on the part of misguided parents is compelled to keep his thoughts in his heart and brood upon his little aproned companions as upon a secret sin. Two things are thereby engendered, stealth and unhealth. If Fred escaped certain youthful pitfalls, it was because he was so repressed that he had learned to hide himself from himself, his thoughts from the mind that produced them.

He was a boy strong and full of blood. The very discipline that had given a gloomy cast to his mind had given strength and fortitude to his body. He was austere, because austerity was all that he had ever known or had a chance of knowing; but too often austerity is but the dam that holds back the flood of potential passion. Not to know the power which rages behind the barricade is to leave the structure weak for a hapless day when, carrying all before it, the flood shall break its bonds and in its fury ruin fair field and smiling mead. It was well for Fred Brent that the awakening came when it did.

In the first days of June, when examinations are over, the annual exhibition done, and the graduating class has marched away proud in the possession of its diplomas, the minds of all concerned turn naturally toward the old institution, the school picnic. On this occasion parents join the teachers and pupils for a summer day's outing in the woods. Great are the preparations for the festal day, and great the rejoicings thereon. For these few brief hours old men and women lay aside their cares and their dignity and become boys and girls again. Those who have known sorrow—and who has not?—take to themselves a day of forgetfulness. Great baskets are loaded to overflowing with the viands dear to the picnicker's palate—sandwiches whose corpulence would make their sickly brothers of the railway restaurant wither with envy, pies and pickles, cheese and crackers, cakes and jams galore. Old horses that, save for this day, know only the market-cart or the Sunday chaise, are hitched up to bear out the merry loads. Old wagons, whose wheels have known no other decoration than the mud and clay of rutty roads, are festooned gaily with cedar wreaths, oak leaves, or the gaudy tissue-paper rosettes, and creak joyfully on their mission of lightness and mirth. On foot, by horse, in wagon or cart, the crowds seek some neighboring grove, and there the day is given over to laughter, mirth, and song. The children roll and tumble on the sward in the intoxication of "swing-turn" and "ring-around-a-rosy." The young women, with many blushes and shy glances, steal off to quiet nooks with their imploring swains. Some of the elders, anxious to prove that they have not yet lost all their youth and agility, indulge, rather awkwardly perhaps, in the exhausting amusement of the jumping-rope. A few of the more staid walk apart in conversation with some favorite pastor who does not decline to take part in the innocent pleasures and crack ponderous jokes for the edification of his followers. Perhaps some of the more daring are engaged in one of the numerous singing plays, such as "Oh, la, Miss Brown," or "Swing Candy, Two and Two," but these are generally frowned upon: they are too much like dancing, and time has been when some too adventurous church-member has been "churched" for engaging in one.

In such a merrymaking was the community which surrounded the high school at Dexter engaged when the incident occurred which opened Fred's eyes to his own state. Both he and Elizabeth had been in the prize ranks that year, and their friends had turned out in full and made much of them. Even Eliphalet Hodges was there, with old Bess festooned as gaily as the other horses, and both Miss Prime and Mr. Simpson were in evidence. The afternoon of the day was somewhat advanced, the dinner had been long over, and the weariness of the people had cast something of a quietus over the hilarity of their sports. They were sitting about in groups, chatting and laughing, while the tireless children were scurrying about in games of "tag," "catcher," and "hide-and-seek."

The grove where the festivities were being held was on a hillside which sloped gently to the bank of a small, narrow stream, usually dry in summer; but now, still feeling the force of the spring freshets, and swollen by the rain of the day before, it was rushing along at a rapid rate. A fence divided the picnic-ground proper from the sharper slope of the rivulet's bank. This fence the young people had been warned not to pass, and so no danger was apprehended on account of the stream's overflowing condition. But the youngsters at Dexter were no more obedient than others of their age elsewhere. So when a scream arose from several childish voices at the lower part of the hill, everybody knew that some child had been disobeying, and, pell-mell, the picnickers rushed in the direction of the branch.

When they reached the nearest point from which they could see the stream, a terrifying sight met their eyes. A girl was struggling in the shallow but swift water. She had evidently stepped on the sloping bank and fallen in. Her young companions were running alongside the rivulet, stretching out their hands helplessly to her, but the current was too strong, and, try as she would, she could not keep her feet. A cry of grief and despair went up from the girls on the bank, as she made one final effort and then fell and was carried down by the current.

Men were leaping the fence now, but a boy who had seen the whole thing from a neighboring hillock was before them. Fred Brent came leaping down the hill like a young gazelle. He had seen who the unfortunate girl was—Elizabeth—and he had but one desire in his heart, to save her. He reached the bank twenty yards ahead of anyone else, and plunged into the water just in front of her, for she was catching and slipping, clinging and losing hold, but floating surely to her death. He struggled upstream, reached and caught her by the dress. The water tugged at him and tried to throw him over, but he stemmed it, and, lifting her up in his arms, fought his way manfully to the bank. Up this he faltered, slipping and sliding in the wet clay, and weak with his struggle against the strong current. But his face was burning and his blood tingling as he held the girl close to him till he gave her unconscious form into her father's arms.

For the moment all was confusion, as was natural when a preacher's daughter was so nearly drowned. The crowd clustered around and gave much advice and some restoratives. Some unregenerate, with many apologies and explanations concerning his possession, produced a flask, and part of the whisky was forced down the girl's throat, while her hands and face and feet were chafed. She opened her eyes at last, and a fervent "Thank God!" burst from her father's lips and called forth a shower of Amens.

"I allus carry a little somethin' along, in case of emergencies," explained the owner of the flask as he returned it to his pocket, with a not altogether happy look at its depleted contents.

As soon as Fred saw that Elizabeth was safe, he struck away for home, unobserved, and without waiting to hear what the crowd were saying. He heard people calling his name kindly and admiringly, but it only gave wings to the feet that took him away from them. If he had thrown the girl in instead of bringing her out, he could not have fled more swiftly or determinedly away from the eyes of people. Tired and footsore, drenched to the skin and chilled through, he finally reached home. He was trembling, he was crying, but he did not know it, and had he known, he could not have told why. He did not change his clothes, but crouched down in a corner and hid his face in his hands. He dreaded seeing anyone or hearing any person speak his name. He felt painfully conscious of a new self which he thought must be apparent to other eyes.

The accident of the afternoon had cast a gloom over the merrymakings, and, the picnic breaking up abruptly, sent the people scurrying home, so that Miss Prime was at the house not far behind her charge.

"Freddie," she called to him as she entered the house, "Freddie, where air you?" And then she found him. She led him out of the corner and looked him over with a scrutinizing eye. "Freddie Brent," she said solemnly, "you've jest ruined yore suit." He was glad. He wanted to be scolded. "But," she went on, "I don't care ef you have." And here she broke down. "You're a-goin' to have another one, fur you're a right smart boy, that's all I've got to say." For a moment he wanted to lay his head on her breast and give vent to the sob which was choking him. But he had been taught neither tenderness nor confidence, so he choked back the sob, though his throat felt dry and hot and strained. He stood silent and embarrassed until Miss Prime recovered herself and continued: "But la, child, you'll take yore death o' cold. Git out o' them wet things an' git into bed, while I make you some hot tea. Fur the life o' me, I never did see sich carryin's-on."

The boy was not sorry to obey. He was glad to be alone. He drank the warm tea and tried to go to sleep, but he could not. His mind was on fire. His heart seemed as if it would burst from his bosom. Something new had come to him. He began to understand, and blushed because he did understand. It was less discovery than revelation. His forehead was hot. His temples were throbbing. It was well that Miss Prime did not discover it: she would have given him horehound to cure—thought!

From the moment that the boy held the form of the girl to his heart he was changed, and she was changed to him. They could never be the same to each other again. Manhood had come to him, in a single instant, and he saw in her womanhood. He began for the first time to really know himself, and it frightened him and made him ashamed.

He drew the covers over his head and lay awake, startled, surprised at what he knew himself and mankind to be.

To Fred Brent the awakening had come—early, if we would be prudish; not too early, if we would be truthful.

Chapter 8

IF FRED BRENT HAD needed anything to increase his consciousness of the new feeling that had come to him, he could not have done better to get it than by going to see Eliphalet Hodges next day. His war of thought had gone on all night, and when he rose in the morning he thought that he looked guilty, and he was afraid that Miss Prime would notice it and read his secret. He wanted rest. He wanted to be secure from anyone who would even suspect what was in his heart. But he wanted to see and to talk to someone. Who better, then, than his old friend?

So he finished his morning's chores and slipped away. He would not pass by Elizabeth's house, but went by alleys and lanes until he reached his destination. The house looked rather silent and deserted, and Mr. Hodges' old assistant did not seem to be working in the garden as usual. But after some search the boy found his old friend smoking upon the back porch. There was a cloud upon the usually bright features, and the old man took his pipe from his mouth with a disconsolate sigh as the boy came in sight.

"I'm mighty glad you've come, Freddie," said he, in a sad voice. "I've been a-wantin' to talk to you all the mornin'. Set down on the side o' the porch, or git a chair out o' the house, ef you'd ruther."

The boy sat down, wondering what could be the matter with his friend, and what he could have to say to him. Surely it must be something serious, for the whole tone and manner of his companion indicated something of import. The next remark startled him into sudden suspicion.

"There's lots o' things made me think o' lots of other things in the last couple o' days. You've grown up kind o' quick like, Freddie, so that a body 'ain't hardly noticed it, but that ain't no matter. You're up or purty nigh it, an' you can understand and appreciate lots o' the things that you used to couldn't."

Fred sat still, with mystery and embarrassment written on his face. He wanted to hear more, but he was almost afraid to listen further.

"I 'ain't watched you so close, mebbe, as I'd ought to 'a' done, but when I seen you yistiddy evenin' holdin' that little girl in yore arms I said to myself, I said, "Liphalet Hodges, Freddie ain't a child no more, he's growed up."" The boy's face was scarlet. Now he was sure that the thoughts of his heart had been surprised, and that this best of friends thought of him as "fresh," "mannish," or even wicked. He could not bear the thought of it; again the tears rose in his eyes, usually so free from such evidences of weakness. But the old man went on slowly in a low, half-reminiscent tone, without looking at his auditor to see what effect his words had had. "Well, that was one of the things that set me thinkin'; an' then there was another." He cleared his throat and pulled hard at his pipe; something made him blink—dust, or smoke, or tears, perhaps. "Freddie," he half sobbed out, "old Bess is dead. Pore old Bess died last night o' colic. I'm afeared the drive to the picnic was too much fur her."

"Old Bess dead!" cried the boy, grieved and at the same time relieved. "Who would have thought it? Poor old girl! It seems like losing one of the family."

"She was one of the family," said the old man brokenly. "She was more faithful than most human beings." The two stood sadly musing, the boy as sad as the man. "Old Bess" was the horse that had taken him for his first ride, that winter morning years before, when the heart of the child was as cold as the day. Eliphalet Hodges had warmed the little heart, and, in the years that followed, man, child, and horse had grown nearer to each other in a queer but sympathetic companionship.

Then, as if recalling his mind from painful reflections, the elder man spoke again. "But it ain't no use a-worryin' over what can't be helped. We was both fond o' old Bess, an' I know you feel as bad about losin' her as I do. But I'm a-goin' to give her a decent burial, sich as a Christian ought to have; fur, while the old mare wasn't no perfessor, she lived the life, an' that's more'n most perfessors do. Yes, sir, I'm a-goin' to have her buried: no glue-man fur me. I reckon you're a-wantin' to know how old Bess dyin' an' yore a-savin' 'Lizabeth could run into each other in my mind; but they did. Fur, as I see you standin' there a-holdin' the little girl, it come me sudden like, 'Freddie's grown now, an' he'll be havin' a girl of his own purty soon, ef he 'ain't got one now. Mebble it'll be 'Lizabeth.'" The old man paused for a moment; his eyes rested on the boy's fiery face. "Tut, tut," he resumed, "you ain't ashamed, air you? Well, what are you a-gitten' so red fur? Havin' a girl ain't nothin' to be ashamed of, or skeered about neither. Most people have girls one time or another, an' I don't know nothin' that'll make a boy or a young man go straighter than to know that his girl's eyes air upon him. Don't be ashamed at all."

Fred still blushed, but he felt better, and his face lightened over the kindly words.

"I didn't finish tellin' you, though, what I started on. I got to thinkin' yesterday about my young days, when I had a girl, an' how I used to ride back an' forth on the pore old horse right into this town to see her; an' as I drove home from the picnic I talked to the old nag about it, an' she whisked her tail an' laid back her ears, jest like she remembered it all. It was on old Bess that I rode away from my girl's house after her first 'no' to me, an' it seemed then that the animal sympathized with me, fur she drooped along an' held down her head jest like I was a-doin'. Many a time after that we rode off that way together, fur the girl was set in her ways, an' though she confessed to a hankerin' fur me, she wanted to be independent. I think her father put the idee into her head, fur he was a hard man, an' she was his all, his wife bein' dead. After a while we stopped talkin' about the matter, an' I jest went an' come as a friend. I only popped the question once more, an' that was when her father died an' she was left all alone.

"It was a summer day, warm an' cheerful like this, only it was evenin', an' we was a-settin' out on her front garden walk. She was a-knittin', an' I was a-whippin' the groun' with a switch that I had brought along to touch Bess up with now an' then. I had hitched her out front, an' she kep' a-turnin' her eyes over the fence as ef she was as anxious as I was, an' that was mighty anxious. Fin'ly I got the question out, an' the girl went all red in a minute: she had been jest a purty pink before. Her knittin' fell in her lap. Fust she started to answer, then she stopped an' her eyes filled up. I seen she was a-weak'nin', so I thought I'd push the matter. 'Come,' says I, gentle like, an' edgin' near up to her, 'give me my answer. I been waitin' a long time fur a yes.' With that she grabbed knittin', apron, an' all, an' put 'em to her eyes an' rushed into the house. I knowed she'd gone in to have a good cry an' settle her nerves, fur that's the way all women-folks does: so I knowed it was no use to bother her until it was done. So I walks out to the fence, an', throwin' an arm over old Bess's back, I told her all about it, jest as I'm a-tellin' you, she a-lookin' at me with her big meltin' eyes an' whinnyin' soft like.

"After a little while the girl come out. She was herself ag'in, but there was a look in her face that turned my heart stone-cold. Her voice sounded kind o' sharp as she said, "Liphalet, I've been a-thinkin' over what you said. I'm only a woman, an' I come purty near bein' a weak one; but I'm all right now. I don't mind tellin' you that ef I was ever goin' to marry, you'd be my choice, but I ain't a-goin' to have my father's sperrit a-thinkin' that I took advantage of his death to marry you. Good-bye, 'Liphalet.' She held out her hand to me, an' I took it. 'Come an' see me sometimes,' she said. I couldn't answer, so I went out and got on old Bess an' we jogged away. It was an awful disappointment, but I thought I would wait an' let my girl come aroun', fur sometimes they do—in fact mostly; but she has never give me a sign to make me think that she has. That was twenty years ago, an' I've been waitin' faithful ever sence. But it seems like she was different from most women an' 'specially good on holdin' out. People that was babies then have growed up an' married. An' now the old companion that has been with me through all this waitin' has left me. I know what it means. It means that I'm old, that years have been wasted, that chances have been lost. But you have taught me my lesson, Bess. Dear old Bess, even in yore last hours you did me a service, an' you, Freddie, you have given me the stren'th that I had twenty years ago, an' I'm a-goin' to try to save what remains of my life. I never felt how alone I was until now." He was greatly agitated. He rose and grasped the boy's arm. "Come, Freddie," he said; "come on. I'm a-goin' ag'in to ask Miss Prime to be my wife."

"Miss Prime!" exclaimed Fred, aghast.

"Miss Prime was my sweetheart, Freddie, thirty years ago, jest like 'Lizabeth is yor'n now. Come along."

The two set out, Hodges stepping with impatient alacrity, and the boy too astounded to speak.

It was a beautiful morning at the end of June. The sense of spring's reviving influence had not yet given way to the full languor and sensuousness of summer. The wind was soft and warm and fragrant. The air was full of the song of birds and the low droning of early bees. The river that flowed between the green hills and down through Dexter was like a pane of wrinkled glass, letting light and joy even into the regions below. Over the streets and meadows and hills lay a half haze, like a veil over the too dazzling beauty of an Eastern princess. The hum of business—for in the passing years Dexter had grown busy—the roar of traffic in the streets, all melted into a confused and intoxicating murmur as the pedestrians passed into the residence portion of the town to the cottage where Miss Prime still lived. The garden was as prim as ever, the walks as straight and well kept. The inevitable white curtains were fluttering freshly from the window, over which a huge matrimony vine drooped lazily and rung its pink and white bells to invite the passing bees.

Eliphalet paused at the gate and heaved a deep sigh. So much depended upon the issue of his present visit. The stream of his life had been flowing so smoothly before. Now if its tranquility were disturbed it never could be stilled again. Did he dare to risk so much upon so hazardous a chance? Were it not better to go back home, back to his old habits and his old ease, without knowing his fate? That would at least leave him the pleasure of speculating. He might delude himself with the hope that some day— He faltered. His hand was on the gate, but his face was turned back towards the way he had come. Should he enter, or should he go back? Fate decided for him, for at this juncture the door opened, and Miss Hester appeared in the doorway and called out, "Do come in, 'Liphalet. What air you a-standin' out there so long a-studyin' about, fur all the world like a bashful boy?"

The shot told. He was a bashful boy again, going fearfully, tremblingly, lovingly, to see the girl of his heart; but there was no old Bess to whinny encouragement to him from over the little fence. If he blushed, even the scrutinizing eyes of Miss Prime did not see it, for the bronze laid on his face by summers and winters of exposure; but he felt the hot blood rush up to his face and neck, and the perspiration breaking out on his brow. He paused long enough to mop his face, and then, saying to Fred, in a low tone, "You stay in the garden, my boy, until it's all over," he opened the gate and entered in the manner of one who leads a forlorn hope through forest aisles where an ambush is suspected. The door closed behind him. Interested, excited, wondering and fearing, doubting and hoping, Fred remained in the garden. There were but two thoughts in his head, and they were so new and large that his poor boy's cranium had room for no more. They ran in this wise: "Miss Prime is Uncle 'Liphalet's girl, and Elizabeth is mine."

Within, Miss Prime was talking on in her usual decided fashion, while the man sat upon the edge of his chair and wondered how he could break in upon the stream of her talk and say what was in his heart. At last the lady exclaimed, "I do declare, 'Liphalet, what kin be the matter with you? You 'ain't said ten words sence you've been a-settin' there. I hope you 'ain't talked yoreself entirely out with Fred. It does beat all how you an' that boy seem to grow thicker an' thicker every day. One 'ud think fur all the world that you told him all yore secrets, an' was afeared he'd tell 'em, by the way you stick by him; an' he's jest as bad about you. It's amazin'."

"Freddie's a wonderful good boy, an' he's smart, too. They ain't none of 'em a-goin' to throw dust in his eyes in the race of life."

"I'm shore I've tried to do my dooty by him the very best I could, an' ef he does amount to anything in this world it'll be through hard labor an' mighty careful watchin'." Miss Hester gave a sigh that was meant to be full of solemnity, but that positively reeked with self-satisfaction.

"But as you say, 'Liphalet," she went on, "Fred ain't the worst boy in the world, nor the dumbest neither, ef I do say it myself. I ain't a-sayin', mind you, that he's anything so great or wonderful; but I've got to thinkin' that there's somethin' in him besides original sin, an' I should feel that the Lord had been mighty favorin' to me ef I could manage to draw it out. The fact of it is, 'Liphalet, I've took a notion in my head about Fred, an' I'm a-goin' to tell you what it is. I've decided to make a preacher out o' him."

"H'm—ah—well, Miss Hester, don't you think you'd better let the Lord do that?"

"Nonsense, 'Liphalet! you 'ain't got no insight at all. I believe in people a-doin' their part an' not a-shovin' everything off on the Lord. The shiftless don't want nothin' better than to say that they will leave the Lord to take care o' things, an' then fold their arms an' set down an' let things go to the devil. Remember, Brother Hodges, I don't mean that in a perfane way. But then, because God made the sunlight an' the rain, it ain't no sign that we shouldn't prune the vine."

Miss Hester's face had flushed up with the animation of her talk, and her eyes were sparkling with excitement.

Eliphalet looked at her, and his heart leaped. He felt that the time had come to speak.

"Miss Hester," he began, and the hat in his hand went round and round nervously.

"'Liphalet, fur goodness' sake do lay yore hat on the table. You'll ruin the band of it, an' you make me as nervous as a cat."

He felt a little dampened after this, but he laid down the offending hat and began again. "I've been thinkin' some myself, Miss Hester, an' it's been about you."

"About me? La, 'Liphalet, what have you been a-thinkin' now?" The "now" sounded as if his thoughts were usually rather irresponsible.

"It was about you an'—an'—old Bess."

"About me an' old Bess! Bless my soul, man, will you stop beatin' about the bush an' tell me what on airth I've got to do with yore horse?"

"Old Bess is dead, Miss Hester; died last night o' colic."

"Well, I thought there was somethin' the matter with you. I'm mighty sorry to hear about the poor old creatur; but she'd served you a long while."

"That's jest what set me a-thinkin': she has served me a long while, an' now she's dead. Do you know what that means, Miss Hester? It means that we're a-gittin' old, you an' me. Do you know when I got old Bess? It was nigh thirty years ago: I used to ride her up to this door an' tie her to that tree out there: it was a saplin' then. An' now she's dead."

The man's voice trembled, and his listener was strangely silent.

"You know on what errands the old horse used to bring me," he went on, "but it wasn't to be—then. Hester," he rose, went over to her, and looked down into her half-averted face, which went red and pale by turns—"Hester, 'ain't we wasted time enough?"

There was a long pause before she lifted her face: he stood watching her with the light of a great eagerness in his eyes. At last she spoke. There was a catch in her voice; it was softer than usual.

"'Liphalet," she began, "I'm right glad you remember those days. I 'ain't never furgot 'em myself. It's true you've been a good, loyal friend to me, an' I thank you fur it, but, after all these years—"

He broke in upon her with something like youthful impetuosity. "After all these years," he exclaimed, "an endurin' love ought to be rewarded. Hester, I ain't a-goin' to take 'no' fur an answer. I've got lots o' years o' life in me yet—we both have—an' I ain't a-goin' on with an empty home an' an empty heart no longer."

"'Liphalet, you ain't a young man no more, an' I ain't a young woman, an' the Lord—"

"I don't care ef I ain't; an' I don't believe in shovin' everything off on the Lord."

"'Liphalet!" It was a reproach.

"Hester!" This was love. He put his arm around her and kissed her. "You're a-goin' to say yes, ain't you? You ain't a-goin' to send me away miserable? You're a-dyin' to say yes, but you're a-tryin to force yoreself not to. Don't." He lifted her face as a young lover might, and looked down into her eyes. "Is it yes?"

"Well, 'Liphalet it 'pears like you're jest so pesterin' that I've got to say yes. Yes, then." And she returned the quiet but jubilant kiss that he laid upon her lips.

"After all these years," he said. "Sorrow may last fur a night, but joy cometh in the mornin'. It was a long night, but, thank the Lord, mornin' 's broke." Then, rising, he went to the door and called joyously, "Freddie, come on in: it's all over."

"'Liphalet, did that boy know what you was a-goin' to say?"

"Yes, o' course he did."

"Oh, my! oh, my! Well, I've got a good mind to take it all back. Oh, my!" And when Fred came in, for the first time in her life Miss Prime was abashed and confused in his presence.

But Eliphalet had no thought of shame. He took her by the hand and said, "Freddie, Miss Hester's consented at last: after thirty years, she's a-goin' to marry me."

But Miss Hester broke in, "'Liphalet, don't be a-puttin' notions in that boy's head. You go 'way, Fred, right away."

Fred went out, but he felt bolder. He went past Elizabeth's house whistling. He didn't care. He wondered if he would have to wait thirty years for her. He hoped not.

Chapter 9

SO GREAT HAS BEEN our absorption in the careers of Fred Brent, Miss Prime, and Eliphalet Hodges that we have sadly neglected some of the characters whose acquaintance we made at the beginning of our story. But nature and Time have been kinder—or more cruel, if you will. They have neither passed over nor neglected them. They have combined with trouble and hard work to kill one of Fred's earliest friends. Melissa Davis is no more, and the oldest girl, Sophy, supplements her day's work of saleswoman in a dry-goods store by getting supper in the evening and making the younger Davises step around. Mrs. Warren, the sometime friend of Margaret Brent and enemy of Miss Prime, has moved farther out, into the suburbs, for Dexter has suburbs now, and boasts electric cars and amusement parks. Time has done much for the town. Its streets are paved, and the mean street that bore the tumbledown Brent cottage and its fellows has been built up and grown respectable. It and the street where Miss Prime's cottage frowned down have settled away into a quiet residential portion of the town, while around to the east, south, and west, and on both sides of the little river that divides the city, roars and surges the traffic of a characteristic middle-West town. Halfway up the hill, where the few aristocrats of the place formerly lived in almost royal luxuriance and seclusion, a busy sewing-machine factory has forced its way, and with its numerous chimneys and stacks literally smoked the occupants out; at their very gates it sits like the commander of a besieging army, and about it cluster the cottages of the workmen, in military regularity. Little and neat and trim, they flock there like the commander's obedient host, and such they are, for the sight of them offends the eyes of wealth. So, what with the smoke, and what with the proximity of the poorer classes, wealth capitulates, evacuates, and, with robes discreetly held aside, passes by to another quarter, and a new district is born where poverty dare not penetrate. Seated on a hill, where, as is their inclination, they may look down, literally and figuratively, upon the hurrying town, they are complacent again, it and the newcomers to the town, the new-rich magnates and the half-rich strugglers who would be counted on the higher level, move up and swell their numbers at Dexter View.

Amid all this change, two alone of those we know remain unaltered and unalterable, true to their traditions. Mrs. Smith and Mrs. Martin, the two ancient gossips, still live side by side, spying and commenting on all that falls within their ken, much as they did on that day when 'Liphalet Hodges took Fred Brent for his first drive behind old Bess. Their windows still open out in the same old way, whence they can watch the happenings of the street. If there has been any change in them at all, it is that they have grown more absorbed and more keen in following and dissecting their neighbors' affairs.

It is to these two worthies, then, that we wish to reintroduce the reader on an early autumn evening some three months after the events narrated in the last chapter.

Mrs. Martin went to her back fence, which was the nearest point of communication between her and her neighbor. "Mis' Smith," she called, and her confederate came hurrying to the door, thimble on and a bit of sewing clutched precariously in her apron, just as she had caught it up when the significant call brought her to the back door.

"Oh, you're busy as usual, I see," said Mrs. Martin.

"It ain't nothn' partic'ler, only a bit o' bastin' that I was doin'."

"You ain't a-workin' on the machine, then, so you might bring your sewin' over and take a cup o' tea with me."

"La! now that's so kind o' you, Mis' Martin. I was jest thinkin' how good a cup o' tea would taste, but I didn't want to stop to make it. I'll be over in a minute, jest as soon as I see if my front door is locked." And she disappeared within the house, while Mrs. Martin returned to her own sitting room.

The invited knew very well what the invitation to tea meant. She knew that some fresh piece of news was to be related and discussed. The beverage of which she was invited to partake was but a pretext, but neither the one nor the other admitted as much. Each understood perfectly, as by a tacit agreement, and each tried to deceive herself and the other as to motives and objects.

There is some subtle tie between tea-drinking and gossip. It is over their dainty cups that women dissect us men and damn their sisters. Some of the quality of the lemon they take in their tea gets into their tongues. Tea is to talk what dew is to a plant, a gentle nourishing influence, which gives to its product much of its own quality. There are two acids in the tea which cultured women take. There is only one in the beverage brewed by commonplace people. But that is enough.

Mrs. Martin had taken her tray into the sitting room, where a slight fire was burning in the prim "parlor cook," on which the hot water was striving to keep its quality when Mrs. Smith came in.

"La, Mis' Martin, you do manage to have everything so cozy. I'm shore a little fire in a settin'-room don't feel bad these days."

"I jest thought I'd have to have a fire," replied Mrs. Martin, "fur I was feelin' right down chilly, though goodness knows a person does burn enough coal in winter, without throwin' it away in these early fall days."

"Well, the Lord's put it here fur our comfort, an' I think we're a-doin' His will when we make use o' the good things He gives us."

"Ah, but Mis' Smith, there's too many people that goes about the world thinkin' that they know jest what the Lord's will is; but I have my doubts about 'em, though, mind you, I ain't a-mentionin' no names: 'no name, no blame.'" Mrs. Martin pressed her lips and shook her head, a combination of gestures that was eloquent with meaning. It was too much for her companion. Her curiosity got the better of her caution.

"Dear me!" she exclaimed. "What is it *now?*"

"Oh, nothin' of any consequence at all. It ain't fur me to be a-judgin' my neighbors or a-talkin' about 'em. I jest thought I'd have you over to tea, you're sich good company."

Mrs. Smith was so impatient that she had forgotten her sewing and it lay neglected in her lap, but in no other way did she again betray her anxiety. She knew that there was something new to be told and that it would be told all in good time. But when gossip has become a fine art it must be conducted with dignity and precision.

"Let me see, I believe you take two lumps o' sugar an' no milk." Mrs. Martin knew perfectly what her friend took. "I don't know how this tea is. I got it from the new grocery over at the corner." She tasted it deliberately. "It might 'a' drawed a little more." Slowly she stirred it round and round, and then, as if she had drawn the truth from the depths of her cup, she observed, "This is a queer world, Mis' Smith."

Mrs. Smith sighed a sigh that was appreciative and questioning at once. "It is indeed," she echoed; "I'm always a-sayin' to myself what a mighty cur'us world this is."

"Have you ever got any tea from that new grocery-man?" asked her companion, with tantalizing irrelevance.

"No: I hain't never even been in there."

"Well, this here's middlin' good; don't you think so?"

"Oh, it's more than middlin', it's downright good. I think I must go into that grocery some time, myself."

"I was in there today, and met Mis' Murphy: she says there's great goin'-ons up at Miss Prime's—I never shall be able to call her Mis' Hodges."

"You don't tell me! She and Brother 'Liphalet 'ain't had a fallin' out already, have they? Though what more could you expect?"

"Oh, no, indeed. It ain't no fallin' out, nothin' o' the kind."

"Well, what then? What has Miss Hester—I mean Mis' Hodges been doin' now? Where will that woman stop? What's she done?"

"Well, you see—do have another cup of tea, an' help yoreself to that bread an' butter—you see, Freddie Brent has finished at the high school, an' they've been wonderin' what to make him."

"Well, what air they a-goin' to make him? His father was a good stone-mason, when he was anything."

"Humph! you don't suppose Miss Hester's been sendin' a boy to school to learn Latin and Greek an' algebry an' sich, to be a stone-mason, do you? Huh uh! Said I to myself, as soon as I see her sendin' him from the common school to high school, says I, 'She's got big notions in her head.' Oh, no; the father's trade was not good enough fur her boy: so thinks Mis' 'Liphalet Hodges."

"Well, what on airth is she goin' to make out of him, then?"

"Please pass me that sugar: thank you. You know Mr. Daniels offered him a place as clerk in the same store where Sophy Davis is. It was mighty kind o' Mr. Daniels, I think, to offer him the job."

"Well, didn't he take it?"

"Well, partly he did an' partly he didn't, ef you can understand that."

"Sally Martin, what do you mean? A body has to fairly pick a thing out o' you."

"I mean that she told Mr. Daniels he might work for him half of every day."

"Half a day! An' what's he goin' to do the other half?"

"He's a-goin' to the Bible Seminary the other half-day. She's a-goin to make a preacher out o' him."

Mrs. Martin had slowly and tortuously worked up to her climax, and she shot forth the last sentence with a jubilant ring. She had well calculated its effects. Sitting back in her chair, she supped her tea complacently as she contemplated her companion's astonishment. Mrs. Smith had completely collapsed into her seat, folded her arms, and closed her eyes. "Laws a massy!" she exclaimed. "What next? Old Tom, drunken Tom, swearin' an' ravin' Tom Brent's boy a preacher!" Then suddenly she opened her eyes and sat up very erect and alert as she broke forth, "Sally Martin, what air you a-tellin' me? It ain't possible. It's ag'in' nature. A panther's cub ain't a-goin' to be a lamb. It's downright wicked, that's what I say."

"An' so says I to Mis' Murphy, them same identical words; says I, 'Mis' Murphy, it's downright wicked. It's a-shamin' of the Lord's holy callin' o' the ministry."

"An' does the young scamp pertend to 'a' had a call?"

"No, indeed: he was mighty opposed to it, and so was her husband; but that woman was so set she wouldn't agree to nothin' else. He don't pertend to 'a' heerd no call, 'ceptin' Miss Hester's, an' that was a command. I know it's all true, fur Mis' Murphy, while she wasn't jest a-listenin', lives next door and heerd it all."

And so the two women fell to discussing the question, as they had heard it, pro and con. It was all true, as these gossips had it, that Miss Hester had put into execution her half-expressed determination to make a preacher of Fred. He had heard nothing of it until the day when he rushed in elated over the kindly offer of a place in Mr. Daniels's store. Then his guardian had firmly told him of her plan, and there was a scene.

"You kin jest tell Mr. Daniels that you kin work for him half a day every day, an' that you're a-goin' to put in the rest of your time at the Bible Seminary. I've made all the arrangements."

"But I don't want to be a preacher," the boy had retorted, with some heat. "I'd a good deal rather learn business, and some day start out for myself."

"It ain't what some of us wants to do in this life; it's what the Lord appoints us to; an' it's wicked fur you to rebel."

"I don't know how you can know so much what the Lord means for me to do. I should think He would give His messages to those who are to do the work."

"That's right, Freddie Brent, sass me, sass me. That's what I've struggled all the best days of my life to raise you fur."

"I'm not sassing you, but—"

"Don't you think, Hester," broke in her husband, "that mebbe there's some truth in what Freddie says? Don't you think the Lord kind o' whispers what He wants people to do in their own ears? Mebbe it wasn't never intended fur Freddie to be a preacher: there's other ways o' doin' good besides a-talkin' from the pulpit."

"I'd be bound fur you, 'Liphalet: it's a shame, you a-goin' ag'in' me, after all I've done to make Freddie material fit for the Lord's use. Jest think what you'll have to answer fur, a-helpin' this unruly boy to shirk his dooty."

"I ain't a-goin' ag'in' you, Hester. You're my wife, an' I 'low 'at your jedgment's purty sound on most things. I ain't a-goin' ag'in' you at all, but—but—I was jest a-wonderin'."

The old man brought out the last words slowly, meditatively. He was "jest a-wonderin'." His wife, though, never wondered.

"Mind you," she went on, "I say to you, Freddie, and to yore uncle 'Liphalet too, ef he upholds you, that it ain't me you're a-rebellin' against. It's yore dooty an' the will o' God that you're a-fightin'. It's easy enough to rebel against man; but do you know what you're a-doin' when you set yourself up against the Almighty? Do you want to do that?"

"Yes," came the boy's answer like a flash. He was stung and irritated into revolt, and a torrent of words poured from his lips unrestrained. "I'm tired of doing right. I'm tired of being good. I'm tired of obeying God—"

"Freddie!" But over the dam the water was flowing with irresistible force. The horror of his guardian's face and the terrible reproach in her voice could not check the boy.

"Everything," he continued, "that I have ever wanted to do since I can remember has been bad, or against my duty, or displeasing to God. Why does He frown on everything I want to do? Why do we always have to be killing our wishes on account of duty? I don't believe it. I hate duty. I hate obedience. I hate everything, and I won't obey—"

"Freddie, be keerful: don't say anything that'll hurt after yore mad spell's over. Don't blaspheme the Lord A'mighty."

'Liphalet Hodges' voice was cool and tender and persuasive. He laid his hand on the boy's shoulder, while his wife sat there motionless, white and rigid with horror.

The old man's words and his gentle touch had a wonderful effect on the boy; they checked his impassioned outburst; but his pent-up heart was too full. He burst into tears and rushed headlong from the house.

For a time he walked aimlessly on, his mind in a tumult of rage. Then he began to come to himself. He saw the people as they passed him. He had eyes again for the street, and he wondered where he was going. He felt an overwhelming desire to talk to someone and to get sympathy, consolation, and perhaps support. But whither should he turn? If 'Liphalet Hodges had been at the old house, his steps would naturally have bent in that direction; but this refuge was no longer his. Then his mind began going over the people whom he knew, and no name so stuck in his fancy as that of Elizabeth. It was a hard struggle. He was bashful. Any other time he would not have done it, but now his great need created in him an intense desperation that made him bold. He turned and retraced his steps toward the Simpson house.

Elizabeth was leaning over the gate. The autumn evening was cool: she had a thin shawl about her shoulders. She was humming a song as Fred came up. His own agitation made her seem irritatingly calm. She opened the gate and made room for him at her side.

"You seem dreadfully warm," she said, "and here I was getting ready to go in because it is so cool."

"I've been walking very fast," he answered, hesitatingly.

"Don't you think you'd better go in, so as not to take cold?"

"Oh, I don't care if I do take cold." The speech sounded rude. Elizabeth looked at him in surprise.

"What's the matter with you?" she asked.

"I'm mad; that's what's the matter."

"Oh, Fred, you shouldn't get mad: you know it's wrong."

He put up his hand as if she had struck him. "Wrong! wrong! It seems I can't hear anything else but that word. Everything is wrong. Don't say any more about it. I don't want to hear the word again."

Elizabeth did not know what to make of his words, so she said nothing, and for a while they stood in strained silence. After a while he said, "Aunt Hester wants me to be a preacher."

"I am so glad to hear that," she returned. "I think you'll make a good one."

"You too!" he exclaimed, resentfully. "Why should I make a good one? Why need I be one at all?"

"Oh, because you're smart, and then you've always been good."

The young man was suddenly filled with disdain. His anger returned. He felt how utterly out of accord he was with everyone else. "Don't you think there is anything else required besides being 'smart' and 'good'?" He himself would have blushed at the tone in which he said this, could he have recognized it. "I'm smart because I happened to pass all my examinations. I got through the high school at eighteen: nearly everyone does the same. I'm good because I have never had a chance to be bad: I have never been out of Aunt Hester's sight long enough. Anybody could be good that way."

"But then older people know what is best for us, Fred."

"Why should they? They don't know what's beating inside of us away down here." The boy struck his breast fiercely. "I don't believe they do know half the time what is best, and I don't believe that God intends them to know."

"I wouldn't talk about it, if I were you. I must go in. Won't you come in with me?"

"Not tonight," he replied. "I must be off."

"But papa might give you some advice."

"I've had too much of it now. What I want is room to breathe in once."

"I don't understand you."

"I know you don't; nobody does, or tries to. Go in, Lizzie," he said more calmly. "I don't want you to catch cold, even if I do. Good-night." And he turned away.

The girl stood for a moment looking after him; her eye was moist. Then she pouted, "Fred's real cross tonight," and went in.

It is one of the glaring sarcasms of life to see with what complacency a shallow woman skims the surface of tragedy and thinks that she has sounded the depths.

Fred continued his walk towards home. He was thinking. It ran in him that Elizabeth was a good deal of a fool; and then he felt horrified with himself for thinking it. It did not occur to him that the hard conditions through which he had come had made him mentally and spiritually older than the girl. He was thinking of his position, how perfectly alone he stood. Most of the people whom he knew would see only blind obstinacy in his refusal to be a minister. But were one's inclinations nothing? Was there really nothing in the "call" to preach? So he pondered as he walked, and more and more the hopelessness of his predicament became revealed to him. All his life had been molded by this one woman's hands. Would not revolt now say to the world, "I am grown now; I do not need this woman who has toiled. I can disobey her with impunity; I will do so."

He went home, and before going in leaned his head long upon the gate and thought. A listless calm had succeeded his storm of passion. He went in and to bed.

At breakfast he seemed almost cheerful, while Mr. Hodges was subdued. His wife had taken refuge in an attitude of injured silence.

"Aunt Hester," said the young man, apparently without effort, "I was wrong yesterday; I am sorry. I will do whatever you say, even to being a preacher." Something came up in his throat and choked him as he saw a brightness come into the face and eyes of his beloved "Uncle 'Liph," but it grew hard and bitter there as Mrs. Hodges replied, "Well, I'm glad the Lord has showed you the errors of your way an' brought you around to a sense o' your dooty to Him an' to me."

Poor, blind, conceited humanity! Interpreters of God, indeed! We reduce the Deity to vulgar fractions. We place our own little ambitions and inclinations before a shrine, and label them "divine messages." We set up our Delphian tripod, and we are the priest and oracles. We despise the plans of Nature's Ruler and substitute our own. With our short sight we affect to take a comprehensive view of eternity. Our horizon is the universe. We spy on the Divine and try to surprise His secrets, or to sneak into His confidence by stealth. We make God the eternal a puppet. We measure infinity with a foot-rule.

Chapter 10

WHEN FATE IS FIGHTING with all her might against a human soul, the greatest victory that the soul can win is to reconcile itself to the unpleasant, which is never quite so unpleasant afterwards. Upon this principle Frederick Brent acted instinctively. What with work and study and contact with his fellow students, he found the seminary not so bad a place, after all. Indeed, he began to take a sort of pleasure in his pursuits. The spirit of healthy competition in the school whetted his mind and made him forgetful of many annoyances from without. When some fellow salesman at the store gibed at him for being a parson, it hurt him; but the wound was healed and he was compensated when in debate he triumphed over the crack speaker of his class. It was a part of his training to do earnestly and thoroughly what he had to do, even though it was distasteful, and it was not long before he was spoken of as one of the most promising members of the school.

Notwithstanding its steady growth toward citydom, Dexter retained many of the traditions of its earlier and smaller days. Among them was that of making the church the center of its social and public life. For this reason the young student came in for much attention on account of his standing in the religious college. Another cause which elicited the praise and congratulations of his friends was his extreme youth. That community which could send out a "boy preacher" always deemed itself particularly favored by Providence. Dexter was no exception, and it had already begun to bestow the appellation upon young Brent, much to his disgust. He knew the species and detested it. It was mostly composed of ignorant and hypocritical young prigs, in whom their friends had seemed to see some especial merit and had forthwith hoisted them into a position that was as foolish as it was distasteful. They were hailed as youthful prodigies and exploited around the country like a patent medicine or a sideshow. What is remarkable at eighteen is not so striking at twenty-eight. So when their extreme youth was no longer a cause for surprise, the boy preachers settled down into everyday dullness, with nothing except the memory of a flimsy fame to compensate the congregations they bored.

Against this Frederick Brent fought with all his strength. He refused invitation after invitation to "talk" or "exhort," on the plea that he wished to be fully prepared for his work before entering upon it.

But his success at school militated against him, for the fame of his oratorical powers was gradually but surely leaking out. The faculty recognized and commended it, so he could not hope long to hide behind his plea, although he dreaded the day when it would no longer serve his purpose.

Some of the "older heads" accused him of an unwarranted fear, of cowardice even, and an attempt to shirk his evident duty. The truth of it was that these same people wanted to hear him and then attack his manner or his doctrine. They could not, would not forget that he was the son of old Tom Brent, the drunkard, and of the terrible, the unspeakable Margaret, his wife. They could not forget that he was born and lived the first years of his life on the "mean" street, when it was a mean street; and when any obstinate old fossil was told of the youth's promise, he would shake his head, as who should say, "What good can come out of that Nazareth?"

But the young man went his way and heeded them not. He knew what they were saying. He knew what they were thinking, even when they held his hand and smiled upon him, and it filled him with a spirit of distrust and resentment, though it put him bravely on his mettle. While he was a man, and in the main manly, sometimes he was roused to an anger almost childish; then, although he did not want to be a preacher at all, he wished and ever prayed to become a great one, just to convince the old fools who shook their heads over him. To his ears had crept, as such tales will creep, some of the stories of his parents' lives, and, while he pitied his mother, there was a great fierceness in his heart against his father.

But as in the old days when Miss Prime's discipline would have turned all within him to hardness and bitterness Eliphalet Hodges stood between him and despair, so now in this crucial time Elizabeth was a softening influence in his life.

As the days came and went, he had continued to go to see her ever since the night when he had stood with her at the gate and felt the bitterness of her lack of sympathy; but all that had passed now, and unconsciously they had grown nearer to each other. There had been a tacit understanding between them until just a few weeks before. It was on a warm spring evening: he had just passed through her gate and started towards the house, when the opening chords of the piano struck on his ear through the opened window and arrested him. Elizabeth had a pleasant little voice, with a good deal of natural pathos in it. As the minister's daughter, the scope of her songs was properly, according to Dexter, rather limited, but that evening she was singing softly to herself a love-song. The words were these:

> If Death should claim me for her own today,
>   And softly I should falter from your side,
> Oh, tell me, loved one, would my memory stay,
>   And would my image in your heart abide?
> Or should I be as some forgotten dream,
>   That lives its little space, then fades entire?
> Should Time send o'er you its relentless stream
>   To cool your heart, and quench for aye love's fire?
> I would not for the world, love, give you pain,
>   Or ever compass what would cause you grief;
> And oh, how well I know that tears are vain!
>   But love is sweet, my dear, and life is brief;
> So, if some day before you I should go
>   Beyond the sound and sight of song and sea,
> 'T would give my spirit stronger wings to know
>   That you remembered still and wept for me.

She was alone in the room. The song was hardly finished when Brent stepped through the window, and laid his hand over hers where they rested on the keys.

"Why do you sing like that, Elizabeth?" he said, tremulously.

She blushed and lowered her eyes beneath his gaze, as if she already knew the words that were on his lips, or feared that her soul lay too bare before him.

"Why do you think of death?" he asked again, imprisoning her hands.

"It was only my mood," she faltered. "I was thinking, and I thought of the song, and I just sang it."

"Were you thinking of anyone in particular, Lizzie?"

Her head drooped lower until her face was hidden, but she did not answer. A strange boldness had come to him. He went on: "I listened as you were singing, and it seemed as if every word was meant for me, Lizzie. It may sound foolish, but I—I love you. Won't you look at me and tell me that I am right in thinking you love me?" She half raised her face to his and murmured one word. In it were volumes; he bent down and kissed her. It was the first time he had ever kissed a girl. He did it almost fearfully. It was a kiss in which reverence struggled with passion.

"You are to be my little sweetheart now, and I am to be in your thoughts hereafter when you sing; only we don't want any more such songs as this one. I don't want to 'remember still and weep for you,' I want to have you always by me and work for you. Won't you let me?"

Elizabeth found her tongue for a moment only, but that was enough for her lover. A happy light gleamed in his eyes: his face glowed. He was transfigured. Love does so much for a man.

From that time forward, when he was harassed by cares and trouble, he sought out Elizabeth, and, even though he could seldom tell her all that was in his heart, he found relief in her presence. He did not often speak of his trials to her, for, in spite of his love for her, he felt that she could not understand; but the pleasure he found in her company put sweetness into his life and made his burdens easier to bear.

Only once had a little shadow come between them, and the fact that so little a thing could have made a shadow shows in what a narrow, constrained atmosphere the two young people lived. Young Brent still had his half-day position in the store, and when the employees of a rival establishment challenged Daniels's clerks to a game of baseball, he was duly chosen as one of the men to uphold the honor of their house upon the diamond.

The young man was not fossilized. He had strength and the capacity for enjoyment, so he accepted without a thought of wrong. The Saturday came, the game was played. Fred Brent took part, and thereby brought a hornets' nest about his ears. It would scarcely have been so bad, but the young man entered the game with all the zest and earnestness of his intense nature, and several times by brilliant playing saved his side from defeat. In consequence, his name was in the mouth of everyone who had seen or heard of the contest. He was going home that evening, feeling pleased and satisfied with himself, when he thought he would drop in a moment on the way and see Elizabeth. He had hardly got into the house before he saw from her manner that something was wrong, and he wondered what it could be. He soon learned. It is only praise that is slow.

"Oh, Fred," said the girl, reproachfully, "is it true that you have been playing baseball?"

"Baseball, yes; what of it? What are you looking so horrified about?"

"Did you think it was right for you, in your position, to play?"

"If I had thought it was wrong I assuredly should not have played," the young man returned.

"Everybody is talking about it, and father says he thinks you have disgraced your calling."

"Disgraced my calling by playing an innocent game?"

"But father thinks it is a shame for a man who is preparing to do such work as yours to have people talking about him as a mere ball-player."

The blood mounted in hot surges to the young man's face. He felt like saying, "Your father be hanged," but he controlled his anger, and said, quietly, "Elizabeth, don't you ever think for yourself?"

"I suppose I do, Fred, but I have been brought up to respect what my elders think and say."

"Don't you think that they, as well as we, can be narrow and mistaken?"

"It is not for me to judge them. My part is to obey."

"You have learned an excellent lesson," he returned, bitterly. "That is just the thing: 'obey, obey.' Well, I will. I will be a stick, a dolt. I will be as unlike what God intended me to be as possible. I will be just what your father and Aunt Hester and you want me to be. I will let them think for me and save my soul. I am too much an imbecile to attempt to work out my own salvation. No, Elizabeth, I will not play ball any more. I can imagine the horrified commotion it caused among the angels when they looked down and saw me pitching. When I get back to school I shall look up the four Gospels' views on ball-playing."

"Fred, I don't like you when you talk that way."

"I won't do that any more, either." He rose abruptly. "Good-bye, Elizabeth. I am off." He was afraid to stay, lest more bitter words should come to his lips.

"Good-bye, Fred," she said. "I hope you understand."

The young man wondered as he walked homeward if the girl he had chosen was not a little bit prim. Then he thought of her father, and said to himself, even as people would have said of himself, "How can she help it, with such a father?"

All his brightness had been dashed. He was irritated because the thing was so small, so utterly absurd. It was like the sting of a miserable little insect—just enough to smart, and not enough to need a strong remedy. The news of the game had also preceded him home, and his guardian's opinion of the propriety of his action did not tend to soothe his mind. Mrs. Hodges forcibly expressed herself as follows: "I put baseball-playin' right down with dancin' and sich like. It ain't no fittin' occupation for anyone that's a-goin' into the ministry. It's idleness, to begin with; it's a-wastin' the precious time that's been given us for a better use. A young man that's goin' to minister to people's souls ought to be consecrated to the work before he begins it. Who ever heerd tell of Jesus playin' baseball?"

Among a certain class of debaters such an argument is always supposed to be clinching, unanswerable, final. But Mr. Hodges raised his voice in protest. "I ain't a-goin' to keep still no longer. I don't believe the boy's done a bit o' harm. There's lots of things the Lord didn't do that He didn't forbid human bein's to do. We ain't none of us divine, but you mark my words, Freddie, an' I say it right here so's yore aunt Hester can hear me too, you mark my words: ef you never do nothin' worse than what you've been a-doin' today, it'll be mighty easy for you to read your title clear to mansions in the skies."

"Omph huh, 'Liphalet, there ain't nothin' so easy as talkin' when Satin's a-promptin' you."

"There you go, Hester, there you go ag'in a-pattin' the devil on the back. I 'low the Old Boy must be tickled to death with all the compliments Christian people give him."

"A body'd about as well be complimentin' the devil as to be a-countenancin' his works, as you air."

The old man stopped with a piece halfway to his mouth. "Now jest listen at that! Hester Prime, ain't you ashamed of yoreself? Me a-countenancin' wrong! Sayin' that to me, an' me ol' enough to be—to be—well, I'm your husband anyway."

In times of excitement he was apt to forget this fact for the instant and give his wife her maiden name, as if all that was sharp in her belonged to that prenuptial period. But this storm relieved the atmosphere of its tension. Mrs. Hodges felt better for having spoken her mind, and for having answered, while the young man was relieved by the championship of his elder, and so the storm blew over. It was several days before Brent saw Elizabeth again; but, thanks to favoring winds, the sky had also cleared in that direction.

It was through such petty calms and storms that Fred passed the days and weeks of his first year at the seminary. Some of them were small annoyances, to be sure, but he felt them deeply, and the sting of them rankled. It is not to be supposed, because there was no specific outburst, that he was entirely at rest. Vesuvius had slumbered long before Pompeii's direful day. His mind was often in revolt, but he kept it to himself or confided it to only one friend. This friend was a fellow-student at the seminary, a man older than Fred by some years. He had first begun a literary career, but had renounced it for the ministry. Even to him Fred would not commit himself until, near the end of the year, Taylor declared his intention of now renouncing the study of theology for his old pursuits. Then Brent's longing to be free likewise drew his story from his lips.

Taylor listened to him with the air of one who had been through it all and could sympathize. Then he surprised his friend by saying, "Don't be a fool, Brent. It's all very nice and easy to talk about striking out for one's self, and all that. I've been through it all myself. My advice to you is, stay here, go through the academic discipline, and be a parson. Get into a rut if you will, for some ruts are safe. When we are buried deep, they keep us from toppling over. This may be a sort of weak philosophy I am trying to teach you, but it is the happiest. If I can save any man from self-delusion, I want to do it. I'll tell you why. When I was at school some fool put it into my head that I could write. I hardly know how it came about. I began scribbling of my own accord and for my own amusement. Sometimes I showed the things to my friend, who was a fool: he bade me keep on, saying that I had talent. I didn't believe it at first. But when a fellow keeps dinging at another with one remark, after a while he grows to believe it, especially when it is pleasant. It is vastly easy to believe what we want to believe. So I came to think that I could write, and my soul was fired with the ambition to make a name for myself in literature. When I should have been turning Virgil into English for classroom, I was turning out more or less deformed verse of my own, or rapt in the contemplation of some plot for story or play. But somehow I got through school without a decided flunk. In the meantime some of my lines had found their way into print, and the little cheques I received for them had set my head buzzing with dreams of wealth to be made by my pen. If we could only pass the pitfalls of that dreaming age of youth, most of us would get along fairly well in this matter-of-fact old world. But we are likely to follow blindly the leadings of our dreams until we run our heads smack into a corner-post of reality. Then we awaken, but in most cases too late.

"I am glad to say that my father had the good sense to discourage my aspirations. He wanted me to take a profession. But, elated by the applause of my friends, I scorned the idea. What, mew my talents up in a courtroom or a hospital? Never! It makes me sick when I look back upon it and see what a fool I was. I settled down at home and began writing. Lots of things came back from periodicals to which I sent them; but I had been told that this was the common lot of all writers, and I plodded on. A few things sold, just enough to keep my hopes in a state of unstable equilibrium.

"Well, it's no use to tell you how I went on in that way for four years, clinging and losing hold, standing and slipping, seeing the prize recede just as I seemed to grasp it. Then came the awakening. I saw that it would have been better just to go on and do the conventional thing. I found this out too late, and I came here to try to remedy it, but I can't. No one can. You get your mind into a condition where the ordinary routine of study is an impossibility, and you cannot go back and take up the train you have laid, so you keep struggling on wasting your energy, hoping against hope. Then suddenly you find out that you are and can be only third- or at best second-rate. God, what a discovery it is! How you try to fight it off until the last moment! But it comes upon you surely and crushingly, and, cut, bruised, wounded, you slip away from the face of the world. If you are a brave man, you say boldly to yourself, 'I will eke out an existence in some humble way,' and you go away to a life of longing and regret. If you are a coward, you either leap over the parapets of life to hell, or go creeping back and fall at the feet of the thing that has damned you, willing to be third-rate, anything; for you are stung with the poison that never leaves your blood. So it has been with me: even when I found that I must choose a calling, I chose the one that gave me most time to nurse the serpent that had stung me."

Taylor ceased speaking, and looked a little ashamed of his vehemence.

"This is your story," said Brent; "but men differ and conditions differ. I will accept all the misery, all the pain and defeat you have suffered, to be free to choose my own course."

Taylor threw up his hands with a deprecatory gesture. "There," he said; "it is always so. I might as well have talked to the wind."

So the fitful calms and Elizabeth's love had not cured Frederick Brent's heart of its one eating disease, the desire for freedom.

Chapter 11

IT WAS NOT UNTIL early in Brent's second year at the Bible Seminary that he was compelled to go through the ordeal he so much dreaded, that of filling a city pulpit. The Dexterites had been wont to complain that since the advent among them of the theological school their churches had been turned into recitation rooms for the raw students; but of "old Tom Brent's boy," as they still called him, they could never make this complaint. So, as humanity loves to grumble, the congregations began to find fault because he did not do as his fellows did.

The rumors of his prowess in the classroom and his eloquence in the society hall had not abated, and the curiosity of his fellow-townsmen had been whetted to a point where endurance was no longer possible. Indeed, it was open to question whether it was not by connivance of the minister himself, backed by his trustees on one side and the college authorities on the other, that Brent was finally deputed to supply the place of the Rev. Mr. Simpson, who was affected by an indisposition, fancied, pretended, or otherwise.

The news struck the young man like a thunderbolt, albeit he had been expecting it. He attempted to make his usual excuse, but the kindly old professor who had notified him smiled into his face, and, patting his shoulder, said, "It's no use, Brent. I'd go and make the best of it; they're bound to have you. I understand your diffidence in the matter, and, knowing how well you stand in class, it does credit to your modesty."

The old man passed on. He said he understood, but in his heart the young student standing there helpless, hopeless, knew that he did not understand, that he could not. Only he himself could perceive it in all the trying horror of its details.

Only he himself knew fully or could know what the event involved—that when he arose to preach, to nine-tenths of the congregation he would not be Frederick Brent, student, but "old Tom Brent's boy." He recoiled from the thought.

Many a fireside saint has said, "Why did not Savonarola tempt the hot plough-shares? God would not have let them burn him." Faith is a beautiful thing. But Savonarola had the ploughshares at his feet. The children of Israel stepped into the Red Sea before the waters parted, but then Moses was with them, and, what was more, Pharaoh was behind them.

At home, the intelligence of what Brent was to do was received in different manner by Mrs. Hodges and her husband. The good lady launched immediately into a lecture on the duty that was placed in his hands; but Eliphalet was silent as they sat at the table. He said nothing until after supper was over, and then he whispered to his young friend as he started to his room, "I know jest how you feel, Freddie. It seems that I oughtn't to call you that now; but I 'low you'll allus be 'Freddie' to me."

"Don't ever call me anything else, if you please, Uncle 'Liph," said the young man, pressing Eliphalet's hand.

"I think I kin understand you better than most people," Mr. Hodges went on; "an' I know it ain't no easy task that you've got before you."

"You've always understood me better than anyone, and—and I wish you knew what it has meant to me, and that I could thank you somehow."

"'Sh, my boy. It's thanks enough to hear them words from you. Now you jest calm yoreself, an' when Sunday comes—I don't know as I'd ought to say it this way, but I mean it all in a Christian sperrit—when Sunday comes, Freddie, my boy, you jest go in an' give 'em fits."

The two parted with another pressure of the hand, and it must be confessed that the old man looked a little bit sheepish when his wife hoped he had been giving Fred good advice.

"You don't reckon, Hester, that I'd give him any other kind, do you?"

"Not intentionally, 'Liphalet; but when it comes to advice, there's p'ints o' view." Mrs. Hodges seemed suspicious of her husband's capabilities as an adviser.

"There's some times when people'd a good deal ruther have sympathy than advice."

"An' I reckon, 'cordin' to yore way o' thinkin' this is one o' them. Well, I intend to try to do my dooty in this matter, as I've tried to do it all along."

"Hester, yore dooty'll kill you yit. It's a wonder you don't git tired a-lookin' it in the face."

"I ain't a-goin' to shirk it, jest to live in pleasure an' ease."

"No need o' shirkin', Hester, no need o' shirkin'; but they's some people that wouldn't be content without rowin' down stream."

"An' then, mind you, 'Liphalet, I ain't a-exchangin' words with you, fur that's idleness, but there's others, that wouldn't row up stream, but 'ud wait an' hope fur a wind to push 'em." These impersonalities were as near "spatting" as Mr. and Mrs. Hodges ever got.

Through all the community that clustered about Mr. Simpson's church and drew its thoughts, ideas, and subjects of gossip therefrom, ran like wildfire the news that at last they were to have a chance to judge of young Brent's merits for themselves. It caused a stir among old and young, and in the days preceding the memorable Sunday little else was talked of.

When it reached the ears of old Dan'l Hastings, who limped around now upon two canes, but was as acrimonious as ever, he exclaimed, tapping the ground with one of his sticks for emphasis, "What! that young Brent preachin' in our church, in our minister's pulpit! It's a shame—an' he the born son of old Tom Brent, that all the town knows was the worst sinner hereabouts. I ain't a-goin' to go; I ain't a-goin' to go."

"Don't you be afeared to go, Dan'l: there ain't no danger that his docterns air a-goin' to be as strong as his father's whisky," said his old enemy.

"Oh, it's fur the likes o' you, Thomas Donaldson, to be a-talkin' o' docterns an' whisky in the same breath. You never did have no reverence," said the old man, testily.

"An' yet, Dan'l, I've found docterns an' whisky give out by the same breath."

Mr. Hastings did not think it necessary to notice this remark. He went on with his tirade against the prospective "supply": "Why can't Elder Simpson preach hisself, I'd like to know, instead o' puttin' up that young upstart to talk to his betters? Why, I mind the time that that boy had to be took out o' church by the hand fur laffin' at me—at *me*, mind you," the old man repeated, shaking his stick; "laffin' at me when I was expoundin' the word."

"That's ter'ble, Dan'l; fur, as fur as I kin ricollec', when you're a-expoundin' the word it ain't no laffin' matter."

"I tell you, Thomas Donaldson, the world's a-goin' down hill fast: but I ain't a-goin' to help it along. I ain't a-goin' to hear that Brent boy preach."

This declaration, however, did not prevent the venerable Dan'l from being early in his seat on the following Sunday morning, sternly, uncompromisingly critical.

As might have been expected, the church was crowded. Friends, enemies, and the merely curious filled the seats and blocked the aisles. The chapel had been greatly enlarged to accommodate its growing congregation, but on this day it was totally inadequate to hold the people who flocked to its doors.

The Rev. Mr. Simpson was so far recovered from his indisposition as to be able to be present and assist at the service. Elizabeth was there, looking proud and happy and anxious. Mrs. Hodges was in her accustomed place on the ladies' side of the pulpit. She had put new strings to her bonnet in honor of the occasion. Her face wore a look of great severity. An unregenerate wag in the back part of the church pointed her out to his companions and remarked that she looked as if she'd spank the preacher if he didn't do well. "Poor fellow, if he sees that face he'll break down, sure." Opposite, in the "amen corner," the countenance of the good Eliphalet was a study in changing expressions. It was alternately possessed by fear, doubt, anxiety, and exultation.

Sophy Davis sat in a front seat, spick and span in a new dress, which might have been made for the occasion. People said that she was making eyes at her young fellow-salesman, though she was older than he. Mrs. Martin and her friend whispered together a little farther back.

A short time before the service began, Brent entered by a side door near the pulpit and ascended to his place. His entrance caused a marked sensation. His appearance was impressive. The youthful face was white and almost rigid in its lines. "Scared to death," was the mental note of a good many who saw him. But his step was firm. As Elizabeth looked at him, she felt proud that such a man loved her. He was not handsome. His features were irregular, but his eyes were clear and fearless. If a certain cowardice had held him back from this ordeal, it was surely not because he trembled for himself. The life he had lived and the battles he had fought had given a compression to his lips that corrected a natural tendency to weakness in his mouth. His head was set squarely on his broad shoulders. He was above medium height, but not loosely framed. He looked the embodiment of strength.

"He ain't a bit like his father," said someone.

"He's like his father was in his best days," replied another.

"He don't look like he's over-pleased with the business. They say he didn't want to come."

"Well, I guess it's purty resky work gittin' up to speak before all these people that's knowed him all his life, an' know where an' what he come from."

"They say, too, that he's some pumpkins out at the college."

"I 'ain't much faith in these school-made preachers; but we'll soon see what he kin do in the pulpit. We've heerd preachers, an' we kin compare."

"That's so: we've heerd some preachers in our day. He must toe the mark. He may be all right at college, but he's in a pulpit now that has held preachers fur shore. A pebble's all right among pebbles, but it looks mighty small 'longside o' boulders. He's preachin' before people now. Why, Brother Simpson himself never would 'a' got a special dispensation to hold the church all these years, ef it hadn't been fur the people backin' him up an' Conference was afraid they'd leave the connection."

"Well, ef this boy is anything, Lord only knows where he gets it, fur everybody knows—"

"'Sh!"

The buzz which had attended the young speaker's entrance subsided as Mr. Simpson rose and gave out the hymn. That finished, he ran his eyes over the front seats of the assembly and then said, "Brother Hastings, lead us in prayer."

The old man paused for an instant as if surprised, and then got slowly to his knees. It was a strange selection, but we have seen that this particular parson was capable of doing strange things. In the course of a supplication of some fifteen minutes' duration, Brother Hastings managed to vent his spleen upon the people and to pay the Lord a few clumsy compliments. During the usual special blessing which is asked upon the preacher of the hour, he prayed, "O Lord, let not the rarin' horses of his youth run away with Thy chariot of eternal truth. Lord, cool his head and warm his heart and settle him firm. Grant that he may fully realize where he's a-standin' at, an' who he's a-speakin' to. Do Thou not let *him* speak, but speak through him, that Thy gospel may be preached today as Thy prophets of old preached it."

Throughout the prayer, but one thought was running through Frederick Brent's mind, and his heart was crying in its anguish, "Oh, my God, my God, why do they hound me so?"

It is a terrible thing, this first effort before the home people, especially when home has not been kind.

When he arose to meet the people's eyes, his face was haggard and he felt weak. But unflinchingly he swept his eyes over the crowd, and that instant's glance brought before him all the panorama of the past years. There before him was the sneaking Billy Tompkins, now grown to the maturity of being called "Bill." Then there was Dan'l Hastings. Oh, that night, years ago, when he had been marched up the aisle with crimson face! In one brief second he lived it all over again, the shame, the disgrace, the misery of it. There, severe, critical, expectant, sat his guardian, the master-hand who had manipulated all the machinery of his life. All this passed through his mind in a flash, as he stood there facing the people. His face changed. The haggard look passed away. His eyes kindled, his cheeks mantled. Even in the pulpit, even in the house of God, about to speak His word, the blood sped hotly through his veins, and anger burned at his heart. But he crushed down his feelings for the moment, and began in a clear ringing voice, "Judge not, that ye be not judged. For with what judgment ye judge, ye shall be judged, and with what measure ye mete, it shall be measured to you again." The lesson he drew from the words was God's recognition of the fallibility of human judgment, and the self-condemnation brought about by ignoring the prohibition in the text. By an effort, he spoke deliberately at first, but the fire in his heart came out more and more in his words as he progressed. "Blinded by our own prejudices," he said, "circumscribed by our own ignorance, we dare to set ourselves up as censors of our fellow-men. Unable to see the whole chain of life which God has forged, we take a single link and say that it is faulty. Too narrow to see His broad plan, we take a patch of it and say, 'This is not good.' There is One who works even through evil that good may come, but we take the sin of our brother, and, without seeing or knowing what went before it or shall come after, condemn him. What false, blind, petty judges we are! You women who are condemning your fallen sisters, you men who are execrating your sinful brothers, if Christ today were to command, 'Let him who is without sin cast the first stone,' look into your own hearts and answer me, how many of you would dare to lift a hand? How many of you have taken the beam out of your own eye before attempting to pluck the mote out of your brother's? O ye pharisaical ones, who stand in the public places and thank God that you are not as other men, beware, beware. The condemnation that surely and inevitably shall fall upon you is not the judgment of Jesus Christ. It is not the sentence of the Father. It is your own self-condemnation, without charity, without forbearance, without love; 'for with what judgment ye judge ye shall be judged.'

"Stand by the wayside if you will. Draw aside your skirts in the vainglory of self-righteousness from the passing multitude. Say to each other, if you will, 'This woman is a sinner: this man is a criminal.' Close your eyes against their acts of repentance, harden your hearts against their pleas for forgiveness, withhold mercy and pardon and charity; but I tell you of One who has exalted charity into the highest and best of virtues. I bring you the message of One whose judgment is tempered by divine love. He is seeing you. He is hearing you. Over the parapets of high heaven the gentle Father leans waiting to take into His soul any breath of human love or charity which floats up to Him from this sin-parched world. What have you done to merit His approval? Have you been kind, or have you been hard? Have you been gentle, or have you been harsh? Have you been charitable, or have you hunted out all the evil and closed your eyes to all the good? You have forgotten, O ye of little faith, you have forgotten, you without charity in your hearts, and you who claim to follow Christ and yet have no love for your fellows—you have forgotten that God is a God of wrath as well as of love; that Christ hath anger as well as pity; that He who holds the hyssop of divine mercy holds also the scourge of divine indignation. You have forgotten that the lash you so love to wield over your brother's back shall be laid upon your own by Him who whipped the money changers from His temple. Listen! The day shall come when the condemnation you are accumulating against yourselves shall overwhelm you. Stop trying to steal the prerogative of heaven. Judge not. God only is just!"

The silence throughout the sermon was intense. During the closing words which have been quoted, it was like a presence in the chapel. The voice of the preacher rang out like a clarion. His eyes looked before him as if he saw into the future. His hand was uplifted as if he would call down upon them the very judgment which he predicted.

Without more words he sat down. No one moved or spoke for an instant. Dan'l Hastings let his cane fall upon the floor. It echoed through the silent place with a crash. Some of the women started and half cried out; but the spell was now partly broken. Mr. Simpson suddenly remembered to pray, and the gossips forgot to whisper when their heads were bowed. There were some pale faces in the crowd, and some which the galling of tears had made red. There was in the atmosphere something of the same tense silence that follows a terrific thunderclap. And so the service ended, and the people filed out of church silent still. Some few remained behind to shake the preacher's hand, but as soon as the benediction was over he hurried out the side door, and, before anyone could intercept him, was on his way home. But he left a willing substitute. Mrs. Hodges accepted all his congratulations with complacent condescension.

"Dan'l," said Thomas Donaldson, as he helped the old man down the church steps, "I was mistaken about the docterns an' the whisky. It was stronger an' better, because it was the pure stuff."

"I 'ain't got a word to say," said Dan'l, "'ceptin' that a good deal of it was jest sass." But he kept mumbling to himself as he hobbled along, "Jedge not, fur you're a-pilin' up sentences on yoreself. I never thought of it that way before; no, I never."

Brent did not come out of his room to dinner that afternoon. Mrs. Hodges was for calling him, but the old man objected. "No, Hester," he said, "Freddie jest wants to be let alone. He's a-feelin' now."

"But, 'Liphalet, he ought to know how nice people talked about his sermon. I tell you that was my kind o' doctern. It's wonderful how a child will learn."

Notwithstanding his belief that his young friend wanted to be left alone, the old man slipped into his room later on with a cup of tea. The young man sat before the table, his head buried in his hands. Eliphalet set the cup and saucer down and turned to go, but he paused at the door and said, "Thank the Lord fur the way you give it to 'em, Freddie. It was worth a dollar." He would have hurried out, but the young man sprang up and seized his hand, exclaiming, "It was wrong, Uncle 'Liph, it was wrong of me. I saw them sitting about me like jackals waiting for their prey; I remembered all that I had been and all that I was; I knew what they were thinking, and I was angry, angry. God forgive me! That sermon was preached from as hot a heart as ever did murder."

The old man stroked the young one's hair as he would a child's. "Never mind," he said. "It don't matter what you felt. That's between you an' Him. I only know what you said, an' that's all I care about. Didn't you speak about the Lord a-whippin' the money-changers from the temple? Ain't lots o' them worse than the money-changers? Wasn't Christ divine? Ain't you human? Would a body expect you to feel less 'n He did? Huh! jest don't you worry; remember that you didn't hit a head that wasn't in striking distance." And the old man pressed the boy back into his chair and slipped out.

Chapter 12

BESIDE AN ABSOLUTE REFUSAL again to supply, Brent made no sign of the rebellion which was in him, and his second year slipped quickly and uneventfully away. He went to and from his duties silent and self-contained. He did not confide in Mr. Hodges, because his guardian seemed to grow more and more jealous of their friendship. He could not confide in Elizabeth, on account of a growing conviction that she did not fully sympathize with him. But his real feelings may be gathered from a letter which he wrote to his friend Taylor some two months after the events recorded in the last chapter.

"MY DEAR TAYLOR," it ran, "time and again I have told myself that I would write you a line, keeping you in touch, as I promised, with my progress. Many times have I thought of our last talk together, and still I think as I thought then— that, in spite of all your disadvantages and your defeats, you have the best of it. When you fail, it is your own failure, and you bear down with you only your own hopes and struggles and ideals. If I fail, there falls with me all the framework of pride and anxiety that has so long pushed me forward and held me up. For my own failure I should not sorrow: my concern would be for the one who has so carefully shaped me after a pattern of her own. However else one may feel, one must be fair to the ambitions of others, even though one is the mere material that is heated and beaten into form on the anvil of another's will. But I am ripe for re-volt. The devil is in me—a restrained, quiet, well-appearing devil, but all the more terrible for that.

"I have at last supplied one of the pulpits here, that of my own church. The Rev. Mr. Simpson was afflicted with a convenient and adaptable indisposition which would not allow him to preach, and I was deputed to fill his place. I knew what a trial it would be, and had carefully written out my sermon, but I am afraid I did not adhere very strictly to the manuscript. I think I lost my head. I know I lost my temper. But the sermon was a nine days' wonder, and I have had to refuse a dozen subsequent offers to supply. It is all very sordid and sickening and theatrical. The good old Lowry tried to show me that it was my duty and for my good, but I have set my foot down not to supply again, and so they let me alone now.

"It seems to me that that one sermon forged a chain which holds me in a po-sition that I hate. It is a public declaration that I am or mean to be a preacher, and I must either adhere to it or break desperately away. Do you know, I feel myself to be an arrant coward. If I had half the strength that you have, I should have been out of it long ago; but the habit of obedience grows strong upon a man.

"There is but one crowning act to be added to this drama of deceit and infamy—my ordination. I know how all the other fellows are looking forward to it, and how, according to all the prescribed canons, I should view the momentous day; but I am I. Have you ever had one of those dreams where a huge octopus ap-proaches you slowly but certainly, enfolding you in his arms and twining his hor-rid tentacles about your helpless form? What an agony of dread you feel! You try to move or cry out, but you cannot, and the arms begin to embrace you and draw you towards the great body. Just so I feel about the day of the ceremony that shall take me into the body of which I was never destined to be a member.

"Are you living in a garret? Are you subsisting on a crust? Happy, happy fel-low! But, thank God, the ordination does not take place until next year, and per-haps in that time I may find some means of escape. If I do not, I know that I shall have your sympathy; but don't express it. Ever sincerely yours,   BRENT."

But the year was passing, and nothing happened to release him. He found himself being pushed forward at the next term with unusual rapidity, but he did not mind it; the work rather gave him relief from more unpleasant thoughts. He went at it with eagerness and mastered it with ease. His fellow-students looked on him with envy, but he went on his way unheeding and worked for the very love of being active, until one day he understood.

It was nearing the end of the term when a fellow-student remarked to him, "Well, Brent, it isn't every man that could have done it, but you'll get your reward in a month or so now."

"What do you mean?" asked Brent. "Done what?"

"Now don't be modest," rejoined the other; "I am really glad to see you do it. I have no envy."

"Really, Barker, I don't understand you."

"Why, I mean you are finishing two years in one."

"Oh, pshaw! it will hardly amount to that."

"Oh, well, you will get in with the senior class men."

"Get in with the senior class!"

"It will be kind of nice, a year before your time, to be standing in the way of any appointive plums that may happen to fall; and then you don't have to go miles away from home before you can be made a full-fledged shepherd. Well, here is my hand on it anyway."

Brent took the proffered hand in an almost dazed condition. It had all suddenly flashed across his mind, the reason for his haste and his added work. What a blind fool he had been!

The Church Conference met at Dexter that year, and they had hurried him through in order that he might be ready for ordination thereat.

Alleging illness as an excuse, he did not appear at recitation that day. The shock had come too suddenly for him. Was he thus to be entrapped? Could he do nothing? He felt that ordination would bind him for ever to the distasteful work. He had only a month in which to prevent it. He would do it. From that day he tried to fall gradually back in his work; but it was too late; the good record which he had unwittingly piled up carried him through, *nolens volens*.

The week before Conference met, Frederick Brent, residing at Dexter, by special request of the faculty, was presented as a candidate for ordination. Even his enemies in the community said, "Surely there is something in that boy."

Mrs. Hester Hodges was delighted. She presented him with his ordination suit, and altogether displayed a pride and pleasure that almost reconciled the young man to his fate. In the days immediately preceding the event she was almost tender with him, and if he had been strong enough to make a resolve inimical to her hopes, the disappointment which he knew failure would bring to her would have greatly weakened it.

Now, Conference is a great event in the circles of that sect of which Cory Chapel was a star congregation, and the town where it convenes, or "sets," as the popular phrase goes, is an honored place. It takes upon itself an air of unusual bustle. There is a great deal of housecleaning, hanging of curtains, and laying of carpets, just prior to the time. People from the rural parts about come into town, and settle for the week. Ministers and lay delegates from all the churches in the district, comprising perhaps half of a large State or parts of two, come and are quartered upon the local members of the connection. For two weeks beforehand the general question that passes from one housewife to another is, "How many and whom are you going to take?" Many are the heartburnings and jealousies aroused by the disposition of some popular preacher whom a dozen members of the flock desire to entertain, while the less distinguished visitors must bide their time and be stuck in when and where they may. The "big guns" of the Church are all present, and all the "little guns" are scattered about them, popping and snapping every time a "big gun" booms.

But of all of the days of commotion and excitement, the climax is ordination day, when candidates for the ministry, college students, and local preachers are examined and either rejected or admitted to the company of the elect. It is common on that day for some old dignitary of the church, seldom a less person than the president of the Conference himself, to preach the sermon. Then, if the fatted calf is not killed, at least the fatted fowls are, and feasting and rejoicing rule the occasion.

This ordination day was no exception. A class of ten stood up before the examining committee and answered the questions put to them. Among them stood Frederick Brent. He wished, he tried, to fail in his answers and be rejected, even though it meant disgrace; but, try as he would, he could not. Force of habit was too strong for him; or was it that some unseen and relentless power was carrying him on and on against his will? He clinched his hands; the beads of perspiration broke out on his brow; but ever as the essential questions came to him his tongue seemed to move of its own volition, without command from the brain, and the murmurs of approval told him that he was answering aright. Never did man struggle harder for brilliant success than this one for ignominious failure. Then some whisper in his consciousness told him that it was over. He felt the laying of hands upon his head. He heard the old minister saying, "Behold, even from the lowliest God taketh His workers," and he felt a flash of resentment, but it was only momentary. He was benumbed. Something seemed to be saying in his mind, "Will the old fool never have done?" But it did not appear to be himself. It was afar off and apart from him. The next he knew, a wet cheek was laid against his own. It was Aunt Hester. She was crying and holding his hand. Afterwards people were shaking hands with him and offering their congratulations; but he answered them in a helpless, mechanical way, as he had answered the questions.

He sat through the sermon and heard it not. But some interest revived in him as the appointments were being read. He heard the president say, "It gives me pain to announce the resignation of one who has so long served in the Master's vineyard, but our dear brother Simpson has decided that he is too old for active work, and has asked to be retired. While we do this with pain and sorrow for the loss— though we do not wholly lose him—of so able a man, we feel that we cannot do better than appoint as his successor in this charge the young man whom you have all seen so brilliantly enter into the ranks of consecrated workers, the Rev. Frederick Brent."

A murmur of approval went round the assembly, and a few open "amens" broke forth as the unctuous old ecclesiastic sat down. It sounded to the ears of the young preacher like the breaking of waves on a far-off shore; and then the meaning of all that had happened sifted through his benumbed intellect, and he strove to rise. He would refuse to act. He would protest. He would tell them that he did not want to preach. But something held him down. He could not rise. The light went blue and green and purple before him. The church, with its sea of faces, spun round and round; his head fell forward.

"He has fainted," said someone.

"The excitement has been too much for him."

"Poor young man, he has been studying too hard, working for this."

They carried him out and took him home, and one of the elders offered a special prayer for his speedy recovery, and that, being recovered, he might bear his new responsibilities with becoming meekness.

When the young minister came to himself, he was lying on the bed in his own room, and Mrs. Hodges, Eliphalet, and a doctor were bending over him.

"He's coming round all right now," said the medical man. "You won't need me any longer." And he departed.

"How are you now, Fred?" asked Mrs. Hodges.

The young man closed his eyes again and did not answer. He had awakened to a full realization of his position, and a dull misery lay at his heart. He wished that he could die then and there, for death seemed the only escape from his bondage. He was bound, irrevocably bound.

"Poor child," Mrs. Hodges went on, "it was awful tryin' on his nerves. Joy is worse 'n sorrow, sometimes; an' then he'd been workin' so hard. I'd never 'a' believed he could do it, ef Brother Simpson hadn't stuck up fur it."

"She knew it, then," thought Fred. "It was all planned."

"I don't think you'd better talk, Hester," said her husband, in a low voice. He had seen a spasm pass over the face of the prostrate youth.

"Well, I'll go out an' see about the dinner. Some o' the folks I've invited will be comin' in purty soon, an' others'll be droppin' in to inquire how he is. I do hope he'll be well enough to come to the table: it won't seem hardly like an ordination dinner without the principal person. Jes' set by him, 'Liphalet, an' give him them drops the doctor left."

As soon as he heard the door close behind her, Brent opened his eyes and suddenly laid his hand on the old man's shoulder. "You won't let anybody see me, Uncle 'Liph? you won't let them come in here?"

"No, no, my boy, not ef you don't want 'em," said the old man.

"I shall have to think it all over before I see anyone. I am not quite clear yet."

"I 'low it was unexpected."

"Did you know, Uncle 'Liph?" he asked, fixing his eyes upon his old friend's face.

"I know'd they was a-plannin' somethin', but I never could find out what, or I would have told you."

A look of relief passed over Brent's face. Just then Mrs. Hodges opened the door. "Here's Elizabeth to see him," she said.

"'Sh," said the old man with great ostentation; and tiptoeing over to the door he partly drew it to, putting his head outside to whisper, "He is too weak; it ain't best fur him to see nobody now."

He closed the door and returned to his seat. "It was 'Lizabeth," he said. "Was I right?"

For answer the patient arose from the bed and walked weakly over to his side.

"Tut, tut, tut, Freddie," said Eliphalet, hesitating over the name. "You'd better lay down now; you ain't any too strong yet."

The young man leaned heavily on his chair, and looked into his friend's eyes: "If God had given me such a man as you as a father, or even as a guardian, I would not have been damned," he said.

"'Sh, 'sh, my boy. Don't say that. You're goin' to be all right; you're—you're—" Eliphalet's eyes were moist, and his voice choked here. Rising, he suddenly threw his arms around Fred's neck, crying, "You are my son. God has give you to me to nurse in the time of your trial."

The young man returned the embrace; and so Mrs. Hodges found them when she opened the door softly and peered in. She closed it noiselessly and withdrew.

"Well, I never!" she said. There was a questioning wonder in her face.

"I don't know what to make of them two," she added; "they couldn't have been lovin'er ef they had been father and son."

After a while the guests began to arrive for the dinner. Many were the inquiries and calls for the new minister, but to them all Eliphalet made the same answer: "He ain't well enough to see folks."

Mrs. Hodges herself did her best to bring him out, or to get him to let some of the guests in, but he would not. Finally her patience gave way, and she exclaimed, "Well, now, Frederick Brent, you must know that you air the pastor of a church, an' you've got to make some sacrifices for people's sake. Ef you kin possibly git up—an' I know you kin—you ought to come out an' show yourself for a little while, anyhow. You've got some responsibilities now."

"I didn't ask for them," he answered, coldly. There was a set look about his lips. "Neither will I come out or see anyone. If I am old enough to be the pastor of a church, I am old enough to know my will and have it."

Mrs. Hodges was startled at the speech. She felt vaguely that there was a new element in the boy's character since morning. He was on the instant a man. It was as if clay had suddenly hardened in the potter's hands. She could no longer mold or ply him. In that moment she recognized the fact.

The dinner was all that could be expected, and her visitors enjoyed it, in spite of the absence of the guest of honor, but for the hostess it was a dismal failure. After wielding the scepter for years, it had been suddenly snatched from her hand; and she felt lost and helpless, deprived of her power.

Chapter 13

As Brent thought of the long struggle before him, he began to wish that there might be something organically wrong with him which the shock would irritate into fatal illness. But even while he thought this he sneered at himself for the weakness. A weakness self-confessed holds the possibility of strength. So in a few days he rallied and took up the burden of his life again. As before he had found relief in study, now he stilled his pains and misgivings by a strict attention to the work which his place involved.

His was not an easy position for a young man. He had to go through the ordeal of pastoral visits. He had to condole with old ladies who thought a preacher had nothing else to do than to listen to the recital of their ailments. He had to pray with poor and stricken families whose conditions reminded him strongly of what his own must have been. He had to speak words of serious admonition to girls nearly his own age, who thought it was great fun and giggled in his face. All this must he do, nor must he slight a single convention. No rules of conduct are so rigid as are those of a provincial town. He who ministers to the people must learn their prejudices and be adroit enough not to offend them or strong enough to break them down. It was a great load to lay on the shoulders of so young a man. But habit is everything, and he soon fell into the ways of his office. Writing to Taylor, he said, "I am fairly harnessed now, and at work, and, although the pulling is somewhat hard, I know my way. It is wonderful how soon a man falls into the cant of his position and learns to dole out the cut-and-dried phrases of ministerial talk like a sort of spiritual phonograph. I must confess, though, that I am rather good friends with the children who come to my Sunday-school. My own experiences as a child are so fresh in my memory that I rather sympathize with the little fellows, and do all I can to relieve the half-scared stiffness with which they conduct themselves in church and the Sunday-school room.

"I wonder why it is we make church such a place of terror to the young ones. No wonder they quit coming as soon as they can choose.

"I shock Miss Simpson, who teaches a mixed class, terribly, by my freedom with the pupils. She says that she can't do anything with her charges any more; but I notice that her class and the school are growing. I've been at it for several weeks now, and, like a promising baby, I am beginning to take an interest in things.

"If I got on with the old children of my flock as well as I do with the young ones, I should have nothing to complain of; but I don't. They know as little as the youngsters, and are a deal more unruly. They are continually comparing me with their old pastor, and it is needless to say that I suffer by the comparison. The ex-pastor himself burdens me with advice. I shall tell him some day that he has resigned. But I am growing diplomatic, and have several reasons for not wishing to offend him. For all which 'shop' pray forgive me."

One of the reasons for not wishing to offend the Rev. Mr. Simpson of which Brent wrote was, as may be readily inferred, his engagement to Elizabeth. It had not yet officially become public property, but few of Dexter's observant and forecasting people who saw them together doubted for a moment that it would be a match. Indeed, some spiteful people in the community, who looked on from the outside, said that "Mr. Simpson never thought of resigning until he saw that he could keep the place in the family." But of course they were Baptists who said this, or Episcopalians, or Presbyterians—some such unregenerate lot.

Contrary to the adage, the course of love between the young people did run smooth. The young minister had not disagreed with the older one, so Elizabeth had not disagreed with him, because she did not have to take sides. She was active in the Sunday-school and among the young people's societies, and Brent thought that she would make an ideal minister's wife. Every Sunday, after church, they walked home together, and sometimes he would stop at the house for a meal. They had agreed that at the end of his first pastoral year they would be married; and both parent and guardian smiled on the prospective union.

As his beloved young friend seemed to grow more settled and contented, Eliphalet Hodges waxed more buoyant in the joy of his hale old age, and his wife, all her ambitions satisfied, grew more primly genial every day.

Brent found his congregation increasing, and heard himself spoken of as a popular preacher. Under these circumstances, it would seem that there was nothing to be desired to make him happy. But he was not so, though he kept an unruffled countenance. He felt the repression that his position put upon him. He prayed that with time it might pass off, but this prayer was not answered. There were times when, within his secret closet, the contemplation of the dead level of his life, as it spread out before him, drove him almost to madness.

The bitterness in his heart against his father had not abated one jot, and whenever these spasms of discontent would seize him he was wont to tell himself, "I am fighting old Tom Brent now, and I must conquer him."

Thus nearly a year passed away, and he was beginning to think of asking Elizabeth to name the day. He had his eye upon a pretty little nest of a house, sufficiently remote from her father's, and he was looking forward to settling quietly down in a home of his own.

It was about this time that, as he sat alone one evening in the little chamber which was his study and bedroom in one, Mr. Simpson entered and opened conversation with him.

For some time a rumor which did violence to the good name of Sophy Davis had been filtering through the community. But it had only filtered, until the girl's disappearance a day or two before had allowed the gossips to talk openly, and great was the talk. The young minister had looked on and listened in silence. He had always known and liked Sophy, and if what the gossip said of her was true, he pitied the girl.

On this particular evening it was plain that Mr. Simpson had come to talk about the affair. After some preliminary remarks, he said, "You have a great chance, dear Brother Brent, for giving the devil in this particular part of the moral vineyard a hard blow."

"I don't clearly see why now, more than before," returned Brent.

"Because you are furnished with a living example of the fruits of evil: don't you see?"

"If there is such an example furnished, the people will see it for themselves, and I should be doing a thankless task to point it out to them. I would rather show people the beauty of good than the ugliness of evil."

"Yes, that's the milk-and-water new style of preaching."

"Well, we all have our opinions, to be sure, but I think it rather a good style." Brent was provokingly nonchalant, and his attitude irritated the elder man.

"We won't discuss that: we will be practical. I came to advise you to hold Sophy Davis up in church next Sunday as a fearful example of evil-doing. You needn't mention any names, but you can make it strong and plain enough."

Brent flushed angrily. "Are there not enough texts in here," he asked, laying his hand upon the Bible, "that I can cite and apply, without holding up a poor weak mortal to the curiosity, scorn, and derision of her equally weak fellows?"

"But it is your duty as a Christian and a preacher of the gospel to use this warning."

"I do not need to kick a falling girl to find examples to warn people from sin; and as for duty, I think that each man best knows his own."

"Then you aren't going to do it?"

"No," the young man burst forth. "I am a preacher of the gospel, not a clerical gossip."

"Do you mean that I am a gossip?"

"I was not thinking of you."

"Let me preach for you, Sunday."

"I will not do that either. I will not let my pulpit be debased by anything which I consider so low as this business."

"You will not take advice, then?"

"Not such as that."

"Be careful, Frederick Brent. I gave you that pulpit, and I can take it away—I that know who you are and what you come from."

"The whole town knows what you know, so I do not care for that. As for taking my pulpit from me, you may do that when you please. You put it upon me by force, and by force you may take it; but while I am pastor there I shall use my discretion in all matters of this kind."

"Sophy's been mighty quiet in her devilment. She doesn't accuse anybody. Maybe you've got more than one reason for shielding her."

Brent looked into the man's eyes and read his meaning; then he arose abruptly and opened the door.

"I'm not accusing—"

"Go," said the young man hoarsely. His face was white, and his teeth were hard set.

"You'll learn some respect for your elders yet, if—"

"Go!" Brent repeated, and he took a step towards his visitor. Mr. Simpson looked startled for a moment, but he glanced back into the young man's face and then passed hurriedly out of the room.

Brent let two words slip between his clenched teeth: "The hound!"

No one knew what had passed between the young pastor and Mr. Simpson, but many mutterings and head-shakings of the latter indicated that all was not right. No one knew? Perhaps that is hardly correct, for on Sunday, the sermon over, when Brent looked to find Elizabeth in her usual place whence they walked home together, she was gone. He bit his lip and passed on alone, but it rankled within him that she had so easily believed ill of him.

But he had not seen the last of the Rev. Mr. Simpson's work. It was the right of five members of the congregation to call a church meeting, and when he returned for service in the evening he found upon the pulpit the written request for such an assembly to be held on Tuesday night. Heading the list of members was the name of the former pastor, although this was not needed to tell the young man that it was his work. In anger he gave out the notice and went on with his duties.

"Somethin' must 'a' riled you tonight, Fred," said Eliphalet when church was out. "You give 'em a mighty stirrin' touch o' fire. It 'minded me o' that old supply sermon." Brent smiled mirthlessly. He knew that the same feelings had inspired both efforts.

On Tuesday evening he was early at church, and in the chair, as was the pastor's place. Early as he was, he did not much precede Mr. Simpson, who came in, followed by a coterie of his choicest spirits.

When the assembly had been duly called to order, Brent asked, "Will someone now please state the object of this meeting?"

Mr. Simpson arose.

"Brothers and sisters," he said, "the object of this meeting is a very simple one. From the time that I began to preach in this church, twenty-five years ago, we had purity and cleanness in the pulpit and in the pew."

Brent's eyes were flashing. Eliphalet Hodges, who had thought that the extra session was for some routine business, pricked up his ears.

Simpson proceeded: "One in this flock has lately gone astray: she has fallen into evil ways—"

"Brother Simpson," interrupted Brent, his face drawn and hard with anger, "will you state the object of this meeting?"

"If the pastor is not afraid to wait, he will see that that is what I am doing."

"Then you are bringing into the church matters that have no business here."

"We shall see about that. We intend to investigate and see why you refused to hold up as a warning one of the sinners of this connection. We propose to ask whom you were shielding—a sinner in the pew, or a sinner in the pulpit as well. We propose—"

"Stop!" The young man's voice broke out like the report of a rifle. "Stop, I say, or, as God sees me, here in His temple, at His very altar, I will do you violence. I speak to you not as your pastor, but as a man: not as an accused man, for you dare not accuse me."

The church was in a commotion. In all its long history, such a scene had never before been enacted within the sacred walls. The men sat speechless; the women shrank far down into their seats. Only those two men, the young and the old, stood glaring into each other's faces.

"Remember, brethren," said someone, recovering himself, "that this is the house of God, and that you are preachers of the gospel."

"I do remember that it is God's house, and for that reason I will not let it be disgraced by scandal that would stain the lowest abode of vice. I do remember that I am a preacher, and for that reason I will not see the gospel made vindictive —a scourge to whip down a poor girl, who may have sinned—I know not—but who, if she did, has an advocate with God. Once before in this place I have told you my opinion of your charity and your love. Once before have I branded you as mockeries of the idea of Christianity. Now I say to you, you are hypocrites. You are like carrion birds who soar high up in the ether for a while and then swoop down to revel in filth and rottenness. The stench of death is sweet to you. Putridity is dear to you. As for you who have done this work, you need pity. Your own soul must be reeking with secret foulness to be so basely suspicious. Your own eyes must have cast unholy glances to so soon accuse the eyes of others. As for the thing which you, mine enemy, have intimated here tonight, as pastor of this church I scorn to make defense. But as a man I say, give such words as those breath again, and I will forget your age and only remember your infamy. I see the heads of some about me here wagging, some that knew my father. I hear their muffled whispers, and I know what they are saying. I know what is in their hearts. You are saying that it is the old Tom Brent in me showing itself at last. Yes, it has smoldered in me long, and I am glad. I think better of that spirit because it was waked into life to resent meanness. I would rather be the most roistering drunkard that ever reeled down these streets than call myself a Christian and carouse over the dead characters of my fellows.

"Tonight I feel for the first time that I am myself. I give you back gladly what you have given me. I am no longer your pastor. We are well quit. Even while I have preached to you, I have seen in your hearts your scorn and your distrust, and I have hated you in secret. But I throw off the cloak. I remove the disguise. Here I stand stripped of everything save the fact that I am a man; and I despise you openly. Yes, old Tom, drunken Tom Brent's son despises you. Go home. Go home. There may be work for your stench-loving nostrils there."

He stood like an avenging spirit, pointing towards the door, and the people who had sat there breathless through it all rose quietly and slipped out. Simpson joined them and melted into the crowd. They were awed and hushed.

Only Mrs. Hodges, white as death, and her husband, bowed with grief, remained. A silent party, they walked home together. Not until they were in the house did the woman break down, and then she burst into a storm of passionate weeping as if the pent-up tears of all her stoical life were flowing at once.

"Oh, Fred, Fred," she cried between her sobs, "I see it all now. I was wrong. I was wrong. But I did it all fur the best. The Lord knows I did it fur the best."

"I know you did, Aunt Hester, but I wish you could have seen sooner, before the bitterness of death had come into my life." He felt strangely hard and cold. Her grief did not affect him then.

"Don't take on so, Hester," said the old man, but the woman continued to rock herself to and fro and moan, "I did it fur the best, I did it fur the best." The old man took her in his arms, and after a while she grew more calm, only her sobs breaking the silence.

"I shall go away tomorrow," said Brent. "I am going out into the world for myself. I've been a disgrace to every one connected with me."

"Don't say that about yoreself, Fred; I ain't a-goin' to hear it," said Eliphalet. "You've jest acted as any right-thinkin' man would 'a' acted. It wouldn't 'a' been right fur you to 'a' struck Brother Simpson, but I'm nearer his age, an' my hands itched to git a hold o' him." The old man looked menacing, and his fist involuntarily clenched.

"'Liphalet," said his wife, "I've been a-meddlin' with the business o' Providence, an' I've got my jest deserts. I thought I knowed jest what He wanted me to do, an' I was more ignorant than a child. Furgive me ef you kin, Fred, my boy. I was tryin' to make a good man o' you."

"There's nothing for me to forgive, Aunt Hester. I'm sorry I've spoiled your plans."

"I'm glad, fur mebbe God'll have a chance now to work his own plans. But pore little 'Lizabeth!"

Brent's heart hurt him as he heard the familiar name, and he turned abruptly and went to his room. Once there, he had it out with himself. "But," he told himself, "if I had the emergency to meet again, I should do the same thing."

The next morning's mail brought him a little packet in which lay the ring he had given Elizabeth to plight their troth.

"I thank you for this," he said. "It makes my way easier."

Chapter 14

THE STORY OF THE altercation between the young minister and a part of his congregation was well bruited about the town, and all united in placing the fault heavily on the young man's shoulders. As for him, he did not care. He was wild with the enjoyment of his newfound freedom. Only now and again, as he sat at the table the morning after, and looked into the sad faces of Eliphalet and his guardian, did he feel any sorrow at the turn matters had taken.

In regard to Elizabeth, he felt only relief. It was as if a half-defined idea in his mind had been suddenly realized. For some time he had believed her unable either to understand him or to sympathize with his motives. He had begun to doubt the depth of his own feeling for her. Then had come her treatment of him last Sunday, and somehow, while he knew it was at her father's behest, he could not help despising her weakness.

He had spent much of the night before in packing his few effects, and all was now ready for his departure as they sat at breakfast. Mrs. Hodges was unusually silent, and her haggard face and swollen eyes told how she had passed the night. All in a single hour she had seen the work of the best part of her life made as naught, and she was bowed with grief and defeat. Frederick Brent's career had really been her dream. She had scarcely admitted, even to herself, how deeply his success affected her own happiness. She cared for him in much the same way that a sculptor loves his statue. Her attitude was that of one who says, "Look upon this work; is it not fair? I made it myself." It was as much her pride as it was her love that was hurt, because her love had been created by her pride. She had been prepared to say, exultingly, "Look where he came from, and look where he is"; and now his defection deprived her for ever of that sweet privilege. People had questioned her ability to train up a boy rightly, and she had wished to refute their imputations, by making that boy the wonder of the community and their spiritual leader; and just as she had deemed her work safely done, lo, it had come toppling about her ears. Even if the fall had come sooner, she would have felt it less. It was the more terrible because so unexpected, for she had laid aside all her fears and misgivings and felt secure in her achievement.

"You ain't a-eatin' nothin', Hester," said her husband, anxiously. "I hope you ain't a-feelin' bad this mornin'." He had heard her sobbing all night long, and the strength and endurance of her grief frightened him and made him uneasy, for she had always been so stoical. "Hadn't you better try an' eat one o' them buckwheat cakes? Put lots o' butter an' molasses on it; they're mighty good."

"Ef they're so good, why don't you eat yoreself? You been foolin' with a half a one for the last ten minutes." Indeed, the old man's food did seem to stick in his throat, and once in a while a mist would come up before his eyes. He too had had his dreams, and one of them was of many a happy evening spent with his beloved boy, who should be near him, a joy and comfort in the evening of his life; and now he was going away.

The old man took a deep gulp at his coffee to hide his emotion. It burned his mouth and gave reason for the moisture in his eye when he looked up at Fred.

"What train air you goin' to take, Fred?" he asked.

"I think I'll catch that eight-fifty flier. It's the best I can get, you know, and vestibuled through, too."

"You have jest finally made up yore mind to go, have you?"

"Nothing could turn me from it now, Uncle 'Liph."

"It seems like a shame. You 'ain't got nothin' to do down in Cincinnaty."

"I'll find something before long. I am going to spend the first few days just in getting used to being free." The next moment he was sorry that he had said it, for he saw his guardian's eyes fill.

"I am sorry, Frederick," she said, with some return to her old asperity, "I am sorry that I've made your life so hard that you think that you have been a slave. I am sorry that my home has been so unpleasant that you're so powerful glad to git away from it, even to go into a strange city full of wickedness an' sin."

"I didn't mean it that way, Aunt Hester. You've been as good as you could be to me. You have done your duty by me, if anyone ever could."

"Well, I am mighty glad you realize that, so's ef you go away an' fall into sinful ways you can't lay none of it to my bringin'-up."

"I feel somehow as if I would like to have a go with sin some time, to see what it is like."

"Well, I lay you'll be satisfied before you've been in Cincinnaty long, for ef there ever was livin' hells on airth, it's them big cities."

"Oh, I have got faith to believe that Fred ain't a-goin' to do nothin' wrong," said Eliphalet.

"Nobody don't know what nobody's a-goin' to do under temptation sich as is layin' in wait fur young men in the city, but I'm shore I've done my best to train you right, even ef I have made some mistakes in my poor weak way an' manner."

"If I do fall into sinful ways, Aunt Hester, I shall never blame you or your training for it."

"But you ain't a-goin' to do it, Fred; you ain't a-goin' to fall into no evil ways."

"I don't know, Uncle 'Liph. I never felt my weakness more than I do now."

"Then that very feelin' will be yore stren'th, my boy. Keep on feelin' that way."

"It'll not be a stren'th in Cincinnaty, not by no means. There is too many snares an' pitfalls there to entrap the weak," Mrs. Hodges insisted.

It is one of the defects of the provincial mind that it can never see any good in a great city. It concludes that, as many people are wicked, where large numbers of human beings are gathered together there must be a much greater amount of evil than in a smaller place. It overlooks the equally obvious reasoning that, as some people are good, in the larger mass there must be also a larger amount of goodness. It seems a source of complacent satisfaction to many to sit in contemplation of the fact of the extreme wickedness of the world. They are like children who delight in a "bluggy" story—who gloat over murder and rapine.

Brent, however, was in no wise daunted by the picture of evil which his guardian painted for him, and as soon as breakfast was over he got his things in hand ready to start. Buoyant as he was with his new freedom, this was a hard moment for him. Despite the severity of his youthful treatment in Dexter, the place held all the tender recollections he had, and the room where he stood was the scene of some memories that now flooded his mind and choked his utterance when he strove to say good-bye. He had thought that he should do it with such a fine grace. He would prove such a strong man. But he found his eyes suffused with tears, as he held his old guardian's hand, for, in spite of all, she had done the best for him that she knew, and she had taken a hard, uncompromising pride in him.

"I hope you'll git along all right, Frederick," she faltered forth tearfully. "Keep out of bad company, an' let us hear from you whenever you can. The Lord knows I've tried to do my dooty by you."

Poor Eliphalet tried to say something as he shook the young man's hand, but he broke down and wept like a child. The boy could not realize what a deal of sunshine he was taking out of the old man's life.

"I'll write to you as soon as I am settled," he told them, and with a husky farewell hurried away from the painful scene. At the gate the old couple stood and watched him go swinging down the street towards the station. Then they went into the house, and sat long in silence in the room he had so lately left. The breakfast-table, with all that was on it, was left standing unnoticed and neglected, a thing unprecedented in Mrs. Hodges' orderly household.

Finally her husband broke the silence. "It 'pears as if we had jest buried someone and come home from the funeral."

"An' that's jest what we have done, ef we only knowed it, 'Liphalet. We've buried the last of the Fred Brent we knowed an' raised. Even ef we ever see him ag'in, he'll never be the same to us. He'll have new friends to think of an' new notions in his head."

"Don't say that, Hester; don't say that. I can't stand it. He is never goin' to furgit you an' me, an' it hurts me to hear you talk like that."

"It don't soun' none too pleasant fur me, 'Liphalet, but I've learned to face the truth, an' that's the truth ef it ever was told."

"Well, mebbe it's fur the best, then. It'll draw us closer together and make us more to each other as we journey down to the end. It's our evenin', Hester, an' we must expect some chilly winds 'long towards night, but I guess He knows best." He reached over and took his wife's hand tenderly in his, and so they sat on sadly, but gathering peace in the silence and the sympathy, until far into the morning.

Meanwhile the eight-fifty "flier" was speeding through the beautiful Ohio Valley, bearing the young minister away from the town of his birth. Out of sight of the grief of his friends, he had regained all his usual stolid self-possession, though his mind often went back to the little cottage at Dexter where the two old people sat, and he may be forgiven if his memory lingered longer over the image of the man than of the woman. He remembered with a thrill at his heart what Eliphalet Hodges had been to him in the dark days of his youth, and he confessed to himself with a half shame that his greatest regret was in leaving him.

The feeling with which he had bidden his guardian good-bye was one not of regret at his own loss, but of pity for her distress. To Elizabeth his mind only turned for a moment to dismiss her with a mild contempt. Something hard that had always been in his nature seemed to have suddenly manifested itself.

"It is so much better this way," he said, "for if the awakening had come later we should have been miserable together." And then his thoughts went forward to the new scenes towards which he was speeding.

He had never been to Cincinnati. Indeed, except on picnic days, he had scarcely ever been outside of Dexter. But Cincinnati was the great city of his State, the one towards which adventurous youth turned its steps when real life was to be begun. He dreaded and yet longed to be there, and his heart was in a turmoil of conflicting emotion as he watched the landscape flit by.

It was a clear August day. Nature was trembling and fainting in the ecstasies of sensuous heat. Beside the railway the trenches which in spring were gurgling brooks were now dry and brown, and the reeds which had bent forward to kiss the water now leaned over from very weakness, dusty and sickly. The fields were ripening to the harvest. There was in the air the smell of fresh-cut hay. The cornstalks stood like a host armed with brazen swords to resist the onslaught of that other force whose weapon was the corn-knife. Farther on, between the trees, the much depleted river sparkled in the sun and wound its way, now near, now away from the road, a glittering dragon in an enchanted wood.

Such scenes as these occupied the young man's mind, until, amid the shouts of brakemen, the vociferous solicitations of the baggageman, and a general air of bustle and preparation, the train thundered into the Grand Central Station. Something seized Brent's heart like a great compressing hand. He was frightened for an instant, and then he was whirled out with the rest of the crowd, up the platform, through the thronged waiting room, into the street.

Then the cries of the eager men outside of "Cab, sir? cab, sir?" "Let me take your baggage," and "Which way, sir?" bewildered him. He did the thing which every provincial does: he went to a policeman and inquired of him where he might find a respectable boardinghouse. The policeman did not know, but informed him that there were plenty of hotels farther up. With something like disgust, Brent wondered if all the hotels were like those he saw at the station, where the guests had to go through the barroom to reach their chambers. He shuddered at it; so strong is the influence of habit. But he did not wish to go to a hotel: so, carrying his two valises, he trudged on, though the hot sun of the mid-afternoon beat mercilessly down upon him. He kept looking into the faces of people who passed him, in the hope that he might see in one encouragement to ask for the information he so much wanted; but one and all they hurried by without even so much a glance at the dusty traveler. Had one of them looked at him, he would merely have said, mentally, "Some country bumpkin come in to see the sights of town and be buncoed."

There is no loneliness like the loneliness of the unknown man in a crowd. A feeling of desolation took hold upon Brent, so he turned down a side-street in order to be more out of the main line of business. It was a fairly respectable quarter; children were playing about the pavements and in the gutters, while others with pails and pitchers were going to and from the corner saloon, where their vessels were filled with foaming beer. Brent wondered at the cruelty of parents who thus put their children in the way of temptation, and looked to see if the little ones were not bowed with shame; but they all strode stolidly on, with what he deemed an unaccountable indifference to their own degradation. He passed one place where the people were drinking in the front yard, and saw a mother holding a glass of beer to her little one's lips. He could now understand the attitude of the children, but the fact, nevertheless, surprised and sickened him.

Finally, the sign "Boarding Here" caught his eye. He went into the yard and knocked at the door. A plump German girl opened it, and, to his question as to accommodation, replied that she would see her mistress. He was ushered into a little parlor that boasted some shabby attempts at finery, and was soon joined by a woman whom he took to be the "lady of the house."

Yes, Mrs. Jones took boarders. Would he want room and board? Terms five dollars per week. Had he work in the city? No? Well, from gentlemen who were out of work she always had her money in advance. But would he see his room first?

Wondering much at Mrs. Jones's strange business arrangement, Brent allowed her to conduct him to a room on the second floor, which looked out on the noisy street. It was not a palatial place by any means, but was not uncomfortable save for the heat, which might be expected anywhere on such a day. He was tired and wanted rest, so he engaged the place and paid the woman then and there.

"You just come off the train, I see. Will you have luncheon at once, Mr.—?"

"Brent," said he. "Yes, I will have some luncheon, if you please."

"Do you take beer with your luncheon?"

"No-o," he said, hesitating; and yet why should he not take beer? Everybody else did, even the children. Then he blushed as he thought of what his aunt Hester would think of his even hesitating over the question. She would have shot out a "no" as if it were an insult to be asked. So without beer he ate his luncheon and lay down to rest for the afternoon. When one has traveled little, even a short journey is fatiguing.

In the evening Brent met some of the other boarders at supper; there were not many. They were principally clerks in shops or under-bookkeepers. One genial young fellow struck up a conversation with Fred, and became quite friendly during the evening.

"I guess you will go out to the 'Zoo' tomorrow, won't you? That is about the first place that visitors usually strike for when they come here."

"I thought of getting a general idea of the city first, so that I could go round better before going farther out."

"Oh, you won't have any trouble in getting around. Just ask folks, and they will direct you anywhere."

"But everybody seems to be in a hurry; and by the time I open my mouth to ask them, they have passed me."

The young clerk, Mr. Perkins by name, thought this was a great joke and laughed long and loudly at it.

"I wish to gracious I could go around with you. I have been so busy ever since I have been here that I have never seen any of the show sights myself. But I tell you what I will do: I can steer you around some on Thursday night. That is my night off, and then I will show you some sights that are sights." The young man chuckled as he got his hat and prepared to return to the shop. Brent thanked him in a way that sounded heavy and stilted even to his own ears after the other's light pleasantry.

"And another thing," said Perkins, "we will go to see the baseball game on Sunday, Clevelands and the Reds—great game, you know." It was well that Mr. Perkins was halfway out of the door before he finished his sentence, for there was no telling what effect upon him the flush which mounted to Brent's face and the horror in his eyes would have had.

Go to a baseball game on Sunday! What would his people think of such a thing? How would he himself feel there—he, notwithstanding his renunciation of office, a minister of the gospel? He hastened to his room, where he could be alone and think. The city indeed was full of temptations to the young! And yet he knew he would be ashamed to tell his convictions to Perkins, or to explain his horror at the proposition. Again there came to him, as there had come many times before, the realization that he was out of accord with his fellows. He was not in step with the procession. He had been warped away from the parallel of everyday, ordinary humanity. In order to still the tumult in his breast, he took his hat and wandered out upon the street. He wanted to see people, to come into contact with them and so rub off some of the strangeness in which their characters appeared to him.

The streets were all alight and alive with bustle. Here a fakir with loud voice and marketplace eloquence was vending his shoddy wares; there a drunkard reeled or was kicked from the door of a saloon, whose noiselessly swinging portals closed for an instant only to be reopened to admit another victim, who ere long would be treated likewise. A quartet of young Negroes were singing on the pavement in front of a house as he passed and catching the few pennies and nickels that were flung to them from the door. A young girl smiled and beckoned to him from a window, and another who passed laughed saucily up into his face and cried, "Ah, there!" Everywhere was the inevitable pail flashing to and fro. Sickened, disgusted, thrown back upon himself, Brent turned his steps homeward again. Was this the humanity he wanted to know? Was this the evil which he wanted to have a go with? Was Aunt Hester, after all, in the right, and was her way the best? His heart was torn by a multitude of conflicting emotions. He had wondered, in one of his rebellious moods, if, when he was perfectly untrammeled, he would ever pray; but on this night of nights, before he went wearily to bed, he remained long upon his knees.

Chapter 15

BRENT FOUND HIMSELF IN a most peculiar situation. He had hated the severe discipline of his youth, and had finally rebelled against it and renounced its results as far as they went materially. This he had thought to mean his emancipation. But when the hour to assert his freedom had come, he found that the long years of rigid training had bound his volition with iron bands. He was wrapped in a mantle of habit which he was ashamed to display and yet could not shake off. The pendulum never stops its swing in the middle of the arc. So he would have gone to the other extreme and reveled in the pleasures whose very breath had been forbidden to his youth; but he found his sensibilities revolting from everything that did not accord with the old Puritan code by which they had been trained. He knew himself to be full of capabilities for evil, but it seemed as if some power greater than his held him back. It was Frederick Brent who looked on sin abstractly, but its presence in the concrete was seen through the eyes of Mrs. Hester Hodges. It could hardly be called the decree of conscience, because so instantaneous was the rejection of evil that there was really no time for reference to the internal monitor. The very restriction which he had complained of he was now putting upon himself. The very yoke whose burden he hated he was placing about his own neck. He had run away from the sound of "right" and "duty," but had not escaped their power. He felt galled, humiliated, and angry with himself, because he had long seen the futility of blind indignation against the unseen force which impelled him forward in a hated path.

One thing that distressed him was a haunting fear of the sights which Perkins would show him on the morrow's night. He had seen enough for himself to conjecture of what nature they would be. He did not want to see more, and yet how could he avoid it? He might plead illness, but that would be a lie; and then there would be other nights to follow, so it would only be a postponement of what must ultimately take place or be boldly rejected. Once he decided to explain his feelings on the subject, but in his mind's eye he saw the half-pitying sneer on the face of the worldly young cityite, and he quailed before it.

Why not go? Could what he saw hurt him? Was he so great a coward that he dared not come into the way of temptation? We do not know the strength of a shield until it has been tried in battle. Metal does not ring true or false until it is struck. He would go. He would see with his own eyes for the purpose of information. He would have his boasted bout with sin. After this highly valorous conclusion he fell asleep.

The next morning found him wavering again, but he put all his troubled thoughts away and spent the day in sightseeing. He came in at night tired and feeling strange and lonesome. "Whom the gods wish to destroy, they first make mad," we used to say; but all that is changed now, and whom the devil wishes to get, he first makes lonesome. Then the victim is up to anything.

Brent had finished his supper when Perkins came in, but he brightened at the young clerk's cherry salute, "Hello, there! ready to go, are you?"

"Been ready all day," he replied, with a laugh. "It's been pretty slow."

"'Ain't made much out, then, seeing the sights of this little village of ours? Well, we'll do better tonight, if the people don't see that black tie of yours and take you for a preacher getting facts for a crusade."

Brent blushed and bit his lip, but he only said, "I'll go up and change it while you're finishing your supper."

"Guess you'd better, or someone will be asking you for a sermon." Perkins laughed good-naturedly, but he did not know how his words went home to his companion's sensitive feelings. He thought that his haste in leaving the room and his evident confusion were only the evidence of a greenhorn's embarrassment under raillery. He really had no idea that his comrade's tie was the badge of his despised calling.

Brent was down again in a few minutes, a gray cravat having superseded the offending black. But even now, as he compared himself with his guide, he appeared somber and ascetic. His black Prince Albert coat showed up gloomy and oppressive against young Perkins's natty drab cutaway relieved by a dashing red tie. From head to foot the little clerk was light and dapper; and as they moved along the crowded streets the preacher felt much as a conscious omnibus would feel beside a pneumatic-tired sulky.

"You can talk all you want to about your Chicago," Perkins was rattling on, "but you can bet your life Cincinnati's the greatest town in the West. Chicago's nothing but a big overgrown country town. Everything looks new and flimsy there to a fellow, but here you get something that's solid. Chicago's pretty swift, too, but there ain't no flies on us, either, when it comes to the go."

Brent thought with dismay how much his companion knew, and felt a passing bitterness that he, though older, had seen none of these things.

"Ever been in Chicago?" asked Perkins; "but of course you haven't." This was uttered in such a tone of conviction that the minister thought his greenness must be very apparent.

"I've never been around much of anywhere," he said. "I've been hard at work all my life."

"Eh, that so? You don't look like you'd done much hard work. What do you do?"

"I—I—ah—write," was the confused answer.

Perkins, fortunately, did not notice the confusion. "Oh, ho!" he said: "do you go in for newspaper work?"

"No, not for newspapers."

"Oh, you're an author, a regular out-and-outer. Well, don't you know, I thought you were somehow different from most fellows I've met. I never could see how you authors could stay away in small towns, where you hardly ever see anyone, and write about people as you do; but I suppose you get your people from books."

"No, not entirely," replied Brent, letting the mistake go. "There are plenty of interesting characters in a small town. Its life is just what the life of a larger city is, only the scale is smaller."

"Well, if you're on a search for characters, you'll see some tonight that'll be worth putting in your notebook. We'll stop here first."

The place before which they had stopped was surrounded by a high vine-covered lattice fence: over the entrance flamed forth in letters set with gaslights the words "Meyer's Beer-Garden and Variety Hall. Welcome." He could hear the sound of music within—a miserable orchestra, and a woman singing in a high strident voice. People were passing in and out of the place. He hesitated, and then, shaking himself, as if to shake off his scruples, turned towards the entrance. As he reached the door, a man who was standing beside it thrust a paper into his hand. He saw others refuse to take it as they passed. It was only the announcement of a temperance meeting at a neighboring hall. He raised his eyes to find the gaze of the man riveted upon him.

"Don't you go in there, young man," he said. "You don't look like you was used to this life. Come away. Remember, it's the first step—"

"Chuck him," said Perkins's voice at his elbow. But something in the man's face held him. A happy thought struck him. He turned to his companion and said, in a low voice, "I think I've found a character here already. Will you excuse me for a while?"

"Certainly. Business before pleasure. Pump him all you can, and then come in. You'll find me at one of the tables on the farther side." Perkins passed on.

"You won't go in, my young friend?" said the temperance man.

"What is it to you whether I go in or stay out?" asked Brent, in a tone of assumed carelessness.

"I want to keep every man I kin from walkin' the path that I walked and sufferin' as I suffer." He was seized with a fit of coughing. His face was old and very thin, and his hands, even in that hot air, were blue as with cold. "I wisht you'd go to our meetin' tonight. We've got a powerful speaker there, that'll show you the evils of drink better'n I kin."

"Where is this great meeting?" Brent tried to put a sneer into his voice, but an unaccountable tremor ruined its effect.

He was duly directed to the hall. "I may come around," he said, carelessly, and sauntered off, leaving the man coughing beside the door of the beer-garden. "Given all of his life to the devil," he mused, "drunk himself to death, and now seeking to steal into heaven by giving away a few tracts in his last worthless moments." He had forgotten all about Perkins.

He strolled about for a while, and then, actuated by curiosity, sought out the hall where the meeting was being held. It was a rude place, in a poor neighborhood. The meeting room was up two flights of dingy, rickety stairs. Hither Brent found his way. His acquaintance of the street was there before him and sitting far to the front among those whom, by their position, the young man took to be the speakers of the evening. The room was half full of the motleyest crew that it had ever been his ill fortune to set eyes on. The flaring light of two lard-oil torches brought out the peculiarities of the queer crowd in fantastic prominence. There was everywhere an odor of work, but it did not hang chiefly about the men. The women were mostly little weazen-faced creatures, whom labor and ill treatment had rendered inexpressibly hideous. The men were chiefly of the reformed. The bleared eyes and bloated faces of some showed that their reformation must have been of very recent occurrence, while a certain unsteadiness in the conduct of others showed that with them the process had not taken place at all.

It was late, and a stuffy little man with a wheezy voice and a very red nose was holding forth on the evils of intemperance, very much to his own satisfaction evidently, and unmistakably to the weariness of his audience. Brent was glad when he sat down. Then there followed experiences from women whose husbands had been drunkards and from husbands whose wives had been similarly afflicted. It was all thoroughly uninteresting and commonplace.

The young man had closed his eyes, and, suppressing a yawn, had just determined to go home, when he was roused by a new stir in the meeting, and the voice of the wheezy man saying "And now, brothers, we are to have a great treat: we are to hear the story of the California Pilgrim, told by himself. Bless the Lord for his testimony! Go on, my brother." Brent opened his eyes and took in the scene. Beside the chairman stood the emaciated form of his chance acquaintance. It was the man's face, now seen in the clearer light, that struck him. It was thin, very thin, and of a deathly pallor. The long gray hair fell in a tumbled mass above the large hollow eyes. The cheekbones stood up prominently, and seemed almost bursting through the skin. His whole countenance was full of the terrible, hopeless tragedy of a ruined life. He began to speak.

"I'll have to be very brief, brothers and sisters, as I haven't much breath to spare. But I will tell you my life simply, in order to warn any that may be in the same way to change their course. Twenty years ago I was a hard-workin' man in this State. I got along fairly, an' had enough to live on an' keep my wife an' baby decent. Of course I took my dram like the other workmen, an' it never hurt me. But some men can't stand what others kin, an' the habit commenced to grow on me. I took a spree, now an' then, an' then went back to work, fur I was a good hand, an' could always git somethin' to do. After a while I got so unsteady that nobody would have me. From then on it was the old story. I got discouraged, an' drunk all the more. Three years after I begun, my home was a wreck, an' I had ill-treated my wife until she was no better than I was; then she got a divorce from me, an' I left the town. I wandered from place to place, sometimes workin', always drinkin'; sometimes ridin' on trains, sometimes trampin' by the roadside. Fin'lly I drifted out to Californy, an' there I spent most of my time until, a year ago, I come to see myself what a miserable bein' I was. It was through one of your Bands of Hope. From then I pulled myself up; but it was too late. I had ruined my health. I started for my old home, talkin' and tellin' my story by the way. I want to get back there an' jest let the people know that I've repented, an' then I can die in peace. I want to see ef my wife an' child—" Here a great fit of coughing seized him again, and he was forced to sit down.

Brent had listened breathlessly to every word: a terrible fear was clutching at his heart. When the man sat down, he heard the voice of the chairman saying, "Now let us all contribute what we can to help the brother on his journey; he hasn't far to go. Come forward and lay your contributions on the table here, now. Someone sing. Now who's going to help Brother Brent?"

The young man heard the name. He grasped the seat in front of him for support. He seized his hat, staggered to his feet, and stumbled blindly out of the room and down the stairs.

"Drunk," said someone as he passed.

He rushed into the street, crying within himself, "My God! my God!" He hurried through the crowds, thrusting the people right and left and unheeding the curses that followed him. He reached home and groped up to his room.

"Awful!" murmured Mrs. Jones. "He seemed such a good young man; but he's been out with Mr. Perkins, and men will be men."

Once in his room, it seemed that he would go mad. Back and forth he paced the floor, clenching his hands and smiting his head. He wanted to cry out. He felt the impulse to beat his head against the wall. "My God! my God! It was my father," he cried, "going back home. What shall I do?" There was yet no pity in his heart for the man whom he now knew to be his parent. His only thought was of the bitterness that parent's folly had caused. "Oh, why could he not have died away from home, without going back there to revive all the old memories? Why must he go back there just at this troublous time to distress those who have loved me and help those who hate me to drag my name in the dust? He has chosen his own way, and it has ever been apart from me. He has neglected and forgotten me. Now why does he seek me out, after a life spent among strangers? I do not want him. I will not see him again. I shall never go home. I have seen him, I have heard him talk. I have stood near him and talked with him, and just when I am leaving it all behind me, all my past of sorrow and degradation, he comes and lays a hand upon me, and I am more the son of Tom Brent tonight than ever before. Is it Fate, God, or the devil that pursues me so?"

His passion was spending itself. When he was more calm he thought, "He will go home with a religious testimony on his lips, he will die happy, and the man who has spent all his days in drunkenness, killed his wife, and damned his son will be preached through the gates of glory on the strength of a few words of familiar cant." There came into his mind a great contempt for the system which taught or preached so absurd and unfair a doctrine. "I wish I could go to the other side of the world," he said, "and live among heathens who know no such dreams. I, Frederick Brent, son of Tom Brent, temperance advocate, sometime drunkard and wife-beater." There was terrible, scorching irony in the thought. There was a pitiless hatred in his heart for his father's very name.

"I suppose," he went on, "that Uncle 'Liph"—he said the name tenderly—"has my letter now and will be writing to me to come home and hear my father's dying words, and receive perhaps his dying blessing—his dying blessing! But I will not go; I will not go back." Anger, mingled with shame at his origin and a greater shame at himself, flamed within him. "He did not care for the helpless son sixteen years ago: let him die without the sight of the son now. His life has cursed my life, his name has blasted my name, his blood has polluted my blood. Let him die as he lived—without me."

He dropped into a chair and struck the table with his clenched fists.

Mrs. Jones came to the door to ask him not to make so much noise. He buried his face in his hands, and sat there thinking, thinking, until morning.

Chapter 16

NEXT MORNING WHEN BRENT went down to breakfast he was as a man who had passed through an illness. His eyes were bloodshot, his face was pale, his step was nervous and weak.

"Just what I expected," muttered Mrs. Jones. "He was in a beastly condition last night. I shall speak to Mr. Perkins about it. He had no right to take and get him in such a state."

She was more incensed than ever when the gay young clerk came in looking perfectly fresh. "He's used to it," she told herself, "and it doesn't tell on him, but it's nearly killed that poor young man."

"Hullo there, Brent," said Perkins. "You chucked me for good last night. Did you lose your way, or was your 'character' too interesting?"

"Character too interesting," was the laconic reply.

"And I'll bet you've been awake all night studying it out."

"You are entirely right there," said Brent, smiling bitterly. "I haven't slept a wink all night: I've been studying out that character."

"I thought you looked like it. You ought to take some rest today."

"I can't. I've got to put in my time on the same subject."

Mrs. Jones pursed her lips and bustled among the teacups. The idea of their laughing over their escapades right before her face and thinking that she did not understand! She made the mental observation that all men were natural born liars, and most guilty when they appeared to be most innocent. "Character," indeed! Did they think to blind her to the true situation of things? Oh, astute woman!

"Strange fellow," said Perkins to his spoon, when, after a slight breakfast, Brent had left the table.

"There's others that are just as strange, only they think they're sharper," quoth Mrs. Jones, with a knowing look.

"I don't understand you," returned her boarder, turning his attention from his spoon to the lady's face.

"There's none so blind as those who don't want to see."

"Again I say, I don't understand you, Mrs. Jones."

"Oh, Mr. Perkins, it's no use trying to fool me. I know men. In my younger days I was married to a man."

"Strange contingency! But still it casts no light on your previous remarks."

"You've got very innocent eyes, I must say, Mr. Perkins."

"The eyes, madam, are the windows of the soul," Perkins quoted, with mock gravity.

"Well, if the eyes are the soul's windows, there are some people who always keep their windows curtained."

"But I must deny any such questionable performance on my part. I have not the shrewdness to veil my soul from the scrutiny of so keen an observer as yourself."

"Oh, flattery isn't going to do your cause one mite of good, Mr. Perkins. I'm not going to scold, but next time you get him in such a state I wish you'd bring him home yourself, and not let him come tearing in here like a madman, scaring a body half to death."

"Will you kindly explain yourself? What condition? And who is 'him'?"

"Oh, of course you don't know."

"I do not."

"Do you mean to tell me that you weren't out with Mr. Brent last night before he came home?"

"I assuredly was not with him after the first quarter of an hour."

"Well, it's hard to believe that he got that way by himself."

"That way! Why, he left me at the door of Meyer's beer-garden to talk to a temperance crank who he thought was a character."

"Well, no temperance character sent him rushing and stumbling in here as he did last night. 'Character,' indeed! It was at the bottom of a pail of beer or something worse."

"Oh, I don't think he was 'loaded.' He's an author, and I guess his eye got to rolling in a fine frenzy, and he had to hurry home to keep it from rolling out of his head into the street."

"Mr. Perkins, this is no subject for fun. I have seen what I have seen, and it was a most disgraceful spectacle. I take your word for it that you were not with Mr. Brent, but you need not try to go further and defend him."

"I'm not trying to defend him at all; it's really none of my business." And Perkins went off to work, a little bit angry and a good deal more bewildered. "I thought he was a 'jay,'" he remarked.

To Brent the day was a miserable one. He did not leave his room, but spent the slow hours pacing back and forth in absorbed thought, interrupted now and then by vain attempts to read. His mind was in a state of despairing apprehension. It needed no prophetic sense to tell him what would happen. It was only a question of how long a time would elapse before he might expect to receive word from Dexter summoning him home. It all depended upon whether or not the "California Pilgrim" got money enough last night for exploiting his disgraceful history to finish the last stage of the journey.

What disgusted the young man so intensely was that his father, after having led the life he had, should make capital out of relating it. Would not a quiet repentance, if it were real, have been quite sufficient? He very much distrusted the sincerity of motive that made a man hold himself up as an example of reformed depravity, when the hope of gain was behind it all. The very charity which he had preached so fiercely to his congregation he could not extend to his own father. Indeed, it appeared to him (although this may have been a trick of his distorted imagination) that the "Pilgrim" had seemed to take a sort of pleasure in the record of his past, as though it were excellent to be bad, in order to have the pleasure of conversion. His lip involuntarily curled when he thought of conversion. He was disgusted with all men and principles. One man offends, and a whole system suffers. He felt a peculiar self-consciousness, a self-glorification in his own misery. Placing the accumulated morality of his own life, against the full-grown evil of his father's, it angered him to think that by the intervention of a seemingly slight quantity the results were made equal.

"What is the use of it all," he asked himself, "my struggle, involuntary though it was, my self-abnegation, my rigidity, when what little character I have built up is overshadowed by my father's past? Why should I have worked so hard and long for those rewards, real or fancied, the favor of God and the respect of men, when he, after a career of outrageous dissipation, by a simple act or claim of repentance wins the Deity's smile and is received into the arms of people with gushing favor, while I am looked upon as the natural recipient of all his evil? Of course they tell us that there is more joy over the one lamb that is found than over the ninety and nine that went not astray; it puts rather a high premium on straying." He laughed bitterly. "With what I have behind me, is it worth being decent for the sake of decency? After all, is the game worth the candle?"

He took up a little book which many times that morning he had been attempting to read. It was an edition of Matthew Arnold's poems, and one of the stanzas was marked. It was in "Mycerinus."

> Oh, wherefore cheat our youth, if thus it be,
> > Of one short joy, one lust, one pleasant dream,
> Stringing vain words of powers we cannot see,
> > Blind divinations of a will supreme?
> Lost labour! when the circumambient gloom
> But holds, if gods, gods careless of our doom!

He laid the book down with a sigh. It seemed to fit his case.

It was not until the next morning, however, that his anticipations were realized, and the telegraph messenger stopped at his door. The telegram was signed Eliphalet Hodges, and merely said, "Come at once. You are needed."

"Needed"! What could they "need" of him? "Wanted" would have been a better word—"wanted" by the man who for sixteen years had forgotten that he had a son. He had already decided that he would not go, and was for the moment sorry that he had stayed where the telegram could reach him and stir his mind again into turmoil; but the struggle had already recommenced. Maybe his father was burdening his good old friends, and it was they who "needed" him. Then it was his duty to go, but not for his father's sake. He would not even see his father. No, not that! He could not see him.

It ended by his getting his things together and taking the next train. He was going, he told himself, to the relief of his guardian and his friend, and not because his father—his father!—wanted him. Did he deceive himself? Were there not, at the bottom of it all, the natural promptings of so close a relationship which not even cruelty, neglect, and degradation could wholly stifle?

He saw none of the scenes that had charmed his heart on the outward journey a few days before; for now his sight was either far ahead or entirely inward. When he reached Dexter, it was as if years had passed since he left its smoky little station. Things did not look familiar to him as he went up the old street, because he saw them with new eyes.

Mr. Hodges must have been watching for him, for he opened the door before he reached it.

"Come in, Freddie," he said in a low voice, tiptoeing back to his chair. "I've got great news fur you."

"You needn't tell me what it is," said Brent. "I know that my father is here."

Eliphalet started up. "Who told you?" he said; "some blockhead, I'll be bound, who didn't break it to you gently as I would 'a' done. Actu'lly the people in this here town—"

"Don't blame the people, Uncle 'Liph," said the young man, smiling in spite of himself. "I found it out for myself before I arrived; and, I assure you, it wasn't gently broken to me either." To the old man's look of bewildered amazement, Brent replied with the story of his meeting with his father.

"It's the good Lord's doin's," said Eliphalet, reverently.

"I don't know just whose doing it is, but it is an awful accusation to put on the Lord. I've still got enough respect for Him not to believe that."

"Freddie," exclaimed the old man, horror-stricken, "you ain't a-gettin' irreverent, you ain't a-beginnin' to doubt, air you? Don't do it. I know jest what you've had to bear all along, an' I know what you're a-bearin' now, but you ain't the only one that has their crosses. I'm a-bearin' my own, an' it ain't light neither. You don't know what it is, my boy, when you feel that somethin' precious is all your own, to have a real owner come in an' snatch it away from you. While I thought yore father was dead, you seemed like my own son; but now it 'pears like I 'ain't got no kind o' right to you an' it's kind o' hard, Freddie, it's kind o' hard, after all these years. I know how a mother feels when she loses her baby, but when it's a grown son that's lost, one that she's jest been pilin' up love fur, it's—it's—" The old man paused, overcome by his emotions.

"I am as much—no, more than ever your son, Uncle 'Liph. No one shall ever come between us; no, not even the man I should call father."

"He is yore father, Freddie. It's jest like I told Hester. She was fur sendin' him along." In spite of himself, a pang shot through Brent's heart at this. "But I said, 'No, no, Hester, he's Fred's father an' we must take him in, fur our boy's sake.'"

"Not for my sake, not for my sake!" broke out the young man.

"Well, then, fur our Master's sake. We took him in. He was mighty low down. It seemed like the Lord had jest spared him to git here. Hester's with him now, an'—an'—kin you stand to hear it?—the doctor says he's only got a little while to live."

"Oh, I can stand it," Brent replied, with unconscious irony. The devotion and the goodness of the old man had softened him as thought, struggle, and prayer had failed to do.

"Will you go in now?" asked Eliphalet. "He wants to see you: he can't die in peace without."

The breath came hard between his teeth as Brent replied, "I said I wouldn't see him. I came because I thought you needed me."

"He's yore father, Freddie, an' he's penitent. All of us pore mortals need a good deal o' furgivin', an' it doesn't matter ef one of us needs a little more or a little less than another: it puts us all on the same level. Remember yore sermon about charity, an'—an' jedge not. You 'ain't seen all o' His plan. Come on." And, taking the young man by the hand, he led him into the room that had been his own. Hester rose as he entered, and shook hands with him, and then she and her husband silently passed out.

The sufferer lay upon the bed, his eyes closed and his face as white as the pillows on which he reclined. Disease had fattened on the hollow cheeks and wasted chest. One weak hand picked aimlessly at the coverlet, and the labored breath caught and faltered as if already the hand of Death was at his throat.

The young man stood by the bed, trembling in every limb, his lips now as white as the ashen face before him. He was cold, but the perspiration stood in beads on his brow as he stood gazing upon the face of his father. Something like pity stirred him for a moment, but a vision of his own life came up before him, and his heart grew hard again. Here was the man who had wronged him irremediably.

Finally the dying man stirred uneasily, muttering, "I dreamed that he had come."

"I am here." Brent's voice sounded strange to him.

The eyes opened, and the sufferer gazed at him. "Are you—"

"I am your son."

"You—why, I—saw you—"

"You saw me in Cincinnati at the door of a beer-garden." He felt as if he had struck the man before him with a lash.

"Did—you—go in?"

"No: I went to your temperance meeting."

The elder Brent did not hear the ill-concealed bitterness in his son's voice. "Thank God," he said. "You heard—my—story, an'—it leaves me—less—to tell. Something—made me speak—to you that—night. Come nearer. Will—you—shake hands with—me?"

Fred reached over and took the clammy hand in his own.

"I have—had—a pore life," the now fast weakening man went on; "an' I have —done wrong—by—you, but I—have—repented. Will you forgive me?"

Something came up into Brent's heart and burned there like a flame.

"You have ruined my life," he answered, "and left me a heritage of shame and evil."

"I know it—God help me—I know it; but won't—you—forgive me, my son? I—want to—call you—that—just once." He pressed his hand closer.

Could he forgive him? Could he forget all that he had suffered and would yet suffer on this man's account? Then the words and the manner of old Eliphalet came to him, and he said, in a softened voice, "I forgive you, father." He hesitated long over the name.

"Thank God for—for—the name—an'—forgiveness." He carried his son's hand to his lips, "I sha'n't be—alive—long—now,—an' my—death—will set— people to talkin'. They will—bring—up the—past. I—don't want you—to—stay an' have to bear—it. I don't want to—bring any more on—you than I have— already. Go—away, as—soon as I am dead."

"I cannot leave my friends to bear my burdens."

"They will not speak—of them—as they—will speak of—you, my—poor— boy. You—are—old—Tom Brent's—son. I—wish I could take—my name—an' all —it means—along—with—me. But—promise—me—you—will—go. Promise—"

"I will go if you so wish it."

"Thank—you. An'—now—good-bye. I—can't talk—any—more. I don't dare —to advise—you—after—all—you—know—of me; but do—right—do right."

The hand relaxed and the eyelids closed. Brent thought that he was dead, and prompted by some impulse, bent down and kissed his father's brow—his father, after all. A smile flitted over the pale face, but the eyes did not open. But he did not die then. Fred called Mrs. Hodges and left her with his father while he sat with Eliphalet. It was not until the next morning, when the air was full of sunlight, the song of birds, and the chime of church bells, that old Tom Brent's weary spirit passed out on its search for God. He had not spoken after his talk with his son.

There were heavy hearts about his bed, but there were no tears, no sorrow for his death—only regret for the manner of his life.

Mrs. Hodges and Eliphalet agreed that the dead man had been right in wishing his son to go away, and, after doing what he could to lighten their load, he again stood on the threshold, leaving his old sad home. Mrs. Hodges bade him good-bye at the door, and went back. She was too bowed to seem hard any more, or even to pretend it. But Eliphalet followed him to the gate. The two stood holding each other's hands and gazing into each other's eyes.

"I know you're a-goin' to do right without me a-tellin' you to," said the old man, chokingly. "That's all I want of you. Even ef you don't preach, you kin live an' work fur Him."

"I shall do all the good I can, Uncle 'Liph, but I shall do it in the name of poor humanity until I come nearer to Him. I am dazed and confused now, and want the truth."

"Go on, my boy; you're safe. You've got the truth now, only you don't know it; fur they's One that says, 'Inasmuch as ye have done it unto one of the least of these, ye have done it unto me.'"

Another hearty handshake, and the young man was gone.

As Fred went down the street, someone accosted him and said, "I hear yore father's home."

"Yes, he's home," said Fred.

Tom Brent was buried on Tuesday morning. The Rev. Mr. Simpson, who, in spite of his age, had been prevailed upon to resume charge of his church, preached the sermon. He spoke feelingly of the "dear departed brother, who, though late, had found acceptance with the Lord," and he ended with a prayer—which was a shot—for the "departed's misguided son, who had rejected his Master's call and was now wandering over the earth in rebellion and sin." It was well that he did not see the face of Eliphalet Hodges then.

Dan'l Hastings nodded over the sermon. In the back part of the church, Mrs. Martin and Mrs. Smith whispered together and gaped at the two old mourners, and wondered where the boy was. They had "heerd he was in town."

Bill Tompkins brought Elizabeth to the funeral.

Chapter 17

IN ANOTHER TOWN THAN Dexter the events narrated in the last chapter would have proved a nine days' wonder, gained their meed of golden gossip, and then given way to some newer sensation. But not so here. This little town was not so prolific in startling episodes that she could afford to let such a one pass with any-thing less than the fullest comment. The sudden return of Tom Brent, his changed life, and his death were talked of for many a day. The narrative of his life was yet to be a stock camp-meeting sermon story, and the next generation of Dexterites was destined to hear of him. He became a part of the town's municipal history.

Fred's disappearance elicited no less remark. Speculations as to his whereabouts and his movements were rife. The storm of gossip which was going on around them was not lost on Eliphalet Hodges and his wife. But, save when some too adventurous inquirer called down upon himself Mrs. Hodges' crushing rebuke or the old man's mild resentment, they went their ways silent and uncommunicative.

They had heard from the young man first about two weeks after his departure. He had simply told them that he had got a place in the office of a packing establishment. Furthermore, he had begged that they let his former fellow-townsmen know nothing of his doings or of his whereabouts, and the two old people had religiously respected his wishes. Perhaps there was some reluctance on the part of Mrs. Hodges, for after the first letter she said, "It does seem like a sin an' a shame, 'Liphalet, that we can't tell these here people how nice Fred's a-doin', so's to let 'em know that he don't need none o' their help. It jest makes my tongue fairly itch when I see Mis' Smith an' that bosom crony o' her'n, Sallie Martin, a-nosin' around tryin' to see what they kin find out."

"It is amazin' pesterin', Hester. I'm su'prised at how I feel about it myself, fur I never was no hand to want to gossip; but when I hear old Dan'l Hastings, that can't move out o' his cheer fur the rheumatiz—when I hear him a-sayin' that he reckoned that Fred was a-goin' to the dogs, I felt jest like up an' tellin' him how things was."

"Why on airth didn't you? Ef I'd 'a' been there, I'd—"

"But you know what Freddie's letter said. I kept still on that account; but I tell you I looked at Dan'l." From his pocket the old man took the missive worn with many readings, and gazed at it fondly. "Yes," he repeated, "I looked at Dan'l hard. I felt jest like up an' tellin' him."

"Well, no wonder. I'm afeard I'd 'a' clean furgot Freddie's wishes an' told him everything. To think of old Dan'l Hastings, as old he is, a-gossipin' about other people's business! Sakes alive! he needs every breath he's got now fur his prayers —as all of us pore mortals do now," added Mrs. Hodges, as she let her eyes fall upon her own wrinkled hands.

"Yes, we're old, Hester, you an' I ; but I'm mighty glad o' the faith I've been a-storin' up, fur it's purty considerable of a help now."

"Of course, 'Liphalet, faith is a great comfort, but it's a greater one to know that you've allus tried to do yore dooty the very best you could; not a-sayin' that you 'ain't tried."

"Most of us tries, Hester, even Dan'l."

"I ain't a-goin' to talk about Dan'l Hastings. He's jest naturally spiteful an' crabbed. I declare, I don't see how he's a-goin' to squeeze into the kingdom."

"Oh, never mind that, Hester. God ain't a-goin' to ask you to find a way."

Mrs. Hodges did not reply. She and her husband seldom disagreed now, because he seldom contradicted or found fault with her. But if this dictum of his went unchallenged, it was not so with some later conclusions at which he arrived on the basis of another of Fred's letters.

It was received several months after the settlement of the young man in Cincinnati, and succeeded a long silence. "You will think," it ran, "that I have forgotten you; but it is not so. My life has been very full here of late, it is true, but not so full as to exclude you and good Aunt Hester. I feel that I am growing. I can take good full breaths here. I couldn't in Dexter: the air was too rarefied by religion."

Mrs. Hodges gasped as her husband read this aloud, but there was the suspicion of a smile about the corners of Eliphalet's mouth.

"You ask me if I attend any church," the letter went on. "Yes, I do. When I first left, I thought that I never wanted to see the inside of a meeting-house again. But there is a young lady in our office who is very much interested in church work, and somehow she has got me interested too, and I go to her church every Sunday. It is Congregational."

"Congregational!" exclaimed Mrs. Hodges. "Congregational! an' he borned an' raised up in the Methodist faith. It's the first step."

"He wasn't borned nothin' but jest a pore little outcast sinner, an' as fur as the denomination goes, I guess that church is about as good as any other."

"'Liphalet Hodges, air you a-backslidin' too?"

"No: I'm like Freddie; I'm a-growin'."

"It's a purty time of life fur you to be a-talkin' about growin'. You're jest like an old tree that has fell in a damp place an' sen's out a few shoots on the trunk. It thinks it's a-growin' too, but them shoots soon wither, an' the tree rots; that's what it does."

"But before it rotted, it growed all that was in it to grow, didn't it. Well, that's all anybody kin do, tree or human bein'." He paused for a moment. "I 'ain't got all my growth yit."

"You kin git the rest in the garden of the Lord."

"It ain't good to change soil on some plants too soon. I ain't ready to be set out." He went on reading:

"'I'm not so narrow as I was at home. I don't think so many things are wrong as I used to. It is good to be like other people sometimes, and not to feel yoreself apart from all the rest of humanity. I am growing to act more like the people I meet, and so I am—'" the old man's hand trembled, and he moved the paper nearer to his eyes—"'I—' What's this he says? 'I am learning to dance.'"

"There!" his wife shot forth triumphantly. "What did I tell you? Going to a Congregational church an' learnin' to dance, an' he not a year ago a preacher of the gospel."

Eliphalet was silent for some time: his eyes looked far out into space. Then he picked up the paper that had fluttered from his hand, and a smile flitted over his face.

"Well, I don't know," he said. "Freddie's young, an' they's worse things in the world than dancin'."

"You ain't a-upholdin' him in that too, air you? Well, I never! You'd uphold that sinful boy ef he committed murder."

"I ain't a-upholdin' nothin' but what I think is right."

"Right! 'Liphalet Hodges, what air you a-sayin'?"

"Not that I mean to say that dancin' is right, but—"

"There ain't no 'buts' in the Christian religion, 'Liphalet, an' there ain't no use in yore tryin' to cover up Freddie's faults."

"I ain't a-tryin' to cover nothin' up from God. But sometimes I git to thinkin' that mebbe we put a good many more bonds on ourselves than the Lord ever meant us to carry."

"Oh, some of us don't struggle under none too heavy burdens. Some of us have a way of jest slippin' 'em off of our shoulders like a bag of flour."

"Meanin' me. Well, mebbe I have tried to make things jest as easy fur myself as possible, but I 'ain't never tried to make 'em no harder fur other people. I like to think of the Master as a good gentle friend, an' mebbe I 'ain't shifted so many o' the burdens He put on me that He won't let me in at last."

"'Liphalet, I didn't say what I said fur no slur ag'in' you. You're as good a Christian man as—well, as most."

"I know you didn't mean no slur, Hester. It was jest yore dooty to say it. I've come to realize how strong yore feelin' about dooty is, in the years we've been together, an' I wouldn't want you to be any different."

The calm of old age had come to these two. Life's turbulent waters toss us and threaten to rend our frail bark in pieces. But the swelling of the tempest only lifts us higher, and finally we reach and rest upon the Ararat of age, with the swirling floods below us.

Eliphalet went on with the letter. "He says some more about that little girl. 'Alice is a very nice and sensible girl. I like her very much. She helps me to get out of myself and to be happy. I have never known before what a good thing it was to be happy—perhaps because I have tried so hard to be so. I believe that I have been selfish and egotistical.' Freddie don't furgit his words," the old man paused to say. "'I have always thought too much of myself, and not enough of others. That was the reason that I was not strong enough to live down the opposition in Dexter. It seems that, after all your kindness to me, I might have stayed and made you and Aunt Hester happy for the rest of your days.' Bless that boy! 'But the air stifled me. I could not breathe in it. Now that I am away, I can look back and see it all—my mistakes and my shortcomings; for my horizon is broader and I can see clearer. I have learned to know what pleasure is, and it has been like a stimulant to me. I have been given a greater chance to love, and it has been like the breath of life to me. I have come face to face with Christianity without cant, and I respect it for what it is. Alice understands me and brings out the best that is in me. I have always thought that it was good for a young man to have a girl friend.'"

For an instant, Mrs. Hodges resumed her old manner. A slight wave from the old flood had reached the bark and rocked it. She pursed her lips and shook her head. "He furgot Elizabeth in a mighty short time."

"Ef he hadn't he'd ought to be spanked like a child. Elizabeth never was the kind of a mate fur Freddie, an' there ain't nobody that knows it better than you yoreself, Hester, an' you know it."

Mrs. Hodges did not reply. The wavelet had subsided again.

"Now jest listen how he ends up. 'I want you and Aunt Hester to come down and see me when you can. I will send for you in a week or two, if you will promise to come. Write to me, both of you. Won't you? Your changed boy, Fred.' Changed, an' I'm glad of it. He's more like a natural boy of his age now than he ever was before. He's jest like a young oak saplin'. Before he allus put me in mind o' one o' them oleander slips that you used to cut off an' hang ag'in' the house in a bottle o' water so's they'd root. We'll go down, won't we, Hester? We'll go down, an' see him."

"Not me, 'Liphalet. You kin go; but I ain't a-goin' nowhere to be run over by the cars or wrecked or somethin'. Not that I'm so powerful afeared of anything like that, fur I do hope I'm prepared to go whenever the Master calls; but it ain't fur me to begin a-runnin' around at my age, after livin' all these years at home. No, indeed. Why, I couldn't sleep in no other bed but my own now. I don't take to no sich new things."

And go Mrs. Hodges would not. So Eliphalet was forced to write and refuse the offered treat. But on a day there came another letter, and he could no longer refuse to grant the wish of his beloved boy. The missive was very brief. It said only, "Alice has promised to marry me. Won't you and Aunt Hester come and see me joined to the dearest girl in the world?" There was a postscript to it: "I did not love Elizabeth. I know it now."

"Hester, I'm agoin'," said Eliphalet.

"Go on, 'Liphalet, go on. I want you to go, but I'm set in my ways now. I do hope that girl kin do something besides work in an office. She ought to be a good housekeeper, an' a good cook, so's not to kill that pore child with dyspepsy. I do hope she won't put saleratus in her biscuits."

"I think it's Freddie's soul that needs feedin'."

"His soul'll go where it don't need feedin', ef his stomach ain't 'tended to right. Ef I went down there, I could give the girl some points."

"I don't reckon you'd better go, Hester. As you say, you're set in yore ways, an' mebbe her ways 'ud be diff'rent; an' then—then you'd both feel it."

"Oh, I suppose she thinks she knows it all, like most young people do."

"I hope she don't; but I'm a-goin' down to see her anyhow, an' I'll carry yore blessin' along with mine."

For the next week, great were the preparations for the old man's departure, and when finally he left the old gate and turned his back on the little cottage it was as if he were going on a great journey rather than a trip of less than a hundred miles. It had been a long time since he had been on a train, and at first he felt a little dubious. But he was soon at home, for his kindly face drew his fellow-passengers to him, and he had no lack of pleasant companions on the way.

Like Fred, the noises of the great station would have bewildered him, but as he alighted and passed through the gate a strong hand was laid on his shoulder, and his palm was pressing the palm of his beloved son. The old carpetbag fell from his hands.

"Freddie Brent, it ain't you?"

"It's I, Uncle 'Liph, and no one else. And I'm so glad to see you that I don't know what to do. Give me that bag."

They started away, the old man chattering like a happy child. He could not keep from feasting his eyes on the young man's face and form.

"Well, Freddie, you jest don't look like yoreself. You're—you're—"

"I'm a man, Uncle 'Liph."

"I allus knowed you'd be, my boy. I allus knowed you'd be. But yore aunt Hester told me to ask you ef—ef you'd dropped all yore religion. She's mighty disturbed about yore dancin'."

Brent laughed aloud in pure joy.

"I knowed you hadn't," the old man chuckled.

"Lost it all? Uncle 'Liph, why, I've just come to know what religion is. It's to get bigger and broader and kinder, and to live and to love and be happy, so that people around you will be happy."

"You're still a first-rate preacher, Freddie."

"Oh, yes, Uncle 'Liph; I've been to a better school than the Bible Seminary. I haven't got many religious rules and formulas, but I'm trying to live straight and do what is right."

The old man had paused with tears in his eyes. "I been a-prayin' fur you," he said.

"So has Alice," replied the young man, "though I don't see why she needs to pray. She's a prayer in herself. She has made me better by letting me love her. Come up, Uncle 'Liph. I want you to see her before we go on to my little place."

They stopped before a quiet cottage, and Fred knocked. In the little parlor a girl came to them. She was little, not quite up to Fred's shoulder. His eyes shone as he looked down upon her brown head. There were lines about her mouth, as if she had known sorrow that had blossomed into sweetness. The young man took her hand. "Uncle 'Liph," he said, "this is Alice."

She came forward with winning frankness, and took the old man's hand in hers. The tears stood in his eyes again.

"This is Alice," he said; "this is Alice." Then his gaze traveled to Fred's glowing face, and, with a sob in his voice that was all for joy, he added, "Alice, I'm glad you're a-livin'."

THE END

THE LOVE
OF LANDRY

Introduction

By CONSENSUS, *The Love of Landry* is Dunbar's least successful novel. Each of the others is considered an accomplished work of art or at least important for historical or stylistic reasons. *Landry*, on the other hand, is seen as ephemeral, a capitulation to the low end of popular tastes, a white man's novel by a talent who should have stuck to his own line, maybe at best a partially successful long short story that should have been published serially. In the second of Dunbar's four novels, the story works out details of problems Dunbar himself was facing at the time and provides additional examples of his attempts to try his hand at literary genres with which he was not altogether comfortable. As is always the case with the complex Dunbar, though, we see him mastering and then modifying generic conventions to his own ends.

Granted, Dunbar's story is predictable to the point of being formulaic and stylistically unworthy of this master of music and rhythms. But as in his poetry, drama, and essays, he is never far from the subtlest of irony, and his mastery of such a wide variety of genres is nothing short of remarkable. This foray into cheesy romance again shows a writer in command of language, comfortable in the creation of stock characters, and most at home in his understatement and ventures into ironic wit.

Having recently been diagnosed with tuberculosis and sent to the Colorado air for medicinal purposes, Dunbar worked out his own anxieties through the dialogue and formulaic action of the story. In *The Love of Landry* Dunbar chose to use white characters partly to suit himself but also because he could never work in this genre of romantic novel had he stayed within the experiences of his own people, as all the critics remarked. Setting aside the double standard—noted by authors from Virginia Woolf to Richard Wright—that women and writers of color are expected to write about their own experiences, Dunbar in *Landry* again demonstrates the astonishing range of an African American writer working within the literary establishment in 1900 in America. Finally, Dunbar speaks through Mildred and Landry as he did through Bob Herrick in his play and through Frederick Brent in *The Uncalled,* giving himself if not the last laugh at least an occasional chuckle. At this late date, it is almost impossible to overestimate how rigidly Dunbar was confined by expectations about his race and how seriously he was challenged by his own choices to try many different literary genres rather than taking refuge in one. He nonetheless repeatedly sprung himself from traps—those set for him and others of his own making—through sheer determination, ingenuity, and linguistic prowess. Even though it may be the least of Dunbar successes, there is much to admire in the perplexing and often inexplicable *Landry*.

Critical reception of the book was mixed and often much better than we would now expect. The *Boston Transcript* felt that Dunbar had forgotten his duty to his race and that he should have written about what he knew best. *Outlook* concluded that the story was light, simple, and prettily told but not as strong in feeling and humor as his other works. The *New York Times* called the work pretty but more conventional than readers had come to expect from Dunbar. The *Grand Rapids (Michigan) Herald* summed up the most common conclusion that *Landry* was not a specimen of Dunbar's best work. Interestingly, the *Boston Journal* observed a recurring problem with Dunbar's enthusiastic but sometimes rushed experimentation that put him in the position of addressing an audience better versed in his subject than he could be. Of course that judgment missed the point that African American artists often understood the actions and motives of whites better than most whites were willing to admit.

Among the favorable reviews for *The Love of Landry*, the *Palladium* of New Haven, Connecticut, celebrated Dunbar's remarkable versatility. The *Buffalo Express* said the story was engagingly told. The *Brooklyn Standard Union* thought the book was engaging and cleverly written. Overall, the *Washington Times* encapsulated the opinion we might still be inclined to accept today when their reviewer contrasted the genius of Dunbar's poetry to the talent in evidence here.

The way Dunbar's novels have been critiqued in our time reinforces the unfortunate split between high and popular art in which we remain mired in spite of all the electronic and cyberspace innovations that are transforming the literary scene. Peter Revell's judgments (in the Twayne Series *Paul Laurence Dunbar*, 1979) are typical. Revell sees the book as a serious disappointment after the modest success of Dunbar's first novel and concludes that the work is "an almost total capitulation to the standards of popular fiction written for the typical reading public" (146). That popular fiction must be a capitulation is asserted but never argued. Revell provides a sensitive reading of the plot, characters, and dialect spoiled by his dismissive references to "faintly promising beginnings" and "increasingly trivial . . . incident" (147).

Critics have tended to agree with Revell's assertion that "Dunbar takes the point of view of his wealthy white characters throughout" (147), missing the ironies much as audiences had overlooked them first in Dunbar's dialect poems and later in the sarcastic lyrics of his musicals. Here Revell is particularly insightful in suggesting that Dunbar identifies with Landry Thayer as he had with Frederick Brent in *The Uncalled* because both reject confinement in favor of "the more natural and joyous responses of the human spirit." No doubt Dunbar created almost exclusively white characters in his first two novels because the genres he was trying out called for them. But perhaps also Dunbar made rebel Frederick Brent and free spirit Landry Thayer white to disprove the assumptions that the author could create only characters of his own race or that a predisposition to being a free spirit was somehow stronger among members of his own race than among Caucasians. In a particularly ironic twist, perhaps Dunbar was striking back against the stereotyping of whites by manipulating the prevailing conventions of genre.

Revell's conclusion provides valuable insights on ways we might reinterpret Dunbar's fiction: "Dunbar, here and elsewhere, finds false values and standards, whatever their origins, to be obstacles to human happiness. Failure on the part of critics to recognize this has led to serious misinterpretation of much of his fiction, and to a largely misleading habit of interpreting his work as a defense of a conservative, agrarian position against a progressive, urban one." (This misdirection in our readings worsens when we come to *The Sport of the Gods*, in which Dunbar's larger targets are often missed in the overemphasis on his attack against the wicked ways of city folk.)

Not only do Dunbar's first two novels provide a closer look at the extent of his social critiques, but they also read well in line with recent developments in our approach to the value of popular writing in our time. The fact that *The Love of Landry* was more favorably received than we would expect may be due to readers' identification with the feelings and values of the mysterious Landry himself. Recent critical approaches to popular culture have urged us to concentrate less on mere sales figures and best-seller lists or on the divide between popular and elite art and instead to focus more on the way readers' preferences express a good deal about who they are and what they value. In conventional terms, quality matters less than an author's sense of audience and how the writing and reading processes give expression to people often deprived of their own voice. Dunbar understood these phenomena a hundred years ago, as evidenced in his experimentation with so many forms of writing and the degree to which he expressed his own and his readers' contrarian values by getting them to identify with characters who were camouflaged stand-ins for himself.

Landry's attack on aspects of civilization would resonate with readers who felt trapped in some way themselves. Loving Landry could be a way of evading the rules we do not accept as valid or at least a way of protesting the limits imposed on us by societal constraints. Even dabbling in popular forms can afford an author the chance to fight back against constraints by which people feel overregulated. This process is often expressed in a Landry-like populism or what John Fiske has called "a democratic version of elite humanism [that] . . . resituates the cultural life of a nation in the popular rather than the highbrow" (*Understanding Popular Culture* [Routledge, 1991], 19).

This approach to popular culture could restore respectability to what might otherwise be called merely popular or folk materials. In many of Dunbar's works —and certainly this is true for *The Love of Landry*—the pleasure of reading lies in more than just passing time; it also invokes the joy of fighting back against powers that restrict. While it is true that the marketplace and advertising have always tried to tell us what will be popular, readers' tastes are often surprising. Although Dunbar enjoyed a diverse following, the official critics still created a set of expectations to which he was to adhere because of youth and race and the popularity of his dialect writing. Fiske helps us further here by showing that liking *The Love of Landry* is for many readers itself a form of empowerment. Popularity that empowers readers is neither degrading nor delimiting but rather a form of high praise, though it often takes more than an author's lifetime for the realizations to hit. One hundred years after Dunbar's death we can at last understand why he undertook so many popular forms, not just because the work was there to do but also because the levels of awareness and pleasure experienced by his readers present opportunities for the evasion and subversion he achieved elsewhere when his characters wore the mask. Like the smile that hides tears, the use of a popular form can mask elements of rebellion. With hindsight we come to understand the achievement this kind of sophisticated masking represents, and the novels at last become not only acceptable and accessible but worthy of praise.

The Love of Landry

To my friend
Major William Cooke Daniels
In Memory of Some Pleasant Days
Spent Over This Little Story

Chapter 1

FOR A TIME, AT LEAST, the Osborne family circle was to be broken up. There were only three of them in the big old house in Gramercy Park: John Osborne, the father, and Helen and Mildred, the daughters. The mother had died when Mildred was less than ten, and since then the three had never been separated for long at a time. Even when they were away for the summer, the father managed to join them every week or two if they were near New York, or, if far away, to spend several weeks with them at the end of the season. But now Mildred, who was a slight girl, had contracted a cough, and the doctor had ordered her away from New York.

"There is, at present, nothing the matter with her lungs," said old Dr. Van Pelt. "Nothing, except a tendency. But a tendency, my dear sir, is a thing that should always be stopped. By all means, always stop a tendency."

"But, Heavens, doctor!" exclaimed Osborne, "where shall I send the child?"

He was usually a very placid old gentleman until something came near one of his doves. Then he was apt to become nervous, and lose his repose.

"Oh, there's the south of France, southern California, Colorado—oh, a dozen places; but for my part," he added, shaking his *pince-nez* thoughtfully, "I should go to Colorado. High, dry air, out-of-door life, and in a year, or maybe two, our young lady comes back, blooming and hearty."

"But, Van Pelt, man, Colorado? why, that seems almost beyond civilization!"

"It isn't, but what matter if it were? You know I'm a doctor of the old school, although I've kept up with the new; and it's one of my old-fogy opinions, sort of left over, as it were, that civilization has always been a foe to good health. When our ancestors painted themselves, and danced impossible things on the sand, who ever heard of weak lungs? But now, after a season of tripping it in a close room in heavy silks, my lady has a cough. But it's no matter, John, it's no matter, it's a slight thing. Pack up the little girl nevertheless, and take her away. Good-morning. Good-morning."

So it was decided that to Colorado Mildred must go. But then the quandary confronted the family, who would go with her? There were many reasons why Helen could not leave, and the father thought of his business. At this juncture they did as they always did, and called in council Aunt Annesley. She was the sister of John Osborne's deceased wife, a widow of fortune, and possessed of very positive views. She came, and the case was laid before her.

"Hum," she mused, "to Colorado. Why not to southern France?"

"The doctor prefers the former place."

"He's an old fogy, and I don't see why you have him, John."

"I beg your pardon, Anna, but he's both an old friend and an excellent physician."

"Oh, I mean no harm to your Van Pelt. He comes of a very excellent old family, and I have no doubt does very well for his age. The question is merely, do you insist upon Colorado?"

"We do."

"Then the matter simply settles itself without further discussion. John, you must go with Mildred."

"But, Anna—"

"You have worked long enough and hard enough to take a year's vacation. The business for that length of time can do without your personal supervision. Now don't interrupt me. You know that Mildred must have some one of her near and dear ones with her. Now, Helen can't go, while Mr. Berkeley—that is, while matters are, as at present, *in statu quo*."

Helen went furiously red, while Mildred laughed behind her hand.

"I would go myself," went on Mrs. Annesley, "if things were otherwise. In fact, I shouldn't mind a trip to France; but Colorado—way out there?—never!"

And so, because there was no gainsaying Mrs. Annesley's word, this much was settled, that John Osborne should accompany his younger daughter out West, while Mrs. Annesley should take charge of Helen and their home.

"And I do hope, my dear," Mrs. Annesley added before going, "that you'll take good care of yourself out there among those cowboys and catamounts and things. It really seems terrible to send you to such a place."

"Why, Aunt Anna, I'm going to wear leggings, and go deer-hunting," laughed Mildred; "and I shall come back wearing a sombrero and a buckskin skirt."

"Don't joke, Mildred, don't joke. It's highly improper, and I'm sure you are joking, for you could never so disgrace your family as to wear leggings and a buckskin skirt."

"Dear Aunt Anna has such an overpowering sense of humor," said Mildred, as the door closed upon their worthy relative.

"You really shouldn't laugh at her, Mildred," returned Helen; "you know she has such a good heart, and it was so good of her to offer to come here and take charge of the house."

"I'd rather it were you than I, though," replied the younger girl. "I'd sooner take my chances with catamounts and cowboys."

More than either her father or sister, Mildred Osborne retained her good spirits in face of the coming separation. She was young, she had only turned twenty, and she had youth's belief in her powers of recuperation. Not for one moment did she doubt what would be the outcome to her health. She saw that the western trip was the inevitable, and, like a little philosopher, accepted it.

It was the night before the day of their departure that she stood in the drawing room, looking out on the dreary September streets. It was early in the month, but a cold rain blew gustily against the pane. Every now and then a bouncing hansom went by, its lamps throwing a silvery glow on the wet streets. A moment before, Mildred had been crying, as she and Helen talked over the morrow's parting. But now her cheery mood had reasserted itself, and she was drumming on the glass, and humming a merry tune to herself. Suddenly she ceased, and pressed her face against the pane with a convulsive motion. "Look there!" she cried, "at that poor child, trudging along with a bundle through this miserably cold rain."

Helen came to the window. "Too bad," she said calmly.

"Oh, why will people send their children out such nights as this?"

"Because they're poor, and have to, I suppose."

"And we're warm and comfortable here in the house, while that poor child is out there stumbling through the rain. Look, she almost fell. I'm going out to her."

"Mildred, you must not; you're not well, and you'll take your death of cold."

"Oh, Helen, don't stop me. I must and I will. It isn't right. I've never thought about it at all until tonight."

As she talked, the girl was hastily throwing a cloak about her shoulders. Against her sister's continued remonstrances, she hurried out into the street, and after the child. The little trudger with the great bundle had gotten some distance beyond the house when Mildred went to find her, and Helen, shivering in the doorway, saw her when she overtook, and stooped to speak to, the midget, and then watched her lift the child's bundle and turn back toward the house.

"Impulsive girl," she said to herself, starting down the steps; but just then she saw a hansom, which was about passing, stop, and a gentleman get out. He took possession of the bundle, placing his umbrella at the disposal of the two. Helen gasped, "Arthur Heathcote!—what will he think?"

It didn't seem to matter much what Arthur Heathcote thought, for it was a very merry party that came up the steps of the Osborne house. Mildred was squeezing the hand of the mite, and laughing, and the young Englishman, looking decidedly awkward with his bundle, smiling down upon them both. Mediæval bravery very commonly risked death for a woman's love, but it remained for nineteenth-century courage to risk ridicule.

"Surely, you're not going to bring her in here? How do you do, Mr. Heathcote?"

"Why not?" this from Mildred.

"Oh, why, she's so draggly. Just drop the bundle right here, Mr. Heathcote."

"The more reason for bringing her in. Come on, little girl."

The Osborne house was old-fashioned enough to have in its drawing room the grate of an earlier period. Of course, in winter, there was furnace heat, and no one shivered about the inadequate open fire as they had done at functions of fifty years before. But then, it looked cheerful, and it showed up the mellow tints of some famous pictures, a Maclise and a Corot among them; and so, when the nights were chill, the fire was duly lit. Before it tonight the little girl was placed, and the wet shawl taken from her head and put out to dry. Nina, the maid, held the garment gingerly between her thumb and forefinger, and sniffed perceptibly, but Mildred beamed on the child, as she sat blinking her round black eyes at the blaze. With her own hands she brought her hot tea, and good things to eat, and the child, half-dazed and wondering, looked up into the girl's face, and took them all in silence, save when they could draw from her lips the reluctant answer to some question.

"I wonder if she's real clean?" asked Helen, timorously approaching.

"Cleanliness in children is abnormal, and should be discouraged," said Mildred, shortly.

"Oh! ha, ha, ha! good, good!" cried Heathcote; "cleanliness abnormal, good! but of course, Miss Mildred, you don't mean it?"

At this juncture the visitor, feeling her dignity offended, made a motion to go. Mildred hastened to wrap her up warmly and to slip something shiny in her hand. The little hard fingers closed around the soft ones, and Mr. Osborne's young daughter received a look from the child's grave eyes that brought the tears into her own, and made her stoop and kiss the grimy face. When she looked up again, Heathcote was standing at the door, hat in hand, and waterproof on.

"I'm going to send the little one home, you know," he explained.

"Oh—" began Helen.

"But it is good of you," said Mildred, softly, and he bowed himself out, helping the child down the steps as if she had been a princess.

"Mildred, how could you?" cried Helen, almost tearfully.

"I couldn't if he hadn't helped me, dear. He didn't do it because I made him, but because it was in him. Helen, I have a slight cough, and everyone is helping and sheltering me. Father is leaving his business to go there across the country with me. That poor little thing, didn't you hear her cough? And yet she is out in the rain alone, and carrying her great burden; couldn't I do that little bit for her?"

"What a queer girl you are, Mildred!"

And then Heathcote came back. His face was glowing with exercise, and no man ever looked less disgraced.

"I put her in a cab, you know, and told the cabby where to go," he said; "some beastly little street down here. Really, you ought to have seen the little beggar; she looked as pleased as a kitten, and hugged her bundle up as tight—" and there was a light in his eyes as he looked down upon Mildred, such as they put in the halo of a saint. "Wasn't it jolly?" he added.

"Jolly? yes," said Mildred, with just the suspicion of a shake in her voice; and then they talked of other things, of commonplaces, until Helen, according to that ancient, and not always respected custom, rose and excused herself.

There was a long silence between them when they were alone. The big Englishman, fair, with the suggestion that the blood was always just ready to come swift to his face, was good to look at, and the girl, with the color in her cheeks, and her thick, brown hair half high upon her head, was a fitting foil for him.

"So you are going tomorrow, Miss Mildred?" he said.

"Yes, tomorrow; but you know tomorrow is the day that never comes."

"I have believed that fallacy until now," he said, "but now I find that it does come, and crushingly soon."

"Yes, I go tomorrow," she added aimlessly; "it's going to be a long journey, isn't it?"

"I wish I might take it for you."

"You are good; you have been so good to me tonight, and I thank you."

"Please don't thank me. I wish I might go on being good to you for a thousand years, even if I had no other reward than hope. Miss Mildred, I don't want to go on boring you, but you know, you know, don't you?"

"I know, of course I do, Arthur, dear Arthur; but can't you understand? It's so hard for me to explain it tonight."

"I'm a brute for making you think of it, instead of trying to make this last night of yours at home pleasant. What a miserable blunderer and brute I am!"

"No, no, it is I who am the brute, who cannot feel—I—"

"I wish Heaven would send me the man who would say so. You can feel, you do feel, only I am not the man. Well, let me see; this is the fifth 'no' I have heard from you since April. Very well, no 'no' that you say shall be final until some other claims you. And now, I must not keep you up. I shall not see you tomorrow."

His tone was cheery, but his face was pale, though the light that was in his eyes when he looked at her had not died out as he left her. She sank down, crying softly, "He is so good, so honest, why cannot I love him?"

Chapter 2

THE RAIN WAS OVER, and the sun, come from his sulking tent, looked bravely on the world again. It was the morning of Mildred's departure. Heathcote had sent flowers, and Mrs. Annesley had already come and begun her matronly duties over John Osborne's house. She was very busy indeed, much more busy than circumstances at all demanded. But she felt that nervous bustle would anyway show the importance of the position she held.

"It's really awful, John, for me to have to leave my dear home and come here, but I knew under just what an affliction you and the dear girls were laboring, and so I determined to make the sacrifice. John, do be careful of Mildred; you know how her poor dear mother went off."

She applied her handkerchief tenderly to her eyes, and shook with ostensible sobs. She had helped worry her sister to death.

"It was very good of you to come here, Anna," said Mr. Osborne, "and I know how you will miss the comforts of your own home." His house was twice as large and a good deal more home-like.

"Of course, you know, John, it's been a dear house to me ever since Annesley died, and you know how attached I am to it, and how hard it is for me to leave it."

When she wasn't at Lenox or at Newport, she was abroad.

"I know all, Anna, I know all, and your kindness shall never be forgotten."

"Oh, well, for myself, I shall be all fears and anxiety for the dear child. But of course, on Helen's account, it wouldn't do to let my feelings get the better of me, and so I had thought that perhaps this winter, not too soon, you know, but if we have good news of our dear Mildred, my grief might make the concession of a few receptions and a ball or two."

"That's right, that's right."

"And it's such a magnificent house for entertaining. That ballroom would accommodate an army."

"Have your army, Anna, and draw on me for supplies."

"Oh, you dear, generous John. What times we shall have, and it's all so necessary for Helen, while Mr. Berkeley—that is, while matters are, as I said before, *in statu quo.*"

"Give Helen any pleasures she wants to keep her spirits up—balls, parties, dances, the theatre."

"Glorious! I'll do it. Oh, could her poor mother have lived to see this day! And, oh, John, do be careful of Mildred among those people out there, and don't let her put on leggings and a buckskin skirt."

John Osborne started away. He could stand it no longer, and a short time later he was locked securely in his library, to spend the hour before train time.

After leaving him, Mrs. Annesley traversed the whole servants' department, awing them into respect for her authority. Then, with a muttered "Now I must go and comfort the girls," she started for her niece's room. But the rustle of her silken skirts upstairs was a herald that preceded her, and just before she reached the top, a door banged to. She kept her way, however, right on to Helen's room. It was deserted. Then she went to Mildred's room, and looked at the grim panels shut against her.

"Poor child," she said, "I know that she hates so to leave me that the sight of my face would be only a grief to her. I won't go in"; and Mrs. Annesley went down into the drawing room to spend the rest of the time alone.

The girls were together in Mildred's room. They had gone there because Helen would not have dared to lock her door upon her aunt. They were in the close intimate converse of girls about to part, and the elder sister was shedding real tears, as she chided the younger for her apparent heartlessness.

"I don't believe you care for me a bit, Mildred, or you surely would show more feeling than you do at leaving me."

"Dearie," said Mildred, "what's the use of my crying, and reddening my eyes, when I know it will be such a short time until we're laughing at the whole thing and at all the funny things we've seen?"

"But, oh, suppose you don't come back?"

"But I am coming back. Now, Nell, don't be a silly goose; did I ever say I was going to do a thing that I didn't do?"

Mildred was bearing up bravely, poor little girl, though there were dark rings about her eyes, and she had to keep swallowing. Fortunately a new matter of interest took hold of her sister's mind, and she asked suddenly, "Arthur Heathcote, did he propose again?"

Instantly Mildred's whole attitude changed. She became at once defiant, and yet with something of sorrow in her manner. The defiance was external, the sorrow personal.

"Yes," she said.

"And you?"

"I gave him the same answer, the only one I can ever give him."

"Oh, Mildred—"

"Please don't let's talk of it, Helen, he's such a good fellow."

"And such a chance."

"I'm looking for love, not chance. Arthur Heathcote demands love, and I cannot give it to him. Such men as Mr. Berkeley make a chance. Oh, forgive me, Helen, you know I didn't mean it," she cried, as Helen had recourse to her rather inadequate handkerchief again. "I didn't mean what I said; I don't know what I'm saying. Arthur Heathcote is so good I came near to surrendering last night. But I know I couldn't give him what he wants, what he deserves, and I wouldn't give him less."

"You can try."

"No," said the girl, dreamily, "there is something else for me. I have known it ever since men talked to me of love. Someone, some prince, maybe," she added, laughing, "will come to claim me, and I have known just how I shall feel when he takes me by the hand."

So many women believe this. It is true of so few.

"That all comes of reading your silly stories, Mildred."

"Oh, no, you goose," and Mildred threw her arms about her sister's neck, "it all comes of reading my silly heart."

"And suppose Prince Charming does not appear?"

"Then I shall marry Arthur, if he is still unwed."

"But what silly talk this is for us, within an hour of parting."

"Helen," said Mildred, gravely, "this is just the kind of talking I want to do, and if you touch that handkerchief again, I'll strangle you with smelling-salts."

The morning was bringing out its most vivid contrast to the night's dreariness as they rolled away to the station. Helen was subdued, but Mildred chattered like a magpie, and her aunt kept pace with her.

"Remember all my warnings," said the latter, as they neared their destination.

"Yes, auntie, dear, I'm to flirt with the cowboys, if they're not a thing of the past, and I suppose they are, in this degenerate age of the world, when everything romantic is past."

"Mildred, don't lay any such thing at my door. I said nothing of the kind."

"And I'm to bring you a little papoose to raise."

"John, listen to the girl. A papoose! why, I wouldn't have such a thing."

"Never mind, Aunt Anna, you're right. A papoose would be troublesome. I'll bring you a great big Indian."

Mrs. Annesley collapsed just as they reached the Grand Central Station. She revived as the carriage drew up, and they found Arthur Heathcote there to help them out.

The others went on up to the train, but he held Mildred back a pace.

"I couldn't help coming," he said; "you know I didn't intend to. But—but you'll forgive me, won't you?"

"Kindness is always easy to forgive; and, oh! thank you for your flowers."

"I am glad if they gave you pleasure, but I shouldn't have come, should I?"

"Do you feel very guilty?" she asked, playfully.

"I am simply bowed with my transgression, you know."

"I shall not scold you, then, since you are sufficiently contrite."

"Then I shall always be contrite before you."

"Really, you are like a Methodist, who is always possessed of 'a lowly and a contrite heart.' But then, when a man has no weapon against a woman, he uses his shield of contrition."

"I hope, at least, this time, it has turned aside your anger." They were approaching the others on the platform then. "Where shall you stop?" he asked abruptly.

"Oh, we're going out on a ranch belonging to one of father's friends, or a company he knows, or something like that. It is situated somewhere between Denver and the setting sun."

"Good-bye," he said gently; "I know this must be a family party, and I cannot claim the pleasure of admittance. Good-bye; I must speak to your father."

He went over and shook Osborne's hand, and then turned away down the platform, looking back every moment with a wistful expression on his face until he had turned the corner and was out of sight.

And then they went into the luxurious coach, Helen as tearful as Nina, the maid and Mildred all gaiety. Mrs. Annesley's handkerchief was in constant use, and John Osborne was very grave. He was taking his child away from her sister, perhaps never to see her again. Then a polite porter said, "All off, please."

Mrs. Annesley kissed her niece quickly on the nose and hurried to the door. But Helen held her sister in one long embrace.

"Oh, Mildred!" was all she could say.

And "Oh, Helen!" was the choking reply; and then the younger girl brightened up as her sister left the car, and waved a frantic farewell to her. Then the blue-coated official waved his arms, and the long train pulled out. Mildred was alone in the stateroom with her father. As they passed from the sight of those on the platform, she threw herself on his breast, crying, "Oh, father, father!" and burst into tears.

Chapter 3

MR. OSBORNE HAD FELT a sort of grieved surprise at his daughter's gaiety in the face of departure from the ties she should have held sacred. But he was more terribly shocked at her utter breakdown. When he saw that instead of being heartless, she had really been brave for her sister's sake, he felt a helpless resentment at his own stupidity that could wrong her, even in thought. He hastened to try to quiet the girl's sorrow, and when Mildred saw that her tears disturbed her father, she dried her eyes, and smiling like an April day, exclaimed, "Oh, what a baby I am! but it was hard, wasn't it, papa, leaving Helen, and everything I love?"

"It was hard, and you are a brave little girl, that's what you are, and I'm an old fool not to have seen it."

"You mustn't call yourself a fool, papa; it isn't at all respectful, and then, there isn't a shade of reason for it."

"Oh, yes, there is. Do you know—" he began.

But she put her hand over his mouth.

"Yes, I know; you thought I was heartless and unfeeling, because I didn't seem to care about leaving, and that's just what I wanted you to think then. I wanted them all to think it. So I'm not so bad at acting, you see."

Her cheeriness warmed her father's heart, and restored his self-respect. He laughed and chatted with his daughter in his old accustomed way, and she responded in such a merry mood that he did not note the tremor in her voice, nor see the cloud that now and then rested on her brow.

"Do you know," he was saying, "I'm glad I had the chance to come with you, Mildred. I feel already like a new man. I suppose I should have stayed on there, just working, with my little summer jaunts for intermission, until I should have dropped in harness. It's strange to me how little enjoyment the rich really get out of their wealth. Talk about the slavery of the poor! It's the rich who are really to be pitied—those people with enjoyment in their grasp, and yet with golden scales upon their eyes that keep them from seeing and grasping their opportunities. I wish Helen could be here."

Just then the porter came in to see if anything was needed. At least that was ostensibly what he came for. In reality, he came because *he* needed or thought he needed something. After he had been dismissed, Mildred asked, "But, papa, don't you think that even the life the wealthy drudge leads is better than the existence dragged out by that poor colored man who just came in here, trying to smile a little fee out of our pockets?"

"Poor colored man! Why, Mildred, that man gets more out of life than I do. He has a greater capacity for enjoyment, with the paradox that less satisfies it. You think it humiliates him to take a tip? Not in the least. That's his business. He courteously fleeces us, and then laughs about it, no doubt. Ha, ha!"

"You're becoming quite a cynic; I'm ashamed of you."

"Well, I guess an old codger who has dropped business and gone racing across the continent with the prettiest little malingerer in the world can afford to be a bit cynical, even contemptuous, in his attitude towards the rest of the world."

Mildred cuddled up close to her father, and so they rattled on.

The train bounded over the rails like a thing of life. It sped over bridges that spanned great rivers, through cities, towns, and hamlets, pausing only at long intervals to take breath, as if weary of its terrific race. Then it stops for a little while at a great city on an inland sea. It is night when they reach there, and the shimmer of the water and the lights of the streets make Mildred sad for a space, for her mind goes back to the bay and the rivers at home, and she thinks of Helen alone there, with just the servants and Aunt Annesley. Then the porter comes again, and she goes to bed to bathe the pillow with tears of homesickness and yearning, while her father goes into the smoking room to brood over his cigar. What a pity it is that women cannot smoke. They would weep less. The puffs that John Osborne took on his cigar that night were the full equivalent of Mildred's tears.

With all the faith one may have in one's self, with all the strong hopefulness of youth, it is yet a terrible thing to be forced away from home, from all one loves, to an unknown, uncared-for country, there to fight, hand to hand with death, an uncertain fight. There is none of the rush and clamor of battle that keeps up the soldier's courage. There is no clang of the instruments of war. The panting warrior hears no loud huzzas, and yet the deadly combat goes on; in the still night, when all the world's asleep, in the gray day, in the pale morning, it goes on, and no one knows it save himself and death. Then if he go down, he knows no hero's honors; if he win, he has no special praise. And yet, it is a terrible lone, still fight.

In the morning both Mildred and her father were in their accustomed good spirits. Their minds had adjusted themselves to the changed situation, and Nature, as if rewarding them for their good behavior, smiled upon them. It was a glorious day. Great masses of white clouds were piled high in the heavens like fairy mountains, and between them stretched long rifts of blue like intervening streams. They were passing through a green rolling land, touched not yet with the yellow hand of decay, although it was September. Much of the land was in pasture, and Mildred laughed as she watched the horses gallop wildly away from the fences as the train flew by, or the placid cows regarding the express with undisturbed equanimity.

So the day passed, and they went through another great city on a lake, and then on again, the country becoming flatter and browner as they proceeded. The rolling green land was succeeded by perfect seas of yellow corn. Corn here, there, and everywhere. It seemed that all the world had been drowned beneath its moving billows. Look to either side she would, the girl saw nothing but the one grain, stretching for miles along the track and on over to the horizon.

"What—what do they do with so much corn, papa?" she asked.

"They bring down prices with so much corn," he answered grimly.

"Yes, but what else do they do with it? Surely it has some other use besides that?"

"It has. They eat it, they feed it to their stock, they mill it, and they corner it."

"I've heard of corners in wheat, but—"

"My dear, there can be a corner in anything that one man has and another man wants. A corner is just the repetition of the act of the dog in the manger in the fable, with the exception that the ox is left the alternative of paying a high price to the dog or going without. Well, even an option is a good thing," and the old man chuckled thoughtfully.

"Papa, were you ever in a corner?"

"Which side, the cornerer or the cornered?"

"The cornerer."

Mr. Osborne smiled again, and patted the girl's head.

"Well, now, if this were the Inquisition, and I had to answer that question or go to the rack, I should be in a very unpleasant situation"; and still laughing, he rose and made his way to that refuge of the wayfaring man—the smoking room.

"I wonder if papa ever cornered anybody," mused Mildred; but finding no answer to the question in the fields that had made it possible, she turned her mind to other things. It did not take long for the other things to drive all thoughts of corn and corners out of her head, for those other things proved to be prairie-dogs, sitting demurely by their houses with their hands up, like devout little boys in prayer. A sudden peal at the bell, so decided, so hurried, that it brought the porter hastening to Mildred as if she were on fire, and he had to hurry to put her out, evinced her interest.

"What is it, miss?" asked the startled servant.

"Tell my father to come here quickly."

"Can I help you?" he was sure something was the matter.

"No, no; just hurry, that's all."

If that porter had been a blackbird instead of a black man, he would have flown, so great was his excitement. As it was, he came as near accomplishing that impossible feat as Nature, a narrow aisle, and a rolling car would allow him. He had to go the length of another car before he found Mr. Osborne, but he seemed to achieve the distance in an incredibly short time. Then he came, guiding back the old gentleman, who was white to the lips.

Mildred stood up as he approached.

"What is it?" he asked an anxious tone.

"Didn't you see them?" and just then they passed another dog-town, and she cried, "There they are! There they are! Oh, papa, look at them!"

Mr. Osborne saw what the excitement was about and collapsed limply into his seat.

"Mildred, Mildred," he said, "is this what you have called me for? Where, oh, where, is your reserve, the fruit of a hundred drawing rooms? What would your Aunt Anna say?" and he bent into a very undignified curve.

"I don't care," Mildred pouted; "they are just as cute as they can be."

"Why, you nearly startled that porter out of his wits. He didn't say it, but he looked as if he thought you might be in a fit."

And, indeed, the colored man was still staring at them with wide, white eyes, and when he saw them burst anew into laughter, he left the door and went back to his place, in disgust no doubt with the thought in his mind that here was another instance of white people trampling on, and making a fool of, the black man.

"I didn't mean to frighten him," said Mildred. "But it was such a new sight to me! I'll give him an extra tip before we leave."

"You should make him pay you for turning him so near white, even for such a short space of time."

"I don't know anything I've enjoyed half so much as those dear little dogs. They are such plump, roly-poly little things. Do you know, papa, they remind me of little Chinese babies?"

"Have mercy on the dogs, Mildred, do."

"I love them."

"That proves you a tenderfoot. I don't believe they are held in such reverence by the people of the West, especially those whose business takes them riding over the prairie."

They were nearing Denver, and it was afternoon.

"There's our first glimpse of Pike's Peak," said Osborne.

"Where? Oh, yes. But look, papa, here's another dog-town."

It was dusk when they rolled into Denver, where they were to stop for a day.

"This is Denver, Denver, and I am West," she said breathlessly.

"You are West, yes, you are West, little girl."

As they alighted at the hotel door, she looked round her once more at the busy streets, the hurrying people, and murmured as if in a dream, "Denver."

Yes, Denver, the city where so many hopes were blighted, where so many dreams came true, where so many fortunes went up and so many lives went down. Denver, over which Nature broods with mystic calm, and through which humanity struggles with hot, strenuous life.

Chapter 4

THE RANCH TO WHICH they were destined lay about one hundred miles south and west of Denver, and after a day's rest they set out therefor. The train took them within eight miles of the place, and at the station they were to take wagon to the end of their journey.

Mildred declared herself better already. The sights were all so new to her— the rolling, illimitable plains, then the great bleak mountains, standing up like hoary sentinels guarding the land.

"It's magnificent!" she breathed; "this is geography realized! The Rockies!"

"Wait until you get to going over those roads in a wagon-team, though."

"Don't pour cold water now, papa; let me go on enjoying when I may, so that I shall have something to remember when I may not."

"Go on, child, and store up numerous memories, for you'll need them," said her father, banteringly.

Every turn of the train disclosed new beauties to the girl's wondering eyes. Before her lay the panorama of mountain and cloud. Time and time again she found herself puzzled to tell which was vapor and which was rock. First, the brown foothills shrouded in a purple haze, and behind them, range after range rising in snow-garmented grandeur.

When they arrived at the station, a young man came forward to meet them. His dress was in no way remarkable—not at all in the extravagant style which the illustrators of fiction had made familiar to Mildred's eyes, and she had time to notice that he had a pleasing face, although it was much browned, and a good gray eye, before he said—

"This is Mr. Osborne?"

"That's my name, sir. I suppose you are Hendrickson?"

"No, Mr. Hendrickson was unable to come, and so sent me in his place. Our buckboard is just here at the end of the platform."

"Unable to come," mused Mildred, mentally. "Hum, that is not dialect, and here's Aunt Annesley's cowboy at last. I wonder where his pistols are."

She laughed to herself as she thought of her aunt looking askance at the young man who was with them. She turned to look at him, and his eyes were fastened on her face.

"Impertinence," thought Mildred; "he'd better attend to his own business. I am right, though; he has got good eyes, such a soft gray."

"Here we are," said the young man quickly, as they approached the vehicle, a large, easy, two-seated affair, to which two wiry horses were harnessed.

He offered Mildred his hand, but she gave her father her arm, and stepped in. Mr. Osborne and the young man followed. The latter clucked to the horses, and they trotted away. The road lay for awhile between widely scattered houses and shacks, then it broke away into the open country, where the bridges across the ditches were precarious, and the sight of a human being a novel thing.

It was a silent party, for a strange embarrassment had fallen on the girl, and she replied to her father's bantering advances with none of her pretty retorts and tricks. Finally, Mr. Osborne turned to the driver and said—

"You've quite a place out here, my friend Hopkins tells me."

"Pretty fair, yes."

"I've known Hopkins for a great many years, even before he had any interests at all in the West."

"Yes."

"I suppose he seldom visits you?"

"Very seldom."

"Whenever he has spoken of his place here, he has always said that this man Hendrickson filled the bill completely."

"Yes, Hendrickson is a good man."

"I suppose you have been in his employ for some time?"

Just the ghost of a smile crossed the young man's brow, as he answered, "Yes, I've been here for some little while."

"What do you do, that is, mostly?" Mildred was nudging her father, but he was determined to be friendly.

"Oh, almost anything. I just knock around generally."

"Oh."

After this unproductive attempt at conversation, Mr. Osborne lapsed into silence. Surely, if the rest of the people on the ranch were no more loquacious, they would have a dull time of it. Well, Mildred had come out for climate, not for conversation.

The young lady herself kept her eyes straight before her. She did not like the taciturnity of their driver in face of her father's genial overtures. "It is all of a piece with the mistaken idea of democracy and equality in the West," she thought. "The idea has run wild. Independence has been superseded by insolence, and every laborer is so afraid of being put upon that his attitude is one of aggression or defiance toward his superiors." And she grew inwardly angry as she felt that the young man was looking at her out of the corner of his eye.

"That's just the trouble," her thoughts went on; "he has been partly educated, and that's what keeps him from knowing his place. Now, in England, it would be different; a servant would be respectful, at least. Even Nina is better. Well, we are different in the East."

"I think you'll like it out here," said the driver, "after you get used to the silence"; and she relented a little towards him. Perhaps he was only embarrassed, after all. Of course there were not many modest men; she had never seen one, but then, she had heard that there were such things.

"I am sure I shall like it," said her father. "I need a little silence after the bustle and buzz of New York."

"I should think you would."

With this little talk, he drew up at the entrance of an enclosure, and leaping down, flung open a long barred gate. Through this the horses walked, and then waited until he closed it, when they resumed their journey up a road the counterpart of the former one, save that it lay through fenced ground. They must have proceeded about a mile when they came to a broad, low house. There was the barking of dogs within as the wagon stopped, and a big man, who would have been fair but for the sun's care, came running out to meet them. He was followed by a plump little woman.

"How do you do, Mr. Osborne?" said the man.

"This is Hendrickson," said the driver as they alighted.

"How do you do, Mr. Hendrickson?" said Mr. Osborne; "and this is my daughter, Miss Mildred Osborne. I have heard much of you from my friend Hopkins."

"We think a great deal of Mr. Hopkins out here, although we don't often see him. This is my wife," he added, as they neared the smiling little woman.

Mr. Osborne bowed, and Mildred shook hands with her. She felt glad to see the face of another woman besides the silent maid. "Come right in." Then Hendrickson went on laughingly—

"I hope you haven't had any trouble with Landry on the road."

"With Landry?" said Mr. Osborne questioningly.

"Oh, yes; I don't reckon he's introduced himself to you. That's just like him, to drive eight miles with people, and never say who he is—Landry."

Mildred turned in time to see the driver, who was about going off with the team, flush beneath his tan. "Will he dare to introduce him? That's what he's going to do," she thought. "Well, this is too much of Western democracy."

The young fellow had left his charges and strolled up, not without a certain grace in his bearing.

"This is our Mr. Landry, Mr. and Miss Osborne."

Mildred's bow was very slight.

"I shall give him special charge of your pleasure and comfort. He's better able to take care of you than I am." So they went into the house, and Landry went about his work.

The plump little woman took charge of Mildred and showed her to their rooms. There were four for her father, herself, and Nina, plainly furnished, but comfortable.

"*Mr.* Landry," mused the girl, as her maid was making her comfortable; "and he is to provide for our pleasure. Nina shall be my proxy there. Even on a ranch one must draw the line somewhere."

Jack, one of the men, was leading the horses away from the wagon, when he turned to Landry and said, "Great gal, I tell you. What a face to—"

"What?"

Jack stopped.

"If ever I hear you speak that way of that young lady again I'll break every bone in your body," said the young man, calmly.

Chapter 5

IF MILDRED HAD EXPECTED the man Landry to force his attentions upon her, she was greatly mistaken. He gave her no occasion whatever to offer Nina's services as proxy. Hendrickson had fulfilled his promise, and left them much to the young ranchman's care. While, indeed, he was all that courtesy or hospitality could demand, all his offers of service were made to Mr. Osborne, and Mildred's presence or participation in the pleasures he provided was a mere incident. He seldom spoke to her except to answer some question, or to point out some place of interest as they journeyed to and fro about the ranch. She had not been there a week before she was compelled to change her ideas of Western democracy, and to admit that she had done Landry himself an injustice. What she could not understand was his attitude toward themselves, and the attitude of the men towards him. The former, while perfectly respectful, had nothing that could suggest the relation of master and servant. While there was nothing of assertiveness about his manner, he seemed to look upon them calmly as equals, and her father had already accepted him as such. But it was harder for the girl. There is, in every woman, a bit of the snob, and while it was at its lowest development in this clean, sweet, American maiden, she could not but feel a certain resentment at the cool way in which he took his acceptability for granted. She could not deny that his manners and his language were those of a gentleman, and she could not withhold a measure of admiration for his sturdy manhood, as she saw him hardy and alert at his labors, or swinging across the plains at the long lope which is the chief charm of the Western rider.

The men treated him with a peculiar mixture of comradeship and respect, which Mildred could attribute to nothing but his superior education, or perhaps his prowess with his fists, which she had always heard was a good foundation for respect in the West.

And while she mused and pondered over Landry, he went calmly on, treating her politely and letting her alone. Now, there was just enough of the coquette in Mildred's make-up for this sort of treatment to pique her. So it was in a spirit entirely feminine that she set out to compel the notice of the man whose attentions she had determined to resent.

With this end in view, she began to talk to Landry more, and to attempt to draw him out.

No one could long resist Mildred's sweetness and charm, and this strange, reticent ranchman was no exception to the rule. He soon responded, and within three weeks the two young people were on a footing of pleasant companionship.

Landry talked more, though not much, but he found time to take the girl about the ranch, showing her things which he did not think Mr. Osborne would care for, and so did not trouble him about. He grew frankly to like her, and made no attempt to conceal it. Mildred often blushed at the honest admiration she saw in his gray eyes, and it gave her a thrill of something between pleasure and fright as she saw how his face would light up at unexpected meetings between them. A man whose face was such a tell-tale might be embarrassing sometimes. But it was pleasant to be liked in such a frank, honest way.

They rode and walked together, and he taught her how to shoot with the rifle. It gave him a quiet delight to saddle her pony for her with his own hands, and he taught her how to guide the intelligent little beast, as the cowboy does, by the mere inclination of her lithe body.

Meanwhile, Mr. Osborne looked on at the growing intimacy between them and made no attempt to check it. He liked Landry and did not see why Mildred should not do so, especially as he was the means of keeping her out in the open air, and the roses were coming back into her cheeks. Of course, this was a man's point of view.

Men are so unpractical about these things. A woman would have looked at the matter differently. Mrs. Annesley, now, for instance, would have scented danger as soon as she saw that Landry did not wear buckskins and a pistol. A man hardly entertains an idea of love in a case where a woman goes forward and postulates it.

So Landry and Mildred rode on toward the dreamland of romance, he consciously, gladly; she unknowing.

It was one golden morning in October that he came to her saying, "I am going out to ride the fence, Miss Mildred. Some of the men report breaks in it somewhere along the west side. Won't you come with me?"

"Really, I ought to write letters this morning, Mr. Landry."

"Oh, please don't 'Mr.' Landry me," he said a little impatiently; "surely you've known me long enough to see that no one gives me 'Mr.,' and to do like them."

She looked at him in surprise.

"You must forgive me for being impatient," he went on. "But you know that 'Mr.' smells to me of civilization, and it makes me feel stuffy."

"All right, I'll 'Mr.' you no more, then, Landry."

He smiled gladly. "And now, won't you come?"

"I oughtn't to, but I will; and we'll throw up the wide windows of the morning to remove the stuffy feeling." She laughed gaily, and went in to put on her strong, gray habit.

They were soon out and in the saddle and galloping away over the plains, the sun in her eyes and the wind in her hair, and the joy of youth and freedom throbbing in her heart.

Landry looked at her in silence, a smile like a sunbeam lying on his lips. The desire to possess her rose up and grew strong in his being. What a glory it would be to hold this light, airy creature against the world, to anticipate all her wants, and to supply them!

The morning was like a song, so sweet it was half sad. The air was like wine, and so clear that the farthest mountain ranges looked near and neighborly. The alfalfa fields, with their deep, dark green, half sprung from the third cutting, stood out in deep contrast to the browns and yellows which are Colorado's prevailing autumn tints. The sky was a dream of blue and white, with a touch of crimson over a peak where the sun had lately come up. The mysterious, ever-changing mountains were clothed in a morning veil of pale opal light, except in the hollows, where the darkness of shadow turned it to lavender and purple.

Mildred looked like the child of the day and rode like the spirit of the wind, and for a long time neither she nor Landry said anything. They were too busy just enjoying what Nature had given them. After awhile she drew rein, and turned to him smiling.

"I wonder what my people at home would say of this weak plant if they could see me now."

"You have thrived in the sunshine, and they could only be thankful."

Just then a jackrabbit flashed across their path, a mere leaping bundle of gray-white, and he laughed aloud at the joy she had in the sight.

"They would say for one thing that your capacity for enjoyment was in no way diminished by coming out here."

"I wonder," Mildred laughed, "if they could believe that there was anything to enjoy in this desert."

"I don't like to hear it called a desert. It is full of teeming life to me; with things to see and things to love and to do."

"Oh, but they would never understand that unless they had seen it for themselves. I know I didn't. Why, I had a letter from my sister in the mail that you brought yesterday, and she asked me if you wore many pistols, or were at all careless in handling firearms. I had written her about you"—blushing.

Landry laughed a good deal longer than the humor of the remark demanded. But he was laughing out of pure joy because she had thought of him and had written about him. The impulse seized him to speak then and know his fate, and he was only able to check it by darting away on the pretended chase of another rabbit. He came back laughing.

"What an awful opinion they must have of us!" he said. "I wonder they let you come out here."

"It was not without many admonitions from my aunt to be careful of cowboys and catamounts—that was quite the nearest to the concrete she could bring the West, and so she seized on that. I really don't believe that she regards this part of the country as civilized."

"Nothing is quite so conceited as what we call civilization; and what does it mean after all, except to lie gracefully, to cheat legally, and to live as far away from God and Nature as the world limit will let. If it must mean that out here, pray God that it may never come to this part of the country. If it does, then some of us will have no refuge."

Mildred looked at him with wide eyes. "Why are you so bitter?" she asked. "Now, I think that civilization is very good when it treats us well. Maybe it didn't treat you well, though. Anyway, I'm glad to know one thing, that papa is wrong. He says that everyone who has a chance to live in the heart of the world, and yet comes here, must be driven either by consumption, cupidity, or crime."

"No, some of us come to get breathing space, when we are stifled back there by meanness and deceit. Some of us come here to look at the great mountains and broad plains, and forget how little man is; to see Nature, and, through it, Nature's God, and so get back to faith."

His face was flushed, and his manner vehement, and Mildred thought she had offended him.

"Oh, you mustn't mind papa's remark; he was only trying to make an epigram. You know it's the fashion to make epigrams now, alliterative, if possible, but epigrams of some kind. They are supposed to be philosophical shortcuts."

"Yes, I know; they are a kind of electric-lighted royal road to truth, but I confess, I never did like electric lights. But you must forgive me for making a shadow on your day."

"You haven't," she said simply.

They had come to one of the breaks in the fence now, and he had dismounted to see what could be done, and, if possible, to make repairs. He went at his work cheerfully, almost joyously. Mildred watched him for a time, and then she asked suddenly, "Do you really like it, Landry?"

He looked up in surprise, "Why, yes; why not?"

"Oh, I don't know," she answered, blushing, "but it doesn't seem like you; it seems so trivial, inadequate, inconsequential; oh, I don't know what I mean."

"Why, it's work; I'm doing something."

"But wouldn't you rather be doing something else?"

"I don't see that I should. I'm not only mending fences out here; that would be trivial perhaps, although even fence-mending has its place, and farther south they have men who do nothing else but ride the fence day after day. But besides this, we are digging a new irrigation ditch, and, altogether, I'm bearing my share in the work of feeding the world. What man can do more?"

"Oh, yes, I know—but—but—" she paused, embarrassed.

Landry laughed and went on: "You see, Miss Mildred, it isn't what a man does, but how he does it. I love work, not for work's sake, but for what it accomplishes, although I do find a certain pleasure in the process."

"But don't you know, Landry, pardon me if I seem impertinent, you might have made a good soldier, or an officer," she said diffidently.

"I don't know that I should want to be," he said calmly; and then dropping his work he went on: "I know it isn't heroic, but I don't know that those fellows, brave as they may be, who are out there fighting a lot of half-naked savages are doing any more for ultimate good than we who are here, fighting the hard conditions of nature. I like a fight, but there are fights and fights, and I'd rather know that this irrigation ditch that I'm digging is going to make the land better and a lot of people happier, than to feel that I was carrying a cartridge-belt full of civilization to folks that didn't want it."

"Oh, shame! shame! you're an anti-expansionist," said Mildred.

"No, I'm not an anti-expansionist, either. I believe in America's spreading out as big and as broad as she can, and doing all the good she can. But whenever I look around me on all this—" he swept his eyes around the horizon—"I cannot help thinking that there's a good deal of expanding to be done at home."

"Would you recall the men from the Philippines?"

"I wouldn't recall anybody or anything. Those fellows for that work, and every man to his liking. But I do say that a good many of those boys who are out there wasting their lives under suns that weren't made to shine on anybody but niggers, might be better employed out here in God's country, where every air is a blessing, helping to make a paradise of this land that's so near it already."

"Why, Landry, you're really eloquent when you get started."

"Pardon me," he said, blushing under his tan; "I've been blowing off a good deal, but I was so full of it."

With Landry's work the morning went quickly, and it was past noon when they started riding leisurely back to the ranch-house.

"I wish you could help me brighten things for the boys out here a little," he said. "Their lives are sometimes dull. I've been thinking of giving them some music one of these nights. I have a violin and a guitar."

"You have?" she exclaimed. "Why, you never told me."

"No, I'm not much of a musician; but you have a banjo, and I could make shift if you could help me. Will you?"

She hesitated. He was so blunt, so direct. Why couldn't he hint at things, and give her a chance?

"Will you?" he repeated.

"Yes," she answered at last.

And as they alighted at the door and he held her hand in saying good-bye, she wondered what manner of man was this Landry, who hated civilization and yet practiced all its graces.

Chapter 6

"Papa," said Mildred when she and her father were alone again, "that Mr. Landry has very queer ideas."

"Is that so, my dear? He surely doesn't maintain that the moon is made of green cheese?"

"No, no; but he does maintain something almost as heretical—the heroism of common labor."

"Oh, he preaches that doctrine, does he, he being the common laborer, eh?"

"Well, he doesn't say quite that either; for, as I remember now, he said that he wasn't heroic, but he claims that the men who make a farm or a ranch better are as good and as great as the men who are fighting in the Philippines."

Mr. Osborne laughed, then said musingly, "I've seen men in my day whom I regard as greater generals than any our war has yet produced, and their battlefields were only offices and counting rooms, too. Landry is right. He has a great deal of sound sense for a man in his station."

"His station? That's just it. Papa, what is his station?"

Mr. Osborne paused and looked at her. "Well, now that is one on me. Come to think of it, I have never considered the matter. He is not a man whose character or manner lends itself to much speculation about station. One feels so sure about his manhood that he forgets to ask about the status of it."

"But I do want very much to know," the daughter pursued. "He has asked me to help him in a little entertainment for the men, and I have told him I would."

"Oh, well, that won't hurt you. It will be a good thing for the men, and out here you can afford to be pretty democratic, although Landry strikes me as being a man one couldn't well be ashamed of anywhere."

It pleased Mildred so to hear her father say this of Landry that she immediately resented both her feeling and his remark.

"I must say, papa, that you do make some sudden and enthusiastic friendships."

"I am seldom wrong, though," the old man returned.

And so the girl's mind was set at rest as to the fitness of her helping Landry in his entertainment for the men, or the "boys," as he more often called them.

Somehow the young man seemed to find even more spare time than usual that week, and much of it was spent in practicing with her. Sometimes it was the violin and the banjo, sometimes it was the banjo alone, and as often it tinkled to the heavier strumming of the guitar, and they laughed and enjoyed it and were glad they had thought of this plan of entertaining the boys.

And so the days went on, and the night of the concert arrived—a moonlight night, with a cool wind blowing down from the mountain after a hot day. The ranch-house was a scene of repressed joy. Repressed, for your ranchman prides himself on his stoicism, and holds the concealment of his emotion a great virtue. Young Tod, though, the youngest of the helpers, had been insane with delight, and was doing fancy steps before the door an hour and a half earlier than the hour set for the festivities.

The general dining room, a long wainscoted chamber, had been fitted up with chairs and settees as the audience hall, and all the lamps and lanterns obtainable had been brought into requisition to make it bright and cheerful. Little less pleased than Tod, Mr. Hendrickson came in as soon as it was decently near the time of beginning and seated himself near the center of the room, smiling and dumb with joy. His wife was flying around, as Tod expressed it, "like a chicken with its head wrung off," very busy putting the finishing touches to things, and saying an admonishing word to the boys, who were dropping in, one by one.

A lamp flared and smoked, and a half-dozen willing pairs of hands were up to attend to it, and as many faces, bronzed and mellow in the light, bent over it, smiling to be of service.

When it was time to begin, Mr. Osborne came in with Mildred and the banjo, and they were greeted with a burst of uproarious applause. The old man looked a little embarrassed and sank quickly into a seat, where he sat smiling upon the scene as if it were all a play and he had been unexpectedly cast for a part. Mildred blushed like a peony, and began tuning her banjo to relieve her confusion. The entrance of Landry a little later with his violin and guitar was the signal for another outburst. The rancher only smiled as he took his seat beside Mildred, and she made the mental comment that surely this man was different from those around him.

In order to get things going, Landry struck a few chords on his guitar, and he and Mildred swung into one of the liveliest of Sousa's marches. It is just possible that none of the musical societies had recommended the banjo and guitar as two instruments especially adapted for such work. But these bronzed, hardhanded fellows, so far away from the pleasures and amusements of the town, isolated from their fellows, the companions of cattle—they were not critics. The music, light though it was, gave them the hint of the better, brighter things outside their own barren lives, and never was a performance so thoroughly enjoyed. Fingers were snapped, and feet were stamped in time to the strain, and some even joined to whistle softly the air.

Encouraged by these signs of appreciation, Mildred's fingers fairly flew over the strings. She had entered heart and soul into the spirit of the affair. Her face was flushed and her eyes were shining. No wonder that Landry could not see the men around him, nor the room, nor hear the applause which greeted the music. All his senses were absorbed in one, and that one was wholly devoted to drinking her in with his eager eyes.

Finally, though, he awakened, and in response to a vociferous encore they began another tune. After this he called out to Tod—

"Come on, now, Tod, and give us your rancher's song."

"Tod! Tod!" chorused the others.

Tod ducked his head and sat still. He was embarrassed by the presence of Mildred who seemed to him like a being from another sphere.

"Come on, Tod," repeated Landry, striking his guitar, "the boys'll join in the chorus. Won't you, boys?"

"That's what!" they shouted, and "You bet!"

Thus adjured, Tod rose from his seat, but at the sight of the faces looking at him, collapsed into it again, like a scared schoolboy on exhibition day.

There was a burst of laughter at this, but it stopped suddenly, for Mildred was standing up, speaking.

"Won't you come on and sing, please?" she was saying. "I should feel very badly if I thought you felt strange before papa and me."

"Go on! you can't refuse the lady," the men urged; and Tod rose again a little less embarrassed and shuffled forward. He bowed awkwardly to Mildred as he came out and gave her a look. It was such a look as one of the rude shepherds, half-startled, half-uplifted, might have bent on the angels with the glad tidings. It was as if the purity of the girl had suddenly metamorphosed the man's whole nature and the light of the change was made manifest in his eyes.

Landry saw the look, and the insane desire took possession of him to get up and hug Tod. But he only said, "Go on," and struck up the tune.

Tod began to sing the "Ranchman's Song," one of the few clean ones in the plainsman's répertoire—

> "The ranchman's life is the life for me—
>   A wild, sweet life indeed;
>   By day, the sun on the mesa free,
>   By night, the mad stampede.
>   CHORUS.

A long lope, and a slow lope,
    That is the gait we ride;
But who would change the life of the range
    For the city and all its pride?

This is the life for the man who feels
    The warm blood in his veins;
To sit him straight when his pony wheels,
    And to skim the melting plains.
        CHORUS.

I have no wife, no kin have I,
    I bide alone and free;
But cattle, plains, and hill and sky
    Are wife enough for me.
        CHORUS.

I have no house, and I have no home,
    So, comrades, when I die
Just plant me here, where the cattle roam,
    And you will still ride by."
        CHORUS.

The men roared the chorus out lustily, and the song ended with a great flourish. Then a banjo solo by Mildred ran the men wild again, and while they were still shouting over the encore she played, Landry began singing to the accompaniment of his own guitar. A hush fell upon the room, and Mildred looked at him in surprise. His voice was a rich baritone—the voice for a man—and he sang with deep feeling, even emotion. It was only a simple ballad—such as one may hear from the ballad-singer any time at a music hall—but the manner of the singing was instant in its effect. The men began clearing their throats and looking down at their boots. Tod got up and stood with his back to the rest, looking at the wall as if he saw a picture there; nor did he turn around when Landry had finished, but swept his sleeve quickly and surreptitiously across his eyes and joined in the hearty applause. The men straightened up and began smiling sheepishly at each other; and not one of them would have admitted to another the presence of the great lump in his throat.

Mildred found her own lashes wet as she joined Landry, and they broke into the inspiriting strains of the "Georgia Camp-Meeting." The change was instantaneous. The men, like great children, were as quickly swayed from grief to joy, or the reverse. The music got into their blood like fire, and the imp of dancing tickled their feet. Tod suddenly left his corner, and springing into the middle of the floor, began to dance wildly, but not ungracefully. There was the hasty pushing back of chairs and a half-dozen men joined him. Embarrassment and restraint were forgotten in the momentary excitement. Even Hendrickson was taken by the infection, and seizing his plump little wife, spun her dizzily about the room. Tod danced his way toward Nina and then paused before her, bowing. The maid gave a startled glance toward Mildred, who nodded, and a moment later she was flying away in the arms of the happy rancher, who laughed at the envious faces of his comrades. When the tune had been played through there were loud cries of "Again! Again!" and it was repeated to the hilarious joy of the dancers. Nina came back breathless from the exertion.

"Oh, Miss Mildred," she gasped, "I don't know what you'll think of me!"

"I'll think you've been enjoying yourself like a sensible girl," replied Mildred.

"Mr. Tod is a nice dancer, of course—"

"I abhor conventionality," interrupted Mildred. Her father heard her and smiled at her. He was satisfied, for she was happy.

They played once more, and then Landry announced that the concert was over. The men took their hats and crowded to the door; but there they stopped and looked hungrily back.

Mildred will never know why she did it, save that something in their eyes compelled it and made her forget herself, and she swung her banjo into position and began playing softly, "Home, Sweet Home."

Landry did not attempt to accompany her, but stood gazing at her in admiration and delight. The men were transfixed. Again Tod turned to the wall, and there were honest tears in the eyes of some of the fellows.

"Good-night, and thanks," they said when she had finished; and then they stepped out as if afraid to disturb something that she had put to sleep within them. But once outside, their restraint fell off like a mantle from their shoulders, and they rent the night air with three cheers for the lady and three more for Landry.

Mildred looked at Landry as she took her father's arm. "What great children they are," she said.

"You have made them very happy tonight," Landry returned, "and I thank you for helping me."

"Don't thank me," she said. "I feel selfish, I am so happy. I am happier than I have ever been."

"I am so glad, and the boys will not forget this, you may rest assured. We always try to have something like this for them before the fall roundup, but there has been none like this."

"The fall roundup, what is that?"

"We get together all the cattle twice a year—in the spring and fall, when we drive them from the ranges down into the valley. Next week is time for the fall driving."

"Oh! may I see it?"

"It is a rather rough experience, but I will try my best to help you to a sight of it. You will go, Mr. Osborne?"

"I shall be greatly interested."

"Oh, thank you, Landry. Good-night."

"Good-night," said Landry, and under his breath, "God bless you!"

Chapter 7

A WHOLE WEEK PASSED, a happy week, full of the joy of outdoor life for Mildred. She saw herself acquiring both gaiety and health, the reward one gains by living near to Nature's heart. She was not yet done babbling of the pleasure the concert had given her, and her father went on, smiling, happy too, and unseeing. The poor man thought it really was the concert that had pleased his daughter, and brought a light into her eyes and a thrill into her voice that he had never known there before now. A girl may be of a very charitable disposition, and Mildred was such a one, but there are certain effects on the feminine nature which even the joy of doing good cannot produce. She had suddenly become more affectionate than usual with her father, and she had fallen into the way of running to him on the impulse of the moment, and throwing her arms around his neck with quick, unaccounted for kisses. Her father called it pecking, took it gladly, and attributed it all to returning health—and the concert.

The girl developed a hundred pretty little ways, which, notwithstanding her charm, she had not possessed before. She was as gay and as joyous as a bird and as irresponsible. She went about the place singing, and the men looked on and blessed her. Little Mrs. Hendrickson adored her, while her husband's admiration seriously interfered with his articulateness whenever the sprightly maiden was around. Meanwhile, Mildred herself had not analyzed her feelings. She was just glad. Glad as a robin is, or a squirrel, and she did not know that it was because Landry was near her that her life was so much like a holiday. She was content to take the joy without questioning whence it came. But she was destined to an unpleasant awakening.

When God is letting a revelation slowly illumine the mind and soul of one of his creatures, there is too often some fool to rush in and anticipate his process. This was the part upon which Mrs. Annesley now entered. Although she was nearly three thousand miles away, she felt what Mr. Osborne on the spot could not see. With the solicitude of the kindly intentioned destroyer, she wrote Mildred:

"MY DEAR CHILD—I feel it my duty [they always do feel it their duty] to mention a thing which both your dear sister and myself have noticed in your last letters. You know, my dear Mildred, I am the last person in the world whom anyone could accuse of being suspicious; but there are certain circumstances which make me feel that I should be doing less than my duty to you as the daughter of my dear deceased sister did I fail to warn you of what I fear. My dear, who is this man Landry, and what are your relations with him? Are you aware, child, that you have spoken of him in every one of your last letters? Do you know that in the very last you called his name six times? [Mildred felt that she knew just the manner in which her aunt would have shot that last question at her could she have been there in person, and her face was suffused with angry blushes. The letter went on.] From what I can understand from your letters, the fellow is a common cowboy, or, I hesitate at the word—cow-puncher, as I have heard them called. Dear, let me beg you not to disgrace your family. I have heard of young girls falling in love with such persons out of a mistaken sense of the romantic. Don't do it, Mildred. Think over what I have said, and confide in me. If necessary, Helen and I will come out to see after you. Helen may come now, as Mr. Berkeley has spoken. I hope that I do not anticipate your sister in telling you this, but she would have told you soon anyway.

"One more thing, my dear niece, and I am done. It has been brought to my ears that the women of Colorado are advocating riding their horses astride. Horrors! And have made an appeal to the country on the score of humanity. Oh, Mildred, I cannot even contemplate the spectacle of a niece of mine astride a horse. [Mrs. Annesley underscored her "astride" as she had done her questions about Landry.] Don't do it, my dear. Propriety in a girl of your station is very much more necessary than humanity. The poor can afford to be humane. The rich cannot afford to be less than proper.

"Ask your dear blind father where his eyes are, and believe me,"

"Your affectionate aunt,"

"ANNE ANNESLEY."

Mildred finished the letter, and flinging it across the room, burst into tears. There should be a penalty imposed upon the old woman who wounds the maiden modesty of a young girl. Mildred cried for very shame, but she was not without the temper to resent her aunt's letter.

"Aunt Annesley," she exclaimed through her tears, "is a meddling, narrow-minded old woman. I in love with Landry, indeed!" And then she blushed so hotly that she hid her face in her arms and wept the more, and in that moment it went very hard for Landry. The sins of Mrs. Annesley were visited upon his head. "He is very presumptuous," Mildred thought, "and no doubt took it for granted that I cared for him, just because I was kind to him. He has been no more than my groom, and I'd as soon think of marrying the butler. Oh, how I hate Aunt Annesley!"

The girl's pride was wounded to the quick, and it is a quality which women and snakes have in common, when wounded, to strike, regardless of reason, at everything near, and so Mildred felt angry with everyone about, as being concerned in her humiliation. She sat down and wrote a brief, curt note to her aunt:

"My dear Aunt [it ran]—I am exceedingly glad to hear that Mr. Berkeley has proposed. It relieves you of one great responsibility. I can assure you also that I am not riding astride, nor am I going to marry Landry, who has been little more than a faithful groom to me."

That was all, and it was unworthy of her; but who can blame a young girl, hurt as she was, for being unjust to everyone about her? She read the note through again and again, and the meanness of it struck her more and more each time. Finally, she tore it into shreds. "I won't send it," she cried, "I won't send it. She may think as she pleases."

Very sad and miserable she felt as she went out-of-doors to the shelving roof which did duty as a porch, and where her father was now sitting with his cigar.

"Why, what is it, my dear?" exclaimed Osborne. "You're not looking well."

"I'm feeling very well," she replied. "But I've been reading letters from home."

"And you're homesick? Well, I don't wonder, child. But Landry shall cheer you up."

It was like a match to the fuse. She turned upon her father, all the pain of her resentment and humiliation flashing in her eyes and thrilling in her voice. "I am sure, papa, I don't see why I must depend upon Landry for amusement," she said angrily.

"Why, I thought you and he were such friends."

"We are not friends. I am surprised that you want your daughter to make friends with the servants. I have ridden with him because there was nothing else to do."

"Why, Mildred," said her father, in surprise, "I am sorry if I have seemed to neglect you. I—I—thought—"

He stopped helplessly.

"Oh, everyone thinks," she said a little brutally And then, there was Landry approaching, swinging along with his swift, easy stride. She gave him one glance and then turned and went into the house.

He saw the action and wondered. What had he done to offend her? He would rather his right arm were cut off than that he should give her pain. He came up awkwardly and stammered a few commonplaces to Mr. Osborne, who was equally puzzled and embarrassed; but his mind was with the girl who had so palpably turned her back upon him.

What had he done? What had he done? He went away cursing himself for a blundering fool, who had stupidly wounded the woman he loved and yet had not sense enough to know how he had done it.

"At least, civilization has that much good in it," he told himself, "that I could not wound a woman without knowing when and how. But I'll find out. I'll find out, damn it, if I have to crawl to her on my knees."

He did not know—how could he?—that he was being made to suffer on account of a meddling old woman three thousand miles away.

When Mildred had gone in, she instantly regretted the act, and suffered in mind little less than Landry himself. After all, it was not his fault. He had possibly never thought of love in connection with her at all. But she was conscious of no great pleasure in the thought. She felt that she ought to be glad, for, of course, it was impossible that she could be anything to him or he to her. But, nevertheless, she was miserable, and it was a miserable dinner that she ate that day. In the afternoon she sat on the porch with her father, and tried to be cheerful, as was her wont; but her cheerfulness had departed, and she made but a sorry feint at it. She wanted to be just to Landry. She wanted to make amends to him, but she feared herself, and was frightened if she even heard his step. Finally, after several false alarms, he did turn the corner of the house, and start towards her. Oh, if she could only fly! Of course he had seen her displeasure of the morning and would be sure to ask the cause of it, and what could she say? She wished he wouldn't be so fearfully direct. He never hinted at a thing. He always spoke straight out, and there was no getting away from the point with him. She had observed this before in him. She bit her lips and waited, because she dared not snub him again. It was awful. She could see his face now. A sort of fascination held her eyes. There were lines of pain about his mouth. She had hurt him, she knew, and she did not know how to tell him why, so the prayer went up from her soul that something might intervene to prevent their meeting.

Mildred's prayer was unexpectedly answered. A wagon rattled up to the entrance, and a man got out and stood for a moment talking to the driver. Then he turned and came hurriedly towards them. Landry had stopped, and as the newcomer drew nearer, turned his eyes first upon him and then upon Mildred. She felt the blood leave her face, and in a moment she seemed to have lived the space of a century. It was Arthur Heathcote.

"Awful of me to drop down on you in this way," said Heathcote, after greeting them; "but you know I've been out this way before, and I thought I'd like to see the country again, so here I am. I'm so glad to see you, Miss Osborne, and you, Mr. Osborne."

He lied very glibly, but his face was red and he looked like a guilty schoolboy.

Osborne was frankly glad to see him, but even Mildred herself realized that her greeting was cold and formal.

"Thought maybe your people might put me up for a week or two. Of course, I didn't know. If they can't, why, I'll be trotting along."

"Of course they can," said Osborne, heartily. "Landry!"

Landry came forward; the two men were introduced. Each eyed the other as if taking stock of his strength and fighting ability.

"Won't you try to help us locate Heathcote?"

"I shall be glad to," said Landry, but his face belied him.

They went into the house, and the Englishman was soon placed. Mrs. Hendrickson was overcome with joy at being able to oblige any friend of Mr. Osborne's, and they could and would put Mr. Heathcote up for as long as he wanted to stay.

So his luggage was brought in from the road, and he settled himself, like the thorough Britisher he was, at home wherever he took off his hat.

After doing what he could for the new arrival, Landry came out of the house again. But this time he did not go toward Mildred. He only bowed to her as he passed, and went with set face out toward the barn.

Mildred could have wept from very grief and vexation. She knew what he must think of her, and her face burned. He would believe that she had known of Heathcote's proposed visit, and had snubbed him that he might be conveniently out of the way. Oh, the shame of it! The meanness of her nature as he must see it! She was glad that he been proud enough to pass her by. She could not respect a man who would stoop to a woman who acted as contemptibly as she appeared to act. But then her thoughts took another turn. He should not have thought it of her. He had no grounds for believing her so low. But then, what did she care? She didn't. She knew she didn't care, for she told herself so several times before Arthur Heathcote came out to talk to her.

Her feelings as she saw him approaching were a study, even to herself. She could not forget the bighearted Englishman's simple kindness that wet September night, when she had made the child the object of her impulsive charity. She liked him, but she was angry at his intrusion. Here she had been living so close to Nature, and, now he had come smelling of civilization—in her thoughts she unconsciously quoted Landry—to break up her paradise. Perhaps her aunt had sent him. Maybe he knew about Landry. Had he come to spy upon her actions? But she dismissed the thought as soon as it was formed. That was not like Heathcote; but oh! she wished he had not come. However, he was here, and coming towards her smiling now. The sky that she had loved had lost its color. The sunset which she had looked at with Landry beside her was devoid of glory. Everything seemed dull and gray to her, and all because a foolish old woman had written a letter, and an unwelcome lover had come at the wrong hour, and a hard-headed girl had refused to listen to the dictates of her heart.

"I am afraid, Miss Mildred, that you will think hardly of my racing out here."

"I cannot blame you for wanting to see the country again. I love it myself."

"Yes; but I mean for coming out here after you."

"Surely that would not be fair, unless you blamed me for coming before you."

"That's so. But now you're laughing at me again. Indeed you are. But, you know, I thought you wouldn't care if I just came."

"I am sure I don't."

Poor fellow! he was helpless and inarticulate after that.

"Of course, you know why I came."

"You have already told me it was because you had been out here before, and you wished to see the country again. A very good reason for coming."

"Oh, come now," Heathcote protested; "you know I was just telling a few then. Mildred, you know why I came. It was because I couldn't stay away from you. I couldn't take no for an answer."

"Arthur," she said sadly, "you make it so hard for me."

"Forgive me?" he broke in, "I don't want to persecute you. Really, I didn't intend speaking until time for me to go away."

"Arthur," she said again, "I do like you, but won't you give up hoping or thinking that I will marry you? I cannot. I cannot."

There was a decided set to Arthur Heathcote's chin as he replied, "I will not give up hope until you are the wife of some other man, but I won't persecute you. I love you, Mildred, and a love like mine is not to be daunted. Now, let's not think any more of it while I am out here. Let's be good friends, for I believe you when you say that you like me, and we can have a pleasant unrestrained time, if you will let me walk with you and ride with you."

"You shall walk with me, and you shall ride with me, Arthur, and I wish I could say more."

"Oh, I have time," he said, and there was a shake in his voice, in spite of the brave ring of it, "and after that, there is eternity." Then he laughed. "Oh, I say, I like your man, Landry, although I can't understand him. A cowboy who talks like a college man is something of a paradox, you know."

"That is not a strange thing. Every American is a paradox, unless he happens to be an Anglomaniac."

"I like the paradoxes better. It's what we expect of Americans. I don't like this sudden turn for friendship and all that between us. We haven't got a soul now, to whet our boys' belligerent appetites against, and whom have you?"

"Oh, we feel our loss as greatly as you do. But then, we have a little trouble on our hands."

"Yes, but that's only a brush. Inferiors never make good enemies. A fellow could never have a real jolly fight with his valet. He might kick the man, but kicking a man is not fighting him."

"Well, you shouldn't complain, at least. England did find metal more attractive among the Boers."

"That's the reason she went to it, like steel to the magnet."

It was in this way that Mildred and Arthur talked on, building up a wall of conversation behind which to hide—the girl, with her torn heart and wounded pride, the man hopeless, in spite of his bravery, saying bantering nothings while his face was white and drawn.

Chapter 8

LANDRY'S FEELINGS WERE SEVERELY hurt when he supposed that Mildred had merely made use of him, and then tossed him away like a soiled glove. It did not seem like her, and his grief was not so much for himself as for the ideal he had had of her, which was now shattered. A man may lose faith in manhood, and his nature suffer a severe wrench, but for him to lose faith in womanhood, which means, to the average man, one woman upon whom he has staked all his beliefs and hopes, often proves the breaking of him.

But, hurt as he was, it would not have been in Landry's nature to sulk long. He was too vigorous and direct, and his love being stronger than his resentment, he would eventually have gone to Mildred, and have had it out with her. But it was reserved for Heathcote, unconsciously, to hasten the event. Unconsciously, yes; not that he would not have done it knowingly had he been aware how matters stood.

It was the morning after his arrival that he sought out Landry where he was wandering disconsolately among the horses, unable to conceal his unrest.

"I say, Mr. Landry," said Heathcote, "I'm afraid I'm bothering you awfully, you know, but I want to see you for a moment."

"Here I am," said Landry, not too pleasantly; and then he added, somewhat to soften the speech, "and at your service."

"I was thinking maybe you might help me to a mount. I don't like to ask Mr. Osborne, you know, as I dropped down on them rather unexpectedly, and it seems mean to trouble them."

Landry in a moment was all alert. "Why, I thought they were expecting you," he said.

"Oh, no, neither of them knew anything about me until I turned up here."

"I shall be glad to help you to a mount, Mr. Heathcote: just come with me." There was a sudden cordiality in Landry's manner that quite took possession of Heathcote. In fact, Heathcote might have had all the horses on the ranch just at that moment with Landry's joyous permission. His troubles fell away from him as the black shadows fall from the mountains before the sun. He was all life and heart again, though he could not but blame himself for having doubted Mildred's honesty, even for a moment. Evidently, he had offended her in some small way, and he would go to her and find out what it was and make it all right. His ideal was reinstated, whole and without a blemish. The goddess was again in her shrine, and he was very happy.

There was a great joy in Heathcote's breast, too, for the mount with which Landry provided him filled him with unspeakable admiration. It was Landry's own horse, so generous was that young man. She was a big roan, raw-boned and strong-limbed. A small, well-formed head was well set on her solid shoulders.

"What a beauty, what a beauty!" said Heathcote.

"You'll find her as good as she is beautiful," said Landry, with pardonable vanity.

"My knees are really itching to be astride of her."

"If you have nothing to do, get on and try her."

The next moment the Englishman was in the saddle, whence he beamed on Landry. The horse moved off at her easy gait. This was too much for Heathcote. The pure air and the wide plain brings out the natural in a man, and it was something of a reversion to primitive instincts when the delighted rider tossed his hand in the air and gave a whoop. He would not have believed it possible had anyone predicted it of him. He felt the enthusiasm of a strong man for fine animals, and dimly, too, something of the influence of the vast life about him. He circled back to Landry, his face glowing, and the gladness of a big, unspoiled boy showing in his eyes.

"I say," he exclaimed, "are you really going to let me ride her? Aren't you depriving yourself now?"

"She's yours as long as you are here," said Landry, "and I'm glad you like her."

"Mr. Landry," said Heathcote, reaching down his hand as solemnly as if it were a ceremonial, "if ever you come to England, you shall have the finest horse in my stable."

"Thank you."

The two men shook hands and were friends from that moment. Three things draw men close—to suffer, to dare, and to enjoy together; and they found a fellow-feeling in their very gladness. Heathcote forgot the traditions of his people, forgot to ask whence Landry came; whether he were cowboy, stableman, or what. He only knew him for a good fellow. They were two strong, clean men, face to face, each drunk with the joy of living and loving. What more was needed to make them friends?

The Englishman rode away towards the ranch-house, and his friend looked after him. He saw a fine rider and a fine man, such a one as might have taken any woman's heart captive.

"It'll be a hard fight," said Landry, musingly, "but it will be a square one; and if I lose, I'll have the satisfaction of losing to a worthy fellow. Oh, well—" and he fell a-thinking.

It was because of all this that Mildred Osborne had the misfortune to grow very angry that morning. Heathcote came riding toward her, and she saw that he sat Landry's horse. Resentment flashed instantly into her heart. "Landry has no right to deprive himself. Maybe he thinks it will please me." Then she stopped saying things to herself, and said "Good-morning" in response to Heathcote's bow.

"Your man, Landry—" he began.

"Pardon me, Mr Heathcote," she broke in, "but he is not my man, Landry. Mr. Landry is a gentleman, and quite our equal." She didn't know why she said it, for she did not know anything about the antecedents of Landry.

"Oh, beg pardon, Miss Mildred, I might have known that. Americans are so eccentric, you know. But the fact of the matter is that I never stopped to think what Landry was. I only knew that he was a fine fellow. I was just going to say that he loaned me his horse. Don't you think she is a fine animal?"

"She is; and he is so attached to her that I really don't know what he'll do without her."

"That's right, and I'm a selfish beast. I'll go straight—"

"Oh, no! no! you won't do anything of the kind. He would feel very much hurt."

"Oh, but I can't help it. It's not fair to take such a mount from a fellow," and he was turning as he spoke.

"Please don't," pleaded Mildred; "please don't, for my sake. That is," she stammered, "he would never forgive me for speaking."

"But he sha'n't know that you have spoken."

He was looking at her keenly, and with a question in his eyes. She blushed furiously under his gaze, and fingered her dress nervously as she spoke.

"Perhaps you don't know, but Landry, Mr. Landry, is very eccentric."

"Indeed?"

"Oh, yes."

If he would only stop looking at her in that way. She knew that her face was guilty, and that she was fast getting angry again, both with herself and with her inquisitor.

"Then if you insist, I shall not take the horse back. I shall go for a spin. Won't you come with me?"

"I shall not ride this morning," she returned.

"Is it wrong for me to remind you of your promise?"

"I have not forgotten my promise, but I shall not ride this morning."

"I must bid you good-morning, then. I cannot lose the pleasure of this horse's gait, even for so fair a lady as yourself," and laughing, he rode away, leaving her there, helplessly embarrassed, and with the idea knocking at her consciousness that she had made something of a fool of herself.

Landry found her still sitting on the porch when he came up a little later. While she would not own it to herself, the girl had practically been waiting and wishing for him, but now she was frightened at his approach.

"May I sit down?" he said, after greeting her.

"To be sure," she answered; "you know we are all generosity here. We give people our horses, and let them sit on their own chairs."

"The horse was nothing, but a chair here is everything. I have offended you. Won't you tell me how, and forgive me?"

"But you have not offended me, Landry. Why should you think so?" She felt how deceitful she was even as she said it.

"I am so glad," he said, humbly; "but you turned your back on me yesterday."

"It was very rude of me, wasn't it? But that was not on account of anything you had done. I had received a letter—" she hesitated "—and it provoked me very much. Of course, I had no right to take it out on you. But then, Landry, you don't know women very well, do you?"

"I don't know anything except that I am the happiest man on earth. Let's go for a ride," he added abruptly.

"No, I don't want to ride since you haven't your horse."

"Then let's walk. It's too glorious to sit still."

He must have meant all he said, for his face showed it.

"I'll walk with you," and she ran into the house to get her hat. Why was the day suddenly bright again, and why were her feet so light? It was because she had righted a wrong, she soberly told herself. That was the reason, too, that she came out singing.

"I've been so miserable," said Landry, as they strolled along the cactus-dotted land. "I—I—had thoughts."

"A very rare thing for a young man," she answered laughingly.

"But you don't know," he went on gravely; "I wronged you greatly in my mind."

"I knew what you thought," she said, "but you were wrong. I am not that kind." She had grown serious in an instant.

"I might have known that you were not. I was blind then, but I am wise now, and because of my wisdom, I know why Mr. Heathcote has come here."

"Mr. Heathcote is a friend of the family."

"Mr. Heathcote loves you, and so do I, and I want to know my fate now. Mildred, will you marry me?"

She had known that it was coming, and yet it was a great shock to her. She could not look at him, as she said tremulously, "I cannot marry you, Mr. Landry."

"Why not?" he asked simply. "Do you love someone else?"

"You have no right to ask that question, but I do not mind answering you. No; but I cannot marry you. First, because I do not love you; why, I hardly know you."

"Then it has meant nothing to you—our companionship? And it meant so much to me. You speak of hardly knowing me, and yet you have so filled my heart and life that I can hardly think of a time when I did not know and love you."

"Oh, Landry, please don't," she cried piteously. "I did so want to be friends with you." Her aunt's letter, and her aunt's horror burned into her mind like a flame. She stole a glance at his face, and it was tender, but sad, so sad.

In the moment a great hatred grew up within her for her aunt, and all the conventions of her set and kind. Even if she had loved Landry, society had set a barrier between them. Here was her aunt's cowboy with a vengeance. The humor of the situation struck her, and she burst out laughing. The man looked at her with sorrow and indignation in his eyes. But in a moment he understood, for she was as quickly possessed by a passion of tears.

"Forgive me," he said; "I have hurt you. I won't say any more about it—now," he added firmly. "Come, let's go back."

She did not answer; she only wept the more, for she felt that all she loved, all she wanted, all that in life was worth having was slipping away from her grasp, but she could not check it. There stood King Convention; this was his decree.

She dried her eyes as they went back toward the house, he walking disconsolately by her side.

She turned to him as they reached the porch. "Landry," she said, "you will always be my friend?"

"I shall always be your friend and lover," he said, taking her hand, and then he turned away toward his own apartment.

Mildred hurried to her room and threw herself upon the bed. The blessed tears came again to relieve her; and then she sat up, crying softly, for fear the very walls would hear, "Landry, Landry, you are worth some woman's love, but who are you?"

Chapter 9

IT WAS STRANGE THAT in Landry's grief at Mildred's refusal of him, there was no anger at the girl herself. He remembered her distress and her tears, and felt only deep pity and a more overwhelming love for her.

"She loves no one else, she said, and I believe her," Landry mused when he was alone. "Well, then, why shouldn't she love me? She doesn't know me, that's true. I might be a horse-thief or a pickpocket for all she knows to the contrary. She's right. She has the right to know more about me, and I was a blundering ass to ask her to take me for granted. But can I tell her everything? Can I explain to her?" A hard wrinkle came into the man's brow as he thought, "The secret is not mine wholly. But I have lost faith in humanity on account of it; now shall I lose the love of my life for this same reason? Great God! is there no limit to what I must suffer —loss, ignominy, shame, and now this?"

He clenched his hands, and the great beads broke out on his forehead. Then, as was his wont when he wished to think, he saddled a horse and went galloping away.

The land was full of the brisk, sweet smells of autumn. The plain fell away in a gray, barren line that held up a turquoise dome. The little ground-birds, scarcely discernible against the grass, so like themselves, skipped away before his horse's feet. But Landry saw nothing, neither landscape, sky, nor birds. He felt nothing, not even the rush of the wind as he swept across the prairie.

Surrounded by the things which he knew and loved and was wont to observe, he was as utterly alone with his own thoughts as if he had suddenly been lifted out of the life of this earth and placed where there were only himself and his soul. He was doubly isolated, in that his was the isolation both of great grief and deep thought. On his face were all the marks of the struggle that was going on within him. His eyes were cold and bright and his cheeks flushed, though his hands held the reins firmly, and there was not the quiver of a muscle in his face. Like a man turned to iron, he rode and rode. Every now and then, unconsciously, he dug his heel into the horse's side, as if, moving swiftly though he was, he could not keep pace with the hard, hot gallop of his thoughts. So he went for an hour, and then, without warning, turned homeward again. The strained look in his eyes was gone, and his whole attitude was one of relaxed force. But there was still on his face the expression of a man who has made a vital decision, and who will carry out his plan to the last extreme. He bent over and stroked the horse's damp neck.

"I will do it," he said. "He shall not take this from me."

With him, when a decision was once made there was no turning back. As soon as he reached his room, he sat down and wrote the following letter:

"DEAR MISS MILDRED—I know now the folly I showed in asking you to marry me, about whom you know absolutely nothing. Five years ago I should have known better, but I have been away from civilization so long that I have forgotten some of its demands and conventions. I had thought that if two people cared for each other, that was all, and there were no other questions to be asked or answered. I confess that I was wrong, and that my theory would only do for a more primitive state of life than this to which you and I belong. But I do not blame you because I blundered, and so, whether or not it affects the issue, I am going to answer the questions, which, if you cared for me, you must have asked.

"I remember that you once repeated the remark that people only came out here on account of crime, cupidity, or consumption. It seems proper that the world should usually take it for granted that the first of these most commonly drives a man to this life. But it was not so in my case. At least, I am not a criminal. The story is a long one, and I should prefer telling it to you to writing it. I should beg your permission to do so, except that when I talk to you I lose my head, and say the things that I do not want to say.

"The secret which I disclose here is not, as you will see, entirely my own, and I need not ask in mercy to all concerned that it go no further than the ear of your father, who also has the right to know.

"In the first place, my name is not Landry, or that is, it is not my surname, but my mother's name, by which I choose to be known out here. My full name is Landry Thayer, and I was born in Philadelphia, twenty-eight years ago. My mother died when I was young, and all my boyish love was given to my elder brother, John, and to my father. My first great grief came with the death of the latter, who had always been a tender and indulgent parent to me.

"I mourned for him sincerely, but the buoyancy of youth soon overcame my sorrow and I turned to my brother, now all that was left to me, with the whole wealth of my affection. He loved me in return; and so it was a great wrench when, finishing my course in the city schools, I went away to the Massachusetts Institute of Technology. We were wealthy. My brother managed the estates but I had my ambition. I was determined to be one of the world's workers, and engineering took my fancy. I wanted to build bridges. I wanted to dig tunnels. I am making irrigation ditches now; but even that is part of my plan. You will laugh at this, won't you? But it's straight.

"Well, before I left for school, I noticed that my brother cared for, or seemed to care for, a very beautiful, frivolous girl who was at that time dominating Philadelphia society, and who had a dozen men in her train. I did not like her, and told my brother so. He flew into a fury, called me an impudent young cub, and bade me never speak her name again. On my knees and with tears in my eyes, I begged his forgiveness. I was younger then. He barely forgave me, and with a sore heart I went to school. One day I received a card that cut me like a knife, and when I came back he was married.

"I hated her; with all my heart I hated her. She had taken from me all that I had—my brother. He was cold and stern with me now, where he had always been loving and kind before. Well, I suppose that I was a young fool, and precipitated matters, but I did not exert myself to be agreeable to my sister-in-law. After a while she told my brother that I was a sullen young fellow, and made her very unhappy. The result was another scene, and my brother, who I believe, loved his wife sincerely, forbade me the house, which he, as the elder, had inherited.

"He packed me out, bag and baggage, and I went into lodgings; but still I did not blame him, and even when I went back to school, I only felt that I was a jealous young fool, who deserved my brother's anger; and God knows I was jealous, for his had been the only love outside a father's that I had ever known. At college there was an allowance ample for all my wants, for I was not extravagant. All went well, and I grew enthusiastic over my work. It is a great work, after all. I was looking forward with joy to my Christmas vacation, when I could go home and be reconciled to him. It was then the blow fell upon me. I received a letter from him, my brother, my only one, saying: 'Since things are as they are, would it not be better if we do not meet? So I would be glad if you spent your vacations from home.' You do not know how it hurt me. Even now I feel the terrible searing of it. My brother, my own brother turned against me, and asking me not to come to my father's house! I had thought the other disagreement only temporary, but this was final.

"I was proud, and I did not go back, nor did I write to him. Occasionally, in the papers, I saw reports of the magnificence of his entertainments, and I was glad, for I loved and trusted him still, though I hated her.

"Then I heard that he had sailed for Europe. I was glad, because he had always wanted to see the wonders of the old world. 'John has gone away,' I told my chum; 'I'm glad, because he always wanted to see the things over there.'

"'It's a pity,' said my chum; 'I'm sorry for his wife.'

"I need not say what I did to Jack Alston; only, since he knows that I did not know then, he has forgiven me and writes to me now, and I love him. He is building a bridge somewhere.

"After Jack had given me this cue, I went and looked further. The papers said that my brother had left suddenly, without his wife, and that there were rumors of irregularities in his handling of my father's estate.

"They were lies, all lies, and I knew it; so I rushed home to refute them. In my father's house, at the door out of which I had seen carried the man who had fathered us both, I met that woman.

"'Oh, it's you,' she said, when the servant had taken her my card. 'It's awful about John, isn't it? Not a thing left.'

"'You're a liar, you're a liar!' I cried, '—and a thief too, and a murderess!' And I flung out of the hall, and down the steps.

"'Heavens, the man is mad!' I heard her say as I was going.

"But the rest is hardly worth the telling. My brother had gone from one excess to another, entertaining, speculating, until he had been tempted to touch what was not his. Then my fortune—I blessed him for sparing me so long—had gone to make up the deficiency. Then he had left. Out of all my father's estate, save what that woman had, there were scarcely five thousand dollars left. I could not stand the grief of it. She showed me a letter from him saying that had I not proved ungrateful—*ungrateful!*—it would have been better. I do not believe he wrote it now.

"With this, and the money that I had left, I came West because I could not bear the sight and sound of the things that had driven my brother to crime. They did drive him. They did drive him, for I knew him when he was square. A year later I heard that he was dead—had shot himself at Monaco. His widow is married.

"That is why I hate civilization, and you are the first one who has ever called me back to it. Do not judge my brother too harshly; he was not so much to blame as the devilish, deceitful, strenuous civilization that drove him to his death.

"With the little money, I have prospered some. Cripple Creek was kind to me, and this ranch calls me one of its masters. Mildred, darling, you know my story. Forgive me if I have given you more than usual of—

"LANDRY."

This letter Mildred received next morning from the hand of Tod. She dropped her tears upon it as she read. Then she arose and went to her father.

"Papa," she said, "Landry has proposed to me, and I—"

"Landry!"

"—and I refused him; here is his letter."

The old man got up, the color in his face rising in anticipation, as it were, of occasion.

"Why—" Then he began to read the letter. As he read, the anger died from his face and the teardrops fell on his ruddy, wrinkled cheeks. They fell as freely as the girl's.

"Do you love him?" he asked, when he had finished.

"No," answered Mildred, firmly; and then, "I don't think I do."

"I am almost sorry," said her father, "for Landry—ah!—Landry is a very big man; but I suppose it's Heathcote. Well—"

"Heathcote!" snapped Mildred, "I hate Heathcote!" and she swept from the room.

"She hates Heathcote!" said Mr. Osborne. "What a remarkable girl! Yesterday it was Landry."

Chapter 10

FOR SOME REASON OR other, quite unrelated to love, Mildred had cried herself to sleep over Landry's letter. She thought it was because she pitied him in his sorrow. When they met again she told him so, and he was more miserable than ever, because she gave him pity when he wanted love.

They tried to resume their old relations, but utterly without success. There was always between them a subtle embarrassment, the shadow of his refusal.

So the days went by until the time for the roundup. Landry kept his promise to Mildred, and saw that arrangements were made for her to ride out to see the cattle when they were to be driven down into the valley. Heathcote had begged to be allowed to ride with the men, and permission had been granted to him. He was as happy as a boy, although he had sacrificed his own inclination and forced Landry to take back his horse for the work.

It was noon of a Monday when the men set out for the broad valley into which the cattle were to be driven down from the ranges. With Heathcote, there were eleven of them in all—brawny, rawboned fellows, bronzed by the sun and wind, hard riders, hard swearers, but faithful to their duty and fearless in the discharge of it. It was near evening when they reached their destination. The horses were unharnessed from the grub-wagon as soon as it came up with them, and after supper they camped for the night, resting for the next day's riding.

They were up the following morning, and with three men left at camp, were away into the hills. All day long they rode the ranges, cleaning them out as with a great ever-moving comb, and the cattle streamed down into the valley. It was an all-day undertaking, and not yet done when Mildred came in the evening. The buckboard brought her and her father, and her pony Jack trotted behind. It was a wonderful sight to her, and she was much grieved that Landry insisted upon her and her father's camping so far away from the herd that night. It seemed to make of them only spectators, when she wished to be part and parcel of it. But Landry knew, and she did not, the words of the songs the cowboy sings as he gallops by night round and round his cattle.

Stirred with the novelty of the situation, Mildred was up in the morning with the earliest of them. It was a glorious day; all golden-browns, yellows, and blues. The mist hung heavy over the mountains, but for miles along the plain the air was as clear as the water of a mountain stream. It was one of those hot days which come to Colorado even as late as November. It was very still, save for the calling of the men one to another as the drove of cattle, eight hundred strong, went milling round and round the valley. All the night before, the men had circled the herd, singing their interminable songs to reassure them. But today the animals were nervous. The smell of water in the bottom of a dry wash, which ran across the end of the valley at its entrance, made them restive, and every now and then one would break away and dash forward, only to be followed by one of the boys and driven back to his fellows. They snorted and bellowed and pushed one upon the other. Their horns crashed and waved, a short, bristling, terrible forest, and their brown or brindled sides gleamed in the sun. It was hard work keeping them together.

To the front and left of the churning herd Landry was riding, his face gloomy and sad. Behind him, on the same side, rode Heathcote, while directly opposite, on her favorite pony, was Mildred. Near her Landry had placed a cowboy, to see that no ill came to her.

He looked uneasily across at Mildred and then glanced at the nervous steers.

"I wish she hadn't come," he muttered. "It's the day and the place for a nasty stampede." A big steer far to the front bellowed and sniffed the air. Landry rode quickly forward, and the long thong of his quirt curled about the great fellow's neck, and the column moved on as before. It was nearly seven o'clock in the morning, and while some of the men were busy keeping the cattle from breaking away, others were preparing to cut out the beef steers for shipping and the late calves for branding.

A wind sprang up, and it seemed that the heat of the atmosphere was about to abate. Landry breathed freer, and again his glance wandered over to the girl he loved. He caught her eye and she smiled at him. He felt as if she had laid a cooling hand upon his brow.

Mildred was a spectacle to call forth the admiration of a man who loved her even less than did Landry. Her gray habit fitted snugly her girlish form, and a soft felt hat with an eagle feather on the side, sat jauntily on her brown head. She was joyous with the movement and life about her, and glad with a feeling of sufficiency which came to her as she turned her pony this way and that.

Her father had felt some misgivings about her coming, but she had pleaded so hard, and had looked so beautiful as she begged, that he had kissed her and told her to go, while he remained with the grub-wagon not far away. He knew that with two such protectors as Landry and Heathcote she could hardly come to harm.

She was going gaily along, and the glow on her face made Landry's heart leap. Then, in a second, it all happened. A bunch of steers broke away toward the water. One by one of the ringing multitude joined them, until in a few minutes the whole herd had joined in the wild rush toward the box-cañon.

"Stampeded!" was the one word that Mildred's cowboy protector expelled from his lips as he galloped away from her side. The cattle were racing like mad down the valley, making a seething caldron of bubbling backs.

The girl saw what had happened. Her face went white. But a sudden thought took her, and digging her heel into the pony's side, with set face she went flying after the maddened steers, bending steadily to the right. She had heard that in such a case the thing to do was first to try and turn them, and then to get the cattle milling, and she felt that she herself might help to do it. But the cattle-men, all forgetful of her, had swept round to the left of the herd and were trying to turn them to the right; for they knew just how far back lay the deep dry run, and what it meant if their raging charges reached that. They had seen such sights before; when the cattle, which made their life and the existence of the ranch possible, went headlong into the steep cut and piled one upon the other, a groaning, bellowing, quivering mass of struggling flesh. They had seen the cut filled until the rear guard of the herd had passed over on a bridge of their dead fellows. So it was no wonder that they forgot the girl, and went galloping wildly to the left of the throng. Even Heathcote became infected with the insanity of the men around him, and the terrible whirl of the whole scene. He put whip and spur to his horse and swept on with them. On, on they went, to the left, bearing the enraged steers to the right, turning them ever from the ditch of death. But Mildred, unconscious of what they were doing, only knowing and feeling the thought that dominated her own soul, raced up behind the herd, still bearing to the right, and on to her death. Let the steers but turn and they would sweep over her, and she would be as utterly lost as a scrap of paper in the mad breath of the cyclone. Only one gray-faced man took in the situation. Landry had started with the men, but two hundred yards down the valley he saw her, and for the time that the glance took him, his heart stood still. "My God!" he cried, "what is the girl doing?" And then, without further time for thought, he cut straight across to the right, behind the herd, and went racing after her. It was only a matter of time, a trial of speed between him and the pony she rode, a race between Love and Death. Down the valley the girl rode, and he after her. The distance between them was wide, for he had to cross the whole width of the herd, but he felt himself gaining at every leap of the roan mare's brawny legs. Then did he thank God that Heathcote had given him back his own good mount. No other horse could have done it, could have overtaken the lithe little pony galloping so madly ahead. "Great God!" he said, "will they yet have time to turn before I reach her?" and he called to his horse with a prayer that was half an oath. The brown prairie burned under the roan's feet. Mildred did not look back. She rode as one rides who has a purpose, and that purpose quickly to be accomplished. They were nearing the cut now. He could see a straggly tree or two which grew upon its sides. "Mildred, Mildred!" he cried out, but the wind blew his voice behind him, and laughed in his face. Then Landry swore deeply, and the next moment uttered a prayer to Heaven, and struck his horse until the spurs drew blood from her foaming sides. On, on, they passed the cattle on the left. The roan flew, and Landry was gasping and his breath came hard between shut teeth. His eyes were wild as he came nearer, nearer. They were turning now, and there were a hundred yards between them. He swept up and stretched out his hand for the pony's bridle; but just then the deep hole of a prairie dog reached out and caught the pony's off forefoot. He stumbled. Mildred swayed in her saddle. Landry's hand forgot the goal to which it had started as he rode up to her side. He threw his arm around her waist and dragged her willy-nilly from her saddle, throwing her rudely, but safe, across the pommel of his own. Then his knees pressed the sides of the roan mare, and she, obedient, turned sharply to the right. They were just in time. Mildred's pony floundered and attempted to rise. Just then the herd swerved suddenly further to the right, and in a moment the little beast who had so lately borne the girl was beaten beneath a hundred hoofs.

With tears of excitement in his eyes, and curses of pure joy that took the place of prayers and thanksgivings on his lips, Landry slowed his horse and rode back toward the grub-wagon. He looked down into Mildred's face. It was white as death itself could have painted it; she had fainted. He bent above her, and a groan forced itself from the depths of his very soul. "I have hurt her," he cried, "but she will live, she will live, thank God!"

He rode as swiftly as he could back to the wagon where her father was waiting. Mr. Osborne saw them coming, Mildred lying as one dead across the saddle. He rose, pale and trembling, as Landry drew up. "What have you done to my child?" he said in a voice so low that it was scarcely audible.

"I have brought her back to you," said Landry; "she is hurt a little, but she is safe. Take her"; and putting the girl into her father's arms, he turned his horse and went swiftly back to his duty.

With the help of the drivers the grub-wagon was cleared, and Mildred was laid on a bed made of the men's coats. Nina was wringing her hands in the excess of helpless grief, but Hendrickson, who had seen it all, rode up, knowing and helpful. Her shoulder was wrenched. It was not a great affair, and he set himself at once to put it in place and to bandage it.

"It is not so much," he said to Mr. Osborne; "she is greatly shaken up, but she is young and will soon be well."

But the old man only bent above his daughter, crying, "Oh, Mildred! Mildred! have I brought you out here for this?"

On the girl's face there was no sign of life, but the set expression still lay about her lips. "Will she live?" asked Mr. Osborne.

"Oh, yes," said Hendrickson, "she will live; she is not greatly hurt. It will be a little painful, but she will live."

"If she recovers from this I shall take her home at once," her father said, his anger at himself growing that he had allowed her to run into such great danger.

"She is a brave young woman," said Hendrickson. "I am glad that Landry saw her in time."

"Landry! Landry! he has saved my daughter to me. I wonder what I can do to reward him."

The big ranch manager smiled. "I think your daughter will know better than you," he said.

Osborne looked at him dully, as if hardly comprehending. "He is a big fellow," he said; "I have always told her so."

Mildred's eyelids fluttered with returning consciousness.

Chapter 11

When Mildred regained consciousness she found herself lying in the grub-wagon, with Nina beside her. The wagon had been substituted for the buckboard, as being easier for her to recline in.

"What has happened, Nina?" she asked. "I remember about the stampede, and—and—Mr. Landry; but was I hurt, was I injured in any way?"

"Not unto death, miss," said Nina, solemnly; "but Mr. Hendrickson, he says your shoulder's out o' place, an' while you was insensible he set it, an' he says you'll soon be all right. But the pony, oh, miss, you should see the pony!"

"It was killed?"

"Ah, Miss Mildred, killed was no name for it. It was pulverized."

"What are they going to do with me now?" asked the girl, a shudder passing over her frame at the thought of the poor animal.

"They're going to start to the ranch-house with you as soon as you dare move."

"Tell them, Nina, that I want to see the spot; don't say pony, whatever you do—the spot where it occurred."

Nina went upon her errand and Mildred settled back with tears of pain and humiliation in her eyes.

"I wanted to do something big because I felt strong and capable; and I knew he looked at me with contempt; and, oh! how it has turned out! It only leaves me his debtor—his debtor," and with repetition the thought did not seem so bitter. "Well, he did his part; he was very brave and noble. Even if I cannot love him, I can respect him."

Then her father put his anxious face in at the door. "So you've come around all right, my dear? Hendrickson said you would. Really, he's quite a surgeon. Are you in much pain?"

"My shoulder does hurt very much, papa, but that doesn't matter. I'm sorry I gave you so much anxiety."

"Don't say a word, my child; I shall have you taken back at once to the ranch-house. But Nina tells me that you want to see the spot where the accident occurred. I don't believe I would if I were you, my dear."

"I want to see it, papa, and if they cannot take me I shall walk."

"There, there, don't excite yourself, my child; you shall see it. We will go by it on our way home."

He signalled to the men, and one galloped ahead, while the other started the horses which had been harnessed to the wagon, to await any turn which Mildred's injury might take.

As Nina sat down beside her mistress, Mildred's face flushed and paled by turns, and she looked into the maid's eyes wistfully.

"What is it, Miss Mildred?" asked Nina, gently.

"Nothing," snapped Mildred, going all red again; "did I ask for anything?"

"No, miss, but I thought you looked like you wanted something."

"No," she replied more gently, "but my shoulder does hurt so."

"You poor, dear child!" said Nina, easing the wounded part.

"I hope," Mildred went on, "that poor Mr. Landry isn't suffering this way."

Deceitful is the human heart, but it's the eye that usually gives it away; and so Nina saw nothing, for at that moment her mistress' eyes were closed in a spasm of pain.

"La, miss!" she exclaimed, "him a-sufferin'? Why, he wasn't hurt at all!"

The eyes suddenly flew open, almost too suddenly for honesty, and the sufferer cried eagerly, "Wasn't he? oh, I'm so glad!" And then a tell-tale look came into her eyes, and they were closed again in pain.

When the wagon had stopped at the spot to which Mildred indicated she wished to go, she raised the flap with her uninjured hand and looked out of the opening. There was nothing there, except the marks of many hoofs and a space covered with grass and sage.

She knew at once what it was.

"Uncover it," she said.

"No, no, Mildred," protested her father. He had sent the man on for that purpose, knowing what the sight would be.

"I want to see him," she persisted.

"But miss," said the man who had ridden on ahead, "it ain't a pleasant sight for a young lady."

"That's why I want to see it."

"Mildred!"

"Papa, must I get out and do it myself?"

Mr. Osborne nodded to the men, and they began to uncover the flat, soft something that had once been the pony. The hoofs of eight hundred cattle had beaten its flesh almost into the soil. Mildred gazed at it. "And I should have been like that," she said. "Thank you. Come, papa"; and she lay down again, very white. "Poor pony! poor little Jack! I rode him to his death, but I hope his spirit will forgive me, for I didn't mean to. I wonder if horses have souls or spirits?" she asked Nina a bit later.

And Nina answered, "I'm sure I don't know, miss, never havin' studied such things."

As soon as they were back at the ranch-house, where much ado was made both of Mildred and of the event of the morning, Mr. Osborne came into his daughter's room to see if she needed anything beyond Nina's ministrations.

"Papa," she asked, "Mr. Landry was very brave today, wasn't he?"

"Not only brave, but decisive, my dear; a moment's delay would have lost you to me forever. That man has the making of a general in him."

"Do you think so?"

"Mildred, my child, you speak of it so apathetically. The man saved your life, and I want you to thank him with all your heart."

"I was just going to suggest something of the kind. Send him to me as soon as he comes. Remember, papa, as soon as he comes."

"Yes, my dear."

"And now I'm going to try to sleep."

She closed her eyes until her father had left the room, then she opened them very wide, and lay gazing into space.

"Poor Jack!" she sighed, "and poor Landry! One I killed and the other I wounded. Well, I shall see him tomorrow."

But it was three days before Landry saw her; for when the message came, he was still away with the cattle, and the captain of the roundup could not, or would not, spare him.

When he arrived and came into her room she was sitting at her window, and rose to greet him. One arm was in a sling, but she extended the well hand to him.

"It was good of you to come," she said, and she felt just how flat and commonplace the words must sound.

"I could not do otherwise," said Landry, a little stiffly; although, after he had dropped her hand his own had gripped convulsively as he looked upon her pain.

"I—I—went up to see the pony. Oh!" She put her hand over her face as if to shut out the sight.

Landry flushed angrily.

"Who was fool enough to take you up there?" he said.

"I made them," she answered.

"I would rather you hadn't seen it. It wasn't a pretty sight."

"But it was an instructive one. It told me what I would have been like had you let my folly take its course."

"I don't know about that. I guess you were all right."

"It told me, too, what you had done for me."

"That was nothing; any fellow that knew anything about horses and cattle—"

She waved him into silence, and he stood abashed, holding his hat like a scolded schoolboy.

"I know, I know," she said; "but what I want you to understand is that it was not all wantonness on my part, my galloping after them as I did. No, hear me out, for you cannot, do not understand. After I saw that they had stampeded, I suddenly remembered what you had once told me of the method to be pursued, and I was possessed with the idea of helping to do it, so I raced after them in hopes that I could turn them or start them—what do you call it?—grinding or ringing."

A shade of a smile came into the man's eyes, but his lip quivered with a deeper emotion, and the impulse was very strong upon him to take the poor little wounded girl into his arms and strain her to his breast. But he remembered Thursday, and held himself back.

"Your ambition was very noble, Miss Mildred," he said; and it sounded very mean to him after it as was out, though, "God knows," he told himself, "I did not intend it so."

"It was very foolish and reckless," Mildred went on; "but then, I did so want to see a roundup, and when I saw those cattle making for the dry wash I knew what it meant, and I wanted to help. Of course, I didn't know how, and I made a silly spectacle of myself; but I did want to do something worthy, and—and—I only made you risk your life."

"That was nothing. You were perfectly right, Miss Mildred, and no one blames you in the least. It was such an accident as might happen anywhere. There are no serious consequences attached to it, save the pain you suffer, but that will pass, and thank God you weren't killed." Landry blurted it out before he could check himself, but in a moment he saw his mistake, and went on calmly, "Your father would never have forgiven us if you had been trampled out there."

"Landry, I know I owe my life to you. How can I thank you? What can I do to pay the debt?"

The young man threw up his head, and there was a light in his eyes that she had never seen there before. Then, with a bow that was his heritage from some old Virginia grandfather, he replied, "Consider the debt canceled, Miss Mildred," and turning hastily on his heel, left the room.

"He is angry with me," Mildred murmured. "I did everything but scorn him"; and she sat down crying softly, but bitterly.

She was filled with both sorrow and anger. She would not admit to herself that she loved Landry, and had done wrong to refuse him. She attributed all her misery to her inability to show him her gratitude. Had the young rancher returned even then and renewed his question, it is doubtful that she would have told him yes. Unconsciously, perhaps, but nevertheless dangerously, she was playing with her own feelings and his.

Her mood of grief was succeeded by one of distinct pettishness. "I am sure," she thought, "I can't go on my knees to him to thank him for what he has done. I do appreciate it, and I have tried to tell him so. What does he expect? Oh, well, I do hope papa will satisfy him, and express all that I cannot."

She knew perfectly that her father couldn't and wouldn't, but it pleased her to be perverse, even to try to deceive herself.

Someone knocked at the door, and Nina came in. "Please, Miss Mildred," she said, "Mr. Heathcote gave me these for you." "These" was a bunch of brilliant red and white roses.

"Put them on the table, Nina."

"Yes, miss; can I do anything for you?"

"No, go."

Evidently, "miss" was cross, and Nina went.

"I suppose he sent all the way to Denver for these," she said, handling the flowers. "I wish he wouldn't. Now if—" she blushed furiously, all alone as she was, and threw the offending flowers into one corner of the room, where they lay, the white and the red, like a pale girl bleeding. She sat down and brooded awhile, and then, relenting, picked up the flowers and replaced them in a vase.

Woman is a strange creature, and there is no accounting for her moods, and this is hereby acknowledged, or else one would be helpless before this one. For suddenly Mildred burst out laughing, and flying to the couch, hid her head in a pillow, rising at last to exclaim, "Well, I don't care if I do," and to sit looking with dreamy eyes into the fire, and a smile on her lips.

Meanwhile, Landry, in passing out, had encountered Mr. Osborne, who was in wait for him.

"My dear Landry," exclaimed the old man, holding out both his hands, "how can I ever thank you for the great thing you have done for me? Words are so poor."

"Don't mention it," said Landry; "it was nothing."

"Perhaps you may regard it as nothing, but it was everything to me." There was deep pathos in Mr. Osborne's voice and great earnestness, and Landry, looking at him, said bitterly in his soul, "Perhaps I do regard it too lightly"; but aloud he said, "I am glad to have been able to serve you, Mr. Osborne."

"I hope my daughter has thanked you."

"Oh, she has thanked me," was the grim reply.

"I fear she has hardly said all that she wishes to say or that she feels. She is like me there, my dear boy; I can't say what I feel. Just take it for granted; and if ever I can do you a service, no matter how great, just call on me. I am your servant."

"Don't mention it," said Landry, hastily, and he bolted.

"That is a very remarkable young man," said Mr. Osborne, gently. "I fear Mildred has not fully expressed her gratitude to him. I must see"; so he went to Mildred.

He found her still musing before the fire, with the smile on her face and a wrinkle between her brows. When he told her his beliefs and fears, she put her arm around his neck and drew him down to her.

"You're a dear old papa," she said; and that was all the answer he ever got.

And Landry went off to be miserable by himself.

Chapter 12

IT WAS NOT EXACTLY anger that had driven Landry from Mildred's presence with high head and flashing eyes. He felt that resentment against fate which a man feels when his sorrows are not the fault of any particular person. He had left the presence of the woman he loved, less because her inadequate thanks provoked him than from the fear that the words which were tugging at his heart would strain up and burst from his lips.

"All that's over now," he told himself bitterly. "I can't go to her now, like the hero of a dime novel, and ask her hand in return for her life. It would be cowardly, and it would be mean." So he went moping miserably about, all his enthusiasm in life dead or dormant.

He consistently avoided Mr. Osborne and Mildred, much to the former's surprise and the latter's grief. Mr. Osborne knew Landry so little as to think now that he had so great a claim that he would renew his suit, and successfully, for he believed that Mildred's gratitude must ripen into love for her savior.

Mildred frankly hoped that he would speak again, but knowing him better, she expected it less. It was strange now that repression intensified her feelings. She saw her lover but little, but she thought of him only the more. The vision of him was ever before her, and she remembered, with a pleasure so keen that it was almost pain, the innumerable little acts of kindness and consideration that had unconsciously endeared him to her. She missed their long rides together, and all the details of their sweet companionship. Fearing that before she had held him too cheaply, she now placed an unwarrantably high value upon him.

So the days went on, and still Landry did not come to her, when one day, her father approached her with a letter in his hand. His face was very grave, and his voice shook as he said—

"Mildred, I have just received a letter from your aunt."

The girl looked up apprehensively.

"Your aunt writes me that she fears that I have not kept a father's eye upon you, and that you are being allowed to be too much in the company of a very low person—in fact, as your aunt puts it, a horrible cowboy."

Mildred was looking angrily at her father now, but her anger was not for him.

"Pray," went on the old man, "whom does she mean?"

"She means the cowboy who saved my life a little while ago."

"She—she—cannot mean Landry?"

"She does, and she has written me before about it."

"Hum," said Mr. Osborne, gently, but with an annoyed look. "Your aunt is a very remarkable person. I shall write to her; I shall tell her," his voice was rising, "that Landry Thayer is a gentleman, and my friend, and the equal of any man I ever knew."

"Oh, papa," and Mildred's head was hidden on her father's waistcoat, somewhere in the region of the heart.

He held her off, and looked at her blushing face.

"Is it so?" he asked.

"Yes, and has been for a long time, but I didn't know."

He took his daughter very gently in his arms, and kissed her, saying, "I am very glad."

Meanwhile Landry, knowing nothing of the happiness in store for him, and hoping nothing, had determined to go further into the mountains for a shoot with Heathcote. That amiable young Englishman still lingered, and rode, drove, and shot with the joy that only a true sportsman can know. The friendship between him and Landry had increased, and when the latter was not mooning about, they were always together.

Mildred had been seeing almost as little of the one as she had of the other. It was Heathcote's plan to give her a respite from his importunities, and maybe, he thought, she would come round to his way of thinking. He had decided now, on his return from his hunting trip to go directly East; so the day before the start was to be made, he came to her once more.

She saw his purpose in his eyes, and would have saved him this final humiliation, but he would speak.

"I hope I'm not boring you too much," he said humbly, "but have kept silent as long as I can, and on my return, I shall go directly East, so I thought maybe you wouldn't mind giving me my answer now."

She looked at him with shining eyes, and he took a moment's hope, which was destined to be dashed immediately.

"Arthur, my good friend," she said, "I will not keep you in suspense. I cannot say to you what I said a little while ago, for now I do love another. I thank you for the honor you do me, for it is an honor to be loved by such a man."

He bowed and she gave him her hand. He was turning away, when suddenly a light broke through the gloom of his face, and he came back to her eagerly.

"I say," he began awkwardly, "it couldn't be old Landry, you know?"

"It is Landry," she said firmly.

"That's good, that's good," he said, with a ring of honesty in his voice; "I'd rather him than anybody else except myself. I congratulate you both." He stood pumping her hand, and smiling down at her, though there lurked a sadness in his eyes.

"There—there—is nothing to congratulate me about. Landry asked me before the stampede, and then I did not know, so I refused him. He has not asked me since."

Heathcote gazed at her for a moment in silence, and then he turned abruptly and left the room.

"What are you going to do?" she cried.

But he did not answer, and she sat down, suddenly laughing and crying, both together.

There was no mistaking Heathcote's purpose, and Mildred was filled with a great gladness, while her heart quivered with fright. Landry would know, he would know that she loved him and would come to her. Had she been unmaidenly to take this method to let him know?

Meanwhile Heathcote was striding along at a great gait. He burst into the door of the room where Landry sat cleaning a gun.

"You blooming ass," cried Heathcote, snatching the rifle from his friend's hands, "You blooming, idiotic ass."

"All right," said Landry, "What's the matter? You're getting your hands full of oil."

"Why don't you go to her?" said Heathcote.

Landry suddenly stood up, his nostrils dilated with excitement.

"What do you mean?" he asked.

"She loves you," blurted the other. "I've just asked for her hand; it's about the seventh time, I think. She'll never marry me, old chap; you're the man."

"How do you know?"

Landry was trembling like a leaf.

"Never mind how I know, I'm not telling secrets," Heathcote had shown remarkable reticence, it must be admitted. "You go to her, and thank your God it's you."

"I can't do it, old man," said the ranchman, sadly taking his seat.

"Can't do it? Why, what the—Why, man, you've got to do it."

"I can't, I can't! And how I wish I could!"

Heathcote stared at him with wide, uncomprehending eyes.

"Well, I'll be—Look here; will you tell me why?"

"Don't you see, Heathcote, that she has made it impossible for me to marry her, or even to ask her. Why, damn it, man, if I should take her now, it would look as if I had bought that sweet girl's life by an act of cheap heroism. Can't you see that?"

In his excitement, Landry sprang up, and seized his friend's arm.

"If anyone else spoke of your act in that tone and that manner," said Heathcote, slowly, "I should knock him down. You did a great thing; a big thing, and you saved a woman's life. Besides, she loves you. Go to her."

"I have told you why I cannot go."

Heathcote put his hands upon his friend's shoulders, and looked him squarely in his eyes.

"You're a damned fool," he said, "and all kinds of an idiot in the bargain, but you're the biggest man I've ever met. You may call me a meddler, or what you please, but I'm not going to let you suffer and make a woman suffer, simply because God did not choose to give you a fair amount of British vanity"; and he was out of the room in an instant.

It was with strangely confused feelings that Mildred saw the Englishman coming back to her. What was the matter? Why did not Landry come to her? Was his pride, after all, stronger than his love for her? Her face burned with shame at the memory of the means she had taken to bring him back, and the longing she had to hear his word of love again. Heathcote did not make matters better as he reached her. He may have always been honest, but it is true that he was seldom tactful.

"He won't come," he blurted out.

"Who sent for him?" said Mildred, rising proudly. "I am sorry, Mr. Heathcote, that you so little respected the confidence I gave you." Her anger was rising, her face was blazing. "An American gentleman," she went on, hotly, "in a like circumstance, would have known how to hold his tongue."

"Oh, come, now," said Heathcote, shamefacedly, "I couldn't help it, you know. Landry's awfully cut up because he couldn't come, but he's got some bally idea about your liking him out of gratitude, and his buying you by cheap heroism. It's all silly rot, you know. But say," he paused in admiration, "that fellow's fine."

The anger had left Mildred's face.

"Does he feel all you say?" she asked.

"All that, and more."

She came down the steps, and put her hand on Heathcote's arm.

"Take me to him," she said, simply.

"Now, that's something like," he said, beaming on her, as if he were not sealing his own death-warrant.

He took her to Landry's door, and left her.

Landry sat alone with his head in his hands. He looked up at her step. Then he sprang to his feet with a glad cry, and rushed toward her. She took a step toward him, and only smiled with a great content as he folded her in his arms. Beyond the one glad cry that had seemed to burst like a flame from the lava crust of his heart, he had said no word, and Mildred, looking up, saw that he was sobbing silently, as only a strong, reticent man can sob, when he does give way.

"Poor Landry," she said, stroking his head, "it's all right now, and we won't misunderstand any more."

Later, they went to Mr. Osborne, hand in hand. But they had no need to ask his consent. He was as happy in their love as they themselves.

When Mrs. Annesley was written to, it is reported on good authority that she fainted at the first lines of the letter, and could only be brought to with much trouble, so that she could finish it. When she found that Landry Thayer was something besides a cowboy, she consented to let the maid cease fanning her. When she found out that Heathcote was to be best man, she quite recovered, and said, bridling, "Well, that will lend distinction to the affair, and, well—it's very original, anyway."

THE FANATICS

Introduction

FOR PAUL LAURENCE DUNBAR, literary protest was an act of sedition. Dunbar, like authors before him and the many to come afterward, have used the mask as the ultimate symbol of survival. Humor is another symbol of survival, employed by Dunbar in fiction and poetry in all of its ironic modes. Protests—whether religious, social, or political—have never been welcomed by the status quo. Thus, masks and humor have become and necessarily remains the acceptable medium for protest.

Accomplished as he was, Dunbar has often been criticized by succeeding generations as an accommodationist for employing dialect, the lyrical sounds of blues and spirituals, and what were perceived as stereotypical Uncle Tom characters.

First, it is incumbent upon us to remember that dialect was the result of slaves' learning English not from book or page but by ear. Also, importantly, we would do well to remember that many laws forbade the teaching of reading and writing to the slave population.

Second, in Dunbar's texts, numerous black males and females, young and old, become models of survival who have to be recognized as human beings. One of those model beings is the narrator/preacher in "An Ante-Bellum Sermon," who remarks to his congregants:

> But I think it would be bettah,
>   Ef I'd pause agin to say,
> Dat I'm talkin' 'bout ouah freedom
>   In a Bibleistic way.

Clearly, to have spoken outright about freedom would have been taken as a threat, and the minister is quick to point out that his sermon and its evocation of freedom are only meant in terms of the Bible. Who would be willing to argue with scripture? Irony saves the day.

In a much more honorable way, the narrator in "When Dey 'Listed Colored Soldiers" reflects on the words her fiancé tells her:

>   his conscience hit was callin' to him so,
> An' he couldn't baih to lingah w'en he had a canst to fight
> For de freedom dey had gin him an' de glory of the right,

The tone here is daring and direct; it is brave and unmasked. It offers no threat because it perceives what freedom entails and is willing to risk everything for it. Dunbar's sympathies are, uncompromisingly, in the voices of his narrators.

The tone in both these quotations suggests that Dunbar was never the accommodationist he was accused of being, for the author knew well that social protest was often met with isolation, ostracism, and even death. Perhaps the greater act of subversion was a masked survival that led to another day of insurrection.

In his professional years of something like a decade and a half, the range of his output was enormous. One can only begin to imagine what he might have written had he lived longer. The modern reader must not fall victim to the same accusations about dialect that plagued Dunbar and cast doubts on his literary reputation.

In *The Fanatics,* Paul Laurence Dunbar imagines a mythical city just above the line of demarcation for free slaves: Dorbury, Ohio. Dunbar writes that the city will be tested for its beliefs:

> Ohio, placed as she was, just on the border of the slave territory, was getting more than her share of this unwelcome population, and her white citizens soon began to chafe at it. Was their free soil to become a haven for escaped Negroes? Was this to be the stopping ground for every runaway black from the South? Would they not become a menace to public safety? Would they not become a public charge and sorely strain that generosity that was needed to encourage and aid the soldiers in the field? These and a thousand such conjectures and questions were rife about the hapless blacks. . . . The cry rose for the enforcement of the law for the restriction of emancipated Negroes, while others went to the extreme of crying for expulsion of all blacks from the state. (158–59)

Dunbar wrestles with the fanaticism that characterizes both black and white, Northern and Southern, rich and poor, learned and unlearned. He forces the reader to consider the question of war in all of its political and religious implications. He takes us literally to the military battlefield but also to the site of conflict in the human soul.

More specifically, *The Fanatics* examines how the Civil War strained the moral and spiritual fabric of the Union, suggesting that slavery burdened the consciousness of the nation. The outcomes of war and slavery caused dissension and damage between families as well as political and religious allies. When Dunbar focuses his attention on the attitudes of the black community, we are forced to see how contemptuous a group of people can be. He observes:

> The free blacks of Dorbury themselves, took it up, and even before they could pronounce the word that disgusted them, they were fighting their unfortunate brothers of the South as vigorously as their white neighbors. "Contraband" became the fighting banter for black people in Ohio. (160–61)

The indictment takes on a larger significance when Dunbar writes about the black religious community:

> In Dorbury, the Negro aristocracy was . . . one founded . . . upon free birth or manumission before the war. . . .
>
> After much difficulty, the Negro contingent in Dorbury had succeeded in establishing a small house of worship in an isolated section known as "the com-

mons." Here, according to their own views, they met Sunday after Sunday to give praise and adoration to the God whom they, as well as the whites, claimed as theirs, and hither, impelled by the religious instincts of their race, came the contrabands on reaching the town. But were they received with open arms? No, the God that fostered black and white alike, rich and poor, was not known to father these poor fugitives, so lately out of bondage. (161–62)

It might be expected that the larger society might turn its back on these newly freed individuals. The irony of the situation, however, becomes even more heartrending when the black religious community fails to "suffer these people to come unto them." Here Dunbar points the finger of accusation at black and white alike. The toll of anger, pain, loss, regret, and even reconciliation is felt not only in this southern Ohio town but in the entire country.

In *The Fanatics,* Dunbar concentrates on several themes: love, allegiance, duty, and the substitution of segregation for slavery. Two types of love in this novel verge on fanaticism: romantic and filial love. They are intertwined and woven into the fabric of this novel. First, there is romantic love between three couples: Mary Waters and Robert Van Doren, Tom and Nannie, and Dolly and Walter. Caught up in fractious demands of war and duty, all three couples are tested in various ways. Then there is the filial love between the ex-slave and his mother that demands from him a certain honor and respect. It is the fathers who, withdrawing their consent for marriage, cause the most damage. It is the principle of the Union or Slavery that makes them so fanatic. What once seemed like a war with a foregone conclusion turns into a more despicable conflict. Mary comes face to face with this sudden reaction when her father tells her: "There is a time when men must separate on the ground of their beliefs, and this house has no dealings with the enemies of the Union, Mary" (10). And he continues a sentence or two later: "We are two families on opposite sides of a great question. We can have no dealings, one with the other" (10). The bond of one's word counts for naught in this instance because the father blatantly asserts: "I'd rather see you marry Nigger Ed, the town crier, than cross my blood with that Van Doren breed" (10).

This is fanaticism on the edge. Clearly, the father has given no thought to miscegenation or the marriage of his daughter to someone of a lower status, let alone a different race. Both of these issues the South was equally opposed to. It is this same determination that sends Robert Van Doren into the arms of the Confederacy. His sensibilities are with the Union, and his hope still to marry Mary keeps him in undecided territory. It is Mary's father who pushes him fanatically into the arms of the South. Would that Bradford Waters could have sensed the acceptance Robert Van Doren was seeking.

Then there is the filial love between the ex-slave and his mother, a love that requires honor and respect. The young man and his mother have just left the South and are seeking refuge in the southern Ohio town of Dorbury. Filial love brings his anger to the fore, resulting in the death of Ray Stothard, who is a different kind of fanatic with an opposing view. Dunbar thus creates a black character of strength and daring, simply referred to as "the young Negro." From his very introduction to us, he is determined and unafraid, with "a light in his eye that was not good to see." Perhaps to defuse this dramatic moment, Dunbar describes the young man's reaction as "the glare of an animal brought to bay."

When these two characters encounter each other a second time, the results are even more ironic and certainly more devastating.

> "Now, boys," said Stothard's voice from the rear, "rush them!" and he sprang forward. But a black face confronted him, its features distorted and its eyes blazing. It was the face of the contraband boy whom he had abused the day before. A knife flashed in the dim light, and in a moment more was buried in the leader's heart. The shriek, half of fear, half of surprise which was on his lips, died there, and he fell forward with a groan, while the black man sped from the room. The wild-eyed boy who went out into the night to be lost forever, killed Stothard, not because he was fighting for a principle, but because the white man had made his mother cry the day before. (176)

Seeking a respite, and some of the freedom promised by this conflict, this family of blacks has come to this mythical southern Ohio town. The resistance of Stothard and many like him forecasts the modern African American "ghetto."

In "the young Negro," Dunbar has created a character willing to stand up and demand respect, even if such an act is attributable to his "primitiveness," taking his vengeance upon the perpetrators even in the face of retribution. He is a new type of character who both literally and figuratively refuses to go back. Although he literally disappears from the action, he is strong and expresses a new kind of humanity that cannot be taken for granted. He has struck a blow for the future; that fact we dare not deny him or his act. In the final analysis, Dunbar questions our goodness and humanity. In each instance we may not meet those requirements.

The Fanatics

To my friend

Edwin Henry Keen

Contents

Chapter 1

Love and Politics

THE WARMTH OF THE April sunshine had brought out the grass, and Mary Waters and Bob Van Doren trod it gleefully beneath their feet as they wended their way homeward from the outskirts of the town, where Mary had gone ostensibly to look for early spring blossoms and where Bob had followed her in quest of a pet setter that was not lost.

The little town was buzzing with excitement as the young people entered it, but they did not notice it, for a sweeter excitement was burning in their hearts.

Bob and Mary had been engaged for three months, a long time in those simple days in Ohio, where marriages were often affairs of a glance, a word and a parent's blessing. The parent's blessing in this case had been forthcoming too, for while the two widowed fathers could not agree politically, Stephen Van Doren being a staunch Democrat, and Bradford Waters as staunch a Republican, yet they had but one mind as to the welfare of their children.

They had loud and long discussions on the question of slavery and kindred subjects, but when it came to shaking hands over the union of Bob and Mary, they were as one. They had fallen out over the Missouri Compromise and quarreled vigorously over the Fugitive Slave Law; but Stephen had told his son to go in and win, for there was not a better girl in the village than Mary, and Bradford had said "Yes" to Bob when he came.

On this day as the young people passed down Main Street, oblivious of all save what was in their hearts, some people who stood on the outskirts of a crowd that was gathered about the courthouse snickered and nudged each other.

"Curious combination," old man Thorne said to his nearest neighbor, who was tiptoeing to get a glimpse into the middle of the circle.

"What's that?"

"Look a-there," and he pointed to the lovers who had passed on down the street.

"Geewhillikens," said the onlooker, "what a pity somebody didn't call their attention; wouldn't it 'a' been a contrast, though?"

"It would 'a' been worse than a contras'; it would 'a' been a broken engagement, an' perhaps a pair o' broken hearts. Well, of all fools, as the sayin' is, a ol fool is the worst."

"An' a Southern fool up North who has grown old in the South," said Johnson, who was somewhat of a curbstone politician.

"Oh, I don't know," said Thorne placidly, "different people has different ways o' thinkin'."

"But when you're in Rome, do as Rome does," returned Johnson.

"Most men carries their countries with them. The Dutchman comes over here, but he still eats his sauerkraut."

"Oh, plague take that. America for the Americans, I say, and Ohio for the Ohioans. Old Waters is right."

"How long you been here from York state?"

"Oh, that ain't in the question."

"Oh, certainly not. It's allus a matter o' whose ox is gored."

The matter within the circle which had awakened Mr. Johnson's sense of contrast was a hot debate which was just about terminating. Two old men, their hats off and their faces flushed, were holding forth in the midst of the crowd. One was Stephen Van Doren, and the other was Bradford Waters.

The former had come up from Virginia sometime in the forties, and his ideas were still the ideas of the old South. He was a placid, gentlemanly old man with a soldierly bearing and courtly manners, but his opinions were most decided, and he had made bitter enemies as well as strong friends in the Ohio town. The other was the typical Yankee pioneer, thin, wiry and excitable. He was shouting now into his opponent's face, "Go back down South, go back to Virginia, and preach those doctrines!"

"They've got sense enough to know them down there. It's only up here to gentlemen like you that they need to be preached."

"You talk about secession, you, you ! I'd like to see you build a fence unless the rails would all stand together—one rail falling this way, and another pulling that."

The crowd laughed.

"I'd like you to show me a hand where one finger wasn't independent of another in an emergency."

"Build a fence," shouted Waters.

"Pick up a pin!" answered Van Doren.

"You're trying to ruin the whole country; you're trying to stamp on the opinions that the country has lived for and fought for and died for—"

"Seven states have seceded, and I think in some of those seven were men who lived and fought and even died for their country. Yes, sir, I tell you, Yankee as you are, to your face, the South has done for this country what you buying and selling, making and trading Yankees have never done. You have made goods, but the South has produced men." The old man was warmed up.

"Men, men, we can equal any you bring."

"Calhoun!"

"Sumner!"

"Clay!"

"Webster!"

"We shall claim Douglass!"

"Lincoln!"

"I should have said the South produced gentlemen, not rail-splitters. We don't make statesmen of them."

"We produce men, and we'd make soldiers of them if it was necessary."

"Well, it may be."

"Oh, no, it won't. Even the state that gave birth to men like you, Stephen Van Doren, wouldn't dare to raise its hand against the Union."

"Wait and see."

"Wait and see! I don't need to wait and see. I know."

"Bah, you're all alike, dreamers, dreamers, dreamers."

"Dreamers, maybe, but my God, don't wake us!"

The crowd began to break as it saw that the argument was over, and the bystanders whispered and laughed among themselves at the vehemence of the two men.

"Wind-bags."

"Time wasted listening."

"War—pshaw!"

Just then a newsboy tore into the square shouting, "Paper, paper!" and every heart stood still with ominous dread at the next words, "Fort Sumter fired on!" The crowd stood still, and then with one accord, formed around the old men.

A slow smile covered Stephen Van Doren's lips as he stood facing Bradford Waters.

"Well, they've done it," he said.

"Yes," replied the other, wavering from the shock, "now what are you going to do about it?"

The old man straightened himself with sudden fire. He took off his hat and his thin white hair blew hither and thither in the cool spring breeze.

"I'll tell you what I'm going to do about it. I'll tell you what I'm going to do, when the call comes, I'm going down there and I'll help whip them out of their boots—and if they won't take me, I'll send a son. Now what are you going to do?"

"Likewise."

Bradford Waters was known as a religious man, but now he turned and raising his hand to heaven said,

"God grant that we or our sons may meet where the right will win, you damned copperhead, you!"

In an instant Van Doren's fist shot out, but someone caught his arm. Waters sprang towards him, but was intercepted, and the two were borne away by different crowds, who were thunderstruck at the awful calamity which had fallen upon the nation.

The two old men sweated to be loosed upon each other, but they were forcibly taken to their homes.

Over the gate of the Waters' cottage, Bob Van Doren leaned, and Mary's hand was in his.

Chapter 2

The Parting of the Ways

"DON'T YOU THINK A little cottage down by the river would be the best thing, Mary?" asked Bob.

"And then you'd be away from me every minute you could spare fishing. I know you, Bob Van Doren."

From the inside of the house Mary's brother Tom "twitted" the two unmercifully.

"I say there, Bob," he called, "you'd better let Mary come in and help about this supper. If you don't, there'll be a death when father comes home."

Mary's father was gentle with her, and this remark of her brother's was so obviously hyperbolic that she burst out laughing as she flung back, "Oh, I guess you've kept Nannie Woods from her work many a time, and there haven't been any deaths in that family yet."

"But there may be in this if Luke Sharples catches you sparking around Nannie," interposed Bob.

"Oh, I can attend to Luke any day."

"That's so, Luke isn't a very fast runner."

Tom threw a corncob out of the door and it struck Bob's hat and knocked it off. "There's an answer for you," he called.

They were still laughing and Mary's face was flushed with love and merriment when Bradford Waters came up and strode silently through the gateway.

"I must go in now," said Mary.

"So soon? Why it's hardly time to put the potatoes on yet."

"Suppose sometimes you should come home and find your supper not ready?"

"Oh, I wouldn't mind if you were there."

Just then Bradford Waters' voice floated angrily out to them,

"What's that young whelp hanging around my gate for?"

The girl turned pale, and her heart stood still, but the young man only laughed and shouted back, "What's the matter, Mr. Waters, you and father been at war again?"

"Yes, we've been at war, and soon we shall all be at war. Some of your dirty kinsmen have fired on Fort Sumter."

"What!"

"Yes, and there'll be hell for this day's work, you mark my words." The old man came to the door again, and his son stood behind him, holding his arm. "Get away from my gate there. Mary, come in the house. I've got better business for you than skylarking with copperheads."

The girl stood transfixed. "What is it, father, what is it?" cried Tom.

"I tell you, those Southern devils have fired on Fort Sumter, and it means war! Get away from here, Bob Van Doren. There is a time when men must separate on the ground of their beliefs, and this house has no dealing with the enemies of the Union, Mary."

But the girl's eyes were flashing, and her lips compressed. "Go in, Mary," said Bob, and he dropped her hand. His face was red and pale by turns. She turned and went into the house, and her lover left the gate and walked down the street.

"Let this be the last time I catch you talking with one of the Van Dorens. We are two families, on opposite sides of a great question. We can have no dealings, one with the other."

"But father, you gave Bob the right to love me, and you can't take it back, you can't."

"I can take it back, and I will take it back. I'd rather see you marry Nigger Ed, the town crier, than to cross my blood with that Van Doren breed. Today, Stephen Van Doren rejoiced because his flag had been fired upon. The flag he's living under, the flag that protects him wherever he goes!"

"That wasn't Bob, father."

"Like father, like son," broke in Tom passionately.

"Why, Tom!" Mary turned her eyes, grief-filled to overflowing upon her brother, "you and he were such friends!"

"I have no friends who are not the friends of my country. Since I know what I know, I would not take Bob Van Doren's hand if he were my brother."

"If he were Nannie Woods' brother?"

"Nannie Woods is a good loyal girl, and her affections are placed on a loyal man. There is no division there."

"Bob is right, Mary. We have come to the parting of the ways. Those who hold with the South must go with the South. Those who hold with the North must stand by the flag. We are all either Union men or we are rebels."

"But father, what of Vallandigham? You have always said that he was a noble man."

"Vallandigham? Let me never hear his name again! In this house it spells treason. I can make some allowance for the Southerner, living among his institutions and drawing his life from them; but for the man who lives at the North, represents Northern people and fills his pockets with the coin which Northern hands have worked for, for him, I have only contempt. Such men hide like copperheads in the grass, and sting when we least expect it. Weed them out, I say, weed them out!"

The old man shook with the passion of his feelings, and his face was ashen with anger. There had been a time when Vallandigham was his idol. He had gone against his party to help vote him into Congress, and then—

It was a strangely silent meal to which the three sat down that night. Tom was feverishly anxious to be out for news, and Mary with tearstained face sat looking away into space. There was a compression about her lips that gave her countenance a wonderful similarity to her father's. She could not eat, and she could not talk, but her thoughts were busy with the events that were going on about her. How she hated it all—the strife, the turmoil, the bickerings and disagreements. The Union, Confederacy, abolition, slavery, the North, the South; one the upper, the other, the lower millstone, and between them, love and the women of the whole country. Why could not they be let alone? Was there not enough to be sacrificed that even the budding flower of love must be brought too? It was hard, too hard. She loved Bob Van Doren. What did she care with which side he sympathized? She loved Bob, not his politics. What had she to do with those black men down there in the South, it was none of her business? For her part, she only knew one black man and he was bad enough. Of course, Nigger Ed was funny. They all liked him and laughed at him, but he was not exemplary. He filled, with equal adaptability, the position of town crier and town drunkard. Really, if all his brethren were like him, they would be none the worse for having masters. Anyhow, her father had not been always so rigid, for he laughed when somebody stole the Bible from the colored folks' meeting-house, and wondered what they could do with a Bible anyhow.

Her reverie was broken by her brother's rising from the table.

"I'm going out to see what's going on," he announced.

"I'll walk up the street with you," said his father.

They took their hats and went out, and with a gray face, but set lips, the daughter went about her evening's work.

When they reached the courthouse a crowd was gathered there, and rumors and stories of all was kinds were passing from lip to lip. Another crowd was gathered on the opposite side of the street, hooting and jeering, while now and then some self-appointed orator harangued it. The assembly was composed of the worst elements of the town, reinforced by the young sports of some of the best families. Altogether, it was a combination of hot blood and lawlessness.

An old friend of the Waters', who had been listening to the noisier crowd, brushed against the two men, and said under his breath, "Come on home, there's hell's work brewing here tonight."

"Then I'll stay and be in it," said the older man.

"There's nothing you can help about," replied the friend. "You'd better come."

"No, we'll stay."

The lawless element, emboldened at the news of Sumter's disaster, determined to have some fun at the expense of their opponents. With one accord, they surged towards the office of the *Republican,* armed with horns, and whistled, hooted and jeered themselves hoarse.

"This is child's play," said Bradford Waters to his son, "if this is all they're going to do, we might as well go home."

They went back to the house, where for hours they could hear the horns and whistles of the crowd.

It was near midnight, when they were awakened by the clanging of a bell, and they heard Nigger Ed as he sped past the house, crying, "Fiah, fiah! De *'Publican* buildin' on fiah, tu'n out!"

The Waters were dressed and out of the house in a twinkling and had joined the crowd of men and boys who, with shouts and grunts, were tugging at the old hose-cart. Then they strained and tore their way to the *Republican* office where the fire had made terrible headway. The hose was turned on the building, and the pumps started. The flames crackled and the water hissed and like an echo there floated to the ears of the toiling men the cry of the rioters far away in another part of the town. They had done their work. It had, perhaps, come about unintentionally. They had only met to jeer; but me finally someone threw a stone. The sound of crashing glass filled them with the spirit of destruction. A rioter cried, "Fire the damned shanty!" There were cries of "No! No!" but the cry had already been taken up, and a brand had been flung. Then madness seized them all and they battered and broke, smashed and tore, fired the place and fled singing with delirious joy.

The work of the firemen was of no avail, and in an hour the building and its contents were a confused mass of ashes, charred beams and' molten metal.

When the Waters reached home, Mary, wide-eyed, white and shivering, sat up waiting for them. She hurried to give them each a cup of coffee, but asked no questions, though her hungry eyes craved the news. She sat and stared at them, as they eagerly drank.

Then her father turned to her. "Well," he said, "here's another sacrifice to the spirit of rebellion in the North. A man ruined, his property destroyed. They have burned the *Republican,* but they can't burn the principle it stood for, and the fire they lighted tonight will leave a flame in the heart of loyal citizens that will burn out every stock and stubble of secession, and disloyalty. Then woe to the copperheads who are hiding in the grass! When the flames have driven them out, we will trample on them, trample on them!" The old man rose and ground his heel into the floor.

Mary gave a cry, and shivering, covered her face with her hands.

Chapter 3

Preparation

THERE WERE MANY OTHER men in Dorbury no less stirred than was Bradford Waters over the events of the night, and the news from Charleston harbor. The next day saw meetings of the loyal citizens in every corner of the little town, which at last melted into one convention at the courthouse. Those who had no southern sympathies had been stung into action by the unwarranted rashness of the rioters, which brought the passions of the time so close to themselves.

The one question was asked on all sides: How soon would the president call for troops to put down this insurrection, and even as they asked it, the men were organizing, recruiting, drilling and forming companies to go to the front. The Light Guards, the local organization, donned their uniforms and paraded the streets. Already drums were heard on all sides, and the shrill cry of the fifes. In that portion of the town where lived a number of wealthy Southerners, there was the quiet and desolation of the grave. Their doors were barred and their windows were shut. Even they could not have believed that it would come to this, but since it had come, it was too soon for them to readjust themselves to new conditions, too soon to go boldly over to the side of the South, or changing all their traditions, come out for the North and the Union, which in spite of all, they loved. So they kept silent, and the turmoil went on around them. The waves of excitement rolled to their very doors, receded and surged up again. Through their closed blinds, they heard the shouts of the men at the public meeting a few blocks away. They heard the tramping of feet as the forming companies moved up and down. The men knew that many of their employees were away, mingling with the crowds and that work was being neglected, but they kept to their rooms and to their meditations.

"Ah," said one, "it's a hard thing to make us choose between the old home and the old flag. We love both, which the better, God only knows."

The children came home from school and told how one of the teachers was preparing to go to war, and it brought the situation up to their very faces. Those were, indeed, terrible times when preceptors left their desks for the battlefield. But still their hearts cried within them, "What shall we do?"

In the afternoon of the day following the convention, Nannie Woods came over for a chat with Mary Waters. They were close friends, and as confidential as prospective sisters should be.

"Do you think they will fight?" asked Nannie.

"The South? Yes, they will fight, I am sure of it. They have already shown what is in them. Father and Tom think it will be easy to subdue them, but I feel, somehow, that it will be a long struggle."

"But we shall whip them," cried the other girl, her eyes flashing.

"I don't know, I don't know. I wish we didn't have to try."

"Why, Mary, are you afraid?"

"Oh, no, I'm not afraid, but there are those I love on both sides and in the coming contest, whichever wins, I shall have my share of sorrow."

"Whichever wins! Why you haven't a single friend in the South!"

"I have no friend in the South—now."

"Oh, you mean Rob Van Doren. Well, if he didn't think enough of me to be on my side, I'd send him about his business."

"A man who didn't have courage enough to hold to his own opinions wouldn't be the man I'd marry."

"A man who didn't have love enough to change his opinions to my side wouldn't be the man for me."

"Very well, Nannie, we can't agree."

"But we're not going to fall out, Mary," and Nannie threw her arms impulsively around her friend's neck. "But oh, I do long to see our boys march down there and show those rebels what we're made of. What do you think? Father says they claim that one of them can whip five Yankees, meaning us. Well, I'd like to see them try it."

"Spoken like a brave and loyal little woman," cried Tom, rushing in.

"Eavesdropping," said Nannie coquettishly, but Mary turned her sad eyes upon him.

"I am no less loyal than Nannie," she said, "and if the worst comes, I know where my allegiance lies, but—but—I wish it wasn't necessary, I wish it wasn't necessary to take sides."

"Never you mind, Mary, it's going to be all right. We'll whip them in a month or two."

"We!" cried Nannie. "Oh, Tom, you're never going?"

"Why, what should I be doing when men are at war?"

"But will there be war?"

"There is war. The South has fallen out of step and we shall have to whip them back into line. But it won't be long, two or three months at most, and then all will be quiet again. It may not even mean bloodshed. I think a display of armed force will be sufficient to quell them."

"God grant it may be so."

Tom turned and looked at his sister in an amused way. "Oh, you needn't be afraid, Mary, Bob Van Doren won't go. Copperheads only talk, they never fight, ha, ha."

"Tom Waters, that's mean of you," Nannie exclaimed, "and it's very little of you, for a day or two ago Bob was your friend." She held Mary closer as she spoke, but Tom Waters was imbued with the madness that was in the air.

"What," he burst out, "Bob Van Doren my friend! I have no friend except the friends of the Union, I tell you, and mark my words, when the others of us march away, you will find him skulking with the rest of his breed in the grass, where all snakes lie."

"Bob Van Doren is no coward," said Mary intensely, "and when the time comes, he will be found where his convictions lead, either boldly on the side of the Union or fighting for the cause which his honor chooses, you—" She broke down and burst into tears.

"Oh, dry up, Mary," Tom said, with rough tenderness, "I didn't mean to hurt your feelings. Rob's a good enough fellow, but oh, I wish he was on our side. Don't cry, Mary, he's a first-rate fellow, and I—I'll be friends with him."

"Tom, you go away," cried Nannie, "you're just like all men, a great big, blundering—don't cry, Mary, don't cry. Mind your own business, Tom Waters, nobody wants you officiating around here, you've put your foot in it, and if you get smart, Mary and I will both turn rebel. Take your arm away."

"A pretty rebel you'd make."

"I'd make a better rebel than you would a soldier."

"All right, I'll show you," and the young man went out and slammed the door behind him.

"Now you've hurt his feelings," said Mary, suddenly drying her tears.

"I don't care, it was all your fault, Mary Waters." Then they wept in each other's arms because they were both so miserable.

Just then, the Negro known as Nigger Ed came running down the street. "Laws, have mussy on us, dey's hangin' Mistah V'landi'ham!"

The hearts of the two girls stood still with horror for the moment, and they clutched each other wildly, but the taint of Eve conquered, and they hurried to the door to get the news.

"Nigger Ed, Nigger Ed!" they called, and the colored man came breathlessly back to them.

"What did you say as you passed the house? They're hanging Mr. Vallandigham?"

"Yes'm, dey's hangin' him up by de co'thouse, a whole crowd o' men's a-hangin' him. Yo' fathah's 'mongst 'em, missy," he said turning to Mary.

"My father helping to hang Vallandigham! Oh, what are we coming to? Isn't it a terrible thing? Why, it's murder!"

Nannie called across to a friend who was passing on the other side of the street, "Oh, Mr. Smith, can it be true that they are hanging Vallandigham?"

The friend laughed. "Only in effigy," he said.

"Get along with you, Ed," said Nannie indignantly; "running around here scaring a body to death; they're only hanging him in effigy."

"Effigy, effigy, dat's whut dey said, but hit don't mek no diffunce how a man's hung, des so he's hung."

"Go along, you dunce, it's a stuffed Vallandigham they're hanging."

"Stuffed!" cried Ed, "I t'ought effigy meant his clothes. Lawd bless yo' soul, missy, an' me brekin' my naik runnin' f'om a stuffed co'pse. I reckon I 'larmed half de town," and Ed went on his way.

"And it's for those people our brothers and fathers are going to war?"

"Oh, no, not at all," said Nannie. "It's for the Union and against states' rights, and—and—everything like that."

"Those people are at the bottom of it all, I know it. I knew when that book by Mrs. Stowe came out. They're at the bottom of all this trouble. I wish they'd never been brought into this country."

"Why, how foolish you are, Mary, what on earth would the South have done without them? You don't suppose white people could work down in that hot country?"

"White people will work down in that hot country, and they will fight down there, and oh, my God, they will die down there!"

"Mary, you cry now at the least thing. I believe you're getting a touch of hysteria. If you say so, I'll burn some feathers under your nose."

"It isn't hysterics, Nannie, unless the whole spirit of the times is hysterical, but it is hard to see families that have known and loved each other for so long suddenly torn asunder by these dissensions."

"But the women folks needn't be separated. They can go on loving each other just the same."

"No, the women must and will follow their natural masters. It only remains for them to choose which shall be their masters, the men at home, or those whom they love outside."

"Well, with most of us that will be an easy matter, for our lovers and the folks at home agree—forgive me, Mary, I mean no reflection upon you, and I am so sorry."

"We are not all so fortunate, but however it comes, our women's hearts will bear the burdens. The men will get the glory and we shall have the grief."

"Hooray!" Tom's voice floated in from the street, and he swung in at the gate, singing gaily, his cap in his hand.

"Oh, what is it, Tom?" cried Nannie, "what's the news?"

"The bulletin says it is more than likely that the president will call for volunteers tomorrow, and I'm going to be the first lieutenant in the company, if the Light Guards go as a body."

"Oh, my poor brother!"

"Poor nothing, boom, boom, ta, ra, ra, boom, forward march!" And Tom tramped around the room in an excess of youthful enthusiasm. He was still parading, much to Nannie's pride and delight, when his father entered and stood looking at him. His eyes were swollen and dark, and there were lines of pain about his mouth.

"Ah, Tom," he said presently, "there'll be something more than marching to do. I had expected to go along with you, but they tell me I'm too old, and so I must be denied the honor of going to the front; but if you go, my son, I want your eyes to be open to the fact that you are going down there for no child's play. It will be full grown men's work. There will be uniforms and shining equipments, but there will be shot and shell as well. You go down there to make yourself a target for rebel bullets, and a mark for Southern fevers. There will be the screaming of fifes, but there will also be the whistling of shot. The flag that we love will float above you, but over all will hover the dark wings of death."

"Oh, father, father," cried Mary.

"It is a terrible business, daughter."

Tom had stood silent in the middle of the floor while his father was speaking, and now he drew up his shoulders and answered, "Don't be afraid of me, father, I understand it all. If I go to the war, I shall expect to meet and endure all that the war will bring, hardships, maybe worse. I'm not going for fun, and I don't think you'll ever have reason to be ashamed of me."

Mary flung herself on her father's breast and clung to him as if fearful that he also might be taken from her. But Nannie, with burning face, ran across and placed her hand in Tom's.

"That's right, Tom, and I'm not afraid for you." The young man put his hand tenderly upon the girl's head, and smiled down into her face.

"You're a brave little woman, Nannie," he said. The deep menace of the approaching contest seemed to have subdued them all.

"I'm not afraid for my son's honor," said Bradford Waters proudly, "but we must all remember that war brings more tears than smiles, and makes more widows than wives."

"We know that," said Nannie, "but we women will play our part at home, and be brave, won't we, Mary?"

The girl could not answer, but she raised her head from her father's shoulder and gripped her brother's hand tightly.

It was strange talk and a strange scene for these self-contained people who thought so little of their emotions; but their very fervor gave a melodramatic touch to all they did that at another time must have appeared ridiculous.

Chapter 4

Sons and Fathers

THE SCENES THAT WERE taking place in Dorbury were not different from those that were being enacted over the whole country. While the North was thunderstruck at the turn matters had taken, there had yet been gathering there a political force which only needed this last act of effrontery to galvanize its intention into action. Everywhere, men were gathering themselves into companies, or like Dorbury, already had their Light Guards. Then like the sound of a deep bell in the midst of potential silence came the president's proclamation and the waiting hosts heard gladly. Lincoln's call for troops could hardly do more than was already done. Volunteering was but a word. In effect, thousands of men were ready, and the call meant only marching orders. The enthusiasm of the time was infectious. Old men were vying with youths in their haste and eagerness to offer their services to the country. As Bradford Waters had said, it was a time for sharp divisions, and men who had been lukewarm in behalf of the Northern cause before, now threw themselves heart and soul into it.

This state of affairs effected Southern sympathizers in the North in two ways. It reduced the less robust of spirit to silence and evasion. The bolder and more decided ones were still also, but between the silence of one and that of the other was a vast difference of motive. One was the conceding silence of fear; the other was a sullen repression that brooded and bided its time.

Among those who came out strongly on the side of the South, was old Colonel Stewart, one of the oldest citizens of the town. He had served with distinction throughout the Mexican war, and was the close friend of Vallandigham. He had come of good old Virginia blood, and could not and would not try to control his utterances. So when the crisis came, his family, fearing the heat and violence of the time, urged him to go South, where his words and feelings would be more in accordance with the views of his neighbors. But he angrily refused.

"No," said he, "I will not run from them a single step. I will stay here, and thrust the truth of what I believe down their throats."

"But it will do no good," said his old wife plaintively. "These people are as set in their beliefs as you are in yours, and you have no more chance of turning them than of stemming the Ohio River.

I am not here to stem the current. Let them go on with it and be swept to destruction by their own madness, but they shall not move me."

"All of your friends are keeping silent, colonel, although they feel as deeply as you do."

"All the more reason for him who feels and dares speak to speak."

"Then, too, you owe it to your family to leave this place. Your views make it hard for us, and they will make it worse as the trouble grows."

"I hope I have a family heroic enough to bear with me some of the burdens of the South."

His wife sighed hopelessly. It seemed a throwing of her words into empty air to talk to her husband. But Emily Stewart took up the cause. She had the subtlety of the newer generation, which in argument she substituted for her mother's simple directness.

"It seems to me, father," she said, "that you owe the most not to your family, but to yourself."

"What do you mean?" he said, turning upon her.

"That if you are going to bear the burdens of the South, you should bear them not half-heartedly, but in full."

"Well, am I not?"

"Let me explain. If trouble should come to the South, if disaster or defeat, it would be easy for you, for any man, to raise his voice in her behalf, while he, himself, rides out and beyond the stress of the storm. If you are on the side of the South, she has a right to demand your presence there; the strength of your personality thrown in with her strength."

The old man thought deeply, and then he said, "I believe you are right. Body as well as soul should be with the South now. Yes, we will go South. But I am sorry about Walter. He has been so bound up in his work. It will be a great disappointment for him to go away and leave it all. But then he may, in fact, I hope he will find consolation for whatever he loses in defending the birthplace of his father against the invasion of vandals."

The two women were silent. They were keener than the man. Women always are; and these knew or felt with a vividness that bordered on knowledge that Walter would not think as his father thought or go his father's way, and here the breach would come. But the colonel never once thought but that his son would enter heartily into all his plans and he prided himself upon the step he was about to take. His wife and daughter went out and left him anxiously awaiting Walter's coming.

They were apprehensive when they heard the young man's step in the hall, and afterwards heard him enter the library where the colonel always insisted that any matter of importance should be discussed.

Heroism, real or fancied, is its own reward, its own audience and its own applause. With continued thought upon the matter, Colonel Stewart's enthusiasm had reached the fever pitch from which he could admit but one view of it. He had bade the servant send his son to him as soon as he came in, and he was walking back and forth across the floor when he heard the young man's step. The old man paused and threw back his head with the spirited motion that was reminiscent of the days when he was a famous orator.

The boy, he was the colonel's only son, was not yet twenty-four—a handsome fellow, tall, well-made and as straight as an arrow. As they stood there facing each other, there was something very much alike in them. Age, experience, and contact with the world had hardened the lines about the old man's mouth, which as yet in the boy's, only indicated firmness.

"Sit down, Walter," said the colonel impressively, "I have something of importance to say to you; something that will probably change your whole life." His son had dropped into a chair opposite to the one which his father had taken. His face was white with the apprehension that would tug at his heart, but his eye was steady and his lips firm.

Alexander Stewart could never quite forget that for two sessions he had been a speaking member of the Ohio legislature, and whenever he had anything of importance to say, he returned involuntarily to his forensic manner.

"Walter, my son," he began, "we have come upon startling times. I have known all along that this crisis would come, but I had not expected to see it in my day. It was inevitable that the proud spirit of the South and the blind arrogance of the North should some day clash. The clash has now come, and with it, the time for all strong men to take a decided stand. We of the South"—the boy winced at the words—"hold to our allegiance, though we have changed our homes, and this is the time for us to show our loyalty. The South has been insulted, her oldest institutions derided, and her proudest names dragged in the dust by men who might have been their owners' overseers. But she does not bear malice. She is not going to wage a war of vengeance, but a holy war for truth, justice and right. I am going back home to help her." The old man's own eloquence had brought him to his feet in the middle of the floor, where he stood, with eyes blazing. "Back home," he repeated, "and you, my son—" he held out his hand.

"Father," Walter also arose; his face was deadly pale. He did not take the proffered hand. His father gazed at him, first in amazement, then as the truth began to reach his mind, a livid flush overspread his face. His hand dropped at his side, and his fingers clenched.

"You," he half groaned, half growled between his teeth.

"Father, listen to me."

"There is but one thing I can listen to from you."

"You can never hear that. The North is my home. I was born here. I was brought up to revere the flag. You taught me that."

"But there is a reverence greater than that for any flag. There is a time when a flag loses its right to respect."

"You never talked to me of any such reverence or told me of any such time, and now I choose to stand by the home I know."

"This is not your home. Your home is the home of your family, and the blood in your veins is drawn from the best in the South."

"My blood was made by the streams and in the meadows; on the hills and in the valleys of Ohio, here; where I have played from babyhood, and father, I can't —I can't. May we not think differently and be friends?"

"No, if you had the blood of a single Yankee ancestor in you, I would impute it to that and forgive the defection; I could understand your weakening at this time, but—"

"It is not weakening," Walter flashed back, "if anything, it is strengthening when a man stands up for his flag, for the only flag he has ever known, when it is attacked by traitors."

"Traitors!" the old man almost shouted the word as he made a step towards the boy.

"Traitors, yes, traitors," said the son, unflinchingly.

"You cur, you mongrel cur, neither Northern nor Southern!"

"Father—"

"Silence! I wish the North joy of your acquisition. The South is well shed of you. You would have been like to turn tail and skulked in her direst extremity. It is well to know what you are from the start."

"Let me say a word, father."

"Don't father me. I'll father no such weak-kneed renegade as you are. From today, you are no son of mine. I curse you—curse you!"

The door opened softly and Mrs. Stewart stood there, transfixed, gazing at the two men. She was very pale for she had heard the last words.

"Husband, Walter—" she said tremulously, "I have intruded, but I could not help it."

Neither man spoke.

"Alexander," she went on, "take back those words. I felt all along it would be so, but you and Walter can disagree with each other and yet be father and son. Walter, come and shake hands with your father." The boy took a reluctant step forward, without raising his head, but his father drew himself up and folded his arms.

"Alexander!"

"I have no son," he said simply.

Walter raised his eyes and answered, "And I no father," and seizing his mother in his arms, he covered her face with kisses, and rushed from the room. Presently they heard the front door close behind him.

"Call him back, husband, call him back, for God's sake. He is our son, the only one left—call him back!"

The colonel stood like a statue. Not a muscle of his face quivered, and his folded arms were like iron in their tenseness. "He has chosen his faith," he said. He relaxed then to receive his wife's fainting form in his arms. He laid her gently on a couch and calling his daughter and the servants, went to his own room.

It is an awful thing to have to answer to a mother for her boy. To see her eyes searching your soul with the question in them, "Where is my child?" But it is a more terrible thing to a father's conscience when he himself is questioner, accuser and culprit in one. Colonel Stewart walked his room alone and thought with agony over his position. He knew Walter's disposition. It was very like his own, and this was not a matter in which to say, "I have been hasty," and then allow it to pass over. How could he meet his wife's accusing eyes? How could he do without Walter? The old man sat down and buried his face in his hands. The fire and enthusiasm of indignation which had held him up during his interview with his son had left him, and he was only a sad, broken old man. If he could but stay in his room forever, away from everybody.

As soon as his wife recovered from her swoon she sent for him, he went tremblingly and reluctantly to her, fearful of what he should see in her eyes. The room, though, was sympathetically darkened when he went in. He groped his way to the bed. A hand reached out and took his and a voice said, "Let us hurry, let us go away from here, Alexander." There was no anger, no reproach in the tone, only a deep, lingering sadness that tore at his heartstrings.

"Margaret, Margaret!" he cried, and flinging his arms about her, held her close while sobs shook his frame.

His wife patted his gray hair. "Don't cry, beloved," she said, "this is war. But let us go away from here. Let us go away."

"Yes, Margaret," he sobbed, "we will go away."

Preparations for the departure of the Stewarts began immediately. Mrs. Stewart busied herself feverishly as one who works to drive out bitter thoughts. But the colonel kept to his room away from the scenes of activity. His trouble weighed heavily upon him. His enthusiasm for the war seemed suddenly to have turned its heat malignantly upon him to consume him. Except when circumstances demanded his presence, he kept away from the rest of the family, no longer through the mere dread of meeting them, for it was the spirit of his conscience to press the iron into his soul; but because he felt that this was a trouble to be borne alone. No one could share it, no one could understand it.

For several days no one outside of the house knew of the breach that had occurred in the Stewart family, nor of their intention to go South. Then they made the mistake of hiring the Negro, Ed, to help them finish their packing.

The servant is always curious; the Negro servant particularly so, and to the Negro the very atmosphere of this silent house, the constrained attitude of the family were pregnant with mystery. Then he did not see the son about. It took but a little time for his curiosity to lead to the discovery that the son was boarding in the town. This, with scraps of information got from the other servants, he put together, and his imagination did the rest. Ed had a picturesque knack for lying, and the tale that resulted from his speculations was a fabric worthy of its weaver.

According to the Negro's version, the colonel, though long past the age for service, was going down South to be a general, and wanted to take his son, Walter, along with him to be a captain. Walter had refused, and he and his father had come to fisticuffs in which the young man was worsted, for Ed added admiringly by way of embellishment, "Do ol' cunnel is a mighty good man yit." After this the young man had left his father's house because he thought he was too old to be whipped.

This was the tale with which Ed regaled the people for whom he worked about Dorbury; but be it said in vindication of their common sense that few, if any, believed it. That there was some color of fact in the matter they could not doubt when it was plainly shown that Walter Stewart was not living at his father's house.

There must have been a breach of some kind, they admitted, but Ed's picture must be reduced about one-half.

The story, however, threw young Stewart into an unenviable prominence. As modest as it is natural for a young man of twenty-three to be, it gave him no pleasure to have people turn around to look after him with an audible, "There he goes!"

At first, his feeling towards his father had been one, not so much of anger as of grief. But he had no confidant, and the grief that could not find an outlet hardened into a grief that sticks in the throat, that cannot be floated off by tears or blown away by curses that will not melt, that will not move, that becomes rebellion. It was all unjust. He thought of the ideas of independence that his father had inculcated in him; how he had held up to him the very strength of manhood which he now repudiated. How he had set before him the very example upon which he now modeled his conduct, and then abased it. He had built and broken his own idol, and the ruins lay not only about his feet, but about his son's. It was a hard thought in the boy's mind, and for a time he felt as if he wanted to hold his way in the world, asking of nothing, is it right or wrong? leaning to no beliefs, following no principles. This was the first mad rebellion of his flowering youth against the fading ideals, against the revelation of things as they are. But with the rebound, which marks the dividing line between youth and manhood, he came back to a saner view of the affair.

It came to him for the first time that now was a period of general madness in which no rule of sane action held good. And yet, he could not wholly forgive his father his unnecessary harshness. The understanding of his unmerited cruelty came to him, but his condemnation of it did not leave. Only once did he ask himself whether the cause for which he stood was worthy of all that he had sacrificed for it; home, mother, comfort and a father's love. Then there came back to him the words his father had uttered on a memorable occasion, "Walter, principle is too dear to be sacrificed at any price," and his lips closed in a line of determination. Resolutely he turned his face away from that path of soft delight. He was no longer his father's son; but he was enough of a Stewart to believe strongly.

He felt sorely hurt, though, when he found that Ed's story, while failing to find a resting place in the ears of the sensible, had percolated the minds of the lower classes of the town. He heard ominous threats hurled at the old copperhead, which he knew to be directed at his father. All that lay in his power to do, he did to stem the tide of popular anger, but he felt it rising steadily, and knew that at any moment it might take the form of open violence or insult to his family. This must be avoided, he determined, and night after night, after he had left home, he patrolled the sidewalk in front of his father's house, and the grief-stricken mother, reaching out her arms and moaning for her son in her sleep, did not know that he was there, watching the low flicker of the night lamp in her room.

It was nearly a week after the memorable evening interview between Walter and his father that the young man received by the hands of the gossiping Ed a note from his mother. It ran, "We expect to go tomorrow evening at seven. Will you not come and tell me good-bye?" Walter was brave, and he gulped hard. This was from his mother, and neither principle nor anything else separated him from her. He would go. He wrote, "I will come in by the side gate, and wait for you in the arbor."

The evening found him there a half hour before the time set, but a mother's fond eagerness had outrun the hours and Mrs. Stewart was already there awaiting him. She embraced her son with tears in her eyes, and they talked long together. From the window of his room, Colonel Stewart watched them. His eyes lingered over every outline of his son's figure. Once, he placed his hand on the sash as if to raise it. Then he checked himself and took a turn round the dismantled room. When he came back to the window, Walter was taking his leave. The old man saw his wife clinging about the boy's neck. He saw the young fellow brush his hand hastily across his eyes. Again, his hand went out involuntarily to the window, but he drew it back and ground it in the other while a groan struggled up from under the weight of his pride and tore itself from his pale lips. Gone, gone, Walter was gone, and with him, his chance of reconciliation. He saw his wife return, but he locked his door and sat down to battle with his pride and grief until it was time to go.

It was a worn-looking old man that came down to step into the carriage an hour later. But Colonel Stewart never looked more the soldier. Walter was at a safe point of vantage, watching to get a last glimpse of his family. He was heavy of heart in spite of his bravery. But suddenly, his sadness flamed into anger. A crowd had been gathering about his father's house, but he thought it only the usual throng attracted by curiosity. As his father stepped into the carriage, he heard a sudden huzza. The people had surrounded the vehicle. A band appeared, and there floated to his ears the strains of the Rogues' march. A red mist came before his eyes, but through it he could not help seeing that they were taking the horses from the shafts. He waited to see no more, but dashed down the street. He forgot his sorrow, he forgot the breach, he forgot everything but his fury. It was his father; his father.

They were drawing the carriage toward him now, and the band was crashing out the hateful music. He reached the crowd and dashed into it like a young bull, knocking the surprised rioters and musicians right and left. He was cursing; he was pale, and his lip was bleeding where he had bitten it. The music stopped. Those who held the shafts dropped them. They were too astonished by the sudden onslaught to move. Then a growl rose like the noise of wild beasts and the crowd began to surge upon the young man. Forward and back they swept him, struggling and fighting. Then the carriage door opened and Colonel Stewart stepped out, his face was the face of an angel in anger, or perhaps of a very noble devil.

"Stop," he thundered, and at his voice, the uproar ceased. "Take up the shafts, my fellow-citizens," he said sneeringly, "this act is what I might have expected of you, but go on. It is meet that I should be drawn by such cattle." Then turning to his son, he said, "Sir, I need no defense from you." There was a joyous cry at this, though it was the young man's salvation. Someone hurled a stone, which grazed the old man's head. Walter was at the coward's side in an instant, and had felled him to the ground. For an instant, something that was not contempt gleamed in the old man's eye, but Walter turned, and lifting his hat to his father, backed from the crowd. They took up the shafts again. The musicians gathered their courage, and with a shout they bore the colonel away to the station.

Walter stood looking after the carriage. He had caught a glimpse of his mother's face from the window for a moment, and to the day of his death he never forgot the look she gave him. It was to be a help to him in the time of his trouble, and strength when the fight was hottest. His anger at his father had melted away in the flash of action. But he could not help wonder if the colonel's insult to him had been sincere, or only for the purpose of accomplishing what it did, the diversion of the crowd. He knew that he had been saved rough handling, and that his father had saved him, and he went home with a calmer spirit than he had known for many days.

Despite the intolerance which kept Stephen Van Doren always at loggerheads with Bradford Waters, he was in reality a fairly reasonable man. He was as deep and ardent a partisan of the South as Colonel Stewart, and if he was not less anxious that his son should espouse her cause, at least he had more patience, and more faith to wait for, his boy to turn to the right path.

From the time that Robert Van Doren was driven from his sweetheart's gate, there had been a silence between father and son as to the latter's intentions. But as the feverish preparations went on, Stephen Van Doren grew more and more uneasy and excited. It was hard not to speak to his son and find out from him where he stood in regard to the questions which were agitating his fellows. But a stalwart pride held the old man back. There were times when he told himself that the boy only waited for a word from him. But that word he determined never to say. The South did not need the arm of anyone who had to be urged to fight for her.

The struggle and anxiety which possessed his father's mind was not lost on the young man, and he sympathized with the trouble, while he respected the fine courtly breeding which compelled silence under it. As for himself, he must have more time to think. This was no light question which he was now called upon to decide. The times were asking of every American in his position, "Are you an American or a Southerner first?" The answer did not hang ready upon his lips. Where foes from without assailed, it was the country, the whole country. Could there arise any internal conditions that would make it different?

Finally, he could not stand the pained question in his father's eyes any longer. A word would let him know that, at least, his son was thinking of the matter which agitated him.

"Father," he said, "you are worrying about me."

The old man looked up proudly, "You are mistaken," was the reply, "I have no need to worry about my son. He is a man."

Robert gave his father a grateful glance, and went on, "You are right, you need not worry. I am looking for the right. When I find it, you may depend upon me to go that way."

"I am sure of it, Bob!" exclaimed the old man, grasping his son's hand, "I am sure you will. You are a man and must judge for yourself. I have confidence in you, Bob."

"Thank you, father."

They pressed each other's hands warmly, the cloud cleared from Van Doren's brow and the subject was dropped between the two.

Between Tom Waters and his father from the very first, there had been only harmony. There vas a brief period of silence between them when Bradford Waters first fully realized that his age put him hopelessly beyond the chance of being beside his son in the ranks. At the first intimation that he was too old, he had scouted the idea, and said that it often took a gray head to manage a strong arm rightly. But when he saw the full quota of militia made up and his application denied, it filled him with poignant grief.

"I had so hoped to be by your side, Tom, in this fight," he said.

"It's best, father, as it is, though, for there's Mary to be taken care of."

"Yes, the fever in our blood makes us forget the nearest and dearest nowadays, but I'm glad that you will be there to represent me anyway."

From that time all the enthusiasm which Waters had felt in the Northern cause was centered upon his son. He watched him on the parade ground with undisguised pride, and when Tom came home in the glory of his new uniform, with the straps upon his square shoulders, Bradford Waters' voice was husky, and there was a moisture in his eyes as he said, "I'm glad now that it's you who are going, Tom, for I understand what a poor figure I must have made among you young fellows."

The son was too joyous to be much affected by the sadness in his father's tone, and he only laughed as he replied, "I tell you, father, those steel muscles of yours would have put many a young fellow to the blush when it came to endurance."

"Well, it isn't my chance. You're the soldier."

The young fellow would have felt a pardonable pride could he have known that his father was saying over and over again, "Lieutenant Thomas Waters, Lieutenant Thomas Waters, why not captain or colonel?" And his pride would have been tempered could he have known also that back of this exclamation was the question, "Will he come back to me?"

For so long a time had Bradford Waters been both father and mother to his son that he had come to have some of the qualities of both parents. And if it were true, as Mary said, that in this war the women's hearts would suffer most, then must he suffer doubly. With the woman's heart of the mother and the man's heart of the father, the ache had already begun for the struggle was on between the tenderness of the one and the pride of the other; between the mother's love and the father's ambition. At the barracks, or on the parade ground, in the blare of the trumpets where Lieutenant Waters strode back and forth, ambition conquered. But in the long still nights when his boy Tom was in his thoughts and dreams, only love and tenderness held him.

Chapter 5

"The Pomp and Circumstance"

THE SHIFTING SCENES IN the panorama of the opening war brought about the day of departure. The company to which Tom Waters belonged was to leave on an afternoon train for Columbus, and Dorbury was alert to see them off; friend and foe swayed by the same excitement. The town took on the appearance and spirit of a gala day. The streets were full of sight-seers, pedestrians, riders and drivers, for the event had brought in the farmers from the surrounding townships. Here and there, the blue of a uniform showed among the crowd and some soldier made his way proudly, the center of an admiring crowd. A troop of little boys fired by the enthusiasm of their elders marched to and fro to the doubtful tune of a shrill fife and an asthmatic drum. People who lived a long distance away, and who consequently, had been compelled to start long before sunrise, now lolled lazily around, munching gingerbread, or sat more decorously in the public square, eating their delayed breakfasts.

About the barracks, which were the quarters of the militia, was gathered a heterogeneous crowd. Within, there was the sound of steady tramping, as the sentinels moved back and forth over their beats. Their brothers without, were doing a more practical duty, for it took all the bravery of their bristling bayonets to keep back the curious. There was a stir among them like the rippling of the sea by the wind when a young man in the uniform of a private of the Light Guards hastened up and elbowed his way towards the door. There was a buzz, a single shout, and then a burst of cheers, as the young man, flushed and hot, leaped up the steps and entered the door. Some who had been his enemies were in the crowd; some who had laid violent hands on him only a few days before, but they were all his friends now. It was Walter Stewart. He had followed the leadings of his own mind and stayed with his company; but somehow the applause of these people who were all his father's enemies, was very bitter to him.

After Stewart, came a figure that elicited a shout from the throng, and a burst of laughter. It was the town crier, Negro Ed, who was to go as servant to the militia captain, Horace Miller.

"Hi, Ed," called one, "ain't you afraid they'll get you and make you a slave?" and "Don't forget to stop at Dorbury when you get to running!"

Ed was usually good-natured, and met such sallies with a grin, but a new cap and a soldier's belt had had their effect on him, and he marched among his deriders, very stern, dignified and erect, as if the arduous duties of the camp were already telling upon him. The only reply he vouchsafed was "Nemmine, you people, nemmine. You got to git somebody else to ring yo' ol' bell now." The crowd laughed. There came a time when they wept at thought of that black buffoon; the town nigger, the town drunkard, when in the hospital and by deathbeds his touch was as the touch of a mother; when over a blood-swept field, he bore a woman's dearest and nursed him back to a broken life. But no more of that. The telling of it must be left to a time when he who says aught of a Negro's virtues will not be cried down as an advocate drunk with prejudice.

To the listeners outside the barracks came the noise of grounding arms, and the talk of men relieved from duty. They were to go to their homes until time to form in the afternoon. The authorities were considerate. If men must go to war, good-byes must be said, women must weep and children cling to their fathers. The last sad meal must be taken. The net of speculation must be thrown out to catch whatever motes of doubt the wind of war may blow, and the questions must fly, "Will he come back? Shall I see him again?"

Yes, women must weep. In spite of all the glory of war they will cling to the neck of the departing husband, brother or son. Poor foolish creatures; they have no eye then for the brave array, the prancing charger and the gleaming arms. They have no ear for the inspiring fife and drum.

The men were soberer than they had yet been when they filed out of the barracks. At last, the reality of things was coming home to them. It was all very well, this drilling on the common in the eyes of the town, but now for the result of their drills.

Midway among them came Tom and Walter side by side, lieutenant and private; they had not yet come to feel the difference in their positions.

"Well, we'll be on the way in a few hours," said Walter as they passed out beyond the borders of the crowd, "and I'm glad of it."

"I'm glad, too, now that we're in it, Walt, and I'm glad to be in it myself. But it means a whole lot, doesn't it?"

"Of course, you're leaving your family," replied Walter tentatively.

"More than that."

Both young men smiled, Walter a little bit sheepishly. He had been Tom's rival for Nannie Wood's affections, and had taken defeat at his hands.

"Oh," pursued Tom, "if the fight is going to be as short as many people think, a mere brush, in fact, we shan't be gone long—but—"

"The people who think this is going to be a mere brush don't know the temper of the South."

"I believe you. There'll be a good many of us who won't come back."

"Oh, well, it's one time or another," and Walter smiled again as they came to the corner, and Tom turned up the street towards Nannie's house. "So long."

"So long, until this afternoon," and then the young lieutenant found himself staring straight into the eyes of Robert Van Doren. For a moment the feeling of antagonism which had shown in his conversation with Mary, surged over him, but in the next, he remembered his promise. He held out his hand.

"Hello, Bob," he said, "I guess it's hello and good-bye together."

Bob grasped his hand warmly. "Well, I reckon nobody'll be gladder to say how-dye-do to you again than I, Tom. Good luck."

"Thanks, Bob."

"Give my regards to Mary."

"I will." Tom started on. Suddenly he turned and found Van Doren watching him with a strange expression on his face. He went back and impulsively seized the other's hand. "Say, Bob, what's what?"

The blood went out of Van Doren's face. "God knows," he said in a pained voice, "that's just what I've been asking myself, and I don't know yet, Tom."

The young man paused ashamed of this show of feeling, then he said, "Well, anyway, Bob, good luck," and they went their ways.

In his heart, Tom believed that Robert Van Doren would eventually go to the Confederacy, and he resented what to him seemed flagrant disloyalty. Ohio was Van Doren's adopted home, and a tender mother she had been to him. Out of her bounty she had given him well. Now to go over to her enemies! The fight in Tom's mind as to his manner of meeting Van Doren had been brief but sharp. The result was less the outcome of generosity than the result of a subtle selfishness. It was, as all putting one's self in another's place is, the sacrifice which we make to the gods of our own desires, the concession we make to our weakness. He forgave Robert, not because Mary loved and was about to lose him, but because he, himself, loved Nannie, and for a time, at least, was about to lose her. The grasp which he gave Bob's hand meant pity for himself as well as for his sister.

There was a flash of pride on Nannie's face, though tears stood in her eyes as she saw her lover approaching. She had been expecting him and was at the gate. The soft April sunshine was playing on her gold-brown hair, and in her simple pink dimity gown she looked akin to the morning glories that blossomed about her. She opened the gate and took the young man's hand, and together they passed around the side of the house, to a rustic bench among the verbenas and sweet williams.

There was a simplicity and frankness about Nannie's love that was almost primitive. It was so natural, so spontaneous, so unashamed. It looked you as squarely in the face as did her coquetry. But there was no sign of coquetry now. Gone were all her whims and quips, her airs and graces. There had come into her life the transmuting element that suddenly makes a maid a woman.

For a time the two sat in silence on her flower-surrounded bench. Tom, afraid to trust his voice, and Nannie finding a certain satisfaction in merely pressing the hand she held.

Finally, he broke silence. "Well, the time is about here, Nannie."

"Yes," she replied, drawing his hand closer and caressing it, "you—you're glad, of course?"

"Glad? Well, that's a hard question. I'm glad, of course, but—but"—he struggled to grasp the elusive idea that was floating ill in his brain—"but there is more than one kind of being glad. I am glad, to be sure, as a citizen, and I'm sorry as a man—"

"You're sorry because—"

"You know why, little girl, I'm sorry to leave you. I'm sorry to take any chance of never being able to call you wife. It may be cowardly, but at such a time, the thought is forced irresistibly upon a man."

"It isn't cowardly, Tom, it isn't. It's manly, I know it is, because you're think-ing about me. Oh, but I shall miss you when you are gone. But I'll pray for you, and I'll try to be as brave up here as you are down there. You are wrong, Tom, you are very brave, braver than the men who do not think to sorrow for the women, but go rushing into this war with a blind enthusiasm that will not let them feel. You're brave, you're brave, and I'm going to be, but I can't help it!" He caught her in his arms, and strained the weeping face to his breast.

"Darling, darling, my brave little girl, don't cry." A man is so helpless, so word-less in these times. He can do nothing but stammer and exclaim lavish caresses.

After the first gust of weeping was over, she raised her tearstained face, and said with a rainy smile, "I want you to understand, Tom, I'm not crying all for grief. It's just as much pride as it is sorrow. Oh, I've been spoiling your uniform." There was somewhat of a return of her old coquetry of manner, and her lover was un-speakably cheered. He had felt in that brief moment of passion as he had never felt before; how near the ocean of tears lay to the outer air and how strong was their surge against the barriers of manhood. But, her change of manner gave him the courage to say the tender good-bye—the farewell too sacred to be spied upon. Ah, how his heart ached within him. How his throat swelled, and she smiled and smiled, though her eyes grew moist again. And he went on inspired by the heroism of a woman's smile, the smile she gives even when she sends her dear ones forth to face death.

He bade good-bye to Nannie's family, and went home to a sad meal and a repe-tition of his leave-takings.

The sister hardly succeeded as well as the sweetheart in hiding her emotions. Her heart was already heavy, and she wept, not only at the fear of death, but with the pain of love. At the very last, when he was going to take his place in the ranks, she broke down, and clung sobbing to her brother. Tom gulped, and the father, wringing his son's hands, took away her arms and comforted her as best he could. His eyes were bright and hard with the stress of the fight he was having with his feelings, but his voice was firm. Bradford Waters showed the mettle of his pasture. A New Englander, born and reared in that section of the country which has pro-duced the most and the least emotional people, men the most conservative and the most radical; the wisest philosophers and the wildest fanatics, he did not disgrace his breeding.

It was easier for Tom, when he was once more in the ranks. Then he felt again the infectious spirit of enthusiasm which swayed his comrades. His heart beat with the drums. He heard the people cheering as they went down the street. Hand-kerchiefs were waving from windows and balconies, and there was a following that half walked, half trotted to keep up with the swinging stride of the soldiers. The train that was to bear them away stood puffing in the station. They crowded on. Here and there, a man dropped into his seat and buried his head in his hands, but most of the heads were out of the windows nodding good-byes. There was an air of forced gaiety over it all. Young fellows with flushed cheeks laughed hard laughs, and bit their lips the moment after. It was as if no one wanted to think and yet thought would come. Children were held up to be kissed, their mothers eyes weeping openly as is a mother's right. Fathers would start a reassuring sentence, and suddenly break off to laugh brokenly, short skeleton laughs that were sadder than tears. Then the bell gave and warning and with a last rousing shout, they were off for the state capital and the chances of war.

Tom caught the last glimpse of the family and Nannie as they stood together on the platform. They were waving to him and he waved back. Nannie and Mary stood with clasped hands watching the long line of cars. On the former's face there was sorrow and pride; sorrow for her lover, pride for her soldier; but with the latter was only grief, for she could not be thoroughly loyal to her brother without feeling disloyalty to her lover. Bradford Waters walked with the crowd, but the two girls stood still, until they heard the train whistle and slacken speed as it crossed the railroad bridge, then they turned and walked back to the town. A few moments before the place had been all movement and life; now it was left to silence and tears.

Chapter 6

A Lone Fight

THERE WAS ONE MAN whom the moving glory of the departing troops filled with no elation. From a distant point, Bob Van Doren saw the blue lines swinging down the streets of Dorbury, and heard the shriek of the fifes. But there was in him no inclination to join in the shouting or to follow the admiring crowd. He was possessed neither by the joyous nor the sorrowing interest of the citizen, nor yet by the cowardly shame of the stay-at-home. While he could not go as far as his father and stay within the closed and shuttered house, yet he felt that he was not a part of the flag-flying, drum-beating throng. Many of the young fellows there were his friends who had eaten and drunk with him. They had laughed and sported together both as men and boys. But now, suddenly, it seemed that something had arisen to make them entirely different, and to put him as far apart from them and their sympathies as if they had been born at opposite poles. What was this impalpable something? he asked himself. Was it in him, in them or outside and beyond them both? Or to get at the bottom of things, did it really exist? Their training and his had been very much the same. They had gone to the same schools, read the same books and adored the same heroes. What, then, was the subtle element that had entered into life to divide them?

These were the questions he was asking himself as he heard the farewell shouts of the departing troops and the clanging of the train bell. Then he turned and with his mind full of harassing inquiries took his way home.

"Well, they're off to help rob the South of its niggers, are they?" said his father.

"They are gone," replied Robert laconically. He was not in the mood to talk.

"Humph, Southern buzzards will be the fatter for them."

"Don't, father, that's horrible. There are a good many of the fellows we both knew and liked among them."

Stephen Van Doren flashed a quick suspicious glance at his son as he remarked, "So much the worse for them."

"I wish it might have been settled some other way," pursued Robert drearily, "I'd rather have let the South secede than institute this orgy of unnatural bloodshed, brother against brother, friend against friend."

Again his father flashed that white questioning look at him. Then he rose abruptly and left the room. Robert hardly noticed the movement, so absorbed was he in his own thoughts, but sat staring blankly before him. He was momentarily aroused from his reverie by the reentrance of his father, who laid an old miniature upon the table before him, and went out again without a word. Robert picked up the picture. It was the portrait of a beautiful young woman painted in the style of forty years before—his mother—and her name was written on a piece of yellow paper stuck in the frame, "Virginia Nelson, Fairfax Courthouse, Virginia." He gazed at the picture and read and re-read the inscription, "Fairfax Courthouse." What a quaint old-fashioned, southern sound it had. It seemed redolent of magnolias and jessamine and soft as the speech of its own citizens. But was that home, or this, the place where his youth and early manhood had been passed? Which was home, the place of memories or the place of action? What makes home; dreams or labor; the hopes of boyhood or the hard reality of later life?

To young Van Doren, the memory of his mother, who had lived only two years after coming North, had been as a guiding star and he knew that it was to recall this that his father had brought him the picture. It was apparent that he must have been strongly moved, for that little worn and faded miniature seldom left the old man's desk. His father felt deeply; so did he. His mother's eyes were pleading with him. Sentiment, said his mind; truth, said his heart.

Finally, he laid the picture face downward on the table. He told himself it must not enter into his thoughts at all. But his mind would not let it go. Eel-like, his consciousness wrapped itself about it and would not let it go. He felt guilty when the thought assailed him that perhaps the face of another woman which was graven on his heart, argued more strongly than the pictured one. "Mary, Mary," his heart said, "is my love for you blinding me to right and justice? While other men decide and do, I stand still here waiting and asking what to do." He thought of Walter Stewart and the apparent ease with which he had made a hard decision, and his anger flashed up against his own impotence; but still his inclination wavered weakly back and forth. The Union, the Confederacy; the place of his boyhood and the home of his manhood.

At last, he asked himself the question which he had so long shunned, What he believed? and he was compelled to answer that his convictions leaned to the side of those who were in arms against the general government. Then there was but one thing to do. He stood up, very pale and sad of countenance, trembling on the verge of a decision. But suddenly as out of nowhere, a voice seemed to sound into his very being, "Has love no right?" "Good God," he cried aloud, "shall I go on this way, forever wavering? Shall I go on being a coward, I who hate cowardice?" His heart was burning with pain, misery and anger and shame at himself, and yet he could not, he dared not say where he stood. The fact that he tried to fight out of recognition, and herein lay his greatest cowardice, was that he did not feel the Southern cause deeply enough to risk losing the woman he loved by its espousal; nor could he leap open-eyed into the Northern movement, for which he had no sympathy. Had he felt either as deeply as did Bradford Waters or his own father, he would not have hesitated where to take his place.

The struggle in his mind had not just begun. From the very moment that the atmosphere had become electric with the currents of opposing beliefs, he had felt himself drawn into the circuit. But, by nature, always inexpressive, he had said nothing, and left those who thought of him to the conviction that he was unmoved by passing events. But the lone nights and the gray dawns knew better. Many a time had he gone to bed after a period of earnest, self-searching, satisfied at last, and saying, "It is true, I shall take my stand," only to wake and find that everything was changed in the light of day. Many a time had morning found him in his chair where he had sat all night, trying to wrench order out of the chaos of his mind. And now, now, it was no better.

There was a step in the hall, and his father looked in on him for a moment and passed on. Robert knew that he was going through an ordeal no less terrible than his own, and he wished that it might be ended, even if it brought strife and separation between them as it had done between Walter Stewart and his father. The thought had hardly left his brain when it was occupied by another. Was he to be watched like a child who was likely to get into mischief? This was too much, too much. He had borne with his father as long as he could. Now he would show him that he was his own master, to go his own way. Anyway, it was his concern alone. With whichever side he went, he must be shot for himself. If he stayed at home, it was he who must bear the sneers and jokes, who must live down the contumely. Whose right was it, then, to institute an annoying surveillance over him? Not even his father's. It had come to a pretty pass when a man might not think without interruption. Bah, he could not call his soul his own. It was only the sign of his nervous condition that he should fall into this state of petulant anger.

Then unaccountably, his whole mental attitude changed, and the appearance of his father's questioning face in the door, struck him only with a ludicrous aspect. He thought of himself as some coquettish but wavering maiden who bade her lover wait outside until she could answer the momentous question, yes or no, and he burst out laughing.

But his mirth was short and unnatural.

"I am either a fool or a brute," he said, "I know that father and Mary are both watching me, but they have a right to watch and they have the right to demand from me the answer in their hearts."

He paused as if a new thought had struck him. Then he rose and took his hat. "I'll do it," he exclaimed passionately, "I'll go to her and let her help me. Why haven't I thought of it before?" He passed out and called to his father as he went, "I'm going out for a while, father."

"All right," was the answer, but the words that followed solemnly were, "The boy is driven out into the street, even as the men possessed of devils spirit were driven to the rocks and the tombs. It is the evil spirit of Northern narrowness working in him."

It was with a heart somewhat lightened by the hope of relief that Robert Van Doren hastened along the street towards the Waters' home. So much had passed in the days since he had last stood at the gate that the little difference between him and the father of the woman he loved appeared as a very small thing. When two great sections of a nation are arrayed against each other, there is no time for the harboring of petty angers. Two thoughts held him. He would see Mary again. She would help him, and his honor should come to its own. These thoughts left no room in his mind for malice.

No misgiving touched him even when he stood at the door and his knock brought Mary to the door. She looked at him with a frightened face, and turned involuntarily to glance at her father who sat within.

"Is anything the matter?" she said in a low, hurried voice.

"Nothing, only I want your advice and help," said Van Doren, stepping across the threshold.

At the voice and step, Bradford Waters rose and faced the visitor, and his face began working with growing anger. "What do you mean by invading my house, again, Robert Van Doren?"

"I came to see Mary."

Waters took his daughter by the hand as if he would put himself between the girl and her lover. "Mary can have no dealings with you or your kind. We do not want you here. I have told you that before. Your way and ours lie apart."

"They have not always lain apart and need not now." Van Doren's surprise was stronger than his resentment as he looked into the old man's passionate face. Could a few days work such a change in a man?

"They must and shall lie apart," Waters took him up hotly. "What you have been to this family, you cannot be again."

"What have I done to forfeit your respect?"

"It isn't what you've done, but what you are."

"How do you know what I am?"

"That's it. At least, your father has the courage to come out and say what he is. You haven't. At least, he is a man—"

"Father, father," cried Mary, "don't say any more!"

"I'm sorry to see a daughter of mine," said Waters, turning upon her, "pleading for one of those whom her brother has gone South to kill." The girl put her hands up quickly as if she would check the words upon her father's lips. Van Doren had turned very white. He stood as one stunned. All his hopes of help had been suddenly checked, and instead of sympathy, he had received hard words. But a smile curved his lips.

"Have I not said enough, Robert Van Doren?"

"Yes," was the reply, still with a quiet smile, "you have said enough," and he turned towards the door.

Mary sprang away from her father. "Robert, Robert, don't go," she cried, "he doesn't mean it. This great trouble has made him mad." Bradford Waters started to speak but stopped as the young man put off the girl's detaining hand. "I must go, Mary," he said, "your father is right. We have come to the parting of the ways. I have not had the courage to say where I stood, but I have it now. I came for help to decide a momentous question. I have got it. Good-bye, Mary, good-bye—Mr. Waters, the Confederacy may thank you for another recruit."

He opened the door and passed out, the old man's voice ringing after him, "Better an open rebel than a copperhead." A hard look came into the girl's eyes.

"You needn't worry," said her father, "it's good riddance." She made no reply.

In spite of all that passed, Robert Van Doren went home in a lighter frame of mind.

"I'm going to leave tomorrow," he said to his father.

"You have made your choice?"

"The South needs me," returned the young man evasively. His father came to him and kissed him on both cheeks. Then he took the miniature from the table and placed it on his breast.

"I knew that your mother would not plead with you in vain," he said, and Robert smiled bitterly.

Chapter 7

Divided Houses

THERE IS A TRAGIC QUIETNESS about a town whose best and bravest have gone to a doubtful battlefield. The whole place seems hushed and on tiptoe as if listening for some sound from the field. The cry of a cricket shivers the silence into splinters of sound, and each one pierces the ear with a sharpness which is almost pain. It was under such a pall of stillness that Dorbury lay immediately after the departure of the troops. It was not altogether the torpor that succeeds an upheaval. Part of it was the breathless silence of expectancy, as when from a height someone hurls a boulder into space and waits to hear it fall. Of course, it would be some time before they could expect to hear from the new soldiers, and yet, Dorbury listened, expectant hand to ear.

The spring sunshine, not yet strong nor violent enough to destroy its own sweetness, fell with a golden caress on the quiet streets. To some, who went to and fro, bowed with anxiety, it seemed strange that in such a time, nature should go on performing her processes as she had always done. Their hearts seemed to stand still, but time went on, the flowers bloomed, the grasses sprung and the restless river sang to the silent town.

The tension of suspense had told greatly upon Bradford Waters' character. From being a gentle father, he had grown to be short, almost harsh to Mary. His love and fear for his soldier son had made him blind to the pain his daughter suffered.

He was so far gone in the earnestness of his views that he could see nothing but a perverse disloyalty in his daughter's feeling towards Robert Van Doren. His friendship for the young fellow had changed with the changing of the times, and he could not understand that a woman's love may be stronger than her politics; her heart truer to its affections than her head to its principles.

It can hardly be said of Mary that she felt more than she thought, but her emotions were stronger than her convictions. It was the worse for her state of mind that for two widely different reasons, the taking of her brother and the estrangement from her lover, she was placed in a resentful position against the cause that she naturally would have espoused.

Still, at first, she kept a certain appearance of loyalty, and when some of the girls with impetuous enthusiasm, started a sewing circle for the soldiers, she joined with them, and began to ply her needle in the interest of the Union troops. But among these friends of undivided interests, it was not always pleasant for Mary. All about her, she heard sentiments that did not comport with the feelings of one who had loved ones on both sides of the great question. Over the lint and flannels that passed through the sewers' hands, were made several hot and thoughtless speeches that seared the very soul of one poor girl. They were not intentional. Most of them, had they known that one among them suffered from their unthinking remarks, would have held their tongues. Others, not more than one or two, be it said, knew that every sneer they cast at the army of the South, every hard wish they expressed, tore like an arrow through the tender heart of the pale sad girl in the corner who bent so silently over her work.

"I do wish," said little Martha Blake one day, "that the whole Southern army was drowned in the depths of the sea. They are so troublesome."

"What would their sisters do?" asked Mary quietly.

"Oh, really, they seem such monsters to me that I never thought of their having sisters."

Mary smiled. "And yet they have," she said, "some of them, perhaps, making just as foolish a wish about our brothers as you have made about them."

"I know it's foolish," Martha pursued, "but it has never seemed to me that those people down there who have done so much to tempt the Northern government are quite the same as we are."

Unconsciously, Mary took the defensive and stepped over into the point of view of the man whom in her heart she was defending.

"But why," she exclaimed, "do you say the Northern government? The very mention of the word denies the principle for which we claim we are fighting—that there is no North, no South, but one country inseparable into sections."

"I had never thought of that," said Martha.

"I don't think any of us have thought of it," put in Anice Crowder, "except those who have very dear friends among the traitors."

Mary turned deadly pale for she knew that Bob Van Doren's decision had just become generally known. She turned a pair of flashing eyes on Anice as she replied,

"No man is a traitor who fights for what he believes to be right."

"Any man is a traitor who lives under one flag and leaves it to fight under another."

"A man is accountable only to his conscience and his God."

"Yes, when he has proved traitor to every other tie, only then."

The words cut Mary like a knife. She rose, work in hand, and stood quivering with passion as she looked down on her insulter.

"Then the woman who cares for such a man, who dares stand up for him is a traitor too?" she cried as she flung her work to the floor.

"Yes," said Anice acidly.

Mary started towards the door, but a chorus of girls' voices checked her.

"Don't go, Mary," they cried, "we know, we don't blame you." But the girl's heart was overburdened, and bursting into tears, she fled from the room. She heard the hubbub of voices as she went hastily out of the house, and even in that moment of grief she was glad that some of the girls there would be quick to defend her. She knew who must have been foremost in this defense when she heard a light step behind her and felt Nannie Woods' arm about her waist.

"Don't cry, Mary," said Nannie soothingly. "No one minds Anice Crowder or anything she says. Anyway, I gave her a good piece of my mind before I left there, and so did some of the rest of the girls. I just told her right to her face that she'd have more feeling for people if she had a lover on either side."

Mary was forced to smile a little at her friend's impetuosity. But from her heart she thanked the girl, and drew her arm tighter about her waist.

"I suppose Anice thinks that I can send my love where I will, and that I am to blame if it does not go in the right, or what she thinks, the right direction."

"She's a cat," was the emphatic rejoinder, "and I for one, will never go to their old sewing-circle. We'll sew together, just you and I, Mary, and while I'm making things for Tom, there's no reason why you shouldn't make a keepsake for Bob to take with him."

Mary gasped.

"Oh, that's all right, I know if I lived down South and it was Tom, I'd—"

"Hush, Nannie," said Mary hurriedly, "you mustn't say those things."

"I will say them and I don't care."

They reached the Waters' gate and the girls parted. There, for Nannie, the incident closed, but it was destined to cause Mary Waters even more suffering.

Women's sewing circles are not usually noted for their reticence, and the institution at Dorbury was no exception. Within an hour after it happened, the whole affair was out to the town, and the story in a highly embellished form reached Bradford Waters' ears.

He went home in a white passion. Mary had got supper and was sitting idly by the window when her father burst into the room. She looked up and saw on the instant that he had heard.

"What is this I hear of you at the sewing circle?"

"I suppose you have heard the truth or part of it."

"So it has come to the pass where my daughter must defend a former copperhead and now an avowed rebel!"

"The man whom I defended, if defense it could be called, was to me neither copperhead nor rebel. He was my lover. I have nothing to do with his politics. The war has nothing to do with my love."

She was calmer than usual, and her very quietness exasperated her father the more.

"I'll have no more of it," he cried passionately, "I'll have no more of it. Love or no love, a house divided against itself cannot stand. My house must be with me. And if my daughter feels called upon to go over to the enemy's side, she must go over to the enemy's house. My house shall not shelter her."

"Father—"

"Enough, I have said my say. You must abide by it. I'll have no more such stories as I have heard today poured into my ears. Either give up that renegade or take your love for him to another roof."

He flung himself petulantly into a chair and fell to his supper. Mary did not answer him, only a look of hard defiance came into her gentle eyes. It might have struck Bradford Waters had he seen it, but he did not look at her again.

A little kindness might have done much to soften the rigor of Mary's feelings, and so changed the course of events; for she was easily swayed through her affections. She would not have given up Van Doren, his hold upon her was too strong. But she would have repressed herself even to the hiding of her feelings, had she not been driven into the open revolt to which her father's harsh treatment goaded her. Now the determination to be true to her lover at all hazards came upon her so strongly that her attitude really became one of aggression.

It was now that the remembrance of Nannie's thoughtless words came to her, and she asked herself, "Why not?" Why should she not make and give Van Doren a keepsake to take into the ranks with him? She had suffered sorrow for his sake; in effect, she had been forcibly, almost involuntarily, cast on his side. She had to withstand contempt and reviling. Would this one show of affection be so much more?

That evening, Mary was very busy sewing, and so part of the next day, until the time when her father came home. Then she hastened to leave her stitching to go about her supper, for in the absorption of her new idea, she had neglected it.

Bradford Waters looked at the work which had stood between him and his meals with an ill-concealed exasperation. Why couldn't women sew at the proper time and leave off properly? Maybe, though, it was something for her brother Tom. If that were so, he did not care. He would go without his meals any time, that Tom might have a single comfort. Bless the brave boy. His face softened, and he looked with filling eyes as his mind dwelt on tender memories of the soldier son. Suddenly the bit of embroidery there on the shelf seemed to take on a new interest for him.

Mary was crossing the floor with a plate in her hand, when he rose and going to the shelf, picked up the work. She made an involuntary motion as if to stop him and take it away, then she paused rigid.

He stood smiling down on the sewing. "Something for Tom," he began, and then the smile froze and the words died on his lips as he turned it over. It was only a little maroon housewife such as any soldier might need in the emergency of camp life, but on its front were embroidered the letters, "R. V. D."

He stood gazing at them for a moment as if they were cabalistic, and the mystery was just filtering through his mind. Then, with trembling hands, he threw it across the room.

"My God," he cried, "and I thought it was for her brother! And it is for the comfort of the enemy!"

"It is only a keepsake," said Mary faintly. She was frightened and weakened by his agitation.

He looked at her as if he saw her but dimly, then he said in a hard voice, "This is the end of all. Pick it up," pointing to the housewife. "Now go. Take the visible evidence of your treason and go, and may God and your poor brother forgive you. I never shall."

At another time, Mary might have pleaded with him, but she was dazed, and before she had recovered her presence of mind, her father had left the house. Then she too, as if still in a dream, picked up the offending gift and went out.

She could not understand her father. She did not know what the gift to the enemy meant to him. How he felt as if a serpent had stung him from his own hearth.

She went mechanically, at first, scarce knowing which way she tended. Then thought came to her, and with the keepsake still in her hand, she turned dry-eyed towards Nannie Woods' house.

"It was such a little thing," she murmured as she went into the house, and then suddenly, unconsciousness came to her.

Chapter 8

As a Man Thinketh in His Heart

WHEN MARY RECOVERED CONSCIOUSNESS, it was to find herself lying in Nannie's own bed and her friend beside her. For a moment, she did not remember what had happened, and then the full flood tide of recollection swept over her mind. She buried her head on Nannie's bosom and sobbed out her story.

"Never mind," said Nannie, "never mind, you're going to come here and stay with me, that's what you are going to do. No hardhearted fathers are going to bother you, that's what they're not."

Say what you will, there is always something of the child left in every woman, and though the soft-hearted girl talked and cooed to Mary as she would have done to a restless child, the heartbroken woman was soothed by it.

"Don't you think father ought to understand, Nannie? It isn't because Robert is a copperhead or a rebel, whichever he is, that I love him, but in spite of it."

"Mary," said Nannie, and her voice was meditative and her face dreamy, "don't you know there never was a man yet who knew how or why a woman loved?" A new wisdom, a half playful wisdom though it was, seemed to have come to the girl. Some women never grow clear-sighted until their eyes are opened to the gray form of an oncoming sorrow. Nannie was of this class. "But," she went on laughing, "it's all the fault of Father Adam. Men are so much the sons of their fathers, and it all comes of giving him the first woman while he was asleep and not letting him know when nor how."

"And yet men do love," said Mary seriously.

"Oh, of course they love, but—" the girls' eyes met and both of them blushed. "It won't last long anyhow, Mary, so what's the use of being sad? Let's talk about them." Nannie cuddled down close to the bed.

"About whom?" was the deceitful question.

"Oh, you minx, you know whom. What's the use of asking? I wonder where Tom is tonight?"

"It's hard telling, they've been delaying them so much along the road."

"I don't think it's right at all. They rushed them off toward Washington, and I think they ought to be allowed to get there. How's a man going to distinguish himself if he can't get anywhere within sight of the enemy?"

"I haven't your spirit, Nannie, I wish I had. I forget all about distinction. I only wonder how it's all going to turn out, and if those I love are coming back to me."

"Oh, Mary, don't be like that. Of course, they're coming back, Tom and Rob and all of them, and we're going to be happy again, and there won't be any such names called as copperhead and rebel and abolitionist. Let me show you what I've made for Tom. I'd have given it to him before he went away, but it was all so sudden. Oh, my!" and for an instant the girl dropped her chin upon her hands and sat staring into Mary's eyes without seeing her. Then she sprang up and darted away. In a few minutes she returned bearing with her some mysterious piece of feminine handiwork over which the two fell into the sweet confidences so dear to their age and sex.

Nannie, light and frivolous as she seemed, had a deep purpose in her mind. She saw clearly that the serious, not to say, morbid cast, of Mary's character, would drive her to lay too much importance upon her father's act and so perhaps, let it prove more injurious to her than was necessary. Without Mary's depth, she saw more clearly than Bradford Waters' daughter that a little space of madness was at hand, and every deed had to be judged not by its face alone, but by its face as affected by the surrounding atmosphere, just as the human countenance shows ghastly in one light and ruddy in another, without really changing. So she strove to draw her companion's thought away from her sorrows and to avert the dangers she anticipated. She succeeded only in part. After awhile, Mary fell into a light sleep, but on the morrow she awoke with a raging fever. The strain on her nerves had been too great and she had succumbed to it.

At the first intimation of danger to his daughter, Nannie had bid her father hasten to notify Bradford Waters.

"It's no use," said Nathan Woods, "Waters is more set in his views than any man I ever saw. If he believes that he had reason to send her out of his house, not even death itself could take her back there unless those reasons were destroyed. I know Bradford Waters, and he's a hard man."

But the young woman insisted, and, as usual, had her way. Her father went to Waters. There was not much tact or finesse about his approach. He found his neighbor sitting down to a lonely breakfast, and depositing his hat on the floor, after an embarrassed silence, he began.

"Kind of lonesome, eh?"

"These are no times for men to be lonesome. The Lord makes every loyal man a host in himself."

"That's good, and yet it isn't the kind of host that crowds on each other's toes and cracks jokes to keep the time a-going."

"You're irreverent, Nathan, and besides, this is no time to be cracking jokes. The hour has come when the cracking of rifles is the only thing."

"I didn't mean to be irreverent, and I'm afraid you don't understand. I've come for your own good, Waters. The little girl sent me. Don't you think you're doing wrong?"

"No, as the god of battles is my judge, no!" Waters' eyes were blazing, and he had forgotten his breakfast.

"Your daughter is at my house, and she is sick, very sick."

"I have no daughter."

"God gave you one."

"He also said that a house divided against itself cannot stand."

"What of that?"

"My house is my son Tom and myself."

"What of your daughter, Mary?"

Waters turned upon him his sad bright eyes, sad in spite of their hardness.

"If thy right hand offend thee, cut it off," he said, with a slashing gesture.

"That's not right," said Nathan Woods. "It's not right, I say, to be using the Scripture to stand between you and your daughter."

"I have no daughter. The daughter I had has gone out after other gods than mine."

The old New England fanaticism, the Puritanical intolerance, was strong in the man.

"My God," exclaimed his opposer, "quit mutilating the Bible to bolster up your own pride. Mary's sick, she's sick enough to die, maybe."

"If she die away from home, it is God's will, perhaps his punishment," said Waters solemnly.

"Is it Jepthah and his daughter?"

"No, it is David and Absalom."

Nathan Woods got up; he looked long and hard at his old friend. Then, taking his hat from the floor, he started for the door. There he paused.

"And the war has done this," he said slowly. "Well, Bradford, I say damn the war."

The lonely father sat down again to his breakfast, but the food disgusted him.

Mary sick and away from home. What would Tom say? What would Tom have done? But then the memory of the whole wrong she had done him and her brother came back upon the old man, and he shut his teeth hard. It was a crime. It was treason. Let her go her way and die among the people who were willing to condone her faults. He could not. It was not flesh and blood, but soul and spirit that counted now. It was not that the South had touched his body, and that Mary had sided with them. It was that a rebellious section had touched not his soul, but the soul of his country, and his daughter had bade them Godspeed. This was the unforgivable thing. This was the thing that put the girl outside the pale of parental pardon. So thinking, he rose from the table and went out of the disordered house.

Dorbury was a town of just the size where anyone's business is everyone's else. So it was an impossibility that the breach between Mary and her father should long remain a secret. A half-dozen neighbors knew the story an hour after the doctor had left Nathan Woods' door, and had told it in varying degrees of incorrectness.

One gossip said that Waters' daughter had sought to elope with Robert Van Doren, had even got as far as the railway station, when her father had found her and brought her back. She was now imprisoned at the Woods', with Nannie to watch her.

Another knew on good authority that Mary had denounced the Union, declared her intention of doing all she could to aid the Confederacy, and had then fled from home to escape from her father's just wrath. Anice Crowder's story of the affair in the sewing-circle gave color to this view of the case.

Still, another, however, told how Robert Van Doren's sweetheart, mad for love of him, and crazed at the choice he had made, went wandering about the streets until friendly hands took her to Nannie's door. One man had helped to take her there.

So the rumors flew from lip to lip like shuttlecocks and the story grew with the telling of it.

It would have been strange then, if it had not reached the ears of the Van Dorens. Indeed, it came to them on the first morning. Stephen Van Doren chuckled.

"You're making a great stir for one poor copperhead," he said to his son. "You've made the wolf's stir in the Waters' sheepfold. If you'll only cause the Yankees as much trouble when you have a musket in your hand, I shall have reason to be proud of my son."

Robert turned angrily upon his father.

"I wish you wouldn't talk that way about the matter, father. I don't like all this talk about Mary, and I wish I could stop it. If the girl is suffering on account of loyalty to me, God bless her. It's as little as my father could do to speak respectfully of her sacrifice."

"You do not understand me, Robert, I do not laugh at the girl. It is at her father and his folly that I laugh."

"My love for his daughter makes the father sacred to me."

"It must be a very strong love that makes Bradford Waters sacred."

"My love for Mary is deeper and stronger than any political prejudice that you or I might have."

"Very well, Bob, very well, go your own way. My business is not with your love, but with your politics; if the latter be all right I shall not worry about the former."

Robert Van Doren spent little time after hearing of Mary's illness, but betook himself immediately to her door. Nannie met him and drew him inside.

"I am so sorry," she began before he could tell his errand, "but you cannot see her. She is very sick and excitable. Oh, Robert, isn't it awful, this war and all that it is bringing to us?"

"I wish it were over. Is Mary delirious?"

"At times, and when she isn't, we could almost wish she were; she is so piteous."

"Her father has been hard upon her."

"Yes, that's because he's delirious too. Everyone is mad, you and I and all of us. When shall we come to our senses?"

"God knows. Will you give Mary this?" He drew off his glove and laid it in Nannie's hand. "Tell her it is forbidden me to say good-bye to her, but I leave this as a pledge, and when I may, I shall come back and redeem it."

There were tears on Nannie's face as he turned toward the door. With an impulsive movement, she sprang forward and laid her hand on his arm. "You may kiss me," she said, "and I will bear it to her, and place it on her lips as you would have done."

Robert paused, and bent over her lips as he might have done over Mary's, and then with a wave of his hand, he was gone and the door behind him closed. Nannie turned and went to Mary's room where she laid the glove on the pillow beside the pale face of the unconscious girl. Her brow was fevered and her hair disheveled, and every now and then incoherent words forced themselves between her parched lips.

"I might have let him see her for a minute, but it was better not to. He would only have gone away with the misery of it in his heart." Then Nannie stooped and kissed her friend's lips. "There, Mary," she said, "it's from him. Oh, my dear, dear girl, if your father could see you now, I believe even his heart would melt towards you."

But Bradford Waters was not to see her then. With bowed head and slow steps, eaten by grief, anger and anxiety, he made his way towards the tobacco warehouse where he spent a large part of the day among his employees. The place never seemed quite the same to him since the first day Tom had been absent from his desk. He was thinking of him now as he went cheerlessly along. What a head for business the boy had. How much more of a success he would be than ever his father had been. How the men loved him already. It was no wonder that Mary—but Mary— He checked his thoughts and set his teeth hard. There was no Mary, no sister any more. She had broken the tie that bound her to Tom and him. He said this to himself because he did not know how women wrench and tear their hearts to keep from breaking ties that war with each other.

He was absorbed in such thoughts when someone hailed him from a doorway.

"What news?" said a gentleman stepping out and joining him in his walk.

"No news, except of delay," said Waters in a dissatisfied tone.

"Where is the gallant First now?"

They were already the "Gallant First" although they had not yet got within powder-smelling distance of the enemy.

"The gallant First is being delayed and played with somewhere between Columbus and Washington."

"Why should that be?"

"It all comes of electing a gentleman governor."

"Why now, Waters," said Davies, smilingly. "There is surely no objection to a governor's being a gentleman?"

"There's some objection to his being nothing else."

"You remind me a good deal of the Methodists and the devil; whatever bad happens, they are never at a loss to know where to put the blame. I sometimes think that maybe the devil is painted a little black, and likewise, maybe, Dennison isn't to blame for everything that goes wrong in the handling of this situation."

Waters took this sally with none too good a grace. Davies was suspected of being lukewarm in the Union cause, and some had even accused him of positive Southern sympathies. He was a wealthy, polished, easygoing man, and his defense of Governor Dennison, whose acts everyone felt free to blame at that time, was more because he sympathized with that gentleman's aristocratic tastes and manners than because he wished delay to the progress of the Union's forces.

"So you think it's Dennison who's delaying the troops, do you?" he went on in a light, bantering tone.

"I think nothing about it, I only know that our boys went rushing away to the state capital, and under the impression that Washington was menaced, were sent flying east half equipped and totally unprepared for the conflict, and I do know that despite their haste, they have not reached their destination yet."

"For which, of course, the devil is to blame?"

"Whoever is to blame, this is no time for a banqueting, bowing, speechmaking governor. We need a man of action in the chair now, if we ever did. Look how things are going at Columbus. Troops flocking there, no provision made for them. Half of them not knowing whether they are to be accepted or not and the dandy who calls himself the chief executive sits there and writes letters. My God, what have we come to!"

"Have you ever thought that even a governor needs time to adjust himself to a great crisis? Is it not true that the authorities of the general government insisted on the regiment in which your son's company is placed going directly to Washington?"

"Then why are they not there instead of dallying about, heaven knows where, while a lot of other fellows are being quartered at the Columbus hotels at extortionate prices which the taxpayers must pay?"

"Are you measuring your patriotism by dollars and cents?"

"I'm measuring my patriotism by the greatest gift that anyone could make to his country, his only son. Have you an equal measure?"

"No, but I have some confidence in my state and my country's officers, and that is worth something in a time like this. Now don't get hot in the collar, Waters, but you wait awhile and give Dennison and the government time."

"Yes, wait, wait, that's been the cry right along. Wait until every road this side the capital of the country is blocked and from Maryland and Virginia the rebels march victorious into Washington. Don't talk to me of waiting, Davies, we have waited too long already, that's what's the matter."

Davies laughed lightly as he turned down the street which led to his own office.

Bradford Waters' intemperance was a great index of the spirit of the time as it was manifested in Ohio. Governor Dennison was too slow for the radicals; too swift for the conservatives, and incompetent in the opinion of both. Nothing could happen, except what was good, nothing could go wrong but that he was blamed for it. All the men who volunteered could not be accepted and Dennison was to blame. The soldiers were delayed en route and Dennison was to blame. Rations were scarce and prices high and Dennison was to blame, and so all the odium that attaches to a great war which strikes a people unprepared for it, fell upon the head of the hapless executive.

Chapter 9

A Letter from the Front

IN THE DAYS WHICH FOLLOWED the separation between Mary and himself, Bradford Waters was indeed a lonely man. He was harassed not only by the breach with the child he loved and the public comments upon it, but torn with anxiety for Tom. He spent his days and nights in brooding that made him harder and bitterer as time went on. His fanatical dislike for Stephen Van Doren grew because this man and his family seemed to him the author of all his woes. He was not only just a copperhead, now, with a son in the Confederate army, he stood as the personification of the whole body of rebellion that had taken Waters' son and daughter and broken up his home. He could have no pride in his soldier boy without cursing Van Doren for being one of those who had driven him into danger. He could not grieve for the loss of Mary without sending his imprecations flying in the same direction. Always to his distorted vision, his old-time enemy appeared as some relentless monster grinning in terrible glee at his distress.

Despite his moroseness, however, there was a wistful, almost plaintive attitude in Waters' conduct towards his acquaintances. He hovered between moods of grief, anxiety and pride. But always, at the last, the innate hardness of his nature triumphed. There were times when his heart cried out for Mary, for someone of his blood to share his grief with him. But he closed his lips and uttered no word to bring her back to him. Always a simple-living man, accustomed to no service save that of his own family, he was compelled to employ a servant, and this galled him, not out of penuriousness, but because he could not bear an alien in his home. He felt her eyes upon him at moments when it seemed that the struggle in his heart must be written large upon his face, and it filled him with dumb, helpless anger.

A change, too, was taking place in Van Doren. Now that he had a son in the field, he had a new feeling for his friend and enemy. Besides being a partisan, he was a father and the paternal instinct prompted him to change his actions towards Waters. Had the two old men let themselves, they would have poured out their fears, hopes and anxieties to each other, and found relief and sympathy. Both affectionate fathers, similarly bereft of sons and similarly alone, they might have been a comfort to each other, but that their passions forbade their fraternizing. Often they met upon the streets and Van Doren would look at Waters with a question in his eyes. It would have been such a natural thing to say, "Any news of Tom?" and to be asked in the same tone, "What of Bob?" But Waters always scowled fiercely although he kept his head averted. So each, smothering down the yearning in his heart for companionship and sympathy passed on his way with a curb bit on his emotions.

It was about this time that dispatches from the front gave warning that a sharp, though brief encounter had taken place between the rebels and a detachment of troops under General Schenck. The news ran like wildfire through Dorbury, for it was at first rumored and then assured that the First, to which the home company belonged, had been engaged and had lost several men. Every home out of which a husband, son or father had gone, waited with breathless expectancy, longing, yet dreading to hear more definite tidings from the field. The people about every fireside clustered closer together with blanched faces, wondering if their circle had been touched. This was war indeed, and with the first fear for their loved ones, came the first realization of what it really meant.

At first, Bradford Waters tried hard to restrain himself. He gripped his hands hard and paced up and down the room. But finally, he could stand it no longer. The house had grown close and unbearable. Its walls seemed to be narrowing in upon him like the sides of a torture chamber. He hurried out into the street and into the telegraph office. There was no further news. Then to the office of the one remaining paper. Their bulletin furnished nothing further. For two hours he paced back and forth between these two places, feverish and disturbed. Van Doren saw him pass back and forth on his anxious tramp, and his own heart interpreted the other's feelings. Once, the impulse came to him to speak to Waters, and he rose from the window where he had been sitting, and went to the door, but the crazed man turned upon him such a gray, haggard face and withal so fierce and unfriendly, that he retreated from his good intentions, and let him pass on unchallenged.

The next day the news was better. The papers said that the casualties had been almost nothing.

Waters' hopes rose, and he showed a more cheerful face to those who saw him. Maybe Tom was safe, after all, maybe he had been gallant in action, and would be promoted. His heart throbbed with joy and pride as if what he wished were already a fact. It is a strange thing about home people in war time that after the first pang of anxiety is over, the very next thought is one of ambition. They seem all to see but two contingencies for their loved ones, death or promotion. It happened that there was not a single engagement of the war, however small or insignificant, but it gave some home circle a thrill of hope that one who was dear to them might have moved up a notch in the notice and respect of his country. It was not narrowness nor was it the lust for personal advancement. It was rather the desire of those who give of their best to serve a beloved cause to have them serve it in the highest and most responsible position possible.

Meanwhile, to Mary slowly recovering her strength and balance, had come much of the anxiety which racked her father. With the inconsistent faith of a woman, she said that God could not have let her brother fall in this first fight, and she prayed that he might be restored to them safe. And even before the breath of her declaration and prayer had cooled on her lips, she wept as she pictured him dead on the roadside.

Later, it is true, these people's hearts came to be so schooled in the terrible lessons of civil war that they let such light skirmishes as this one at Vienna give them little uneasiness. But then, they did not know.

Bradford Waters' great joy came to him two days after the papers had lightened his care. There was a list of the wounded and killed, and Tom's name was not among them. Then came his letter.

"DEAR FATHER," it ran, "I suppose you've been in horrible suspense about me, and a good deal of it is my fault. But when a fellow is learning entirely new things, among them how to write without any sort of writing materials under the sun, it isn't easy, is it? Then, too, I've been trying to learn to be a soldier. It's awfully different, this being a militiaman and a soldier. In the first place, a militiaman may curse his governor. A soldier must not. It's been hard refraining, but I haven't cursed Dennison as I wanted to. Some of the fellows say he's all right, but we've been delayed on the way here by first one thing and then another until the patience of all of us is worn out. If it isn't Governor Dennison's fault, whose is it? I wish you'd find out. We fellows don't know, and can't find out anything. The generals just take us wherever they please and never consult us about anything. But I'm used to that now.

"Of course, you've heard about the trouble at Vienna, and I was afraid you'd be considerably worried. It wasn't anything much. Only it was different from a muster day. Some rebels fired on our train unexpectedly, but we tumbled out helter-skelter and fired back at them, and so they let us alone. It didn't seem quite fair to jump on a fellow when he wasn't looking, but I guess this is war.

"There isn't a thing to do about Washington these days. It's as safe as a meeting-house. There are some New York troops here that I have got acquainted with, but we don't any of us do anything but look pretty. Some of the fellows are already looking forward to the mustering out day. But mustered out or not, I'm going to hang around here, for there's no telling when things are going wrong, and for my part, I expect more trouble. A set of fellows who will fire on their own flag as they did at Sumter are perfectly capable of lying low until they quiet our suspicions and then raising the very dickens.

"Give Mary my love, and tell her she ought to see Washington and all the pretty girls here that cheer us as we go along the streets. (Tell her to read this part of the letter to Nannie. I'm going to write her anyway in a day or two, but now it's all go, go, go, learn, learn, learn.) Take care of yourself, father, or rather let Mary take care of you, for you would never think of it. I'll write you again when I get a chance.

"Your son,

"Tom."

Bradford Waters could have wept for joy over his son's letter, but that he felt weeping to be unworthy of a soldier's father. The battle of Vienna had been fought and his son had come out safe. He thought of it as a Thermopylae when it was only a petty skirmish. A few rebels fired at a few Unionists, who lined themselves up against their cars and returned the fire. This was all, but he preferred to think of his son as one of a band of heroes who at great odds had repelled the assailants of their country's flag, and held the day against armed treason.

One thing grieved him greatly, the reference to Mary. He could not tell her nor talk it over with her. She take care of him! What would her brother think if he knew how they were living, and he was going to write to Nannie? Would she not tell him all, and what encouragement would this be to the boy in the field when he knew how matters were going at home? Bradford Waters' hand trembled and the letter burned in his fingers.

Notwithstanding his perplexity, when Waters appeared on the streets that day, Stephen Van Doren seeing him, did not need to inquire to know that the Unionist had received a welcome letter from his son, and secretly, he rejoiced at it. Knowing as he did, that the time would come when anxiety for his own boy would tear at his heart, he could not begrudge the other man his joy. He was pleased, too, because as he passed Waters and looked into his beaming face, there seemed almost an inclination on his part to stop and speak.

Indeed, the old Unionist did want to stop and say, "Stephen, I've heard from Tom, and he's all right." He did not, and the repression only made him long the more for Mary. He wanted her to see his letter, to know that her brother was being cheered by the women of Washington, and to feel what he felt. But would she feel so? Had not her heart already gone too strongly to the other side? The question came again to him, and he hardened again in face of it.

He would not tell her nor send the letter to her. She was a traitor. But he would let her know that he had received it. So that afternoon, he talked much of his letter in the places where men congregate, and told what Tom had said, and Mary heard of it from others and burned with eagerness.

That night, as soon as darkness had fallen, eluding Nannie's vigilance, she crept out of the house. She made her way to her own home, and back and forth before the door, she walked and kept vigil. Maybe her father would see her and come out and tell her more of Tom. Maybe he would understand and forgive her and she could go back to him again. But she wished in vain, and after a time, her heart unsatisfied, she went back to Nannie's, and silently let herself in.

It was after midnight, when Waters crept out of his house, and with feverish steps made his way to the Woods' door. For a long time he walked up and down before the place even as Mary had done, and then, as if struck with a sudden determination, he opened the gate and going to the door, slipped the letter under it. Then he turned away home, feeling lighter and better because he had shared his joy with his daughter.

Chapter 10

Sorrow May Last for a Night

IT WAS OF A PIECE with the proverbial blindness of man that Nathan Woods should have stepped over the letter as he went out in the morning without taking note of it, just as it was natural to the keen sight of woman that Nannie should see it the first thing as she came down in the morning. She ran swiftly towards it and cast her eye over the address. At first she gasped, then she awoke the echoes with a joyous shriek and went flying up to Mary's room. Mary sat up in bed in dumb amazement which was only increased when the enthusiastic girl threw her arms about her and began sobbing and laughing alternately.

"Oh, Mary," she cried, "it's come, it's come, and he's all right."

"What is it, Nannie? What's come, and who's all right?"

"Your father's been here, oh!"

"My father? When? What did he say?"

"Nothing, oh, I didn't see him, he didn't say anything."

"I don't understand you, Nannie. You say my father didn't say anything at all?"

"Why, how could he? He came at night, and he didn't say anything because he couldn't, you know. We were all asleep, but he left this." She broke off her violent demonstrations long enough to thrust the letter into Mary's hand, then she immediately resumed them with such a degree of fervor that her friend found it impossible to get a glimpse of the missive she held in her hand. Gently, at last, she put her hand aside, and then trembling with anticipation, glanced at the letter. Her face fell.

"But this is not addressed to me," she said.

"Oh, you great goose, don't you see, that it's to your father and from Tom and that he wanted you to know? Else why should he have slipped it under the door?"

"Do you think he did it, really?"

"Of course, he did, who else? He couldn't lose it crawling into our hallway, and that's the only other way it could have got there."

"I wonder if I ought to read it?" mused Mary fingering the envelope eagerly, but nervously.

"Mary Waters!" exclaimed Nannie, "if you don't read that letter this instant, I'll take it from you and read it myself."

"That's right, do, Nannie, you're braver than I am," and Mary proffered the letter. But Nannie sprang back with sudden timidity.

"No, I won't," she said. "It's for you, but if it were my brother's letter, I'd have read it long before now."

"Well, I'll read it, if you'll stay and hear it," and she took the penciled sheets out and began the perusal of the words which had brought so much joy to her father's heart. As she read, the color came back to her faded cheeks and the light to her eyes. Her bosom heaved with pleasure and pride. Nannie was no less delighted. As the reading went on, she continued to give Mary little encouraging hugs, and she was radiant.

Then came the passage about the girls.

"Humph," said Nannie, "is that all a soldier has to write about? I should think he'd be thinking more about the safety of his country than about the girls he sees."

"Oh, you know he's only funning, Nannie, and then he says Washington's as safe as a meeting-house."

"I don't believe it. I believe the rebels are waiting to swoop down on the city at any time and capture all our state papers, and archives and things, wherever they keep them, while our soldiers go around looking pretty for the girls to cheer. Humph!"

Mary kissed her and laughed, and the rest of the reading proceeded without demonstrations from Tom's sweetheart. At its close, she made no comment whatever, but sat upon the bed swinging her feet with pronounced indifference.

"Aren't you glad to hear from him?" said Mary merrily, "and to find him in such good spirits? Dear old Tom. And wasn't it good of father to bring his letter to me? Didn't I tell you, Nannie, that my father didn't mean half he said?"

"No you didn't, Mary Waters. You thought the end of everything had come, even after I tried to convince you that it hadn't, and as for being glad, to be sure, I'm glad you've heard from your brother. Anyone with relatives in the field must be very anxious."

"But you know, he said he was going to write to you, Nannie."

"It's very kind in him; I wonder he can take time from his Washington girls to write."

Then Mary laughed. "It can't be that you are jealous, Nannie, girl," she said affectionately taking her friend in her arms. "You know Tom is teasing you."

"I jealous!" oh how the little woman sniffed! "I can assure you that I'm not jealous, but I have the interests of my country at heart, and I cannot but feel sorry to see our soldiers giving themselves up to trivial amusements when she is in danger of—oh, just the most awful things. I'm not jealous, oh, no, but I'm ashamed of Tom."

"Why, Nannie, how can you?" said Mary reddening.

"Well, I am, and I mean it, and it's awful, that's what it is."

"I'm sorry my brother has offended you."

"Oh, Mary," Nannie was always inarticulate in her emotion, but Mary understood the burst of tears as Nannie threw herself on her bosom, and forgave her disparagement of Tom.

"What a little silly you are. You know he was only joking."

"Joking! Such a letter isn't any joke. It's brutal, that's what it is. Pretty girls cheering him! I hate those Washington girls. I just know they're bold, brazen things, and they didn't look at another man but Tom."

"Never you mind, you'll have a letter soon."

"I don't want it."

"All right. Maybe it won't come. The mails are very irregular now."

"Mary Waters, how can you say such a mean thing?"

"I didn't think you'd mind it."

"But I do mind it. You know the mails are regular here. It's not the mails that I'm worrying about."

She must have worried about something though, for when her father came in with the morning paper, she was eager to know if he had been to the post office, and on receiving a negative answer, was downcast for fully five minutes.

"The mail wouldn't have been sorted yet, anyhow," said her father, "and Banes's boy's going to bring it when he goes for theirs."

"The mail is very slow in Dorbury, isn't it?" Nannie proffered a little later, and was angry because Mary laughed again.

The promise of a letter was at least two days away, but Nannie ate very little that morning. She fastened her eyes upon the window which commanded the walk up which the Banes boy must come. Finally, when he hove in sight, she sprang away from the table with a cry, of "Oh, there he is!" and everyone knew why her appetite had lapsed.

Fate was kind. It was kind two days ahead of promise, a strange thing, but this was her off day. There was a letter, and it was for Nannie and from Tom. She came directly to the table with it, because she didn't know any better, and there were no daws about to peck at an exposed heart. She read and smiled and bridled and blushed while the rest of the assembly neglected their eggs.

"Oh, give us some of it," said her father banteringly.

"I won't," she answered, and it was a good thing Tom couldn't see her smile and blush, for if he had been any sort of man, he would have deserted at once.

"Isn't there anything he says that we may hear?"

"Oh, do let me alone," she answered, and—well, it's hard to tell, but she giggled.

"What a softy he must be," said her little brother, "just writing about no-account things, when you'd think he'd be saying something about fighting. 'Tain't polite to read letters before folks anyhow."

"You hush up, Reuben," said Nannie indignantly, "don't you suppose a soldier can talk about anything but the horrors of war?"

"I knew it was from Tom," said Reuben jeeringly.

"Keep quiet, Reuben," said his father, "no telling when you'll be putting on fresh ties every night, an' tryin' to find out an excuse to be out to a 'literary' or a singing school."

Reuben grew red and was silent. His particular tone of red was what is denominated Turkey, and it was relieved by freckles.

"Well, I'll just read you a little of it," said Nannie finally. "I'm not going to tell you what he calls me in the beginning. That's none of their business, is it, Mary?" and she ran over and kissed Tom's sister for Tom's sake. Then she looked at the letter again.

"Well, he says, 'Dear little—' no I'm going to leave that out. He sends his love to you, papa, but of course, that's at the last."

"Would it hurt you to be consecutive?" asked Nathan Woods drily.

"Oh, now, don't tease, just listen. He says, oh, Mary, he doesn't say another word about those Washington girls. It was only a joke, don't you think it was? I knew Tom couldn't be thinking very seriously just of girls when there was something very, very important to do. You know I told you so, Mary."

"No," said Mary tantalizingly, "I don't think that you did tell me just that."

"And of course," said her father, "you may not know it isn't, but this is not. I maintain, this is not hearing the letter."

"Oh, well, he says he's in Washington. How perfectly charming it must be in Washington. I know that must be a great town with the government and senators and such things about you. Dear, how I should like to be there, and oh, Mary, don't you remember about the Potomac in the geography, just think, Tom's seen the Potomac!"

"I know about the Potomac," said Reuben.

"That's not the letter yet," was her father's comment.

"Well, if you'd only stop, father, I'd get to it," said Nannie.

"We are dumb."

"Oh, papa, now, please don't joke, it's really very, very serious."

"Has one among them been taken?"

"That's just it, that's just it. The rebels tried to take them, and they didn't, and Tom—Tom—I think he ought to be promoted for it. It's wonderful."

"What did Tom do? Save his whole brigade?"

"Well, I don't know that he did that, but he says that he shot and shot, and that the bullets spit up against the car behind him. Think of it!"

"It would have been a good deal worse if they had spit up against him," said Woods. He had been in the Mexican war and unfortunately had lost his romance. "Now, daughter, for the letter."

"All right, you won't mind omissions, will you?"

"No, if you'll only omit your pauses and exclamations."

"'We are here, at last at the capital, and I tell you, it's a great place. I don't wonder in the least that men want to be congressmen when they can live in a town like this. Why, I'd be willing to take all the cares of the government on my shoulders just to live in a town like this. But you know, the voters have never pressed upon my shoulders the affairs of state, and so thy willingness to be unselfish goes for nothing!' Now isn't that bright of Tom?"

"Oh, Nannie, for heaven's sake, go on." Nathan Woods was both short and impatient. "What we want is news, news about the troops and their condition there."

"I'm afraid, papa," said Nannie ruefully, "that there isn't much news. But never mind, listen. 'I got to see Lincoln the other day, and I don't think much of him. He's a big raw-boned fellow with a long face and an awfully serious look. But for any kind of polish I'll bet old Dennison could give him a good many lessons, although I don't think much of Dennison. My own—' Oh, no, there's where I've got to make an omission, but he goes on to say, 'People are saying that the rebellion is going to be a good deal bigger thing than we think, and that three months' service is hardly going to begin the fighting, others say different. Well, I don't care. I'm in it to stay, and you needn't expect to see me until we've licked the boots off these fellows. Do you know what they say? They boast that one Southerner can lick five Yankees. Well, I'd like to see them try it. Oh, isn't that just like Tom? He always was in for experiments."

"Go on, Nannie, and omit comment."

"'But as old man Wilson used to say in geometry class, if they proceed upon this hypothesis, they will be wrong.' Oh, Mary, don't you remember old Mr. Wilson, and how often Tom used to tell us about his funny expressions. How awfully clever of him to think of it now. But I know you're waiting to hear the rest. Oh, I can't read this, papa, not a bit of it. Nor the rest, oh, I wouldn't read that for anything. Tom is so enthusiastic. You know how he is. That's just what is going to make a good soldier out of him. He says, 'I've seen General Schenck, and he's just what you would expect from the Schenck family. It seems as if those people kept themselves busy making decent men. The boys all like him, although they have not got generally trained into liking generals yet. Say, Nannie—' and that's all," said the young girl with a guilty blush.

"How abruptly your brother ends his letters," said Nathan Woods, turning to Mary with a quizzical smile. "It may be striking, but it's not a good literary style."

"You must always consider the collaborator, Mr. Woods," said Mary.

"In this case, I'm not sure that it has been collaboration. It may have been interpretation, or even, heaven help us, expurgation."

"Papa," said Nannie with a very red face, then she gathered up the loose sheets of her letter and fled from the table.

"Mary," said Nathan Woods, "what has happened this morning has made me very happy, but don't count too much upon it. No man respects your father more than I do. But the oyster opens his shell for a little and then shuts it as tight as ever.

So I would advise you to stay with us a while longer. Had he wanted you at home, now this is plain, he would have come to you openly; but in putting the letter under the door, he only made a sacrifice on account of his love for Tom. Don't cry, little girl."

"No, I'm going to be brave, for I am glad even of this kindness from him— but—"

"Aren't we treating you pretty well?"

"Yes, but Mr. Woods, you know, don't you?"

"Yes, I believe I do understand how you feel about it, but just keep on waitin', your time'll come."

Chapter 11

At Home

WITH THE INCIDENTS THAT immediately succeeded the skirmish at Vienna, this story has little to do. Notwithstanding the enlistment of only three-months-men, the country had begun to settle down to the realization of war, not insurrection, not only rebellion any longer, but war, stern, implacable, and perhaps to last longer than had at first been expected. As the days passed, there was talk of reorganization. The first was not behindhand in the matter, and by the August following work among the men had begun.

On the day that the men came home, Dorbury, complacent because no casualty had as yet attacked her ranks, was out in full force to meet them. They, too, recognized the state of war, but as yet, it was only a passive condition, and when they saw their unbroken lines come back, three months' veterans, their pride and joy knew no bounds. That many of their men would return to the field, would go back to soldiers' deaths and soldiers' graves, did not disturb them then. Sufficient unto the day is the evil thereof. So they put away all thought of further disaster, and reveled only in the present.

Among those who came back, proud and happy, none was more noticeable than "Nigger Ed." The sight of camps, the hurry of men and the press of a real responsibility had evoked a subtle change in the Negro, and though his black face showed its accustomed grins, and he answered with humor the sallies made at him, he capered no more in the public square for the delectation of the crowd that despised him. He walked with a more stately step and the people greeted him in more serious tones, as if his association with their soldiers, light though it had been, had brought him nearer to the manhood which they still refused to recognize in him.

Perhaps the least joyous of them all was Walter Stewart, who had given up his family for a principle. While the other boys returned to eager relatives, he came home to no waiting mother's arms, and no sweetheart was there to greet him with love and pride in her eyes. There were friends, of course, who gave him hearty handclasps. But what were friends compared with one's own family?

His mood was not improved when less than two days after the return there came a telegram calling him to the bedside of his dying father. It was a great blow to the young fellow, and coming as it did, seemingly as a reproof of his career, it may be forgiven him, if in his grief, his heart grew lukewarm towards the cause he had espoused. As soon as he was able, he hastened away to Virginia and his father's bedside, torn with conflicting emotions of remorse, love and sorrow.

On an open space topping a hill near Dorbury, the white tents of the reorganizing regiment had begun to settle like a flock of gulls on a green sea. Most of the men who had been out were going back again, and the town took on a military appearance. It came to be now that the girl who had not a military lover or relative was one to be pitied, and the one who had, stood up with complacent Phariseeism and thanked her Creator that she was not as other maidens were.

It was now that the sewing-circle exerted itself to the utmost, both in their natural province and in entertainment for the soldiers. Everything now, had the military prefix to it. There were soldiers' balls, soldiers' teas, soldiers' dinners and soldiers' concerts. Indeed, the sentiment bade fair to run to a foolish craze, and those who felt most deeply and looked forward with fear to what the days might bring forth, beheld this tendency deprecatingly.

Many of the volunteers, from being decent, sensible fellows, had developed into conceited prigs. The pride of their families and the adulation of indiscreet women and none-too-well balanced men, combined to turn their thoughts more upon the picturesqueness of their own personalities than upon the seriousness of what was yet to be done. They were blinded by the glare of possible heroism, and sometimes lost sight of the main thing for which they had banded themselves together. It would be entirely false to say that at their first realization of what they had gone into they did not rise to all that was expected of them. But such was for a time the prevailing spirit, and for a while it called forth the sneers of old men who had not forgotten 1812 and 1846, at these three months' soldiers.

There were others, too, who smiled at the behavior of the young soldiers with less generous thoughts. Among them, Stephen Van Doren, who watched from behind closed blinds their comings and goings.

"Do they expect to whip the South, which is all fire and passion, with their stripling dandies, who go about the streets posing for a child's wonder and a woman's glance? Bah, the men who have gone into the field from the states of rebellion, have gone to fight for a principle, not to wear a uniform. They are all earnestness and self-sacrifice, and that's what's going to take the South to victory."

His old housekeeper, who was alone with him on the place, heard with admiration and belief, for she shared her master's opinion of the relative worth of the two sections of the country. Neither one of them knew that the young men of the South were taking their valets into the service with them; entering it as gallants with the traditionary ideas of the day, and leaving college for the field, because they believed it would be a famous lark.

It was perfectly true of both sections that neither looked upon the contest at first with a great amount of seriousness. But it is equally true that the fact might have been forgiven the youth of a country whose sons hitherto had made a common cause against a general enemy.

Unlike Van Doren, who stayed between walls and chuckled at the coming discomfiture of the Union arms, Bradford Waters was much upon the streets, and at Camp Corwin, as if the sight of these blue-coated defenders of the flag gave him courage and hope. He had a good word for every soldier he met, and his eyes sparkled as they told him of Tom, and the few experiences they had had together.

Tom, true to his promise, had not returned with the rest, but had preferred to remain near the seat of war, and to join his regiment after its reorganization. The old man took pride, even, in this fact. To him, it was as if Tom were staying on the field where he could guard the safety of his country in an hour of laxity on the part of his comrades. He longed to see him, of course, but there was joy in the pain he felt at making a sacrifice of his own desires. He had not loaned his son to the cause. He had given him freely and fully.

The difference in attitude, between Van Doren and Waters, was the difference between regard for traditions and a personal faith. The Southerner said, "What my people have done," the Yankee, "What a man must do." Said one, "Coming from the stock he does, Bob must fight well." Said the other, "If they all fight like Tom, we're bound to whip." It all came to the same thing at last, but the contrast was very apparent then.

At news of the safety of his enemy's son, the copperhead had lost any sympathy he may have had for his Union antagonist, and the other no longer looked wistfully at his foreman's face when they chanced to meet.

It was not unnatural that the two girls, Nannie and Mary, should be affected by the hero-worshiping spirit of the town, and being deprived of the objects of their immediate affection, enter heartily into the business of spoiling all the other young men they could. To Nannie, it was all very pleasant, and something of coquetry entered into her treatment of the soldiers. But with Mary it was different. Her thoughts and motives were serious, and her chief aim was to do something for Tom's old associates, for Tom's sake.

There was no abatement of the rigor of the estrangement between her and her father, for although, after the incident of the letter, she had expected him to call her home, he had made no further sign, nor had she. She had yielded not one whit in her devotion and loyalty to Robert Van Doren. But she took pleasure in doing little kindnesses for the men whom she knew hated him for the choice he had made. The time soon came, when even this pleasure, gentle as it was, was denied her.

The story went round among the soldiers that old Waters' daughter was the sweetheart of a rebel soldier, and that in spite of all her good work, she had left home for love of him and his cause, and they grew cold towards her. Some were even rude.

It hurt the girl, but she continued her ministrations, nevertheless. Then one day as she passed through the camp where the girls sometimes went, she heard a voice from a tent singing derisively,

> "Father is a Unionist, so is Brother Tom,
>   But I, I'm making lots o' things
>   To keep a rebel warm."

Mary flushed and hurried on, but the voice sang after her:

> "Never mind my Union home, never mind my flag,
>   What's the glorious stars and stripes
>   Beside Jeff Davis' rag?
>   Damn my home and family, damn my Northern pride,
>   So you let me go my way to be a rebel's bride."

The song which some scalawag had improvised, cut Mary to the heart, but though no man would have dared sing it openly, she never took the chance of hearing it again. In spite of Nannie's pleadings, she would not go again where soldiers were congregated. Nor would she tell her reason, not that she felt shame in her love, but that there seemed some shade of truth in the song. She did want to go her way and she did want to be Robert's bride, even though they called him by such a name as rebel. She loved him and what had the stars and stripes or love of country to do with that? What he believed was nothing to her, it was only what he was.

She had heard from Robert but once since his departure; a brief but brave and loving letter, in which he told her that he was safe within the Confederate lines, and spoke of John Morgan, whom he had already begun to admire. Now in the dark moment of her sorrow, when every hand seemed turned against her because she loved this man, she dreamed over his letter as if it were a sacred writing, and so dreaming kept to herself whenever she could. Even old Nathan Woods began to look askance at her when her visits and ministrations to the soldiers ceased. But he comforted himself with the philosophy that "A woman is an unreasonable creature and never is responsible for her actions," and however false this may be in fact, it satisfied him towards Mary, and kept him unchanged to her. He was influenced, too, by Nannie's stalwart faith. While she could not understand Mary, could not enter into the secret chambers of her soul and see what was within there, she believed in her, and faith is stronger than knowledge.

"Never mind," she said one day after roundly scolding her friend for remaining so close to the house, "I know you've got some good reason, though I'm sure it's something fanciful. It's so like you, Mary." This may have been a bit inconsistent in the young girl, but it was expressive of her trust in Mary, and the burdened girl was grateful for it.

So, with bicker, prejudice, adulation, discontent and a hundred other emotions that must come to human beings, the stream of days went on, and the reorganization of the First was an accomplished fact. Still from the South there came news of battle and from Cincinnati there were tidings of Kentucky's threatening attitude. West Virginia had been rescued for the Union, but what if this even more powerful state went over to the Confederacy. Men were of many minds. Some were wondering at the president for his tardiness, and others cursing Dennison for his rashness. It became the fashion to damn Lincoln on Sunday and Dennison on Monday. It was from such a hotbed of discontent that the First finally tore itself, and left Dorbury on the last day of October for the southernmost city of the state.

Chapter 12

A Journey South

THE CONDITION OF MIND in which young Walter Stewart left Dorbury was not calculated to bring him back hastily for the reorganization of his old regiment. His thoughts were more of seeing his father alive, and of settling their differences, than of the righteousness of his cause. Indeed, as the train sped southward, his busy mind sometimes questioned if he had done right. If the North and South were one people as he claimed, would not neutrality have been the better course? Surely two brothers have the right to differ without the whole family's putting in. Is the love of country, which we call patriotism, a more commendable trait than filial affection and obedience, and can one deficient in the latter be fully capable of comprehending the former? Had he not by the very act of disobeying his father's wishes and refuting his wisdom in a case where right and wrong were so nearly related, demonstrated his inability for a high devotion and obedience to his country? These, and like sophistries, raced through the young man's mind in the first heat of his remorse, and for the time, he forgot that his choice meant not less love for his father, but a broader devotion to his country. It was not for the sake of disobedience that he had cast his lot with the North, but in pursuance of an idea of a larger allegiance. But this he could not see, and as he worried and speculated, his distress grew.

When he reached Washington, he had anticipations of some difficulty in securing passage through the lines. There was every possibility of his being taken for
a spy or an informer by one side or the other, and the fact that he was a lately mustered out soldier would make him an object of suspicion to both Unionist and
Confederate. For the time being, his anxiety to be away, across the Potomac and
into Virginia drove every other thought out of his head. Fortunately for him, he
was known in Washington, and influential friends procured for him passes through
the Union lines. His progress, after he reached the rebel outposts, was less speedy.
But foreseeing this, he conceived that discretion would be the better part of valor,
and so waited for night, and then the laxity of the few pickets scattered about
helped him, and the stables of Falls Church were kind to him, and within an hour
after darkness had fallen, he was galloping down the road towards Rockford.

The night was dark and the road none too even, but he rode as speedily as
caution would allow. The way was unfamiliar to him, but he followed the directions
he had received, trusting somewhat to the instincts of his horse to keep the path.
Now and then, as the animal's hoofs clattered over the wooden bridge of river or
streamlet, he held his breath lest he should rouse some lurking foeman. Once as
he sped along a road beside which the trees grew thickly, a voice called to him to
halt, but he only dug his spurs into the mare's flank, and leaning low over her neck,
urged her on. Two shots spit vainly in the darkness as the road fell away under his
horse's feet.

"Suppose I should miss the path," he said to himself, "and daylight find me
still upon the way? Well, it's only a thing to chance now, and I must see father before he dies. I must see him!" The cry died away between clinched teeth, and leap
after leap, the blackness swallowed him, and vomited him forth again. The branches
of the trees underneath which he passed, reached out and caught at him as if they
would detain him from his errand. The wind and the cricket and all the voices of
the night called to him. The horse stumbled and her rider lurched forward, but the
good steed was up and on again with scarcely a break in her pace, as if she knew
that the man upon her back was crying in an agony of fear, "Father, father, live till
I come!"

As the distance lessened, Walter's mind was in a tumult of emotions. Again
and again, the picture of his father already dead came before him. The white cov-
ering of the bed, the stark form and the weeping women all were vivid to him as
actuality. He saw a light ahead of him, and checking the speed of his horse, he
rode towards it. But he found that it came from a house up one of two roads which
forked before him. He paused and looked helplessly at the diverging paths. He
knew there was no time to be lost, and chafed at the delay. His indecision, however, did not last long. He turned the animal's head up the road on which the light
was shining.

Proceeding cautiously, he found that the rays which had guided him came from
the curtained, but unshuttered window of a little house standing back from the
roadside, on a terrace. The place itself, did not look formidable, but there was no

telling what elements of further delay were behind the closed door. Nevertheless, he reined in, and bringing his horse just inside the side gateway, hastened up the terrace and knocked at the door. There was the shuffling of feet within, and then the soft, swift scurrying as of someone hastening from the room. A moment later, the back door slammed, and a horse and rider clattered around the side of the house and out of the gate.

In spite of his haste and anxiety, Walter could but smile at the grim humor of the situation. That he, who stood there on the threshold, dreading what he should encounter beyond, should prove a source of terror to anyone else, was but an illustration of the intermittent comedy which treads upon the heels of tragedy in the stern melodrama of war.

His reflections took but a moment; all that had passed, had hardly taken more time, but before the impressions were out of his mind, he found himself again knocking at the door.

"Who is there?" came a woman's voice.

"A stranger, but a friend."

"How do I know that you are a friend?"

"You need not know, you need not even open the door, only answer my question. I am hunting the house of Colonel Stewart, and am not sure that I am on the right road. Can you direct me?"

"You have missed your way," said the hidden woman in a voice that bespoke relief from some fear. "You should have taken the road to the right at the forks. The house is about two miles beyond on the right side. You can tell it without trouble. It is a large house, and there will be lights about it, for the colonel is very sick."

Walter did not wait to hear the woman's closing words, but with a hearty word of thanks, hurried away towards the gate. He was almost blithe with the thought that his journey would soon be over, and hope rose again in his heart. His father might be alive. He would be alive. He must be. So he went from hope to certainty as he passed with flying steps across the lawn and terrace to the gate. There he stopped with a gasp of alarm. His horse was no longer there. Gone, and the distance between him and his father lessened by many minutes when every second counted.

It all came to him in a flash. The frightened rider who had dashed away from the house in a flash, fearing pursuit, had taken the horse with him, or the animal, itself, had become frightened and followed involuntarily.

Walter halted hardly a moment, but turned swiftly back to the house. To his knock, came the woman's voice again in question.

"Someone has taken my horse," he cried.

"It is not so far to walk from here to Colonel Stewart's," said the woman coldly.

"But I cannot walk, I am pressed for time."

"I do not know you," was the reply, "nor do I know your business, but I warn you that I am armed, and you had better go away."

"My God!" cried Walter, "I mean you no harm, but can't you help me to a horse, or must I take one wherever I can find it? I am Colonel Stewart's son, and my father is dying. I must see him." A dry sob broke in his throat.

An exclamation was uttered from within. Something that was very like the thud of a gun butt sounded on the carpeted floor. The bolts were shot and a woman stood in the flood of yellow light.

In the first instant, Walter saw the form of a tall young woman with fair hair, and behind her, the room disordered as by hasty movements. A gun stood against the wall. Further details he did not take note of.

"Come in for a moment," said the woman, "you need have no fear. I can help you to a horse." She was hastening into a wrap and hood as she spoke. "We already know of you, my brother and I; you are Colonel Stewart's Unionist son."

Walter flushed, but raised his head defiantly.

The young woman laughed as she hastened out of the room and came back with a lantern and key. "You need have no fear, there are no ambushes here. Come." She led the way around the house, where Walter could see the low outlines of the outbuildings.

"You gave us quite a fright; I may tell you, now that I know who you are. Brother is suspected of Unionist sentiments and has been looking to be arrested every moment. Tonight, we took you for a Confederate officer, come to exercise that unpleasant commission, and it was he who must have frightened off your horse as he rode away. He's on Blue Grass, and if your horse keeps up with him, they're farther away now than you would care to follow."

During the last words she was unlocking the barn door. Then she handed the lantern to Walter, and called softly, "Come, Beth, come." A whinny answered her, and she went forward and quickly took the halter from a sleek brown mare. Walter started in to put the bridle on, but the girl waved her hand.

"No," she said, "I'll do it myself. Beth is my own particular pet, and is somewhat averse to strangers. You'll have to ride bareback too, as there isn't another man's saddle about. But she'll carry you safe when she's once on the road, and she'll turn in the right gate, for she knows the way."

The young man was stammering his thanks as the girl led the horse out. He would have walked with her back to the house, but upon an assurance that she was not afraid, he leaped to the mare's back and was off.

But it was not written that the object of his heart should be so easily obtained. He had scarcely gone half way to the crossroads, when the ominous word, "Halt!" sounded again in his ears, and several mounted men rose as from the road before him. Again, he gave spur to his horse, but this time, it was only for a moment that he moved, and then he came crash into another horseman, and felt the cold muzzle of a pistol pressed against his face, while a hand seized his bridle.

"Steady, my boy, steady, unless you want to get hurt. We don't want to do you any harm, but you mustn't move."

"Are you hurt, sergeant?" asked a voice from the darkness.

"No, cap'n, not particular. I may be a little strained, and this horse may be a little bruised up, but I was ready for the shock. I knew the youngster was game."

Just now the man addressed as captain rode up.

"Well, youngster," he said, "we've got a little business with you, and I reckon we're just in time."

Walter's head was whirling with the shock of his collision and he had a mean pain in the leg that had struck the other man's saddle. But he spoke up hotly.

"What's the meaning of this outrage?" he asked. "Cannot a man and a Virginian at that, ride his own roads in safety by night and by day?"

"Hoity-toity, not so fast, my young Union peacock, not so fast. Any Virginian may go his way in Virginia until he becomes dangerous to Virginia's cause. Then he comes with us as you do."

"What right have you to take me in this highhanded way?"

"We needn't bandy words, but I can say that we have the right that any state has to arrest within its borders any citizen who is suspected of working or attempting to work against its interest and safety. We have been watching you for a long time, Etheridge, and we know what your plans are."

They had been standing for the few moments that they talked, but now the company started to move off.

"Stop," cried Walter, as the name was called, "whom do you take me for?"

"We know who you are," said the captain grimly.

"But my name is not Etheridge, you are mistaken."

"What is this, sergeant? " asked the officer in charge of the party and who had done most of the talking.

"I know the horse, captain, it's his sister's."

"Come on, then, don't delay any further. It's no use denying your identity."

"But I can prove to you that I'm not the man you're seeking, nor is this horse mine. Having lost my own, I borrowed it at a house a little way up the road here."

"A very likely story."

"But if there is anyone here who knows Etheridge, let him look at me and see."

The sergeant leaned forward and striking a match looked into Walter's face.

"Whew, captain," he whistled, "it's true, we've caught the wrong bird. This is not Nelson Etheridge. He's a stranger."

"Well, who the devil are you?" asked the captain shortly. "Strangers without credentials are not very welcome about here these times."

"My name is Walter Stewart, and my father is Colonel Stewart who lives about two miles from here."

"Stewart—Walter Stewart, hurrah, boys!" cried the captain, "we've lost one good bird but caged another! This is Colonel Stewart's Yankee soldier son. You'll do, come on."

"But, captain, I'm not in the service now, and my father is dying. A few minutes' delay may keep me from ever seeing him alive."

"I am sorry," was the captain's reply, "but you have been a Union soldier. We take you leaving a suspected house, and find you as you tacitly admit within our lines and without credentials. It may be hard for you, but you are our prisoner."

"Very well, but cannot I be paroled at once? If necessary, send a soldier with me to my house, and keep me under guard."

The captain halted. "I know your father," he said coldly, "and he is a brave man and a Southern gentleman who has not forsaken the South. For his sake, I will do as you say, even though I exceed my authority. I will send two men with you. You will remain under guard until I secure your parole, if that may be done."

"I thank you," said Walter.

"Sergeant Davis!" The sergeant saluted.

"You and Private Wilkins will take charge of the prisoner. When his parole has been secured, you will be relieved. Until then, the closest vigilance."

"I am a soldier and a gentleman," said Walter calmly.

The officer vouchsafed no answer, but with his remaining associates spurred on into the darkness, leaving the prisoner to ride away with his captors.

Chapter 13

A Stewart Comes to His Own

As WALTER APPROACHED HIS father's house, he saw lights moving about in the upper chambers, and he began to fear the worst.

"Have you heard any news of my father?" he asked the sergeant.

"None, except that he is a pretty sick man and not expected to last long."

"How did the captain and all of you come to know about me?"

"The servants will talk and it's few family secrets they don't know and tell. Your father invested in some niggers as soon as he got here in order to show his contempt for the Yankees' invasion, but they're too new to have any of the family pride that the old ones used to have. Why an old family servant would rather die than tell any of the happenings at the big house, but these darkies of your father's have blown his business broadcast."

Walter shivered at the man's tone and his revelations.

In order not to alarm the house unduly they dismounted at the gate and left the private to lead the horses around to the stables while the sergeant went with Walter.

Their ring brought a servant to the door, who stood in white-eyed astonishment as he saw the young man, worn and haggard with anxiety and beside him, an officer in gray.

"W'y, w'y, gent'men, dis hyeah's a confede'ate house."

"Shut up and let us in. Make as little stir as possible, and bring my mother to the parlor. Sergeant, this will be a family meeting."

"You know my orders, sir."

"I do, and I am enough of a soldier not to want you to disobey them; but I prefer seeing my family alone. Examine the room where I shall talk with my mother, and have the places of egress guarded. I think the windows let out on a veranda."

"There may be more than one outlet, and I have not enough men to guard them if there is."

"You forget, sergeant," said Walter haughtily, "that I am a soldier and a gentleman."

"I'm not much of either yet," returned the non-commissioned officer calmly, "but I'm learning enough of a soldier's business to know how to obey orders."

"You are right," said the younger man blushing. "Come, let's examine the room together and see what dispositions we can make."

At this period, Private Wilkins came in from his errand. They stationed him outside and passed into the room. It was a large apartment, with three long windows, opening, as Walter had surmised, on the veranda.

"You see," pursued the sergeant, "it's just as I said. You have too many places by which to leave, though I do not doubt your honor."

"Let us see," said Walter going to the door. "Ah, this will serve you," and he held up a key. "Lock this door that shuts off one outlet. One of you patrol the veranda and the other hold the hall. Will that suit you?"

"Perfectly." And the sergeant proceeded to do as directed. He stationed Wilkins in the hall, and then as he was about to step out upon the veranda, turned, and on a sudden impulse, saluted the young private as if he were an officer.

He had hardly left the room, when Mrs. Stewart came rushing in.

"Walter, Walter, my boy!"

"Dear little mother."

"Oh, you are well, you are well, aren't you?"

"In body, yes, mother, but—but—am I in time?"

"Thank God, yes."

The young man bowed his head and the gesture itself, was a prayer of thanksgiving that God understood.

"I have so much that I want to say to you, mother, but take me to him at once. I am afraid that it will be too late. You shall have a talk with me afterwards." He put his arm affectionately about his mother's waist.

"Wait a moment, Walter," she said. "He is yet conscious. Oh, Walter, Walter, humor him, humor him in his dying moments. Promise, whatever he asks."

"Whatever he asks? Why, what can he ask?"

"Perhaps one great thing. Your father has not changed, even in the hands of death."

"I shall promise what I can without lying."

"If necessary, my son, lie, to ease your father's heart. Have I ever given you such advice before? Will you do it?"

He looked at her fondly for a moment, and then answered firmly, "I will lie, if need be. Take me to him."

They started out but Walter turned back to call the sergeant.

"I am going to my father's room," he said.

"I will come as far as the door," he said, "for the rest, I leave that to you. Go on."

As they passed up the broad steps, Mrs. Stewart asked in some agitation, "What does the presence of those soldiers mean?"

"Don't disturb yourself, mother, but I was taken on the way here after I had passed the reb—the Confederate lines, and I am a prisoner."

She grasped him by the arm. "A prisoner?" she gasped.

"Don't be alarmed," he went on soothingly, "I shall be paroled, the captain has as good as promised it, and then I shall be here with you."

"That is almost good," she replied, "and you will have less to promise."

The light was turned low in the sickroom, and a nurse glided out as they entered. Walter's sister passed out also, and in passing pressed his hand.

Mrs. Stewart left her son at the door and went forward to the bed, a shadowy, gliding form in the dim room.

"Here is Walter," she said softly.

The sick man opened his eyes, and said weakly, but with some of his old coldness, "Raise the light, and let me see him."

"Father!" the boy stood over the bed.

The eyes that even then death was glazing, grew brighter as the colonel looked upon his son, but the words that he whispered huskily were, "Thank God, he does not wear their uniform. Walter!"

The young man threw his arms about his father and held him close to his heaving breast. His eyes were tearless, but his bronzed face was pale and his throat throbbed convulsively. "Father, I am so sorry to have grieved you, so sorry."

"You're a Stewart," said the old man weakly, but dotingly. "They always were —they always were strong-headed. But you won't go back to them, will you, Walter? Will you? For your father's sake, for the sake of Virginia, you won't go back to the—Yankees?"

"I cannot lie to you, father, now," the filming eye formed a new light, and his mother started forward.

"What!"

"I could not go back to them if I would. I was taken on the way here, and am a prisoner in the hands of our own people."

The old man settled back with a glad sigh.

"This is very good," he said, "very good. They can never have your services again. Better a prisoner in the camp of our people—our people—you said, Walter, than a general of those—aliens. Now I am content."

"Would you not better rest now?" asked his son gently.

"Yes, yes, I will rest," and he relaxed again upon his pillow.

Walter was easing his arms from underneath the gray head, when the muscles of the dying man took on strength again. His eyes opened.

"Would you," he said almost fiercely, "would you go back to them again if you could?"

Walter cast one agonizing look at his mother's appealing eyes, then he answered firmly, "No, father, not if I could."

His father smiled. "I knew it," he murmured. "He is a Stewart, and a Stewart must come back to his own. Now I shall rest."

He sank into a soft slumber, and mother and son left the room on tiptoe.

"Come, you will go and see Emily now," said his mother.

"Let them come to my room," he said, "wherever you have placed me. We must make it as easy for Sergeant Davis as possible."

The morrow proved that the colonel had been right. He had rested, and the rest was one that should be eternally unbroken.

As soon as he found that the home was a place of death and mourning, the sergeant, be it said to his credit, relaxed some of his vigilance, and Walter was allowed to attend to the duties connected with his father's funeral with greater freedom. The same day, his parole was granted, and the house given over again to privacy.

In spite of a natural sorrow for his father's loss, Walter felt a sense of peace, even joy, at the reconciliation. The words, "Now I shall rest," rang in his head with soothing cadence. It was so much better this way than that his father should have gone from him in anger and reproach.

The joy Walter felt in coming back into the family circle proved how much his heart must have been hungering for it. Drawn by a strong enthusiasm for what he deemed the right, he had gone off into the wilderness to face death. But he had not ceased to look back with longing eyes towards the fleshpots of Egypt. Being back to them, he was not prone to question why he came. The fact in itself, was sufficiently pregnant of content. Somehow, he did not feel ashamed of the satisfaction he felt in having the parole solve a vexing problem. He had lied to his father, had he not, in saying that he would not go back if he could? And then, he began to quibble with himself. Had he lied, after all? Was it not merely the premature assertion of a condition of mind that was to be? Would he go back if he could? He was not sure. His father had called him a Stewart, and that meant much. It was sweet to be there, with his own family, in the great old place. Going to the window, his eyes swept the surrounding landscape with restful satisfaction.

There was the broad sweep of lawn, and across that, rugged against the sky, the dark row of outbuildings, the kitchen, the stables and the Negro cabins, and beyond that, the woods. It was fine and manorial, and appealed to the something in Walter which is in every Anglo-Saxon, the love of pomp and circumstance and power. After all, it was for this he had been dragged from the camp and from the hardships of war, and was it not a pleasant change? Fate had been kind to him. There were many young fellows who would envy him, so why should he repine?

While he was still in the midst of his meditations, his mother came into the room.

"Brooding again?" she said. "You must not do this, my son."

He blushed and raised his hand in protest, but his mother went on, "I know you were influenced by a strong principle, my son, a principle so deeply rooted that you were willing to give up everything for it, and you are longing to be back again. But yours are, after all, only the common fortunes of war."

The young man's face was burning, and all the thoughts that had just passed through his mind came surging back in an accusing flood. He saw that he had weakened on the side of his affections, and that for a little while he had put home and ease and mother-love before the cause for which he had once been so hot. His shame seethed in his face.

"You know what I told father," he said, "that I would not go back if I could?"

"Yes, yes, I know, and I understand what the falsehood cost you, but weighed against what it brought to your father and me, it seems justifiable. Why, Walter, don't you see that even a lie that softens a father's deathbed is a noble sacrifice?"

"I should feel the better if it were that way, but it is not a lie. It is coming to be true."

"Your heart is really coming over to the South?"

"Not to the South so much as to you and Emily and home and father's memory"

"Walter, Walter," she cried, embracing him, "this is nothing to hang your head about; this is true nobility!"

Her mother-love blinded her sight to his moral defection, but he saw and saw clearly, and was ashamed.

"It is strange," Mrs. Stewart mused, "how things have balanced. If the South has gained an adherent in you, the North has just taken one of Virginia's own sons."

"What do you mean?"

"The news came to us this morning that Nelson Etheridge has not returned, but has gone over to the Union lines."

"How do you know that?" cried Walter, starting up.

"We sent Caesar with the horse this morning."

"Oh, I wanted to take it over myself and thank Miss Etheridge in person."

"You will have many chances to thank her," said his mother. "She is a great friend of Emily's and is often here."

"I am very glad," he stammered, "that is, on Emily's account."

When his mother left him, he too, went from the room, and sought the room where his father lay. He drew back the cloth and looked at the calm face, as stern and white as a figure in marble. Even in death, the lips had found their old line of compression, and the chin had not lost its decision.

"Oh, my father," said Walter, "I am a weaker man than you, but I am more your son than I knew." He replaced the cloth and went sadly away.

The funeral of Colonel Stewart was a piteous affair. The remnants of the families about came to pay their respects to the dead. But mostly, they were women or old men. The army had taken the rest. The clergyman who conducted the services wore the gray under his gown, and as soon as his work was done, left his vestments and rode back to the regiment of which he was chaplain.

People looked askance at Walter or did not look at him at all. To them, he had the shame of being a Unionist on parole, but within him there was a greater shame —that he was neither with them nor against them.

Chapter 14

The Contrabands

IT WAS NOW THAT a new unpleasantness began to harass the already burdened people of Ohio. The decree of General Butler making all slaves who came into camp contraband of war, affected the Negroes not only in his immediate vicinity, but wherever there was a Union camp. Drunk with the dream of freedom, at the first intimation of immunity, they hastened to throw off their shackles and strike for the long-coveted liberty. Women, children, young, able-bodied men and the feeble and infirm, all hastened towards the Union lines. Thence, it was usually an easy matter, or at least, one possible of accomplishment, to work their way North to the free states.

Hardly a camp, hardly a column in which the officers were not reputed vigorously to oppose the admission of slaves but presented a strange and varied appearance. In the rear, but keeping close to their saviors always, straggled a lot of half-clad, eager Negroes of all ages and conditions, bearing every conceivable form of movable property—bags, bundles, bedclothes, cooking utensils, and even an occasional calf or sheep trailed along. Many, indeed, found employment as the servants of officers, where their traditional qualifications as cooks or valets came into full play. But for the most part, they simply hung on, worrying and embarrassing the soldiers with their importunities, sickening and dying from fatigue and exposure, and conducting themselves altogether, like the great, helpless, irresponsible children that they were.

To those, who only a few years ago, primed with the prejudices of their masters, had looked upon the Yankees as monsters, there had come a great change, and every man who wore the blue had become as God's own vicegerent. They had been told that the Yankees had horns, and many of them believed it, but on contact, the only horn that they had found was the horn of plenty, and their old faith in their masters' infallibility died.

They were not all a burden, though. In the gloom of the dark hours, their light-heartedness cheered on the march; their pranks, their hymns and their ditties made life and light. Through the still watches of the night, the lonely sentinel on his beat, heard their singing and sometimes he thought of home with a choking at his throat, and had a vision of a tender mother singing to the babe upon her breast, and he looked up to the stars, and was alone no more.

The poor blacks, wandering in the darkness of their ignorance were as frightened children in the night. They had lost faith in their masters, but it was not lost to them entire, only transferred to these new beings, who mastered them by the power of love. Is it any wonder that they shouted and sang, and that often their songs were "Out of Old Egypt," "De Promised Lan'," and "Go Down Moses"?

One of the principal songs they sang, ran thus, a low minor melody at first, then breaking in the improvisation into a joyous shout:

> "In Egypt I sang a moun'ful song,
>   Oh, Lawd, de life was ha'd;
> Dey said yo' bondage won't be long,
>   Oh, Lawd, de life was ha'd.
> Dey preached an' dey prayed, but de time went on,
>   Oh, Lawd, de life was ha'd;
> De night was black w'en dey talked of dawn,
>   Oh, Lawd, de life was ha'd:
> We t'ought 'twas day in de lightin' flash,
>   Oh, Lawd, de life was ha'd,
> But night come down wid de mastah's lash,
>   Oh, Lawd, de life was ha'd."

And, then, some clear voice would break into further improvisation,

> "But de Yankees come and dey set us free,
>   T'ank Gawd, hit's bettah now,
> De Yankee man is de man fu' me,
>   T'ank Gawd, hit's bettah now—
> He gi' me braid an' he gi' me meat,
>   T'ank Gawd, hit's bettah now,
> Eatin' nevah did seem so sweet,
>   T'ank Gawd, hit's bettah now."

For them it was better now, though they toiled and struggled and fell by the wayside. The abstract idea of freedom which they did not yet understand, had become a fetish to them. And over the burning sands, or through the winter's snow where they trudged with bleeding feet, they kept their stalwart faith in it. They were free at last, and being free, no evil thing could hurt them.

It was strange that most of them should not have become discouraged and gone back to the fleshpots still in Egypt. The Union officers did not understand these great children who flocked so insistently about their heels. Some were harsh to them, and others who would have been kind, did not know how. But they staid on and on, clinging to the garments of the army, going from camp to camp, until they swept like a plague of locusts into some Northern town.

Ohio, placed as she was, just on the border of the slave territory, was getting more than her share of this unwelcome population, and her white citizens soon began to chafe at it. Was their free soil to become the haven for escaped Negroes? Was this to be the stopping ground for every runaway black from the South? Would they not become a menace to the public safety? Would they not become a public charge and sorely strain that generosity that was needed to encourage and aid the soldiers in the field? These and a thousand such conjectures and questions were rife about the hapless blacks. The whole gamut of argument that had been used in '49, '50 and '51 was run again. The menace of Maryland with her free Negroes was again held we up. The cry rose for the enforcement of the law for the restriction of emancipated Negroes, while others went to the extreme of crying for the expulsion of all blacks, from the state.

Since 1829, there had been a gradual change for the better in the attitude of Ohio towards her colored citizens, but now, all over the state, and especially in the southern counties and towns there had come a sudden revulsion of feeling, and the people rose generally against the possibility of being overwhelmed by an influx of runaway slaves. Their temper grew and ominous mutterings were heard on every side. The first great outburst of popular wrath came when Negro men began offering themselves for military service, and some extremists urged the policy of accepting them.

"Take them," said the extremists, "and you break the backbone of the South's power. While the Southern men are in the field, fighting against the government their Negro slaves are at home raising supplies for them, and caring for their families. When we enlist them, whom have they to leave for such duties?"

But all the North held up its hands and cried, "What, put black men beside our boys to fight? Let slaves share with them the honor and glory of military service? Never!"

The army itself hurled back its protest, "We are fighting for the Union; we are not fighting for niggers, and we will not fight with them."

From none of the states came a more pronounced refusal than from Ohio. She had set her face against men of color. What wonder then, that their coming into the state aroused all her antagonistic blood? Here, for the time, all party lines fell away, and all the people were united in one cause—resistance to the invasion of the black horde. It was at this time that Butler's proclamation struck through the turmoil like a thunderbolt, and the word "Contraband" became a menace to the whites and a reproach to the blacks.

The free blacks of Dorbury themselves, took it up, and even before they could pronounce the word that disgusted them, they were fighting their unfortunate brothers of the South as vigorously as their white neighbors. "Contraband" became the fighting banter for black people in Ohio. But the stream kept pouring in. In spite of resistance, abuse and oppression, there was a certain calm determination about these fugitive slaves that was of the stuff that made the Puritans. As far North as Oberlin and Cleveland, they did not often make their way. If it was their intention to stop in Ohio at all, they usually ended their journey at the more Southern towns. While the spirit in the Northern towns was calmer, it was, perhaps, just as well that they were not overrun. In Cleveland, especially, numerous masters of the south, averse to making slaves of their own offspring, had colonized their discarded Negro mistresses and their illegitimate offspring, and these people, blinded by God knows what idea of their own position, in the eyes of the world, had made an aristocracy of their own shame.

In Dorbury, the Negro aristocracy was not one founded upon mixed blood, but upon free birth or manumission before the war. Even the church, whose broad wings are supposed to cover all sorts and conditions of men, turned its face against the poor children of a later bondage.

After much difficulty, the Negro contingent in Dorbury had succeeded in establishing a small house of worship in an isolated section known as "the commons." Here, according to their own views, they met Sunday after Sunday to give praise and adoration to the God whom they, as well as the whites, claimed as theirs, and hither, impelled by the religious instincts of their race, came the contrabands on reaching the town. But were they received with open arms? No, the God that fostered black and white alike, rich and poor, was not known to father these poor fugitives, so lately out of bondage. The holy portals were closed in their faces, and dark skinned pastors, not yet able to put the "H" in the educational shibboleth, drew aside their robes as they passed them.

Opposition was even expressed to their fellowship with the Christian body. It reached its height when, on a memorable Sunday—a quarterly meeting day in fact, three families of the despised, presented themselves for membership in the Wesleyan chapel. The spirit had been running high that day, and there had been much shouting and praising the Lord for his goodness. But at this act of innocent audacity, the whole tone of the meeting changed. From violent joy, it became one of equally violent anger and contempt. These outcast families seeking God, had stepped upon the purple robes of these black aristocrats, and they were as one for defiance.

One aged woman, trembling with anger and religious excitement, tottered up, and, starting for the door, hurled this brief condemnation of the culprits who dared desire membership in her church: "W'y, befo' I'd see dis chu'ch, dis chu'ch dat we free people built give up to dese conterbands, I'd see hit to' down, brick by brick."

She hurried down the stairs, and a number followed her. But some stayed to remonstrate with the unreasoning contrabands. They were told to form a church of their own and to worship together.

"But," said their spokesman, who had preached down on the plantation, "whyn't we jes' ez well wo'ship wid you? We's all colo'ed togethah."

The pastor tried in vain to show them the difference between people who had been freed three or four years before and those just made free, but somehow, the contraband and none of his company could see it, and the meeting was broken up. The rejected Christians, seeking their poor shanties in amazement, and the aristocrats gathering to talk among themselves over the invasion of their temple.

With both white and black against them, it could not be long before the bad feeling against these poor people must break out into open attack. Theirs was a helpless condition, but they were not entirely alone. In all the town, they had no stronger friend than Stephen Van Doren. A Southerner by birth and education, he understood these people, who had for two centuries been the particular wards of the South. While he had no faith in the ultimate success of the Union arms, and believed that all these blacks must eventually go back into slavery whence they had come, yet he reasoned that they were there, and such being the case, all that was possible, ought to be done for them.

The Negroes were quick to recognize a friend, and his house soon became the court to which they took all their grievances. He had been keeping indoors, but now he began to circulate among his Southern friends, and to do what he could to help his poor protégés.

It was then that the first inklings of a contemplated attack upon them came to his ears. Some of the citizens of Dorbury, inspired by the public spirit which barroom speeches arouse, had determined to rise and throw off the stigma of Negro invasion. The embers of the people's passions had long smouldered, and when a pseudo-politician in the glow of drink had advised them to rise and drive the black plague beyond their borders, they had determined to do so.

The conduct of the whole matter had been put into the hands of Raymond Stothard, for the politician declined to lead such an assault, upon the plea that it was hardly the proper thing for a man who aspired to the legislature.

Stothard was chosen, first, because he was the brother of the prosecuting attorney, which would give the movement prestige, and next, because he was capable of doing anything when he was drunk. He usually was drunk or becoming so. He was drunk when he made the speech which instantly made him the leader of the aggressive movement.

"Gen'lemen," he said, "you all know me, and you know that I ain't the man to try to lead you into an unjust fight, now am I?" He was almost plaintive and the crowd about him cried, "No, no!"

"Thank you," he went on, swaying at his table. "Thanks, I'm glad to see that you per—preciate my motives. You all know my brother, he's a straight—straight man, ain't he? You all know Philip Stothard. Now I'm a peaceable man, I am. But tonight, I say our rights and liberties are being invaded, that's what they are. All the niggers in the South are crowding in on us, and pretty soon, we won't have a place to lay our heads. They'll undercharge the laborer and drive him out of house and home. They will live on leavings, and the men who are eating white bread and butter will have to get down to the level of these black hounds.

"I don't like 'em, anyhow. None of us like 'em. The whole war is on their account. If it hadn't been for them, we'd have been friends with the South today, but they've estranged us from our brothers, rent the country asunder, and now they're coming up here to crowd us out of our towns. Gentlemen, I won't say any more. It shall never be said that Ray Stothard was instrumental in beginning a revolt against law and order. My brother's prosecuting attorney, you know, and we stand for the integrity of the law. But if I had my way, I'd take force, and clear this town of every nigger in it. Gentlemen, drink with me."

His final remark was the most eloquent plea he could have made. The gentlemen drank with Mr. Stothard and voted his plan for saving their homes and workshops a good one.

One man in passing had heard the sound of speechmaking within, and out of idle curiosity had paused at the saloon door in time to hear Stothard's stirring remarks. Stephen Van Doren listened with horror to what the drunken rowdy proposed, and then went with all speed to his brother.

"You're too sensible a man, Van Doren," said the prosecuting attorney, "to believe that I have anything to do with this matter or would countenance it. But I can do nothing whatever with this brother of mine; there is only one thing to do, and that is to warn the Negroes."

"They are not used to fighting for themselves. They would be as helpless as children and could be killed like sheep in a pen."

"They have their freedom, taken as you and I both believe, illegally, let them rise to the occasion which liberty demands," and so the lawyer dismissed the subject, although Van Doren gave back the answer that what these blacks had to meet was not the result of liberty, but the mockery of it.

Leaving Philip Stothard's house, Stephen Van Doren went his way, torn between conflicting opinions as to his duty. Would he be proving a traitor to his fellow-citizens if he told the Negroes of the designs against them? But were these men of the lowest social stratum, loafers, ignoramuses and fanatics his fellow-citizens? Was it not right that these poor fellows, slaves as they had been, and would be again doubtless, should be allowed the chance of defending themselves against assault? He argued with himself long and deeply that night, and in the end he decided that the blacks must be warned. He did not know when the attack would take place. Indeed, he felt sure that it would wait upon inspiration and opportunity, but the intended victims could be put upon their guard and then be left to look out themselves. He could do no more. Perhaps he had already done too much.

On the morrow, he saw some of the blacks, and after cautioning them to secrecy as to what they should hear, told them of their danger. They heard him with horror and lamentation. They were bitterly disappointed. Was this the freedom for which they had toiled? Was this the welcome they received from a free state? They already knew how the church had greeted them. But they were the more shocked because they found out for the first time that politics could be as hard as religion.

One advantage which the Negroes were to have was that in the sudden passion against their race the whites made no distinction as to bond or free, manumitted or contraband. This, of necessity, drew them all together, and they grew closer to each other in sympathy than they had yet known.

The drawing together was not one of spirit only, but of fact. They began to have meetings at night after the warning, and a code of signals was arranged to call all of them together at the first sign of danger.

Meanwhile, Stothard and his confederates, believing that all their workings had been done in profoundest secrecy, only waited an opportunity to strike effectively and finally.

The leader's first open act occurred one day when he seemed to have found an audience of sympathizers. He was strolling along busy with his usual employment of doing nothing, when he noticed a crowd gathered at a point upon the street that led from the railway station. He sauntered towards it, but quickened his pace when he found that the center of the group was a small family of black folk who had just arrived from some place south of the river. There were a father and mother, both verging on old age, a stalwart, strong-limbed son, apparently about twenty, and two younger children. They were all ragged, barefoot and unkempt. They had paused to inquire the way to the Negro portion of the town, and immediately the people, some with animosity, some with amusement, had gathered around them.

"What's all this?" asked the attorney's brother, as he reached the group. None of the whites vouchsafed him an answer, and he turned his attention to the Negroes.

"More niggers," he exclaimed. "Why in hell don't you people stay where you belong?"

The blacks eyed him in silence.

"Why don't you answer when I talk to you?" He took a step forward, and the outcasts cowered before him, all save the son. He did not move a step and there was a light in his eye that was not good to see. It was the glare of an animal brought to bay. Stothard saw it and advanced no further, but went on.

"If I had you across the line, I'd teach you manners." The old woman began to cry.

"We come up hyeah," said the young Negro, "'cause we hyeahed it was a free state."

"It's free for white people, not for niggers."

"We hyeahed it was free fu' evahbody, dat's de reason we come, me an' mammy an' pappy an' de chillun. We ain't a bothahin' nobody. We jes' wants to fin' some of ouah own people."

"There's enough of your people here now, and too many, and we don't want any more. You'd better go back where you come from."

"We cain't go back thaih. Hit's been a long ways a comin', an' we's 'bout wo' out."

"That's none of our business; back you go. Gentlemen, unless we put our foot down now, we shall be overrun by these people. I call you to act now. Turn them back at the portals of the city. Ohio as a state and Dorbury as a town does not want these vagabonds."

Unseen by Stothard, another man attracted by the gathering had joined the crowd, and now his voice broke the silence. "Who made you, Ray Stothard, the spokesman for the people of Ohio?"

The aristocratic loafer turned to meet the eye of Stephen Van Doren, and his face went red in a second.

"I don't know what right you've got to speak, Van Doren, you've done everything you could to hurt the Union."

"It is to the Union's greatest discredit that it has such men as you on its side."

"So you're in favor of letting the niggers overrun the town?"

"I'm in favor of fair play, and I intend to help these people find their fellows."

"Humph, what are you anyhow? First a copperhead, then a rebel, then the champion of contrabands. You're neither fish, flesh, fowl nor good red herring."

"Whatever I may be, I'm not a conspirator." Stothard blanched at the word. "Nor," went on the old man, "am I a barroom orator and leader of ruffians. Come, boys," he said addressing the Negroes, and they grinned broadly and hopefully at the familiar conduct and manner of address of the South which they knew and loved. Away they went behind Van Doren.

"Go on, Steve Van Doren," Stothard crowed after the old man like a vanquished cock. "But you may have more work to do before you get through with your nigger pets."

"All right," was the sturdy answer. "Whenever you and your hounds come for me, you'll find me waiting, and by heaven, you'll leave me weightier men by a few ounces than you've ever been before."

The younger man attempted to raise a jeer as the other man passed down the street. But the crowd refused to join him. There was something too majestic in the carriage of the old copperhead. He commanded an inevitable, if reluctant respect. The same independent habit of thought and sturdy disregard of consequences that made him a copperhead, made him a friend to these poor helpless blacks.

Stothard, however, was not done. He was inflamed with anger at his defeat and the shame put upon him. He hurriedly left the crowd, and went at once to the rendezvous of his confederates. All that day and night he harangued them as they came in one by one, setting before them the alleged dangers of the case, and painting the affair of the afternoon in lurid colors. By midnight, drunken men who mistook intoxication for patriotism, talked solemnly to each other of the "Black invasion," and shook hands in the unity of determination to resent this attack upon the dignity of the state.

All the next day there was an ominous quiet in Dorbury. Men who had no other occupation than lounging about the courthouse corner and in the barrooms were not to be seen. There were no violent harangues in the livery stables and groceries. Mr. Raymond Stothard was not out.

About dusk the clans began to gather. One by one they came from their holes and hiding-places and made their way to the rendezvous. Over their drinks, they talked in whispers and the gaslight flared on drawn, swollen, terrible faces. Their general had found the wherewithal to buy liquor and he plied them well.

Meanwhile on old McLean Street, where stood the house of one of Dorbury's free black citizens another gathering equally silent, equally stealthy and determined was taking place. The signal had gone forth, the warning had been received and free Negro and contraband were drawing together for mutual protection. Not a word was spoken among them. It was not the time for talk. But they huddled together in the half-lit room and only their hard, labored breathing broke the silence. To the freemen, it meant the maintenance of all that they had won by quiet industry. To the contrabands, it meant the life or death of all their hopes of manhood. Now all artificial lines were broken down, and all of them were brothers by the tie of necessity. Contraband and the man who a few days ago had looked down upon him with supreme contempt, now pressed shoulder to shoulder a common grayness in their faces, the same black dread in their hearts. In the back room sick with fear, waited the women and children. Upon the issue of the night depended all that they had prayed for. Was it to be peace and home or exile and slavery? Their mother hearts yearned over the children who clustered helpless about their feet. "If not for us, God, for these, our little ones," they prayed. Their minds went back to the plantation, its pleasures and its pains. They remembered all. There had been the dances and the frolics, and the meetings, but these paled into insignificance before the memory of the field, the overseer and the lash. Often, oh, too often, they had bared their backs to the cruel thongs. Day by day they had toiled and sweated under the relentless sun. But must these, the products of their poor bodies, do likewise? Must they too, toil without respite, and labor without reward? They clasped their children in their arms with a hopelessness that was almost aggression.

The little black babies that night did not know why their mothers hugged them with such terrible intensity or hushed them with such fierce tenderness when they cried.

It was nearly midnight when the whisper ran round the circle in the front room, "They are coming, they are coming!" and the men drew themselves closer together. The sound of the shuffling of many feet and the noisy song of a drunken mob awoke the echoes of the quiet street. Then, of a sudden, the songs ceased as if some authoritative voice had compelled silence. Nearer and nearer moved the feet, softer now, but with drunken uncertainty. They paused at the gate. The lock clicked. The men within the room were tense as bended steel. Then came a thunderous knock at the door. No answer.

There was a pause, and apparently a silent conference. The rioters had sought several other suspected houses, the chapel among them, and found them empty. Here then, was the place which they had definitely settled as the Negroes' stronghold.

"Open in the name of the law," came a voice.

The blacks huddled closer together. Then came a blow upon the door as from the stock of a gun.

"Gently," said the voice, "gently." But the spirit of violence having once been given rein could not be controlled, and blow after blow rained upon the none too strong door, until it yielded and fell in with a crash. But here, the mob found themselves confronted by a surprise. Instead of a cowering crowd of helpless men, they found themselves confronted by a solid black wall of desperate men who stood their ground and fought like soldiers. At first, it was fist, stave, club and the swift, silent knife, and only the gasp of forced breath and the groan of some fallen man told that the terrible fight went on. Then a solitary shot rang out, and the fusillade began. The blacks began to retreat, because they had few weapons, putting their women-folks behind them. Gradually, the white horde poured into the room and filled it.

"Now, boys," said Stothard's voice from the rear, "rush them!" and he sprang forward. But a black face confronted him, its features distorted and its eyes blazing. It was the face of the contraband boy whom he had abused the day before. A knife flashed in the dim light, and in a moment more was buried in the leader's heart. The shriek, half of fear, half of surprise which was on his lips, died there, and he fell forward with a groan, while the black man sped from the room. The wild-eyed boy who went out into the night to be lost forever, killed Stothard, not because he was fighting for a principle, but because the white man had made his mother cry the day before. His ideas were still primitive.

The rout of the Negroes was now complete, and they fled in all directions. Some ran away, only to return when the storm had passed; others, terrified by the horror of the night, went, never to return, and their homes are occupied in Dorbury today by the men who drove them from them.

The whites, too, had had enough, and their leader being killed, they slunk away with his body into the night which befriended them.

Chapter 15

License or Liberty

IN THE DAYS THAT ensued after the mustering out of Tom's regiment neither he nor Dorbury had time for idleness. The events attending the conflict both in the field and at home had followed each other too swiftly for that. Tom had found military service under the government in a capacity that gave him larger experience in the world of men. His letters had given his father exceeding joy and Mary and Nannie were inordinately proud of him. His messages to them were read over and over again as the girls prepared themselves for sleep or sat half-robed upon their bedsides.

The gossips had still spared the brother the story of the breaking up of his home and he went on with his work happy in his unconsciousness. When the final reorganization of the First took place in November, he relinquished his other duties and joined his comrades at Louisville, whence they set out on their journey further South.

In the meantime, Dorbury had continued to seethe as before, with the conflicting elements within its narrow borders. Patriotism and prejudice ran riot side by side, and it was a hard race between them. One set of men talked of the glory of righteous war, while another deplored the shedding of fraternal blood. The war Republicans hurled invectives at the peace advocates, and the latter hurled back invectives and reproaches.

Before the First went back into the field an incident occurred which showed the temper of both parties. A meeting was being held in the square in front of the courthouse. Its object was to protest against what the opponents of the war called the attempted coercion of free citizens. Mr. Vallandigham, whose position, both as a prominent citizen and former congressman gave weight to whatever he said, had spoken and the hearts of his hearers were inflamed with bitterness. Another speaker, half-hearted and little trusted rose to address the assembly. He was a fiery demagogue and depended for his influence upon his power to work upon the passions of the lower element. His audience knew this. He knew it, and for an instant, paused in embarrassment.

Just at that moment, "Nigger Ed" strolled up and joined the crowd. The eye of the orator took him in, and lighted with sudden inspiration. Here was all the text he needed. Raising his tall, spare form, he pointed in silence until every face was turned upon the Negro. Then he said, "Gentlemen, it is for such as that and worse that you are shedding your brothers' blood." Without another word, he sat down. It was the most convincing speech he had ever made. The unhappy advent of the Negro had put a power into the words of a man who otherwise would have been impotent. It was the occasion and the man to take advantage of it. It may have been clap-trap. But in the heated spirit of the time, it was a shot that went straight to the mark. The crowd began to murmur and then broke into hisses and jeers. Rude jests with more of anger than humor in them were bandied back and forth.

One side was furious that blood should be spilled for such as the Negro bell-ringer, while the other was equally incensed at being accused of championing his cause.

"Nigger-stealers! Abolitionists!" shouted one.

"Copperheads!" shouted the other, while some of them tried fruitlessly to explain that they had no interest in niggers.

"He even wears your army cap!" someone cried. "Why don't you give him a gun?"

The stentorian voice of Bradford Waters rose over the storm. "Your friends, the rebels," he said, "have got the niggers digging trenches, and tilling the fields at home to help them in food."

"Ah, that's their business," was the reply.

"I don't know that a gun is any better than a spade."

Back and forth the controversy raged, each party growing hotter and hotter. Negro Ed stood transfixed at the tempest he had raised. He looked from face to face but in none of them found a friend. Both sides hated him and his people. He was like a shuttlecock. He was a reproach to one and an insult to the other.

"Gent'men, gent'men," he began to stammer to the men about him who were hustling him.

"Knock him down, he's been serving the men who fought our brothers."

"Tear off his cap, the black hound, it's the same our soldiers wear."

"Kill him; if it wasn't for his kind, we'd have had no trouble!"

"What's he doing here, anyhow? This is a white man's Union. Down with niggers!"

And so the bewildered black man was like to be roughly handled by both parties, but that an opportune interruption occurred. The gravel sounded sharp and harsh and someone was speaking.

"Let Ed alone," the speaker said. "He has done nothing to you. He has rung our bells, followed our fires, amused our children and always been harmless."

The crowd began to remember that all this was true.

"He is not his people, nor the father of them. The trouble is not with him but with us. It's not without, it's within. It's not what he is but what we believe."

Stephen Van Doren's voice had arrested the activities of the mob and they gave him absolute attention. In the respite, the Negro, glad of his release, slipped away with the insulted cap in his hand. What he felt is hardly worth recording. He was so near the animal in the estimation of his fellows (perhaps too near in reality) that he could be presumed to have really few mental impressions. He was frightened, yes. He was hurt, too. But no one would have given him credit for that much of human feeling. They had kicked a dog and the dog had gone away. That was all. Yet Ed was not all the dog. His feeling was that of a child who has tried to be good and been misunderstood. He should not have felt so, though, for he knew Dorbury and the times by an instinct that was truer than conscious analysis, and he should have known, if he did not, that the people who mistreated him, were not sane and accountable. But the under dog does not stop to philosophize about his position. So Ed went his way in anger and in sorrow.

After Van Doren's interruption, the meeting went on in a somewhat more moderate strain, though the speeches that were made were bitter enough. A new, but vigorous and efficient governor was in the chair, and at times the people chafed under the enforcement of measures which, in a state of war, he deemed necessary. No great disaster had yet come to their own troops to unite the people in one compact body, or to make them look farther than themselves or their fancied personal grievances. The sight of the wounded and the news of the dead had net yet thrilled them into the spirit for self-sacrifice. This was to come later. It was to come when the soil of the state was threatened by hostile invasion; when Pittsburg Landing had told its bloody story, and the gloom of death hung over their homes.

But now all was different. After the first enthusiasm for war had passed, a reaction had set in. Recruiting went on slowly, while the citizens looked on with but languid interest. On the other hand, they flamed with anger at every hint that their personal rights were being trampled on. When men, lacking both honor and loyalty, wrote seditious letters; when others, more earnest than prudent, talked in the public highways or harangued from platforms, it was all free speech, the fetish so dear to American worshippers, and they resented any attempt to restrain or abridge it.

A man might live and work under the flag whose soldiers he counseled to desert. That was all within his private right. Another might assail the motives and powers of the government under which he lived, sneer at its chief executive, and pour out the vials of his wrath against the unholy war which the Union was waging, and still, it was only his right. Any attempt to check disaffection within its borders was construed into coercion. Where now and then, some too bold speaker was arrested by the authorities, war Democrat, and peace Democrat united in denouncing the act as high-handed and unwarranted, and Republican joined with them or was silent.

Upon one thing they were all united, and that was their hatred and disdain for the hapless race which had caused the war. Upon its shoulders fell all the resentment and each individual stood for his race. If their boys suffered hardships in the field, they felt that in some manner they avenged them by firing a Negro's home or chasing him along the dark streets as he made his way home from church. It became an act of patriotism to push a black woman from the sidewalks.

It only needed the knowledge that free men of color had offered their services to the state to bring out a storm of invective and abuse against the "impudent niggers." There were some who expressed fear that the governor might yield to their plea, and threatened if he did, that they would call their sons and brothers from the army, and resent the insult by withholding all aid from the Union arms. But they need have had no fear of their governor. Strong as he was and independent, he was too wise a man not to know and to respect the trend of popular sentiment, and he heard with unyielding heart the prayer of the Negroes to be put in the blue. But the time did come when the despised race was emancipated and they were accepted in the field as something other than scullions. The time came, yes, but this governor was not one of the men who helped to hasten it. It may have been his personal feeling, rather than his acquiescence to the will of the people that prompted his reply to the Massachusetts recruiting agent. The New England commonwealth was recruiting her black regiments and was drawing men of color from every state. When the chief executive of Ohio was consulted, he was so far from objecting to the use of his Negroes by another state that he expressed himself to the effect that he would be glad if they would take "every damned nigger out of the state." It may have been irritation at the anxiety and annoyance that this unwelcome population had caused the good governor which brought forth this strong expression. Whether it was this or not, the fact remains that many black men of Ohio went into the Massachusetts regiments, and when they had made for themselves a record that shamed contempt, it was to that state that popular belief gave the honor of their deeds.

This forecasting of events would be entirely out of place but that it serves in some manner to show the spirit of the times in a loyal and non-slaveholding state at a crucial moment of the nation's life; it was a moment when only a spark was needed to light the whole magazine of discontent and blow doubt and vacillation into a conflagration of disloyalty.

The spark was near being supplied on a Monday night in May. Upon the flint of Dorbury's public pride and prejudice the blow was struck and for a time the flash seemed imminent. For a long time a brave and rugged citizen of the little town, a man having the courage of his convictions and deeply trusted by his fellow-men, had been outspoken in his denunciation of the war. Wherever he was, he did not fear to express his belief in its illegality and unrighteousness. He was a strong man and an earnest one, and in his strength and earnestness lay his power over his fellow-men. He had represented them in Congress and he had done well. They believed in him, and now when he dared to say of the nation struggling for its very life that it was wrong, he found many followers, though some, like Bradford Waters, had already fallen from Vallandigham's side. For a while, he went his way unmolested, until one speech, a thought too bold in expression, brought down upon him the wrath—a wrath rather restraining than vindictive—of the government.

It was near midnight when a small company of soldiers from Cincinnati went to the door of Vallandigham's Dorbury home. The inmates of the house were abed, and all was darkness and silence. There was no reply to the thunderous summons on the panels, some inkling of the object of this midnight visit having leaked out or been suspected. The summons was repeated and while the men talked in low whispers below, a head was put out of an upstairs window and a voice called aloud some apparently meaningless words, which, however, were construed into a signal for aid. From this time, the soldiers delayed no longer, for in the present state of feeling the approach of reinforcements to those within would possibly result in bloodshed. This they were anxious to avoid, so making their way into the house they went from room to room, frequently having to break open locked and barred doors until they found the object of their search, and in spite of threat and protest, hurried away with him to a waiting train.

A small crowd collected, and followed the soldiers to the station, but with the exception of a stone occasionally hurled, it confined itself to threats and abuse.

"This will be heard from," said one.

"It will do more to make Ohio fight against the war than anything else."

"Kidnappers! kidnappers!" was the cry.

On the morrow the excitement in Dorbury was intense, but history has dealt sufficiently with all that was done then, with the speeches that were made, the bombastic letters that were written—the damage that was inflicted upon private property.

The town, iron-clad in its personal pride, gave itself up to an orgy of disloyalty. A tempest in a teapot, someone will say. But the spirit that raged in the teapot showed the temper of the larger cauldron which seethed over the same fire.

"What do you think of this later bit of work?" asked Davies on the way to the office the morning after the arrest.

"I think what I have always thought, that whatever is good for the Union is right." But his tone was not so assured as usual.

"You used to think a great deal of Vallandigham, though."

"In such a time as this, I have no time for personal feelings. I have said that before."

"Yes, it seems about true, we all seem to have taken leave of our senses and to have suspended the operations both of our country's constitution and of our natural affections."

"It is a strange time and we must change with the times."

"It is a horrible, a fanatical time, and I shall thank God when it is over, however the end may come, through Union or peaceful separation."

"I would rather see the country drenched in blood than the latter."

"Waters," said Davies slowly, as if the light were just dawning upon him, "I'm afraid you're a fanatic, I'm afraid you're a fanatic."

But Waters went on moodily and did not reply.

Chapter 16

Dolly and Walter

DOWN THERE IN VIRGINIA, where Walter had now settled into staying with a certain self-satisfaction, the tides of war flowed with vigor but did not reach and submerge the house where he kept the even tenor of his days. There were, of course, midnight visits at times from the soldiers of both sides. But the place enjoyed a peculiar exemption from molestation by either Confederate or Unionist. To the one, it was the home of old Colonel Stewart, an ardent Southerner. To the others, it was the place of abode of a paroled Union prisoner. Walter's position was anomalous, and although he was forced into it, he felt keenly that he was playing a double role. He no longer yearned to be with the Northern forces, but would it not be foolish to proclaim his defection from the housetops? The Southern soldiers and his neighbors looked upon him as a Unionist chafing at restraint, and they laughed at him for a caged bantam. Had their surmises been true, he would have scorned their laughter, but as it was, it cut him like a whip, because to his shame, what they laughed at, did not exist. Nor could he tell them this. They would have thought even less of him as a renegade who changed his allegiance and views under the stress of imprisonment.

Now and then, rather too frequently than he cared to own, he felt a thrill of envy for Nelson Etheridge, who had flung himself body and soul into the Union cause, and from whom he heard occasionally when he rode over to see Miss Etheridge, or when she and his sister Emily exchanged visits. "Here's a man for you," he would say to himself. "One who has not only dared, but continues to dare, one who, placed as I am placed, would feel the galling bonds of his restraint and do something besides feel ridiculously comfortable."

Perhaps it was because he was so young—and youth takes itself seriously, being in its own eyes either God or devil, hero or craven—that Walter was so hard upon his own failings. Sometimes, however, the truth that his position was not of his own seeking, forced itself upon his mind. But unwilling to accept this excuse, he questioned himself if he were not glad that things had turned out as they had. To this he must answer yes, and so he fell again to cursing his own complacency.

It is not to be supposed, however, that he lived constantly in a state of self-condemnation. Other moods were frequent and lasting. It took him a very short time to fall into the ways of a gentleman farmer, and he took a boyish pleasure in directing the work of the Negroes about the place. His moments of greatest happiness were when he was riding about the fields on some duty or other, and he would be joined by Emily or Miss Etheridge. But his greatest moments of depression would follow when he saw, or thought he saw, a question or a reproach in the girl's eyes.

Since his arrival at his father's house, he had come to see more and more of this radiant Southern beauty, and a frank friendship had grown up between them. Friendship, he called it, for cherishing in his heart the memory of his regard for Nannie, he did not dream that love could touch him. But slowly and reluctantly, he began to compare the image in his heart with the fair girl at his side and the image suffered. Finally, he began to say that Nannie had appealed strongly to his boyish fancy, while this woman reached his maturer manhood. In spite of his self-questionings, Walter failed to see the humor implied in the fact that without any great moral, mental or spiritual cataclysm, this maturer manhood had come to him in a very short time after he had looked into Dolly's gray eyes.

She often rallied him about their first romantic meeting, and she would laugh the most musical of laughs as he told her about his trepidation as he approached the house. When she forgot herself, and was merry among friends, she had the habit of falling into the soft-Southern manner of speech.

"It's right down mean," she said to Walter in one of her bantering moods, "that you didn't let a body know you were coming. I reckon you and my brother Nelson would have had a mighty nice time together, but you were entirely too startling."

"If I had known that I was going to find friends behind those doors," he bent his gaze tenderly upon her, "I should have acted differently, knocked easily, or roared me as gently as a sucking dove."

"Poor Nelson, I don't reckon many folks would have stayed on and dared capture like he did; but Nelson always was such a daring boy."

Walter winced. He thought he saw the question in her eyes, and something veiled in what she said.

Did she despise him after all, and only give him the semblance of friendship for his sister's sake? The thought made him miserable, although he never stopped to tell himself what logical reason there was for his being miserable, if the girl whom he had known but a few weeks did despise him.

"The Union has gained a gallant man in your brother," he said, because his head was in a tumult, and he could not say anything else. She did not recognize the commonplaceness of his remark, however. It was praise for her brother, and so, sublime.

"Oh, I wish you could have known him," she went on. "You'd have been sure to love him. Don't you know," she said, with a sudden impulse, "since I've known you, I've always thought of you and him in the same company, marching and fighting together. I don't care in what uniform, blue or gray. There, there, now," she added, gravely, "I've made you feel bad, but don't let's think of it. Yours is the fortune of war, just as whatever happens to him will be."

Walter was pale from forehead to lips and it was the knowledge of this that checked the girl with the belief that she had pained him by touching the subject of his detention.

"I'm afraid you're not a very good Unionist," said the young man somewhat recovering himself.

"I'm a woman, Mr. Stewart, and I reckon you're too young to know just what that implies. I'm in favor of the Union, because Nelson's fighting for it, and he wouldn't do anything that he didn't think was right. But I am a southern girl, and I love the South. Now what am I going to do? You don't know, though, for it's only women who let their affections run against principle."

He gave her a quick, suspicious glance. She was unconscious. He was on the rack.

"It isn't only women," he said.

"You only say that to be polite, and because it's so different with you, but I know better."

He rose quickly and on the plea of some obligation moved away, leaving her to Emily's company and conversation.

The rest of the day was a trying time for Walter. It was now unmistakable. Dolly Etheridge had seen through him, had seen his weakness and his defection, and in her contempt for him delighted to stab him with her quiet sarcasm. What a thing he must be to call forth the girl's disgust. How she must look down upon him when she compared him with her brother, such a brother; and in fancy, he saw Nelson Etheridge sweeping the enemy before him to the huzzas of a great nation. Well, anyway, Dolly could not think less of him than he thought of himself.

He would rather not have seen her any more that night. But he had promised to go with Emily to take her home. He appeared at supper with the best grace possible, and when it was over, joined the girls for the ride in the moonlight. It would have been pleasant to him, this cantering by Dolly's side, with the moon, a silver globe above them, and the scent of magnolias coming sweetly to their senses, but that his mind was sadly busy with what she must be thinking of him. He kept a moody silence while the girls chattered on. Sometimes, even, in his desperation, he thought of violating his parole, but his face grew hot with shame, and the thought went as quickly as it came.

Dolly and Emily, because they both believed Walter immersed in sad thoughts, respected his silence, and when he had helped the girl alight at her door, and given the horse to a black servant aroused from somewhere, the former gave him her hand with a little sympathetic pressure that made his heart leap. But then, the next moment he was saying, "Bah, she is only sorry for having stabbed me so cruelly, but the reason for the stabbing remains."

As they turned their horses homeward again, Walter seemed in no better mood for talking than before. But the moonlight and the sweetness of the soft night seemed to have got into his sister's tongue. She drew her horse close to her brother's and laid her hand gently on his.

"I'm afraid you're not well, tonight, Walter. What's the matter?"

"Oh, nothing, nothing. I'm really very well."

"But you have been so silent, and I really believe Dolly expected you to talk to her."

"I hardly think she could have cared much, either one way or the other," he said bitterly.

"If you can say that, you know very little about Dolly, or in fact, about women at all. You must know that she likes you, and likes you very well."

"I don't believe it," said Walter doggedly, but something he did just at the moment to the horse he was riding, made her arch her neck and step out as daintily as a lady.

"But she does like you, and if she didn't, you would soon know it. She's very peculiar and as open as the day. She can never conceal her thoughts and feelings. Some people call it a fault, but I call it a virtue."

"One would think at times that she was sarcastic or spoke under a veil." He was making a great effort to be indifferent, but the bridle in his hand grew tense.

"Why, she's as innocent of such things as a child. How stupid you are, Walter. I never knew you to be so before, and I did so hope you would be good friends."

"Well, well, haven't we been?"

"It seemed so for awhile, but you were so different tonight."

"Was I? Did she notice it?" The question was eager.

"Being a woman, she could scarcely help noticing it."

"Well, I was thinking," he said lamely, and then burst out, "What a glorious night it is, and how sweet those magnolias are. I didn't notice it before. Why, Emily, it's good to be alive."

"One wouldn't have thought it of you a little while ago, you were so quiet and subdued."

"Oh, well, there are times when the beauty of a night sinks into our souls too deep for words." Walter winced in spirit at his own hypocrisy.

"There, I told Dolly that you felt more than you said."

"You told her that? She talks about me to you?"

"Oh sometimes you come up in the course of conversation."

"What a wonderful girl she is."

"You—do you think so?"

"That is, she shows a deep affection for her brother, which is commendable."

"Oh—but—don't most sisters?"

"There are very few such sisters as I imagine Miss Etheridge and know you to be."

She forgave him instantly. "You dear old Walter."

"And you think she likes me?" It was sweet to him to say it after his bitter thoughts.

"I know she does, and you should have known it too."

"Her brother must be a fine fellow."

"You would like him, I know."

"Let's sit out and talk awhile. It's altogether too lovely to go in," said the young man, as they turned in at the gate.

"I shall like it," said Emily, and giving their horses to a groom, they sat down on the veranda steps. For a few moments there was a silence between them, and both sat gazing at the starry heavens. Then Walter said falteringly,

"I—I—really—I am very much interested in Miss Etheridge's brother. Tell me more about him."

Then his sister laughed, not teasingly nor banteringly, as some sisters would have done, but with a little satisfied note, and she said, "Brother mine, there is only one thing more transparent than glass," and her brother caught her about the waist, and kissed her for some reason not quite clear to himself. So they sat together long that night and talked of the Etheridges, brother and sister.

In the young man, his fellow-soldier, Walter evinced a polite and conservative interest, but he was apt to bring the conversation back to the sister when it seemed to have a tendency to remain too long away from her. If he found no more pertinent remark to make, he would turn to Emily and say, "So you think she likes me?" and this was sufficient to start the stream of talk flowing in proper channel.

When, finally, they sought their rooms that night, and the young man dropped asleep, there was a smile on his lips, and the words on his tongue, "She likes me, she likes me."

Chapter 17

When Love Stands Guard

WHAT SURPRISED WALTER WHEN the morning brought with waking a review of the night's happenings, was that Emily, simple Emily, who had never had a love affair in her life that he knew, should have discovered to him his own secret. Or maybe she had discovered nothing that really existed at the time. Perhaps the train had been laid, the fuse set, and her remark only been the match to set the whole agoing. However, it made no matter at all how or when it happened. It was true. Now to let Dolly know. It was remarkable how soon and how easily all his fears and misgivings had disappeared. It was as if this state of exultation had been waiting for him and he had but to step into it. Why had he delayed so long?

The days that followed were filled with softer sounds than the sounds of war, and doings that had no shadow or show of the harshness of the camp. Walter, dazzled by the glory of the new world that had opened up before him, forgot the hardness of his lot, forgot, perhaps, even the deeper sympathy that should have gone from him to the men in the field—for love is a jealous mistress. He walked and rode much with his sweetheart, by the grass-grown bridle paths and under the ancient trees. His heart sang a song to hers, and hers replied in kind. Emily, like a good sister, knew when to be judiciously absent, and Dolly understood all that he would say to her long before he dared speak.

It was not until the warm southern November was painting the hills and valleys that he told her of his love and his hope.

"It seems, somehow, Dolly, that I have no right to speak to you, placed as I am, but what am I to do? The message beats at my heart until at times I think you must hear it. I love you and have loved you from the very first night that we met."

"Are you sure?" she asked quietly, but with just a suspicion of mirth.

"I was never surer of anything in my life."

"Did you always know that you loved me?"

"I did not always say it to myself as I say it now, sometimes tremblingly, sometimes with exultation, but I must always have known it, else why should your lightest word have had the power of making me happy or miserable?"

They were walking slowly over the crisp pine needles in the copse not far from the house. She drew closer to his side, and her hand slipped into his.

"Poor Walter," she said, "I used to make you miserable. I never wanted to do that because—"

"Because?" he said eagerly.

"Because I do love you."

He took her in his arms and held her close to him. His head bowed humbly.

"What am I to be worthy of this?" he said at last.

"You are Walter, my Walter, my hero."

Even in that moment of ecstasy he winced at the word hero. He was not of the material of which heroes are made and he knew it. But he would not shadow their happiness now. Let her think well of him if she could. Later, he would try to deserve her, and after all, what man is so good, so upright as the woman who loves him believes?

Later, when the deep solemnity of the first betrothal had given way to a gayer mood, she asked him, "What will my Virginia friends say to my marrying a Yankee?"

"What can they say when you are more than half Yankee yourself?"

"I declare I'm not. I'm Southern clear through."

He took her hands and laughed down into her eyes. "No, you're not. You're just—just a woman, and I'm only a man and we're both more lovers than anything else, so let your friends say what they will," and the answer seemed to satisfy her. Walter, himself, was very well satisfied, and when two young people are perfectly satisfied with themselves and each other, the world is shut from their vision, and time trips a merry pace.

"Let us keep our sweet secret for awhile," she said when the lengthening shadows warned them that it was time even for a lover's tête-à-tête to be done.

"Let us," he assented, "if we can. It seems so much more our own, but, can we?"

"Oh, I can, I know, and you can of course, for it's only women who are untrustworthy with secrets."

"Yes, that's true, but there are secrets and secrets. There never was such a one as this before, so we have no foundation upon which to make a conclusion."

"You are a goose," she said, and then paid him for being one. Walter was right though. They went into supper and had not been at table five minutes before everyone knew. Something in their faces or manner or the way they played with the food, laughed inconsequently, cast glances at each other, told more plainly than words what had happened. Love had put on them his subtle sign.

Of course, Walter being a man, thought that he was carrying off his part with wonderful grace and shrewdness. But when Emily teased Dolly as they were passing out on the veranda, the newly betrothed hid her blushing face and cried, "Oh, Emily, how did you know?"

It was within a few days after this that reports began to come to the residents in and about Fairfax of the presence of guerillas, foraging and marauding bands in the neighborhood and frequently greatly exaggerated accounts were given of their depredations. Walter heard them all with a sinking at the heart for the safety of his betrothed. She was alone there with only three or four black servants in whose valor or faithfulness he had little or no belief. The first night or two that the rumors were current, he contented himself with getting to horse, and in silence and secrecy patroling the road in front of the Etheridge cottage. Nothing occurred, but as the rumors grew darker, his state of mind became more perturbed and he decided upon more vigorous measures. But Dolly's danger had not occurred to him alone, and before he could break the subject to his sister, she had come to him with a troubled face.

"Walter," she said, "won't you excuse me—I—haven't been spying on you, but I've guessed where you've been the last two nights."

A thrill half of shame and half of pride in himself shook him.

"Well, wasn't I right, Emily?" he asked

"Of course, you were, for the time being; but do you think it is enough? You know we had word from Miss Mason that the guerillas visited her place last night and if it hadn't been for the servants they would have been rude or worse. Now Dolly is poor and has so few Negroes about her."

"Well, what can we do?"

"I wouldn't trust those black folks anyhow, since they've got notions of freedom in their heads."

"Nor I, but I can't go over there and stay."

"Dolly could come here."

"Would she? Do you think she would?"

"Of course she would. Mother and I both agree that this is altogether the best plan, and we wondered if you'd mind riding over for her tonight."

"Would I mind?"

The tone was quite sufficient, and nothing more was needed to be said.

The moon was at the full, and flooded the landscape with silvery light when accompanied by Sam, a slave boy to whom he had become greatly attached, and bearing the invitation from his mother and sister, Walter set out for Dolly's house. For a time they went their way in silence, and then Sam, with the uncontrollable desire of his race for lyric expression broke into a song that woke the echoes. The young man, he was hardly yet a master, even in his thoughts, listened with pleasure, until he saw a dark form beside the road rise up, gaze at them for a moment, and then disappear into the surrounding wood.

"Sh," said Walter, without mentioning what he had seen, "I don't believe I'd sing any more, Sam. There's no telling what we might start up."

"Wisht to de Lawd it 'ud be a 'possum," said Sam, chuckling with easy familiarity, but he hushed his song.

"If we started up anything, it might not be something so pleasant for you as a 'possum."

"Not pleasant fu' me," replied Sam, "huh uh, you do' know dis hoss."

"So you'd leave me, would you, you rascal? Well, you're a great one."

"'Spec's I'd have to leave you ef I couldn't tek you erlong."

As they approached their destination, Walter suddenly drew rein and laid his hand on his companion's bridle. He pointed quickly and silently to the form of a man clearly outlined in the moonlight. He was standing at the front of the cottage window attempting to peer into the room through a crack between the lower blind and the sill. So intent was he upon his spying that he had not noticed the approach of the others.

"Dismount here," said Walter, "and tie the horses under the shadow of that mulberry tree. I believe there's mischief going on."

The Negro did as he was bidden and hastened back to his companion's side, just as the intruder walked up and began knocking at the door. After some delay, the voice of a Negro from within, questioned, "Who's dat?"

"Never mind," was the answer, "you open up."

The silent watcher was breathless with interest, but he kept cool enough to say, "Sam, you slip around to the cabins, and rouse what Negroes you can. Be ready for whatever happens, for there's no telling how many of them there are." Without a thought of his joke about desertion, Sam slipped away, leaping across the moonlit places from shadow to shadow while Walter crept nearer to the man at the door.

It had not been opened, but a Negro came from a side entrance and confronted the intruder.

"Why don't you open the door?" was the harsh question fired at the dark Cerberus.

"Well, suh, I didn't jes' know who you was, an' I t'ought mebbe I could tell you whutevah you wanted to know."

"It's none of your damn business who I am. I'm here in the name of the law, and you'd better open up all-fired quick or it'll be the worse for you."

The Negro went back around the house and in a few minutes the door opened. As he passed the light, Walter saw that he wore the uniform of a Confederate officer.

The door closed behind him, but Stewart becoming spy in turn, came near enough to hear what was said within.

"Where is your mistress?" in the officer's voice.

"She done retahed, suh."

"Tell her I wish to see her."

"She done retahed."

"Very well, let her get up. Tell her that her brother is supposed to be skulking within the lines, and that I am sent to search the house for him."

"You kin such de house."

"I shall begin with her room."

"Dey is no one in huh room, but huh, suh."

"How dare you talk back to me, you black hound?"

The harsh voice was suddenly checked, and then Walter heard another that made his heart leap within his throat.

"Never mind, Mingo," it said, "I am out of my room now Lieutenant Forsythe," went on Dolly calmly, "you are at liberty to begin there now, and search where you please." The tone reeked with scorn.

"You will go with me," was the reply.

"A trusted servant may accompany you."

"You will go with me, I said."

"As you will, lieutenant, but this is the way you pay your scores—come when there is no man in the house save a servant, to take revenge for a woman's no."

"We will not discuss that matter now, Miss Etheridge."

Walter had pushed the door open and he saw that the man's face went red and white at Dolly's words. He saw too, the fierce eyes of the black servant fixed on Forsythe, and for one instant, he wondered if he were needed. In the next, he had flung the door open and stepped into the room. Every eye turned upon him, and he said clearly, "And why, Lieutenant Forsythe, must the lady go with you?"

"Oh, Walter," Dolly cried, and then checked herself with a sigh of relief. The lieutenant was livid.

"And who in hell are you?" he asked in a tense voice.

"I am Walter Stewart, at your service, lieutenant."

"The paroled Yankee, eh? Oh, I see," he said in a tone that put murder in Walter's heart. "It is thus that you are protected, Miss Etheridge?"

"You may go on with your search, lieutenant, that you have a perfect right to do, but Miss Etheridge, protected or not, will not leave this room."

The two men stood glaring into each other's faces, while Mingo, relaxed from his vigilance, was chuckling in a corner. On a sudden, there was a rush of feet without, and four brawny men sprang into the room. The open door and the loud voices had attracted Forsythe's minions, who had been placed at a convenient distance. The lieutenant smiled grimly as his men surrounded Walter.

"I reckon, Mr. Stewart," he said with a sneer, "that you'll go a bit slower now."

"I'm not so sure of that, lieutenant," said Walter, and as he spoke, four Negroes, led by Sam, and bearing stout clubs swept into the room. The soldiers, if such the ragged guerillas whom Forsythe had taken as his accomplices could be called, were completely taken by surprise, and wilted as the threatening blacks, now man to man lined up beside them.

While the disappointed officer stood there chewing his mustache with rage, Walter had time for a few reflections upon the fidelity of a people whom he so little trusted because their fidelity militated against themselves, and it settled something in his mind that made his eyes flash and his lips press close together.

"You may proceed with your search now, lieutenant," said Dolly sweetly.

"It is unnecessary now. I suppose our bird has flown, and I shall not put myself to the trouble of searching your empty rooms."

"Are you sure that you did not know before you came, lieutenant, that you would not find my brother here?"

"I am sure that I have found out some things that I did not know before," he answered, glancing meaningly at the girl's protector. And then, the devil, which is in every man, became strong in Walter. It overcame him. His fist shot out, and Lieutenant Forsythe's lips spilled blood. The officer's eyes grew green and his hand went quickly to his holster, and then, the veneering that had cracked and shown the brute in him, closed again, and wiping the blood from his mouth, he said with the calmness of intense anger, "What this calls for, Mr. Stewart, is entirely beyond the limits of my present official duty. Will you grant me the pleasure of a few minutes' private conversation?" They stepped outside and a brief whispered conversation ensued. They were equally placid when they returned.

"Attention! about face! forward, march!" and without further word or sign, Forsythe and his minions marched away.

"Follow them quietly, Sam, and see that they are up to no mischief, and you, Miss Etheridge, get your things on, for you must go with me." He had forgotten all about the formal invitation.

"When is it to be?" she asked in reply.

He would have tried to evade, but she looked at him so steadfastly and earnestly that he could not.

"Tomorrow morning," he said simply, "but it is to be taken up as a merely personal matter, so I beg that you say nothing about it. Now go."

She pressed his hand quickly.

"Come 'long, Miss Dolly," said Mingo, still chuckling with glee, "hyeah 'Mandy stan'in' behime de do' wid a flatiron. I reckon ef Mas' Stewa't hadn' 'a' come, she'd a' to' dat game roostah up 'fo' I could a' said Jack Robinson."

When Sam had returned and reported all well, they got to saddle and started on their way, two of the Negroes mounting and coming behind to prevent treachery. Dolly and Walter rode side by side, and Sam, who rode before, had neither eyes nor ears.

"Do you really believe he was looking for Nelson?" she asked.

"Do you?"

"Oh, Walter, he has a grudge, and he is relentless. He proposed to me once, and he has pursued me ever since."

"For that reason, if no other, I shall try to kill him tomorrow," and the shadow being convenient, he kissed her.

There was some commotion in the house when the party reached home, and the story was told in its entirety. But nothing save praise fell to Walter's lot for his action. Dolly respected his wishes and said nothing of the impending duel, though her heart ached for her lover.

"I shall see you before you go in the morning," she said when they were alone for a moment before parting that night.

"I shall be leaving very early, before you are up."

"Before I am up! Walter, what can you be thinking of me? Why, I shall not go to bed."

"You must, dear, for I shall, and I shall sleep well."

"As you say, but I shall see you in the morning, nevertheless."

Walter called Sam to him as he went up to his room.

Chapter 18

An Affair of Honor

THE ARRANGEMENTS FOR THE meeting between Walter Stewart and Lieutenant Forsythe were as simple as the brevity of their conversation indicated. The whole matter was to be kept a profound secret as much on account of Walter's position as a paroled prisoner as because of the other's place in the army. They were to face each other in a small open space under the trees that lined a little creek about three miles from the Etheridge cottage. They were both familiar with the place and agreed upon it with equal readiness. Because of the secrecy which they wished maintained, there were to be no witnesses beside the two seconds, but each might bring with him a trusted friend or servant. Thus promptly, they arranged the affair leaving only to the assistants yet to be chosen the task of marking the ground and giving the signal. Pistols were the weapons.

When, after parting with Dolly, Walter called Sam to his room, it was to dispatch him on a delicate and doubtful errand. Recognizing the peculiar attitude of his neighbors towards him, he had formed but few friendships and these only of the most tentative kind. Now, in this emergency, he needed a friend and a confidant. His mind turned to but one person, a young Dr. Daniel, whose frank manner had won him as much as he dared yield himself. He now sent the servant to bring to him this man upon the plea of most pressing business.

In less than an hour, the young physician was with him. He was an open-faced, breezy looking young man of nine-and-twenty, or thereabouts, with the assured manner of perfect self-possession and self-reliance.

He came into the room with a soft though brisk step, but stopped in surprise to see Walter pacing up and down the room.

"Come in, doctor."

"Why, why, man, from the expression of that rascal of yours, I expected to find you in bed tossing with a raging fever or laid up with a broken leg."

"I shall not be your patient, tonight, doctor, tomorrow, who can say?"

"Eh, what's this? Not thinking of suicide, are you?"

"I'm thinking of how good a shot my opponent may be. The fact is, Dr. Daniel, I called you here on a business that is almost, if not wholly impertinent. But I hope you will pardon and help me, for there is no one else to whom I may turn." He then recounted to him the events of the night; the physician's face, already inclined to ruddiness, growing redder and angrier as he went on.

"Now, doctor," concluded Walter, "I am sure that Forsythe's intentions were neither honest nor official, and I have only tried to do my duty. Is it too much if I ask you to forget what I am politically, and to be my friend and second in this matter?"

"Forget what you are? Damn what you are, Stewart. I'll tell you what I'll do, man, I'll change places with you. I'll let you be my second."

"It's my fight."

"But don't you see it's a nasty business, and might get you into complications."

"I am willing to risk all that."

"Oh, come now, be sensible. The lady's brother is a good friend of mine."

"The lady is a good friend of mine."

"But I know the whole story; how he has tried to annoy that girl ever since she rejected him two years ago as any girl of decency and spirit would have done. I know he has always kept just outside the limit that would give her brother the right to fill his carcass full of lead. He has overstepped it now, and I want a chance to get a shot at the dirtiest hound in all Virginia. Give it to me."

"Wish I could, old man, but I want it myself."

"Oh, well, I always was a selfish dog. It's your say and if you won't, you won't; but anyhow, I'm with you, and I'll be in at the death if I can't have the brush."

"Thank you, doctor, your kindness is even greater than I could have hoped for, even from you."

"Yours isn't, or you'd have given me a shot at that cur; but remember if he happens to hit you, and God forbid that, I get the next chance at his hide."

"I wouldn't want to leave the business to a better man, and now, let us complete our arrangements, and then you may get to bed."

They talked for a short time longer, and then Walter conducted the physician to his room, while he gave his attention to one or two other duties. The last words the buoyant young Southerner said to him as he began to undress were, "Um, you're a lucky dog—a shot at Forsythe!"

It was before the darkness of the night had given way to the morning's gray that the men were up and ready for the saddle. Dr. Daniel had already reached the lawn where Sam was holding the horses. Walter loitered down the hallway, half expecting, yet half doubting that he should see Dolly.

"She's asleep, of course," he told himself, "and I'm glad of it. How could I expect her to get up after such a night as she has had. I was a brute to think of it." Nevertheless, there was a dissatisfied feeling tugging at his heart as he stepped out on the veranda. But his foot had scarcely touched the floor when his eye caught the flash of a woman's white shawl up under some vines that overhung the porch. His heart, suddenly relieved from its tension, gave a great leap as he hastened towards her.

"Dolly," he said, "I was afraid you wouldn't come. Indeed, I didn't want you to, dear."

"I had to come, if only to bid you Godspeed, Walter. Come back to me, you will, won't you?"

"To answer that, lies beyond me, my darling, but I will try. If I don't—"

"Don't say that—you will."

"Good-bye, now."

"Good-bye, Walter, good-bye, and strength to you and a safe return. Good-bye."

She went back and he hastened down and swung into the saddle.

"We must not keep the gentlemen waiting," he said to the doctor as they rode away slowly until out of earshot of the house.

"It will be enough to leave him lie waiting afterwards, and I hope you will leave him for a long wait, after it's all over."

"Well, it's a chance, you know, and I'm willing to take it; if he leaves me, instead, I guess Sam here, can take me home across his horse."

Sam was trailing along, carrying the pistol case, but he caught the words, and spurred up to his master.

"Mas' Waltah," he said solemnly, "ef dat man hits you, dey kin bu'n me er hang me, but he ain' gwine leave dis place alive."

The doctor suddenly halted horse and turned on the Negro.

"Now look here, Sam," he said, "it's all right for you to be protecting your master, but whatever happens, if you raise a hand against John Forsythe, I'll kill you on the instant. When your master is done with him, he's my meat, and he'll hardly take the reckoning of us both."

Sam looked appealingly to his master.

"That's right," the latter replied, "you're not in this part of it, Sam, but you did your share last night. Anyhow, I'm not counting on leaving work for anybody this morning."

For the rest of the journey, they rode in silence, but Walter's thoughts were busy with the events that had filled his life, in the weeks since he had left Ohio. He reviewed the change that had come to him in his feelings towards the cause he had espoused. He saw how remorse for the disagreement with his father, his affection for his family and the glamour of the South had all combined to win him from a righteous allegiance, and made him lukewarm or indifferent to what he had once felt to be the absolute right. He saw that in spirit, if not in deed, he was as much a deserter as the veriest renegade, who stole from the marching ranks to hide in the thickets and by ways until his comrades had passed on. He saw how much weaker a man he was now than on the day when he had gone out from his father's house in Dorbury, though he did not see that the weakening process had been ex-cusable, even inevitable. Though he held himself mercilessly up to his own criticism, the very fact that he was able to see these things in himself clearly, was evidence of the approach of a new state of mind, a change subtler than either of the others had been. He had begun to get back to himself, to be a man stronger than his sur-roundings, with a spirit independent of his affections.

At first contact with it, to him, as to many others beyond his years, the con-dition of the South, its life and its people, had seemed all chivalry and romance. The events of the past and the present day's business, had done more to tear aside this veil than anything else could have done. It was clear to him now that they were not all gods and goddesses in Dixie—that if it were an Eden, at least it was not free from serpents. He had received a royally good shaking up, and now he began to perceive that some hasty conclusions which he had reached were not based upon fact. One of these was that the North was eaten up by commercialism while the South was free from it; another that Northern honor and Southern honor were two essentially different things; both these beliefs died an early death as he reflected that here too, men bought and bartered, sold and intrigued. The occurrences which had taken place within the last few months under his eyes now reacted one upon the other with the result of placing him surely, strongly and logically where his first enthusiasm had placed him, and for the first time since he had been paroled, the irksome hatefulness of his situation was borne in upon him. Now he chafed to be in the field again. Now he felt the thrill of fighting for a great cause. His eyes were flashing and his teeth clenched hard when the voice of the doctor called him to the business at hand.

"Here we are," he cried as gaily as though they were a party reaching the pic-nic grounds, "and we're the first here, of course."

They dismounted and tied their horses, and then began examining the ground. It was a plot of greensward, well surrounded by trees, and sloping with a slow in-cline to a little creek that ran gurgling past—a quiet, pretty enough place, but its very seclusion had made it the recipient of many a bloody secret in those days when men settled affairs of honor according to the code. Two trees stood opposite each other about twenty paces apart, and these had won the name of the "dueling trees," because the distance between them being paced, the principals were usually placed, one under each, and many a deadly combat had been waged beneath their softly sighing branches.

The gray dawn had given way to the warmer hues of morning when two other riders cantered into the circle of trees and halted.

"It's Forsythe," said the doctor.

"And he only brings one of his troopers with him as second."

"If it is true that he went on that errand last night without authority, it is just as well that he does not have too many in his secret," was the rejoinder.

The men greeted each other with the utmost formality, though there was a touch of brusqueness in the physician's recognition of the lieutenant. While the two principals walked apart, their seconds paused for a brief conference as to conditions. In a little while, Dr. Daniel came to Walter.

"Are you ready and steady, old man?"

"Both," was the calm reply.

"The conditions are these; you are to be stationed at twenty paces, back to back. At the word, you are to turn and fire where you stand, then each has the privilege of advancing, firing until one or the other is hit. Are you satisfied?"

"Perfectly."

"Very well, we are ready," said the doctor to Forsythe's trooper, and together they paced off the ground, already so well known. Then the men were put in their places, and each second saw to the condition of his principal's weapon. Dr. Daniel stationed himself to the left, and midway the ground, while the trooper took a like position to the right.

"Are you ready, gentlemen?" said the latter.

"We are ready."

"One."

Then the clatter of horses' hoofs broke the morning stillness, and he paused. Both men waited with manifest impatience, but neither spoke.

"Go on," said the doctor "Quick!"

"Two."

Forsythe half turned, but it was too late. A squad of horsemen in gray uniform burst into the enclosure and rode between the men.

"Walter Stewart," said the sergeant, "I arrest you upon the charge of violating your parole."

"Can you not wait just one moment until this business can be dispatched," said Walter calmly.

But the officer spurred away from him with a curt, "Your business is not ours."

"Never mind, Forsythe," screamed Daniel, "I'll take the job off of Stewart's hands."

"Lieutenant Forsythe is also under arrest," said the sergeant.

Forsythe went very white, but stood calm as a statue.

"You took a miserable, cowardly way to save yourself," he said when he and Walter were brought together.

"You are mistaken, lieutenant," said the sergeant breaking in, "one of your own men was the informant."

The lieutenant bit his lip. The three prisoners, for the trooper was also put under arrest, mounted their horses and were surrounded by a close guard.

"Why am I too not arrested?" stormed the doctor.

"We had no orders regarding you, sir," was the reply, and the little cavalcade cantered away, leaving the physician swearing with feeling and distinction.

"Never mind," he said at last. "Let's go home, Sam. If that old trooper had been a bit quicker, Virginia might have been rid of the meanest sneak that ever scourged her; but instead of that, the party is broken up and nobody gets out of the mess but the doctor and the darky, neither one worth arresting. Come, let's go home."

Chapter 19

Justice

AFTER THE ARREST OF Walter, the doctor and Sam rode back over their tracks one as disconsolate as the other. It was not a pleasant duty that loomed up before them in the all too near future. Walter was gone. He would be missed and questions would be asked. Then what?

"Oh, Lord," sighed the doctor, "Sam, what are we going to do? What are we going to say to them when they ask for him?"

"Well, hit don' seem dey's nuffin else fu' me to do but to tell de trufe."

"My Lord, you are in desperate straits, that's always a man's last resort. Now, for my part, I'd a good deal rather lie if it would do any good. But the devil's going to be raised, and they'll be sure to find out. Biff! there goes my reputation. I tried to persuade your master to let me take this business on my hands. It would have been a good deal better to have faced Forsythe and have shot him or been shot than to face these bereaved women. But I'm in for it now, so come along, Sam. You take a hint from me. If I decide to tell the truth, you tell it. If I decide to lie, you fall in and outlie the devil and stick to it."

As they neared the Stewart home, the spirits of both of them sank lower still. The sun was now overhead, and was fast drying the dew-laden grass by the roadside. The day was clear and bright, or they might have taken for an apparition the white faced figure that stepped out in the road before them.

The doctor drew in his horse with an exclamation, and Sam's eyes threatened to leave their sockets.

"Where is he? Where is he?" cried Dolly. "What has happened to him?"

The dumbfounded men gazed first at the misery-distraught woman, and then, helplessly at each other.

"Oh, don't keep me in suspense. Tell me, where is Walter?" She had thrown aside all reserve and false modesty, and stood before them, self-confessed, a woman distressed for the safety of her lover.

"Why—why—Miss Etheridge," stammered Daniel.

"You tell me, Sam. I command you to tell me the truth. I see, in Dr. Daniel's eyes his intention to hide something from me."

The slave looked at his companion for guidance, but getting no help from him, he mumbled, "Mas' Walter, w'y, he went wid de lootenant."

"Went with him? What do you mean? Was he hurt? Have you deserted him? Oh, doctor, please, please tell me. It was for me that he went into this."

Daniel dismounted, and throwing his bridle over his arm, he began leading the girl towards the house.

"I'll tell you the truth," he said, and as briefly and gently as possible, he related what had taken place.

She heard him through in silence, and then asked, "What will they do with him?"

"That I cannot tell, Miss Etheridge, but I don't see how they can do much when the truth is known."

"But will the truth be known?"

"I cannot vouch for that, either, but whatever I can do to make it known, shall be done. I am going up home to arrange my affairs, so that I may be away, and then I shall start for Colonel Braxton's headquarters, whither he will be taken."

"Will you take a letter for me?"

"With pleasure."

"Thank you, doctor, thank you for your kindness to him and to me. I will have the letter ready when you return. Good-bye until then."

She was hastening away, but he detained her. "I am going up to the house," he said.

"You must not, I will break it to them as you cannot."

"But do you think it quite right?" he asked with a look of relief that belied his anxious tone.

"I can do it better than you. So do not wait for me. Mount and lose no time." She hurried on, and he rejoined Sam.

"It's all right, Sam. Just keep your mouth shut. The telling will be done for us better than we can do it.

"By Jove," he said later, as he left the servant at the gate and rode on past. "If I could find a woman who loved me like that, I'll be hanged if I wouldn't risk it. I would."

With swift, but reluctant steps, Dolly made her way homeward and sought out Emily and her mother. Her face was pale and drawn with pain and her girl-companion saw at once that something was wrong.

"What is it, Dolly?" she asked hastening to her.

"Let me sit down, I don't know what you will say to me, Mrs. Stewart, and you, Emily, how you will feel towards me."

"Nothing can ever change us towards you, Dolly, so be calm," said Emily, putting her arms around her.

"I should have told you last night, but he wouldn't let me, he was afraid you would be worried."

"Is it about Walter?" exclaimed his mother. "What has happened to him?"

"He is at Colonel Braxton's headquarters, under arrest."

"Under arrest?" cried the two women.

"But Dolly," said Emily, "how could they arrest him? He was paroled."

"Oh, you will think that I am a wicked, heartless girl, for it is all my fault."

"Your fault? How?" Emily's tone was colder, and she withdrew her arm from Dolly's waist.

"Don't leave me, Emily, till you understand. There was a personal encounter last night between Walter and Lieutenant Forsythe, and it resulted in a meeting between them this morning."

"A duel?"

"It would have been, but they were both arrested by a squad this morning and taken away."

"Why did you not tell us this before, Dolly, so that we might have stopped it?" said Mrs. Stewart sternly.

"Walter forbade me and I could not violate his confidence."

"There are times when even a violation of confidence might be justifiable."

The girl raised her tearstained face to the older woman's. "You do not understand," she said. "He was involved on my account, and he trusted me. Suppose I had violated this trust, told you and the matter had been stopped by you? What would they have said? 'His mother intervened to save him.' Mrs. Stewart, Walter's honor is as dear to me as to you or Emily, and I could not do that."

"Forgive me, child, you are right, but this is very hard."

"I know it. But though I could not save him then without dishonor, I shall try to help him now, by writing the whole story to Colonel Braxton."

"Who will take it?"

"Dr. Daniel is going to the camp to intercede for Walter, and will call for my letter soon. I will go now and write it. Do try to be calm. They can't be hard upon him when they know what a hero he has been."

Mrs. Stewart patted the girl's hand gently and said, "His mother and sister will try to be as brave as—"

"His sweetheart," cried Dolly, blushing, and taking the gray-haired woman in her arms, she kissed her and sped from the room. Emily laughed.

"Why, daughter, how can you laugh at such a time?" asked her mother.

"Because I feel so sure that Walter is safe, and will come back to us unharmed and without dishonor."

"Don't be sanguine, dear. The conditions of war are very different from those of peace."

"I know, mother, but would you have had him do less?"

"I don't know, and, yes, I do; your father's son could have done no less."

It was not long before Dr. Daniel came hastening back, but quick as he was, Dolly Etheridge was ready with her letter.

"I want you to forgive me," he said, "for my part in this affair, but you must understand that I am not greatly to blame. I begged Stewart to let me chip in, but he's an awfully proud fellow, you see, and he wouldn't let me do it. I was particularly anxious to get a chance at Forsythe. But your son, Mrs. Stewart, said it was his quarrel, and I could only play second fiddle. To be sure, I might have locked him in his room and gone as proxy, but I didn't think he'd like it."

"Why that would have been horrible," exclaimed Emily.

"Yes, but you'd have had your brother with you now."

"We should not have wanted him at that cost," was the sister's reply.

"No, Walter has been perfectly right," added the mother.

"Perhaps I did the best thing, after all," said the doctor ruefully; "but it's pretty hard to see such a chance escape never to return."

"Had you any quarrel with Lieutenant Forsythe?"

"Oh, no, no special quarrel. It was just general principles with me. I really believe the Confederate army would have voted your son a medal if he had rid them of a hound who gained his position through the worst influence, and holds it through duplicity. But I mustn't stand here chattering all morning. I am quite ready to take your letter, Miss Dolly, and I am sure it will do as much good as you want it to do."

Miss Etheridge handed him her missive with a blush. "Bring him back with you," she said.

"Well, I won't promise to do just that, but if I don't, I'll bring you good news anyhow, and I won't spare any time in getting this into the proper hands. Good-morning to you, ladies, and good cheer," and the good doctor leaped into his saddle and cantered away, leaving behind him a cheerier household than he had found.

It was ten miles to his destination, but he made short work of it, sent his message through the lines and received safe conduct to the colonel. This officer was a grizzled veteran who had seen service in the Mexican war, and who was bent on doing for the raw material that he had in hand what years of service had done for him. He was as kind of heart as he was brusque of manner. To him, Dr. Daniel came with his own story and Dolly's letter, which the colonel read grimly.

"You are a friend of the prisoner's, I suppose?"

"Yes, I haven't known him long, but I have learned to like him right well."

"Do you know that this liking of yours and your connection with the affair is likely to involve you in difficulty?"

"Well, now, I hadn't thought of that, but it doesn't matter in the least."

The colonel bent industriously over the paper in his hand, and a smile flickered through his gray mustache.

"Are you acquainted also with Lieutenant Forsythe?"

Daniel straightened himself up angrily. "I know Forsythe."

"I said Lieutenant Forsythe."

"Beg pardon, colonel, but—"

"Enough, suh. Who is this Miss Etheridge?"

"She's a daughter of old Nelson Etheridge, of Rockford, sir."

"Who was related, I believe, to the Etheridges of Mecklenbu'g county?"

"Well, sir, I'm not just up on genealogy, and all that sort o' thing, but I dare say you're right. Most all Virginians are related, you know. It's become a state habit."

Again the colonel had recourse to the papers to hide his amusement. When he looked up again, he said,

"I shall have to detain you, Dr. Daniel, until I look further into this case. Discipline has been altogether too lax here of late, and while disaffection has not become common in Virginia, there is altogether too great a tendency towards it."

"I hope you don't feel any doubt about me, colonel?"

"It isn't a matter of personal feeling."

"Of course not, I ought to have known that. In fact, I did know it, and yet I feel that you are saying, 'What is an able-bodied fellow like that doing at home?' Well, I'm not home for choice or for all time. Yet there are some things to be done before I can go where the rest of the fellows of my age are. There are women and children to be looked after and dosed. Until now, there have been things outside of the army that I could do for Virginia, hut as soon as a breathing time comes, I shall be where I should be."

The colonel's eyes were very bright as he looked at the young man, but he only said, "No doubt," and called an officer to take Daniel away.

"There's a man who would make a good fighter, but a damned bad soldier," was the veteran's mental comment. "He's too free and easy."

"Bring in the prisoner, Stewart," was his command to the orderly.

The appearance of Walter was hardly that of a felon when he came into the presence of the commanding officer. His eyes were clear, his head high and his step firm. There was no sign of fear in the manner in which he met his judge's gaze.

"Your name is—?"

"Walter Stewart."

"And you were until first taken, a soldier of the Northern army?"

"I was."

"You were taken when within the Confederate lines, and were paroled when you might have been dealt with as a spy."

"My business within your lines was perfectly clear."

"That does not alter the case. You were paroled and violated the parole."

"I do not feel that the latter is the case, sir."

"What?" cried the colonel sternly. "Do you dare to deny it?"

"I deny none of the facts of the case, sir, I only question their construction."

"You have no right to question, suh, you are a prisoner to be judged. The case to my mind is perfectly clear against you."

"You are the judge," said Walter calmly.

"You were found, suh, in the very act of an encounter with a Confederate officer, after having assaulted him on the night before. We consider, suh, that you have violated your parole, and broken your word of honor."

"When Virginia thinks that by protecting a defenseless woman, a man tarnishes his honor or forfeits his word, I begin to feel sorry for my father's state."

"Suh, you are not the guardian of Virginia's honah."

"I am the custodian of my own, though."

"Then you should have seen better to it than to have broken your parole. You know the consequences."

"I am not afraid of the consequences. I am willing to abide by them. But I do not think that I have violated my parole. I have not taken up arms against the Confederate states, unless they are warring against their own defenseless women. Nor have I given aid or comfort to your enemies, unless you consider as an enemy, a woman who has never by word or deed shown anything but allegiance to the South she loves."

"Ahem!" said the colonel.

"Furthermore, my quarrel, my encounter, was not against your government, but against the injustice of one man. It was not an encounter involving national views, but a purely personal encounter."

"In troublous times like these, no encounter with an officer of ours can be considered as personal."

"I hope, sir, that you have not also suspended the rule in regard to respect for women."

"You are pleased to be impertinent, and yet I answuh that I hope Virginia will never be guilty of that." Walter bowed.

"I understand that you are a son of the late Colonel Stewart, a Virginia gentleman?"

"I was never more his son than now."

"I doubt that. I knew your father."

"My father, placed in the same position I was, would, I believe, have acted as I did."

"Without doubt—I beg your pardon," the colonel checked himself. "But yours are rules of civil life, and your laws are for civilians; at present, we are under military rule."

"Having been a soldier, I understand that. I am in your hands."

"Sergeant of the guard, you will hold the prisoner under arrest until further orders. I will look into your case and consider it further. Retire. A moment, sergeant." The non-commissioned officer paused just out of earshot of Walter, and the colonel whispered, "Treat him well, sergeant, he's a Stewart cleah through."

After the dismissal of Walter, Lieutenant Forsythe was brought into the colonel's presence. The conference between him and his superior officer was short and decisive.

"Lieutenant Forsythe, you gave as your reason for entering the house of Miss Etheridge, that you were on a search for her brother."

"I did."

"You were not aware that her brother had been for some time in the Union army?"

"I had received reliable information that led me to believe that he had returned and was in hiding at home."

"After gaining entrance into the house, why did you insist upon Miss Etheridge's accompanying you in your search?"

Forsythe hesitated and turned color under the colonel's glance.

"I wished to be able to watch her face and so tell when I was upon the scent."

"Why, when you had the chance to search the house without her, did you not do it?"

"I was sure her brother had been given time and opportunity to escape."

"Now, Lieutenant Forsythe, will you tell me by whose orders you went upon this search for Nelson Etheridge?"

"I thought that the capture of an enemy—"

"Will you answer my question?"

"Upon no one's specific orders, but—"

"No buts about it. I am answwuhed. Were you ever a suitor for Miss Etheridge's hand?"

"I consider that a personal question, sir."

Forsythe saw that the hope for him was gone and he could be no worse off by taking a stand on dignified effrontery.

"Oh, you consider it a personal question?"

"I do, and one that has nothing to do with my service."

"And as such, you refuse to answwuh it? Very well. You have no doubt understood the rules of this command in regard to the treatment of women?"

"Yes—but—"

"That will do, Lieutenant Forsythe. A court-martial will attend to your case."

The lieutenant saluted and was taken away under guard. Walter and Dr. Daniel were then summoned.

"Young man," said the colonel to the former, "I regret that I find cause neither to hold nor to punish you. I regret, too, that you have chosen a course alien to your father's traditions and beliefs. But that, of course, is not my affair. I advise you, in the future, however, to keep cleah of collisions with our officers, or the next time you may not get off so easily."

Walter felt it the part of wisdom to make no reply, and so merely bowed.

"You, Dr. Daniel," said the colonel, turning to the physician, "will always find a welcome here, and whenever, if ever, you choose to throw your lot in with us, I hope to have you in my command."

"Thank you, colonel, thank you, sir."

The two men were conducted safely away from camp and set on their homeward way.

"By Jove, Stewart," said the doctor heartily, "I wish you weren't a Yankee!"

"I'm hardly a Yankee, doctor, as you use the term. But knowing Ohio, and knowing Virginia through such men as you, I am more than ever for the Union that will keep two such states together, let that Union be bought at whatever price it may."

The two men clasped hands across their saddlebows. The physician took Walter's praise as ingenuously as a child.

"I wish," he said, "that more Northerners knew us Southerners."

"If the two sections did know each other better, a deal of blood might be saved."

It was a grave ride home, but the rejoicings at the end of the journey compensated for all the serious thought along the way.

"Bless you, Dr. Daniel," said Mrs. Stewart fervently.

"Oh, don't thank me, Mrs. Stewart. I'm not a drop in the bucket. It was Miss Dolly's letter that fixed everything."

"Dolly's letter!" cried Walter.

The girl blushed, and the doctor added, "Maybe I'm telling tales out of school."

"You shall tell me about it, Dolly," said Walter with glowing eyes. This was perhaps only an excuse to lead her away from the rest for a walk in the arbor. What excuse Dr. Daniel gave for leading Emily in an opposite direction matters not, but it must have been satisfactory, for Mrs. Stewart found the housewife's excuse of her work to leave them, and the doctor stayed to supper.

Chapter 20

The Vision of the Black Rider

DESPITE THE APPARENT CHEERFULNESS with which Mary Waters went her way in the Woods household, she was not entirely her own old self. There was an air about her not so much of sadness as of repression. She tried, as well as the circumstances of the household allowed, to be alone, although Nannie, feeling that brooding over her experiences must be unprofitable to her friend, attempted to correct this tendency in her. She was not always successful, for notwithstanding the pliancy of her disposition with those whom she loved, Bradford Waters' daughter had something of a will of her own, and there were times when she would elude Nannie's vigilance or repel her advances and wander away to indulge her moods to herself.

As the midsummer approached, she grew restless and preoccupied and often she would awake Nannie at night by starting up with cries of terror. But on being questioned, the only reply she would make was that she had been dreaming. Her dreams she would not tell at first.

Finally, the fancy so grew upon her that Nannie began to tax her with keeping something back. Mary continued reticent, but worn and weak, she at last surrendered to her friend's stronger nature.

"You've just got to tell me what it is, Mary Waters," said Nannie. "Something is troubling your mind, and you are troubling mine."

"But it's such a foolish thing, Nannie."

"I don't care. Folly is none the worse for being shared with someone."

"Do you believe in dreams?"

"I don't know, tell me yours, and I'll see. If I believe it means anything, I'll tell you, honestly, I will."

"Well, I have the vision of a black rider that continually comes to me in a sort of stupor that I experience between sleeping and waking. I cannot describe what I mean nor the feeling of it. But I know I am not asleep nor yet awake. The rider is always going along a dark road, and he comes up and holds out his arms to me. His face is covered, but I know him. It is the form of Robert Van Doren. But before I can touch his hand, he is gone, and when I call out after him, everything grows utterly black and I am awake with a terrible misgiving at my heart. Oh, I am afraid something has happened to him."

The girl seldom let herself out so fully, and Nannie saw that she was terribly wrought up.

"It is nothing, Mary," she said. "You've been brooding too much and it has made you nervous and sleepless. It will all come right if you try not to worry and wonder too much."

"I knew you would say that and I would rather not have told you."

"Don't be offended, dear. What I say is only for the best. It is what Tom would say to you if he were here."

"Yes, that's true, for he would understand no better than you, Nannie. There is with me something more than the dream—a feeling here," she pressed her hand to her breast, "a peculiar ache that isn't so much an ache as a premonition of one. You don't know what I mean, but I do."

"I think I almost understand. It's the same feeling that I have in my feet just before I step on the jack in your father's warehouse."

Mary looked up quickly to see if her friend was joking, but the eyes that met her own were perfectly serious, and though she could not vouch for the correctness of the likeness, she felt that somehow, Nannie understood.

"But," the latter pursued, "I never let the feeling in my foot get the better of me, and neither must you give way to that in your heart. It may be there, and it may seem something, but just keep on going."

"That's hardly necessary advice," smiled Mary. "It's the one thing that we have to do in life, keep on going. No matter how many presentiments you have, you've got to go on to their fulfillment. That's one thing that gives me the horrors at times until I want to shriek aloud—this unending forward movement. If one could only stop sometimes—but we can't."

"Don't, Mary, don't; there are some things that we must neither think nor talk about, some things that we must leave to a Higher Intelligence than ours."

"But suppose that one does think about them, that one cannot help it—that everything suggests these thoughts?"

"Oh, in that case, one goes out into the open air with me, walks down to the shop, and as she has a quick eye, helps me match some goods," and seeking to divert her mind from the gloomy thoughts that were taking possession of it, Nannie hurried Mary into her hat and out upon the streets.

The day was full of sunshine, but the air was limpid with the suggestion of rain, and a soft breeze blew up from the river. The town was humming and drowsing comfortably, and there was nothing in its appearance to indicate that just a little below the surface there smoldered volcanic fires of discontent and unrest. The whole place was the embodiment of peace. The blinds of the houses were closed to keep out the garish sunlight and the most active sign of life upon the resident streets was the young children playing in the gutters and on the pavements.

Something of the restfulness of the scene possessed Mary and for the time drove the clouds from her mind. The bright day and her forebodings did not set well together. Could it be true that on such a morning as this with such a sky overhead men could be hating each other and seeking each others' lives? Her mind rejected the incongruity. After all, the darkest hour is just before dawn. She had been going through her dark hour and now all the brightness and beauty about her were but the promise of the better time coming. She went into the shop with Nannie stepping lightly and with a smile on her face.

Though poetry has told us that coming events cast their shadows before them, science has not troubled itself to deal largely with this subject of premonition, nor is it believable that those shadows are cast upon all hearts But there is little doubt that to some there is given the added sorrow of feeling the approach of catastrophe some time before the fact. Call it presentiment or what you will, there are those who are capable of feeling disaster before it comes. Of these, was Mary Waters, and bright as her face had been when she entered the shop with Nannie the clouds had settled upon it again when she emerged.

"Let us walk up Main Street," she said, and her companion agreed.

Nannie chatted on cheerfully because she had not noted Mary's return to her former depression. Had she only looked at her companion's gloomy face, her flow of talk would have been checked. Mary's eyes were fastened upon a knot of people surrounding a bulletin board in front of the *Diurnal* office.

"Something is wrong," said Mary suddenly, breaking in on her friend's talk.

"Why do you think so?" asked the surprised girl.

"Look at the crowd up there. Let us go and see."

Reluctantly Nannie complied and they were soon on the outskirts of the growing crowd. They could not get near enough to see the words on the board, but someone read aloud for the benefit of the latecomers the words that made Mary pale with terror and turn hastily away. "John Morgan with his cavalry has crossed the river and is advancing into Ohio."

"John Morgan is in Ohio, and Robert is with him—my vision, the Black Rider." The disjointed words beat time to the throbbing of her heart. "John Morgan is in Ohio and Robert is with him."

The news spread like wildfire and already the town was alive with people hastening to the center of intelligence. The drowsy summer quiet had gone from the streets as if by magic, and instead there were the shuffling of feet and the babble of many tongues. But Mary did not speak and Nannie gave her the sympathy of silence. Only when they were in the house again did she say, "I shall never question your feelings again. Never." Then with rare good sense, she left Mary to herself.

The shock, coming as it had, as a confirmation of her fears and holding in it unknown possibilities for trouble had a severe effect upon the girl. She was distressed for the safety of her lover, but not only that, for a new element had entered into her feelings. Heretofore, she had had little or no doubt as to the righteousness of her loyalty to Robert. But now it was a very different thing. He was no longer a brave man exiled and driven into the army of the enemy. He was now the invader of his own home and hers. As long as he fought on the soil of his father's state against invasion, he might still have her love and sympathy; but did he not, by this last act, forfeit both? Reasoning with a woman's narrow vision, she admitted his right to defend himself and those he loved against the government, but questioned his privilege to attack it. It is not to be denied that sentiment had much to do with Mary's point of view. In one rôle, Robert was the prince, in the other, the ogre, and she could not quite reconcile herself to sympathy with the ogre. It was rather a nice question to ask her to decide whether the right of defense did not carry with it the right of attack. There was something of horror in the picture she drew of him, riding a marauder over the fields of the state that had so long sheltered him. In her mind, the whole invasion was narrowed down to one man. It was not Morgan and his men—it was Robert—Robert, for whom she had left home, for whom she had suffered contempt. What did it matter to her that John Morgan was with him? What did it matter to her that he was one of two thousand? Then her trend of thought began to change. Had he not been forced to go where he was? She remembered his words to her father on that memorable night. "The Confederacy may thank you for another recruit!" Must he not do then as his comrades did? Would it not be cowardice in him to refuse to go where they went? Would he do wrong consciously? She could not believe it. After all, she loved him and she would trust him blindly, whatever happened. The inevitable thing occurred. Her love triumphed. She need have asked herself no perplexing questions had she only begun with, "Is my love for him strong enough to overlook all shortcomings?" With Nannie in the same case, it would have been different. There would have been no questions at all. She would merely have said, "Well, if *he* does it, it must be right," and gone on with a contented mind. Even Mary was happier for her decision, though she reached it after much doubt.

Dorbury heard of the rebel general's daring dash into Ohio with an astonishment that was only equaled by its anger and terror. There had been threats and rumors of some danger from Kentucky, but the possibility of it had been beyond belief. Now that the thing had really come, men stood aghast. Men who had scoffed before, now became suddenly serious. Men who had wavered in their allegiance, now spoke out boldly for the Union when their homes were menaced. On every side was the cry "The Home Guards, the Home Guards," and old men, middle-aged men and beardless youths went flocking into the armory. "Be sure," said some, "if he dares cross into Ohio, there are more behind him, and it means that they intend to overwhelm the state!" Others said, "They will burn Cincinnati, strike here, unless we can check them, march on and destroy the capital."

On any corner, sane men, fanatics and demagogues could secure audiences to listen to their oratory, in which they adjured their hearers to rise in their might and drive the invader from their sacred soil.

There were some men in the town who smiled and added, "It is a feint, let Morgan come. He will not come far." There were not many of them. There were others who gathered behind the closed blinds of Stephen Van Doren's house to talk of this new development. To them Van Doren spoke confidentially. "I deplore this move," he said. "It will take away sympathy from the cause of the South, although Morgan is only doing what Lincoln has done in the South. It is a sorry matter all through, for we have been plunged into a war that might have been averted by able statesmanship. If worst comes to worst, we have only our government to thank, and yet it is a bad thing, for nothing will do more to cement a feeling of clannishness in the North and give these fanatics something to point to than this same attempt to fight the devil with fire."

Among all the crowding men, the believers in different creeds, walked Bradford Waters like an Elijah among the prophets of Baal. The news was to him as the battle-smoke to the nostrils of the war-horse. He seemed like one inspired, and it was as if the things that he had longed for had been done. There was a look of exaltation on his face, but his was an emotion too deep for words, though none who saw him needed speech of him.

In her bedroom, his daughter sat staring silently out of her window, not thinking—hardly dreaming—and so night fell on Dorbury.

Chapter 21

A Vague Quest

IT IS DOUBTFUL HOW long Mary would have sat staring out into the darkness had not the entrance of Nannie and her preparations for bed disturbed her reverie. She also disrobed and was soon lying in bed, her eyes wide open and her thoughts busy with the events of the day. She did not want to talk and so made but brief replies to Nannie's proffers of conversation. Finally, from feigning sleep, she fell into a light doze from which she started crying, "The Black Rider! The Black Rider!"

The experiences of the last few hours had exhausted Nannie, and though it was yet early in the evening, she was sleeping soundly. Mary recovered herself, and finding that she was not observed, crept stealthily from the bed. She paused for awhile beside the window, and then dressed with feverish haste as if spurred by a definite purpose. When she was fully clothed she stepped quietly down the stairway, and past the sitting room where some of the family were still up, and glided out of the house. Why she was doing so, she herself could not have told, but something was dragging or driving her on, on, towards the station. She had yet no fixed idea where she was going, but she felt in her pocket for money and it never occurred to her until she found the amount of her fare that from the beginning she had intended to go to Cincinnati, though that she did not yet know, the tendency towards a definite act being rather subconscious than apprehended. There was just time to catch the half-past ten train. She reached the station, bought her ticket and sank breathless and dazed into a seat.

There was a moment's delay, and then the train sped away into the darkness. The sum of all her impressions was that the Black Rider whose face was still concealed from her, flitted ever by the side of the coach and just at her window. The lights of the town faded from view and the river lay behind her a line of sinuous silver. The sky overhead was besprent with pale stars, but she saw only the cloaked and muffled man, riding, riding as one rides in a nightmare. The train whistled, wheezed and paused at stations, and then went panting on, and Mary, knowing as little, feeling hardly more than the dumb mechanism that carried her, went on upon a vague, unknown quest, for what, she could not have told.

Prompting her action there was apparently no cause or intelligence. Scarcely was there even volition. Some force, stronger and wiser than she, good or malignant, impelled her forward whether she would or no. She went on not because she would, but because she must.

The night became suddenly overcast, the sky darkened, the stars went out, and as the train flew on its way southward, a peal of thunder broke from the heavens, and sharp rain began pattering against the window. She crouched lower in her seat and stared ever out through the pane where she could see the mantled figure riding, riding. She could hear his horse's hoofbeats above the sound of the storm, and her eyes sought vainly his face, though she knew and could not be deceived in the form.

When the coach drew into Cincinnati, she alighted and still blind, dazed and apparently without direction, hastened out and took a car. The night was one of inky blackness, the rain was coming down in torrents, while intermittent flashes of lightning showed her the wet and shining streets and the roadways through which she was passing. At the call, Avondale, she left the car and went on blindly into the night.

Terror now seized her, terror of the unknown, of the darkness, of the mystery in her own wild act; but she could not stop nor turn back. Was she fleeing from or to something? Once in a moment of consciousness, she asked herself the question, but hurried on without answering or attempting to answer it. On, through the little suburban village and out upon a country road, a mile out; the last house had been passed, the last light had flickered out of her sight, and then drenched, exhausted, she paused under a huge oak and turned her eyes back over the way she had come. It was not weariness that made her stop, it was a sense of waiting, waiting for something, the thing for which she had come. It was perhaps a half hour that she had stood there, and then the sound of clattering hoofs struck her ear. She pressed closer to the tree. A company of cavalrymen were approaching. They came at a smart canter. Breathlessly, she awaited. They were near to her. They were passing, first close together, then with gaps between, then scatteringly. With her physical ear she heard the sound of their hoofbeats in the soft, slushy mud, but with her inner sense, she heard the sound of one horse on dry ground, and her eyes saw but one rider, still the black mantled figure of her dreams. She heard him, saw him coming nearer, nearer, then a flash of lurid lightning lit the whole scene, and starting forward from the tree, she cried, "Robert, Robert!"

As if but one man had heard her, as if her voice had been intended to reach but one, a figure shrouded in a dark cloak, whirled and rode from the straggly ranks up to the side of the road and dismounted. She stretched her arms out. Another flash of lightning showed the trooper the white face of the girl beside the tree, and with a cry he caught her to him as she fell forward.

"Mary, Mary," he cried, "can it be you? Are you flesh or spirit? My God, what does it mean?" But she was lying cold in his arms. The cavalry passed on, stragglers and all. He stood there helplessly holding her, one hand clutching his horse's bridle. The rain from the leaves dripped in her face, and she revived.

"Robert," she said faintly.

"What are you doing here?" he asked.

"I—I—don't know. I dreamed of you and I came. Where am I?"

"On the road out of Cincinnati, about two miles from Avondale. Who came with you?"

"I came alone."

"Where are you going?"

"I don't know. Something sent me to you."

"You are very weak," he said.

"I must go back now," she replied.

"Where will you go?"

"I don't know."

The power that had driven her out, that had guided her seemed suddenly to have left her helpless and without direction.

The men now were entirely passed, and without a word, he lifted her to his saddle and springing up behind her, turned his horse's head back towards the town.

"God knows what brought you here, darling," he whispered close to her ear, "but it was something stronger and wiser than us both. It has been a long, hard ride with me, and I was losing hold, but you have given me strength again. People have heard our horses and are aroused, but I will take you back where you will be safe. Another day," he bent over and kissed her brow, "when all of this is over, you shall tell me how and why you came to me, love of my heart."

She nestled closer to him and did not answer. There was nothing for her to say, she did not understand, he did not understand. He rode straight into the town. Dark forms were gathering upon the corners. Here and there a torch flared.

"I must leave you now, Mary," he said, "the power that brought you will care for you. I must join my company. God be with you."

He set her down and was wheeling away, when a torch beside him flared. A man cried, "Here's one of them!"

Van Doren struck spurs to his horse and the animal dashed away. A hue and cry arose. There was a volley of shots, and the night swallowed the Black Rider. A crowd surrounded Mary and led her speechless and confused to the nearest house. A few of the bolder spirits followed the rider on foot, until the sound of his horse's hoofs had died away into the distance.

The girl could not give any clear account of herself except that she had come from Dorbury and had wandered out of her way. Kind matrons put her to bed where she fell asleep like a child, though she would have rested less easily had she known that Robert was swaying, white-faced in his saddle, his arm shattered by a bullet.

All night long, men full of alarm patrolled the streets of the village fearing and expecting an attack, while women stayed up and brewed tea and talked of their night visitor. When Mary awoke in the morning, the events of the night before were like a dream to her, and though the women questioned her closely and eagerly she was able to give them little or nothing of the satisfaction for which they longed. It was all so strange, so unbelievable, that she did not dare tell them all that had really happened. There were some who said that she must be a spy, and there were threats of detaining her, but she made it clear where she lived, mentioning the names of people whom several of them knew, and so they put her down as some demented or half-witted creature who had lost her way and been rescued by the trooper in gray.

"Well, the hound will have one thing to his credit," said the husband of the woman at whose house she had slept.

Her head clear, the girl was anxious now to return to her home. The busy little matron, still suspecting her sanity, insisted on going with her as far as the train, where with many head-shakes and mysterious comments, she put Mary in charge of the conductor and went away trembling for the safety of her protégée.

The whole Woods household was in an uproar of excitement and Nannie was blaming herself keenly for negligence when Mary walked in.

"Oh, Mary, Mary," cried her friend at sight of her, "where have you been? You've given us such a fright. We've searched everywhere for you."

But Mary only smiled and kept her counsel. "I had to go away," she said.

"What time did you leave?"

Mary smiled again. A little later a message came from Bradford Waters saying, "Have you found Mary yet?"

Nannie blushed. "We thought you had gone home, and so we went there."

"I was not at home," was the only answer.

Whatever it may have meant, the girl herself was never able to explain it, but Mary saw no more visions and she was happier.

The puzzle was deep in Robert's mind as he rode away from the girl, leaving her to the mercies of the gaping townspeople. He had no doubt that they would treat her kindly and send her home in safety. But the thought that held him and made him forget even the pain in his arm that grew and grew was how she had come there. How had she known where to find him, when even the troopers themselves did not know whither they were tending? Who gave the simple, emotional girl the information that the governor of Ohio would have given so much to have? There was nothing in the range of Robert's experience to explain the phenomenon, so although he hugged the memory of her presence to his consciousness, he gave up speculation to wait for that later day when he had said she would tell him. His thoughts now had time to revert to his wound, and he found that his sleeve was soaked with blood that was fast stiffening in spite of the constant downpour. The absorption of his attention no longer kept his misery in subordination. He began to feel fainter and fainter, but clenched his teeth and laid his head upon the neck of his good mare. A mile more, and the sound of moving men came to his ears. Then he gained upon them faster and knew that they had halted for the night. His head was ringing like a chime of bells. His heart throbbed painfully and his tongue was parched. Heavier and heavier he lay upon the mare's neck, and when finally the animal halted in the hastily improvised camp, it was an inert body that had to be lifted from her back.

Already Mary was quietly sleeping in the friendly house and no dream or vision told her of the lover who was to ride no more with John Morgan, but unknown, was to be nursed back to life by a good-hearted farmer and his wife.

Chapter 22

The Homecoming of the Captain

THROUGH THE NEWSPAPERS, AND an occasional letter from the field, Bradford Waters was kept advised of the movements of his son. With his regiment, he had taken part in the engagements at Pittsburg Landing, and in all the active operations of the Army of Ohio, or, as it was finally rechristened, the Army of the Cumberland. He had distinguished himself in the terrible fight of the 19th of July, and it was as a captain that he lay with his company at Chattanooga Creek, encouraging his men by example not to flinch under the awful fire which the Confederate batteries poured upon them.

Dorbury knew the privations through which her boys were going, the long marches when both rest and refreshment were denied, the hardships of camp and field and the heroism of patient endurance. Then began that gradual turn of sentiment and feeling for which the battle of Pittsburg Landing and Morgan's raid had proved the cue. Another wave of enthusiasm for her patriotic sons swept over the town, and this time, had permanent effect. Even Davies scoffed no longer and spoke of "our boys" in a tone that led Waters to forgive all his past transgressions.

Tom had always been a favorite at home, but men spoke his name now with a new affection. After each new engagement in which his regiment was known to have taken a part, there were numerous inquiries at the Waters house as to how "the captain" had fared. He was no longer a family idol. He had become a public hero.

This pride in a young man's success, is, after all, of the vanity which is human. Something of credit seems to accrue to the man himself when he can say, "What! Captain—, why I knew him when he was a boy!"

Behind closed doors, Stephen Van Doren sat and read the papers. He had the largeness of heart that made him respect a brave man wherever placed, and now he felt a real pride in the son of his enemy. To be sure, in his heart, he had misgivings and wished time and again that he might read something of his own son of whose whereabouts he knew nothing. There had come one brief letter some time before the raid, and since that, nothing. Why couldn't his Bob be a captain, too? His anxiety was shared in some degree by Mary, but the pride which she took in her brother and which Nannie constantly nourished, left her little time for brooding.

The summer wore away amid rumors of battles, reconnoissances, and skirmishes. The golden autumn came, and although so many of the husbandmen were away reaping strange harvests in a strange land, the land smiled with the fullness of things, and the ring of scythes could be heard afield. Over the little town, over the fair meadows that surrounded it, the sun of plenty hung and drove away the darkness that the preceding summer had known. Morgan had come and gone and they felt no fear of another such invasion. Terror was dead and the people bent themselves joyously to the task of supplying whatever wants those at the front expressed. They rested in a content and security that even the imminence of a battle at Mission Ridge in which their "Own" might be engaged failed wholly to destroy. Orchard Knob had dealt kindly with them, and they began to think of their soldiers as each an Achilles with the vulnerable heel secure. Then like a tempest from a cloudless sky came the news of the battle of November 25th, and Dorbury was silent from sheer amazement. Could this thing really have happened to them and theirs? They looked down the list of the dead and wounded again. So many of the names were familiar. So many were those whom they thought to see again. Tom Waters, Captain Tom, could it be? Their young hero? They began to awake, and with the awakening the place became as a house of mourning. The bulletin boards were surrounded by hushed, awestricken men, while women with white faces hastened up to hear the latest from the field.

It was Davies, who having heard the news, went over to break it to Bradford Waters. He had not left his office at the warehouse, and only knew from vague rumors that a battle had taken place. He was hastening through to get out and hear the particulars, when Davies entered, his white face speaking for him before his lips could utter a sound. Waters sprang to his feet, and then sank back into a chair.

"There has been a battle, they tell me," he said.

"Yes," said Davies, with dry lips.

"Was—was—Tom's name mentioned?" He asked the question mechanically as if he already knew the answer that was coming.

Davies was trembling, the tears filled his eyes as he went over and laid his hand on the other's shoulder.

"Yes," he answered. "Tom—the captain's name, Waters, is among the killed."

An ashen pallor spread over Waters' seamed face and his hard hands gripped the desk in front of him fiercely. He breathed heavily but did not speak.

"Come, Bradford, come out in the air with me."

Waters rose, but there was a knock at the door, and opening it a messenger confronted him. It was a telegram from Tom's colonel. The old man could hardly read the words, his hand trembled so. But he made out that they were sending him home. Then Davies saw the man's form straighten up and his eye flash as with a clear voice he read, "Killed, while leading a gallant charge." "Thank God, Davies, he died like a soldier."

There was not a tear in Waters' eye, though pride and grief struggled for mastery in his voice. Davies, who under all his cynical indifference was as soft-hearted as a woman, was weeping like a child.

"I gave him unreservedly," the bereaved father went on, "and he has given me nothing to regret. Come on, I must go home, I must set my house in order to receive my son, the captain."

They went out of the house together, Bradford Waters' face set and firm. Men looked at him shyly upon the street and greeted him briefly. They knew how deeply he had loved his son, and feared a break down of his self-control. Men are always cowards in the face of grief. But their caution was unnecessary. Waters returned their civility with a poise of manner almost stern. What had he to weep for? He had laid his son upon the altar, and he had proven an acceptable sacrifice. Other men might weep for craven sons who had left the fighting to others or who had trembled under fire. As for him, he must be strong. He must walk among men with a high head and a step that showed him worthy to be the father of such a son.

Davies left him at the door of his house. He heard him say as he entered, "You must look sharp, Martha, and have everything in good order. The captain is coming home."

The light was fast fading from the room where Waters sat down, but a ray of gold came in through the window and touched the pictured face of the dead soldier in its place on the mantel. The father rose and taking it down held it close to his breast. "I gave you to them, boy," he murmured, "and they took you, but they cannot, they can never take the memory of you from me."

Someone knocked, and a moment later Martha came in, saying, "A gentleman to see you, Mr. Waters."

With perfect self-possession he passed into the next room, where in the dimness a man stood awaiting him.

"I have dared to come, Bradford," said Stephen Van Doren's voice, "because I knew, and we both loved the boy. I thought maybe we could shake hands over the memory of a brave soldier."

Waters' form trembled like an aspen. He paused in silence, and the moment was full of import. It was to say what the course of his whole future life would be. Whether the iron of his nature would be melted or annealed by the fire through which he was passing. He took a step forward and grasped Van Doren's outstretched hand.

"I am glad you came, Stephen," he said; "he was a brave boy, and you loved him, too."

"No one could help loving him. He was one man among a thousand who was fine enough for the sacrifice. Whether my son be alive or dead, may I always have as little right to sorrow for him as you have for yours tonight."

Stephen Van Doren's voice was low, earnest and impressive, and it broke down something that had stood up very hard and stern in Bradford Waters' spirit. The tears welled up into his eyes and fell unheeded down his cheeks. He wrung Van Doren's hand.

"You must stay and talk to me of him, of both of them. Our boys fought on different sides, Stephen, but they were both ours."

"In a time like this, before an example of bravery, we forget sides and differences and only remember our boys and our love for them."

For awhile they sat and talked of the dead, and of him of whose whereabouts they as yet knew nothing, and Waters' heart was lightened and softened.

"You must go away," he said at last to his visitor, "I have another thing that I must do. Maybe, after all, Stephen, there is a deeper meaning in this sacrifice than either of us yet sees."

"May God grant it," was the fervent response.

"When you hear from Bob, let me know at once. You know he was Tom's friend," he added, almost joyously.

As soon as Van Doren was gone, he gave the servant some directions, and then set out for Nathan Woods' house, which was no less than his own a place of bereavement. The entire household was grief-stricken. The two girls had mingled their tears and sought vainly to comfort each other in their sorrow. Mary was fairly exhausted from her grief, and Nannie, seeing that, recovered herself sufficiently to minister to the weaker girl.

When Mary found out that her father was below and asking for her, she sprang up with wild eyes and fluttering heart.

"Oh, he has come to reproach me," she said. "He will never forgive me."

"There is no reproach in his face, Mary. I think he wants you to be with him when Tom comes home."

Nannie's voice reassured her, and together they went down band in hand. When his daughter came into the room, Bradford Waters held forth his arms, and with a cry that was half grief, half joy, she flung herself into them.

"Father, father," she sobbed, "what shall we do without him?"

"What would his country have done without him, my dear? It has taken him, and we must give him ungrudgingly."

Nannie was leaving the room, but with a new softness, a quality his voice had never known, he put out his hand to her.

"Come, my other daughter," he said, "you loved him too."

For the three, then, there was no past, no difference, no wrong. They were all members of one family bound more strongly by a great love and a great grief. There was a strange similarity apparent in the attitude of Nannie and Bradford Waters towards Tom's death. While Mary thought almost solely of the brother she had lost, they both seemed to say, "We are glad to give him, since we may give him thus."

"Come, let us go home," said Waters, "there is much to do. Mary, come. Nannie, you must go with us. We must go and make ready to receive the captain."

And together they went with him to receive the captain.

The strange idea took Bradford Waters to prepare for his son's homecoming as if the dead could know. Perhaps there did remain to him some of the mysticism to which his New England birth and ancestry gave him right. It would not have assorted illy with his bleak nature. Perhaps he believed that Tom would know. However it was, he had determined that all should be quite as the young man would have liked it had he come home with conscious eyes to see and light with pleasure at what he saw.

To Mary the house was very desolate, and a rush of sad emotions swept over her as she looked at the familiar things arranged by an alien hand.

"Tom would hardly know the place now, if he could see it," she told her father.

But he replied, "Never mind, never mind, it shall all be set right before he comes. He shall find nothing to his distaste."

The saddest duty they had was the arrangement of his room. The old man still followed his strange whim, and had the chamber arranged as if a living guest were to occupy it. The bed was laid as Tom would have had it laid, and the fresh sheets turned back as if to receive his tired form. In the vases was the late golden-rod, always a great favorite with him. But on his pillows were the marks of tears which Nannie had shed as she smoothed their soft whiteness, and knew that his brown head would never press them again.

To her a great change had come. In spite of the pride and fortitude which bore her up, the light and spontaneity had gone out of her life. She might laugh again, but it would never be with the old free ring. In spirit, she was already Tom's wife, and she was now as much widowed as any woman who had followed her husband to the grave. That she bore her burden better than Mary, was largely due to the practical strength of her love for Tom. Had he lived, she would have been glad to welcome and help him. As he was dead, she was no less his and waited the time when she might join him. Mary might weep for him, but she would wait for him, believing that no such love as hers was given to mortals to wither and die without fruition. This love held her so utterly above ordinary opinions and conventions that she did not think to ask what would be said of her entering her lover's house as one of the family. It was nothing to her. It was a matter of course. There was a certain joy in feeling that she had the right to help and in seeing hour after hour that Tom's father and sister leaned more and more upon her strength.

It was on the third day after the news of the battle that Tom's body was brought home, one mute mourner accompanying it—Nigger Ed. Those were strenuous times and there was no opportunity for fine courtesies, for escorts and officer pall-bearers, even for that brave one, but the flag was wrapped around him, the flag he had fought and died for.

His father was very calm as he looked at the boyish face so cold and still before him. Death had been kind to the soldier and had come quickly, leaving him almost unaltered. He lay as if he had fallen asleep with bright dreams of a purposeful tomorrow. There was none of the horror or dread of battle impressed upon his marble countenance, nothing that could cause the woman who loved him best of all to shrink from him.

Bradford Waters stooped and kissed his son's brow. There was a smile on his own lips. Even Mary forgot to weep. This was the majesty, the beauty of death. Nannie hovered over him as she would over a flower. They were alone together— these three, when a knock, soft and hesitating, fell upon the door. Bradford opened it to find without the Negro Ed. He silently motioned him to enter.

"Dey tol' me to gin you dis when you was settled," he said. He handed Waters a letter. It was from Colonel Bassett, Tom's commanding officer, and ran,

"Dear Sir, I wish I knew how to pay tribute to the finest man and most gallant gentleman I ever knew—your son. I wish I might have shown him the respect that I feel and come with his body to see it laid in its last resting-place, but this is war. I would condone with you, sir, but that I know the father of such a son must be proud to have had him die where and as he did."

It was a soldier's letter and though Waters read it with trembling voice, his eyes glowed and he looked at the still form as if to say, "I would not have had it otherwise."

Ed was still standing, waiting for the father to speak. But Waters said nothing. The Negro shifted uneasily, then he said anxiously, "Is you mad at me, Mistah Watahs? Has de cunnel said anythin'? Dey wouldn't have sont me home wid him, but I baiged, 'cause I kinder thought you'd ravah have somebody—dat knowed him—bring him back."

Waters reached out and grasped the black man's hand. "Why, God bless you forever and ever," he said.

The privacy of the family even with its dead could not long be maintained. Dorbury had suspended business. This hero was theirs as well as his family's. They filled the sidewalks, they surged at the doors. They would see him. They would bring their flowers to lay beside his bier. He belonged to them, to them, who had helped to send him forth and had cheered his departure. Bradford Waters should not be selfish in his grief. The boys from the factories and ware-houses came, and also from the shops, those who had known him and those who had not. All men know a hero. And the father said, "Let them come in, he will be glad to see them."

And so "the captain" came home.

Chapter 23

A Troublesome Secret

FOR A LONG TIME curiosity was rampant in a little country district not very far from Cincinnati. It was the proverbial rural locality where everyone knows or wishes to know the business of everyone else, and is offended if he doesn't. In this particular place, the object of interest was a white farmhouse set forward on the road, and fronting ample grounds both of field and garden. It was the home of John Metzinger, a prosperous German husbandman and his good wife, Gretchen. They were pleasant, easygoing people, warmhearted and generous. Their neighbors had always looked upon them with favor, until one day—it was early in August, the eye of suspicion fell upon the house. Those who had lived near the Metzingers, and those who merely passed upon the road to and from town began to point questioning fingers at the place and to look askance at it. The gossips shook their heads and whispered together.

It all began with one woman who had unceremoniously "dropped in" on the couple; "dropping in" consisting of pushing open the door and entering unannounced by the formality of a knock. The easygoing neighbor had pursued this course only to find the door of an inner room hastily closed and the good wife profuse in embarrassed expostulations. Mrs. Metzinger was not good at dissimulation, and her explanation that the room was all torn up for she was housecleaning served but to arouse her visitor's suspicion. In her own words as she told it many times later, she said with fine indignation, "Think o' her sayin' to me that she was cleanin' house, an' she with as spick an' span a white apron on as ever you see. Says I to her, 'Ain't you pickin' out a funny time to clean, Mrs. Metzinger?' and she says with that Dutch brogue o' hers, 'Oh, I cleans anydimes de place gets dirty.' Then I says ca'm like, because I've allus liked that woman, 'I should think you'd get yer apron dirty,' an' all of a sudden she jerked it off an' stood there grinnin' at me; but that was what give her away, for lo, an' behold, her dress was as clan as my bran' new calico. Then I says, 'Well, never min', I'll just come in an' help you,' an' would you believe it, that woman got right in my way an' wouldn't let me go in that room, all the time jabbering something about 'Nod troublin' me.' Right then an' there, thinks I, there's something wrong in that room."

She closed her remarks as one who says, "There's murder behind that door."

Her hearers were struck by her tragic presentation of the case, and they too, began to watch for signs of guilt in the Germans. These were soon plentiful. None was more convincing than that a room that had always been open to the light had now its blinds closed. Someone had said too, that they had seen the doctor's gig at the door one night, and had waited for him to come out. But on questioning him, as any man has a right to do, "Who's sick, doctor?" he had sprung into his vehicle, put whip to his horse and dashed away without answering. This in itself, looked dark. For why should a doctor of all men, refuse to be questioned about his patients? The little scattered community for three or four miles and even further up and down the road was awestruck and properly indignant. Such communities have no respect for reticence.

Meanwhile the trouble went on, and the Metzingers grew in disfavor. What had been friendly greetings degenerated into stiff nods or grew into clumsily veiled inquiries. While their neighbors lost sleep asking each other what horror was going on behind those closed doors, the simple couple went on about their duty and kept their counsel. It was really not so much the horror that the community resented but that the particulars of it were being kept from them.

If the Metzingers could have told their story, it would have proved, after all, a very short and simple one. It would have been to the effect that late one night towards the end of July, they had been awakened by the tramping of feet and a knocking upon their door. Going thither, they had found four men unkempt and mud-stained, who bore between them another, evidently wounded. They had brought him and laid him upon the sofa, and then with promises, that were half threats, had left him in their care. They came then to know who their visitors were; some of "Morgan's terrible men." Their promises to respect the farmer's stock had not been needed to secure attention for their wounded comrade, for the good wife's heart had gone out already to the young fellow who lay there so white and drabbled with blood.

John Metzinger would have told, though his good wife would never have mentioned it, how all that night and the next day, Gretchen had hovered over the wounded man, bandaging his arm, bathing it, and doing what she could to ease the pain, while the sufferer muttered strange things in his sleep and tossed like a restless child.

They could not get a doctor until the next night, for they knew that all must proceed with secrecy, and when the physician came, the fever had already set in and the chances for the man's recovery seemed very slight.

They could have told too, of the doctor's long fight with the fever, and what the gossips did not know, how one night two physicians came and amputated the wounded arm at the elbow. Then of the long fight for life through the hot August days, of the terrible nights when Death seemed crowding into the close room and the sufferer lay gasping for breath. But they told nothing. Silently they went their way, grieved by the distrust of those about them, but unfaltering in their course. And when Van Doren first looked up weakly enough into the German woman's face, his eyes full of the gratitude he could not speak, both she and her John were repaid for all that they had suffered.

The woman fell upon her knees by the bedside saying, "Dank Got, dank Got, he vill gid vell now, Shon," and "Shon" who was very big and very much a man, pressed his wife's hand and went behind the door to look for something that was not there.

With the cooler weather of autumn came more decided convalescence to the young trooper, but the earliest snows had fallen before he was able to creep to the door that looked out upon the road. He was only the shadow of his former self. Mrs. Metzinger looked at him, full of pity.

"I guess you petter led de toctor wride by your home now. Dey vill vant to hear from you."

"Not yet, not yet," he protested. "It would cause my father too much anxiety, and some others perhaps, too much joy to know how I am faring."

"Your poor fader, dough, he vill be vorried aboud you."

"Father knows the chances of war and he will not begin to worry yet. It would grieve him so much more to know that I am out of it all so soon."

"Mister Robert," said the woman impressively, "you don't know faders. Dey vas yoost like modders, pretty near, und modders, alvays vants to know; if he is vell, she is glad und she dank Got for dat. If he is det, she vants to gry und gry ofer dose leedle shoes dot he used to vear."

"He shall know, he shall know, Mrs. Metzinger, and very soon, for I am going home to him and his joy will make him forget how long he has waited."

"Yes, I guess maype dot is so."

Robert had divined more by instinct than by any outward demonstration of his hosts that his secret stay in the house had aroused in their neighbors some sort of feeling against these people. He was perfectly sure that should he write to his father, he would come to him in spite of everything, and at any stir or unusual commotion about the house, what was only smoldering now might burst into flame. So, although it wrung his heart to do so, living within sixty miles of his father, he kept his lips closed and gave no sign. His heart had gone out to these people who had sacrificed so much for him, and he wanted to do something in return for them. At first, because of his very weakness, they had forborne to question him about his home and people, and when he was strong enough to act, he had unconsciously accepted this silence as his sacrifice, without divining that he was not the real sufferer, not the real bearer of the burden.

He had promised that he would go home soon, but the case had been a severe one, and it was December before he dared to venture out beyond the gate. Sometimes, when the days were warm and bright, he would sit wrapped up on the porch at the side, for the need of secrecy gone, the Metzingers were openly and humanly unhumble. They bowed proudly, even jauntily to their detractors, while the priest and the Levites passed by on the other side. There were no good Samaritans about save the Metzingers themselves, and their little devices might have gone unobserved, but that the priest and the Levites were curious people, and at last, came over to question.

"Who is the sick young man?" they questioned.

"He is a friend of ours from de var," Mrs. Metzinger answered them.

"We'd like to talk to him," they volunteered.

"No, he must not talk to beoples, not yet," was the answer.

"Why don't he wear his uniform?" Robert wore a suit of "Shon's" jeans.

"It was yoost ruint and all spoilt mit blood."

But they looked at Robert askance, and the gossip which for awhile from inaction had faltered, sprang up anew. Who was he? Why so little about him? Why had they kept the secret so long?

The good people saw with dismay what they had done. They had only aroused the trouble which they had hoped to allay. Van Doren saw their trouble and determined immediately to relieve them.

"I am going home now," he told them one day.

"You are not yet so strong."

"Oh, yes I am. I'm quite a giant now."

"Vat you dinks Shon? Iss he strong enough?"

"I dinks he gan stay here so long as he vants."

"But I am going, my good friends, it's best for us all."

"Vy?"

"I have seen how the neighbors look at me and I have seen how they look at you. You shan't hurt yourselves any longer."

"Dat iss not right. We care nodings for de neighbors. Ve minds our own business."

Mrs. Metzinger's husband said something under his breath, only a word it was, but it made his wife gasp and cry, "Shon, for shame on you!"

"I'm going," Robert went on, "either with your consent or without. I don't know how I'm ever going to thank you. You've both been so good. It's nasty in a case like this to think of pay. I can't do it decently, but I'm going to do it. It's the nearest way a brute of a man can come to showing his appreciation."

"No pay," said John.

"Not vun cent," said his wife.

"Ve had some gompany," Gretchen put in.

Robert smiled on; they were so like big children.

"I am not going to let you two cheat me out of showing my gratitude by any such excuse."

Gretchen wept and John caused his wife to exclaim again, but it was of no use, and just at dusk, the old carryall took him away to the station, still in his host's suit, the empty sleeve turned up, and the stump of arm flapping at his side.

It was about an hour after John had gone with Robert to the station, that Mrs. Metzinger heard footsteps, and going to the door saw several men without.

"We want that man that's stayin' here," said the leader.

"He's yoost gone to his home in Dorbury."

"In Dorbury—why we thought—what side was he on?"

Mrs. Metzinger drew herself up in dignified anger and said, "I don'd dink Got has any sides, Deacon Callvell," then she slammed the door, and the deacon and his "Committee" went away feeling small, and glad that it was dark, while Mrs. Metzinger rocked out her pious anger until the floor cried again.

Chapter 24

Robert Van Doren Goes Home

THERE WAS NO BLARE of trumpets, no popular acclaim to greet Robert Van Doren's homecoming. He entered Dorbury alone and unwelcomed, weary and sick at heart. It was half-past eight o'clock when his train drew into the familiar station, and the winter night had settled heavy and black. A familiar form came towards him as he walked down the platform, and sadly changed as he was, he saw the light of recognition in the man's eyes. The next instant, he was looking at the stern lines of an averted face. He shuddered and hurried on as rapidly as his weakness would allow. Although he had often in his moments of convalescence pictured dimly how he would be received at home, yet the actuality was so much stronger and harsher than any anticipation of it could be that he was quite unmanned. For the first time it came to him that he was an alien in the land of his adoption, and even upon the dark streets, he shrank from the people he met because he knew his face would be to them as a leper's, and even the empty sleeve, the badge of honor to so many of them, would read only to these people, "Unclean, unclean."

He was bending his steps towards his father's house, absorbed in bitter thoughts, when a sort of divination, rather than the appearance of things roused him from his reverie. He looked around upon the place, the houses, the lawns, and then a lighted window caught his eye and he realized that he was passing Bradford Waters' house.

"I wonder if she is back at home?" he said. "I caused her so much grief." He passed through the gate, and crept up to the window. The light shone through a thin shade, but he could see nothing within the house. After a short while, however, he heard the sound of women's voices, and one was hers. Without warning, all the pent-up feeling of the past three years burst forth in the cry, "Mary!"

"What's that?" cried someone within, but there was no answer save the hurried tread of feet across the floor. Aware of what he had done, he was hurrying away, when the front door was thrown open, and he saw her before him standing in a flood of light. Then he could not go. He stood transfixed until she walked down the steps to him crying, "Robert, Robert, I was sure you would come!" And all he could do was to bow his head and murmur, "Thank God."

She took him by the hand and led him into the house, he unresisting.

"Here is Robert," she said to Nannie. "Did I not tell you he would come?"

"Yes, and I am glad with you." Her greeting of Robert was tender, almost sisterly. As soon as she could do so tactfully, she left the room, and Van Doren's glance followed her questioningly. He could not understand her subdued manner, her sad face. Mary saw the look in his eyes and asked,

"Do you not know, then?"

"No," he answered, "what is it?"

"Tom."

"Tom—not—dead?"

"Dead, yes."

"Killed?"

"Yes, at Mission Ridge, nearly a month ago," and she told of all that had happened, while he sat like one dazed.

Finally he broke in, "Tom dead, I living, why is this? Why this choice of the brave instead of the lukewarm, the soldier instead of the raider?"

"Robert, Robert, you are not yourself. I weep for my brother, but you, I have you still."

For answer he raised his empty sleeve.

"Ah, Robert, you don't know. I love you. Here are two arms—yours."

He kissed her cheek silently, and then a sound made them start apart and stare into each other's faces with parted lips. Someone was on the step. There was but one person whom it could be.

"Quick, quick," said Mary, opening a door into the next room. "In here." And Robert hurried in just as Bradford Waters entered, finding Mary troubled and embarrassed. He stood looking at her with a sad face, and then he said,

"Mary, you grieve me very much. Has all the past been so hard that you cannot forget it? Has not the past month proven that I am a changed man and that you need hide nothing from me?"

"Yes, father, forgive me." And going to the door she called, "Robert!"

Van Doren came in with a defiant look on his face which vanished at sight of Waters' outstretched hand.

"Why—why—Mr. Waters," he stammered confusedly.

"Yes, yes, I know, my boy, but I'm glad to see you back, Robert."

Robert grasped the old man's hand and wrung it warmly. "I'm so glad you're reconciled to me, you didn't like me before."

"No more of that, no more of that. I always liked you, but I didn't like your principles. I've seen sorrow though, and I look at things differently."

"Mary has told me and it grieved me much."

"You know then, that the captain has come home?"

"Yes, would to God that I might have come like that."

"Tut, Tut, have you been home?"

"No, I was on my way there, when I heard Mary's voice and stopped."

"You must go to him at once now, he will be overjoyed."

"Do you think I dare go to him myself? I'm afraid he thinks me dead."

"I have no doubt. Let Mary go with you and break the news to him. Go on."

Mary hastened to put on her hat and cloak, and together the two went out, leaving the old man standing by the mantel looking at them with strange tenderness. Robert turned at the door and looked back. "You will never know what you have done, Mr. Waters, to make my homecoming less than a tragedy to me," he said huskily.

"It was Tom, not I," said Waters gently.

The house looked very dismal as Mary and Robert approached it, and the latter's heart failed him.

"Has my father seemed to grieve much?" he asked.

"He has been absorbed and preoccupied, but his faith was like mine. We knew you would come back."

"I have heard of the faith that is stronger than death, but I always thought it a meaningless phrase until now. Bless you both."

Stephen Van Doren was drowsing by his library fire when Mary was admitted, but with the courtesy of his kind, he rose and went nimbly to meet her, apologizing meanwhile for his dressing-gown and slippers.

"But, my dear child," he exclaimed, "what brings you here at this hour?"

"Mr. Van Doren," Mary faltered, her face all aglow.

"Stop," he exclaimed, "whether the dead can come to life or not, no girl can show a face like that, unless she has seen her lover. What is it?"

"I have seen him, he is here in the hall."

Van Doren took a step forward, and then stood trembling, but Robert had thrown the door open and rushed to his father.

"Father!"

"My boy!"

This was in the days before men grew too old to embrace their fathers, and bearded cheeks and lips met. The father's arms were about his son and the empty sleeve fell under his hand. He held it up and then pushed his son from him. His head drooped sadly for a moment, but there was a look of exaltation on his face.

"Father—father, don't let that grieve you. I—I—lost it honorably."

Stephen Van Doren's head went up like a bull's when he scents resistance. "Grieve me," he cried, and then turning to Mary, he said, "Now, my dear, I can show your father that and talk to him upon more nearly equal terms. Why, boy, you've won your spurs, if you haven't got them. To us of the newer land, an empty sleeve, when gallantly won is what the Victoria Cross is to an Englishman."

Robert flushed and moved away a pace further from his father. "But you do not know all."

"All? You said it was won honestly—that is enough."

The young soldier looked appealingly at Mary. "I shall have to tell you all," he said.

"I will go, Robert," she said; "it was wrong for me to stay so long, but this meeting has given me such joy as I have never known before." She turned towards the door.

"You must not go," he cried, detaining her, "it is for you also to know. It belongs to you."

"To me?"

"To you—yes."

"How?"

"You remember that night of nights," he asked her softly. "Do they know of it?"

"No, I have never dared to tell them so wild a story."

"I will tell it now, then."

"You may, Robert, they will believe you, everyone will."

Then briefly Robert told his father of the strange meeting with Mary that had resulted in his wound. "I don't know what you will say," he ended, "and I don't know what it means."

"It means God," said his father solemnly. "He sent her. Think of it as an old man's fancy if you will, but he lighted one of his own torches at the moment that you might see each other's faces."

"Oh, Robert," cried Mary. "Then it was for me?"

"Yes, darling. Father forgive us, but Mary is glad."

"Why, Mary, child, you show more sense than that great hulking, one-armed hero."

"Hero—father!"

"The man who is old enough to have done a noble deed and is not old enough to know it, should be sent into a closet like a child."

"He does know it—he must know it. Robert, you must see it."

"Hero" was the word running through young Van Doren's brain and he did not understand. He felt Mary's arms about him, he felt his father's hand pressing his own and his thoughts grew hazy. "Hero," how could he be a hero when he was lying helpless when the best fighting was going on, when—though he dared not say it—he did not even know if his heart were wholly with the cause.

His father's voice broke in upon his reverie. "Bob, you are the—well, look here, don't you see what kind of a man he must be who dares to ride away from his comrades and into the face of the enemy, and alone, to save a woman?"

"Yes, don't you see, Rob?" said Mary eagerly.

"Why, I loved her," said Robert. "I loved her, and forgive me, father, more than my cause."

"Unless you had had that in you that made your cause strong and noble, you could not have done it even for love."

"Have I pleased you?"

"I am proud to be your father."

"And Mary, I didn't want to tell you—are you hurt?"

"Hurt with the sort of a hurt that a woman—" she started impulsively towards her lover and then paused abashed.

"Never check a good impulse," said old Van Doren. "I am now looking at the portrait of my grandfather."

The two young people improved the opportunity. The old man showed consideration in the length of time he spent admiring the portrait. But a hurried knock on the door recalled their attention.

A servant with a frightened face entered. "There's a lot of men at the door," he said.

"What do they want?" asked Van Doren sternly.

"They—they say that there is a rebel in here, and they want him."

"Go back to them and say," said the old man, his voice ringing like a trumpet, "that there is no rebel here, but a soldier and the son of a soldier, and if they want to see him, he is at their service when he knows their business with him." The servant retired.

"The hounds have begun to bay already," said Robert, his face set and dogged, though he patted Mary's hair as she clung fearfully to him.

"The hounds!" said his father, bringing from his desk a brace of pistols that had seen service, "you mean the curs. The hounds know their true game. Can you use your left hand?"

"As well as my right."

The father tried vainly to hide his satisfaction as he handed his son a weapon. Outside a clamor arose, which grew louder and louder, and the servant came flying back. "They say you must come out."

"So they are afraid to chance it where there's a man's chance," said Robert. "Come, father, let us go to them. You are right, they are curs, not hounds, after all."

Mary moved forward with them.

"No, dear, stay here."

"I will not, Robert, I have no fear for myself. I am going with you. If you die, I do not want to live. I am going."

"Think of your father."

"Do you think of my brother? Would he have me do less?"

The cries were growing fiercer every moment, and the father at the door cried, "Come on," and stepped out as if eager to meet a crowd of enthusiastic admirers. They passed along the hall, threw open the front door and stepped out into the blaze of light which fell from the chandelier within. At their appearance a hoarse cry rose from the lips of the mob, for mob it was, low, ignorant, infuriated.

"There he is—the rebel!"

"Rebel's too good for him—copperhead's the name!"

"Traitor!"

"Coward!"

They stood calmly upon the steps, the three. Robert, pale but dauntless; his father as fixed as a statue, and Mary just behind them, like a spirit of Justice, with eyes unbound.

When their attitude had somewhat quieted the tumult, Stephen Van Doren spoke, and his voice was calm and hard. "Well, gentlemen," he said, "what is it that you want of us?"

"We want your son. We want that damned copperhead that's joined the rebels and been killing our boys. That's what we want," came the reply in fifty voices.

"There is no traitor and no copperhead here," Van Doren went on. "My son, it is true, is here," and he bowed to Robert as if he were delivering a complimentary address, "but he is none of the things which you name. He is a man who has fought for his convictions, and has returned here where he has as good a right as any of you. He is here, I say, and if any or all of you want him, damn you, come and take him!"

The old man's voice had risen, and at the moment both he and Robert, as if by a preconcerted signal, raised their pistols and leveled them at the foremost ranks of the mob. Intimidated at this defiance, the crowd fell back. Just then a rock hurtled past Van Doren's head, and crashed through a window. The noise was like an electric shock to the rabble's failing energies, and with the cry, "Come on, rock them!" they started forward again, those behind forcing the front ranks.

"Try not to kill any of the fools," the father whispered briefly to his son.

They were both pressing their triggers and the forward men were on the first step, when a new cry, "Waters, Waters!" checked their advance, and a man with flowing white hair who had been thrusting his way through the crowd, also mounted the step. The mob thought it had found a new champion, and again yelling, "Waters, Waters!" rushed forward, but Waters turned and faced them, waving his arms.

"Back, back, you cowards!" he cried. They paused in amazement, as he backed slowly up the steps. When they took in his meaning, they attempted another rush, but he stood above them, and suddenly from beneath his coat he tore a long whip with leaden tipped thongs.

"Back," he cried, wielding it with terrific force into the faces and over the heads of the leaders. "Take this, this is for dogs. Back to your kennels, I say!"

His face was terrible, and the men in front quickly turned and began fighting their way to the rear. Others followed, and a panic seized upon them. When Waters stood alone, and the mob at a safe distance began sullenly to gather, someone shouted, "If it wasn't for your son's sake, Waters, we'd kill you."

Waters indicated that he wished to speak, and they became silent with the silence of watchful beasts.

"If it were not for my son's sake!" he said. "I gave him for the cause of right and decency, and I am willing to give myself. What right has any of you who joins so cowardly an attack as this to take upon his lips the name of a brave man? Let never a man who was in this mob tonight utter my son's name again, or by the God who rules over us, I will kill him!" A breath like a shudder passed over the rabble, and Waters went on, "I have lost and I have the right to demand the full worth of my sacrifice, and you who know my loss, have no right, to deny me this." He moved up beside Robert, and putting his hand on his shoulder, said, "This man shall stand to me in lieu of the son I have lost, and his empty sleeve shall be the sign of an eternal compact between us, the badge of honor which it is. He is mine, not yours. Mine, by the blood of my son, mine by the void in my heart. Touch him, if you dare! Go home," and he began moving down the steps, his whip grasped tightly in his hand. "Go home, I say, or I'll whip you there."

The mob fell back, and just then the orderly tramping of feet was heard and a rush was made in an opposite direction as the police arrived on the scene, late and reluctant.

The four turned and went silently into the house. They sat silent, too, in the library, all too tense for speech, until Waters said, "Come, Mary, let us go. You need have no fear of further trouble, Bob, the captain will be about. Steve, I disagree with you very much in your last article in the *Diurnal*. You are all wrong, but I'll talk to you about that tomorrow. Good-night. Come, Mary. It is strange how fanatical some men will be on a subject."

Chapter 25

Conclusion

IN THE AFTER DAYS, it was as Bradford Waters had said, and Robert Van Doren experienced no further trouble at the hands of the mob. Indeed, no man was willing to be known as having been a member of the party. When it was talked about in public, men turned their faces away and did not meet each others' eyes. In so small a town, it was inevitable that many of the participants in such an affair should be known, but no name was ever mentioned, and the matter was not pressed. However, there was something suspicious about the manner in which some men avoided Bradford Waters, and kept silent when others spoke his son's name.

In the close counsels which took place between the two families, formerly so far apart, Robert had suggested that perhaps it would be better for him to go away from Dorbury to some place where he was not known; but both Waters and his father strenuously objected to that.

"No," said the latter, "there are times when concessions must be made to the prejudices of people. There are other times when it is no less than righteous to ride them down."

"Your father is right. Had I lived in the South with my early training and bent of thought, I should have had no better sense than to stand up for my principles just as he did. I should have resented any Southerner's question of my right to do so. The trouble with us all is that we will not allow others the right which we demand for ourselves."

"I think the trouble with us all is that we talk a great deal about free thought and free speech, meaning that others shall have both as long as they think and speak as we do. No, Rob, you stay right here. Dorbury's got to accept you just as you are."

And Robert stayed. There were those who looked askance at him, and those who could not be reconciled to him, but no one troubled him. As the war drew to a close, and the continued victories of the Union filled the people with enthusiasm, they even began to grow friendly towards him, but he was slow to receive their advances. He was much with Mary and the stream of their love that had been so turbulent, now flowed smoothly and sweetly. Together, they tried to cheer Nannie. "Cheer" is hardly the word either, for she had never lost a certain lightness of spirit that would not let her be entirely cast down. But they tried to bring back the old gaiety of her manner that had been her chief charm. She was now back and forth between the Waters' and her own home, and was full of the sweetness of good words and good works on every hand. She was called "Little Miss Nannie," and men had already begun to pay to her that delicate deference which is given to a woman who will never marry. She was always, and would always be "Miss Nannie."

"I wish, Nannie," Mary said to her one day, "that I could give you a part of my happiness." Nannie laughed.

"You poor child," she said, "don't you know that I am very happy. I am happier than anyone could ever imagine. I have a lover who will always be young and a love that cannot grow cold. Don't worry about me, I am blest beyond most women."

So they let her go her way and their hearts ceased to ache for her as they saw how cheerful she grew with the joy of doing good. So Nannie began, and so she went on through the years until the end, like a fair flower dying away in its own perfume. There was no selfishness in her subdued sweetness, for when the soldiers came back no one was dearer to them than their dead captain's sweetheart.

The horror of the war has been written of, the broken homes and the broken hearts, but many a life was made sweeter for the fiery trial through which it passed. Stephen Van Doren was stern and implacable until the end. Robert was with him when the news of the surrender came. A shiver passed over his body as if he himself were the Confederacy which was dying. Then he took his son's hand, and said with a smile, "Well, a principle has been tested and failed. We must submit to the inevitable. From now on—it is the Union," and he opened his window to hear the bells and whistles that proclaimed the people's rejoicings.

The war was ended, but there were gaping wounds to bind up and deep sores that needed careful nursing. The country had been drenched with fraternal blood and the stench of it was an ill savor in the nostrils of both North and South. Grant was a hero, but men were asking, "What is McClellan?" The homecoming soldiers, worn and weary with the long campaign, were being dropped along the wayside from every train. Some homes wore hung with evergreens for gladness and others were draped with cypress for those who would never come back. Dorbury had its share of joy and grief. There were returns and there were messages from those who would not return; from lovers, husbands, fathers and brothers. But above the note of sadness was one of joy, for joy is more persistent than grief, if shorter lived.

A little after Appomattox, Robert and Mary were married and went to live in a little home of their own where the two fathers were destined to come many an evening thereafter to fight over the war, talk politics and wrangle as heartily as ever.

Down in Virginia wounded and broken and sore, her heart bleeding for her lost cause and her lost sons; her fields devastated, and her resources depleted, a solemn tone characterized the thanksgiving for the war's end. Walter Stewart thanked God for the triumph of the Union; but wept for the grief of his state. Just about the time that Robert and Mary were united, he and Dolly were married in the little vine-covered church by the rector who had looked askance at him a few years before.

And they were happy with the happiness of youth. Nelson Etheridge had come back safe. Dr. Daniel, now with a major's stripes, walked much in the garden with Emily, from whom, before going away, he had gained a certain promise.

Stewart had indeed come to his own again, and he would have been a delight to his father's eyes could the old colonel have seen him riding about the plantation among the Negroes who remained, and directing the repair of the damages which the war had made. He would never go back to Dorbury now, but his memory oft reverted to the old scenes and old acquaintances. His description of Nigger Ed had so pleased Dolly that it resulted in the receipt of the following letter by that gentleman one day in Dorbury:

"MY DEAR ED—You will remember me as one of the boys who used to run around the streets after you years ago, and later as one of the First, *when you were in command.* If you will come down here where there are lots of your people, I'll give you a position on my plantation where you won't be teased. Let me know if you will come. It will be much better than going about ringing an old bell.
"WALTER STEWART."

With this letter the Negro marched into the office of one of Dorbury's young lawyers one day. The lawyer had been with the First.

"I want you to read dis an' answeh it, mistah—'scuse me—lootenant."

The young fellow took it and his face flushed as he read it.

"Uh huh," said Ed, "now you answer it, please suh."

"All right," the young fellow scribbled for a moment, and then turned saying, "I think you'd better make it a telegram, Ed."

"Wha' fu'?"

"Shorter, more expressive."

"Les' hyeah it."

The young man picked up the slip of paper and read slowly and carefully, "Mr. Walter Stewart, Stewart House, Rockford Co., Virginia. You be damned."

Ed started as if he had been shot, and then said hastily, "Oh, no, lootenant. I reckon I won't send dat. A telegram's too 'spressive."

"How dare he send for you?" the young man broke in. "You belong to Dorbury. You're a part of it."

"Yes, co'se I is, but I wants to be 'spressive and curtchus too. Jes' you write an' tell him some'p'n 'bout me wanting to 'tain my 'ficial position."

This advice was taken and the result was that Walter threw the household into convulsions over an epistle couched in the most elegant language which informed Mr. Stewart that while he appreciated the very kind offer, the writer—Ed couldn't write a line—preferred to retain his official position, in view of the fact that the emoluments thereof had been materially increased.

And it was true. There were men who had seen that black man on bloody fields, which were thick with the wounded and dying, and these could not speak of him without tears in their eyes. There were women who begged him to come in and talk to them about their sons who had been left on some Southern field, wives who wanted to hear over again the last words of their loved ones. And so they gave him a place for life and everything he wanted, and from being despised he was much petted and spoiled, for they were all fanatics.

THE SPORT OF
THE GODS

Introduction

OF DUNBAR'S FOUR NOVELS, only the final one, *The Sport of the Gods,* remains in print and is read with any regularity in college courses or studied extensively by scholars. As a significant contribution to the naturalistic writing and the African American literature of its time, *The Sport of the Gods* has been seen, almost without question, as Dunbar's best novel. Few have found the story cheerful or uplifting, but many have admired the author's subversion of the plantation and minstrel traditions. Many have also appreciated the skillfulness with which he created the grimly fatalistic setting and action at the core of the naturalistic tradition. In pairing the two parallel families of the Hamiltons and Oakleys in plot and thematic networks, Dunbar undermined the conventions of plantation fiction, even as he advanced past many of the novelists of the time by portraying, with pinpoint accuracy, the duplicity and brutality facing African Americans who migrated to Northern cities.

Less than four years before his death and nearly a decade after the triumph of his dialect poems, *The Sport of the Gods* at last freed Dunbar from the bonds of problematic plantation stories and coon show dialect, and marked him as a forerunner of novels by Claude McKay, Wallace Thurman, and Richard Wright. In spite of its achievements, even *The Sport of the Gods* has not received the critical acclaim it deserves. For too long the novel has been read in isolation from the earlier novels and with little regard for the plays, essays, and short stories Dunbar wrote around the same time.

The narrator's opening sentence sets the tone and direction for the action and social commentary to follow: "Fiction has said so much in regret of the old days when there were plantations and overseers and masters and slaves, that it was good to come upon such a household as Berry Hamilton's, if for no other reason than it afforded a relief from the monotony of tiresome iteration." Twenty years after the emancipation of slaves in 1865, Berry and Fannie Hamilton and their children live in what would be considered "the home of a typical, good-living Negro." Instead of being rewarded with freedom and the American dream, however, Berry is falsely accused of stealing and is condemned without a hearing, and the Hamiltons' world rapidly falls apart.

Perhaps Dunbar subsequently places too much blame on wicked city life as the culprit in the family's misfortune, as the novel invites us to see that everything, everywhere, has always been stacked against them. Life in New York does appear to offer hope, but Dunbar soon reveals that what seems to be an opportunity is filled with hypocrisy and indifference. Hopes for a new beginning turn into monstrosities that soon multiply. To protect his family honor, Oakley conceals the true identity of the thief. Through the efforts of a diligent reporter, Hamilton is exonerated. Freed at last from jail, Berry tries unsuccessfully to reunite his family. By the novel's end, he and Fannie have returned to live in the South once more. Hand in hand, they listen to Oakley's shrieks of madness and endure the cruel jokes until the gods at last tire of their sport. The famous concluding passage is typical of Dunbar's understatement, but the proverbial mask has been dropped: "It was not a happy life, but it was all that was left to them, and they took it up without complaint, for they knew they were powerless against some Will infinitely stronger than their own."

In this pivotal work, Dunbar is still experimenting with a variety of literary conventions new to him. Typically, he masters those conventions quickly, stretches them in new directions, and modifies or even undermines likely expectations. Paramount in his accomplishments completed over a short career was his propensity to experiment, his degree of success with little experience, and the way he managed to walk a very fine line between what might be accepted or even liked and the full range of his penetrating analysis and satiric wit. He used many conventions of literature in his time, only to subvert them to his own ends.

In line with many postbellum writers who were encouraged to see daily life progressing in accord with what they saw to be good on the plantations, *The Sport of the Gods* presents Maurice Oakley as caring and supportive of his former slave, Berry Hamilton, and his family. To suggest the alleged benefits of life on the plantation, Dunbar uses the literary device of mirroring: Maurice and Berry are not only on good terms but apparently alike in many of their ways of thinking and acting. Maurice sees himself as a model for Berry to follow. "There is no telling," he says with pride, "when Berry will be following my example and be taking a wife unto himself." When the money disappears, however, Maurice concludes that Berry is not to be trusted, and the accusations are quickly accepted as fact. Even though Oakley later learns who stole the money, he wants foremost to protect his own and ignores the advice of the detective he has hired: "I should advise . . . no open proceedings against this servant until further evidence to establish his guilt is found." Even Maurice's brother, the actual thief, urges Oakley to avoid extreme action: "Promise me you won't be too hard on him, Maurice. Give him a little scare and let him go." Finally his wife pleads: "Don't be revengeful, Maurice." Of course, legal proceedings would not be available to them, and nothing short of condemnation and cover-up are the goals from the beginning. The story is thus laced with ironies; the reader knows the guilty party all along, as Berry good-naturedly or naively allows himself to be reduced to something less than human and, in essence, to be returned to a form of slavery. While critical interpretation of the novel emphasizes the harsh and uncaring city, the Hamiltons' fate is sealed long before they migrate North in this undermining of the trust and mutual interdependence that is so often claimed as characteristic of the plantation tradition.

The indifference of the naturalistic tradition is found in both the opportunism that bludgeons the Hamiltons in New York and the total violation of values perpetrated by Oakley. "He is gone and will never know what happens," he assures his wife about his brother Frank's request for clemency toward Berry, "so I may be as revengeful as I wish." The fierce determination and perversity of Oakley's action leads to his own insanity when he discovers the truth and chooses to protect his family and the old order they represent. At the same time, Berry falls into a trap after he asks Oakley how he can possibly suspect him, given his long-standing honesty, dependability, and loyalty. Hamilton's curse, though understandable, appears to create a self-inflicted wound, again adding to the layers of irony Dunbar creates: "Den, damn you! damn you! ef dat's all dese yeahs counted fu', I wish I had a-stoled it." The troubles the Hamiltons are about to endure within the communities of their own people introduce yet another dimension of satire that in many ways shows Dunbar to be a social critic far ahead of his time. Perhaps not totally surprised by Oakley's betrayal of his mentee, Hamilton might expect at least some level of support from his community. Instead the disapprobation of his own people is added to his jail sentence. Dunbar's satire extends to the fear and jealousy of Berry's neighbors who rejoice at his misfortune because somehow his being taken down raises them up. When even the members of their religious congregation turn their backs, Fannie Hamilton and her children look to the glimmer of hope offered by a move to New York.

Readers of Dunbar understand that his sympathies lie more with rural values than with the sophisticated and seductive, but likely much more corrupt, big city. In his essay "The Race Question Discussed," Dunbar underscores the dangers of the city and adds another level of satire on the state into which his people all too quickly fell: "The gist of the whole problem lies in the flocking of ignorant and irresponsible Negroes to the great city. But how is it to be done? They say they have no rights in the South; but better the restrictions there than *a seeming liberty which blossoms noxiously into license*" (emphasis added). At this point Dunbar is sounding much less like the naturalistic novelist decrying the grotesque indifference and evil of the big city and more like the social critic we know (from his essays, stories, plays, and poems) who exposes the corruption inside and outside the communities of people seeking betterment.

In *The Sport of the Gods,* New York (and the whole of the attempt to jump headlong into life after slavery) is, at best, a roller-coaster ride. For Joe, the loops up and down end in despair and violence. We are also left to wonder if Kitty will have the wherewithal to survive after she is warned by the more experienced Hattie. Even more devastatingly, Fannie loses her husband, son, daughter, and then herself to an abusive marriage. In the details of their lives in New York, Dunbar directs sharp satire as well at the black intellectual communities as a group of lower-class, unrefined individuals who will also take advantage of Berry and his family. The gamblers and night owls of the Banner Club, for example, instead of being exemplary of racial uplift protagonists, actually lead to the main character's downfall. Indeed, the club contributes to Joe Hamilton's moral decline, upon which, according to Kevin Gaines, "the gamblers continued to sermonize in their unlikely role as the purveyors of the moral discourse of Darwinian determinism and social control, cynically abdicating responsibility for their exploitation of Joe" (*Uplifting the Race* [University of North Carolina Press, 1996], 193). Far from being a formulaic naturalistic tract against deterministic entrapment, Dunbar's novel undermines naturalism itself by suggesting a human cause for what is often seen as mere indifference.

Even though *The Sport of the Gods* was written before Dunbar was thirty years old, we are accustomed to the maturity of his later writings. Now that we can read his last novel alongside the other three, we can see how he experimented with new literary conventions and genres, mastering them with speed and precision, and then manipulating them to his own ends. Usually that meant undermining or subverting themes, beliefs, and literary techniques with which he had been too quickly identified.

The Sport of the Gods

Contents

Chapter 1

The Hamiltons

FICTION HAS SAID so much in regret of the old days when there were plantations and overseers and masters and slaves, that it was good to come upon such a household as Berry Hamilton's, if for no other reason than that it afforded a relief from the monotony of tiresome iteration.

The little cottage in which he lived with his wife, Fannie, who was housekeeper to the Oakleys, and his son and daughter, Joe and Kit, sat back in the yard some hundred paces from the mansion of his employer. It was somewhat in the manner of the old cabin in the quarters, with which usage as well as tradition had made both master and servant familiar. But, unlike the cabin of the elder day, it was a neatly furnished, modern house, the home of a typical, good-living Negro. For twenty years Berry Hamilton had been butler for Maurice Oakley. He was one of the many slaves who upon their accession to freedom had not left the South, but had wandered from place to place in their own beloved section, waiting, working, and struggling to rise with its rehabilitated fortunes.

The first faint signs of recovery were being seen when he came to Maurice Oakley as a servant. Through thick and thin he remained with him, and when the final upward tendency of his employer began his fortunes had increased in like manner. When, having married, Oakley bought the great house in which he now lived, he left the little servant's cottage in the yard, for, as he said laughingly, "There is no telling when Berry will be following my example and be taking a wife unto himself."

His joking prophecy came true very soon. Berry had long had a tenderness for Fannie, the housekeeper. As she retained her post under the new Mrs. Oakley, and as there was a cottage ready to his hand, it promised to be cheaper and more convenient all around to get married. Fannie was willing, and so the matter was settled.

Fannie had never regretted her choice, nor had Berry ever had cause to curse his utilitarian ideas. The stream of years had flowed pleasantly and peacefully with them. Their little sorrows had come, but their joys had been many.

As time went on, the little cottage grew in comfort. It was replenished with things handed down from "the house" from time to time and with others bought from the pair's earnings.

Berry had time for his lodge, and Fannie time to spare for her own house and garden. Flowers bloomed in the little plot in front and behind it; vegetables and greens testified to the housewife's industry.

Over the door of the little house a fine Virginia creeper bent and fell in graceful curves, and a cluster of insistent morning-glories clung in summer about its stalwart stock.

It was into this bower of peace and comfort that Joe and Kitty were born. They brought a new sunlight into the house and a new joy to the father's and mother's hearts. Their early lives were pleasant and carefully guarded. They got what schooling the town afforded, but both went to work early, Kitty helping her mother and Joe learning the trade of barber.

Kit was the delight of her mother's life. She was a pretty, cheery little thing, and could sing like a lark. Joe too was of a cheerful disposition, but from scraping the chins of aristocrats came to imbibe some of their ideas, and rather too early bid fair to be a dandy. But his father encouraged him, for, said he, "It's de p'opah thing fu' a man what waits on quality to have quality mannahs an' to waih quality clothes."

"'T ain't no use to be a-humo'in' dat boy too much, Be'y," Fannie had replied, although she did fully as much "humo'in'" as her husband; "hit sho' do mek' him biggety, an' a biggety po' niggah is a 'bomination befo' de face of de Lawd; but I know 't ain't no use a-talkin' to you, fu' you plum boun' up in dat Joe."

Her own eyes would follow the boy lovingly and proudly even as she chided. She could not say very much, either, for Berry always had the reply that she was spoiling Kit out of all reason. The girl did have the prettiest clothes of any of her race in the town, and when she was to sing for the benefit of the A. M. E. church or for the benefit of her father's society, the Tribe of Benjamin, there was nothing too good for her to wear. In this too they were aided and abetted by Mrs. Oakley, who also took a lively interest in the girl.

So the two doting parents had their chats and their jokes at each other's expense and went bravely on, doing their duties and spoiling their children much as white fathers and mothers are wont to do.

What the less fortunate Negroes of the community said of them and their offspring is really not worth while. Envy has a sharp tongue, and when has not the aristocrat been the target for the plebeian's sneers?

Joe and Kit were respectively eighteen and sixteen at the time when the preparations for Maurice Oakley's farewell dinner to his brother Francis were agitating the whole Hamilton household. All of them had a hand in the work: Joe had shaved the two men; Kit had helped Mrs. Oakley's maid; the mother had fretted herself weak over the shortcomings of a cook that had been in the family nearly as long as herself, while Berry was stern and dignified in anticipation of the glorious figure he was to make in serving.

When all was ready, peace again settled upon the Hamiltons. Mrs. Hamilton, in the whitest of white aprons, prepared to be on hand to annoy the cook still more; Kit was ready to station herself where she could view the finery; Joe had condescended to promise to be home in time to eat some of the good things, and Berry —Berry was gorgeous in his evening suit with the white waistcoat, as he directed the nimble waiters hither and thither.

Chapter 2

A Farewell Dinner

MAURICE OAKLEY WAS NOT a man of sudden or violent enthusiasms. Conservatism was the quality that had been the foundation of his fortunes at a time when the disruption of the country had involved most of the men of his region in ruin.

Without giving anyone ground to charge him with being lukewarm or renegade to his cause, he had yet so adroitly managed his affairs that when peace came he was able quickly to recover much of the ground lost during the war. With a rare genius for adapting himself to new conditions, he accepted the changed order of things with a passive resignation, but with a stern determination to make the most out of any good that might be in it.

It was a favorite remark of his that there must be some good in every system, and it was the duty of the citizen to find out that good and make it pay. He had done this. His house, his reputation, his satisfaction, were all evidences that he had succeeded.

A childless man, he bestowed upon his younger brother, Francis, the enthusiasm he would have given to a son. His wife shared with her husband this feeling for her brother-in-law, and with him played the role of parent, which had otherwise been denied her.

It was true that Francis Oakley was only a half-brother to Maurice, the son of a second and not too fortunate marriage, but there was no halving of the love which the elder man had given to him from childhood up.

At the first intimation that Francis had artistic ability, his brother had placed him under the best masters in America, and later, when the promise of his youth had begun to blossom, he sent him to Paris, although the expenditure just at that time demanded a sacrifice which might have been the ruin of Maurice's own career. Francis's promise had never come to entire fulfillment. He was always trembling on the verge of a great success without quite plunging into it. Despite the joy which his presence gave his brother and sister-in-law, most of his time was spent abroad, where he could find just the atmosphere that suited his delicate, artistic nature. After a visit of two months he was about returning to Paris for a stay of five years. At last he was going to apply himself steadily and try to be less the dilettante.

The company which Maurice Oakley brought together to say good-bye to his brother on this occasion was drawn from the best that this fine old Southern town afforded. There were colonels there at whose titles and the owners' rights to them no one could laugh; there were brilliant women there who had queened it in Richmond, Baltimore, Louisville, and New Orleans, and every Southern capital under the old régime, and there were younger ones there of wit and beauty who were just beginning to hold their court. For Francis was a great favorite both with men and women. He was a handsome man, tall, slender, and graceful. He had the face and brow of a poet, a pallid face framed in a mass of dark hair. There was a touch of weakness in his mouth, but this was shaded and half hidden by a full mustache that made much forgivable to beauty-loving eyes.

It was generally conceded that Mrs. Oakley was a hostess whose guests had no awkward half-hour before dinner. No praise could be higher than this, and tonight she had no need to exert herself to maintain this reputation. Her brother-in-law was the life of the assembly; he had wit and daring, and about him there was just that hint of charming danger that made him irresistible to women. The guests heard the dinner announced with surprise—an unusual thing, except in this house.

Both Maurice Oakley and his wife looked fondly at the artist as he went in with Claire Lessing. He was talking animatedly to the girl, having changed the general trend of the conversation to a manner and tone directed more particularly to her. While she listened to him, her face glowed and her eyes shone with a light that every man could not bring into them.

As Maurice and his wife followed him with their gaze, the same thought was in their minds, and it had not just come to them, Why could not Francis marry Claire Lessing and settle in America, instead of going back ever and again to that life in the Latin Quarter? They did not believe that it was a bad life or a dissipated one, but from the little that they had seen of it when they were in Paris, it was at least a bit too free and unconventional for their traditions. There were, too, temptations which must assail any man of Francis's looks and talents. They had perfect faith in the strength of his manhood, of course; but could they have had their way, it would have been their will to hedge him about so that no breath of evil invitation could have come nigh to him.

But this younger brother, this half ward of theirs, was an unruly member. He talked and laughed, rode and walked, with Claire Lessing with the same free abandon, the same show of uninterested good comradeship, that he had used towards her when they were boy and girl together. There was not a shade more of warmth or self-consciousness in his manner towards her than there had been fifteen years before. In fact, there was less, for there had been a time, when he was six and Claire three, that Francis, with a boldness that the lover of maturer years tries vainly to attain, had announced to Claire that he was going to marry her. But he had never renewed this declaration when it came time that it would carry weight with it.

They made a fine picture as they sat together tonight. One seeing them could hardly help thinking on the instant that they were made for each other. Something in the woman's face, in her expression perhaps, supplied a palpable lack in the man. The strength of her mouth and chin helped the weakness of his. She was the sort of woman who, if ever he came to a great moral crisis in his life, would be able to save him if she were near. And yet he was going away from her, giving up the pearl that he had only to put out his hand to take.

Some of these thoughts were in the minds of the brother and sister now.

"Five years does seem a long while," Francis was saying, "but if a man accomplishes anything, after all, it seems only a short time to look back upon."

"All time is short to look back upon. It is the looking forward to it that counts. It doesn't, though, with a man, I suppose. He's doing something all the while."

"Yes, a man is always doing something, even if only waiting; but waiting is such unheroic business."

"That is the part that usually falls to a woman's lot. I have no doubt that some dark-eyed mademoiselle is waiting for you now."

Francis laughed and flushed hotly. Claire noted the flush and wondered at it. Had she indeed hit upon the real point? Was that the reason that he was so anxious to get back to Paris? The thought struck a chill through her gaiety. She did not want to be suspicious, but what was the cause of that tell-tale flush? He was not a man easily disconcerted; then why so tonight? But her companion talked on with such innocent composure that she believed herself mistaken as to the reason for his momentary confusion.

Someone cried gaily across the table to her: "Oh, Miss Claire, you will not dare to talk with such little awe to our friend when he comes back with his ribbons and his medals. Why, we shall all have to bow to you, Frank!"

"You're wronging me, Esterton," said Francis. "No foreign decoration could ever be to me as much as the flower of approval from the fair women of my own State."

"Hear!" cried the ladies.

"Trust artists and poets to pay pretty compliments, and this wily friend of mine pays his at my expense."

"A good bit of generalship, that, Frank," an old military man broke in. "Esterton opened the breach and you at once galloped in. That's the highest art of war."

Claire was looking at her companion. Had he meant the approval of the women, or was it one woman that he cared for? Had the speech had a hidden meaning for her? She could never tell. She could not understand this man who had been so much to her for so long, and yet did not seem to know it; who was full of romance and fire and passion, and yet looked at her beauty with the eyes of a mere comrade. She sighed as she rose with the rest of the women to leave the table.

The men lingered over their cigars. The wine was old and the stories new. What more could they ask? There was a strong glow in Francis Oakley's face, and his laugh was frequent and ringing. Some discussion came up which sent him running up to his room for a bit of evidence. When he came down it was not to come directly to the dining room. He paused in the hall and dispatched a servant to bring his brother to him.

Maurice found him standing weakly against the railing of the stairs. Something in his air impressed his brother strangely.

"What is it, Francis?" he questioned, hurrying to him.

"I have just discovered a considerable loss," was the reply in a grieved voice.

"If it is no worse than loss, I am glad; but what is it?"

"Every cent of money that I had to secure my letter of credit is gone from my bureau."

"What? When did it disappear?"

"I went to my bureau tonight for something and found the money gone; then I remembered that when I opened it two days ago I must have left the key in the lock, as I found it tonight."

"It's a bad business, but don't let's talk of it now. Come, let's go back to our guests. Don't look so cut up about it, Frank, old man. It isn't as bad as it might be, and you mustn't show a gloomy face tonight."

The younger man pulled himself together, and re-entered the room with his brother. In a few minutes his gaiety had apparently returned.

When they rejoined the ladies, even their quick eyes could detect in his demeanor no trace of the annoying thing that had occurred. His face did not change until, with a wealth of fervent congratulations, he had bade the last guest good-bye.

Then he turned to his brother. "When Leslie is in bed, come into the library. I will wait for you there," he said, and walked sadly away.

"Poor, foolish Frank," mused his brother, "as if the loss could matter to him."

Chapter 3

The Theft

FRANK WAS VERY PALE when his brother finally came to him at the appointed place. He sat limply in his chair, his eyes fixed upon the floor.

"Come, brace up now, Frank, and tell me about it."

At the sound of his brother's voice he started and looked up as though he had been dreaming.

"I don't know what you'll think of me, Maurice," he said, "I have never before been guilty of such criminal carelessness."

"Don't stop to accuse yourself. Our only hope in this matter lies in prompt action. Where was the money?"

"In the oak cabinet and lying in the bureau drawer. Such a thing as a theft seemed so foreign to this place that I was never very particular about the box. But I did not know until I went to it tonight that the last time I had opened it I had forgotten to take the key out. It all flashed over me in a second when I saw it shining there. Even then I didn't suspect anything. You don't know how I felt to open that cabinet and find all my money gone. It's awful."

"Don't worry. How much was there in all?"

"Nine hundred and eighty-six dollars, most of which, I am ashamed to say, I had accepted from you."

"You have no right to talk that way, Frank; you know I do not begrudge a cent you want. I have never felt that my father did quite right in leaving me the bulk of the fortune; but we won't discuss that now. What I want you to understand, though, is that the money is yours as well as mine, and you are always welcome to it."

The artist shook his head. "No, Maurice," he said, "I can accept no more from you. I have already used up all my own money and too much of yours in this hopeless fight. I don't suppose I was ever cut out for an artist, or I'd have done something really notable in this time, and would not be a burden upon those who care for me. No, I'll give up going to Paris and find some work to do."

"Frank, Frank, be silent. This is nonsense. Give up your art? You shall not do it. You shall go to Paris as usual. Leslie and I have perfect faith in you. You shall not give up on account of this misfortune. What are the few paltry dollars to me or to you?"

"Nothing, nothing, I know. It isn't the money, it's the principle of the thing."

"Principle be hanged! You go back to Paris tomorrow, just as you had planned. I do not ask it, I command it."

The younger man looked up quickly.

"Pardon me, Frank, for using those words and at such a time. You know how near my heart your success lies, and to hear you talk of giving it all up makes me forget myself. Forgive me, but you'll go back, won't you?"

"You are too good, Maurice," said Frank impulsively, "and I will go back, and I'll try to redeem myself."

"There is no redeeming of yourself to do, my dear boy; all you have to do is to mature yourself. We'll have a detective down and see what we can do in this matter."

Frank gave a scarcely perceptible start. "I do so hate such things," he said; "and, anyway, what's the use? They'll never find out where the stuff went to."

"Oh, you need not be troubled in this matter. I know that such things must jar on your delicate nature. But I am a plain hard-headed business man, and I can attend to it without distaste."

"But I hate to shove everything unpleasant off on you. It's what I've been doing all my life."

"Never mind that. Now tell me, who was the last person you remember in your room?"

"Oh, Esterton was up there awhile before dinner. But he was not alone two minutes."

"Why, he would be out of the question anyway. Who else?"

"Hamilton was up yesterday."

"Alone?"

"Yes, for a while. His boy, Joe, shaved me, and Jack was up for a while brushing my clothes."

"Then it lies between Jack and Joe?"

Frank hesitated.

"Neither one was left alone, though."

"Then only Hamilton and Esterton have been alone for any time in your room since you left the key in your cabinet?"

"Those are the only ones of whom I know anything. What others went in during the day, of course, I know nothing about. It couldn't have been either Esterton or Hamilton."

"Not Esterton, no."

"And Hamilton is beyond suspicion."

"No servant is beyond suspicion."

"I would trust Hamilton anywhere," said Frank stoutly, "and with anything."

"That's noble of you, Frank, and I would have done the same, but we must remember that we are not in the old days now. The Negroes are becoming less faithful and less contented, and more's the pity, and a deal more ambitious, although I have never had any unfaithfulness on the part of Hamilton to complain of before."

"Then do not condemn him now."

"I shall not condemn anyone until I have proof positive of his guilt or such clear circumstantial evidence that my reason is satisfied."

"I do not believe that you will ever have that against old Hamilton."

"This spirit of trust does you credit, Frank, and I very much hope that you may be right. But as soon as a Negro like Hamilton learns the value of money and begins to earn it, at the same time he begins to covet some easy and rapid way of securing it. The old Negro knew nothing of the value of money. When he stole, be stole hams and bacon and chickens. These were his immediate necessities and the things he valued. The present laughs at this tendency without knowing the cause. The present Negro resents the laugh, and he has learned to value other things than those which satisfy his belly."

Frank looked bored.

"But pardon me for boring you. I know you want to go to bed. Go and leave everything to me."

The young man reluctantly withdrew, and Maurice went to the telephone and rung up the police station.

As Maurice had said, he was a plain, hard-headed business man, and it took very few words for him to put the Chief of Police in possession of the principal facts of the case. A detective was detailed to take charge of the case, and was started immediately, so that he might be upon the ground as soon after the commission of the crime as possible.

When he came he insisted that if he was to do anything he must question the robbed man and search his room at once. Oakley protested, but the detective was adamant. Even now the presence in the room of a man uninitiated into the mysteries of criminal methods might be destroying the last vestige of a really important clue. The master of the house had no alternative save to yield. Together they went to the artist's room. A light shone out through the crack under the door.

"I am sorry to disturb you again, Frank, but may we come in?"

"Who is with you?"

"The detective."

"I did not know he was to come tonight."

"The chief thought it better."

"All right in a moment."

There was a sound of moving around, and in a short time the young fellow, partly undressed, opened the door.

To the detective's questions he answered in substance what he had told before. He also brought out the cabinet. It was a strong oak box, uncarven, but bound at the edges with brass. The key was still in the lock, where Frank had left it on discovering his loss. They raised the lid. The cabinet contained two compartments, one for letters and a smaller one for jewels and trinkets.

"When you opened this cabinet, your money was gone?"

"Yes."

"Were any of your papers touched?"

"No."

"How about your jewels?"

"I have but few and they were elsewhere."

The detective examined the room carefully, its approaches, and the hallways without. He paused knowingly at a window that overlooked the flat top of a porch.

"Do you ever leave this window open?"

"It is almost always so."

"Is this porch on the front of the house?"

"No, on the side."

"What else is out that way?"

Frank and Maurice looked at each other. The younger man hesitated and put his hand to his head. Maurice answered grimly, "My butler's cottage is on that side and a little way back."

"Uh huh! and your butler is, I believe, the Hamilton whom the young gentleman mentioned some time ago."

"Yes."

Frank's face was really very white now. The detective nodded again.

"I think I have a clue," he said simply. "I will be here again tomorrow morning."

"But I shall be gone," said Frank.

"You will hardly be needed, anyway."

The artist gave a sigh of relief. He hated to be involved in unpleasant things. He went as far as the outer door with his brother and the detective. As he bade the officer good-night and hurried up the hall, Frank put his hand to his head again with a convulsive gesture, as if struck by a sudden pain.

"Come, come, Frank, you must take a drink now and go to bed," said Oakley.

"I am completely unnerved."

"I know it, and I am no less shocked than you. But we've got to face it like men."

They passed into the dining room, where Maurice poured out some brandy for his brother and himself. "Who would have thought it?" he asked, as he tossed his own down.

"Not I. I had hoped against hope up until the last that it would turn out to be a mistake."

"Nothing angers me so much as being deceived by the man I have helped and trusted. I should feel the sting of all this much less if the thief had come from the outside, broken in, and robbed me, but this, after all these years, is too low."

"Don't be hard on a man, Maurice; one never knows what prompts him to a deed. And this evidence is all circumstantial."

"It is plain enough for me. You are entirely too kind-hearted, Frank. But I see that this thing has worn you out. You must not stand here talking. Go to bed, for you must be fresh for tomorrow morning's journey to New York."

Frank Oakley turned away towards his room. His face was haggard, and he staggered as he walked. His brother looked after him with a pitying and affectionate gaze.

"Poor fellow," he said, "he is so delicately constructed that he cannot stand such shocks as these;" and then he added: "To think of that black hound's treachery! I'll give him all that the law sets down for him."

He found Mrs. Oakley asleep when he reached the room, but he awakened her to tell her the story. She was horror-struck. It was hard to have to believe this awful thing of an old servant, but she agreed with him that Hamilton must be made an example of when the time came. Before that, however, he must not know that he was suspected.

They fell asleep, he with thoughts of anger and revenge, and she grieved and disappointed.

Chapter 4

From a Clear Sky

THE INMATES OF THE Oakley house had not been long in their beds before Hamilton was out of his and rousing his own little household.

"You, Joe," he called to his son, "git up f'om daih an' come right hyeah. You got to he'p me befo' you go to any shop dis mo'nin'. You, Kitty, stir yo' stumps, miss. I know yo' ma's a-dressin' now. Ef she ain't, I bet I'll be aftah huh in a minute, too. You all layin' 'roun', snoozin' w'en you all des' pint'ly know dis is de mo'nin' Mistah Frank go 'way f'om hyeah."

It was a cool Autumn morning, fresh and dew-washed. The sun was just rising, and a cool clear breeze was blowing across the land. The blue smoke from the "house," where the fire was already going, whirled fantastically over the roofs like a belated ghost. It was just the morning to doze in comfort, and so thought all of Berry's household except himself. Loud was the complaining as they threw themselves out of bed. They maintained that it was an altogether unearthly hour to get up. Even Mrs. Hamilton added her protest, until she suddenly remembered what morning it was, when she hurried into her clothes and set about getting the family's breakfast.

The good-humor of all of them returned when they were seated about their table with some of the good things of the night before set out, and the talk ran cheerily around.

"I do declaih," said Hamilton, "you all's as bad as dem white people was las' night. De way dey waded into dat food was a caution." He chuckled with delight at the recollection.

"I reckon dat's what dey come fu'. I wasn't payin' so much 'tention to what dey eat as to de way dem women was dressed. Why, Mis' Jedge Hill was des' mo'n go'geous."

"Oh, yes, ma, an' Miss Lessing wasn't no ways behin' her," put in Kitty.

Joe did not condescend to join in the conversation, but contented himself with devouring the good things and aping the manners of the young men whom he knew had been among last night's guests.

"Well, I got to be goin'," said Berry, rising. "There'll be early breakfas' at de 'house' dis mo'nin', so's Mistah Frank kin ketch de fus' train."

He went out cheerily to his work. No shadow of impending disaster depressed his spirits. No cloud obscured his sky. He was a simple, easy man, and he saw nothing in the manner of the people whom he served that morning at breakfast save a natural grief at parting from each other. He did not even take the trouble to inquire who the strange white man was who hung about the place.

When it came time for the young man to leave, with the privilege of an old servitor Berry went up to him to bid him good-bye. He held out his hand to him, and with a glance at his brother, Frank took it and shook it cordially. "Good-bye, Berry," he said. Maurice could hardly restrain his anger at the sight, but his wife was moved to tears at her brother-in-law's generosity.

The last sight they saw as the carriage rolled away towards the station was Berry standing upon the steps waving a hearty farewell and god-speed.

"How could you do it, Frank?" gasped his brother, as soon as they had driven well out of hearing.

"Hush, Maurice," said Mrs. Oakley gently; "I think it was very noble of him."

"Oh, I felt sorry for the poor fellow," was Frank's reply. "Promise me you won't be too hard on him, Maurice. Give him a little scare and let him go. He's possibly buried the money, anyhow."

"I shall deal with him as he deserves."

The young man sighed and was silent the rest of the way.

"Whether I fail or succeed, you will always think well of me, Maurice?" he said in parting; "and if I don't come up to your expectations, well—forgive me— that's all."

His brother wrung his hand. "You will always come up to my expectations, Frank," he said. "Won't he, Leslie?"

"He will always be our Frank, our good, generous-hearted, noble boy. God bless him!"

The young fellow bade them a hearty good-bye, and they, knowing what his feelings must be, spared him the prolonging of the strain. They waited in the carriage, and he waved to them as the train rolled out of the station.

"He seems to be sad at going," said Mrs. Oakley.

"Poor fellow, the affair of last night has broken him up considerably, but I'll make Berry pay for every pang of anxiety that my brother has suffered."

"Don't be revengeful, Maurice; you know what brother Frank asked of you."

"He is gone and will never know what happens, so I may be as revengeful as I wish."

The detective was waiting on the lawn when Maurice Oakley returned. They went immediately to the library, Oakley walking with the firm, hard tread of a man who is both exasperated and determined, and the officer gliding along with the catlike step which is one of the attributes of his profession.

"Well?" was the impatient man's question as soon as the door closed upon them.

"I have some more information that may or may not be of importance."

"Out with it; maybe I can tell."

"First, let me ask if you had any reason to believe that your butler had any resources of his own, say to the amount of three or four hundred dollars?"

"Certainly not. I pay him thirty dollars a month, and his wife fifteen dollars, and with keeping up his lodges and the way he dresses that girl, he can't save very much."

"You know that he has money in the bank?"

"No."

"Well, he has. Over eight hundred dollars."

"What? Berry? It must be the pickings of years."

"And yesterday it was increased by five hundred more."

"The scoundrel!"

"How was your brother's money, in bills?"

"It was in large bills and gold, with some silver."

"Berry's money was almost all in bills of a small denomination and silver."

"A poor trick; it could easily have been changed."

"Not such a sum without exciting comment."

"He may have gone to several places."

"But he had only a day to do it in."

"Then someone must have been his accomplice."

"That remains to be proven."

"Nothing remains to be proven. Why, it's as clear as day that the money he has is the result of a long series of peculations, and that this last is the result of his first large theft."

"That must be made clear to the law."

"It shall be."

"I should advise, though, no open proceedings against this servant until further evidence to establish his guilt is found."

"If the evidence satisfies me, it must be sufficient to satisfy any ordinary jury. I demand his immediate arrest."

"As you will, sir. Will you have him called here and question him, or will you let me question him at once?"

"Yes."

Oakley struck the bell, and Berry himself answered it.

"You're just the man we want," said Oakley, shortly.

Berry looked astonished.

"Shall I question him," asked the officer, "or will you?"

"I will. Berry, you deposited five hundred dollars at the bank yesterday?"

"Well, suh, Mistah Oakley," was the grinning reply, "ef you ain't de beatenes' man to fin' out things I evah seen."

The employer half rose from his chair. His face was livid with anger. But at a sign from the detective he strove to calm himself.

"You had better let me talk to Berry, Mr. Oakley," said the officer.

Oakley nodded. Berry was looking distressed and excited. He seemed not to understand it at all.

"Berry," the officer pursued, "you admit having deposited five hundred dollars in the bank yesterday?"

"Sut'ny. Dey ain't no reason why I shouldn't admit it, 'ceptin' erroun' ermong dese jealous niggahs."

"Uh huh! well, now, where did you get this money?":

"Why, I wo'ked fu' it, o' co'se, whaih you s'pose I got it? 'T ain't drappin' off trees, I reckon, not roun' dis pa't of de country."

"You worked for it? You must have done a pretty big job to have got so much money all in a lump?"

"But I didn't git it in a lump. Why, man, I've been savin' dat money fu mo'n fo' yeahs."

"More than four years? Why didn't you put it in the bank as you got it?"

"Why, mos'ly it was too small, an' so I des' kep' it in a ol' sock. I tol' Fannie dat some day ef de bank didn't bus' wid all de res' I had, I'd put it in too. She was allus sayin' it was too much to have layin' 'roun' de house. But I des' tol' huh dat no robber wasn't goin' to bothah de po' niggah down in de ya'd wid de rich white man up at de house. But fin'lly I listened to huh an' sposited it yistiddy."

"You're a liar! you're a liar, you black thief!" Oakley broke in impetuously. "You have learned your lesson well, but you can't cheat me. I know where that money came from."

"Calm yourself, Mr. Oakley, calm yourself."

"I will not calm myself. Take him away. He shall not stand here and lie to me."

Berry had suddenly turned ashen.

"You say you know whaih dat money come f'om? Whaih?"

"You stole it, you thief, from my brother Frank's room."

"Stole it! My Gawd, Mistah Oakley, you believed a thing lak dat aftah all de yeahs I been wid you?"

"You've been stealing all along."

"Why, what shell I do?" said the servant helplessly. "I tell you, Mistah Oakley, ask Fannie. She'll know how long I been a-savin' dis money."

"I'll ask no one."

"I think it would be better to call his wife, Oakley."

"Well, call her, but let this matter be done with soon."

Fannie was summoned, and when the matter was explained to her, first gave evidences of giving way to grief, but when the detective began to question her, she calmed herself and answered directly just as her husband had.

"Well posted," sneered Oakley. "Arrest that man."

Berry had begun to look more hopeful during Fannie's recital, but now the ashen look came back into his face. At the word "arrest" his wife collapsed utterly, and sobbed on her husband's shoulder.

"Send the woman away."

"I won't go," cried Fannie stoutly; "I'll stay right hyeah by my husband. You sha'n't drive me away f'om him."

Berry turned to his employer. "You b'lieve dat I stole f'om dis house aftah all de yeahs I've been in it, aftah de caih I took of yo' money an' yo' valybles, aftah de way I've put you to bed f'om many a dinnah, an' you woke up to fin' all yo' money safe? Now, can you b'lieve dis?"

His voice broke, and he ended with a cry.

"Yes, I believe it, you thief, yes. Take him away."

Berry's eyes were bloodshot as he replied, "Den, damn you! damn you! ef dat's all dese yeahs counted fu', I wish I had a-stoled it."

Oakley made a step forward, and his man did likewise, but the officer stepped between them.

"Take that damned hound away, or, by God! I'll do him violence!"

The two men stood fiercely facing each other, then the handcuffs were snapped on the servant's wrist.

"No, no," shrieked Fannie, "you mustn't, you mustn't. Oh, my Gawd! he ain't no thief. I'll go to Mis' Oakley. She nevah will believe it." She sped from the room.

The commotion had called a crowd of curious servants into the hall. Fannie hardly saw them as she dashed among them, crying for her mistress. In a moment she returned, dragging Mrs. Oakley by the hand.

"Tell 'em, oh, tell 'em, Miss Leslie, dat you don't believe it. Don't let 'em 'rest Berry."

"Why, Fannie, I can't do anything. It all seems perfectly plain, and Mr. Oakley knows better than any of us, you know."

Fannie, her last hope gone, flung herself on the floor, crying, "O Gawd! O Gawd! he's gone fu' sho'!"

Her husband bent over her, the tears dropping from his eyes. "Nevah min', Fannie," he said, "nevah min'. Hit's boun' to come out all right."

She raised her head, and seizing his manacled hands pressed them to her breast, wailing in a low monotone, "Gone! gone!"

They disengaged her hands, and led Berry away.

"Take her out," said Oakley sternly to the servants; and they lifted her up and carried her away in a sort of dumb stupor that was half a swoon.

They took her to her little cottage, and laid her down until she could come to herself and the full horror of her situation burst upon her.

Chapter 5

The Justice of Men

THE ARREST OF BERRY HAMILTON on the charge preferred by his employer was the cause of unusual commotion in the town. Both the accuser and the accused were well known to the citizens, white and black—Maurice Oakley as a solid man of business, and Berry as an honest, sensible Negro, and the pink of good servants. The evening papers had a full story of the crime, which closed by saying that the prisoner had amassed a considerable sum of money, it was very likely from a long series of smaller peculations.

It seems a strange irony upon the force of right living, that this man, who had never been arrested before, who had never even been suspected of wrongdoing, should find so few who even at the first telling doubted the story of his guilt. Many people began to remember things that had looked particularly suspicious in his dealings. Some others said, "I didn't think it of him." There were only a few who dared to say, "I don't believe it of him."

The first act of his lodge "The Tribe of Benjamin," whose treasurer he was, was to have his accounts audited, when they should have been visiting him with comfort, and they seemed personally grieved when his books were found to be straight. The A. M. E. church, of which he had been an honest and active member, hastened to disavow sympathy with him, and to purge itself of contamination by turning him out. His friends were afraid to visit him and were silent when his enemies gloated. On every side one might have asked, Where is charity? and gone away empty.

In the black people of the town the strong influence of slavery was still operative, and with one accord they turned away from one of their own kind upon whom had been set the ban of the white people's displeasure. If they had sympathy, they dared not show it. Their own interests, the safety of their own positions and firesides, demanded that they stand aloof from the criminal. Not then, not now, nor has it ever been true, although it has been claimed, that Negroes either harbor or sympathize with the criminal of their kind. They did not dare to do it before the sixties. They do not dare to do it now. They have brought down as a heritage from the days of their bondage both fear and disloyalty. So Berry was unbefriended while the storm raged around him. The cell where they had placed him was kind to him, and he could not hear the envious and sneering comments that went on about him. This was kind, for the tongues of his enemies were not.

"Tell me, tell me," said one, "you needn't tell me dat a bird kin fly so high dat he don' have to come down some time. An' w'en he do light, honey, my Lawd, how he flop!"

"Mistah Rich Niggah," said another. "He wanted to dress his wife an' chillen lak white folks, did he? Well, he foun' out, he foun' out. By de time de jedge git thoo wid him he won't be hol'in' his haid so high."

"W'y, dat gal o' his'n," broke in old Isaac Brown indignantly, "w'y, she wouldn' speak to my gal, Minty, when she met huh on de street. I reckon she come down off 'n huh high hoss now."

The fact of the matter was that Minty Brown was no better than she should have been, and did not deserve to be spoken to. But none of this was taken into account either by the speaker or the hearers. The man was down, it was time to strike.

The women too joined their shrill voices to the general cry, and were loud in their abuse of the Hamiltons and in disparagement of their high-toned airs.

"I knowed it, I knowed it," mumbled one old crone, rolling her bleared and jealous eyes with glee. "W'enevah you see niggahs gittin' so high dat dey own folks ain' good enough fu' 'em, look out."

"W'y, la, Aunt Chloe, I knowed it too. Dem people got so owdacious proud dat dey wouldn't walk up to de collection table no mo' at chu'ch, but allus set an' waited twell de basket was passed erroun'."

"Hit's de livin' trufe, an' I's been seein' it all 'long. I ain't said nuffin', but I knowed what 'uz gwine to happen. Ol' Chloe ain't lived all dese yeahs fu' nuffin', an' ef she got de gif' o' secon' sight, 't ain't fu' huh to say."

The women suddenly became interested in this half assertion, and the old hag, seeing that she had made the desired impression, lapsed into silence.

The whites were not neglecting to review and comment on the case also. It had been long since so great a bit of wrongdoing in a Negro had given them cause for speculation and recrimination.

"I tell you," said old Horace Talbot, who was noted for his kindliness towards people of color, "I tell you, I pity that darky more than I blame him. Now, here's my theory." They were in the bar of the Continental Hotel, and the old gentleman sipped his liquor as he talked. "It's just like this: The North thought they were doing a great thing when they come down here and freed all the slaves. They thought they were doing a great thing, and I'm not saying a word against them. I give them the credit for having the courage of their convictions. But I maintain that they were all wrong, now, in turning these people loose upon the country the way they did, without knowledge of what the first principle of liberty was. The natural result is that these people are irresponsible. They are unacquainted with the ways of our higher civilization, and it'll take them a long time to learn. You know Rome wasn't built in a day. I know Berry, and I've known him for a long while, and a politer, likelier darky than him you would have to go far to find. And I haven't the least doubt in the world that he took that money absolutely without a thought of wrong, sir, absolutely. He saw it. He took it, and to his mental process, that was the end of it. To him there was no injury inflicted on anyone, there was no crime committed. His elemental reasoning was simply this: This man has more money than I have; here is some of his surplus—I'll just take it. Why, gentlemen, I maintain that

that man took that money with the same innocence of purpose with which one of our servants a few years ago would have appropriated a stray ham."

"I disagree with you entirely, Mr. Talbot," broke in Mr. Beachfield Davis, who was a mighty hunter.—"Make mine the same, Jerry, only add a little syrup.—I disagree with you. It's simply total depravity, that's all. All niggers are alike, and there's no use trying to do anything with them. Look at that man, Dodson, of mine. I had one of the finest young hounds in the State. You know that white pup of mine, Mr. Talbot, that I bought from Hiram Gaskins? Mighty fine breed. Well, I was spendin' all my time and patience trainin' that dog in the daytime. At night I put him in that nigger's care to feed and bed. Well, do you know, I came home the other night and found that black rascal gone? I went out to see if the dog was properly bedded, and by Jove, the dog was gone too. Then I got suspicious. When a nigger and a dog go out together at night, one draws certain conclusions. I thought I had heard bayin' way out towards the edge of the town. So I stayed outside and watched. In about an hour here came Dodson with a possum hung over his shoulder and my dog trottin' at his heels. He'd been possum huntin' with my hound—with the finest hound in the State, sir. Now, I appeal to you all, gentlemen, if that ain't total depravity, what is total depravity?"

"Not total depravity, Beachfield, I maintain, but the very irresponsibility of which I have spoken. Why, gentlemen, I foresee the day when these people themselves shall come to us Southerners of their own accord and ask to be re-enslaved until such time as they shall be fit for freedom." Old Horace was nothing if not logical.

"Well, do you think there's any doubt of the darky's guilt?" asked Colonel Saunders hesitatingly. He was the only man who had ever thought of such a possibility. They turned on him as if he had been some strange, unnatural animal.

"Any doubt!" cried Old Horace.

"Any doubt!" exclaimed Mr. Davis.

"Any doubt?" almost shrieked the rest. "Why, there can be no doubt. Why, Colonel, what are you thinking of? Tell us who has got the money if he hasn't? Tell us where on earth the nigger got the money he's been putting in the bank? Doubt? Why, there isn't the least doubt about it."

"Certainly, certainly," said the Colonel, "but I thought, of course, he might have saved it. There are several of those people, you know, who do a little business and have bank accounts."

"Yes, but they are in some sort of business. This man makes only thirty dollars a month. Don't you see?"

The Colonel saw, or said he did. And he did not answer what he might have answered, that Berry had no rent and no board to pay. His clothes came from his master, and Kitty and Fannie looked to their mistress for the larger number of their supplies. He did not call to their minds that Fannie herself made fifteen dollars a month, and that for two years Joe had been supporting himself. These things did not come up, and as far as the opinion of the gentlemen assembled in the Continental bar went, Berry was already proven guilty.

As for the prisoner himself, after the first day when he had pleaded "Not guilty" and been bound over to the Grand Jury, he had fallen into a sort of dazed calm that was like the stupor produced by a drug. He took little heed of what went on around him. The shock had been too sudden for him, and it was as if his reason had been for the time unseated. That it was not permanently overthrown was evidenced by his waking to the most acute pain and grief whenever Fannie came to him. Then he would toss and moan and give vent to his sorrow in passionate complaints.

"I didn't tech his money, Fannie, you know I didn't. I wo'ked fu' every cent of dat money, an' I saved it myself. Oh, I'll nevah be able to git a job ag'in. Me in de lock-up—aftah all dese yeahs!"

Beyond this, apparently, his mind could not go. That his detention was anything more than temporary never seemed to enter his mind. That he would be convicted and sentenced was as far from possibility as the skies from the earth. If he saw visions of a long sojourn in prison, it was only as a nightmare half consciously experienced and which with the struggle must give way before the waking.

Fannie was utterly hopeless. She had laid down whatever pride had been hers and gone to plead with Maurice Oakley for her husband's freedom, and she had seen his hard, set face. She had gone upon her knees before his wife to cite Berry's long fidelity.

"Oh, Mis' Oakley," she cried, "ef he did steal de money, we've got enough saved to mek it good. Let him go! let him go!"

"Then you admit that he did steal?" Mrs. Oakley had taken her up sharply.

"Oh, I didn't say dat; I didn't mean dat."

"That will do, Fannie. I understand perfectly. You should have confessed that long ago."

"But I ain't confessin'! I ain't! He didn't—"

"You may go."

The stricken woman reeled out of her mistress's presence, and Mrs. Oakley told her husband that night, with tears in her eyes, how disappointed she was with Fannie—that the woman had known it all along, and had only just confessed. It was just one more link in the chain that was surely and not too slowly forging itself about Berry Hamilton.

Of all the family Joe was the only one who burned with a fierce indignation. He knew that his father was innocent, and his very helplessness made a fever in his soul. Dandy as he was, he was loyal, and when he saw his mother's tears and his sister's shame, something rose within him that had it been given play might have made a man of him, but, being crushed, died and rotted, and in the compost it made all the evil of his nature flourish. The looks and gibes of his fellow-employees at the barbershop forced him to leave his work there. Kit, bowed with shame and grief, dared not appear upon the streets, where the girls who had envied her now hooted at her. So the little family was shut in upon itself away from fellowship and sympathy.

Joe went seldom to see his father. He was not heartless; but the citadel of his long desired and much vaunted manhood trembled before the sight of his father's abject misery. The lines came round his lips, and lines too must have come round his heart. Poor fellow, he was too young for this forcing process, and in the hot-house of pain he only grew an acrid, unripe cynic.

At the sitting of the Grand Jury Berry was indicted. His trial followed soon, and the town turned out to see it. Some came to laugh and scoff, but these, his ene-mies, were silenced by the spectacle of his grief. In vain the lawyer whom he had secured showed that the evidence against him proved nothing. In vain he produced proof of the slow accumulation of what the man had. In vain he pleaded the man's former good name. The judge and the jury saw otherwise. Berry was convicted. He was given ten years at hard labor.

He hardly looked as if he could live out one as he heard his sentence. But Nature was kind and relieved him of the strain. With a cry as if his heart were bursting, he started up and fell forward on his face unconscious. Someone, a bit more brutal than the rest, said, "It's five dollars' fine every time a nigger faints," but no one laughed. There was something too portentous, too tragic in the degra-dation of this man.

Maurice Oakley sat in the courtroom, grim and relentless. As soon as the trial was over, he sent for Fannie, who still kept the cottage in the yard.

"You must go," he said. "You can't stay here any longer. I want none of your breed about me."

And Fannie bowed her head and went away from him in silence.

All the night long the women of the Hamilton household lay in bed and wept, clinging to each other in their grief. But Joe did not go to sleep. Against all their entreaties, he stayed up. He put out the light and sat staring into the gloom with hard, burning eyes.

Chapter 6

Outcasts

WHAT PARTICULARLY IRRITATED Maurice Oakley was that Berry should to the very last keep up his claim of innocence. He reiterated it to the very moment that the train which was bearing him away pulled out of the station. There had seldom been seen such an example of criminal hardihood, and Oakley was hard-ened thereby to greater severity in dealing with the convict's wife. He began to urge her more strongly to move, and she, dispirited and humiliated by what had come to her, looked vainly about for the way to satisfy his demands. With her natural protector gone, she felt more weak and helpless than she had thought it possible to feel. It was hard enough to face the world. But to have to ask something of it was almost more than she could bear.

With the conviction of her husband the last five hundred dollars had been confiscated as belonging to the stolen money, but their former deposit remained untouched. With this she had the means at her disposal to tide over their present days of misfortune. It was not money she lacked, but confidence. Some inkling of the world's attitude towards her, guiltless though she was, reached her and made her afraid.

Her desperation, however, would not let her give way to fear, so she set forth to look for another house. Joe and Kit saw her go as if she were starting on an expedition into a strange country. In all their lives they had known no home save the little cottage in Oakley's yard. Here they had toddled as babies and played as children and been happy and care-free. There had been times when they had complained and wanted a home off by themselves, like others whom they knew. They had not failed, either, to draw unpleasant comparisons between their mode of life and the old plantation quarters system. But now all this was forgotten, and there were only grief and anxiety that they must leave the place and in such a way.

Fannie went out with little hope in her heart, and a short while after she was gone Joe decided to follow her and make an attempt to get work.

"I'll go an' see what I kin do, anyway, Kit. 'T ain't much use, I reckon, trying to get into a bahbah shop where they shave white folks, because all the white folks are down on us. I'll try one of the colored shops."

This was something of a condescension for Berry Hamilton's son. He had never yet shaved a black chin or put shears to what he termed "naps," and he was proud of it. He thought, though, that after the training he had received from the superior "Tonsorial Parlours" where he had been employed, he had but to ask for a place and he would be gladly accepted.

It is strange how all the foolish little vaunting things that a man says in days of prosperity wax a giant crop around him in the days of his adversity. Berry Hamilton's son found this out almost as soon as he had applied at the first of the colored shops for work.

"Oh, no, suh," said the proprietor, "I don't think we got anything fu' you to do; you're a white man's bahbah. We don't shave nothin' but niggahs hyeah, an' we shave 'em in de light o' day an' on de groun' flo'."

"W'y, I hyeah you say dat you couldn't git a paih of sheahs thoo a niggah's naps. You ain't been practicin' lately, has you?" came from the back of the shop, where a grinning Negro was scraping a fellow's face.

"Oh, yes, you're done with burr-heads, are you? But burr-heads are good enough fu' you now."

"I think," the proprietor resumed, "that I hyeahed you say you wasn't fond o' grape pickin'. Well, Josy, my son, I wouldn't begin it now, 'specially as anothah kin' o' pickin' seems to run in yo' fambly."

Joe Hamilton never knew how he got out of that shop. He only knew that he found himself upon the street outside the door, tears of anger and shame in his eyes, and the laughs and taunts of his tormentors still ringing in his ears.

It was cruel, of course it was cruel. It was brutal. But only he knew how just it had been. In his moments of pride he had said all those things, half in fun and half in earnest, and he began to wonder how he could have been so many kinds of a fool for so long without realizing it.

He had not the heart to seek another shop, for he knew that what would be known at one would be equally well known at all the rest. The hardest thing that he had to bear was the knowledge that he had shut himself out of all the chances that he now desired. He remembered with a pang the words of an old Negro to whom he had once been impudent, "Nevah min', boy, nevah min', you's bo'n, but you ain't daid!"

It was too true. He had not known then what would come. He had never dreamed that anything so terrible could overtake him. Even in his straits, however, desperation gave him a certain pluck. He would try for something else for which his own tongue had not disqualified him. With Joe, to think was to do. He went on to the Continental Hotel, where there were almost always boys wanted to "run the bells." The clerk looked him over critically. He was a bright, spruce-looking young fellow, and the man liked his looks.

"Well, I guess we can take you on," he said. "What's your name?"

"Joe," was the laconic answer. He was afraid to say more.

"Well, Joe, you go over there and sit where you see those fellows in uniform, and wait until I call the head bellman."

Young Hamilton went over and sat down on a bench which ran along the hotel corridor and where the bellmen were wont to stay during the day awaiting their calls. A few of the blue-coated Mercuries were there. Upon Joe's advent they began to look askance at him and to talk among themselves. He felt his face burning as he thought of what they must be saying. Then he saw the head bellman talking to the clerk and looking in his direction. He saw him shake his head and walk away. He could have cursed him. The clerk called to him.

"I didn't know," he said—"I didn't know that you were Berry Hamilton's boy. Now, I've got nothing against you myself. I don't hold you responsible for what your father did, but I don't believe our boys would work with you. I can't take you on."

Joe turned away to meet the grinning or contemptuous glances of the bellmen on the seat. It would have been good to be able to hurl something among them. But he was helpless.

He hastened out of the hotel, feeling that every eye was upon him, every finger pointing at him, every tongue whispering, "There goes Joe Hamilton, whose father went to the penitentiary the other day."

What should he do? He could try no more. He was proscribed, and the letters of his ban were writ large throughout the town, where all who ran might read. For a while he wandered aimlessly about and then turned dejectedly homeward. His mother had not yet come.

"Did you get a job?" was Kit's first question.

"No," he answered bitterly, "no one wants me now."

"No one wants you? Why, Joe—they—they don't think hard of us, do they?"

"I don't know what they think of ma and you, but they think hard of me, all right."

"Oh, don't you worry; it'll be all right when it blows over."

"Yes, when it all blows over; but when'll that be?"

"Oh, after a while, when we can show 'em we're all right."

Some of the girl's cheery hopefulness had come back to her in the presence of her brother's dejection, as a woman always forgets her own sorrow when someone she loves is grieving. But she could not communicate any of her feeling to Joe, who had been and seen and felt, and now sat darkly waiting his mother's return. Some presentiment seemed to tell him that, armed as she was with money to pay for what she wanted and asking for nothing without price, she would yet have no better tale to tell than he.

None of these forebodings visited the mind of Kit, and as soon as her mother appeared on the threshold she ran to her, crying, "Oh, where are we going to live, ma?"

Fannie looked at her for a moment, and then answered with a burst of tears, "Gawd knows, child, Gawd knows."

The girl stepped back astonished. "Why, why!" and then with a rush of tenderness she threw her arms about her mother's neck. "Oh, you're tired to death," she said; "that's what's the matter with you. Never mind about the house now. I've got some tea made for you, and you just take a cup."

Fannie sat down and tried to drink her tea, but she could not. It stuck in her throat, and the tears rolled down her face and fell into the shaking cup. Joe looked on silently. He had been out and he understood.

"I'll go out tomorrow and do some looking around for a house while you stay at home an' rest, ma."

Her mother looked up, the maternal instinct for the protection of her daughter at once aroused. "Oh, no, not you, Kitty," she said.

Then for the first time Joe spoke: "You'd just as well tell Kitty now, ma, for she's got to come across it anyhow."

"What you know about it? Whaih you been to?"

"I've been out huntin' work. I've been to Jones's bahbah shop an' to the Continental Hotel." His light-brown face turned brick red with anger and shame at the memory of it. "I don't think I'll try any more."

Kitty was gazing with wide and saddening eyes at her mother.

"Were they mean to you too, ma?" she asked breathlessly.

"Mean? Oh Kitty! Kitty! you don't know what it was like. It nigh killed me. Thaih was plenty of houses an' owned by people I've knowed fu' yeahs, but not one of 'em wanted to rent to me. Some of 'em made excuses 'bout one thing er t' other, but de res' come right straight out an' said dat we'd give a neighborhood a bad name ef we moved into it. I've almos' tramped my laigs off. I've tried every decent place I could think of, but nobody wants us."

The girl was standing with her hands clenched nervously before her. It was almost more than she could understand.

"Why, we ain't done anything," she said. "Even if they don't know any better than to believe that pa was guilty, they know we ain't done anything."

"I'd like to cut the heart out of a few of 'em," said Joe in his throat.

"It ain't goin' to do no good to look at it that a-way, Joe," his mother replied. "I know hit's ha'd, but we got to do de bes' we kin."

"What are we goin' to do?" cried the boy fiercely. "They won't let us work. They won't let us live anywhaih. Do they want us to live on the levee an' steal, like some of 'em do?"

"What are we goin' to do?" echoed Kitty helplessly. "I'd go out ef I thought I could find anythin' to work at."

"Don't you go anywhaih, child. It 'ud only be worse. De niggah men dat ust to be bowin' an' scrapin' to me an' tekin' off dey hats to me laughed in my face. I met Minty—an' she slurred me right in de street. Dey 'd do worse fu' you."

In the midst of the conversation a knock came at the door. It was a messenger from the "House," as they still called Oakley's home, and he wanted them to be out of the cottage by the next afternoon, as the new servants were coming and would want the rooms.

The message was so curt, so hard and decisive, that Fannie was startled out of her grief into immediate action.

"Well, we got to go," she said, rising wearily.

"But where are we goin'?" wailed Kitty in affright. "There's no place to go to. We haven't got a house. Where'll we go?"

"Out o' town someplace as fur away from this damned hole as we kin git." The boy spoke recklessly in his anger. He had never sworn before his mother before.

She looked at him in horror. "Joe, Joe," she said, "you're mekin' it wuss. You're mekin' it ha'dah fu' me to baih when you talk dat a-way. What you mean? Whaih you think Gawd is?"

Joe remained sullenly silent. His mother's faith was too stalwart for his comprehension. There was nothing like it in his own soul to interpret it.

"We'll git de secon'-han' dealah to tek ouah things to-morrer, an' then we'll go away some place, up No'th maybe."

"Let's go to New York," said Joe.

"New Yo'k?"

They had heard of New York as a place vague and far away, a city that, like Heaven, to them had existed by faith alone. All the days of their lives they had heard of it, and it seemed to them the center of all the glory, all the wealth, and all the freedom of the world. New York. It had an alluring sound. Who would know them there? Who would look down upon them?

"It's a mighty long ways off fu' me to be sta'tin' at dis time o' life."

"We want to go a long ways off."

"I wonder what pa would think of it if he was here," put in Kitty.

"I guess he'd think we was doin' the best we could."

"Well, den, Joe," said his mother, her voice trembling with emotion at the daring step they were about to take, "you set down an' write a lettah to yo' pa, an' tell him what we goin' to do, an' to-morrer—to-morrer—we'll sta't."

Something akin to joy came into the boy's heart as he sat down to write the letter. They had taunted him, had they? They had scoffed at him. But he was going where they might never go, and some day he would come back holding his head high and pay them sneer for sneer and jibe for jibe.

The same night the commission was given to the furniture dealer who would take charge of their things and sell them when and for what he could.

From his window the next morning Maurice Oakley watched the wagon emptying the house. Then he saw Fannie come out and walk about her little garden, followed by her children. He saw her as she wiped her eyes and led the way to the side gate.

"Well, they're gone," he said to his wife. "I wonder where they're going to live?"

"Oh, some of their people will take them in," replied Mrs. Oakley languidly.

Despite the fact that his mother carried with her the rest of the money drawn from the bank, Joe had suddenly stepped into the place of the man of the family. He attended to all the details of their getting away with a promptness that made it seem untrue that he had never been more than thirty miles from his native town. He was eager and excited. As the train drew out of the station, he did not look back upon the place which he hated, but Fannie and her daughter let their eyes linger upon it until the last house, the last chimney, and the last spire faded from their sight, and their tears fell and mingled as they were whirled away toward the unknown.

Chapter 7

In New York

To the provincial coming to New York for the first time, ignorant and unknown, the city presents a notable mingling of the qualities of cheeriness and gloom. If he have any eye at all for the beautiful, he cannot help experiencing a thrill as he crosses the ferry over the river filled with plying craft and catches the first sight of the spires and buildings of New York. If he have the right stuff in him, a something will take possession of him that will grip him again every time he returns to the scene and will make him long and hunger for the place when he is away from it. Later, the lights in the busy streets will bewilder and entice him. He will feel shy and helpless amid the hurrying crowds. A new emotion will take his heart as the people hasten by him—a feeling of loneliness, almost of grief, that with all of these souls about him he knows not one and not one of them cares for him. After a while he will find a place and give a sigh of relief as he settles away from the city's sights behind his cozy blinds. It is better here, and the city is cruel and cold and unfeeling. This he will feel, perhaps, for the first half-hour, and then he will be out in it all again. He will be glad to strike elbows with the bustling mob and be happy at their indifference to him, so that he may look at them and study them. After it is all over, after he has passed through the first pangs of strangeness and homesickness, yes, even after he has got beyond the stranger's enthusiasm for the metropolis, the real fever of love for the place will begin to take hold upon him. The subtle, insidious wine of New York will begin to intoxicate him. Then, if he be wise, he will go away, any place—yes, he will, even go over to Jersey. But if he be a fool, he will stay and stay on until the town becomes all in all to him; until the very streets are his chums and certain buildings and corners his best friends. Then he is hopeless, and to live elsewhere would be death. The Bowery will be his romance, Broadway his lyric, and the Park his pastoral, the river and the glory of it all his epic, and he will look down pityingly on all the rest of humanity.

It was the afternoon of a clear October day that the Hamiltons reached New York. Fannie had some misgivings about crossing the ferry, but once on the boat these gave way to speculations as to what they should find on the other side. With the eagerness of youth to take in new impressions, Joe and Kitty were more concerned with what they saw about them than with what their future would hold, though they might well have stopped to ask some such questions. In all the great city they knew absolutely no one, and had no idea which way to go to find a stopping-place.

They looked about them for some colored face, and finally saw one among the porters who were handling the baggage. To Joe's inquiry he gave them an address, and also proffered his advice as to the best way to reach the place. He was exceedingly polite, and he looked hard at Kitty. They found the house to which they had been directed, and were a good deal surprised at its apparent grandeur. It was a four-storied brick dwelling on Twenty-seventh Street. As they looked from the outside, they were afraid that the price of staying in such a place would be too much for their pockets. Inside, the sight of the hard, gaudily upholstered installment-plan furniture did not disillusion them, and they continued to fear that they could never stop at this fine place. But they found Mrs. Jones, the proprietress, both gracious and willing to come to terms with them.

As Mrs. Hamilton—she began to be Mrs. Hamilton now, to the exclusion of Fannie—would have described Mrs. Jones, she was a "big yellow woman." She had a broad good-natured face and a tendency to run to bust.

"Yes," she said, "I think I could arrange to take you. I could let you have two rooms, and you could use my kitchen until you decided whether you wanted to take a flat or not. I has the whole house myself, and I keeps roomers. But latah on I could fix things so's you could have the whole third floor ef you wanted to. Most o' my gent'men's railroad gent'men, they is. I guess it must 'a' been Mr. Thomas that sent you up here."

"He was a little bright man down at de deepo."

"Yes, that's him. That's Mr. Thomas. He's always lookin' out to send someone here, because he's been here three years hisself an' he kin recommend my house."

It was a relief to the Hamiltons to find Mrs. Jones so gracious and home-like. So the matter was settled, and they took up their abode with her and sent for their baggage.

With the first pause in the rush that they had experienced since starting away from home, Mrs. Hamilton began to have time for reflection, and their condition seemed to her much better as it was. Of course, it was hard to be away from home and among strangers, but the arrangement had this advantage—that no one knew them or could taunt them with their past trouble. She was not sure that she was going to like New York. It had a great name and was really a great place, but the very bigness of it frightened her and made her feel alone, for she knew that there could not be so many people together without a deal of wickedness. She did not argue the complement of this, that the amount of good would also be increased, but this was because to her evil was the very present factor in her life.

Joe and Kit were differently affected by what they saw about them. The boy was wild with enthusiasm and with a desire to be a part of all that the metropolis meant. In the evening he saw the young fellows passing by dressed in their spruce clothes, and he wondered with a sort of envy where they could be going. Back home there had been no place much worth going to, except church and one or two people's houses. But these young fellows seemed to show by their manners that they were neither going to church nor a family visiting. In the moment that he recognized this, a revelation came to him—the knowledge that his horizon had been very narrow, and he felt angry that it was so. Why should those fellows be different from him? Why should they walk the streets so knowingly, so independently, when he knew not whither to turn his steps? Well, he was in New York, and now he would learn. Some day some greenhorn from the South should stand at a window and look out envying him, as he passed, red-cravated, patent-leathered, intent on some goal. Was it not better, after all, that circumstances had forced them thither? Had it not been so, they might all have stayed home and stagnated. Well, thought he, it's an ill wind that blows nobody good, and somehow, with a guilty under-thought, he forgot to feel the natural pity for his father, toiling guiltless in the prison of his native State.

Whom the Gods wish to destroy they first make mad. The first sign of the demoralization of the provincial who comes to New York is his pride at his insensibility to certain impressions which used to influence him at home. First, he begins to scoff, and there is no truth in his views nor depth in his laugh. But by and by, from mere pretending, it becomes real. He grows callous. After that he goes to the devil very cheerfully.

No such radical emotions, however, troubled Kit's mind. She too stood at the windows and looked down into the street. There was a sort of complacent calm in the manner in which she viewed the girls' hats and dresses. Many of them were really pretty, she told herself, but for the most part they were not better than what she had had down home. There was a sound quality in the girl's make-up that helped her to see through the glamour of mere place and recognize worth for itself. Or it may have been the critical faculty, which is prominent in most women, that kept her from thinking a five-cent cheesecloth any better in New York than it was at home. She had a certain self-respect which made her value herself and her own traditions higher than her brother did his.

When later in the evening the porter who had been kind to them came in and was introduced as Mr. William Thomas, young as she was, she took his open admiration for her with more coolness than Joe exhibited when Thomas offered to show him something of the town some day or night.

Mr. Thomas was a loquacious little man with a confident air born of an intense admiration of himself. He was the idol of a number of servant-girls' hearts, and altogether a decidedly dashing back-area-way Don Juan.

"I tell you, Miss Kitty," he burst forth, a few minutes after being introduced, "they ain't no use talkin', N' Yawk'll give you a shakin' up 'at you won't soon forget. It's the only town on the face of the earth. You kin bet your life they ain't no flies on N' Yawk. We git the best shows here, we git the best concerts—say, now, what's the use o' my callin' it all out?—we simply git the best of everything."

"Great place," said Joe wisely, in what he thought was going to be quite a man-of-the-world manner. But he burned with shame the next minute because his voice sounded so weak and youthful. Then too the oracle only said "Yes" to him, and went on expatiating to Kitty on the glories of the metropolis.

"D'jever see the statue o' Liberty? Great thing, the statue o' Liberty. I'll take you 'round some day. An' Cooney Island—oh, my, now that's the place; and talk about fun! That's the place for me."

"La, Thomas," Mrs. Jones put in, "how you do run on! Why, the strangers'll think they'll be talked to death before they have time to breathe."

"Oh, I guess the folks understan' me. I'm one o' them kin' o' men 'at believe in whooping things up right from the beginning. I'm never strange with anybody. I'm a N' Yawker, I tell you, from the word go. I say, Mis' Jones, let's have some beer, an' we'll have some music purty soon. There's a fellah in the house 'at plays 'Rag-time' out o' sight."

Mr. Thomas took the pail and went to the corner. As he left the room, Mrs. Jones slapped her knee and laughed until her bust shook like jelly.

"Mr. Thomas is a case, sho'," she said; "but he likes you all, an' I'm mighty glad of it, fu' he's mighty curious about the house when he don't like the roomers."

Joe felt distinctly flattered, for he found their new acquaintance charming. His mother was still a little doubtful, and Kitty was sure she found the young man "fresh."

He came in pretty soon with his beer, and a half-dozen crabs in a bag.

"Thought I'd bring home something to chew. I always like to eat something with my beer."

Mrs. Jones brought in the glasses, and the young man filled one and turned to Kitty.

"No, thanks," she said with a surprised look.

"What, don't you drink beer? Oh, come now, you'll get out o' that."

"Kitty don't drink no beer," broke in her mother with mild resentment. "I drinks it sometimes, but she don't. I reckon maybe de chillen better go to bed."

Joe felt as if the "chillen" had ruined all his hopes, but Kitty rose.

The ingratiating "N' Yawker" was aghast.

"Oh, let 'em stay," said Mrs. Jones heartily; "a little beer ain't goin' to hurt 'em. Why, sakes, I know my father gave me beer from the time I could drink it, and I knows I ain't none the worse fu' it."

"They'll git out o' that, all right, if they live in N' Yawk," said Mr. Thomas, as he poured out a glass and handed it to Joe. "You neither?"

"Oh, I drink it," said the boy with an air, but not looking at his mother.

"Joe," she cried to him, "you must ricollect you ain't at home. What 'ud yo' pa think?" Then she stopped suddenly, and Joe gulped his beer and Kitty went to the piano to relieve her embarrassment.

"Yes, that's it, Miss Kitty, sing us something," said the irrepressible Thomas, "an' after while we'll have that fellah down that plays 'Rag-time.' He's out o' sight, I tell you."

With the pretty shyness of girlhood, Kitty sang one or two little songs in the simple manner she knew. Her voice was full and rich. It delighted Mr. Thomas.

"I say, that's singin' now, I tell you," he cried. "You ought to have some o' the new songs. D'jever hear 'Baby, you got to leave'? I tell you, that's a hot one. I'll bring you some of 'em. Why, you could git a job on the stage easy with that voice o' yourn. I got a frien' in one o' the comp'nies an' I'll speak to him about you."

"You ought to git Mr. Thomas to take you to the th'ater some night. He goes lots."

"Why, yes, what's the matter with to-morrer night? There's a good coon show in town. Out o' sight. Let's all go."

"I ain't nevah been to nothin' lak dat, an' I don't know," said Mrs. Hamilton.

"Aw, come, I'll git the tickets an' we'll all go. Great singin', you know. What d' you say?"

The mother hesitated, and Joe filled the breach.

"We'd all like to go," he said. "Ma, we'll go if you ain't too tired."

"Tired? Pshaw, you'll furgit all about your tiredness when Smithkins gits on the stage. Y' ought to hear him sing, 'I bin huntin' fu' wo'k'! You'd die laughing."

Mrs. Hamilton made no further demur, and the matter was closed.

Awhile later the "Rag-time" man came down and gave them a sample of what they were to hear the next night. Mr. Thomas and Mrs. Jones two-stepped, and they sent a boy after some more beer. Joe found it a very jolly evening, but Kit's and the mother's hearts were heavy as they went up to bed.

"Say," said Mr. Thomas when they had gone, "that little girl's a peach, you bet; a little green, I guess, but she'll ripen in the sun."

Chapter 8

An Evening Out

FANNIE HAMILTON, TIRED AS she was, sat long into the night with her little family discussing New York—its advantages and disadvantages, its beauty and its ugliness, its morality and immorality. She had somewhat receded from her first position, that it was better being here in the great strange city than being at home where the very streets shamed them. She had not liked the way that their fellow lodger looked at Kitty. It was bold, to say the least. She was not pleased, either, with their new acquaintance's familiarity. And yet, he had said no more than some stranger, if there could be such a stranger, would have said down home. There was a difference, however, which she recognized. Thomas was not the provincial who puts every one on a par with himself, nor was he the metropolitan who complacently patronizes the whole world. He was trained out of the one and not up to the other. The intermediate only succeeded in being offensive. Mrs. Jones' assurance as to her guest's fine qualities did not do all that might have been expected to re-assure Mrs. Hamilton in the face of the difficulties of the gentleman's manner.

She could not, however, lay her finger on any particular point that would give her the reason for rejecting his friendly advances. She got ready the next evening to go to the theater with the rest. Mr. Thomas at once possessed himself of Kitty and walked on ahead, leaving Joe to accompany his mother and Mrs. Jones—an arrangement, by the way, not altogether to that young gentleman's taste. A good many men bowed to Thomas in the street, and they turned to look enviously after him. At the door of the theater they had to run the gantlet of a dozen pairs of eyes. Here, too, the party's guide seemed to be well known, for someone said, before they passed out of hearing, "I wonder who that little light girl is that Thomas is with tonight? He's a hot one for you."

Mrs. Hamilton had been in a theater but once before in her life, and Joe and Kit but a few times oftener. On those occasions they had sat far up in the peanut gallery in the place reserved for people of color. This was not a pleasant, cleanly, nor beautiful locality, and by contrast with it, even the garishness of the cheap New York theater seemed fine and glorious.

They had good seats in the first balcony, and here their guide had shown his managerial ability again, for he had found it impossible, or said so, to get all the seats together, so that he and the girl were in the row in front and to one side of where the rest sat. Kitty did not like the arrangement, and innocently suggested that her brother take her seat while she went back to her mother. But her escort overruled her objections easily, and laughed at her so frankly that from very shame she could not urge them again, and they were soon forgotten in her wonder at the mystery and glamour that envelops the home of the drama. There was something weird to her in the alternate spaces of light and shade. Without any feeling of its ugliness, she looked at the curtain as at a door that should presently open between her and a house of wonders. She looked at it with the fascination that one always experiences for what either brings near or withholds the unknown.

As for Joe, he was not bothered by the mystery or the glamour of things. But he had suddenly raised himself in his own estimation. He had gazed steadily at a girl across the aisle until she had smiled in response. Of course, he went hot and cold by turns, and the sweat broke out on his brow, but instantly he began to swell. He had made a decided advance in knowledge, and he swelled with the consciousness that already he was coming to be a man of the world. He looked with a new feeling at the swaggering, sporty young Negroes. His attitude towards them was not one of humble self-depreciation any more. Since last night he had grown, and felt that he might, that he would, be like them, and it put a sort of chuckling glee into his heart.

One might find it in him to feel sorry for this small-souled, warped being, for he was so evidently the jest of Fate, if it were not that he was so blissfully, so conceitedly, unconscious of his own nastiness. Down home he had shaved the wild young bucks of the town, and while doing it drunk in eagerly their unguarded narrations of their gay exploits. So he had started out with false ideals as to what was fine and manly. He was afflicted by a sort of moral and mental astigmatism that made him see everything wrong. As he sat there tonight, he gave to all he saw a wrong value and upon it based his ignorant desires.

When the men of the orchestra filed in and began tuning their instruments, it was the signal for an influx of loiterers from the door. There were a large number of colored people in the audience, and because members of their own race were giving the performance, they seemed to take a proprietary interest in it all. They discussed its merits and demerits as they walked down the aisle in much the same tone that the owners would have used had they been wondering whether the entertainment was going to please the people or not.

Finally the music struck up one of the numerous Negro marches. It was accompanied by the rhythmic patting of feet from all parts of the house. Then the curtain went up on a scene of beauty. It purported to be a grove to which a party of picnickers, the ladies and gentlemen of the chorus, had come for a holiday, and they were telling the audience all about it in crescendos. With the exception of one, who looked like a faded kid glove, the men discarded the grease paint, but the women under their make-ups ranged from pure white, pale yellow, and sickly greens to brick reds and slate grays. They were dressed in costumes that were not primarily intended for picnic going. But they could sing, and they did sing, with their voices, their bodies, their souls. They threw themselves into it because they enjoyed and felt what they were doing, and they gave almost a semblance of dignity to the tawdry music and inane words.

Kitty was enchanted. The airily dressed women seemed to her like creatures from fairy-land. It is strange how the glare of the footlights succeeds in deceiving so many people who are able to see through other delusions. The cheap dresses on the street had not fooled Kitty for an instant, but take the same cheese-cloth, put a little water starch into it, and put it on the stage, and she could see only chiffon.

She turned around and nodded delightedly at her brother, but he did not see her. He was lost, transfixed. His soul was floating on a sea of sense. He had eyes and ears and thoughts only for the stage. His nerves tingled and his hands twitched. Only to know one of those radiant creatures, to have her speak to him, smile at him! If ever a man was intoxicated, Joe was. Mrs. Hamilton was divided between shame at the clothes of some of the women and delight with the music. Her companion was busy pointing out who this and that actress was, and giving jelly-like appreciation to the doings on the stage.

Mr. Thomas was the only cool one in the party. He was quietly taking stock of his young companion—of her innocence and charm. She was a pretty girl, little and dainty, but well developed for her age. Her hair was very black and wavy, and some strain of the South's chivalric blood, which is so curiously mingled with the African in the veins of most colored people, had tinged her skin to an olive hue.

"Are you enjoying yourself?" he leaned over and whispered to her. His voice was very confidential and his lips near her ear, but she did not notice.

"Oh, yes," she answered, "this is grand. How I'd like to be an actress and be up there!"

"Maybe you will some day."

"Oh, no, I'm not smart enough."

"We'll see," he said wisely; "I know a thing or two."

Between the first and second acts a number of Thomas's friends strolled up to where he sat and began talking, and again Kitty's embarrassment took possession of her as they were introduced one by one. They treated her with a half-courteous familiarity that made her blush. Her mother was not pleased with the many acquaintances that her daughter was making, and would have interfered had not Mrs. Jones assured her that the men clustered about their host's seat were some of the "best people in town." Joe looked at them hungrily, but the man in front with his sister did not think it necessary to include the brother or the rest of the party in his miscellaneous introductions.

One brief bit of conversation which the mother overheard especially troubled her.

"Not going out for a minute or two?" asked one of the men, as he was turning away from Thomas.

"No, I don't think I'll go out tonight. You can have my share."

The fellow gave a horse laugh and replied, "Well, you're doing a great piece of work, Miss Hamilton, whenever you can keep old Bill from goin' out an' lushin' between acts. Say, you got a good thing; push it along."

The girl's mother half rose, but she resumed her seat, for the man was going away. Her mind was not quiet again, however, until the people were all in their seats and the curtain had gone up on the second act. At first she was surprised at the enthusiasm over just such dancing as she could see any day from the loafers on the street corners down home, and then, like a good, sensible, humble woman, she came around to the idea that it was she who had always been wrong in putting too low a value on really worthy things. So she laughed and applauded with the rest, all the while trying to quiet something that was tugging at her away down in her heart.

When the performance was over she forced her way to Kitty's side, where she remained in spite of all Thomas's palpable efforts to get her away. Finally he proposed that they all go to supper at one of the colored cafés.

"You'll see a lot o' the show people," he said.

"No, I reckon we'd bettah go home," said Mrs. Hamilton decidedly. "De chillen ain't ust to stayin' up all hours o' nights, an' I ain't anxious fu' 'em to git ust to it."

She was conscious of a growing dislike for this man who treated her daughter with such a proprietary air. Joe winced again at "de chillen."

Thomas bit his lip, and mentally said things that are unfit for publication. Aloud he said, "Mebbe Miss Kitty 'ud like to go an' have a little lunch."

"Oh, no, thank you," said the girl; "I've had a nice time and I don't care for a thing to eat."

Joe told himself that Kitty was the biggest fool that it had ever been his lot to meet, and the disappointed suitor satisfied himself with the reflection that the girl was green yet, but would get bravely over that.

He attempted to hold her hand as they parted at the parlor door, but she drew her fingers out of his clasp and said, "Good-night; thank you"; as if he had been one of her mother's old friends.

Joe lingered a little longer;

"Say, that was out o' sight," he said.

"Think so?" asked the other carelessly.

"I'd like to get out with you some time to see the town," the boy went on eagerly.

"All right, we'll go some time. So long."

"So long."

Some time. Was it true? Would he really take him out and let him meet stage people? Joe went to bed with his head in a whirl. He slept little that night for thinking of his heart's desire.

Chapter 9

His Heart's Desire

WHATEVER ELSE HIS VISIT to the theater may have done for Joe, it inspired him with a desire to go to work and earn money of his own, to be independent both of parental help and control, and so be able to spend as he pleased. With this end in view he set out to hunt for work. It was a pleasant contrast to his last similar quest, and he felt it with joy. He was treated everywhere he went with courtesy, even when no situation was forthcoming. Finally he came upon a man who was willing to try him for an afternoon. From the moment the boy rightly considered himself engaged, for he was master of his trade. He began his work with heart elate. Now he had within his grasp the possibility of being all that he wanted to be. Now Thomas might take him out at any time and not be ashamed of him.

With Thomas, the fact that Joe was working put the boy in an entirely new light. He decided that now he might be worth cultivating. For a week or two he had ignored him, and, proceeding upon the principle that if you give corn to the old hen she will cluck to her chicks, had treated Mrs. Hamilton with marked deference and kindness. This had been without success, as both the girl and her mother held themselves politely aloof from him. He began to see that his hope of winning Kitty's affections lay, not in courting the older woman but in making a friend of the boy. So on a certain Saturday night when the Banner Club was to give one of its smokers, he asked Joe to go with him. Joe was glad to, and they set out together. Arrived, Thomas left his companion for a few moments while he attended, as he said, to a little business. What he really did was to seek out the proprietor of the club and some of its hangers on.

"I say," he said, "I've got a friend with me tonight. He's got some dough on him. He's fresh and young and easy."

"Whew!" exclaimed the proprietor.

"Yes, he's a good thing, but push it along kin' o' light at first; he might get skittish."

"Thomas, let me fall on your bosom and weep," said a young man who, on account of his usual expression of innocent gloom, was called Sadness. "This is what I've been looking for for a month. My hat was getting decidedly shabby. Do you think he would stand for a touch on the first night of our acquaintance?"

"Don't you dare? Do you want to frighten him off? Make him believe that you've got coin to burn and that it's an honor to be with you."

"But, you know, he may expect a glimpse of the gold."

"A smart man don't need to show nothin'. All he's got to do is to act."

"Oh, I'll act; we'll all act."

"Be slow to take a drink from him."

"Thomas, my boy, you're an angel. I recognize that more and more every day, but bid me do anything else but that. That I refuse: it's against nature"; and Sadness looked more mournful than ever.

"Trust old Sadness to do his part," said the portly proprietor; and Thomas went back to the lamb.

"Nothin' doin' so early," he said; "let's go an' have a drink."

They went, and Thomas ordered.

"No, no, this is on me," cried Joe, trembling with joy.

"Pshaw, your money's counterfeit," said his companion with fine generosity. "This is on me, I say. Jack, what'll you have yourself?"

As they stood at the bar, the men began strolling up one by one. Each in his turn was introduced to Joe. They were very polite. They treated him with a pale, dignified, high-minded respect that menaced his pocketbook and possessions. The proprietor, Mr. Turner, asked him why he had never been in before. He really seemed much hurt about it, and on being told that Joe had only been in the city for a couple of weeks expressed emphatic surprise, even disbelief, and assured the rest that anyone would have taken Mr. Hamilton for an old New Yorker.

Sadness was introduced last. He bowed to Joe's "Happy to know you, Mr. Williams."

"Better known as Sadness," he said, with an expression of deep gloom. "A distant relative of mine once had a great grief. I have never recovered from it."

Joe was not quite sure how to take this; but the others laughed and he joined them, and then, to cover his own embarrassment, he did what he thought the only correct and manly thing to do—he ordered a drink.

"I don't know as I ought to," said Sadness.

"Oh, come on," his companions called out, "don't be stiff with a stranger. Make him feel at home."

"Mr. Hamilton will believe me when I say that I have no intention of being stiff, but duty is duty. I've got to go down town to pay a bill, and if I get too much aboard, it wouldn't be safe walking around with money on me."

"Aw, shut up, Sadness," said Thomas. "My friend Mr. Hamilton'll feel hurt if you don't drink with him."

"I cert'n'y will," was Joe's opportune remark, and he was pleased to see that it caused the reluctant one to yield.

They took a drink. There was quite a line of them. Joe asked the bartender what he would have. The men warmed towards him. They took several more drinks with him and he was happy. Sadness put his arms about his shoulder and told him, with tears in his eyes, that he looked like a cousin of his that had died.

"Aw, shut up, Sadness!" said someone else. "Be respectable."

Sadness turned his mournful eyes upon the speaker. "I won't," he replied. "Being respectable is very nice as a diversion, but it's tedious if done steadily." Joe did not quite take this, so he ordered another drink.

A group of young fellows came in and passed up the stairs. "Shearing another lamb?" said one of them significantly.

"Well, with that gang it will be well done."

Thomas and Joe left the crowd after a while, and went to the upper floor, where, in a long, brilliantly lighted room, tables were set out for drinking-parties. At one end of the room was a piano, and a man sat at it listlessly strumming some popular air. The proprietor joined them pretty soon, and steered them to a table opposite the door.

"Just sit down here, Mr. Hamilton," he said, "and you can see everybody that comes in. We have lots of nice people here on smoker nights, especially after the shows are out and the girls come in."

Joe's heart gave a great leap, and then settled as cold as lead. Of course, those girls wouldn't speak to him. But his hopes rose as the proprietor went on talking to him and to no one else. Mr. Turner always made a man feel as if he were of some consequence in the world, and men a deal older than Joe had been fooled by his manner. He talked to one in a soft, ingratiating way, giving his whole attention apparently. He tapped one confidentially on the shoulder, as who should say, "My dear boy, I have but two friends in the world, and you are both of them."

Joe, charmed and pleased, kept his head well. There is a great deal in heredity, and his father had not been Maurice Oakley's butler for so many years for nothing.

The Banner Club was an institution for the lower education of Negro youth. It drew its pupils from every class of people and from every part of the country. It was composed of all sorts and conditions of men, educated and uneducated, dishonest and less so, of the good, the bad, and the—unexposed. Parasites came there to find victims, politicians for votes, reporters for news, and artists of all kinds for color and inspiration. It was the place of assembly for a number of really bright men, who after days of hard and often unrewarded work came there and drunk themselves drunk in each other's company, and when they were drunk talked of the eternal verities.

The Banner was only one of a kind. It stood to the stranger and the man and woman without connections for the whole social life. It was a substitute—poor, it must be confessed—to many youths for the home life which is so lacking among certain classes in New York.

Here the rounders congregated, or came and spent the hours until it was time to go forth to bout or assignation. Here too came sometimes the curious who wanted to see something of the other side of life. Among these, white visitors were not infrequent—those who were young enough to be fascinated by the bizarre and those who were old enough to know that it was all in the game. Mr. Skaggs, of the New York *Universe,* was one of the former class and a constant visitor—he and a "lady friend" called "Maudie," who had a penchant for dancing to "Rag-time" melodies as only the "puffessor" of such a club can play them. Of course, the place was a social cesspool, generating a poisonous miasma and reeking with the stench of decayed and rotten moralities. There is no defense to be made for it. But what do you expect when false idealism and fevered ambition come face to face with catering cupidity?

It was into this atmosphere that Thomas had introduced the boy Joe, and he sat there now by his side, firing his mind by pointing out the different celebrities who came in and telling highly flavored stories of their lives or doings. Joe heard things that had never come within the range of his mind before.

"Aw, there's Skaggsy an' Maudie—Maudie's his girl, y' know, an' he's a reporter on the N' Yawk *Universe.* Fine fellow, Skaggsy."

Maudie—a portly, voluptuous-looking brunette—left her escort and went directly to the space by the piano. Here she was soon dancing with one of the colored girls who had come in.

Skaggs started to sit down alone at a table, but Thomas called him, "Come over here, Skaggsy."

In the moment that it took the young man to reach them, Joe wondered if he would ever reach that state when he could call that white man Skaggsy and the girl Maudie. The newcomer soon set all of that at ease.

"I want you to know my friend, Mr. Hamilton, Mr. Skaggs."

"Why, how d' ye do, Hamilton? I'm glad to meet you. Now, look a here; don't you let old Thomas here string you about me bein' any old 'Mr!' Skaggs. I'm Skaggsy to all of my friends. I hope to count you among 'em."

It was such a supreme moment that Joe could not find words to answer, so he called for another drink.

"Not a bit of it," said Skaggsy, "not a bit of it. When I meet my friends I always reserve to myself the right of ordering the first drink. Waiter, this is on me. What'll you have, gentlemen?"

They got their drinks, and then Skaggsy leaned over confidentially and began talking.

"I tell you, Hamilton, there ain't an ounce of prejudice in my body. Do you believe it?"

Joe said that he did. Indeed Skaggsy struck one as being aggressively unprejudiced.

He went on: "You see, a lot o' fellows say to me, 'What do you want to go down to that nigger club for?' That's what they call it—'nigger club.' But I say to 'em, 'Gentlemen, at that nigger club, as you choose to call it, I get more inspiration than I could get at any of the greater clubs in New York.' I've often been invited to join some of the swell clubs here, but I never do it. By Jove! I'd rather come down here and fellowship right in with you fellows. I like colored people, anyway. Its natural. You see, my father had a big plantation and owned lots of slaves—no offense, of course, but it was the custom of that time—and I've played with little darkies ever since I could remember."

It was the same old story that the white who associates with Negroes from volition usually tells to explain his taste.

The truth about the young reporter was that he was born and reared on a Vermont farm, where his early life was passed in fighting for his very subsistence. But this never troubled Skaggsy. He was a monumental liar, and the saving quality about him was that he calmly believed his own lies while he was telling them, so no one was hurt, for the deceiver was as much a victim as the deceived. The boys who knew him best used to say that when Skaggs got started on one of his debauches of lying, the Recording Angel always put on an extra clerical force.

"Now look at Maudie," he went on; "would you believe it that she was of a fine, rich family, and that the colored girl she's dancing with now used to be her servant? She's just like me about that. Absolutely no prejudice."

Joe was wide-eyed with wonder and admiration, and he couldn't understand the amused expression on Thomas's face, nor why he surreptitiously kicked him under the table.

Finally the reporter went his way, and Joe's sponsor explained to him that he was not to take in what Skaggsy said, and that there hadn't been a word of truth in it. He ended with, "Everybody knows Maudie, and that colored girl is Mamie Lacey, and never worked for anybody in her life. Skaggsy's a good fellah, all right, but he's the biggest liar in N' Yawk."

The boy was distinctly shocked. He wasn't sure but Thomas was jealous of the attention the white man had shown him and wished to belittle it. Anyway, he did not thank him for destroying his romance.

About eleven o'clock, when the people began to drop in from the plays, the master of ceremonies opened proceedings by saying that "The free concert would now begin, and he hoped that all present, ladies included, would act like gentlemen, and not forget the waiter. Mr. Meriweather will now favor us with the latest coon song, entitled 'Come back to yo' Baby, Honey.'"

There was a patter of applause, and a young Negro came forward, and in a strident, music-hall voice, sung or rather recited with many gestures the ditty. He couldn't have been much older than Joe, but already his face was hard with dissipation and foul knowledge. He gave the song with all the rank suggestiveness that could be put into it. Joe looked upon him as a hero. He was followed by a little, brown-skinned fellow with an immature Vandyke beard and a lisp. He sung his own composition and was funny; how much funnier than he himself knew or intended, may not even be hinted at. Then, while an instrumentalist, who seemed to have a grudge against the piano, was hammering out the opening bars of a march, Joe's attention was attracted by a woman entering the room, and from that moment he heard no more of the concert. Even when the master of ceremonies announced with an air that, by special request, he himself would sing "Answer"—the request was his own—he did not draw the attention of the boy away from the yellow-skinned divinity who sat at a near table, drinking whiskey straight.

She was a small girl, with fluffy dark hair and good features. A tiny foot peeped out from beneath her rattling silk skirts. She was a good-looking young woman and daintily made, though her face was no longer youthful, and one might have wished that with her complexion she had not run to silk waists in magenta.

Joe, however, saw no fault in her. She was altogether lovely to him, and his delight was the more poignant as he recognized in her one of the girls he had seen on the stage a couple of weeks ago. That being true, nothing could keep her from being glorious in his eyes—not even the grease-paint which adhered in unneat patches to her face, nor her taste for whiskey in its unreformed state. He gazed at her in ecstasy until Thomas, turning to see what had attracted him, said with a laugh, "Oh, it's Hattie Sterling. Want to meet her?"

Again the young fellow was dumb. Just then Hattie also noticed his intent look, and nodded and beckoned to Thomas.

"Come on," he said, rising.

"Oh, she didn't ask for me," cried Joe, tremulous and eager.

His companion went away laughing.

"Who's your young friend?" asked Hattie.

"A fellah from the South."

"Bring him over here."

Joe could hardly believe in his own good luck, and his head, which was getting a bit weak, was near collapsing when his divinity asked him what he'd have? He began to protest, until she told the waiter with an air of authority to make it a little "'skey." Then she asked him for a cigarette, and began talking to him in a pleasant, soothing way between puffs.

When the drinks came, she said to Thomas, "Now, old man, you've been awfully nice, but when you get your little drink, you run away like a good little boy. You're superfluous."

Thomas answered, "Well, I like that," but obediently gulped his whiskey and withdrew, while Joe laughed until the master of ceremonies stood up and looked sternly at him.

The concert had long been over and the room was less crowded when Thomas sauntered back to the pair.

"Well, good-night," he said. "Guess you can find your way home, Mr. Hamilton"; and he gave Joe a long wink.

"Goo'-night," said Joe, woozily, "I be a' ri'. Goo'—night."

"Make it another 'skey," was Hattie's farewell remark.

IT WAS LATE THE next morning when Joe got home. He had a headache and a sense of triumph that not even his illness and his mother's reproof could subdue.

He had promised Hattie to come often to the club.

Chapter 10

A Visitor from Home

MRS. HAMILTON BEGAN TO question very seriously whether she had done the best thing in coming to New York as she saw her son staying away more and more and growing always farther away from her and his sister. Had she known how and where he spent his evenings, she would have had even greater cause to question the wisdom of their trip. She knew that although he worked he never had any money for the house, and she foresaw the time when the little they had would no longer suffice for Kitty and her. Realizing this, she herself set out to find something to do.

It was a hard matter, for wherever she went seeking employment, it was always for her and her daughter, for the more she saw of Mrs. Jones, the less she thought it well to leave the girl under her influence. Mrs. Hamilton was not a keen woman, but she had a mother's intuitions, and she saw a subtle change in her daughter. At first the girl grew wistful and then impatient and rebellious. She complained that Joe was away from them so much enjoying himself, while she had to be housed up like a prisoner. She had receded from her dignified position, and twice of an evening had gone out for a car-ride with Thomas; but as that gentleman never included the mother in his invitation she decided that her daughter should go no more, and she begged Joe to take his sister out sometimes instead. He demurred at first, for he now numbered among his city acquirements a fine contempt for his woman relatives. Finally, however, he consented, and took Kit once to the theater and once for a ride. Each time he left her in the care of Thomas as soon as they were out of the house, while he went to find or to wait for his dear Hattie. But his mother did not know all this, and Kit did not tell her. The quick poison of the unreal life about her had already begun to affect her character. She had grown secretive and sly. The innocent longing which in a burst of enthusiasm she had expressed that first night at the theater was growing into a real ambition with her, and she dropped the simple old songs she knew to practice the detestable coon ditties which the stage demanded.

She showed no particular pleasure when her mother found the sort of place they wanted, but, went to work with her in sullen silence. Mrs. Hamilton could not understand it all, and many a night she wept and prayed over the change in this child of her heart. There were times when she felt that there was nothing left to work or fight for. The letters from Berry in prison became fewer and fewer. He was sinking into the dull, dead routine of his life. Her own letters to him fell off. It was hard getting the children to write. They did not want to be bothered, and she could not write for herself. So in the weeks and months that followed she drifted farther away from her children and husband and all the traditions of her life.

After Joe's first night at the Banner Club he had kept his promise to Hattie Sterling and had gone often to meet her. She had taught him much, because it was to her advantage to do so. His greenness had dropped from him like a garment, but no amount of sophistication could make him deem the woman less perfect. He knew that she was much older than he, but he only took this fact as an additional sign of his prowess in having won her. He was proud of himself when he went behind the scenes at the theater or waited for her at the stage door and bore her off under the admiring eyes of a crowd of gapers. And Hattie? She liked him in a half-contemptuous, half-amused way. He was a good-looking boy and made money enough, as she expressed it, to show her a good time, so she was willing to overlook his weakness and his callow vanity.

"Look here," she said to him one day, "I guess you'll have to be moving. There's a young lady been inquiring for you today, and I won't stand for that."

He looked at her, startled for a moment, until he saw the laughter in her eyes. Then he caught her and kissed her. "What're you givin' me?" he said.

"It's a straight tip, that's what.'

"Who is it?"

"It's a girl named Minty Brown from your home."

His face turned brick-red with fear and shame. "Minty Brown!" he stammered.

Had that girl told all and undone him? But Hattie was going on about her work and evidently knew nothing.

"Oh, you needn't pretend you don't know her," she went on banteringly. "She says you were great friends down South, so I've invited her to supper. She wants to see you."

"To supper!" he thought. Was she mocking him? Was she restraining her scorn of him only to make his humiliation the greater after a while ? He looked at her, but there was no suspicion of malice in her face, and he took hope.

"Well, I'd like to see old Minty," he said. "It's been many a long day since I've seen her."

All that afternoon, after going to the barbershop, Joe was driven by a tempest of conflicting emotions. If Minty Brown had not told his story, why not? Would she yet tell, and if she did, what would happen? He tortured himself by questioning if Hattie would cast him off. At the very thought his hand trembled, and the man in the chair asked him if he hadn't been drinking.

When he met Minty in the evening, however, the first glance at her reassured him. Her face was wreathed in smiles as she came forward and held out her hand.

"Well, well, Joe Hamilton," she exclaimed, "if I ain't right-down glad to see you! How are you?"

"I'm middlin', Minty. How's yourself?" He was so happy that he couldn't let go her hand.

"An' jes' look at the boy! Ef he ain't got the impidence to be waihin' a mustache too. You must 'a' been lettin' the' cats lick yo' upper lip. Didn't expect to see me in New York, did you?"

"No, indeed. What you doin' here?"

"Oh, I got a gent'man friend what's a porter, an' his run's been changed so that he comes hyeah, an' he told me, if I wanted to come he'd bring me thoo fur a visit, so, you see, hyeah I am. I allus was mighty anxious to see this hyeah town. But tell me, how's Kit an' yo' ma?"

"They're both right well." He had forgotten them and their scorn of Minty.

"Whaih do you live? I'm comin' roun' to see 'em."

He hesitated for a moment. He knew how his mother, if not Kit, would receive her, and yet he dared not anger this woman, who had his fate in the hollow of her hand.

She saw his hesitation and spoke up. "Oh, that's all right. Let by-gones be by-gones. You know I ain't the kin' o' person that holds a grudge ag'in anybody."

"That's right, Minty, that's right," he said, and gave her his mother's address. Then he hastened home to prepare the way for Minty's coming. Joe had no doubt but that his mother would see the matter quite as he saw it, and be willing to temporize with Minty; but he had reckoned without his host. Mrs. Hamilton might make certain concessions to strangers on the score of expediency, but she absolutely refused to yield one iota of her dignity to one whom she had known so long as an inferior.

"But don't you see what she can do for us, ma? She knows people that I know, and she can ruin me with them."

"I ain't never bowed my haid to Minty Brown an' I ain't a-goin' to do it now," was his mother's only reply.

"Oh, ma," Kitty put in, "you don't want to get talked about up here, do you?"

"We'd jes' as well be talked about fu' somep'n we didn't do as fu' somep'n we did do, an' it wouldn' be long befo' we'd come to dat if we made frien's wid dat Brown gal. I ain't a-goin' to do it. I'm ashamed o' you, Kitty, fu' wantin' me to."

The girl began to cry, while her brother walked the floor angrily.

"You'll see what'll happen," he cried; "you'll see."

Fannie looked at her son, and she seemed to see him more clearly than she had ever seen him before—his foppery, his meanness, his cowardice.

"Well," she answered with a sigh, "it can't be no wuss den what's already happened."

"You'll see, you'll see," the boy reiterated.

Minty Brown allowed no wind of thought to cool the fire of her determination. She left Hattie Sterling's soon after Joe, and he was still walking the floor and uttering dire forebodings when she rang the bell below and asked for the Hamiltons.

Mrs. Jones ushered her into her fearfully upholstered parlor, and then puffed upstairs to tell her lodgers that there was a friend there from the South who wanted to see them.

"Tell huh," said Mrs. Hamilton, " dat dey ain't no one hyea wants to see huh."

"No, no," Kitty broke in.

"Heish," said her mother; "I'm goin' to boss you a little while yit."

"Why, I don't understan' you, Mis' Hamilton," puffed Mrs. Jones. "She's a nice-lookin' lady, an' she said she knowed you at home."

"All you got to do is to tell dat ooman jes' what I say."

Minty Brown downstairs had heard the little colloquy, and, perceiving that something was amiss, had come to the stairs to listen. Now her voice, striving hard to be condescending and sweet, but growing harsh with anger, floated up from below:

"Oh, nevah min', lady, I ain't anxious to see 'em. I jest called out o' pity, but I reckon dey 'shamed to see me 'cause de ol' man's in penitentiary an' dey was run out o' town."

Mrs. Jones gasped, and then turned and went hastily downstairs.

Kit burst out crying afresh, and Joe walked the floor muttering beneath his breath, while the mother sat grimly watching the outcome. Finally they heard Mrs. Jones' step once more on the stairs. She came in without knocking, and her manner was distinctly unpleasant.

"Mis' Hamilton," she said, "I've had a talk with the lady downstairs, an' she's tol' me everything. I'd be glad if you'd let, me have my rooms as soon as possible."

"So you goin' to put me out on de wo'd of a stranger?"

"I'm kin' o' sorry, but everybody in the house heard what Mis' Brown said, an' it'll soon be all over town, an' that 'ud ruin the reputation of my house."

"I reckon all dat kin be 'splained."

"Yes, but I don't know that anybody kin 'splain your daughter allus being with Mr. Thomas, who ain't even divo'ced from his wife." She flashed a vindictive glance at the girl, who turned deadly pale and dropped her head in her hands.

"You daih to say dat, Mis' Jones, you dat fust interduced my gal to dat man and got huh to go out wid him? I reckon you'd bettah go now."

And Mrs. Jones looked at Fannie's face and obeyed.

As soon as the woman's back was turned, Joe burst out, "There, there! see what you've done with your damned foolishness."

Fannie turned on him like a tigress. "Don't you cuss hyeah befo' me; I ain't nevah brung you up to it, an' I won't stan' it. Go to dem whaih you larned it, an' whaih de wo'ds soun' sweet." The boy started to speak, but she checked him. "Don't you daih to cuss ag'in or befo' Gawd dey'll be somep'n fu' one o' dis fambly to be rottin' in jail fu'!"

The boy was cowed by his mother's manner. He was gathering his few belongings in a bundle.

"I ain't goin' to cuss," he said sullenly, "I'm goin' out o' your way."

"Oh, go on," she said, "go on. It's been a long time sence you been my son. You on yo' way to hell, an' you is been fu' lo dese many days."

Joe got out of the house as soon as possible. He did not speak to Kit nor look at his mother. He felt like a cur, because he knew deep down in his heart that he had only been waiting for some excuse to take this step.

As he slammed the door behind him, his mother flung herself down by Kit's side and mingled her tears with her daughter's. But Kit did not raise her head.

"Dey ain't nothin' lef' but you now, Kit"; but the girl did not speak, she only shook with hard sobs.

Then her mother raised her head and almost screamed, "My Gawd, not you, Kit!" The girl rose, and then dropped unconscious in her mother's arms.

Joe took his clothes to a lodging-house that he knew of, and then went to the club to drink himself up to the point of going to see Hattie after the show.

Chapter 11

Broken Hopes

WHAT JOE HAMILTON LACKED more was someone to kick him. Many a man who might have lived decently and become a fairly respectable citizen has gone to the dogs for the want of someone to administer a good resounding kick at the right time. It is corrective and clarifying.

Joe needed especially its clarifying property, for though he knew himself a cur, he went away from his mother's house feeling himself somehow aggrieved, and the feeling grew upon him the more he thought of it. His mother had ruined his chance in life, and he could never hold up his head again. Yes, he had heard that several of the fellows at the club had shady reputations, but surely to be the son of a thief or a supposed thief was not like being the criminal himself.

At the Banner he took a seat by himself, and, ordering a cocktail, sat glowering at the few other lonely members who had happened to drop in. There were not many of them, and the contagion of unsociability had taken possession of the house. The people sat scattered around at different tables, perfectly unmindful of the bartender, who cursed them under his breath for not "getting together."

Joe's mind was filled with bitter thoughts. How long had he been away from home? he asked himself. Nearly a year. Nearly a year passed in New York, and he had come to be what he so much desired—a part of its fast life—and now in a moment an old woman's stubbornness had destroyed all that he had builded.

What would Thomas say when he heard it? What would the other fellows think? And Hattie? It was plain that she would never notice him again. He had no doubt but that the malice of Minty Brown would prompt her to seek out all of his friends and make the story known. Why had he not tried to placate her by disavowing sympathy with his mother? He would have had no compunction about doing so, but he had thought of it too late. He sat brooding over his trouble until the bartender called with respectful sarcasm to ask if he wanted to lease the glass he had.

He gave back a silly laugh, gulped the rest of the liquor down, and was ordering another when Sadness came in. He came up directly to Joe and sat down beside him. "Mr. Hamilton says 'Make it two, Jack,'" he said with easy familiarity. "Well, what's the matter, old man? You're looking glum."

"I feel glum."

"The divine Hattie hasn't been cutting any capers, has she? The dear old girl hasn't been getting hysterical at her age? Let us hope not."

Joe glared at him. Why in the devil should this fellow be so sadly gay when he was weighted down with sorrow and shame and disgust?

"Come, come now, Hamilton, if you're sore because I invited myself to take a drink with you, I'll withdraw the order. I know the heroic thing to say is that I'll pay for the drinks myself, but I can't screw my courage up to the point of doing so unnatural a thing."

Young Hamilton hastened to protest. "Oh, I know you fellows now well enough to know how many drinks to pay for. It ain't that."

"Well, then, out with it. What is it? Haven't been up to anything, have you?"

The desire came to Joe to tell this man the whole truth, just what was the matter, and so to relieve his heart. On the impulse he did. If he had expected much from Sadness he was disappointed, for not a muscle of the man's face changed during the entire recital.

When it was over, he looked at his companion critically through a wreath of smoke. Then he said: "For a fellow who has had for a full year the advantage of the education of the New York clubs, you are strangely young. Let me see, you are nineteen or twenty now—yes. Well, that perhaps accounts for it. It's a pity you weren't born older. It's a pity most men aren't. They wouldn't have to take so much time and lose so many good things learning. Now, Mr. Hamilton, let me tell you and you will pardon me for it, that you are a fool. Your case isn't half as bad as that of nine-tenths of the fellows that hang around here. Now, for instance, my father was hung."

Joe started and gave a gasp of horror.

"Oh, yes, but it was done with a very good rope and by the best citizens of Texas, so it seems that I really ought to be very grateful to them for the distinction they conferred upon my family, but I am not. I am ungratefully sad. A man must be very high or very low to take the sensible view of life that keeps him from being sad. I must confess that I have aspired to the depths without ever being fully able to reach them.

"Now look around a bit. See that little girl over there? That's Viola. Two years ago she wrenched up an iron stool from the floor of a lunchroom, and killed another woman with it. She's nineteen—just about your age, by the way. Well, she had friends with a certain amount of pull. She got out of it, and no one thinks the worse of Viola. You see, Hamilton, in this life we are all suffering from fever, and no one edges away from the other because he finds him a little warm. It's dangerous when you're not used to it; but once you go through the parching process, you become inoculated against further contagion. Now, there's Barney over there, as decent a fellow as I know; but he has been indicted twice for pocket-picking. A half-dozen fellows whom you meet here every night have killed their man. Others have done worse things for which you respect them less. Poor Wallace, who is just coming in, and who looks like a jaunty ragpicker, came here about six months ago with about two thousand dollars, the proceeds from the sale of a house his father had left him. He'll sleep in one of the club chairs tonight, and not from choice. He spent his two thousand learning. But, after all, it was a good investment. It was like buying an annuity. He begins to know already how to live on others as they have lived on him. The plucked bird's beak is sharpened for other's feathers. From now on Wallace will live, eat, drink, and sleep at the expense of others, and will forget to mourn his lost money. He will go on this way until, broken and useless, the poorhouse or the potter's field gets him. Oh, it's a fine, rich life, my lad. I know you'll like it. I said you would the first time I saw you. It has plenty of stir in it, and a man never gets lonesome. Only the rich are lonesome. It's only the independent who depend upon others."

Sadness laughed a peculiar laugh, and there was a look in his terribly bright eyes that made Joe creep. If he could only have understood all that the man was saying to him, he might even yet have turned back. But he didn't. He ordered another drink. The only effect that the talk of Sadness had upon him was to make him feel wonderfully "in it." It gave him a false bravery, and he mentally told himself that now he would not be afraid to face Hattie.

He put out his hand to Sadness with a knowing look. "Thanks, Sadness," he said, "you've helped me lots."

Sadness brushed the proffered hand away and sprung up. "You lie," he said, "I haven't; I was only fool enough to try"; and he turned hastily away from the table.

Joe looked surprised at first, and then laughed at his friend's retreating form. "Poor old fellow," he said, "drunk again. Must have had something before he came in."

There was not a lie in all that Sadness had said either as to their crime or their condition. He belonged to a peculiar class—one that grows larger and larger each year in New York and which has imitators in every large city in this country. It is a set which lives, like the leech, upon the blood of others—that draws its life from the veins of foolish men and immoral women, that prides itself upon its well-dressed idleness and has no shame in its voluntary pauperism. Each member of the class knows every other, his methods and his limitations, and their loyalty one to another makes of them a great hulking, fashionably uniformed fraternity of indolence. Some play the races a few months of the year; others, quite as intermittently, gamble at "shoestring" politics, and waver from party to party as time or their interests seem to dictate. But mostly they are like the lilies of the field.

It was into this set that Sadness had sarcastically invited Joe, and Joe felt honored. He found that all of his former feelings had been silly and quite out of place; that all he had learned in his earlier years was false. It was very plain to him now that to want a good reputation was the sign of unpardonable immaturity, and that dishonor was the only real thing worth while. It made him feel better.

He was just rising bravely to swagger out to the theater when Minty Brown came in with one of the club-men he knew. He bowed and smiled, but she appeared not to notice him at first, and when she did she nudged her companion and laughed.

Suddenly his little courage began to ooze out, and he knew what she must be saying to the fellow at her side, for he looked over at him and grinned. Where now was the philosophy of Sadness? Evidently Minty had not been brought under its educating influences, and thought about the whole matter in the old, ignorant way. He began to think of it too. Somehow old teachings and old traditions have an annoying way of coming back upon us in the critical moments of life, although one has long ago recognized how much truer and better some newer ways of thinking are. But Joe would not allow Minty to shatter his dreams by bringing up these old notions. She must be instructed.

He rose and went over to her table.

"Why, Minty," he said, offering his hand, "you ain't mad at me, are you?"

"Go on away f'om hyeah," she said angrily; "I don't want none o' thievin' Berry Hamilton's fambly to speak to me."

"Why, you were all right this evening."

"Yes, but jest out o' pity, an' you was nice 'cause you was afraid I'd tell on you. Go on now."

"Go on now," said Minty's young man; and he looked menacing.

Joe, what little self-respect he had gone, slunk out of the room and needed several whiskeys in a neighboring saloon to give him courage to go to the theater and wait for Hattie, who was playing in vaudeville houses pending the opening of her company.

The closing act was just over when he reached the stage door. He was there but a short time, when Hattie tripped out and took his arm. Her face was bright and smiling, and there was no suggestion of disgust in the dancing eyes she turned up to him. Evidently she had not heard, but the thought gave him no particular pleasure, as it left him in suspense as to how she would act when she should hear.

"Let's go somewhere and get some supper," she said; "I'm as hungry as I can be. What are you looking so cut up about?"

"Oh, I ain't feelin' so very good."

"I hope you ain't lettin' that long-tongued Brown woman bother your head, are you?"

His heart seemed to stand still. She did know, then.

"Do you know all about it?"

"Why, of course I do. You might know she'd come to me first with her story."

"And you still keep on speaking to me?"

"Now look here, Joe, if you've been drinking, I'll forgive you; if you ain't, you go on and leave me. Say, what do you take me for? Do you think I'd throw down a friend because somebody else talked about him? Well, you don't know Hat Sterling. When Minty told me that story, she was back in my dressing-room, and I sent her out o' there a-flying, and with tongue-lashing that she won't forget for a month o' Sundays."

"I reckon that was the reason she jumped on me so hard at the club." He chuckled. He had taken heart again. All that Sadness had said was true, after all, and people thought no less of him. His joy was unbounded.

"So she jumped on you hard, did she? The cat!"

"Oh, she didn't say a thing to me."

"Well, Joe, it's just like this. I ain't an angel, you know that, but I do try to be square, and whenever I find a friend of mine down on his luck, in his pocketbook or his feelings, why, I give him my flipper. Why, old chap, I believe I like you better for the stiff upper lip you've been keeping under all this."

"Why, Hattie," he broke out, unable any longer to control himself, "you're— you're—"

"Oh, I'm just plain Hat Sterling, who won't throw down her friends. Now come on and get something to eat. If that thing is at the club, we'll go there and show her just how much her talk amounted to. She thinks she's the whole game, but I can spot her and then show her that she ain't one, two, three."

When they reached the Banner, they found Minty still there. She tried on the two the same tactics that she had employed so successfully on Joe alone. She nudged her companion and tittered. But she had another person to deal with. Hattie Sterling stared at her coldly and indifferently, and passed on by her to a seat. Joe proceeded to order supper and other things in the nonchalant way that the woman had enjoined upon him. Minty began to feel distinctly uncomfortable, but it was her business not to be beaten. She laughed outright. Hattie did not seem to hear her. She was beckoning Sadness to her side. He came and sat down.

"Now look here," she said, "you can't have any supper because you haven't reached the stage of magnificent hunger to make a meal palatable to you. You've got so used to being nearly starved that a meal don't taste good to you under any other circumstances. You're in on the drinks, though. Your thirst is always available. —Jack," she called down the long room to the bartender, "make it three.—Lean over here, I want to talk to you. See that woman over there by the wall? No, not that one—the big light woman with Griggs. Well, she's come here with a story trying to throw Joe down, and I want you to help me do her."

"Oh, that's the one that upset our young friend, is it?" said Sadness, turning his mournful eyes upon Minty.

"That's her. So you know about it, do you?"

"Yes, and I'll help do her. She mustn't touch one of the fraternity, you know." He kept his eyes fixed upon the outsider until she squirmed. She could not at all understand this serious conversation directed at her. She wondered if she had gone too far and if they contemplated putting her out. It made her uneasy.

Now, this same Miss Sterling had the faculty of attracting a good deal of attention when she wished to. She brought it into play tonight, and in ten minutes, aided by Sadness, she had a crowd of jolly people about her table. When, as she would have expressed it, "everything was going fat," she suddenly paused and, turning her eyes full upon Minty, said in a voice loud enough for all to hear—

"Say, boys, you've heard that story about Joe, haven't you?"

They had.

"Well, that's the one that told it; she's come here to try to throw him and me down. Is she going to do it?"

"Well, I guess not!" was the rousing reply, and every face turned towards the now frightened Minty. She rose hastily and, getting her skirts together, fled from the room, followed more leisurely by the crestfallen Griggs. Hattie's laugh and "Thank you, fellows," followed her out.

MATTERS WERE LESS EASY for Joe's mother and sister than they were for him. A week or more after this, Kitty found him and told him that Minty's story had reached their employers and that they were out of work.

"You see, Joe," she said sadly, "we've took a flat since we moved from Mis' Jones,' and we had to furnish it. We've got one lodger, a race-horse man, an' he's mighty nice to ma an' me, but that ain't enough. Now we've got to do something."

Joe was so smitten with sorrow that he gave her a dollar and promised to speak about the matter to a friend of his.

He did speak about it to Hattie.

"You've told me once or twice that your sister could sing. Bring her down here to me, and if she can do anything, I'll get her a place on the stage," was Hattie's answer.

When Kitty heard it she was radiant, but her mother only shook her head and said, "De las' hope, de las' hope."

Chapter 12

"All the World's a Stage"

KITTY PROVED HERSELF JOE'S sister by falling desperately in love with Hattie Sterling the first time they met. The actress was very gracious to her, and called her "child" in a pretty, patronizing way, and patted her on the cheek.

"It's a shame that Joe hasn't brought you around before. We've been good friends for quite some time."

"He told me you an' him was right good friends."

Already Joe took on a new importance in his sister's eyes. He must be quite a man, she thought, to be the friend of such a person as Miss Sterling.

"So you think you want to go on the stage, do you?"

"Yes, 'm, I thought it might be right nice for me if I could."

"Joe, go out and get some beer for us, and then I'll hear your sister sing."

Miss Sterling talked as if she were a manager and had only to snap her fingers to be obeyed. When Joe came back with the beer, Kitty drank a glass. She did not like it, but she would not offend her hostess. After this she sang, and Miss Sterling applauded her generously, although the young girl's nervousness kept her from doing her best. The encouragement helped her, and she did better as she became more at home.

"Why, child, you've got a good voice. And, Joe, you've been keeping her shut up all this time. You ought to be ashamed of yourself."

The young man had little to say. He had brought Kitty almost under a protest, because he had no confidence in her ability and thought that his "girl" would disillusion her. It did not please him now to find his sister so fully under the limelight and himself "up stage."

Kitty was quite in a flutter of delight; not so much with the idea of working as with the glamour of the work she might be allowed to do.

"I tell you, now," Hattie Sterling pursued, throwing a brightly stockinged foot upon a chair, "your voice is too good for the chorus. Gi' me a cigarette, Joe. Have one, Kitty?—I'm goin' to call you Kitty. It's nice and homelike, and then we've got to be great chums, you know."

Kitty, unwilling to refuse anything from the sorceress, took her cigarette and lighted it, but a few puffs set her off coughing.

"Tut, tut, Kitty, child, don't do it if you ain't used to it. You'll learn soon enough.

Joe wanted to kick his sister for having tried so delicate an art and failed, for he had not yet lost all of his awe of Hattie.

"Now, what I was going to say," the lady resumed after several contemplative puffs, "is that you'll have to begin in the chorus anyway and work your way up. It wouldn't take long for you, with your looks and voice, to put one of the 'up and ups' out o' the business. Only hope it won't be me. I've had people I've helped try to do it often enough."

She gave a laugh that had just a touch of bitterness in it, for she began to recognize that although she had been on the stage only a short time, she was no longer the all-conquering Hattie Sterling, in the first freshness of her youth.

"Oh, I wouldn't want to push anybody out," Kit expostulated.

"Oh, never mind, you'll soon get bravely over that feeling, and even if you didn't it wouldn't matter much. The thing has to happen. Somebody's got to go down. We don't last long in this life: it soon wears us out, and when we're worn out and sung out, danced out and played out, the manager has no further use for us; so he reduces us to the ranks or kicks us out entirely."

Joe here thought it time for him to put in a word. "Get out, Hat," he said contemptuously; "you're good for a dozen years yet."

She didn't deign to notice him save so far as a sniff goes.

"Don't you let what I say scare you, though, Kitty. You've got a good chance, and maybe you'll have more sense than I've got, and at least save money—while you're in it. But let's get off that. It makes me sick. All you've got to do is to come to the opera-house tomorrow and I'll introduce you to the manager. He's a fool, but I think we can make him do something for you."

"Oh, thank you, I'll be around tomorrow, sure."

"Better come about ten o'clock. There's a rehearsal tomorrow, and you'll find him there. Of course, he'll be pretty rough, he always is at rehearsals, but he'll take to you if he thinks there's anything in you and he can get it out."

Kitty felt herself dismissed and rose to go. Joe did not rise.

"I'll see you later, Kit," he said; "I ain't goin' just yet. Say," he added, when his sister was gone, "you're a hot one. What do you want to give her all that con for? She'll never get in."

"Joe," said Hattie, "don't you get awful tired of being a jackass? Sometimes I want to kiss you, and sometimes I feel as if I had to kick you. I'll compromise with you now by letting you bring me some more beer. This got all stale while your sister was here. I saw she didn't like it, and so I wouldn't drink any more for fear she'd try to keep up with me."

"Kit is a good deal of a jay yet," Joe remarked wisely.

"Oh, yes, this world is full of jays. Lots of 'em have seen enough to make 'em wise, but they're still jays, and don't know it. That's the worst of it. They go around thinking they're it, when they ain't even in the game. Go on and get the beer."

And Joe went, feeling vaguely that he had been sat upon.

Kit flew home with joyous heart to tell her mother of her good prospects. She burst into the room, crying, "Oh, ma, ma, Miss Hattie thinks I'll do to go on the stage. Ain't it grand?"

She did not meet with the expected warmth of response from her mother.

"I do' know as it'll be so gran'. F'om what I see of dem stage people dey don't seem to 'mount to much. De way dem gals shows demse'ves is right down bad to me. Is you goin' to dress lak dem we seen dat night?"

Kit hung her head.

"I guess I'll have to."

"Well, ef you have to, I'd ruther see you daid any day. Oh, Kit, my little gal, don't do it, don't do it. Don't you go down lak yo' brothah Joe. Joe's gone."

"Why, ma, you don't understand. Joe's somebody now. You ought to 've heard how Miss Hattie talked about him. She said he's been her friend for a long while."

"Her frien', yes, an' his own inimy. You needn' pattern aftah dat gal, Kit. She ruint Joe, an' she's aftah you now."

"But nowadays everybody thinks stage people respectable up here."

"Maybe I'm ol'-fashioned, but I can't believe in any ooman's ladyship when she shows herse'f lak dem gals does. Oh, Kit, don't do it. Ain't you seen enough? Don't you know enough already to stay away f'om dese hyeah people? Dey don't want nothin' but to pull you down an' den laugh at you w'en you's dragged in de dust."

"You mustn't feel that away, ma. I'm doin' it to help you."

"I do' want no sich help. I'd ruther starve."

Kit did not reply, but there was no yielding in her manner.

"Kit," her mother went on, "dey's somep'n I ain't nevah tol' you dat I'm goin' to tell you now. Mistah Gibson ust to come to Mis' Jones's lots to see me befo' we moved hyeah, an' he's been talkin' 'bout a good many things to me." She hesitated. "He say dat I ain't noways ma'ied to my po' husban', dat a pen'tentiary sentence is de same as a divo'ce, an' if Be'y should live to git out, we'd have to ma'y ag'in. I wouldn't min' dat, Kit, but he say dat at Be'y's age dey ain't much chanst of his livin' to git out, an' hyeah I'll live all dis time alone, an' den have no one to tek keer o' me w'en I git ol'. He want me to ma'y him, Kit. I love yo' fathah; he's my only one. But Joe, he's gone, an' ef yo go, befo' Gawd I'll tell Tawm Gibson yes."

The mother looked up to see just what effect her plea would have on her daughter. She hoped that what she said would have the desired result. But the girl turned around from fixing her neck-ribbon before the glass, her face radiant. "Why, it'll be splendid. He's such a nice man, an' race-horse men 'most always have money. Why don't you marry him, ma? Then I'd feel that you was safe an' settled, an' that you wouldn't be lonesome when the show was out of town."

"You want me to ma'y him an' desert yo' po' pa?"

"I guess what he says is right, ma. I don't reckon we'll ever see pa again an' you got to do something. You got to live for yourself now."

Her mother dropped her head in her hands. "All right," she said, "I'll do it; I'll ma'y him. I might as well go de way both my chillen's gone. Po' Be'y, po' Be'y. Ef you evah do come out, Gawd he'p you to baih what you'll fin'." And Mrs. Hamilton rose and tottered from the room, as if the old age she anticipated had already come upon her.

Kit stood looking after her, fear and grief in her eyes. "Poor ma," she said, "an' poor pa. But I know, an' I know it's for the best."

On the next morning she was up early and practicing hard for her interview with the managing star of "Martin's Blackbirds."

When she arrived at the theater, Hattie Sterling met her with frank friendliness.

"I'm glad you came early, Kitty," she remarked, "for maybe you can get a chance to talk with Martin before he begins rehearsal and gets all worked up. He'll be a little less like a bear then. But even if you don't see him before then, wait, and don't get scared if he tries to bluff you. His bark is a good deal worse than his bite."

When Mr. Martin came in that morning, he had other ideas than that of seeing applicants for places. His show must begin in two weeks, and it was advertised to be larger and better than ever before, when really nothing at all had been done for it. The promise of this advertisement must be fulfilled. Mr. Martin was late, and was out of humor with everyone else on account of it. He came in hurried, fierce, and important.

"Mornin', Mr. Smith, mornin', Mrs. Jones. Ha, ladies and gentlemen, all here?"

He shot every word out of his mouth as if the aftertaste of it were unpleasant to him. He walked among the chorus like an angry king among his vassals, and his glance was a flash of insolent fire. From his head to his feet he was the very epitome of self-sufficient, brutal conceit.

Kitty trembled as she noted the hush that fell on the people at his entrance. She felt like rushing out of the room. She could never face this terrible man. She trembled more as she found his eyes fixed upon her.

"Who's that?" he asked, disregarding her, as if she had been a stick or a stone.

"Well, don't snap her head off. It's a girl friend of mine that wants a place," said Hattie. She was the only one who would brave Martin.

"Humph. Let her wait. I ain't got no time to hear anyone now. Get yourselves in line, you all who are on to that first chorus, while I'm getting into sweat-shirt."

He disappeared behind a screen, whence he emerged arrayed, or only half arrayed, in a thick absorbing shirt and a thin pair of woollen trousers. Then the work began. The man was indefatigable. He was like the spirit of energy. He was in every place about the stage at once, leading the chorus, showing them steps, twisting some awkward girl into shape, shouting, gesticulating, abusing the pianist.

"Now, now," he would shout, "the left foot on that beat. Bah, bah, stop! You walk like a lot of tin soldiers. Are your joints rusty? Do you want oil? Look here, Taylor, if I didn't know you, I'd take you for a truck. Pick up your feet, open your mouths, and move, move, move! Oh!" and he would drop his head in despair. "And to think that I've got to do something with these things in two weeks—two weeks!" Then he would turn to them again with a sudden reaccession of eagerness. "Now, at it again, at it again! Hold that note, hold it! Now whirl, and on the left foot. Stop that music, stop it! Miss Coster, you'll learn that step in about a thousand years, and I've got nine hundred and ninety-nine years and fifty weeks less time than that to spare. Come here and try that step with me. Don't be afraid to move. Step like a chicken on a hot griddle!" And some blushing girl would come forward and go through the step alone before all the rest.

Kitty contemplated the scene with a mind equally divided between fear and anger. What should she do if he should so speak to her? Like the others, no doubt, smile sheepishly and obey him. But she did not like to believe it. She felt that the independence which she had known from babyhood would assert itself, and that she would talk back to him, even as Hattie Sterling did. She felt scared and discouraged, but every now and then her friend smiled encouragingly upon her across the ranks of moving singers.

Finally, however, her thoughts were broken in upon by hearing Mr. Martin cry: "Oh, quit, quit, and go rest yourselves, you ancient pieces of hickory, and let me forget you for a minute before I go crazy. Where's that new girl now?"

Kitty rose and went toward him, trembling so that she could hardly walk.

"What can you do?"

"I can sing," very faintly.

"Well, if that's the voice you're going to sing in, there won't be many that'll know whether it's good or bad. Well, let's hear something. Do you know any of these?"

And he ran over the titles of several songs. She knew some of them, and he selected one. "Try this. Here, Tom, play it for her."

It was an ordeal for the girl to go through. She had never sung before at anything more formidable than a church concert, where only her immediate acquaintances and townspeople were present. Now to sing before all these strange people, themselves singers, made her feel faint and awkward. But the courage of desperation came to her, and she struck into the song. At the first her voice wavered and threatened to fail her. It must not. She choked back her fright and forced the music from her lips.

When she was done, she was startled to hear Martin burst into a raucous laugh. Such humiliation! She had failed, and instead of telling her, he was bringing her to shame before the whole company. The tears came into her eyes, and she was about giving way when she caught a reassuring nod and smile from Hattie Sterling, and seized on this as a last hope.

"Haw, haw, haw!" laughed Martin, "haw, haw, haw! The little one was scared, see? She was scared, d' you understand? But did you see the grit she went at it with? Just took the bit in her teeth and got away. Haw, haw, haw! Now, that's what I like. If all you girls had that spirit, we could do something in two weeks. Try another one, girl."

Kitty's heart had suddenly grown light. She sang the second one better because something within her was singing.

"Good!" said Martin, but he immediately returned to his cold manner. "You watch these girls close and see what they do, and tomorrow be prepared to go into line and move as well as sing."

He immediately turned his attention from her to the chorus, but no slight that he could inflict upon her now could take away the sweet truth that she was engaged and tomorrow would begin work. She wished she could go over and embrace Hattie Sterling. She thought kindly of Joe, and promised herself to give him a present out of her first month's earnings.

On the first night of the show pretty little Kitty Hamilton was pointed out as a girl who wouldn't be in the chorus long. The mother, who was soon to be Mrs. Gibson, sat in the balcony, a grieved, pained look on her face. Joe was in a front row with some of the rest of the gang. He took many drinks between the acts, because he was proud.

Mr. Thomas was there. He also was proud, and after the performance he waited for Kitty at the stage door and went forward to meet her as she came out. The look she gave him stopped him, and he let her pass without a word.

"Who'd 'a' thought," he mused, "that the kid had that much nerve? Well, if they don't want to find out things, what do they come to N' Yawk for? It ain't nobody's old Sunday-school picnic. Guess I got out easy, anyhow."

Hattie Sterling took Joe home in a hansom.

"Say," she said, "if you come this way for me again, it's all over, see? Your little sister's a comer, and I've got to hustle to keep up with her."

Joe growled and fell asleep in his chair. One must needs have a strong head or a strong will when one is the brother of a celebrity and would celebrate the distinguished one's success.

Chapter 13

The Oakleys

A YEAR AFTER THE ARREST of Berry Hamilton, and at a time when New York had shown to the eyes of his family so many strange new sights, there were few changes to be noted in the condition of affairs at the Oakley place. Maurice Oakley was perhaps a shade more distrustful of his servants, and consequently more testy with them. Mrs. Oakley was the same acquiescent woman, with unbounded faith in her husband's wisdom and judgment. With complacent minds both went their ways, drank their wine, and said their prayers, and wished that brother Frank's five years were past. They had letters from him now and then, never very cheerful in tone, but always breathing the deepest love and gratitude to them.

His brother found deep cause for congratulation in the tone of these epistles.

"Frank is getting down to work," he would cry exultantly. "He is past the first buoyant enthusiasm of youth. Ah, Leslie, when a man begins to be serious, then he begins to be something." And her only answer would be, "I wonder, Maurice, if Claire Lessing will wait for him?"

The two had frequent questions to answer as to Frank's doing and prospects, and they had always bright things to say of him, even when his letters gave them no such warrant. Their love for him made them read large between the lines, and all they read was good.

Between Maurice and his brother no word of the guilty servant ever passed. They each avoided it as an unpleasant subject. Frank had never asked and his brother had never proffered aught of the outcome of the case.

Mrs. Oakley had once suggested it.

"Brother ought to know," she said, "that Berry is being properly punished."

"By no means," replied her husband. "You know that it would only hurt him! He shall never know if I have to tell him."

"You are right, Maurice, you are always right. We must shield Frank from the pain it would cause him. Poor fellow! he is so sensitive."

Their hearts were still steadfastly fixed upon the union of this younger brother with Claire Lessing. She had lately come into a fortune, and there was nothing now to prevent it. They would have written Frank to urge it, but the both believed that to try to woo him away from his art was but to make him more wayward. That any woman could have power enough to take him away from this jealous mistress they very much doubted. But they could hope, and hope made them eager to open every letter that bore the French postmark. Always it might contain news that he was coming home, or that he had made a great success, or, better, some inquiry after Claire. A long time they had waited, but found no such tidings in the letters from Paris.

At last, as Maurice Oakley sat in his library one day, the servant brought him a letter more bulky in weight and appearance than any he had yet received. His eyes glistened with pleasure as he read the postmark. "A letter from Frank," he said joyfully, "and an important one, I'll wager."

He smiled as he weighed it in his hand and caressed it. Mrs. Oakley was out shopping, and as he knew how deep her interest was, he hesitated to break the seal before she returned. He curbed his natural desire and laid the heavy envelope down on the desk. But he could not deny himself the pleasure of speculating as to its contents.

It was such a large, interesting-looking package. What might it not contain? It simply reeked of possibilities. Had anyone banteringly told Maurice Oakley that he had such a deep vein of sentiment, he would have denied it with scorn and laughter. But here he found himself sitting with the letter in his hand and weaving stories as to its contents.

First, now, it might be a notice that Frank had received the badge of the Legion of Honor. No, no, that was too big, and he laughed aloud at his own folly, wondering the next minute, with half shame, why he laughed, for did he, after all, believe anything was too big for that brother of his? Well, let him begin, anyway, away down. Let him say, for instance, that the letter told of the completion and sale of a great picture. Frank had sold small ones. He would be glad of this, for his brother had written him several times of things that were a-doing, but not yet of anything that was done. Or, better yet, let the letter say that some picture, long finished, but of which the artist's pride and anxiety had forbidden him to speak, had made a glowing success, the success it deserved. This sounded well, and seemed not at all beyond the bounds of possibility. It was an alluring vision. He saw the picture already. It was a scene from life, true in detail to the point of very minuteness, and yet with something spiritual in it that lifted it above the mere copy of the commonplace. At the Salon it would be hung on the line, and people would stand before it admiring its workmanship and asking who the artist was. He drew on his memory of old reading. In his mind's eye he saw Frank, unconscious of his own power or too modest to admit it, stand unknown among the crowds around his picture waiting for and dreading their criticisms. He saw the light leap to his eyes as he heard their words of praise. He saw the straightening of his narrow shoulders when he was forced to admit that he was the painter of the work. Then the windows of Paris were filled with his portraits. The papers were full of his praise, and brave men and fair women met together to do him homage. Fair women, yes, and Frank would look upon them all and see reflected in them but a tithe of the glory of one woman, and that woman Claire Lessing. He roused himself and laughed again as he tapped the magic envelope.

"My fancies go on and conquer the world for my brother," he muttered. "He will follow their flight one day and do it himself."

The letter drew his eyes back to it. It seemed to invite him, to beg him even. "No, I will not do it; I will wait until Leslie comes. She will be as glad to hear the good news as I am."

His dreams were taking the shape of reality in his mind, and he was believing all that he wanted to believe.

He turned to look at a picture painted by Frank which hung over the mantel. He dwelt lovingly upon it, seeing in it the touch of a genius.

"Surely," he said, "this new picture cannot be greater than that, though it shall hang where kings can see it and this only graces the library of my poor house. It has the feeling of a woman's soul with the strength of a man's heart. When Frank and Claire marry, I shall give it back to them. It is too great a treasure for a clod like me. Heigho, why will women be so long a-shopping?"

He glanced again at the letter, and his hand went out involuntarily towards it. He fondled it, smiling.

"Ah, Lady Leslie, I've a mind to open it to punish you for staying so long."

He essayed to be playful, but he knew that he was trying to make a compromise with himself because his eagerness grew stronger than his gallantry. He laid the letter down and picked it up again. He studied the postmark over and over. He got up and walked to the window and back again, and then began fumbling in his pockets for his knife. No, he did not want it; yes, he did. He would just cut the envelope and make believe he had read it to pique his wife; but he would not read it. Yes, that was it. He found the knife and slit the paper. His fingers trembled as he touched the sheets that protruded. Why would not Leslie come? Did she not know that he was waiting for her? She ought to have known that there was a letter from Paris today, for it had been a month since they had had one.

There was a sound of footsteps without. He sprang up, crying, "I've been waiting so long for you!" A servant opened the door to bring him a message. Oakley dismissed him angrily. What did he want to go down to the Continental for to drink and talk politics to a lot of muddle-pated fools when he had a brother in Paris who was an artist and a letter from him lay unread in his hand? His patience and his temper were going. Leslie was careless and unfeeling. She ought to come; he was tired of waiting.

A carriage rolled up the driveway and he dropped the letter guiltily, as if it were not his own. He would only say that he had grown tired of waiting and started to read it. But it was only Mrs. Davis's footman leaving a note for Leslie about some charity.

He went back to the letter. Well, it was his. Leslie had forfeited her right to see it as soon as he. It might be mean, but it was not dishonest. No, he would not read it now, but he would take it out and show her that he had exercised his self-control in spite of her shortcomings. He laid it on the desk once more. It leered at him. He might just open the sheets enough to see the lines that began it, and read no further. Yes, he would do that. Leslie could not feel hurt at such a little thing.

The first line had only "Dear Brother." "Dear Brother"! Why not the second? That could not hold much more. The second line held him, and the third, and the fourth, and as he read on, unmindful now of what Leslie might think or feel, his face turned from the ruddy glow of pleasant anxiety to the pallor of grief and terror. He was not halfway through it when Mrs. Oakley's voice in the hall announced her coming. He did not hear her. He sat staring at the page before him, his lips apart and his eyes staring. Then, with a cry that echoed through the house, crumpling the sheets in his hand, he fell forward fainting to the floor, just as his wife rushed into the room.

"What is it?" she cried. "Maurice! Maurice!"

He lay on the floor staring up at the ceiling, the letter clutched in his hands. She ran to him and lifted up his head, but he gave no sign of life. Already the servants were crowding to the door. She bade one of them to hasten for a doctor, others to bring water and brandy, and the rest to be gone. As soon as she was alone, she loosed the crumpled sheets from his hand, for she felt that this must have been the cause of her husband's strange attack. Without a thought of wrong, for they had no secrets from each other, she glanced at the opening lines. Then she forgot the unconscious man at her feet and read the letter through to the end.

The letter was in Frank's neat hand, a little shaken, perhaps, by nervousness.

"DEAR BROTHER," it ran, "I know you will grieve at receiving this, and I wish that I might bear your grief for you, but I cannot, though I have as heavy a burden as this can bring to you. Mine would have been lighter today, perhaps, had you been more straightforward with me. I am not blaming you, however, for I know that my hypocrisy made you believe me possessed of a really soft heart, and you thought to spare me. Until yesterday, when in a letter from Esterton he casually mentioned the matter, I did not know that Berry was in prison, else this letter would have been written sooner. I have been wanting to write it for so long, and yet have been too great a coward to do so.

"I know that you will be disappointed in me, and just what that disappointment will cost you I know; but you must hear the truth. I shall never see your face again, or I should not dare to tell it even now. You will remember that I begged you to be easy on your servant. You thought it was only my kindness of heart. It was not; I had a deeper reason. I knew where the money had gone and dared not tell. Berry is as innocent as yourself—and I—well, it is a story, and let me tell it to you.

"You have had so much confidence in me, and I hate to tell you that it was all misplaced. I have no doubt that I should not be doing it now but that I have drunken absinthe enough to give me the emotional point of view, which I shall regret tomorrow. I do not mean that I am drunk. I can think clearly and write clearly, but my emotions are extremely active.

"Do you remember Claire's saying at the table that night of the farewell dinner that some dark-eyed mademoiselle was waiting for me? She did not know how truly she spoke, though I fancy she saw how I flushed when she said it: for I was already in love—madly so.

"I need not describe her. I need say nothing about her, for I know that nothing I say can ever persuade you to forgive her for taking me from you. This has gone on since I first came here, and I dared not tell you, for I saw whither your eyes had turned. I loved this girl, and she both inspired and hindered my work. Perhaps I would have been successful had I not met her, perhaps not.

"I love her too well to marry her and make of our devotion a stale, prosy thing of duty and compulsion. When a man does not marry a woman, he must keep her better than he would a wife. It costs. All that you gave me went to make her happy.

"Then, when I was about leaving you, the catastrophe came. I wanted much to carry back to her. I gambled to make more. I would surprise her. Luck was against me. Night after night I lost. Then, just before the dinner, I woke from my frenzy to find all that I had was gone. I would have asked you for more, and you would have given it; but that strange, ridiculous something which we misname Southern honor, that honor which strains at a gnat and swallows a camel, withheld me, and I preferred to do worse. So I lied to you. The money from my cabinet was not stolen save by myself. I am a liar and a thief, but your eyes shall never tell me so.

"Tell the truth and have Berry released. I can stand it. Write me but one letter to tell me of this. Do not plead with me, do not forgive me, do not seek to find me, for from this time I shall be as one who has perished from the earth; I shall be no more.

"Your brother,
        "FRANK."

By the time the servants came they found Mrs. Oakley as white as her lord. But with firm hands and compressed lips she ministered to his needs pending the doctor's arrival. She bathed his face and temples, chafed his hands, and forced the brandy between his lips. Finally he stirred and his hands gripped.

"The letter!" he gasped.

"Yes, dear, I have it; I have it."

"Give it to me," he cried. She handed it to him. He seized it and thrust it into his breast.

"Did—did—you read it?"

"Yes, I did not know—"

"Oh, my God, I did not intend that you should see it. I wanted the secret for my own. I wanted to carry it to my grave with me. Oh, Frank, Frank, Frank!"

"Never mind, Maurice. It is as if you alone knew it."

"It is not, I say, it is not!"

He turned upon his face and began to weep passionately, not like a man, but like a child whose last toy has been broken.

"Oh, my God," he moaned, "my brother, my brother!"

"'Sh, dearie, think—it's—it's—Frank."

"That's it, that's it—that's what I can't forget. It's Frank—Frank, my brother."

Suddenly he sat up and his eyes stared straight into hers.

"Leslie, no one must ever know what is in this letter," he said calmly.

"No one shall, Maurice; come, let us burn it."

"Burn it? No, no," he cried, clutching at his breast. "It must not be burned. What! burn my brother's secret? No, no, I must carry it with me—carry it with me to the grave."

"But, Maurice—"

"I must carry it with me."

She saw that he was overwrought, and so did not argue with him.

When the doctor came, he found Maurice Oakley in bed, but better. The medical man diagnosed the case and decided that he had received some severe shock. He feared too for his heart, for the patient constantly held his hands pressed against his bosom. In vain the doctor pleaded; he would not take them down, and when the wife added her word, the physician gave up, and after prescribing, left, much puzzled in mind.

"It's a strange case," he said; "there's something more than the nervous shock that makes him clutch his chest like that, and yet I have never noticed signs of heart trouble in Oakley. Oh, well, business worry will produce anything in anybody."

It was soon common talk about the town about Maurice Oakley's attack. In the seclusion of his chamber he was saying to his wife:

"Ah, Leslie, you and I will keep the secret. No one shall ever know."

"Yes, dear, but—but—what of Berry?"

"What of Berry?" he cried, starting up excitedly. "What is Berry to Frank? What is that nigger to my brother? What are his sufferings to the honor of my family and name?"

"Never mind, Maurice, never mind, you are right."

"It must never be known, I say, if Berry has to rot in jail."

So they wrote a lie to Frank, and buried the secret in their breasts, and Oakley wore its visible form upon his heart.

Chapter 14

Frankenstein

FIVE YEARS IS BUT A short time in the life of a man, and yet many things may happen therein. For instance, the whole way of a family's life may be changed. Good natures may be made into bad ones and out of a soul of faith grow a spirit of unbelief. The independence of respectability may harden into the insolence of defiance, and the sensitive cheek of modesty into the brazen face of shameless-ness. It may be true that the habits of years are hard to change, but this is not true of the first sixteen or seventeen years of a young person's life, else Kitty Hamilton and Joe could not so easily have become what they were. It had taken barely five years to accomplish an entire metamorphosis of their characters. In Joe's case even a shorter time was needed. He was so ready to go down that it needed but a gen-tle push to start him, and once started, there was nothing within him to hold him back from the depths. For his will was as flabby as his conscience, and his pride, which stands to some men for conscience, had no definite aim or direction.

Hattie Sterling had given him both his greatest impulse for evil and for good. She had at first given him his gentle push, but when she saw that his collapse would lose her a faithful and useful slave she had sought to check his course. Her threat of the severance of their relations had held him up for a little time, and she began to believe that he was safe again. He went back to the work he had neglected, drank moderately, and acted in most things as a sound, sensible being. Then, all of a sud-den, he went down again, and went down badly. She kept her promise and threw him over. Then he became a hanger-on at the clubs, a genteel loafer. He used to say in his sober moments that at last he was one of the boys that Sadness had spo-ken of. He did not work, and yet he lived and ate and was proud of his degrada-tion. But he soon tired of being separated from Hattie, and straightened up again. After some demur she received him upon his former footing. It was only for a few months. He fell again. For almost four years this had happened intermittently. Finally he took a turn for the better that endured so long that Hattie Sterling again gave him her faith. Then the woman made her mistake. She warmed to him. She showed him that she was proud of him. He went forth at once to celebrate his vic-tory. He did not return to her for three days. Then he was battered, unkempt, and thick of speech.

She looked at him in silent contempt for a while as he sat nursing his ach-ing head.

"Well, you're a beauty," she said finally with cutting scorn. "You ought to be put under a glass case and placed on exhibition."

He groaned and his head sunk lower. A drunken man is always disarmed.

His helplessness, instead of inspiring her with pity, inflamed her with an unfeeling anger that burst forth in a volume of taunts.

"You're the thing I've given up all my chances for—you, a miserable, drunken jay, without a jay's decency. No one had ever looked at you until I picked you up and you've been strutting around ever since, showing off because I was kind to you, and now this is the way you pay me back. Drunk half the time and half drunk the rest. Well, you know what I told you the last time you got 'loaded'? I mean it too. You're not the only star in sight, see?"

She laughed meanly and began to sing, "You'll have to find another baby now."

For the first time he looked up, and his eyes were full of tears—tears both of grief and intoxication. There was an expression of a whipped dog on his face.

"Do'—Ha'ie, do'—" he pleaded, stretching out his hands to her.

Her eyes blazed back at him, but she sang on insolently, tauntingly.

The very inanity of the man disgusted her, and on a sudden impulse she sprang up and struck him full in the face with the flat of her hand. He was too weak to resist the blow, and, tumbling from the chair, fell limply to the floor, where he lay at her feet, alternately weeping aloud and quivering with drunken, hiccoughing sobs.

"Get up!" she cried; "get up and get out o' here. You sha'n't lay around my house."

He had already begun to fall into a drunken sleep, but she shook him, got him to his feet, and pushed him outside the door. "Now, go, you drunken dog, and never put your foot inside this house again."

He stood outside, swaying dizzily upon his feet and looking back with dazed eyes at the door, then he muttered: "Pu' me out, wi' you? Pu' me out, damn you! Well, I ki' you. See 'f I don't"; and he half walked, half fell down the street.

Sadness and Skaggsy were together at the club that night. Five years had not changed the latter as to wealth or position or inclination, and he was still a frequent visitor at the Banner. He always came in alone now, for Maudie had gone the way of the half-world, and reached depths to which Mr. Skaggs's job prevented him from following her. However, he mourned truly for his lost companion, and tonight he was in a particularly pensive mood.

Someone was playing rag-time on the piano, and the dancers were wheeling in time to the music. Skaggsy looked at them regretfully as he sipped his liquor.

It made him think of Maudie. He sighed and turned away.

"I tell you, Sadness," he said impulsively, "dancing is the poetry of motion."

"Yes," replied Sadness, "and dancing in rag-time is the dialect poetry."

The reporter did not like this. It savored of flippancy, and he was about entering upon a discussion to prove that Sadness had no soul, when Joe, with bloodshot eyes and disheveled clothes, staggered in and reeled towards them.

"Drunk again," said Sadness. "Really, it's a waste of time for Joe to sober up. Hullo there!" as the young man brought up against him; "take a seat." He put him in a chair at the table. "Been lushin' a bit, eh?"

"Gi' me some'n' drink."

"Oh, a hair of the dog. Some men shave their dogs clean, and then have hydrophobia. Here, Jack!"

They drank, and then, as if the whiskey had done him good, Joe sat up in his chair.

"Ha'ie's throwed me down."

"Lucky dog! You might have known it would have happened sooner or later. Better sooner than never."

Skaggs smoked in silence and looked at Joe.

"I'm goin' to kill her."

"I wouldn't if I were you. Take old Sadness's advice and thank your stars that you're rid of her."

"I'm goin' to kill her." He paused and looked at them drowsily. Then, bracing himself up again, he broke out suddenly, "Say, d' ever tell y' 'bout the ol' man? He never stole that money. Know he di' n'."

He threatened to fall asleep now, but the reporter was all alert. He scented a story.

"By Jove!" he exclaimed, "did you hear that? Bet the chap stole it himself and's letting the old man suffer for it. Great story, ain't it? Come, come, wake up here. Three more, Jack. What about your father?"

"Father? Who's father. Oh, do' bother me. What?"

"Here, here, tell us about your father and the money. If he didn't steal it, who did?

"Who did? Tha' 's it, who did? Ol' man di' n' steal it, know he di' n'."

"Oh, let him alone, Skaggsy, he don't know what he's saying."

"Yes, he does, a drunken man tells the truth."

"In some cases," said Sadness.

"Oh, let me alone, man. I've been trying for years to get a big sensation for my paper, and if this story is one, I'm a made man."

The drink seemed to revive the young man again, and by bits Skaggs was able to pick out of him the story of his father's arrest and conviction. At its close he relapsed into stupidity, murmuring, "She throwed me down."

"Well," sneered Sadness, "you see drunken men tell the truth, and you don't seem to get much guilt out of our young friend. You're disappointed, aren't you?"

"I confess I am disappointed, but I've got an idea, just the same."

"Oh, you have? Well, don't handle it carelessly; it might go off." And Sadness rose. The reporter sat thinking for a time and then followed him, leaving Joe in a drunken sleep at the table. There he lay for more than two hours. When he finally awoke, he started up as if some determination had come to him in his sleep. A part of the helplessness of his intoxication had gone, but his first act was to call for more whiskey. This he gulped down, and followed with another and another. For a while he stood still, brooding silently, his red eyes blinking at the light. Then he turned abruptly and left the club.

It was very late when he reached Hattie's door, but he opened it with his latch-key, as he had been used to do. He stopped to help himself to a glass of brandy, as

he had so often done before. Then he went directly to her room. She was a light
sleeper, and his step awakened her.

"Who is it?" she cried in affright.

"It's me." His voice was steadier now, but grim.

"What do you want? Didn't I tell you never to come here again? Get out or I'll
have you taken out."

She sprang up in bed, glaring angrily at him.

His hands twitched nervously, as if her will were conquering him and he were
uneasy, but he held her eye with his own.

"You put me out tonight," he said.

"Yes, and I'm going to do it again. You're drunk."

She started to rise, but he took a step towards her and she paused. He looked
as she had never seen him look before. His face was ashen and his eyes like fire and
blood. She quailed beneath the look. He took another step towards her.

"You put me out tonight," he repeated, "like a dog."

His step was steady and his tone was clear, menacingly clear. She shrank back
from him, back to the wall. Still his hands twitched and his eye held her. Still he
crept slowly towards her, his lips working and his hands moving convulsively.

"Joe, Joe!" she said hoarsely, "what's the matter? Oh, don't look at me like
that."

The gown had fallen away from her breast and showed the convulsive fluttering of her heart.

He broke into a laugh, a dry, murderous laugh, and his hands sought each other
while the fingers twitched over one another like coiling serpents.

"You put me out—you—you, and you made me what I am." The realization
of what he was, of his foulness and degradation, seemed just to have come to him
fully. "You made me what I am, and then you sent me away. You let me come back,
and now you put me out."

She gazed at him fascinated. She tried to scream and she could not. This was
not Joe. This was not the boy that she had turned and twisted about her little finger.
This was a terrible, terrible man or a monster.

He moved a step nearer her. His eyes fell to her throat. For an instant she lost
their steady glare and then she found her voice. The scream was checked as it began.
His fingers had closed over her throat just where the gown had left it temptingly
bare. They gave it the caress of death. She struggled. They held her. Her eyes prayed
to his. But his were the fire of hell. She fell back upon her pillow in silence. He had
not uttered a word. He held her. Finally he flung her from him like a rag, and sank
into a chair. And there the officers found him when Hattie Sterling's disappearance had become a strange thing.

Chapter 15

"*Dear, Damned, Delightful Town*"

WHEN JOE WAS TAKEN, there was no spirit or feeling left in him. He moved me-chanically, as if without sense or volition. The first impression he gave was that of a man over-acting insanity. But this was soon removed by the very indifference with which he met everything concerned with his crime. From the very first he made no effort to exonerate or to vindicate himself. He talked little and only in a dry, stupefied way. He was as one whose soul is dead, and perhaps it was; for all the little soul of him had been wrapped up in the body of this one woman, and the stroke that took her life had killed him too.

The men who examined him were irritated beyond measure. There was noth-ing for them to exercise their ingenuity upon. He left them nothing to search for. Their most damning question he answered with an apathy that showed absolutely no interest in the matter. It was as if someone whom he did not care about had committed a crime and he had been called to testify. The only thing which he no-ticed or seemed to have any affection for was a little pet dog which had been hers and which they sometimes allowed to be with him after the life sentence had been passed upon him and when he was awaiting removal. He would sit for hours with the little animal in his lap, caressing it dumbly. There was a mute sorrow in the eyes of both man and dog, and they seemed to take comfort in each other's pres-ence. There was no need of any sign between them. They had both loved her, had they not? So they understood.

Sadness saw him and came back to the Banner, torn and unnerved by the sight. "I saw him," he said with a shudder, "and it'll take more whiskey than Jack can give me in a year to wash the memory of him out of me. Why, man, it shocked me all through. It's a pity they didn't send him to the chair. It couldn't have done him much harm and would have been a real mercy."

And so Sadness and all the club, with a muttered "Poor devil!" dismissed him. He was gone. Why should they worry? Only one more who had got into the whirl-pool, enjoyed the sensation for a moment, and then swept dizzily down. There were, indeed, some who for an earnest hour sermonized about it and said, "Here is another example of the pernicious influence of the city on untrained Negroes. Oh, is there no way to keep these people from rushing away from the small villages and country districts of the South up to the cities, where they cannot battle with the terrible force of a strange and unusual environment? Is there no way to prove to them that woolen-shirted, brown-jeaned simplicity is infinitely better than broad-clothed degradation?" They wanted to preach to these people that good agriculture is better than bad art—that it was better and nobler for them to sing to God across the Southern fields than to dance for rowdies in the Northern halls. They wanted to dare to say that the South has its faults—no one condones them—and its disadvantages, but that even what they suffered from these was better than what awaited them in the great alleys of New York. Down there, the bodies were restrained, and they chafed; but here the soul would fester, and they would be content.

This was but for an hour, for even while they exclaimed they knew that there was no way, and that the stream of young Negro life would continue to flow up from the South, dashing itself against the hard necessities of the city and breaking like waves against a rock—that, until the gods grew tired of their cruel sport, there must still be sacrifices to false ideals and unreal ambitions.

There was one heart, though, that neither dismissed Joe with gratuitous pity nor sermonized about him. The mother heart had only room for grief and pain. Already it had borne its share. It had known sorrow for a lost husband, tears at the neglect and brutality of a new companion, shame for a daughter's sake, and it had seemed already filled to overflowing. And yet the fates had put in this one other burden until it seemed it must burst with the weight of it.

To Fannie Hamilton's mind now all her boy's shortcomings became as naught. He was not her wayward, erring, criminal son. She only remembered that he was her son, and wept for him as such. She forgot his curses, while her memory went back to the sweetness of his baby prattle and the soft words of his tenderer youth. Until the last she clung to him, holding him guiltless, and to her thought they took to prison, not Joe Hamilton, a convicted criminal, but Joey, Joey, her boy, her first-born—a martyr.

The pretty Miss Kitty Hamilton was less deeply impressed. The arrest and subsequent conviction of her brother was quite a blow. She felt the shame of it keenly, and some of the grief. To her, coming as it did just at a time when the company was being strengthened and she more importantly featured than ever, it was decidedly inopportune, for no one could help connecting her name with the affair.

For a long time she and her brother had scarcely been upon speaking terms. During Joe's frequent lapses from industry he had been prone to "touch" his sister for the wherewithal to supply his various wants. When, finally, she grew tired and refused to be "touched," he rebuked her for withholding that which, save for his help, she would never have been able to make. This went on until they were almost entirely estranged. He was wont to say that "now his sister was up in the world, she had got the big head," and she retorted that her brother "wanted to use her for a 'soft thing.'"

From the time that she went on the stage she had begun her own life, a life in which the chief aim was the possession of good clothes and the ability to attract the attention which she had learned to crave. The greatest sign of interest she showed in her brother's affair was, at first, to offer her mother money to secure a lawyer. But when Joe confessed all, she consoled herself with the reflection that perhaps it was for the best, and kept her money in her pocket with a sense of satisfaction. She was getting to be so very much more Joe's sister. She did not go to see her brother.

She was afraid it might make her nervous while she was in the city, and she went on the road with her company before he was taken away.

Miss Kitty Hamilton had to be very careful about her nerves and her health. She had had experiences, and her voice was not as good as it used to be, and her beauty had to be aided by cosmetics. So she went away from New York, and only read of all that happened when someone called her attention to it in the papers.

Berry Hamilton in his Southern prison knew nothing of all this, for no letters had passed between him and his family for more than two years. The very cruelty of destiny defeated itself in this and was kind.

Chapter 16

Skaggs's Theory

THERE WAS, PERHAPS, MORE depth to Mr. Skaggs than most people gave him credit for having. However it may be, when he got an idea into his head, whether it were insane or otherwise, he had a decidedly tenacious way of holding to it. Sadness had been disposed to laugh at him when he announced that Joe's drunken story of his father's troubles had given him an idea. But it was, nevertheless, true, and that idea had stayed with him clear through the exciting events that followed on that fatal night. He thought and dreamed of it until he had made a working theory. Then one day, with a boldness that he seldom assumed when in the sacred Presence, he walked into the office and laid his plans before the editor. They talked together for some time, and the editor seemed hard to convince.

"It would be a big thing for the paper," he said, "if it only panned out; but it is such a rattle-brained, harum-scarum thing. No one under the sun would have thought of it but you, Skaggs."

"Oh, it's bound to pan out. I see the thing as clear as day. There's no getting around it."

"Yes, it looks plausible, but so does all fiction. You're taking a chance. You're losing time. If it fails—"

"But if it succeeds?"

"Well, go and bring back a story. If you don't, look out. It's against my better judgment anyway. Remember I told you that."

Skaggs shot out of the office, and within an hour and a half had boarded a fast train for the South.

It is almost a question whether Skaggs had a theory or whether he had told himself a pretty story and, as usual, believed it. The editor was right. No one else would have thought of the wild thing that was in the reporter's mind. The detective had not thought of it five years before, nor had Maurice Oakley and his friends had an inkling, and here was one of the New York *Universe*'s young men going miles to prove his idea about something that did not at all concern him.

When Skaggs reached the town which had been the home of the Hamiltons, he went at once to the Continental Hotel. He had as yet formulated no plan of immediate action and with a fool's or a genius' belief in his destiny he sat down to await the turn of events. His first move would be to get acquainted with some of his neighbors. This was no difficult matter, as the bar of the Continental was still the gathering-place of some of the city's choice spirits of the old régime. Thither he went, and his convivial cheerfulness soon placed him on terms with many of his kind.

He insinuated that he was looking around for business prospects. This proved his open-sesame. Five years had not changed the Continental frequenters much, and Skaggs's intention immediately brought Beachfield Davis down upon him with the remark, "If a man wants to go into business, business for a gentleman, suh, Gad, there's no finer or better paying business in the world than breeding blooded dogs—that is, if you get a man of experience to go in with you."

"Dogs, dogs," driveled old Horace Talbot, "Beachfield's always talking about dogs. I remember the night we were all discussing that Hamilton nigger's arrest, Beachfield said it was a sign of total depravity because his man hunted 'possums with his hound." The old man laughed inanely. The hotel whiskey was getting on his nerves.

The reporter opened his eyes and his ears. He had stumbled upon something, at any rate.

"What was it about some nigger's arrest, sir?" he asked respectfully.

"Oh, it wasn't anything much. Only an old and trusted servant robbed his master, and my theory—"

"But you will remember, Mr. Talbot," broke in Davis, "that I proved your theory to be wrong and cited a conclusive instance."

"Yes, a 'possum-hunting dog."

"I am really anxious to hear about the robbery, though. It seems such an unusual thing for a Negro to steal a great amount."

"Just so, and that was part of theory. Now—"

"It's an old story and a long one, Mr. Skaggs, and one of merely local repute," interjected Colonel Saunders. "I don't think it could possibly interest you, who are familiar with the records of the really great crimes that take place in a city such as New York."

"Those things do interest me very much, though. I am something of a psychologist, and I often find the smallest and most insignificant-appearing details pregnant with suggestion. Won't you let me hear the story, Colonel?"

"Why, yes, though there's little in it save that I am one of the few men who have come to believe that the Negro, Berry Hamilton, is not the guilty party."

"Nonsense! nonsense!" said Talbot; "of course Berry was guilty, but, as I said before, I don't blame him. The Negroes—"

"Total depravity," said Davis. "Now look at my dog—"

"If you will retire with me to the further table I will give you whatever of the facts I can call to mind."

As unobtrusively as they could, they drew apart from the others and seated themselves at a more secluded table, leaving Talbot and Davis wrangling, as of old, over their theories. When the glasses were filled and the pipes going, the Colonel began his story, interlarding it frequently with comments of his own.

"Now, in the first place, Mr. Skaggs," he said when the tale was done, "I am lawyer enough to see for myself how weak the evidence was upon which Negro was convicted, and later events have done much to confirm me in the opinion that he was innocent."

"Later events?"

"Yes." The Colonel leaned across the table and his voice fell to a whisper. "Four years ago a great change took place in Maurice Oakley. It happened in the space of a day, and no one knows the cause of it. From a social, companionable man, he became a recluse, shunning visitors and dreading society. From an open-hearted, unsuspicious neighbor, he became secretive and distrustful of his own friends. From an active business man, he has become a retired brooder. He sees no one if he can help it. He writes no letters and receives none, not even from his brother, it is said. And all of this came about in the space of twenty-four hours."

"But what was the beginning of it?"

"No one knows, save that one day he had some sort of nervous attack. By the time the doctor was called he was better, but he kept clutching his hand over his heart. Naturally, the physician wanted to examine him there, but the very suggestion of it seemed to throw him into a frenzy; and his wife too begged the doctor, an old friend of the family, to desist. Maurice Oakley had been as sound as a dollar, and no one of the family had had any tendency to heart affection."

"It is strange."

"Strange it is, but I have my theory."

"His actions are like those of a man guarding a secret."

"Sh! His Negro laundress says that there is an inside pocket in his undershirts."

"An inside pocket?"

"Yes."

"And for what?" Skaggs was trembling with eagerness.

The Colonel dropped his voice lower.

"We can only speculate," he said; "but, as I have said, I have my theory. Oakley was a just man, and in punishing his old servant for the supposed robbery it is plain that he acted from principle. But he is also a proud man and would hate to confess that he had been in the wrong. So I believed that the cause of his first shock was the finding of the money that he supposed gone. Unwilling to admit this error, he lets the misapprehension go on, and it is the money which he carries in his secret pocket, with a morbid fear of its discovery, that has made him dismiss his servants, leave his business, and refuse to see his friends."

"A very natural conclusion, Colonel, and I must say that I believe you. It is strange that others have not seen as you have seen and brought the matter to light."

"Well, you see, Mr. Skaggs, none are so dull as the people who think they think. I can safely say that there is not another man in this town who has lighted upon the real solution of this matter, though it has been openly talked of for so long. But as for bringing it to light, no one would think of doing that. It would be sure to hurt Oakley's feelings, and he is of one of our best families."

"Ah, yes, perfectly right."

Skaggs had got all that he wanted; much more, in fact, than he had expected. The Colonel held him for a while yet to enlarge upon the views that he had expressed.

When the reporter finally left him, it was with a cheery "Good-night, Colonel. If I were a criminal, I should be afraid of that analytical mind of yours!"

He went upstairs chuckling. "The old fool!" he cried as he flung himself into a chair. "I've got it! I've got it! Maurice Oakley must see me, and then what?" He sat down to think out what he should do tomorrow. Again, with his fine disregard of ways and means, he determined to trust to luck, and as he expressed it, "brace old Oakley."

Accordingly he went about nine o'clock the next morning to Oakley's house. A gray-haired, sad-eyed woman inquired his errand.

"I want to see Mr. Oakley," he said.

"You cannot see him. Mr. Oakley is not well and does not see visitors."

"But I must see him, madam; I am here upon business of importance."

"You can tell me just as well as him. I am his wife and transact all of his business."

"I can tell no one but the master of the house himself."

"You cannot see him. It is against his orders."

"Very well," replied Skaggs, descending one step; "it is his loss, not mine. I have tried to do my duty and failed. Simply tell him that I came from Paris."

"Paris?" cried a querulous voice behind the woman's back. "Leslie, why do you keep the gentleman at the door? Let him come in at once."

Mrs. Oakley stepped from the door and Skaggs went in. Had he seen Oakley before he would have been shocked at the change in his appearance; but as it was, the nervous, white-haired man who stood shiftily before him told him nothing of an eating secret long carried. The man's face was gray and haggard, and deep lines were cut under his staring, fish-like eyes. His hair tumbled in white masses over his pallid forehead, and his lips twitched as he talked.

"You're from Paris, sir, from Paris?" he said. "Come in, come in."

His motions were nervous and erratic. Skaggs followed him into the library, and the wife disappeared in another direction.

It would have been hard to recognize in the Oakley of the present the man of a few years before. The strong frame had gone away to bone, and nothing of his old power sat on either brow or chin. He was as a man who trembled on the brink of insanity. His guilty secret had been too much for him, and Skaggs's own fingers twitched as he saw his host's hands seek the breast of his jacket every other moment.

"It is there the secret is hidden," he said to himself, "and whatever it is, I must have it. But how—how? I can't knock the man down and rob him in his own house." But Oakley himself proceeded to give him his first cue.

"You—you—perhaps have a message from my brother—my brother who is in Paris. I have not heard from him for some time."

Skaggs's mind worked quickly. He remembered the Colonel's story. Evidently the brother had something to do with the secret. "Now or never," he thought. So he said boldly, "Yes, I have a message from your brother."

The man sprung up, clutching again at his breast. "You have? you have? Give it to me. After four years he sends me a message! Give it to me!"

The reporter looked steadily at the man. He knew that he was in his power, that his very eagerness would prove traitor to his discretion.

"Your brother bade me to say to you that you have a terrible secret, that you bear it in your breast—there—there. I am his messenger. He bids you to give it to me."

Oakley had shrunken back as if he had been struck.

"No, no!" he gasped, "no, no! I have no secret."

The reporter moved nearer him. The old man shrunk against the wall, his lips working convulsively and his hand tearing at his breast as Skaggs drew nearer. He attempted to shriek, but his voice was husky and broke off in a gasping whisper.

"Give it to me, as your brother commands."

"No, no, no! It is not his secret; it is mine. I must carry it here always, do you hear? I must carry it till I die. Go away! Go away!"

Skaggs seized him. Oakley struggled weakly, but he had no strength. The reporter's hand sought the secret pocket. He felt a paper beneath his fingers. Oakley gasped hoarsely as he drew it forth. Then raising his voice gave one agonized cry, and sank to the floor frothing at the mouth. At the cry rapid footsteps were heard in the hallway, and Mrs. Oakley threw open the door.

"What is the matter?" she cried.

"My message has somewhat upset your husband," was the cool answer.

"But his breast is open. Your hand has been in his bosom. You have taken something from him. Give it to me, or I shall call for help."

Skaggs had not reckoned on this, but his wits came to the rescue.

"You dare not call for help," he said, "or the world will know!"

She wrung her hands helplessly, crying, "Oh, give it to me, give it to me. We've never done you any harm."

"But you've harmed someone else; that is enough."

He moved towards the door, but she sprang in front of him with the fierceness of a tigress protecting her young. She attacked him with teeth and nails. She was pallid with fury, and it was all he could do to protect himself and yet not injure her. Finally, when her anger had taken her strength, he succeeded in getting out. He flew down the hallway and out of the front door, the woman's screams following him. He did not pause to read the precious letter until he was safe in his room at the Continental Hotel. Then he sprang to his feet, crying, "Thank God! thank God! I was right, and the *Universe* shall have a sensation. The brother is the thief, and Berry Hamilton is an innocent man. Hurrah! Now, who is it that has come on a wild-goose chase? Who is it that ought to handle his idea carefully? Heigho, Saunders my man, the drinks'll be on you, and old Skaggsy will have done some good in the world."

Chapter 17

A Yellow Journal

MR. SKAGGS HAD NO qualms of conscience about the manner in which he had come by the damaging evidence against Maurice Oakley. It was enough for him that he had it. A corporation, he argued, had no soul, and therefore no conscience. How much less, then, should so small a part of a great corporation as himself be expected to have them?

He had his story. It was vivid, interesting, dramatic. It meant the favor of his editor, a big thing for the *Universe,* and a fatter lining for his own pocket. He sat down to put his discovery on paper before he attempted anything else, although the impulse to celebrate was very strong within him.

He told his story well, with an eye to every one of its salient points. He sent an alleged picture of Berry Hamilton as he had appeared at the time of his arrest. He sent a picture of the Oakley home and of the cottage where the servant and his family had been so happy. There was a strong pen-picture of the man, Oakley, grown haggard and morose from carrying his guilty secret, of his confusion when confronted with the supposed knowledge of it. The old Southern city was described, and the opinions of its residents in regard to the case given. It was there— clear, interesting, and strong. One could see it all as if every phase of it were being enacted before one's eyes. Skaggs surpassed himself.

When the editor first got hold of it he said "Huh!" over the opening lines— a few short sentences that instantly pricked the attention awake. He read on with increasing interest. "This is good stuff," he said at the last page. "Here's a chance for the *Universe* to look into the methods of Southern court proceedings. Here's a chance for a spread."

The *Universe* had always claimed to be the friend of all poor and oppressed humanity, and every once in a while it did something to substantiate its claim, whereupon it stood off and said to the public, "Look you what we have done, and behold how great we are, the friend of the people!" The *Universe* was yellow. It was very so. But it had power and keenness and energy. It never lost an opportunity to crow, and if one was not forthcoming, it made one. In this way it managed to do a considerable amount of good, and its yellowness became forgivable, even commendable. In Skaggs's story the editor saw an opportunity for one of its periodical philanthropies. He seized upon it. With headlines that took half a page, and with cuts authentic and otherwise, the tale was told, and the people of New York were greeted next morning with the announcement of—

"A BURNING SHAME!
A POOR AND INNOCENT NEGRO MADE TO SUFFER
FOR A RICH MAN'S CRIME!
GREAT EXPOSÉ BY THE 'UNIVERSE'!
A 'UNIVERSE' REPORTER TO THE RESCUE!
THE WHOLE THING TO BE AIRED THAT THE
PEOPLE MAY KNOW!"

Then Skaggs received a telegram that made him leap for joy. He was to do it. He was to go to the capital of the State. He was to beard the Governor in his den, and he, with the force of a great paper behind him, was to demand for the people the release of an innocent man. Then there would be another write-up and much glory for him and more shekels. In an hour after he had received his telegram he was on his way to the Southern capital.

MEANWHILE IN THE HOUSE of Maurice Oakley there were sad times. From the moment that the master of the house had fallen to the floor in impotent fear and madness there had been no peace within his doors. At first his wife had tried to control him alone, and had humored the wild babblings with which he woke from his swoon. But these changed to shrieks and cries and curses, and she was forced to throw open the doors so long closed and call in help. The neighbors and her old friends went to her assistance, and what the reporter's story had not done, the ravings of the man accomplished; for, with a show of matchless cunning, he continually clutched at his breast, laughed, and babbled his secret openly. Even then they would have smothered it in silence, for the honor of one of their best families; but too many ears had heard, and then came the yellow journal bearing all the news in emblazoned headlines.

Colonel Saunders was distinctly hurt to think that his confidence had been imposed on, and that he had been instrumental in bringing shame upon a Southern name.

"To think, suh," he said generally to the usual assembly of choice spirits—"to think of that man's being a reporter, suh, a common, ordinary reporter, and that I sat and talked to him as if he were a gentleman!"

"You're not to be blamed, Colonel," said old Horace Talbot. "You've done no more than any other gentleman would have done. The trouble is that the average Northerner has no sense of honor, suh, no sense of honor. If this particular man had had, he would have kept still, and everything would have gone on smooth and quiet. Instead of that, a distinguished family is brought to shame, and for what? To give a nigger a few more years of freedom when, likely as not, he don't want it; and Berry Hamilton's life in prison has proved nearer the ideal reached by slavery than anything he has found since emancipation. Why, suhs, I fancy I see him leaving his prison with tears of regret in his eyes."

Old Horace was inanely eloquent for an hour over his pet theory. But there were some in the town who thought differently about the matter, and it was their opinions and murmurings that backed up Skaggs and made it easier for him when at the capital he came into contact with the official red tape.

He was told that there were certain forms of procedure, and certain times for certain things, but he hammered persistently away, the murmurings behind him grew louder, while from his sanctum the editor of the *Universe* thundered away against oppression and high-handed tyranny. Other papers took it up and asked why this man should be despoiled of his liberty any longer? And when it was replied that the man had been convicted, and that the wheels of justice could not be stopped or turned back by the letter of a romantic artist or the ravings of a madman, there was a mighty outcry against the farce of justice that had been played out in this man's case.

The trial was reviewed; the evidence again brought up and examined. The dignity of the State was threatened. At this time the State did the one thing necessary to save its tottering reputation. It would not surrender, but it capitulated, and Berry Hamilton was pardoned.

Berry heard the news with surprise and a half-bitter joy. He had long ago lost hope that justice would ever be done to him. He marveled at the word that was brought to him now, and he could not understand the strange cordiality of the young white man who met him at the warden's office. Five years of prison life had made a different man of him. He no longer looked to receive kindness from his fellows, and he blinked at it as he blinked at the unwonted brightness of the sun. The lines about his mouth where the smiles used to gather had changed and grown stern with the hopelessness of years. His lips drooped pathetically, and hard treatment had given his eyes a lowering look. His hair, that had hardly shown a white streak, was as white as Maurice Oakley's own. His erstwhile quick wits were dulled and imbruted. He had lived like an ox, working without inspiration or reward, and he came forth like an ox from his stall. All the higher part of him he had left behind, dropping it off day after day through the wearisome years. He had put behind him the Berry Hamilton that laughed and joked and sang and believed, for even his faith had become only a numbed fancy.

"This is a very happy occasion, Mr. Hamilton," said Skaggs, shaking his hand heartily.

Berry did not answer. What had this slim, glib young man to do with him? What had any white man to do with him after what he had suffered at their hands?

"You know you are to go New York with me?"

"To New Yawk? What fu'?"

Skaggs did not tell him that, now that the *Universe* had done its work, it demanded the right to crow to its heart's satisfaction. He said only, "You want to see your wife, of course?"

Berry had forgotten Fannie, and for the first time his heart thrilled within him at the thought of seeing her again.

"I ain't hyeahed f'om my people fu' a long time. I didn't know what had become of 'em. How's Kit an' Joe?"

"They're all right," was the reply. Skaggs couldn't tell him, in this the first hour of his freedom. Let him have time to drink the sweetness of that all in. There would be time afterwards to taste all of the bitterness.

Once in New York, he found that people wished to see him, some fools, some philanthropists, and a great many reporters. He had to be photographed—all this before he could seek those whom he longed to see. They printed his picture as he was before he went to prison and as he was now, a sort of before-and-after-taking comment, and in the morning that it all appeared, when the *Universe* spread itself to tell the public what it had done and how it had done it, they gave him his wife's address.

It would be better, they thought, for her to tell him herself all that happened. No one of them was brave enough to stand to look in his eyes when he asked for his son and daughter, and they shifted their responsibility by pretending to themselves that they were doing it for his own good: that the blow would fall more gently upon him coming from her who had been his wife. Berry took the address and inquired his way timidly, hesitatingly, but with a swelling heart, to the door of the flat where Fannie lived.

Chapter 18

What Berry Found

HAD NOT BERRY'S YEARS of prison life made him forget what little he knew of reading, he might have read the name Gibson on the door-plate where they told him to ring for his wife. But he knew nothing of what awaited him as he confidently pulled the bell. Fannie herself came to the door. The news the papers held had not escaped her, but she had suffered in silence, hoping that Berry might be spared the pain of finding her. Now he stood before her, and she knew him at a glance, in spite of his haggard countenance.

"Fannie," he said, holding out his arms to her, and all of the pain and pathos of long yearning was in his voice, "don't you know me?"

She shrank away from him, back in the hallway.

"Yes, yes, Be'y, I knows you. Come in."

She led him through the passageway and into her room, he following with a sudden sinking at his heart. This was not the reception he had expected from Fannie.

When they were within the room he turned and held out his arms to her again, but she did not notice them. "Why, is you 'shamed o' me?" he asked brokenly.

"'Shamed? No! Oh, Be'y," and she sank into a chair and began rocking to and fro in her helpless grief.

"What's de mattah, Fannie? Ain't you glad to see me?"

"Yes, yes, but you don't know nothin', do you? Dey lef' me to tell you?"

"Lef' you to tell me? What's de mattah? Is Joe or Kit daid? Tell me."

"No, not daid. Kit dances on de stage fu' a livin', an', Be'y, she ain't de gal she ust to be. Joe—Joe—Joe—he's in pen'tentiary fu' killin' a ooman."

Berry started forward with a cry, "My Gawd! my Gawd! my little gal! my boy!"

"Dat ain't all," she went on dully, as if reciting a rote lesson; "I ain't yo' wife no mo'. I's ma'ied ag'in. Oh Be'y, Be'y, don't look at me lak dat. I couldn't he'p it. Kit an' Joe lef' me, an' dey said de pen'tentiary divo'ced you an' me, an' dat you'd nevah come out nohow. Don't look at me lak dat, Be'y."

"You ain't my wife no mo'? Hit's a lie, a damn lie! You is my wife. I's a innocent man. No pen'tentiay kin tek you erway f'om me. Hit's enough what dey 've done to my chillen." He rushed forward and seized her by the arm. "Dey sha'n't do no mo', by Gawd! dey sha'n't, I say!" His voice had risen to a fierce roar, like that of a hurt beast, and he shook her by the arm as he spoke.

"Oh, don't, Be'y, don't, you hu't me. I couldn't he'p it."

He glared at her for a moment, and then the real force of the situation came full upon him, and he bowed his head in his hands and wept like a child. The great sobs came up and stuck in his throat.

She crept up to him fearfully and laid her hand on his head.

"Don't cry, Be'y," she said; "I done wrong, but I loves you yit."

He seized her in his arms and held her tightly until he could control himself. Then he asked weakly, "Well, what am I goin' to do?"

"I do' know, Be'y, 'ceptin' dat you'll have to leave me."

"I won't! I'll never leave you again," he replied doggedly.

"But, Be'y, you mus'. You'll only mek it ha'der on me, an' Gibson'll beat me ag'in."

"Ag'in!"

She hung her head: "Yes."

He gripped himself hard.

"Why cain't you come on off wid me, Fannie? You was mine fus'."

"I couldn't. He would fin' me anywhaih I went to."

"Let him fin' you. You'll be wid me, an' we'll settle it, him an' me."

"I want to, but oh, I can't, I can't," she wailed. "Please go now, Be'y, befo' he gits home. He's mad anyhow, 'cause you're out."

Berry looked at her hard, and then said in a dry voice, "An' so I got to go an' leave you to him?"

"Yes, you mus'; I'm his'n now."

He turned to the door, murmuring, "My wife gone, Kit a nobody, an' Joe, little Joe, a murderer, an' then I—I—ust to pray to Gawd an' call him 'Ouah Fathah.'" He laughed hoarsely. It sounded like nothing Fannie had ever heard before.

"Don't, Be'y, don't say dat. Maybe we don't un'erstan'."

Her faith still hung by a slender thread, but his had given way in that moment.

"No, we don't un'erstan'," he laughed as he went out of the door. "We don't un'erstan'."

He staggered down the steps, blinded by his emotions, and set his face towards the little lodging that he had taken temporarily. There seemed nothing left in life for him to do. Yet he knew that he must work to live, although the effort seemed hardly worth while. He remembered now that the *Universe* had offered him the under janitorship in its building. He would go and take it, and someday, perhaps— He was not quite sure what the "perhaps" meant. But as his mind grew clearer he came to know, for a sullen, fierce anger was smoldering in his heart against the man who through lies had stolen his wife from him. It was anger that came slowly, but gained in fierceness as it grew.

Yes, that was it, he would kill Gibson. It was no worse than his present state. Then it would be father and son murderers. They would hang him or send him back to prison. Neither would be hard now. He laughed to himself.

And this was what they had let him out of prison for? To find out all this. Why had they not left him there to die in ignorance? What had he to do with all these people who gave him sympathy? What did he want of their sympathy? Could they give him back one tithe of what he had lost? Could they restore to him his wife or his son or his daughter, his quiet happiness or his simple faith?

He went to work for the *Universe*, but night after night, armed, he patrolled the sidewalk in front of Fannie's house. He did not know Gibson, but he wanted to see them together. Then he would strike. His vigils kept him from his bed, but he went to the next morning's work with no weariness. The hope of revenge sustained him, and he took a savage joy in the thought that he should be the dispenser of justice to at least one of those who had wounded him.

Finally he grew impatient and determined to wait no longer, but to seek his enemy in his own house. He approached the place cautiously and went up the steps. His hand touched the bell-pull. He staggered back.

"Oh, my Gawd!" he said.

There was crape on Fannie's bell. His head went round and he held to the door for support. Then he turned the knob and the door opened. He went noiselessly in. At the door of Fannie's room he halted, sick with fear. He knocked, a step sounded within, and his wife's face looked out upon him. He could have screamed aloud with relief.

"It ain't you!" he whispered huskily.

"No, it's him. He was killed in a fight at the race-track. Some o' his frinds are settin' up. Come in."

He went in, a wild, strange feeling surging at his heart. She showed him into the death-chamber.

As he stood and looked down upon the face of his enemy, still, cold, and terrible in death, the recognition of how near he had come to crime swept over him, and all his dead faith sprang into new life in a glorious resurrection. He stood with clasped hands, and no word passed his lips. But his heart was crying, "Thank God! thank God! this man's blood is not on my hands."

The gamblers who were sitting up with the dead wondered who the old fool was who looked at their silent comrade and then raised his eyes as if in prayer.

WHEN GIBSON WAS LAID away, there were no formalities between Berry and his wife; they simply went back to each other. New York held nothing for them now but sad memories. Kit was on the road, and the father could not bear to see his son; so they turned their faces southward, back to the only place they could call home. Surely the people could not be cruel to them now, and even if they were, they felt that after what they had endured no wound had power to give them pain.

Leslie Oakley heard of their coming, and with her own hands re-opened and refurnished the little cottage in the yard for them. There the white-haired woman begged them to spend the rest of their days and be in peace and comfort. It was the only amend she could make. As much to satisfy her as to settle themselves, they took the cottage, and many a night thereafter they sat together with clasped hands listening to the shrieks of the madman across the yard and thinking of what he had brought to them and to himself.

It was not a happy life, but it was all that was left to them, and they took it up without complaint, for they knew they were powerless against some Will infinitely stronger than their own.